Story of Naples = & legacy of the
old exfacist uncle

A LAST LAMP BURNING

A LAST LAMP

Gwyn Griffin

BURNING

A Novel

G. P. Putnam's Sons   New York

VENERATION OF IMAGES

Thou man, first-comer, whose wide arms entreat,
  Gather, clasp, welcome, bind,
Lack, or remember; whose warm pulses beat
  With love of thine own kind:

Unlifted for a blessing on yon sea,
  Unshrined on this highway,
O flesh, O grief, thou too shalt have our knee,
  Thou rood of every day!

                                   —MEYNELL

Homecoming

ᵉᵍ 1

IN the end they brought the coffin down the fire escape. They had tried, against the advice of the cook and her husband, to carry it down the narrow inside staircase but it had jammed hopelessly at the first bend, tearing off one of its baroque metal corners and deeply scarring the sea-blue distemper of the wall. During the straining, sweating and softly swearing minutes while it was being extricated and taken back into the bedroom it suffered further superficial damage and the imitation-bronze crucifix on the lid, somehow working loose, swung round to hang blasphemously by its feet, disclosing its cheap tin interior. Also the body must have shifted, for as they staggered down the iron steps of the fire escape—the one indubitably well-constructed fitting in the shoddy seaside villa—the whole weight of the coffin seemed concentrated on its left side.

Below them the black varnish and polished nickel-plate of the ancient hearse gleamed and sparkled in the vivid summer sunlight, the huge, foliated lanterns at the corners reflecting blinding flashes from each glinting death's-head, extinguished torch and weeping angel. Then a last few stumbling paces across the soft sand, an ultimate heave of aching arms, and the oiled rollers in the hearse's floor took the coffin and slid it smoothly between the engraved glass sides.

They stood back panting—Gennaro, in his long black coat edged with tarnished gold braid and the peaked cap which came down over his ears, the cook's husband, red-faced in shirtsleeves, and the two boatmen who had been pressed into service and now stood smiling a little deprecatingly and waiting to be paid for their efforts. The lawyer from Pescara, a handsome dark man in a neat suit, looked meaningly at Gennaro and then at the boatmen. "These people who have been so kindly helping. Perhaps you . . . ?"

Gennaro smiled, equally polite but firm. "It was certainly very kind of them. But of course I am only the driver—an employee."

"But are you not also the grandson of the undertaker? Signor Giuseppe Sanbrenedetto telephoned that the undertaker was sending his grandson. . . ."

"Yes, but I am only an employee. I work for my grandfather."

The lawyer nodded irritably. It was intolerably hot standing here on burning white sand with sea and sky glaring back the sunlight in vast expanses of blue and gold. He thought longingly of his cool flat and the glass of iced beer which his wife would have waiting for him on his return. "Yes, yes, yes. But the undertaker is naturally responsible for all the financial arrangements; that is always understood. Since your grandfather supplied no men to carry down the deceased, and since these kind people have willingly left their work . . ." The boatmen shifted their bare feet in the sand; they were embarrassed but they would not leave without remuneration.

Gennaro mentally balanced the chances of the lawyer employing the firm in future business against the pleasure of retaining the two hundred lire he had ready in one of the pockets of his coat, and reluctantly came down on the side of the former. It was not very likely that the lawyer would have many clients who, dying on the Adriatic coast, would wish to be taken across Italy for burial at Naples— But it could happen. Visitors who were drowned while bathing, perhaps. . . . So he smiled placatingly, took the two coins from his pocket and slipped them into the broad brown hands of the boatmen. "Many thanks for your kind help."

Then it was merely a question of signing a couple of documents for the lawyer, climbing into the hearse's cab and starting the heavy old engine. He reversed onto the hot macadam of the road, the lawyer took off his hat, the two boatmen, the cook and her husband crossed themselves, and Gennaro let in the clutch and drove slowly away along the dead-straight coast road, a somber figure in his shabby black coat and cap.

After three kilometers, the longing to swim which had been growing upon him ever since he reached the coast nearly two hours ago became insupportable. There was a convenient clump of high bamboos—tall, thick, pale green canes of the sort whose fibrous, spear-shaped leaves were used for wrapping wine flasks—just on the side of the road. It was enough to partially screen the hearse and Gennaro edged carefully into its shade and drew up. He slid out of the driving seat and glanced up and down the long, straight road; there was nothing to be seen, no movement at all. The tarred surface narrowed away into the distance to vanish, finally, into quivering, watery mirages of corrugated air. In the bamboo thicket beside him a cicada shrilled its single, high-pitched note; nothing else broke the afternoon silence.

Gennaro unbuttoned his coat and threw it, with his driver's cap, onto the floor of the cab; his black hair fell damply across his forehead and his striped beach-shirt clung to his back and chest. He kicked off his shoes, unbuckled his belt and with some difficulty pulled the sticky shirt over his head. Stepping out of his jeans he stood for a moment in his cheap blue underpants among the broken shadows of the bamboos and then ran quickly across twenty meters of burning-hot sand and plunged into the sea.

The Adriatic took him caressingly, lifting and lowering him on its gentle swell. It was very shallow and Gennaro turned over twice, rolling like a porpoise, and then started to swim out toward the horizon where sea and sky melted almost imperceptibly into each other. He swam with slow, regular strokes, the water, cut by his cheek and chin, streaming slickly along his body, between his legs, to be thrust back by his kicking feet. This was the first time he had swum in the Adriatic and after the dirty, narrow beaches of Mergellina and San Giovanni he was enchanted by its vast sunlit emptiness. After a little he dived, swimming down and careening over the sandy, sun-dappled floor across which small crabs scuttled jerkily away from his sliding shadow; then, breaking surface in a spatter of silver spray, he was back once more in a tranquil, silent world, blue and sunlit. Huge curving sky, spotless and shining, great empty

placid sea; suddenly it came to Gennaro that this was peace—
something entirely different from the disciplined, folded-hands
quiescence enjoined by the Ferrara monks or, later, that intimi-
dating darkness of eternal rest at whose portals he was a shabby
but enthusiastic servitor—this vast, bright, contented calmness,
perpetual, without either past or future and with oneself held
forever in the middle of it, embedded yet completely free, completely alone yet completely happy. Slowly he turned over onto
his back, breathing deeply, filled with a delight he had never
known before and could not possibly express even to himself; a
supreme moment, one of those instances, rare and indescrib-
able, when the quickened senses store up impressions which
may become a secret key to beauty and inspire a lifetime. The
peace that passes all understanding—and yet for that moment
Gennaro understood it very well.

He was a long way out. Too far. He began to paddle slowly
back, his eyes sweeping the long, empty shoreline, focusing at
last on the clump of bamboos which hid the hearse and shook
and quivered in the heat-haze almost as though someone was
moving about among them. Yet only old Ercole Sanbrenedetto
lay there, bulbous, disfigured by old age and illness, in the
shoddy but pretentious coffin upon which Gennaro had lavished
the last four "antique silver" corner clasps which he had been
keeping for just such a chance. And the interior was lined with
genuine imitation-velvet, too—cloth, not paper. The firm was
making twenty thousand lire on that coffin; four times as much
as the profit on their usual product.

At the thought of that unexpected windfall Gennaro came
suddenly to life, turned a somersault in the water and diving,
zigzagged across the sandy floor, grabbed at a small crab and
started a whirlpool of sun-shot sand. Shooting again to the surface he felt the midafternoon sun striking hotly on his dripping
face and shoulders and wondered what the temperature could
be in the hearse—far too high, certainly, for the proper preservation of a newly dead body. They didn't want a blowup. He
remembered that there had been blowups in the past—luckily
he had never experienced one himself, but his grandfather had
—and he knew that it meant a lot of extra work, hurried, furtive, revoltingly unpleasant.

It spoiled his swim, that thought. He turned over, dived,

chased another crab—but to no avail; that pristine glory of endless, shining blue happiness eluded him and would not return. Reluctantly he set out for the shore.

⤳ 2

WHEN he parted the bamboos he found two heavily uniformed traffic police standing beside the hearse and going through the pockets of his clothes. Their big, red motorcycles were parked a few yards away on the verge of the road. They must have ridden up while he was diving or he would certainly have heard them. Overwhelmed by the disaster, he stood for a moment completely taken aback, thin, dripping, his underpants clinging to his narrow thighs, glancing hopelessly from the hot, gleaming hearse to the hot, red-faced policemen. They stared back at him malignly.

"Are you the driver of this vehicle?"

Gennaro nodded wordlessly. "Can I have my trousers, please?"

"Is it in use?"

"You mean—?"

"We mean, is that coffin occupied?"

"Well—yes, it is."

"Let's see the certificate."

"Can I have my trousers?"

"Get the certificate."

Swallowing, Gennaro went to the hearse, opened the cab and brought out the papers relating to the body. He handed them to the policemen and stood, shifting from one bare foot to the other, as they were slowly examined. Once he put out a tentative hand toward his jeans but one of the policemen, taking notes on a small pad, knocked it away.

It seemed an age before they finished. Were they, perhaps, not going to . . . ? Was it possible that, after all, they would not ask for . . . ? But no, they were bound to—they always did. The seawater had dried from his skin, the sun was hot on his back and shoulders; he wriggled his toes miserably in the dusty earth, bitterly regretting his foolishness in stopping for a swim.

At last the tallest of the policemen grunted and folded the papers in one hand. "Well," he said heavily "you're not supposed to stop in the course of transporting a body. It's a contravention against the hygiene laws. You know that?"

"No."

"How old are you?"

"Eighteen," said Gennaro, trying to keep the despair out of his voice.

One policeman grunted disgustedly and muttered something about "ought to have more sense . . ." but the other looked Gennaro up and down, frowning. "Come here." He ran a finger thoughtfully along the side of Gennaro's smooth jaw. "Eighteen, eh? Let's see your license—and your identity card while we're about it."

So that was that. The policemen seemed less surprised than Gennaro had expected. They even grinned with a derisive triumph. "Sixteen and a half—and only licensed to drive a motorcycle. Instead of which you take out a hearse with a body in it —and then go bathing. You're a boy with ideas of your own, you are. Did you steal it?"

"No, of course not. It belongs to my grandfather. That's his name on the side."

"L. P. Quong?" The policeman examined Gennaro's identity card again. "I don't understand this. Fulvio Quong is given as your father. Your name is Gualtierra. Why aren't you Quong? And why *Quong,* of all un-Christian names?"

"I work for my grandfather. It's his hearse. The man who usually drives it didn't come. We were in a hurry."

"Yes, yes. So you took a chance and got caught. But I asked about your name."

Gennaro shrugged sullenly and the policeman suddenly stamped hard beside his bare foot, the heavy boot thudding into the soft sand, spurting dust. "Come on—or the next one's on your toes!"

In a dead voice Gennaro said, "My grandfather came from China. His name's Quong. My father died in Russia with the army. My—my mother's name was Gualtierra. They weren't married."

The policeman re-examined the identity card. "I see. Yes." He glanced up questioningly. "And your father never officially recognized you—so you keep your mother's name?"

Gennaro nodded while a small bomb of hate exploded soundlessly in the back of his mind. The second policeman contemptuously tossed him his clothes and he began to dress with hands that shook.

"Driving while under age and without a license; contravening the state hygiene laws—" The first policeman tapped his lips with his pencil. "We could get him for bathing like that, too —without proper trunks. Indecent exposure?"

The second policeman pondered and shook his head. "Not at sixteen. Not from Naples. They'd let it go. Anyway there's enough as it is. Does he take it back?"

"The hearse—? He shouldn't, certainly. But on a day like this—and with a body—"

"Better let him. We don't want it here. We'll take him to the province boundary and give him a ticket saying the matter's being taken up. Then if anything goes wrong it's not our fault."

For the next half-hour Gennaro drove, wooden-faced, between his escort of the two red motorcycles just as if he was carrying the body of a high state official—a provincial prefect or someone. On two occasions the small cortege was stopped by other policemen anxious to know what was happening and each time, the explanation was accompanied and received with derisive laughter. Red-faced, Gennaro stared straight in front of him, letting in the clutch violently as soon as the signal to proceed was given. By the time they reached the border of the Pescara province the policemen were in a good humor with themselves. "Right. You go on alone from here. Don't stop until you get to Naples. Drive carefully and slowly. And look—we'll tear up the hygiene contravention charge." Gennaro nodded with a pretense of humble gratitude he did not feel. The hygiene charge was as nothing compared with driving under age and without a proper license. For a moment he thought desperately of appealing to them to tear up that charge, too. If he explained about his grandfather, about the dwindling business . . . how much this commission meant to them. . . . If there had been only one policeman he might have tried it, but with two he knew it would be no good; neither would trust the other to remain silent—and they had talked to colleagues on the road as well. . . . "And if you are stopped again show them this." A stamped paper was thrust through the window of the cab and he was waved on.

The road beyond Pescara seemed, to Gennaro, to be alive with the field-gray figures of policemen though probably there were but few more than usual. He was not stopped again for hearses, as he was well aware, were practically never halted. If only he had not yielded to that overwhelming desire to swim out into the empty blue sea everything would have been all right and he would have been half an hour farther on his way home now, free and happy. . . . He thrust down on the accelerator, forcing the old hearse along at top speed. He was not at all sure if the right headlamp worked and he must try to get back to Naples before dark in case it did not. He had not put on his driving coat or cap but sat, glowering and spiky-haired, in his open shirt of green-and-yellow stripes. He drove badly on purpose, bumping and jolting over rough patches in the road, swerving dangerously around corners. For he was more than half convinced that his deceased passenger had somehow summoned those policemen to punish him for his truancy in the sea and he was going to make sure that the journey to Naples should be the most uncomfortable any corpse had ever had.

After Pescara the road turned inland toward the mountains, the great ridge of the Apennines which lay like a serrated dorsal-fin along Italy's backbone. The road twisted into them between the looming cliffs of the Popoli pass and then Gennaro was driving through the long, fertile Peligna valley, hemmed in on either side by mountains and with the towering rock of the Gran Sasso soaring to the pale sky behind him, still snow-covered even on this last day of May. This was Abruzzi country and the slow ox-wagons of the coastal plain gave place to panniered pack mules, herds of jerkily trotting goats and narrow, high-wheeled donkey carts. At the roadside peasants crossed themselves dubiously as the hearse rattled past. They could not really believe that it contained a body—not at the speed it was going and with the disheveled driver smoking at the wheel—but the quick dabs of their fingers across chests and foreheads were more in the nature of signs warding off ill luck than symbolic affirmations of the Christian faith. From the cab

Gennaro eyed them with the contempt of the initiated. They were frightened of all the ritual trappings and appurtenances of death—heaven alone knew why, since most of them lived into their nineties—whereas he himself had dwelt joyfully for the past five years in an atmosphere of cut-rate coffins, cheap wreaths, black crepe and mourning notices.

At the end of the valley the hearse began to climb as the road, curving upward in great loops, left the fields and orchards, the vineyards and little towns that lay scattered like toys on the valley floor to bask away the last of their long, hot, breathless Italian afternoon under the westering sun. Despite the police warning, Gennaro stopped half an hour later at a small mountain village clinging to the rocky slopes and bought himself a large, stale bread roll and a thick slice of mortadella sausage to put in it; then he drove on slowly behind a great trailer-truck whose air brakes hissed and banged like fireworks at every change in the gradient.

The bread and sausage lasted until they were over the crest of the first range of mountains and running along the high plateau of Cinque Miglia where the cool air, smelling of pine trees and mountain grass, blew brightly through the stuffy cab. Then down once more to the valley of the river Sangro where a regiment of infantry was on maneuvers, hindered by a quantity of interested cows, and where white-helmeted Carabinieri motorcyclists shot up and down the road on tactical errands or lounged beside their machines on the grassy verge. Two of them —for want of anything better to do, presumably—stopped Gennaro, examined his papers, laughed at his misfortune and gave him a cigarette; they were big, friendly young men not many years older than himself.

Another range of mountains, bare and craggily purple under the falling sun, the French war cemetery before Venafro with its tricolor floating above the regimented rows of white crosses, and then a sudden emergence onto the plain of the Campania stretching flat and golden into the late-afternoon haze. Gennaro breathed deeply and flung a cigarette butt from the window. This was home country; Naples lay somewhere over the horizon at the end of the road and despite the increased traffic he thrust still harder upon the accelerator and the old hearse responded shakily as if it, too, knew that home was not far off.

Once again, with the long journey nearly over, Gennaro's thoughts turned toward his passenger. For of course old Ercole Sanbrenedetto was coming home, too; making his ultimate return in the last, golden light of this late May afternoon. Even though he had left Naples nearly twenty years ago to live in his bleak villa on the Adriatic coast, Ercole Sanbrenedetto was a Neapolitan and his last wish had been to be taken back for burial in the city where he had been born—born eighty-six years ago in the Quarter of San Lorenzo, in the hot, throbbing heart of the city, a stone's throw from the Porta Capuana. With the hearse rolling smoothly now along the wide road, Gennaro squinted his eyes against the level sunbeams that struck through the cab windows and wondered what life had been like in San Lorenzo some seventy years ago when the worn old body lying three feet behind him had been a strong, heavy-shouldered sixteen-year-old. In those days the Camorra had still ruled throughout the poorer quarters of the city; there were still old men who could recall times when naked *lazzaroni* had lounged about the narrow alleys, and there would be few of middle age who did not remember the last Bourbon king and Garibaldi's spectacular entry from the south.

A far distant time. Gennaro, searching his own memory, found it contained little but Americans; since the last war they had taken the place of both Bourbons and Piedmontese. American warships, gray and lean and powerful, lay in Naples roads to guard Europe from the menacing East while the Shore Patrol, tall and grim and burly, strode the Naples streets to guard Europeans from the American Navy—and out at Posilippo was the great NATO base full of eagle-bedecked uniforms, long black cars and nasal voices. It was said to be the Americans who had driven old Sanbrenedetto away or, more probably, been the cause of his self-exile. They had requisitioned some of his property after the war and his grim, sardonic manner, coupled with his political past, had not assisted him to get it back.

Ercole Sanbrenedetto had been a Fascist from the earliest days—or so it was commonly said. He had never risen particularly high in the party, being more concerned to use its political backing to further his financial affairs, but nevertheless he had been a true believer, if an unfanatical one, and the defeat and destruction of the regime had come as a shock from which, unlike other more implicated but younger and more resilient men, he had never fully recovered. But then he had never really tried to do so; had made no effort to accommodate himself either to occupied, or later to democratic, Italy. With part of his Neapolitan property smashed by American bombs and much of the rest requisitioned for American uses, he had moved out, crossed the peninsula to the other shore, built his ugly concrete villa on the long, flat sands of the Adriatic coast some thirty kilometers south of Pescara and settled down there with his two servants and that endless view of sea and sky.

He had never once revisited Naples. In due time the Americans had released the requisitioned property, but to the old man staring out to sea on that other, so dissimilar, coast it had become a matter of indifference and only after slow and half-unwilling negotiations had he rented the various houses on long and unprofitable leases. The bombed part of the property he had refused to touch—despite the cajolings of his nearest relative, a nephew who had returned to Naples after long years as a prisoner-of-war in Britain—and it remained, a great block of broken building of which only the central section was habitable, taking up the westward end of a narrow *piazza* behind the Porta Capuana. Though this square had, in the early nineteen-fifties, been renamed the Piazza Vittime Civili di Guerra —largely for the sake of the families who had perished in the bombing of the Sanbrenedetto property—the original name, Piazza Giovanni Nicòtera, remained inscribed upon a cracked marble slab on the wall of the still standing portion of the shattered building. It was sometimes a cause of confusion to strangers but the Municipality had at last grown tired of writing unanswered requests for its removal.

The still habitable section contained two small shops: C. BUONAFEDE—*Alimentari* and L. P. QUONG—*Pompe Funebre*. The names were painted in faded gilt above their doorways —a garage for Quong's hearse, a stable for a cab horse and some decayed living accommodation above and in the rear. Both ends of the section terminated in crumbled walls, cascades of weed-grown stones, splintered pantiles and broken bricks. Over this rubble the children of the *piazza* played interminable, raucous games of gang warfare; under it, in the dark, empty cellars half full of refuse, the older ones acted out the ritual sexual experiments of adolescence. In the summer the ruins were covered in dust and flies, in the winter they were brackish with pools and mud—all the year long they smelled mildly but persistently of putrefaction. But now there would be changes, now that Ercole Sanbrenedetto was coming back, at last, to Naples.

❧ 3

GENNARO threw away the stub of his last cigarette as Vesuvius, gray and broken-capped, loomed up from the south to greet him through the softly falling evening. He slowed to the respectful pace suitable to his vehicle and its occupant and swinging right at the Capua intersection passed the iron gates of the airport. A great airliner, gilded to incandescence by the last rays of the all-but-sunken sun, was coming in to land, moving with seemingly incredible slowness as it swung in a wide, lazy arc over Vesuvius. Then the lava flagstones, the blocks of iron-hard *piperno* which formed the city streets, were jolting under the hearse and as Gennaro turned to descend the Via Nuova beside the Capodichino Cemetery, the whole of Naples suddenly spread itself below him in the last evening light. Domes and spires, the high, white monolith of the Cattòlica, the scaffolded skeletal sky signs, UPIM and STANDA and CIM glowing above a thousand streets and squares, a myriad flat or pantiled roofs, countless teeming courts and alleys. To the south the oil and methane works of Poggioreale glittered in ugly aluminum and the perpetual flame from the ITOLGAS waste burner flared brutally among the smoking chimneys. To the northwest the castle of Sant' Elmo, high on the hill of Vomero, reflected the ultimate scarlet of the sunset upon its weatherbeaten façade, and even the trees lining the slope below it took on a hard, coppery tint as if sprayed with fire-bronze lacquer.

The city sprawled round the crimson waters of the gulf—a newly decapitated giant, its arms extended in the great pool of its own blood—and there was no peace; no hint of evening hush or calm. Night brought none of its blessings here, neither rest nor surcease from toil nor coolness after the heat of the day.

Even the weary sky, magnificent over Capri in rose and fading gold, would soon reflect only the hot, pulsing beat of neon and sodium light and the static glare of the great arc lamps along the docks blotting out moon and stars. Naples never slept nor rested except in isolated spots and corners.

For a moment, as the hearse rolled down toward the city, Gennaro had a quick vision of the Adriatic as he had swum in it that afternoon and as it must be now—still and breathless and stretching out endlessly, emptily, to dim horizons under the great vault of softening sky. For a single second his young heart was touched by an odd stab of yearning, an almost imperceptible nostalgia for something briefly encountered, half understood—lost. Something that, in some ill-defined way, made up for his calamitous encounter with the police and all the trouble yet to stem from it; something that could not be taken from him and would remain when the rest had fallen far back into the perpetually receding past.

He swung the hearse into the Piazza Re Carlo III among the sparking, hissing trams and *filobuses,* the vans, trucks and scooters tangled as always in a hooting, fuming confusion of grinding gears, shouting drivers and gesticulating policemen. For a moment the great silver lanterns at the old car's corners glittered out between a green bus and a yellow tanker-truck, and then one set of lights changed abruptly and like a tidal wave the traffic surged forward bearing the hearse away, sucking it along to vanish quickly into the great maw of the city.

Crocifissa

≈§ 1

"SANCTA Maria, madre di Dio, prega per noi peccatori, adesso e nell'ora della nostra morte. . . . Così sia." She rose sighing from her knees and sat resting an instant on the chair behind her, blinking up the nave, empty except for the austerely erect forms of two praying nuns and one shabby old man crouched in some obscure personal supplication in a corner beside a pillar. At the end of the nave the high altar glowed with electric candles, gilt and polished brass, a shining matrix for the gold-embroidered white silk curtain of the tabernacle, closed now but glittering with imitation gems. There was a mass in half an hour but it would be impossible to leave the shop then, with the workers trailing home from the factories, lounging heavily across from Tenerini's for their little packets of anchovies, salami or mortadella. Even so, she would have liked to remain sitting here, resting her heavy bulk, closer in church to Gianangelo and her long-dead parents—above all closer to Dino, closer even than in her own room behind the shop where his photograph smiled down at her from the wall. But she had already been here more than a quarter of an hour and from experience she knew that it was unsafe to leave Gigi in charge of the shop for any longer than that. Not that he didn't do his best, poor little thing, but the older boys came and teased him, picked things up and pretended to walk off with them, driving him into shrill ecstasies of despair and rage. She sighed once more and rising ponderously, adjusted the black lace scarf

on her head and left the church, absently dipping three fingers in the stoup of holy water beside the porch.

And once out on the steps beyond the swing-doors she found her misgivings confirmed. Gigi's voice, rising above the cries of peddlers and cobble-rattle of carts, reached her in high-pitched vituperation from the other side of the twilit square, and there seemed to be a crowd of them around the shop this time— loiterers, unemployed or half-employed youths from the Porta Capuana. Crocifissa descended the shallow stone steps with dangerous speed for someone of her shape and size and began a panting, shambling trot across the rough *piperno* blocks. She guessed that the basin of fish was the cause of the trouble this time, the bowl of tiny anchovies, fried and then preserved in vinegar, which she had turned out of their two-kilo can to be ready for sale later in the evening. Really, it was too bad! You had to leave things ready and then Gigi's tormentors came, pretending just to taste them, and ate one after another and of course Gigi became frantic. Those fish were expensive, too, a luxury almost—at least for the people of San Lorenzo. Next time she would . . . Gigi's voice, rising in a stream of dangerous, back-street obscenities was suddenly silenced; someone had hit him. Crocifissa started to run faster and already as she swayed past the filigree iron screen of the urinal in the middle of the *piazza* she was shouting hoarsely, "Leave him *alone!* I'll call the police! Let him alone, I tell you! Gigi—I'm coming! I'm coming, Gigi!"

As she struggled across the last few yards, gasping for breath, fiery pains shooting up her varicosed legs, the *piazza* lights, dusty, cracked globes on old swan-necked standards, glowed into golden life, dispelling the soft lavender dusk of early evening. A quick glance at the open shop front showed a confused clutter where one of the high towers of canned meat which Gigi loved to build had been knocked down and lay in scattered and glinting disorder among the bottles and loaves and plaited horse-tails of garlic. A round ball of cheese had rolled off into the gutter, a broken bottle of tomato sauce dripped its gore over some sliced sausage and little silvery anchovies lay everywhere.

But Gigi was not there; he was somewhere against the broken wall beyond the shop front, behind a gang of youths dressed in grubby singlets and worn jeans. With her remaining strength Crocifissa kicked and punched at their muscled backs; gasping, shouting breathless imprecations, and suddenly aware of her presence they moved rapidly aside, sliding eel-like into the shadows, laughing at her uneasily or in jeering, ringing mock-defiance. There must have been six or seven of them and as they parted she saw Gigi at last. He was crouched dazedly under a streetlight in the dirt at the foot of the wall upon which a great Church poster depicted a dying, crucified Christ above the words *Amami—sono morte per te*. He was covered in anchovies and vinegar while a heavy-shouldered boy stood over him with the basin, trying to thrust a further handful of broken fish into the front of the child's torn shirt.

Crocifissa seized the basin and kicked the boy viciously on the ankle. "What are you doing? Pig! Thief! Assassin!" With one pudgy hand she struck him across the forehead, her big topaz ring scratching a groove which suddenly gleamed crimson as he turned a face, snarling and white with fury, toward her. "Did you hear what he called me—this little *pupe?* What he said? If he had been older I would have killed him!" But confronted with Crocifissa's own rage his anger began to die. She stormed at him in a tirade of abuse. "Yes, if he was older! But he is only eleven—you know that well. You start it! Always you start it by taunting him—you and your worthless, idle friends! You are thieves, all of you—petty thieves, every one! By rights you should all be in the *casa di correzione*. You came to steal and because he stops you— Give me that basin. . . . Look—practically empty! And it held eighteen hundred lire's worth of fish! *Porca misèria!* How can one live? How can one make even an existence!"

People were clustering round now, coming over from other parts of the square; the girls from the hairdresser's at the corner of the Via Buonuomini, two of Clemente's children from the fish *trattoria* in the Piazza San Francesco, a couple of dirty old men with piles of brown paper clasped under their arms, Raimondo Tenerini, tall, bovine and smart in his soldier's uniform, even the little crippled girl who sometimes helped make wreaths for the Quongs. They stood, saying little; interested spectators watching one of the never-ending Neapolitan sideshows; the constant, evil little explosions of rage and shame and pain that were sparked off continually by the flash-point tensions of this overcrowded city in which there were never less than two hundred thousand unemployed, and often many more. In a moment they would take sides: but not quite yet, for they knew that they were of the same highly combustible material as the protagonists gasping and shouting before them and, vicariously, they too had been insulted, beaten, robbed.

But the scene, as often happened, flickered out as the energy to sustain it waned in the contestants. The youth let go of the basin, growling sullenly, and rubbed a hand across his bleeding forehead. Despite his broad shoulders and bronzed arms he was, like all his friends, underfed and chronically overtired, living permanently in a state bordering on nervous exhaustion, and Crocifissa's blow had sobered him. Pride demanded one last gesture, however; he flung the crushed handful of fish full into Gigi's upturned, tear-stained face and aimed a halfhearted kick at the kneeling child. Crocifissa caught hold of the front of his singlet, the cheap cotton ripped apart in her hand, and for a moment they all three remained panting in the golden glow of the streetlamp—the fat old woman in black clutching her almost empty basin, the half-naked, bloody-faced youth, the kneeling, sobbing little boy scrabbling in the dirt for the scattered fish—below the gaunt, expiring Christ whose sad face from the Cross saw only this after the passion of two thousand years. *"Love me—I died for you."*

Then it was all over. The youth turned, shrugging with hangdog defiance, and walked away spitting once over his shoulder while Crocifissa put a hand under Gigi's shoulder and lifted him to his feet. Still panting heavily she asked, "Are you hurt, little one? Did they hurt you?— No, no, don't put them back in the basin, we can't sell them now. We'll give them to Otello and keep a few for Baldissera." She led him back to the shop while a trail of small silvery fish fell from his blond head, his torn shirt and even from the legs of his crumpled shorts.

As she suspected, when she had him in the room behind the shop, he had not been really hurt; there were a few scratches and bruises on his face and legs but nothing more. But he was covered in vinegar and fish and she fetched a bucket of water and began the slow task of cleaning him up—Gigi was still too shaken to do it himself—while Otello, her big black cat, ate the remains of the crushed anchovies. During the cleaning process she chided the little boy, grumbling and gentle. "You really must be more careful what you say. You *know* there are expressions you must never use. Men—grown men—were stabbed to the heart for saying just those things in the days when I was your age. I've told you so often before, Gigi. . . ."

She sighed, knowing that it was no use. Gigi lived with his young mother in an alleyway beside the Church of the Annunziata on the opposite side of the *piazza*. He was the son of a soldier—or perhaps a sailor or an airman—an American, almost certainly. Crocifissa often thought that she could remember which one, but she was never certain—so many Americans visited Gigi's mother that one could not keep count. And when there was trouble in the quarter, or indeed in other parts of the city, between American servicemen and the natives, and American prestige slumped sharply into jealousy and contempt, Gigi became a temporary butt for the other children. In self-defense he let fly with the most insulting obscenities he had managed to collect—and he had managed, during his eleven years, to collect an astonishingly pungent variety. In the ensuing struggles he seldom came to much harm but it was one thing to provoke a fight with children of his own age and quite another to do the same with fully grown youths. Perhaps it was a mistake to employ him, but he was quick and remembered the prices of things, and he obtained such pleasure from the work. Still . . . "Gigi, it's serious, what I'm telling you. Look what happened this evening. I know it wasn't your fault, but practically all the fish are gone, and there's a bottle of sauce broken —and all that mess. . . ." Someone outside in the shop coughed and rattled a coin noisily on the marble meat slab and Crocifissa hurriedly pushed the cloth into the child's hand. "Now wash yourself properly, Gigi—wherever those fish went. You can take your clothes off; nobody's going to come in here. You don't want to go home smelling like . . . Yes, yes, I'm coming! *Vengo subito!*"

But it was not a customer awaiting her in the tiny, cluttered shop with its four holy pictures ranged above the counter, miniature electric lamps glowing warmly beneath their crimson celluloid hearts, but only old Biagio Bonitatibus, who rented the stable and the single dark, cavernous room behind it. Despite the heat of the early summer evening he still wore a shabby jacket under his still shabbier cabman's coat, his peaked cap was pulled down over his forehead and his greasy whip hung over his shoulder. Outside, gaunt, swaybacked and with every rib barred in the lamplight, Baldissera stood motionless, head hanging, between the shafts of the battered *carròzza*. "What's this I heard just now about the old man? He's dead, then?"

Crocifissa sighed and put her hand to her head. The affair of Gigi and the fish-stealers had put the recent news from her mind and now it flooded back with all its forebodings and looming implications of future difficulties. "Yes, indeed—yesterday. Gennaro told me early this morning. He went off to get the body. Signor Giuseppe had sent a message last night asking for it to be done. But I think those people on the Adriatic might have sent me a telegram. After all, my husband worked for the *padrone* for years—and so did I. I cooked for him long before *she* did.—There are some bread crusts and bits of fish for Baldissera if you want them—those over there."

Biagio nodded and slowly filled his pockets, his old lips mumbling soundlessly in the same way as those of his horse— some people said Baldissera had started it and his owner had caught the habit, and some that it was the other way about. "It's true then? If Quong's boy told you?"

"Of course it's true." Biagio had doubted everything he was told since that terrible morning forty-five years ago and a week after Caporetto when the Carabinieri captain had gone down the ranks of soldiers, counting in tens, while his policemen seized each tenth man and pulled him from the line to straddle a chair with his back to the firing squad. The captain had tapped Biagio—by mistake, for he was number nine—and it was only after a grudging recount, during which Biagio and his friend Francesco Dozzi, the real number ten, had stared at each other in wordless, ashen horror that Biagio had stumbled back into line while Francesco had been dragged away to the chairs. Since then Biagio had required considerable confirmation of even the most self-evident fact—even death.

"What will happen to this place, then?"

Crocifissa began to pick up the scattered cans of meat. She did not build a crenellated tower as Gigi would have done but arranged them in a squat block like a fortress. "I suppose he'll sell it as a building site."

"The nephew?"

"He wanted to before. He tried to make the *padrone,* but . . ."

"Perhaps it won't get left to the nephew."

"There is no one else—not really. Only a married niece and the *padrone* would never . . ."

"The Municipality may not let him."

"Pull it down? They *want* it down. They tried to make the *padrone* do it, only . . ."

"Then they ought to find us somewhere else. If they go and . . ."

"Ought, ought, ought!" Crocifissa sighed tiredly. "They'll say we must wait our turn. There are all those people down by the docks, for a start." She thought momentarily of that conglomeration of wooden and corrugated zinc hovels crowded in hideous squalor on the old bomb sites opposite the Mercato Ittico; six, seven, eight people sleeping jammed together on mattresses on the floors. When one of them died the others continued to sleep with the corpse until it could be removed. Painted in huge, sprawling letters on the wall that hemmed them in a ghetto far filthier and more crowded than any in mediaeval Poland were the despairing words WE ALSO ARE ITALIAN CITIZENS AND NEED HOMES. They had not been given them, however.

For a few moments the old cabdriver stood mumbling his lips, frowning undecidedly with that querulous mixture of resentment and suspicion which so often sours the faces of the elderly poor. He watched Crocifissa rearrange a further pile of canned sardines and then clearing his throat noisily prepared to spit. Since he could not spit in the shop he went outside and spat, and once outside he climbed onto the driving seat of his groaning *carròzza,* flicked his whip over Baldissera's skinny rump and clip-clopped off through the pools of yellow lamplight.

He would not go far, as Crocifissa knew; only to the south side of the square to retail the news to his old friend Tenerini in the tobacco shop, and soon everybody would know—know that Ercole Sanbrenedetto was dead and that the decomposing building which had stood so long, sagging, discolored and flanked by bomb ruins, on the west side of the *piazza* was to go at last. For go it would, of course. Privately Crocifissa had no doubts about that and as chief tenant-caretaker-rent-collector—of the dead old man, let alone being his ex-cook and widow of his one-time manservant, she knew more about the Sanbrenedetto family, or what was left of it, than anyone else in the locality.

2

A *filobus* from Poggioreale and Barra, its swept-back twin antennae hissing and sparking along the overhead wires, rolled up to the middle of the *piazza* and stopping opposite the urinal disgorged a crowd of overalled men and boys, sweaty, sulky and exhausted from their long day's work in the heat and fumes of the methane factories. They fanned out slowly across the *piazza*, fishing in their pockets for cigarettes, unfolding the *Corriere dello Spòrt,* exchanging shouts of farewell, their heavy boots clattering over the rough flagstones. The majority made for the Via Buonuomini which led direct to the Piazza San Francesco and the Porta Capuana, but a handful moved over to Tenerini's and four or five who lived either in the *piazza* itself or in one of the adjoining alleys wandered across to the shop. *"Buona sera, Crocifissa"*—*"Buona sera, buona sera"*; dark faces smiled tiredly, square, work-roughened hands were thrust into pockets for handfuls of small change, and the ranged stock was given the careful, considering scrutiny of people who knew the value of a ten-lire piece and had few enough of them to spend. At home—in the small, overfurnished single rooms which signified "home" to the great majority of Neapolitan workers—these men's womenfolk would have the evening meal ready and waiting and in the main it would be substantial enough—thick soup of fish or beans, piled plates of *pasta,* perhaps even a stew of cheap meat and vegetables—but it was up to the men themselves to provide, if they felt they could afford it, the *antipasto,* the first small course of sliced salami and cucumber, of smoked ham or eel or pickled peppers. It was in preparation for just these people that Crocifissa had turned the two-kilo can of preserved anchovies into a basin an hour ago. And indeed the remaining handful were soon sold to the first customers and those behind looked disappointedly at the oily basin. "No more *alici* tonight? You've sold out quickly, Crocifissa." Crocifissa merely shrugged and smiled. She would have liked to have explained the whole story of the anchovies with voluble and righteous indignation and to have received the equally voluble, righteous and indignant sympathy of her customers. But Gigi was beside her now, small, damp, clean and subdued in a new white apron and she could not embarrass the poor child in front of these neighbors.

The sales were all very small—a single hectogram was the average—and the profit was consequently tiny. Crocifissa's pudgy hands were becoming a little stiff for the manipulation of such miniature packages but Gigi made them up with neatness and dispatch, working silently, solemnly, quickly, trying somehow to atone for the loss of Crocifissa's fish which, in fact, he felt a thousand times more keenly than she did—an agonizing ache of distress in his heart.

A mendicant monk, a bearded Capuchin in a shabby brown habit, pressed in among the customers and smilingly opened a sack already half full of battered fruit and vegetables from the Porta Capuana. With a brief sigh Crocifissa, engaged in slicing mortadella for an elderly workman, thrust a can of pickled gherkins at Gigi, who quickly dropped it into the sack. A hand nearly black with grime was lifted to pat his face and the beard parted in a great gash of a grin. "Thank you, my daughter. God bless you." "And you, father," Crocifissa replied automatically, thinking that she had just parted with nearly half the profits of the last fifteen minutes' sales and trying to reprove herself for the thought—after all, the monks were God's servants.

All too soon the modest stream of customers thinned to a trickle as the workmen sought their homes and their dinners and in a little while the shop was empty. Crocifissa turned to Gigi who was cleaning the long sausage knife on a dirty cloth. "All right. That will be all tonight. You can go now, Gigi." While he was taking off his apron and folding it carefully she took the knife and cut a thick slice of coarse, rubbery brawn— a mass of skin and offal set solidly in glassy brown gelatine of the consistency of Indiarubber which the Neapolitan poor called *ciccìoli*—and thrust it into a split loaf. She pushed it into the child's hand and patted his shoulder. "Off you go now. And don't forget what I told you—about your language."

"*Grazie assai, signora*. Am I to come tomorrow?"

"Of course, *carino*."

Gigi gave her a quick smile of gratitude and left the shop. As he went out into the street clutching his big sandwich she saw that he was limping slightly—perhaps those boys had hurt him after all. For a moment she thought of calling him back, knowing well that his own mother would do nothing—she was the sort who would hardly notice if Gigi came home with a wooden leg —but the child had disappeared before she had a chance to move after him and someone else was entering the shop. This was a girl in her late teens, dark-haired, disheveled and handsome in the traditional, full-figured, heavy-breasted Neapolitan way. She carried a sleeping baby in her arms and her firm, round belly pressing tautly against her cotton frock showed that she was soon to have another. She smiled at Crocifissa with almost as much timidity as Gigi but said only one word, "Renato?"

"Not yet. But he's often late, isn't he? Perhaps he's got some overtime." The girl shook her head. "He hardly ever gets that— not paid overtime. But there are all the societies and committees and things. They're always calling sudden meetings after work."

Crocifissa pursed her lips but made no answer. She disapproved of Renato's political work but the young couple were her closest neighbors—they had a single room in the first house beyond the bomb ruins on the left—and she seldom criticized other inhabitants of the *piazza*. Instead she pushed the single, wooden chair forward and the girl sank down in it gratefully. "He does too much. I'm always telling him that. And it's not only the works committees he's on but all other things as well. But I just thought he might have come in and then gone over to Tenerini's to fill in his coupon."

Crocifissa smiled. "But he always goes home to you first, doesn't he?"

The girl laughed apologetically. "Yes. But in the evenings, when I'm waiting upstairs—sometimes I begin to think of accidents and then I get worried and the time goes so slowly. . . ."

"You should buy a clock. But Renato's just as bad. As soon

as he gets out of the *filobus* he rushes over here and shouts, 'Is Rosalba all right? Has she been here? Has she gone home?' He knows perfectly well that you're waiting with his dinner."

The child in the girl's arms awoke with a small cry and at once she opened the front of her dress and pulled out one big, milk-heavy breast.

Crocifissa said mildly, "It's said to be best to feed them at regular hours. Foreigners do so, I'm told."

"Do they?" Rosalba looked up over the sucking child with surprised interest. "We never do that here. It seems a strange way. Don't the babies cry a lot? Filomena hardly cries at all."

"Cry a lot? Foreign babies do seem to cry a lot, yes. At least the ones I've ever seen did. But I fed Dino whenever he was hungry. The trouble was, I wasn't like you; I had very little milk. I was the thin sort when I was young. You wouldn't think it now to look at me but when I was twenty I was just as slim as —as Signora Giansante."

Rosalba shook her head sadly. "And hers is due in October, isn't it? And without her husband here or anything—poor creature. Renato was only saying yesterday how much he would like to help; to start what he calls 'popular agitation'."

"*Oh Santo Cielo!*" Crocifissa looked shocked. "He mustn't do that whatever happens. Iole Giansante has relatives— friends, too—who could easily do all that was possible if—"

"But they won't, will they? They won't help her at all."

"Not her immediate relatives, perhaps, but she has many acquaintances in high positions. She's always writing to friends in Rome. And she gets replies from them, too. I see all the letters that come here. The postman gives them to me—naturally. And every week there are at least—" She broke off, listening.

From close by outside came an odd rhythmic noise, something heard through, rather than above, the multiplicity of jangling sounds and cries of the hot city night; a clank of metal striking stone followed by a soft yet penetrating thud, clank and thud . . . clank and thud. Crocifissa and the girl in the chair looked up together as something emerged slowly from the half-dark and began to cross the illuminated patch of roadway in front of the shop. It was a creature that at first sight could not be taken for human at all, but merely another of the bulging ragged sacks of old mattress stuffing which were always being wheeled to obscure destinations through the alleys of the *bassifondi*. But there were no wheels below this shapeless bundle, only two crumpled, sliding, blackish pads, and the jumble of dirty gray stuffing that broke and fell from its neck was a mass of tangled human hair. It was bent in the middle—completely bent at right angles—so that it progressed head first, the top half of its body horizontal with the roadway half a meter below. Its back was one high hump, the tousled head a neckless ball set between shoulders which lifted above invisible ears, and it propelled itself forward with a short stick padded with the head of an old mop while its other sooty claw grasped the handle of the battered zinc bucket which clashed rhythmically, in alternate time with the mop, over the *piperno* blocks.

"La Gobba"—in Naples, birthplace of Pulcinello, there were hundreds of hunchbacks, but in the whole Quarter of San Lorenzo—and in parts of San Giuseppe, Pendino and Porto as well—"La Gobba" meant this one only; this untouchably filthy old creature who thumped and clanked slowly and with a peculiar, obscurely frightening purposefulness up and down the alleys and across the *piazza* in search of the cigarette butts which she sold by the hundred to the buyers at the Porta Capuana. Despite the fact that she had been an inhabitant of the Quarter for longer than most people could remember, she had no home but slept scantily in various nooks and crannies of the ancient buildings, grimy holes and cracks into which a normally shaped person could probably not have forced his body but into which she would wriggle rapidly like an earwig, drawing in her bucket and mop after her, vanishing completely into the fetid, clammy dark. Sometimes she made mysterious disappearances for days on end. No one discovered where she went on these occasions but she invariably returned as suddenly as she had gone and as unchanged, with the same shapeless rags, the same bucket, the same mop.

No other city in the civilized world would have tolerated her presence for a day and the few foreigners who visited the Quarter often complained indignantly; it was disgraceful, they said —and they were met by the inevitable smile and shrug, the inevitable answer "She does no harm." In fact the inhabitants

of San Lorenzo were wrong, for La Gobba was as much a menace to their health as the continual misuse of the public urinals
or the heaps of flyblown garbage in the alleys and, though they
knew nothing of sanitation, the San Lorenzini knew, at least,
that they were lying to the foreigners, for they themselves believed that La Gobba had the *malòcchio*—the evil eye—and a
consquently broad capacity for occult evil.

This evening as she passed the shop front Crocifissa
reached below the counter and touched the pair of cow's horns
—painted the traditional scarlet by Gennaro—that lay there
out of sight; then remembered, too late, the disapproval of Father Ambrosio and crossed herself repentantly, kissing her
thumb. Rosalba had given a gasp of distress and whipped
round in her chair, shielding her baby from the dark radiations
of woe and dread which emanated from La Gobba, and quickly
made the sign of the horns with the first and last fingers of her
left hand. "Do you—do you think she looked at Filomena?"

"She never looks at anyone—only at the ground for cigarette ends. I do not think she can turn her head."

"I had a cousin—she lived in the country near Campobasso
—and my uncle told me that once, on the road—"

Brusquely Crocifissa said, "Don't be stupid, Rosalba! You're
starting to talk like an old Abruzzi peasant woman. You're
young. We live in the twentieth century; you've had a school
education and your husband's a Communist and doesn't believe
in God—or *says* he doesn't. Yet you still talk of the evil eye."

But surprisingly Rosalba neither blushed nor looked
abashed. Instead she said, "I don't see why not. Those things
have nothing to do with each other."

Crocifissa was obscurely shocked. "But *you're* a good Catholic, aren't you, girl?"

"Of course." But Rosalba sounded unconvinced. On an impulse Crocifissa reached up above the shelf where the red hearts
of the holy pictures throbbed rhythmically and took down the
wooden crucifix. She approached Rosalba and laid the carved
figure against the baby's forehead. "There!" And now Rosalba
got up smiling. "I must go. I've a lot of mending to do. Tell
Renato the dinner's been ready more than half an hour. Make
him hurry home."

"I will, I will."

✦§ 3

RENATO ran in ten minutes later. Crocifissa was serving a small girl with *cicciòli*—it was amazing how much the children liked it: she herself when young had detested the gristly, rubbery stuff; but then she had had a fastidious appetite, she remembered—and the heavy-shouldered, grinning young workman had to wait, teetering impatiently on his toes, until she had finished. Even so he remembered to wish her good evening—a thing Gennaro invariably forgot—addressing her as *"signora."*

"And Rosalba? She's been here?"

"Yes. And she tells you to hurry. Your dinner's been ready more than half an hour."

He smiled widely, pushing a hand through his thick, rumpled hair and Crocifissa added, "She was in here with Filomena only a few minutes ago. She is progressing well—the baby."

Renato nodded, pleased yet a little impatient. "Yes, yes. And there will be another soon."

"I know."

They looked at each other with complicity; the young man, strong and stocky in his open-necked, sweat-stained workshirt with its red sickle-and-hammer badge above the breast pocket, and the fat old woman in her shiny black—both thinking the same thing and both knowing each other's thoughts. Suddenly they both laughed and Crocifissa said, "Every night, Renato?"

"Every single night. Two—three times on Sundays." There was no embarrassment in the young man's voice, only a warm, contented pride and he lightly tapped the front of his trousers as a jovial well-fed man will pat his bulging stomach.

Crocifissa shared his approval. "You're a true young bull, aren't you?" And indeed he did look like a bull, standing there in the bright light of the shop front, squarely heavy, a little short in the leg but well-built and very powerful, his muscled arms bulging below the tightly rolled sleeves of his shirt. Crocifissa felt a glow of affection for him. Despite his Communism of which, as a devout Catholic, she disapproved deeply, she knew him to be a hardworking, honest boy and a good, if somewhat officious, neighbor. He was the ideal mate for Rosalba, too; no wonder they were so happy together and could never have enough of each other. She said, "The next one—let us hope it will be a boy."

"Senz' altro!" Renato thrust a hand into his pocket, his eyes roaming around the shop. *"Lonza,"* he said at last, *"one etto,* please."

Crocifissa reached down the smoked pork fillet dangling from its hook in the ceiling and sliced it neatly with her long knife. She weighed and wrapped the pile of wafer-thin pieces and as Renato held out a pocketful of small change she closed his hand back over the coins. "No, no— I don't want to be paid."

"But *signora,* please!" He sounded genuinely distressed. "If you won't let me pay you how can I continue to come here?"

"Just for tonight, anyway. You and Rosalba are my friends and one likes to— Anyway, it is nothing."

"It is a hundred grammes of *lonza,*" he reminded her practically. "You are too kind to us."

She smiled. "Well, I may not be living here much longer" and saw with a painful pleasure the sudden shock and dismay written clearly on his sunburned face.

"Not live *here!* But you've always lived here. Why—where else should you go?"

"The *padrone's* dead."

"The *padrone?*" Never very quick mentally, Renato looked puzzled and Crocifissa saw that for a moment he thought she meant his own *padrone*—the managing director of the great *ITOLGAS* plant out at Poggioreale.

"Old Signor Sanbrenedetto, who owned this place. You must have heard of him surely—old Don Ercole? He lived over on the other side beyond Pescara. Anyway he died yesterday and now the property passes to someone else—his nephew, I imagine."

"Oh—I understand. And that will alter things for you, you think? The new owner will want changes? Want to raise the rents? In that case . . ."

Crocifissa shook her head. "I don't think Signor Giuseppe Sanbrenedetto will raise the rents. I think he will consider selling the whole property; this house and the ruined ones on either side."

"But"—Renato stared at her stupidly—"who could possibly want to buy them? Look at the state of this place. And then— bomb ruins!"

"For a site," said Crocifissa a little impatiently. "A building site. They'd pull this place down—which wouldn't be difficult for it's on the point of falling down of its own accord—and clear away the remains of the others. Then they'd put up something new. Offices, a small factory, a hotel—anything. You should remember that we are right in the center of Naples. This site is very valuable, I daresay."

Weighing the little packet of *lonza* in one hand Renato said angrily, "And turn you out. And the Quongs and—and Signora Giansante?"

"And Biagio and his horse," added Crocifissa smiling. "Don't forget them. Biagio was around here earlier about that."

Renato grinned reluctantly. "But they'll have to find you somewhere else. I mean there's you and this shop; and old Quong can't work now and Gennaro's only a boy, and the Signora's husband . . ."

"It won't be easy. We're an odd lot."

"Then they should let you alone!" His voice was sullenly angry. "It is always the same with the capitalists—they don't care what happens to anyone except themselves. This Giuseppe Sanbrenedetto should be made to—"

"Signor Giuseppe is not at all a bad man. I was his nurse when he was a baby. He has had a hard life, too. He will do what he can."

"He'd better! We can make trouble enough here if necessary. I know you don't like Communists, Signora Crocifissa, but we'd never treat you like this. Under Communism you'd be taken proper care of—all the time."

Crocifissa smiled slightly, a little ironically, glancing at his hot, angry face. "Yes, Renato, I know. An Old Woman's Home for me; an Old Man's Home for Biagio; an Institute for Incurables for Quong; some sort of apprentice school or young worker's unit for Gennaro—and the glue factory for poor Baldissera. I would rather take my chance as things are."

"*I* wouldn't do that," said Renato sulkily. "And anyway—"

"I know *you* wouldn't." Crocifissa sighed a little distractedly and rubbed her forehead above the left eye where a small neuralgic pain throbbed insistently. "It's just that we're not going to be easy to help, I'm afraid. But I'm grateful to you, Renato—I really am. You're a good boy—always wanting to help people. Rosalba told me what you said about trying to do something for Signora Giansante, but really, you mustn't interfere there. Not unless she asks you, anyway. You might only make things worse."

Renato nodded somberly. "Yes. I only said it to Rosalba. I didn't really think that . . ." But at the mention of his wife's name the bitterness left his voice and he grinned suddenly, disarmingly. "I must go. Or she'll think I've been killed in an accident. Good night, Signora Crocifissa"—he held up the little packet of sliced meat—"and true thanks for this!"

◄§ 4

AFTER he had left the shop there was silence for a moment; even the ordinary evening noises of the *piazza* seemed temporarily hushed. Crocifissa lifted the cheese which had rolled into the gutter during Gigi's fracas with the youths and found that the bottom was embedded with sharp pieces of grit. She began to dig them out with a skewer, but even so half the cheese remained pitted with holes and gashes; that meant that she would have to sell it at reduced price. An old woman whom she only knew vaguely by sight tottered in and bought half a kilo of *fagioli cotti*, the big yellow beans which simmered for long hours every morning on Crocifissa's kitchen stove, and chaffered, purse in hand, over the price. Clemente's youngest—he could not have been a day over four—ran up breathlessly with a note in his father's spidery writing asking for two hundred grams of Hag caffeine-free coffee. There was no money enclosed but that was all right; Clemente never forgot to pay his debts—any more than he forgot to claim them. Raimondo Tenerini strolled óver and stood, two hundred pounds and six feet two inches of Bersagliere, making the shop seem lilliputian by comparison, while Crocifissa made him a big sandwich of the inevitable *cicciòli*. Fair-haired, pink-faced, he looked little different at twenty-one from the huge, lumbering boy of eighteen he had so recently been. Though the army had smartened him up and taught him how to carry himself he was as shy as ever and his large appetite, which was surely only natural, embarrassed him keenly. Even asking Crocifissa for the sandwich was an effort for him. He must have known about old Sanbrenedetto's death for Biagio practically lived in his father's shop, but he said nothing about it.

It was getting late now; not really late by Neapolitan standards, of course, but still . . . Crocifissa moved about the shop adjusting the stock and the price cards, telling herself that she was becoming as bad now, in her old age, as she had been thirty years ago when she could never let Dino out of her sight without imagining him crushed under the wheels of a bus, trampled below the hoofs of a runaway horse or felled to the flagstones by a falling tile. Yes, she had been an anxious, clucking hen of a mother, she remembered, smiling at herself. It was probably because Dino had been her only child and after his birth she had known that she could never have another. Dear Dino— funny little boy, with his odd questions, his serious smile. It was nearly twenty years now since the *Bartolomeo Colleoni* had gone down in fire and smoke and the roar of exploding ammunition under the crashing salvoes of the British cruser *Sydney*; the news had nearly killed her at the time—had, in fact, killed a part of her, or so she always thought. If Dino had been alive today, he would . . . And then she heard the unmistakable sound of the hearse's approach, the labored grinding of the old engine, the rattle of the great corner lanterns and the gear change as it slowed to enter the garage next to Quong's workroom. She waited, motionless, behind the counter and in less than a minute Gennaro was in the doorway smiling widely, a little shyly, the lamplight glinting on his uncombed black hair, bringing back memories of that first entrance five years ago when he had come in out of the night, a little boy of eleven in black clothes clutching a yellow canary in a tiny cage, to fill the empty void in Crocifissa's life which Dino had left there so long before.

She moved round the counter, her heart swelling as always at the sight of him, noting with all her aroused maternal instincts that his smile was a tired one, that his shoulders sagged wearily under his bright shirt. "My dear—you're safe home! I wondered . . ."

"How is Quong?"

"Quite well. I've been in to see him several times." Despite herself Crocifissa felt the small pang of jealousy which Gennaro's obsessive affection for his grandfather always aroused in her. "He's had his supper. I've got yours ready for you. I expect you need it."

"*Senz' altro.*" His smile widened and she put her hand out and lifting his chin—they were the same height now but it was a relic of the days when he had been small—kissed him lightly. "*Poverino* . . . it was such a long way."

He nodded somberly and she saw at once that something was wrong. "What happened? What is it, *caro mio?*"

For a second he stood silently with his eyes lowered, then his shoulders rose and fell in an abrupt, hopeless gesture of despair, his hands opened. "The police."

"They—found out?"

"It was my fault." He shook his head and began to explain with a weary anger, with that unyouthful bitterness which Crocifissa knew as the corollary of his more frequent moods of excited ebullience. She listened, her eyes wide with distress, understanding too well what this, the second blow in less than two months, must mean to him; half hoping that now, at last, he would see reason and half fearing that he might.

". . . and I never knew about not stopping—that it was illegal. But of course it was stupid. I ought to have known." He stiffened suddenly, turning toward the door. "Crocifissa—did you hear that?" Something had moved, had tumbled, rattling, in the narrow lumber room which, separating the shop and the funeral parlor, was used by both.

"Only a bit of your wood falling, Gennà." Silence. Then the scrape of footsteps passed the front of the shop and turning they saw a beggar shuffling by. A gaunt, unshaven face stared hungrily in at the piled foodstuffs and for a moment Crocifissa's eyes met the glance of a pair of fierce black ones before the man had moved off into the shadows. She shrugged; the Quarter was full of beggars who hung furtively around such shops as hers, edging in occasionally to ask for stale bread or damaged food that might otherwise be thrown out. But with a sudden exclamation Gennaro swung around to the door and stared out into the alternate pools of darkness and lamplight which fell over the ruins beyond the house. He came back grinning and shaking his head.

"That man—I didn't realize it at once—he was wearing Quong's old overalls!"

"No!"

"*Vero!* He must have gone into the workroom and taken them off the hook behind the door. Well—it doesn't matter."

"As long as he took nothing else. Hadn't you better go and see?"

Gennaro shook his head "There's nothing else to take except a few planks, and he hadn't got those. Anyway he's gone now. I'll look tomorrow."

"Then I'll shut the shop." Crocifissa took a long iron hook from beside the wall and began to pull the rolled metal shutter down into place across the open shop front. When she turned from thrusting home the bolts, Gennaro was leaning against the counter smiling at her sleepily, his hands in the pockets of his jeans, and there was something about his stance, the loose, easy, relaxed posture of youth, that worked the old invariable spell. Her eyes met his own slightly almond-shaped ones—and for a moment the years fell away and he became Dino. It was a metamorphosis which had occurred often before and not always with Gennaro, although he was its most constant medium. Any dark-haired boy up to eighteen was apt, for a single, tranced second, to change into Dino. A look, the sudden smile of youth, or one of the many uncertain, half-timid, half-brusque gestures of adolescence—any of these was enough to effect that stabbing, bittersweet transformation of what was someone else's into what had been hers. But tonight, deeper than the warm ache of love that filled her, was the bleak realization that the darkness was gathering closer. She had hoped to see Gennaro grow up, to watch him pass through his nineteenth year where Dino had stopped so abruptly and become the man Dino would otherwise have become, exorcising in his progress the ghost of the boy whose photograph hung in the next room. But the sale and destruction of this crazy old house would prevent that. The loss of the house would inevitably mean the loss of Gennaro—and then for her there would be nothing left at all, forever.

"Quong's"

～§ 1

PERUGIA, waking as the first rays of sun slanted through the window and slid between the brass wires of his cage, blinked rapidly, stretched one yellow wing then the other, bowed twice, hopped to the next perch and began to sing. As the sun heightened, his song rose quickly from a muted chirp to a high, sustained twittering and then to a soaring, piercing trill.

Gennaro stirred and his eyes opened to narrow slits. Colored Chinese dreams blew about his bed, billowed out, ballooning into the air, fading into the past night. For a long minute he lay frowning up at the cracked ceiling remembering yesterday in a mixture of blue seascape and self-reproach, mountain scenery and chagrin. There would be a fine which he could not pay and they would prevent him from driving the hearse—without which it would be more than ever difficult to continue running the business. The hearse was his most important asset. People who would not have dreamt of burying a relation in one of his cut-rate coffins were quite content to hire his hearse. It had been his own idea to lay off the last driver, Suzzo, and take on the job himself. Not only had Suzzo been most unsatisfactory—he was a well-known atheist and a drunken one at that—but the payment of his wages had strained the Quong business to its limit. Twice—once in March and once in April—Suzzo had failed to arrive at the appointed time and Gennaro, desperate in case of a lost commission, had put on the old drunkard's funereal driving coat and cap and himself collected the deceased and headed the procession slowly, carefully through the streets to the Capodichino cemetery. It had been so simple—the police, far from questioning him, had cleared a way through the crowded streets and saluted respectfully as he went by—that he had seen no reason not to continue the practice permanently. Suzzo had been fired after an insulting, drunken interview during which he had used such obscene expressions about Quong and his grandson that the latter, beside himself, with rage, had threatened the old man with a chisel; and Gennaro had become the hearse driver.

It was the last of many such self-appointments for he was also managing director, sales representative ("Funeral Arrangements by QUONG'S—Decorous, Dignified, Modestly Priced") and carpenter, wreath-maker and general handyman in the workshop. He *was* "Quong's" in fact and no one could have been more deeply aware of it. That "Quong's Funeral Pomps," even in its best days, had been merely a small dirty shop run by an old immigrant Chinese with the help of a little casual labor meant nothing to Gennaro. To him "Quong's" was "the firm," "our business," "us"—and whether in the hearse, dressed in the drivers greasy, gold-braided coat and cap, or attempting to sell cheap funeral insurance from door to door wearing his lavender-colored suit with socks and tie to match, or sawing and planing down in the coffin shop clad in old blue dungarees, he always thought of himself as a plural entity and spoke of "we." Once he had even been overheard, answering a telephone call in Tenerini's, saying that "we" would send round "our chief representative, Signor Gualtierra, without delay," and now Gennaro could never buy a cigarette or one of the black Toscana cigars which Quong used to smoke without being asked where Signor Gualtierra was presently working.

Gennaro kicked off the sheet and lay in only his underpants watching a bar of early light cross his bare feet. He was waiting for the sun to reach the white horse and considering whom he might employ to drive the hearse at today's funeral. He wondered momentarily whether Raimondo Tenerini would do it. Raimondo had an army license and could drive a truck; what was more, he would do the job as a neighborly favor and for the fun of boasting to his comrades about it afterwards. But hearses should not be driven like army lorries. Raimondo might forget

the correct speed and any extra pressure on the accelerator
could start the mourners and wreath-bearers practically running to keep up, thus ruining the dignity of the proceedings and
jeopardizing the future of the firm. What was much more important, Suzzo's old coat and cap were far too small for Raimondo's massive figure. No, Gennaro came down regretfully
but firmly on the side of employing a paid driver. He might perhaps pick up a fairly reliable man for a thousand lire from
amongst the unemployed or semi-employed who haunted Clemente's fish eating-house on the Piazza San Francesco.

The sunlight—moving across the windowsill over a few old
books, the remnants of Gennaro's childhood, *Il Gatto degli
Stivali,* D'Amicis's *Cuore,* Verga's *Mastro Don Gesualdo,* his
stamp collection and *Nuda Ogni Giorno* (the story of an artist's
model which Savoldi, the timber merchant, had given him in the
hope of a later discussion of his sex life)—at last reached the
Chinese horse. And then the opaque jade was transformed into
clouded, icy fire—a sunburst of white light that was at once a
glittering sparkle and a frigid glow. The horse, rearing on its
back legs from the pedestal of rosewood, arched its neck, tossing its head and pawing at the sky, and there was nothing about
it of the lean fine-boned Arab or the heavy, gentle beast of the
European countryside: slit-eyed, thick-necked and short-backed,
it was all Mongolian, wild, savage and free. A horse of the sighing red deserts and the Tartar steppes—the last of a dozen
pieces of such work which Quong had brought with him from
his native Pekin more than half a century ago. Gennaro kept it
on the windowsill, finding that the stain of even the ugliest
dream could be erased by the delight of its dawn-irradiated
beauty.

Now he rose and padded over to the corner where, in distress-
ing contrast to the blazing jade horse, a cheap, mass-produced
plaster statuette of the Virgin stood on a shelf below a wooden
crucifix. He dropped onto both knees and sank back to sit on
his heels, his hands folded in his lap, his head raised, staring
up at the plaster figure. It was a curiously oriental posture for
Christian prayer. *"Ave Maria, gratia plena, Dominus tecum
benedicta tu in mulieribus et benedictus fructus ventris tui, Jesus . . ."* Ave, Pater, Gloria—Gennaro, unlike most other
laymen, prayed in singsong Latin like a priest.

But then he had been reared by priests. For when, some seventeen years ago, Quong's son Fulvio, wearing the gray-green of an Italian soldier, had left a Ferrara staging depot on his way to war and death in Russia, he had also left his seed in the body of a local girl whose scandalized peasant parents had subsequently forced her to hand the baby over to a convent foundling's home. Gennaro's first six years had been spent under the care of nuns, the next five under that of monks. Both had been extremely good to him and so at the age of eleven, and as soon as he found out he had anywhere to run to, he had run away.

It was an administrative oversight on the part of an overworked lay brother, burdened by a colleague's illness, which had caused an office door to be left open, a confidential file to be lying on a table, just when Gennaro was passing along the corridor. But two or three pages turned in alphabetical order had shown him that "Gualtierra, Gennaro" was the illegitimate son of a fallen soldier named Quong whose sole living relative, traced through army administration channels, was his father, L. P. Quong, undertaker, resident of the San Lorenzo Quarter of Naples. "Gualtierra, Emilia Maria" and her relatives were also listed, but Gennaro was as uninterested in her as he presumed she was in him. He knew only that she had handed him over to the Church and—since the monks believed in a kindly, guarded, but sensible frankness with their charges on such matters—he also knew why.

Two evenings later, when the monk on duty at the front door was absent, Gennaro had slipped out of the Collegio di San Francesco into the misty lamplight of a quiet Ferrara street along which nothing but a peasant's cart, in from the Bassa with a load of cabbages, creaked gently through the damp winter twilight. Standing hesitantly at the bottom of the Corso della Giovecca a few minutes later he had been offered a lift by a truck driver who was taking a cargo of heavy steel wire to Perugia and whose mate was staying the night with his family in Ferrara. Gennaro had admitted at once that he was escaping from a monastic college and the truck driver, a fervent anticlerical of Communist sympathies, had agreed that it was an excellent thing to do. Gennaro had slept all night in the bunk behind the front seats and wakened next morning in Perugia where the truck driver had thrust five hundred lire into his pocket, told him where to get a lift to Naples, shaken his hand warmly and driven away.

Within half an hour Gennaro was on his way to Naples in the station wagon of a traveling salesman dealing in dog foods and bird seed. The entire back of the car was taken up with packets of dog biscuits, cans of balanced meat diet and packages of seed, but upon all these rested a multitude of tiny cages piled to the roof and each containing a twittering canary—a private form of enterprise on the part of the salesman. He was a burly, gray-haired man, ruminative rather than garrulous, and though from time to time he cast speculative glances at the small boy beside him who with no luggage, with apparently nothing but the black jersey and trousers in which he was dressed, wanted to go all the way to Naples, he asked no questions but instead relied upon oblique remarks which shortly brought out Gennaro's story. As the car rose and fell, swooping along the Tuscan hills toward L'Aquila and the Central Apennines, the salesman listened and nodded and began to look perturbed.

"You're sure that this Signor Quong *is* your grandfather?"

"Yes. I've seen it written down in the book they keep."

"And that he's still alive?"

"They'd have crossed him out and put the date if he'd died. They'd done that with his wife—not with him."

"And—you think he'll be pleased to see you?"

"Of course. I'm his grandson," had replied Gennaro simply.

That evening after dark they reached Naples and, with considerably more difficulty and after much misdirection due to its recent change of name, the Piazza Vittime Civili di Guerra. When eventually they drew up before the half-ruined building on its west side and Gennaro put a hand tentatively on the door handle the salesman stopped him abruptly. "Wait in the car. I'll find out if your grandfather's at home." Gennaro had nodded politely and had waited confidently in the dark car until the salesman had returned, relief apparent on his florid face. "It's quite true. Signor Quong does live here. He's out at present but there's an old woman in the shop next door who will look after you until he gets back. Come on—" Then, suddenly moved by a new thought, he had plunged one arm into the back of his vehicle, brought out a canary in a tiny traveling cage and pushed it gently into Gennaro's hands. "You've never had one before, have you? It's a male. You'll need a bigger cage for him as soon as you can find one. Come, now. . . ." He had put a hand on Gennaro's shoulder and led him into the shop. "This is him— Gennaro Gualtierra." . . . And Gennaro had stood blinking in the bright light, a black-dressed boy holding a bright yellow bird in his hands, while an old woman had risen smiling from among the piled groceries, lifting a big cat from her lap, advancing toward him saying, "Gennaro? That is your name? Then you are doubly welcome in Naples, child, for this is the city of your patron saint."

⊸§ 2

IN a ground-floor room on the other side of Croci-fissa's shop, a dark, untidy, malodorous cave, old Biagio opened his eyes, groaned and sighed. He had been dreaming about the war, the 1915-1918 war, for he never thought about the events of 1940-1945 by the same name; then there had been fighting of a sort, it was true, fighting shockingly mismanaged and ending in national disaster—but not *war*. And now, as the rattle of Austrian machine guns along the Isonzo disclosed itself to be the passage of a donkey cart across the cobbles outside, he groaned again and swung his legs from his tousled blankets. Biagio never used sheets; even in the height of summer it was possible down here in the dank coolness of his cavern to sleep with a blanket. His blood was thin; sheets needed washing which cost good money and it was simple enough to affect to scorn them as un-soldierly.

Biagio's attitude to soldiers, the army, all military life, was, like that of his close friend and wartime comrade Napoleone Tenerini, ambivalent and consistently contradictory. Both old men alternately cursed their military pasts as being the ruin of their lives and the damnation of their souls, yet both took every opportunity of talking endlessly of the campaigns of the Carso, the Isonzo and the Piave, of bragging over their exploits and of displaying faded, tattered photographs of themselves as young men in uniform. In their cups they sang bawdy soldier songs and boasted of apocryphal feats of bravery. When sober they became maudlin and self-pitying, informing everyone that they had saved the nation, ruining their health and prospects in the process, and received neither recompense nor recognition. They were a couple of rather tiresome old men and even Father Ambrosio who, in common with most Neapolitan priests, tolerated every sort of eccentricity amongst his parishioners, had been heard to refer to them sardonically as "our two national heroes."

Biagio had little dressing to do since he habitually went to bed in his trousers. Pouring himself a glass of wine he rasped his other hand over his bristly gray chin, pondered on whether to get a shave and decided to wait until tomorrow. He was well aware that his appearance discouraged possible customers but even if he had remedied this there was nothing he could do about Baldissera and little enough to the old cab. Nonetheless when, at busy times of the day or during the evening rush hour, there was no other cab or taxi available he was reluctantly hired. After all, he represented "transport," and though a passenger might not accomplish his journey in Biagio's *carròzza* much more quickly than upon his own feet he could at least perform it sitting down. Biagio was well aware that his passengers regarded him, in the last resort, as only slightly preferable to the shove and jostle of the crowded sidewalks and he reacted accordingly with a surly taciturnity and a propensity to become quarrelsome over the fare. In a way it was his revenge against the world which had tried—and very nearly succeeded—in shooting him after Caporetto.

When he had finished his wine he threw on his driving coat, picked up his whip and opening the adjoining door, went into Baldissera's windowless stable. Since this place was in perpetual darkness Baldissera was asleep. Of all the inhabitants of the building Baldissera was the last to awake in the mornings as Perugia, high up in Gennaro's sun-filled attic, was the first. Now, with the stable door onto the street flung open, the old horse awoke with a groan and a sigh that duplicated its master's. It, too, must once have been young—a furry foal, all legs, frolicking in some pasture of the Campania—but now, looking at its swayback, thin neck and gaunt haunches, it was impossible to believe it. Biagio grumbled at it tonelessly and it snuffled a rubbery snort in response; then together the two old creatures moved blinkingly out into the sunlight.

ᥣ৯ 3

"COSI SIA . . ." Gennaro crossed himself, lifted
both hands palm outward in the peculiar gesture, at once au-
thoritative and supplicatory, of a priest at mass and rising to his
feet put the small coffeepot on the kerosene burner in the corner.
Then he opened the door into the next room and went to look at
Quong.

It was a room so small as to be almost a cupboard but the figure of the old, old man who lay on the bed was proportioned to
it; even standing he was no higher than a twelve-year-old child
and now, lying huddled on his left side, he appeared doll-like.
One stick-thin arm of pale yellow ivory lay outside the sheet and
his sleeping face, curiously smooth and unlined for so ancient
a man, smiled from the pillow.

Gennaro watched intently, gripped in his usual morning fear
that Quong might have died in his sleep, but the wide Chinese
nostrils, moving gently in the softest breathing, reassured him.
Quong, despite the stroke that had paralyzed his right side last
March, striking him dumb, leaving him a helpless cripple, still
lived—his spirit tranquil, unafraid and serene within that tiny
broken body. The prospect of death did not perturb him and
when he thought of it at all it was with the smiling, very slightly
amused Confucian calm with which he regarded all things—not
least his grandson.

Gennaro's passion for Quong could not truly be said to have
been earned, even though it was entirely reciprocated. Quong
had always been good to him, but then so had the Ferrara nuns
and monks and so had Crocifissa; yet though he unfailingly sent
the former cards of greeting at Christmas, Easter and the Feast
of St. Francis, though he was sincerely fond of the latter, his
heart had long been given to his grandfather. Nor was there anything dutiful or filial about this love—it was a simple posses-
sive obsession. Quong fascinated Gennaro because he was so
small, so Chinese, had come from such a remote country and
such an exotic past, because of his delicate, intricate skill as a
carver of wood and because of his timeless, smiling patience—

but most of all because he was Gennaro's own grandfather in the same way that Perugia was Gennaro's own canary.

For his first eleven years Gennaro had been denied all personal possessions; like the monks among whom he lived even his clothes were not his own but belonged to the Order and were issued, exchanged and renewed impersonally as wear or growth dictated. Then everything had changed overnight. Perugia had been the first extraneous object he had ever owned but had only beaten Quong to this position by the short lead of twenty-five minutes. Since then a varied assortment of possessions had followed in all of which he took an intense pleasure and which in their own way were ramifications of his personality and for that reason prized quite out of proportion to their intrinsic value. For Gennaro was often acutely aware that his appearance in the world had been a chance affair—the result of a squalid incident in the chaos of a continent plunging into catastrophic defeat—something unhoped for, undesired, totally unnecessary. Only by taking his place as a person in his own right, freely, and of equal importance with the rest of mankind, could that drab fact be pressed into the unimportant limbo of the past. His possessions were the outward and visible sign of this desired position. His lavender-colored suit, his stamp collection, Perugia—but above all else his grandfather. Quong was the anchor of his life. Because of Quong he had his own small corner of the world; he was himself at last, an individual, unique and from the hand of God. Quong and he were "us."

Gennaro stared down at his grandfather for a long minute and then softly closed the door and returned to the other room. Quong would sleep another two hours at least, probably longer —and meanwhile there was the whole of Ercole Sanbrenedetto's funeral to arrange. The thought of organizing and carrying out an entire funeral on his own was still a joy which even yesterday's disaster could not too greatly dim. Funeral posters . . . with large black borders and a cross in the center . . . or a broken pillar with a weeping angel? No, a cross, for after all no one could consider that Ercole Sanbrenedetto had been cut off in the prime of life. The body must be registered at the Demographic office at Porta Capuana . . . the chief sexton up at Capodichino for the key of the Sanbrenedetto family mausoleum . . . wine for the mason's men . . . two wreaths had been ordered and must be made.

Gennaro drank his coffee standing at the stove and wondering how cheaply he could pick up a few bunches of damaged flowers in the Via Antonio Abate. That, and a call at the printer's, must be his first jobs. From a box below the window he took a sulphur-colored shirt and a pair of bright blue overalls and began to dress. He had bought these recently at a small shop in the Via Duchesca IX and they were the clothes of a sort of middle position somewhere between the executive in the lavender-colored suit and the down-to-earth coffinmaker in the dungarees. Dressed in them he was neither "our representative, Signor Gualtierra," nor the firm's carpenter but merely "the boy from Quong's" and as such he made calls on associated tradesmen and did minor manual work—wreath-making and the laying-out of an occasional corpse.

But the clothes were, in fact, the standard uniform of AGIP service station employees and all over Italy today men and boys dressed in the same yellow and blue would be working gasoline pumps, checking motorists' oil levels, cleaning windshields and peering under hoods. The six-legged dog alone was missing from the front of Gennaro's overalls since they had been stolen or illegally sold to the shop from which he had bought them.

For a moment he glanced at himself in the small mirror above the washstand and made a halfhearted attempt to comb his hair. Coarse, thick and blue-black it was the last and only undeniable inheritance of the Chinese blood which ran in his veins and nothing—neither hours of brushing by nuns, continual mild rebukes from monks, nor any of the cheap preparations sold in the barbershops of San Lorenzo—had ever been able to tame its springy exuberance. In his moments of gaiety it gave its owner something of the appearance of a genial golliwog; in times of anger and frustration the look of a bad-tempered porcupine. Suzzo—in the drunken anger of his dismissal—had referred to it when he had called Gennaro "a Chinese sea-urchin."

Quong sleeping peacefully, the firm's business to be carried on—and outside the sun was shining brightly. Heartened by his coffee and the thought of death's-heads, crosses and funeral pomps in general, Gennaro left his room, pocketed the key and made his way downstairs.

∞§ 4

IOLE heard Gennaro's step on the stairs as he passed her door and pushed her handkerchief into her mouth to stifle her sobs. Then he was gone and it was too late to call to him and ask him, as she had intended, to buy her a quarter of a kilo of cuttlefish if they were to be had cheaply at the Porta Capuana. Now she would have to do it herself and the stall-holders would automatically overcharge her, sensing at once that she was from the upper class—a bourgeois who should not really be shopping at their stalls—and presuming that she was doing a little private checking on the price her servants paid, would raise their own accordingly. Gennaro, with his overalls and his grin and his springy hair, could buy at the open markets for almost half what she was charged. But she could not call him in while she was red-eyed and exhausted with weeping; she had missed her chance—as she was always missing them, it seemed.

"Ah, signora, if only you had come yesterday . . . last week . . . last month . . . I could have bought it. I had someone looking for just such stones. But now—alas!" . . . "Of course I remember your uncle extremely well, Iole. And of course I will do what I can. But unfortunately, since the recent government reshuffle I am no longer in a position to make that sort of request." . . . "Dear Signora Giansante, the General asks me to acknowledge your letter. Regrettably, and owing to circumstances recently arisen and quite beyond his control . . ." And now, with summer coming again, Iole was beginning to realize fully, for the first time, that probably no one *was* going to help her. Even when, as a last resort, she had tried Peter Henderson at the American Embassy, a man with whom she had had a mild affair two years ago and who was still a friend, the result had been the same. *"I know it's a real, God-awful mess, Iole; but, honestly, there's nothing I can do. We're absolutely forbidden to interfere in that sort of thing. I don't want to sound callous, but it just isn't our business. A lot of people here think we interfere too much as it is. However unofficial we made it we'd just get slapped down. . . ."*

No one was going to help. And now, waking morning after morning in this dirty little room over the food shop, feeling the child's growing weight in her belly, Iole invariably started the day in despair and tears. Later, as the sun rose higher, these turned to the reasoned inward anger which had sustained her so long, but for the first vulnerable half-hour after waking she only knew that she was young and alone and very poor and utterly wretched.

"You read too many books," her father had once said dryly, picking up the latest of the middle-to-highbrow novels with which his daughter beguiled her long, idle, Roman days. "Foreign translations—and not particularly edifying ones, either, I should say." Perhaps they had not been, but then Iole needed to keep up with something and modern fiction seemed as good as anything else. If an upper-class Roman girl was neither remarkably beautiful nor distinctly rich, then she was expected to be intelligent—one must have something to offer a prospective husband. But until she was twenty-four no prospective husband had appeared in the life of Iole De Quilio and by the standards of modern Roman society a girl of twenty-four was beginning to move beyond her prime, her chances of marriage slipping away with every month that passed.

Then, coming home one evening from a staid shopping expedition to the Piazza Barberini, she had found Evaldo at the top of the lane which led to the De Quilio garage. He had just been engaged in what she soon discovered was his usual evening recreation—fighting—and he appeared to be bleeding to death. Iole had never seen so much blood. She ran to the garage, brought the first-aid kit from the car and patched up the worst of his gashes. The smell of blood and sweat and hot male skin reminded her of the descriptions in some of her novels. She felt it should excite her, and it did. A few days later Evaldo came round to thank her. He brought her, appropriately enough, some blood-red carnations and she was startled by his looks, which had been hidden in the darkness and blood at their first encounter. Evaldo's face was unusual, almost unearthly, although there was nothing celestial about it and her father thought him physically repulsive. But to Iole the combination of ash-blond hair, great black eyes, small snub nose and broad, slightly everted lips was for some reason delightful. And he, for his part, seemed equally attracted to her.

They met again and a third time and then knew themselves

to be in love. It was a genuinely sincere passion on both sides, one of those mutually hypnotic fascinations which cannot be explained and so often arouse hostility and suspicion in persons who have never experienced them.

Since Evaldo was nearly five years younger than herself, a garage electrician planning to emigrate to Australia to avoid his military service, Iole had put off introducing him to her father for as long as possible. For Signor De Quilio was a well-to-do lawyer, a wartime artillery captain who possessed all the rigid class-consciousness of the Roman bourgeoisie. And when, eventually, Evaldo was produced, fairly clean except for the fingernails but sullen and a little scared in the unusual surroundings of the De Quilio villa, the impression he made was worse than even Iole had feared. "It's not," her father had said afterwards, and speaking with the controlled, reasoned calm which he generally used to his more obtuse clients, "that he is lowborn and completely uneducated, for the first can sometimes be overlooked if the second is suitably rectified—though in this case I should imagine that impossible—but that I do not believe he is entirely sane. There was something about him that struck me as being—well, berserk. All the time I talked to him I could feel a current of violence. It was like conversing—if one could do such a thing—with a wild animal in a cage. There were bars between us, I'm glad to say; the invisible bars of the law and our civilization—or as much of it as he is aware of—"

"Evaldo's not a criminal! You're talking as if he was! He's never done anything or been in any trouble."

"No, no. I'm not saying he's a criminal. Frankly I doubt if he's clever enough to commit more than the simplest larceny. No—it's just that he's violent. He may not have a criminal mind but he has certain subhuman instincts which I very much doubt if he can effectually control."

"I don't think so."

"You don't know. And he wants to go to Australia. That only bears out my theory."

"Are they all . . . ?" queried Iole, interested despite herself.

"Undoubtedly. I saw them in the war. No, no, Iole. The whole thing is too bizarre. In a moment you'll be telling me that you want to marry this lunatic and go to Australia with him in order to breed a horde of little murderers."

"I *do* want to. That is, I mean . . ."

"Don't talk rubbish, girl!"

Iole did not argue any further—what was the use of arguing with a trained lawyer? Instead she continued to see Evaldo, but secretly and in various parts of the city where she was unknown. It was a strange relationship between the nineteen-year-old electrician who had come to Rome from Potenza seeking the higher wages of the capital, and the lawyer's daughter from the comfortable villa on the Via Lombardia. And yet it was simple enough, and beneficial to both of them. Iole ceased to feel bored and frustrated; Evaldo's innate capacity for dangerous, uncontrolled rage into which the smallest affront or annoyance was apt to precipitate him calmed down, sinking below the smiling, somewhat sleepy surface of a nature which otherwise had much to commend it.

For to her delight and unadmitted surprise, Iole found that he was industrious, forward-looking and thrifty. Even at such an early age he was a very skilled artisan and received high wages —a large proportion of which he saved for his Australian project. Of this he spoke to her often. He had cousins in Brisbane with whom he corresponded regularly, and they would have no difficulty in finding him a job. After a year, or as soon as he had mastered sufficient English, he would buy a small business of his own which he would then set about expanding. The possibilities open to him in Australia were indeed limitless. All he wanted now was to include Iole in this future.

And it was all she wanted, too. It was astonishing to Iole, who possessed a humble heart, that anyone as handsome, as able and as ambitious as Evaldo Giansante could love her and want to marry her; she carried the fact always with her, a continual bright light illuminating the cold gray Roman winter which surrounded them both. But it was summer in Australia. "Let's go!" Evaldo urged constantly. "Let's just get married and go." But Iole, older, more conventional, hung back. Her father, for whom since her mother's death three years before, she had kept house, relied upon her. In her own way she loved him greatly. But beyond, and deeper than this, was the instinctive Italian feeling of family obligation—something inherited from centuries of semi-tribal feuds and alliances, arranged marriages and planned inheritance. "Give him time, Evaldo. Let him get used to the idea, then it will be all right. I'm always telling him about you. In time he will get used to the idea."

"What does he say?"

"Well—not very much at present." Iole had blushed a little, for though her father's words were few they were caustic in the extreme. Had she but known it, he was taking precisely the same attitude over the matter as his daughter. Give her time, he thought to himself as he dressed, ate, drove to his office on the Via Tritone. Give her time; say little; don't argue and she'll get over it. It's preposterous in any case but—give her time.

Evaldo waited, impatiently but with admirable self-control, as the winter drew its wet, gray, snail-like track through the dead end of the year. He had booked their passages to Brisbane long ago but at Iole's pleas for more time he postponed them once, and again—and a third time.

Then it was too late. Abruptly, unexpectedly, Evaldo's draft papers came. There was no chance of escape. Strong, healthy, without any dependents to support, he had no smallest legal excuse to dodge the army. For the next eighteen months he would cease to be a skilled electrician earning five to six thousand lire a day and become a conscript soldier at the derisory pay of one hundred and fourteen. Almost as bad was the knowledge that the passage to Australia for which he had saved so long to pay would be forfeit long before he was released from his military servitude.

White-faced, with a thin veneer of calm, he explained all this to Iole before setting out for a recruit training camp near Verona and she, overcome by the disaster she had brought upon them both, left home the next day and followed him. They went through a form of civil marriage—there was neither the time nor the money for a church one—on his first free afternoon. Only then did Iole write coldly to her father to tell him what she had done—receiving a reply of such raging incoherence that she felt he must have gone mad.

It was not until a fortnight after the marriage that Iole and Evaldo were able to sleep together for the first time—a single evening in the small bedroom of a cheap hotel—and from then on the army seemed bent on frustrating further marital intercourse. Evaldo, as a recruit, was made to keep the hours of a schoolboy and punished with confinement to barracks if he was as much as a minute late in checking past the gates. His first weeks in the army were stormy and soon his only means of communicating with his wife, living in a furnished room less than half a kilometer away, was by post. It was a situation which called up all the latent wildness and savagery in Evaldo's unstable nature. He fought back instinctively like an animal caged for the first time and throwing itself repeatedly at the steel bars which must eventually bruise and batter it to submission or to death.

The first time he struck an N.C.O. he was punished with *tavaloccio*—a light enough penalty considering the gravity of his offense—by his company commander who felt that a short, sharp lesson rather than a long, useless period in detention barracks might have a corrective effect. So for four days Evaldo lay strapped to a flat wooden table in an empty cell. There was a hole in the table with a bucket beneath it and twice a day his right hand was released for five minutes in order that he might eat. He spent most of the four days planning to desert and when he emerged he wrote the details of his plan to Iole. It was not a foolproof one for, as Iole's father had foreseen, Evaldo was not particularly intelligent, but it might have worked, if, five minutes after leaving the barracks and changing into smuggled civilian clothes, Evaldo had not run straight into his company commander in a narrow, fatally deserted back street.

Captain Santorelli was a very ordinary career officer, neither a martinet nor a crank, but to Evaldo he represented the army. He had been directly responsible for those four days on the table and now he was going to block the path to freedom—to Iole— to Australia. All the red rage of which Evaldo was capable broke to the surface and he flung himself upon the captain like a leopard upon its prey. Three minutes later, breathing hard, he heaved Santorelli's battered body down a rubbish chute and ran through the streets to Iole's room, to a panic of packing, a dreadful night of fear and flight and a final bleak dawn arrest at the border.

There was no possible excuse; nothing to be said in mitigation. The facts spoke for themselves. A consistently disobedient and insubordinate soldier had, while attempting desertion, brutally assaulted a superior officer without the slightest provocation, breaking his arm in two places, fracturing his jaw and impairing the sight of one eye. The court-martial would have been fully justified in imposing a sentence of eighteen years' imprisonment, but being Italians and naturally inclined toward mercy even in the most undeserving cases, the members agreed upon twelve.

Evaldo had looked across the courtroom at Iole—one last look of utter, blank despair—and turned away between his guards toward the door, the waiting, steel-barred truck and the grim military fortress-prison that crowned the rocky promontory of Gaeta.

Iole belonged to the well-to-do Italian upper class; the managers, the contrivers, the adjusters of laws and modifiers of regulations. Also she had a little money of her own. She did not despair entirely but followed her husband—the word still sounded strange to her—south to his prison. But she could not live at Gaeta. The sight of that huge castle looming on its rock, the knowledge that somewhere behind those immense walls Evaldo lay shut from the daylight in a stone cell, helpless and alone, were too much for her to bear. More practically she realized that she must live nearer the center of power in order to work, as she intended to work, relentlessly and steadily, for his release. But to Rome she would not go for fear of meeting her father. An hour down the coast lay Naples—an hour, only, from Evaldo. And Naples would be much cheaper; that was immensely in its favor for every lira she possessed would be needed in the fight to which she was pledged.

To Naples she came and true to her vow of thrift took the shabbiest horse cab outside the station, asking its sour old driver if he knew of some cheap lodgings—very cheap, just a single room in a poor quarter was all she required. And he had nodded ruminatively, cleared his throat, spat, looked her up and down and said, at last, that he knew of a vacant room over a shop in the same building in which he stabled his horse. It was very cheap, certainly, but—well, the Signora could see it and decide for herself. . . .

So for the last five weeks Iole had been a tenant in the old house, living in a low-ceilinged room three meters by two and a half, with a cracked window looking out on the public urinal. And from the small table at the foot of the bed she had begun the struggle to rescue Evaldo. Letters to friends and to friends of friends, to lawyers and to authorities both civil and military, to anyone who might be interested in the soldier walled-up in that great Angevin castle on its rock above the sea. And replies came in—sympathetic, embarrassed, seldom hopeful. The kindest was from poor Captain Santorelli, still suffering considerable pain and in fear of being invalided from the Service due to the eye damage he had sustained, but stating that he bore her husband no malice for an action undoubtedly taken during a "brainstorm" and saying that he had already made this clear to the military authorities.

Once, too, there had been a letter from her father, very short and to the point. He refused to accept the fact of a civil marriage as a properly binding tie; it could easily be annulled and if his daughter would agree to this she might come home whenever she chose. If a child was imminent—and he sincerely hoped that this was not the case—then suitable arrangements would have to be made after its birth. Iole assumed he meant some sort of church orphanage like the one from which Gennaro had run away and, tearing the letter to shreds, returned the pieces to the sender. Evaldo was her legal husband, the coming child would be his as much as hers and if, she thought repeatedly and bitterly, she had taken less account of her father and more of her lover, she and Evaldo would be together in Brisbane at this very moment. But as it was . . .

This morning she had another appointment with her lawyer in the Via Roma—the main shopping street of the city, which the Neapolitans still confusingly called the Via Toledo—and they would spend half an hour, at a cost of some two thousand lire, discussing the possibilities of a psychiatrical examination of Evaldo. It was old and depressing ground, for the army was stolidly unwilling to countenance such a thing on an already sentenced prisoner while Iole knew that it meant giving full assent to the view that her husband was partly insane. At best it could only mean a transfer from prison to a military hospital— at any rate, to start with.

She rose reluctantly from her bed and a wave of nausea made her groan and hold to the table, sick and heavy. She clung there sweating for a moment and as the sickness ebbed away the noises of the *piazza* were borne in to her from below the window—the shouts of the emergent workmen greeting each other at the bus stop, the cries of the newspaper vendors who sold them the *Corriere dello Spòrt*, the rattle of donkey carts on the rough stones. Another day was starting here in Naples for the thousands who must earn a living, buy their husbands' dinner, get their children off to school. But for Iole it began only with the clank and rattle of bolts and locks and the stamping of a changing guard in a prison she could not see but which nonetheless held her heart chained, frightened and hopeless within its stony gloom.

ᵉᵍ 5

"TELL me about it."

"There isn't really anything to tell. It went off all right."

"Who was there?"

"Nobody—just me."

"None of the Lords and Ladies?"

"None, I'm thankful to say. It would have been extremely embarrassing if any of them had arrived. But naturally they wouldn't. They're obviously enraged. Galo sent a wreath."

"I know."

"Did you? How? I was most surprised, myself."

"He came to the flat at six to collect that packet he left last March. Then we called in to see Nicola and then I came on here. But go on about what happened."

Beppo sighed, smiling at his daughter across the restaurant table, and then glanced over the dusky sea toward the twinkling lights of Sorrento on the gulf's southern shore. "Nothing *happened*. I went down to San Lorenzo in a taxi and everything was ready. Quong's did the whole thing—the old man's grandson seemed to be in charge. It was rather pathetic, really. There was this shabby old hearse and a really dreadful old *carròzza* to carry the wreaths—mine, Galo's, and one from old Crocifissa Buonafede—and Quong's boy as pleased as Punch in a bright mauve suit with a huge black velvet rose in his buttonhole! But after all, they were his tenants and I can't see why they shouldn't have the job. Well, then we all moved off very slowly with a priest behind the hearse and I in my taxi bringing up the rear. And before we had even got to the Piazza Volturno we stopped

and Quong's boy got out of the hearse, where he'd been riding
with the driver, and came back and asked me if I would mind
taking the Reverend Father the rest of the way in my taxi because his feet were giving out. So I had this priest all the way to
Capodichino, and he stank to heaven—garlic, tobacco or snuff,
and sheer old age."

"Couldn't you have put him in the *carròzza* with the
wreaths?"

"I wish I'd thought of it at the time. Well, then we arrived and
they'd got the family mausoleum open and a catafalque inside
covered with a pall with huge death's-heads done in silver se-
quins—it looked more like a pirate's flag than anything else, I
must say. And then the prayers were said, or I suppose they
were; at any rate the priest gabbled some incantations and
Quong's boy kept crossing himself at what I imagine he knew
to be the right moments, and then the coffin was heaved up into
its niche and as we came out a mason went in to wall it up. So
now old Ercole lies where he always wanted to be—next to the
great Vittorio—and that's that. I left as soon as I decently could
and got away before the priest could ask me for a lift back to
town— Now, what are we going to eat? I'm going to start with
oysters, myself."

"So will I, then."

"You've never eaten them before, Mina. They might make
you ill. Why not try their 'assortment'? It will be mussels and
sea-dates and clams as well, and—"

"And then I can be really ill. All right."

Beppo smiled affectionately at his daughter and beckoning
one of the red-shirted waiters gave the order. But instead of going toward the serving tables at the back of the restaurant the
man approached the edge of the jetty and signaled with his napkin. And at once a small, bright rowboat with the restaurant's
name, O SOLE MIO, painted on the bow, moved across the private pool—a pool carefully designed to represent a miniature
fishing harbor—and sidled up closely to their table. It was piled
with shellfish; and the oysters, sea-dates and mussels were
handed up bedded on plates of damp green seaweed. Mina was
impressed and Beppo, touched at her obvious pleasure, remarked,
"I've been meaning to try this place ever since they started
building it last winter. They've only been open a month but"—

he glanced around at the crowded tables among which waiters dressed as fishermen moved deftly between anchors, crab-pots and artistically draped russet nets—"they seem to be doing very well."

"I'm sure it's horribly expensive."

"So am I. It's a tourist trap really, of course—and somebody's going to make a lot of money out of it. But sometimes, while these places are still new and hoping to make a reputation of sorts, you can get quite a good dinner. Anyway this is a celebration—we can afford it."

Mina started carefully but with some difficulty to eat her sea-dates. After a moment she said, "Did you see the lawyers again?"

"Yes. Everything's quite in order; there's no mistake. I inherit everything. Shall we have mullet after this, or sole?"

"Sole. I've bought mullet for tomorrow's dinner. Well, I bought it for today's really, but now it's in the icebox— What's 'everything' mean?"

Beppo finished his oysters and wiped his mouth. "Well, briefly it means about thirty million lire in various stocks and bonds; a block of good property in the Pendino Quarter; that old ruin in the Piazza Nicòtera—the Vittime Civili di Guerra, they call it now—and the Adriatic villa. There's some furniture and odds and ends besides and, I think, some of Vittorio's relics —particularly the sword Garibaldi gave him after the fall of Messina and the famous pistol ball, carefully preserved in a red velvet case."

"The one that he got in the way of instead of Garibaldi?"

"Allegedly. And they cut it out while he shouted 'Viva l'Italia!' and Garibaldi held his hand and wept—or that's the story. Personally, I've never believed a word of it."

"It might be true. People did behave very oddly then. Though of course they often behave very oddly now, too. I often wonder what peculiar pranks my own dear Vittorio got up to when he had his flesh—if he is a 'he,' of course."

"My dear Mina, I've seen enough of war—not much, but quite enough—to know that soldiers don't get in the way of bullets meant for other people if they can possibly help it. No, no; my own version of the story is much more likely. Vittorio was fooling around with his chief's pistols, which as unofficial

A.D.C. and general Ganymede to the staff it was his duty to keep clean—and shot himself in the leg. While he was yelling his head off with fright and pain Garibaldi dashed out of his tent in a rage and shouted, 'For God's sake shut up! How can I remake Italy with that infernal noise going on outside!' "

Mina spluttered joyfully. "You've never told me that before!" And Beppo, grinning, settled his heavy, black-rimmed glasses more firmly on his bridgeless nose. "My dear, I'd never have dared to breathe a word of criticism about Vittorio while old Ercole was alive. You know what he thought of his father. If he'd found out about what you call *your* Vittorio—and who might easily be a woman anyway, as far as I can see . . . And you know what happened when I urged him to sell the property in San Lorenzo. Just because Vittorio lived there. . . ."

"You'll sell it now, I suppose?"

"Assuredly. It's by far the most valuable part of the whole inheritance. And it has no sentimental ties for *me*. Hurry up with those things, Mina. The sole is coming."

"I can't get the wretched things out of their shells." Mina glanced up from her plate. "What about the people living there?"

"Old Crocifissa Buonafede?" Beppo's mild, round face clouded momentarily "Poor old woman. She attended your christening, if I remember rightly. She certainly saw you several times while you were still a baby. It's odd to think that she was once my nurse. Only for about a year, though; I can't really remember her. Then she went to work for old Ercole—oh, ages ago while I was still a child before the war and when he was living here. Her husband, too. Anyway, the husband died and since Ercole needed a married couple to look after him, he let her have that shop in the Nicòtera. Her boy was killed in the war, too. Yes, she's had a hard life."

"You'll have to do something about her."

"I know. I'll have to think."

"And the Quongs. And that old cabman."

"Them, too. I'll go down to San Lorenzo tomorrow if I can manage it; I've got to give them the statutory three-month notice in any case. I won't make any sort of promises but I'll try to find out how they are situated. I imagine— Oh." Beppo broke off as a tall man in black trousers and a white jacket, the maître d'hôtel himself, perhaps, walked up beside Mina and gently shook his head.

"This is your first encounter with sea-dates, signorina, I think." Without looking around he clicked his fingers and one of the two waiters hovering behind him placed a small silver fish knife in his hand. "Now let me show you. . . . The shells are so fragile, are they not? A certain skill is required. It can only come with practice." Under his large, clean, square-nailed fingers the delicate shellfish opened simply; a touch with the silver knife and the rose-pink flesh was detached from its narrow, nacreous case. Carefully he repeated the process, and a third time.

Beppo and Mina were both embarrassed. They very seldom took meals outside their small Vomero flat and when they did so they were not accustomed to complimentary attentions from high restaurant personnel. Beppo attempted some thanks but he was disregarded. Only when the last sea-date was extricated did the tall man lift his head and glance across the table. Beppo saw a long, smooth, heavy face below almost colorless hair worn stiffly *en brosse,* and pale eyes behind rimless pince-nez. Once more he said, "Many thanks. As you say, they are not easy things to open."

"It is a knack one acquires in time." And as the man moved away unhurriedly between the tables Beppo caught the eye of a waiter and asked, "Who was that? Your chief?"

"*Si, signore. Il padrone.*"

"The *owner?*"

"Yes. Signor Bighencomer."

And Beppo, duly flattered, stared after that tall, stiff back as it disappeared casually between the farther tables. Then he turned with increased pleasure to his sole.

◄§ 6

THE small man in the shabby overalls read the lettering on the ground-glass panel of the office door: F. BIGHENCOMER. He glanced quickly up and down the empty corridor lit softly by shell-shaped wall lamps; from an open window at the far end the noises of the restaurant below floated in mingled with those of the late night traffic changing gear and accelerating as it swung into the Via Mergellina. He knocked deferentially, a voice called *"Entrate,"* and he opened the door. The writer at the big desk in the center of the room did not look up but went on working; his face was partly in shadow, his strong white hands brilliantly illuminated under the hard glare of a powerful desk lamp. "Well—what is it?"

The man in the overalls cleared his throat. "Signor Bighencomer?"

"Yes, yes." Still the writer did not raise his eyes from his work. "Ferenc?"

And immediately the right hand that held the pen ceased its quick, precise movements across the paper and froze. "No—Francesco."

"Francesco? I see. As you wish, then." The man in the overalls came forward grinning, holding out a small, dirty bluntnailed hand. It was taken, pressed quickly and released. From behind the broad desk Signor Bighencomer smiled briefly. "Yes, I read about you. I suppose I should congratulate you. I *do* congratulate you."

"I'm hoping you'll do more than that. Didn't you think I'd come here?"

"I didn't expect you to get this far." Signor Bighencomer rose, switched on the room's main lighting and turned off the desk lamp. He seemed taller than ever, confronting the little man in the stained overalls who still smiled broadly, disclosing a crooked, undershot jaw which lent him an oddly canine look —a little comic yet savage, too. "However, since you are here you had better have a drink. Whisky or cognac?"

"Whisky? No, I've never drunk it. I'd like some beer."

"Very well." Bighencomer opened a wall cabinet and took out the drinks but did so in such a manner that his back was never entirely turned on the small man standing in the middle of the room.

"You've changed, Ferenc, a lot. You've aged."

"You've done neither. But then prison generally has a preserving effect. How old are you now, Duilio? No—don't tell me. Thirty-one. You were eighteen when you went in. Yes, it's remarkable. You could easily pass as twenty-four or twenty-five. Is that the first beer you've had for thirteen years?"

"No. Every Christmas they gave us some—also at Easter, sometimes."

Bighencomer put his whisky glass gently on his desk. "You've come for help, I suppose." His voice was matter-of-fact, expressing neither hostility nor reluctance.

"Yes, yes—naturally."

"What sort of help?"

"That depends what you're doing now."

"I'm doing nothing in your line. I own this restaurant and run it myself. I also direct a real estate company and do a little buying and selling on the stock exchange."

"Petrol—flour—American stores?" The pug-dog grin widened, and Bighencomer smiled in return but without warmth, "Things have changed in thirteen years, Duilio. Our country's back on its feet again now and—"

"*Our* country?"

"Yes. I became a citizen seven years ago."

"And—why 'Bighencomer'?"

"My mother's name. She was a Swiss."

"Do the Jugoslavs know you're here?"

Bighencomer had been half sitting on the edge of his desk. Now he rose abruptly. "Duilio, I'm going to do what I can to help you. But please remember this—the war and its aftermath are both over. Quite over. Italy is, today, a country of which you obviously cannot be expected to know anything. I, and many other men of my age have—"

And suddenly the other was raging. It was as if a great internal fire flared abruptly within him. His face glowed a dark red, the grin became a ferocious snarl and the dark eyes widened into a glare of hate. "I don't want to hear! I'm not interested! What happened thirteen years ago is all I care about. It was you who decided—"

"It was not. You know perfectly well that I was against it—insofar as I knew about it at all. It was Sollier—and he's dead."

"You let him believe that—"

"Keep your voice *down!* I did nothing—had nothing to do with it at all. I was always against that sort of thing—as anybody but young Italian fools would have been! Sollier and people like you who had been in the Black Brigades when you should have been at school—"

"And while you were murdering Jugoslavs!"

Coldly, with his eyes narrowed behind his rimless glasses, Bighencomer said, "War is war, Duilio. I've told you—all that is past. Forgotten. And as far as murder goes—it is *you* who have been serving a twenty-eight-year term for it—and would have got life if you'd been a year older. No! Ah!" He staggered back under the sudden furious assault, recovered himself and reaching behind him seized a long steel paper knife and thrust the point at his attacker's eyes. Under the threat of that thin pointed blade the smaller man drew back, glowering. Bighencomer breathed deeply. "No—I was right. You haven't changed —not at all. But the world has changed, Duilio. There are no Black Brigades—or black markets—any longer and the last bandit was killed in Sicily years ago. I'm not sure it wouldn't be better if I handed you over to the police—from everyone's point of view, and perhaps even your own."

"You do that—and see what happens to you!"

"There's been a general amnesty. In fact I think there have been several."

"Not for people like you, Ferenc."

"On the contrary—expressly for people like me. But not for people like you. But I've said I'll help you and I will. You want to get out of this country?"

"Yes."

"All right." Bighencomer's voice became brisk. "It will take a little time. Surprising as it may seem to you, people need papers today and they are neither easy nor cheap to come by. Fortunately I know one or two places in Rome. . . . Meanwhile you'd better become some sort of worker here in the restaurant where I can keep an eye on you."

The pug-dog grin was back again now, triumphant, knowing. "Where we can keep an eye on each other, Ferenc."

"Please remember not to use that name in public—or in private either, if possible. I'm Francesco Bighencomer today. What do you call yourself now?"

"Domenichelli."

"All right. Duilio Domenichelli—there's no reason to change your first name. Take another beer if you want one."

In an atmosphere still tense and watchful but with the surface calm restored, Bighencomer waited until the beer had been poured out. Then he said, "Tell me—how did you get away?"

"In a garbage bin."

"So? I'm surprised they're not on to that old trick."

"Are you? Well, you needn't be. The garbage bins are collected and emptied automatically into the incinerator through a concrete chute." Domenichelli took a long drink of beer and shuddered. "Sometimes they turn the blowtorch on before the bins are in—sometimes after. If it's done afterwards there's just time to get out of the air-vent at the other end."

"And if it's done before?"

"You burn. The chances are about equal. You can't tell beforehand."

"My God!"

"After thirteen years one is ready to risk it. At least I was. No, I got out all right but before I could get properly away I was seen. I knew they would cordon everything off for at least a dozen kilometers. I was in a marsh for nearly thirty hours up to my neck in water. Then I got away at night and after about eight kilos I crossed the coast road and hid in an old storm-water drain right down by the sea in a great clump of bamboos. I slept for hours. When I woke up I didn't see how I could get much farther. Police were up and down the road all the time. Next afternoon a hearse turned off the road and pulled in among the bamboos, and—"

"A *hearse?*"

"Yes—with a coffin in it. The driver—he was only a boy— apparently wanted a swim. Well, he got out and undressed only about three meters from where I was watching him, and ran off into the sea. At first I thought I would take his clothes— I needed clothes more than anything—and then drive off in the hearse. But it was too dangerous. I would never have got to Pescara. The boy in the sea would have run out yelling his head off and stopped the first car that passed."

"So?"

Domenichelli set down his empty glass and wiped his mouth. "He was right out to sea, diving and fooling around. The hearse was practically screened from the road and it was a quiet time of day. I opened the back and unscrewed the coffin with a screwdriver from the tool kit. There was a body in it—an old man. I

got him out, pulled him down into the storm-water drain, stuffed
him as far down as he'd go and covered him with sand. I would
have liked his clothes but I guessed there wouldn't be time. I was
right, too. I got in the hearse, closed the back, got in the coffin
and pulled the lid on. I put the screws in my pocket first. About
a couple of minutes later I heard two motorcycles draw up. I
guessed they were police all right. When the boy got back from
his swim he was in trouble. Stopping while carrying a body and
so on. . . . I could hear it all—or most of it. Then they found
he was under age and didn't have a license. That worried me
badly because I thought they might take the hearse back to police headquarters in Pescara. But they decided to let him go on
—he was going to Naples. I think they came with him past
Pescara and then let him go. I thought of getting out of the
coffin somewhere in the hills, hitting the boy over the head and
getting away before we reached Naples, but of course I couldn't
see out of the coffin and I couldn't tell where we were or what
we might be passing. And there might have been traffic behind
us, too.

"No, I decided to stay where I was and hope for the best.
Then eventually we got to Naples; the hearse stopped and the
boy got out. I was ready to grab him if he examined the coffin.
It seemed silent and I guessed we were alone. If he lifted the lid
I planned to grab his throat. He'd have been too surprised to
do anything. Afterwards I would have taken his clothes, put him
in the coffin and screwed it down. He would have made a good
substitute body. But I heard him move away and shut a door—
then nothing. I got out. It was dark but there was a light from a
streetlamp outside. The first thing I found was this pair of old
overalls on a hook. They were too small but they covered my
stripes. I went out of a door at the back meaning to get away
fast. I was in a ruin of old walls and broken stones and weeds.
Then I thought of something. I guessed that after what had
happened the boy wasn't coming back that evening. But I
needed something to put in that coffin—otherwise they would
trace the whole thing back and find the body in the bamboos
and guess that I was in Naples. I had plenty of time because—
isn't there some sort of law against funerals at night? I don't
know; I've heard something like that. So I filled the coffin with

some rocks from the place at the back—about what I judged the corpse's weight to have been. Then I screwed back the lid. I expect they buried it today."

He grinned widely and saw for the first time a look of admiration on his listener's face. "Well—there you are."

Bighencomer shook his head. "Yes, Duilio, I see. You haven't changed at all. Not a nerve in your body, eh?"

Domenichelli nodded—portentously, a little ominously—standing small, dark and squat before the desk. "That's how it always was. That's how it is now—and that's how it's going to stay."

Beppo

⌘ 1

THROUGHOUT his forty years he had never been "Giuseppe" to anyone. He had been named, not for the earthly father of Christ, but for the blond man in the red shirt who had made Italy and under whom his grandfather had fought from Sicily to Naples.

It was unlikely that any of Garibaldi's romantically informal staff would have taken liberties with their General's first name —certainly not the ardent young Vittorio who had held the General's bridle and galloped with the General's dispatches and echoed the famous cry *"Qui se fa l'Italia o se mori!"* before Calatafimi. But Giuseppe Sanbrenedetto, unlike his imposing namesake, had been "Peppino," "Pinino," "Pepe" and eventually "Beppo" to everyone all his life—except for his years as a prisoner-of-war when they had called him "Joe."

He was forty; and now at last he was free—free of all the dismal little economic worries of workaday life which had haunted him so long. Forty years of ill-conducted struggle against a constantly shifting combination of more or less adverse circumstances with which Beppo was singularly unfitted to cope had ended at last. It was surprising that they had left so few marks on the small man who now lay asleep in his apartment on the Vomero hill. The light from the high-slung streetlamp, shining through the gaps in the bedroom window curtains, was kinder to that relaxed, round face with the squashed nose than the hard glare of the Neapolitan sunlight, but even by day

Beppo never looked entirely adult, and when he slept, the child who was still largely the true Beppo—the Beppo who seldom saw life steadily and never saw it whole—became physically visible once more.

In the predawn darkness Vittorio's portrait, hanging in its heavy gilt frame beside the door, was only a black square against the paler surface of the wall, but had it been taken quietly down from its hooks and held against Beppo's sleeping face the likeness—that astonishing similarity between the boy soldier of a hundred years ago and the failed businessman turned school-teacher of today—would have shone out at once. It was a similarity which had dogged the latter's youth and if Beppo could ever be said to have hated anyone—and hate of any sort was foreign to his unaggressive nature—that person was his long-dead grandfather.

Despite the fact that the portrait was of some value, Beppo would have parted with it long since if it had not been for Mina. But Mina liked it and had a not unnatural pride in the fact that her great-grandfather had been a Garibaldino. Hanging it in the bedroom was a compromise between her desire to display it properly in the lounge and her father's wish to put it in a trunk in the lumber room.

Beppo seldom looked at the picture, but on the occasions when it caught his eye he was filled with momentarily melancholy remembrances of his childhood years when Vittorio was held up as a continual reproach and example. Visitors to the old house at Bagnuoli had so often remarked on that depressing physical resemblance. So often had his parents—and particularly Uncle Ercole—shaken their heads and sighed, "Yes, yes, but I fear it is only in looks that Beppo takes after him."

For Vittorio had laid the foundations of the modest fortune which he had bequeathed unequally to his three sons and four daughters at his death in 1912. Bald, heavily bearded, stern, portentous, there had been nothing during those last years to connect the old man with the young desperado of the Risorgimento if it had not been for that regrettable picture and when he was gone the picture lived on, a source of pride or reproach to those of his descendants, particularly Beppo, who had failed to make a success of life.

Beppo was not as superstitious as his fellow citizens but he sometimes felt that when he had bad dreams—and these had occurred more and more frequently since, on his wife's death four years ago, they had moved to the Vomero flat—they might be traced to the accusing nocturnal gaze of Vittorio from the wall beside the door. As a soldier Vittorio had been a liberating conqueror whereas Beppo had dropped his rifle and surrendered at the first opportunity. It was true that as a subject of the Kingdom of the Two Sicilies, Vittorio had been a rebel whose surrender would have taken him to the gallows, or worse, the galleys at Gaeta, whereas Beppo's capitulation took him to light and not unpleasant work on an English chicken farm; but against that stood the fact that Vittorio had fought through choice while his grandson had been a most unwilling "volunteer," urged and threatened into the National Militia by Uncle Ercole. Sometimes Beppo would stare irritably at the picture and remark mentally that had Vittorio lived in the modern era he would certainly have exchanged that red shirt for a black one and ended a shorter life hanging upside down beside a less heroic leader in Milan. Then, too, in civilian life Vittorio had been such a success. A Sicilian by birth he had made his home and his fortune in Naples after helping to conquer it. Starting with nothing, he had worked incredible hours and saved every centesimo; shrewd, grasping, hardheaded, businesslike, whereas Beppo . . . No wonder the picture gave him bad dreams.

Tonight they were at their worst; perhaps the ghost of Vittorio, affronted that with the death of Ercole the major part of the Sanbrenedetto fortune and possessions had descended to Beppo, was having a last revenge. At all events Beppo was luridly reliving the most terrifying and miserable time of his life, stumbling, sick and exhausted, in a guarded column of prisoners across the African desert. Burning, glaring heat by day, frigid cold when the temperature dropped like a stone at sunset. It had not been one of the huge, interminably long columns snaking slowly back along the great coastal road under the laconic eyes of British riflemen, but a half-battalion of blackshirts from a surrendered fort deep in the interior making a forced march across open desert guarded by Dominion troops.

There had been very little water and practically no food. After three days Beppo's boots had cracked and broken and begun to come apart. Like most of the other prisoners he had no blanket and could only sleep in short, shivering snatches, awakening sick and stiff and blue with cold to limp on ever more slowly under the growing menace of the guards. After four days the progress of the column had been such that these had removed the slings from their rifles and used them to flog the rear ranks forward through the soft sand or across the hard stony shale. . . . The wheeling arc of the sun expanding to a huge ball of fire, striking down in showers of red-hot arrows among which the brass-tipped rifle slings, cracking over backs and shoulders, had urged the staggering column toward a continually receding horizon that shimmered and gleamed and never came any nearer. . . .

Beside Beppo a grimy, coughing Calabrian, still smaller than himself, had swayed and caught his arm. They both fell down and were kicked upright—Beppo, by a boot in his face which broke his nose near its bridge, covering him with blood—and herded on. The next time the Calabrian reeled toward him Beppo had evaded the groping arm and staggered on alone. Turning he had seen the guards in a small group about the fallen prisoner—then came the sound of a shot and they were running back to their places leaving a crumpled body on the ground. Crossing the next rise Beppo had cast a quick, frightened glance behind. Yes, there it was, very small and alone, dark and still upon the pale sand. A guard had sworn furiously and Beppo had half run, half fallen down the other side of the dune.

That had been the first time. Next day there had been four shots; the day after, seven. Then he had lost count, filled only with a dull surprise that he was still alive and that his leaden feet in their tattered boots still somehow shuffled forward. One evening—the eighth? the tenth?—the guards had tied a prisoner's hands behind him and dropping a live grenade into the front of his black shirt had beaten him into a stumbling run over the sand before flinging themselves flat on their faces, followed in this by most of the other prisoners. A shattering explosion and a cloud of sand and dirt mixed with bloody pieces of flesh. . . . For three nights it had become an evening ritual, the victim being selected from among those who had lagged in the rear during the day. The pace had increased perceptibly; more men fell out and more shots sounded but the rear of the column kept closed up. Then for two days the shots and evening killings ceased and then the great barbed-wire cages appeared at last.

But in his dreams Beppo never got to the cages; they ended— he awoke—after a desperate, dry-mouthed pleading with the guards as they tied his hands and removed the pin from a ser- rated grenade which glinted hotly in the desert sunset. . . . Tonight it was the same. In the final, irrevocable agony as the grenade was thrust into his open shirt collar, hard and cold against his sweating skin, he awoke with a groan and a shud- der and turned on his back. Dawn had come and gone and the room was filled with light and Vittorio stared down mockingly from the wall beside the door, red-shirted, smiling, one hand on the big muzzle-loading pistol thrust dramatically into his tri- color sash.

◄§ 2

The smile of the Sun for pardon.
Bird-song in the trees for mirth;
One is nearer God's heart in a Garden
Than anywhere else on Earth.

THE calendar bore a brightly colored picture of an English cottage garden impenetrably packed with bril- liant flowers; hollyhocks and rambler roses conspicuously to the fore. *To dear Joe with all best wishes for Xmas and the New Year from Esmond and Penelope Pinniger—*

Beppo, leaning across the table in the small, sun-filled kitchen, removed the May leaf. He had forgotten to do this yes- terday morning so now June came officially to the kitchen twen- ty-four hours late. Yet perhaps that was not a bad thing for at this hour yesterday Uncle Ercole was still unburied; but now, with the old man's body firmly in its niche behind a marble slab in Capodichino, there was no longer reason for doubt or worry or pretended sorrow. Nothing need interfere now with the joy- ful expectancy of freedom and a new start in life.

Mina slid two eggs from the frying-pan onto a plate and set it before her father. Ever since his P.O.W. days on the Pin- nigers' chicken farm Beppo had insisted on an English breakfast—eggs and toast and marmalade. He smiled up at his daughter—how tall she was for fifteen, at least as tall as himself. She had inherited that, and the un-Italian slenderness of her figure, from her otherwise very Italian mother. From himself she appeared to have inherited little save mild myopia. Beppo's deep affection for Mina lay at the center of his life— or at any rate he believed it did. She rescued him from his own inconsequence. Like many men who have failed, by early middle age, to make a success of their lives Beppo thankfully grasped the opportunity to shift the burden of the future onto the shoulders of his child. It excused him from the dismal occupation of considering his own. "I live entirely for Mina now," he would sometimes say to acquaintances and though he had no precise idea what he really meant by this, the phrase sounded noble and resigned and a little sad. And when he had been rejected for a position in the Post Office, when his wholesale cheese business failed, when his travel agency was sold over his head, and he was fired from a minor position on a local newspaper it had been somehow comforting to say, "For myself I don't mind so much—it is only for my daughter that I exist at all."

Now, eating his eggs, drinking his tea, he smiled happily across the table. "Tomorrow we can get up when we like. I shall be free. No more work, no more rush and hurry in the mornings."

"But until the will is proved—?"

"We can always get credit from the bank, cara mia. Once they've seen the will and know that I've been left everything . . ." Beppo shook his head. "I wouldn't go down today if it wasn't just to say good-bye to the boys. After all, they've always treated me well. The Commandant asked me to stay on until someone else was found, but I said no. I said, 'I've always understood that you were not very satisfied with my work, Colonel.' That put him in a difficult position. 'Come, come, Sanbrenedetto,' he said, going a bit red. 'I've never said that.' As a matter of fact he has said it—on several occasions, too, but I didn't contradict him. 'I'm sorry,' I said, 'if it's inconvenient. But I've just inherited a lot of property and much of it has been badly neglected. I'll have a great deal to see to now. I shall be a very busy man.' He didn't like that at all." Beppo rose, wiping his mouth, and took his briefcase from the kitchen dresser. "What's in this?"

"Your brown shoes—they need new heels. And your lunch."

"I don't need lunch. I'll be back for lunch."

"Then take it out and leave it on the dresser," said Mina patiently. "And don't forget the shoes." She glanced from the window across the sunny morning street and let out a wail of despair. "Oh, *look!* They've taken his hands off again—and his left arm all the way to the elbow. I do hate it when they do that. He looks so sad."

"He always looks hideously happy—" Beppo gazed over the Via Raffaele Morghen toward the window of the medical school from which Mina's Vittorio, the articulated skeleton in the anatomy classroom, grinned back at him. "If he really looked sad I'd take him down to the Nunziatella with me and leave him in that dreadful vestibule where they keep all their beastly trophies. And I'd put a little placard round his neck with the words *The sole object of this establishment is to reduce humanity to my condition as speedily as possible.*—I don't think the Commandant would be so eager to retain my services after that."

Vomero's wide, clean streets were full of plane trees;· their broad leaves lent a sense of coolness to the summer morning as they swayed under a light breeze from the sea. Beppo, the shoes left at the cobbler's, caught the funicular at the top of the steps on the Via Raffaele Morghen and began the creaking, jolting, eight-minute descent to the Piazza Dante. Disregarding the printed request not to do so he placed both feet on the opposite seat. Even if the conductor was offended it did not matter, for he would have a car soon and cease to use the funicular from that moment.

A car—and many other things as well. So many other things. For perhaps the fiftieth time since the news of his uncle's death Beppo went quickly over the main portions of his inheritance. Firstly the stock to the value of some thirty million lire, mostly invested at a steady, solid five and a half percent. Well, death duties would take a large lump out of that but even so he should be able to count on an income of a million a year, which was a little more than his present salary as an English teacher. Then there was the villa and its furniture on the Adriatic coast.

During the summer that would bring in a good rent—at least sixty thousand a month—if he did not want to use it himself as a holiday house. And, of course, better than all these was the Naples property itself. Ercole had owned a block of three houses in the Pendino Quarter which brought in, altogether, three quarters of a million in rentals. They should by rights bring in much more, those three houses, but regrettably the government rent laws held landlord's profits down to a completely false level based on prewar values.

Best of all was the ruined property in San Lorenzo. Beppo once more blessed the planes which had smashed it. Had some English or American aviator pressed his bomb-release button a second sooner or later, that block would still be classed as "habitable residential property" and he, the new owner, would be forced to keep it in good repair while accepting a ridiculously uneconomical return and paying heavy taxes. But eighteen years ago a young Allied bombardier, lying on his stomach in the nose of a roaring, shuddering plane, tossed by flak, blinded by searchlights, had jabbed a button with his gloved thumb and in releasing his bombs had today released Beppo from the government's rigorous restrictions.

Old Ercole had known the value of the site but had not touched it. It had been his father's first Neapolitan acquisition and his own birthplace and he would not part with it while he lived. Five years ago Beppo had been visited by a representative from a firm which was interested in acquiring the place as the site for a department store. The firm had approached Ercole and been rebuffed but had not given up hope. It had sought out the old man's nephew and suggested that if he would use his good offices to win over his uncle a substantial commission would be forthcoming. Beppo had taken the next train to Pescara, and hired a car all the way to the bleak villa on the sandy coast. Gray skies, leagues of wet sand under the whistling winter wind; Ercole, sour and rheumatic, hunched in his drafty house among the dunes, had not been pleased to see him and had treated his carefully veiled hints about the San Lorenzo property with a total lack of interest. Too frightened of his uncle to press the matter further Beppo had left, unsuccessful and disappointed, on the long return journey. The trip had cost him more than he could afford and had been fruitless; another of the failures and humiliations to add to the long line which stretched depressingly back to his childhood.

But the matter turned out to have far graver consequences than that. The commercial firm he had attempted to help was more stubborn than he had imagined. At a directors' meeting they raised their offer spectacularly and sent their vice-president himself to convey it to the old man on the faraway coast. At this interview the businessman had innocently brought up the subject of Beppo's previous visit and Ercole had realized for the first time that his nephew was in league with this annoying and intrusive firm who bothered his self-imposed exile with undesired requests and promises. As soon as the vice-president had been dismissed with a curt refusal, Ercole had sat down at his desk and written Beppo a letter in which he stated plainly that he was disinheriting his nephew, cutting him completely out of his will. And Beppo had never heard from him again.

It was not until two days ago that he had discovered that the old man had not carried out his threat—probably he had never intended to—and that the will had remained unchanged.

✑ 3

"IN the October of—of one thousand eight hundred fifty-nine while Garibaldi was having his general quarter to Rimini—"

"No, no, *no*! How many more times have I got to tell you about the misuse of the definite article? In English one does not say '*the* October.' Also they pronounce dates in the same way as we pronounce telephone numbers—in a double set of two figures. And surely you can see that this is an occasion in which the Saxon genitive may correctly be used. Listen—in October eighteen fifty-nine, *when* Garibaldi's headquarters were *at* Rimini. . . . All right?"

"*Si, signore.*"

"In *English,* please!"

"Yes, sir."

"Then carry on . . . *gli accade spesso andare in carròzza a Bologna e poi tornasene.*" Beppo sat back tapping a pencil gently against his lips and waiting while the boy standing at the

end of the third row struggled to construe. "Come, come, Pavan, it is not all that difficult, surely? All right then, sit down.
Now, let's see—Bianchi? Corrodino? Della Rocca?"

Della Rocca rose, clearing his throat nervously. "It occurred
often to go by—by wagon to Bologna and after to return himself."

Beppo sighed exaggeratedly and Della Rocca grinned, a little abashed.

"Isn't that right, Professor?"

"It is not, I'm afraid. I've asked you to render this freely in
English. Not to make a word-for-word literal translation." But
what was the good? The class had never been to England. They
had never heard English spoken by the natives nor been taught
—tutored individually, painstakingly, by a well-read, patient
and intelligent Englishman. Twenty years flashed backward
in Beppo's mind and he was sitting once more—hardly any
older than young Della Rocca here—in Mr. Pinniger's study
and Mr. Pinniger was saying in his slow careful voice, "Now
Joe, here is another characteristically illogical construction
which we must examine together . . ." A stab of sorrow, of
nostalgia for the distant past, caused a momentary catch in
Beppo's breath. He had been so happy in England; the Pinnigers had treated him just like a son—considerably better, in
point of fact, than his own parents. He had been back to see
them once and as soon as the will was proved he would visit
them again. They must be getting old by now. . . .

Reluctantly he returned to the present; to the books on his
desk and the class of boys in their smartly pressed, pale summer khaki ranged at the benches before him. "Well—does
anyone want to try the next sentence? What about Lecco?
Lecco, your father took you on a visit to London last year,
didn't he?"

"Yes, Professor. But it was only for a fortnight."

"You must have heard a lot of English spoken, nonetheless."

"Not really. We stayed at the Embassy, you see." Lecco's father was a general and had been in London on official business. Beppo felt, as he had often felt before, a vague yet all-
pervading helplessness, a sense of impotent frustration. He
knew that none of the class really wanted to learn to speak English. They wanted to acquire just sufficient grammar to gain a

pass in the written subject and they were willing enough to work hard to achieve this. But they saw no reason to speak the language—it would not be part of their duties when they became army officers in a few years' time.

Beppo had been very pleased when a family connection had successfully helped him to this post of assistant English teacher at the Nunziatella a year ago. Before that he had been teaching in a small secondary school at Bagnuoli at a salary so low that he had been forced to augment it by private lessons and Sunday work in the travel agency which had once been his own. His mixed classes at the secondary school, too, had been rowdy and ill-disciplined and Beppo was bad at keeping order. He had, at first, been delighted with the changed circumstances in which he found himself: the big, well-lighted classrooms, the rows of quiet, polite, industrious boys. Yet he had soon found that the industry, though genuine enough in one sense, was completely mechanical. At the secondary school there had always been two or three pupils who really wanted to learn and were sincerely interested in the language. Here, at the famous military academy, it was merely a question of securing a pass in examinations.

And the atmosphere, at least to someone of Beppo's disposition and with his memories of war, was so depressing—military, cold and formal. At his previous school those members of the class who were not attending to him—about forty percent, generally—were engaged in passing scurrilous notes to each other or making obscene drawings in their exercise books, but only once had he caught a boy not attending—drawing in his notebook at the Nunziatella. It had been young Ricci, not yet sixteen and therefore still without the silver State stars on his collar that marked out anyone over that age. Beppo had called him up, expecting to find some silly picture and to administer a mild rebuke. Instead, in beautiful detail, colored with crayons, he had been shown the half-section diagram of a hand-grenade. He had glanced from the diagram to the boy before him— a cold-eyed, closemouthed, immaculately uniformed little Prussian even by Nunziatella standards. Suddenly he had had a vision of Ricci pulling the pin from this grenade and thrusting it into the shirt of a weeping, trembling prisoner. He had shuddered and handed the book back. "You must not continue your military studies during English lessons. Please remember that. All right—go and sit down."

Now he looked across the class to where Ricci sat beside the taller figure of Galo. They were friends he believed, though he could never think what they could find in common; Ricci with his stiffness and cool ability and Galo with his great, wide faun's eyes, his air of a continual distrait desire to please. But boys were odd creatures; one never knew what liasons they would make. Lecco, despite his seniority, was a friend of Galo's, too.

"Well—has *anybody* done any more? We've been told, with some difficulty and without much enthusiasm, that when Garibaldi had his headquarters at Rimini in October 1859 he often happened to go by carriage to Bologna and then return. So far, so good. Let us see, however, whether we can struggle a little further. Ricci will construe the next two lines for us, I'm sure."

Ricci rose at once. "*Si, signore.*"

"*English,* Ricci!"

"Yes, sir. *Allora*—in—in those most rapid journeys, wear—wearisome beyond all telling, the Colonel Malenchini, I and another officer accompanied."

"*Accompagnarlo. AccompagnarLO!*"

"Oh—yes! Accompanied him."

"Thank you, Ricci. Very good. Now—" Beppo sighed. It wasn't really fair after Ricci, but one had to avoid any open hint of favoritism. "Colavolpe will give us the next sentence—I hope. *La corsa, per lo più, si faceva di notte e coi cavalli della posta*—not very difficult, really."

Galo rose, smiling uncertainly. "The race, for most—one was making—was made—*si*—one made on night-horses to the post? *No, scusi, signore*—at the post."

Beppo rubbed one hand across his forehead. "Look, let us try to be a little less surrealistic over this small, unimportant, but quite rational incident in the life of our national hero. Garibaldi, Colonel Malenchini and some of his staff officers, among whom is the narrator, are making frequent and tiresome journeys between Rimini and Bologna. Even if it had not been explicitly stated that these were undertaken in a carriage, do you seriously imagine that they would have raced each other madly down the road on 'night-horses'—whatever they may be? The

English have a word 'nightmare'— Can anyone tell me what it means? No?—Well anyway, it would fit your translation appropiately enough, Colavolpe. And surely, anything else apart, we all know that *'della'* means 'of the.' "

He shook his head, sighing. It was not as if Galo was unintelligent, either. He was merely a nervous type who could not concentrate or connect his thoughts properly. But then with that background and that family—the Lords and Ladies, as Mina called them—it was amazing that he was not a gibbering idiot.

As so often before, Beppo did his best to encourage him. "*Corsa* can certainly mean a race. But in this case it means 'the journey.' So we get 'The journey—*per lo più*—'for the most.' We add the word 'part' to make it good English. The journey, for the most part—*si faceva*—was made—you were quite right there, Colavolpe—*di notte*—by night. And now we come to these horses. What are—or rather, were—'*cavalli della posta'?*"

Still smiling, but pink-faced, Galo thought a moment. "Post horses?"

"Exactly! Good. 'The journey for the most part was made by night and with post horses.' All right. Now, Rannaletta, you go on. . . ."

The lesson moved forward more quickly now but at the back of Beppo's mind was the small, sad, nagging worry that whoever took the place he himself was vacating today could hardly be expected to be as patient with Galo or to surreptitiously give him better marks than he ever earned. Of course for himself there had been a strong tie of obligation in the matter since Galo's deplorable mother was his widowed cousin and Galo's still more deplorable uncle—the mutilated war hero, Major Concezio Colavolpe—had been instrumental in getting him this job. A Gold Medal and the loss of a leg and a hand could still do wonders in acquiring military favors, and the fact that Concezio Colavolpe was stupid, brutal and profligate could be entirely overlooked in the remembrance of his ten terrific days of desperate fighting as commander of a rearguard in Russia. Otherwise, of course, he would never have been able to arrange his nephew's entry into the Nunziatella, for Galo was not up to the high standards demanded of all other entrants into the academy. Beppo had at first believed that the strain of trying, and inevitably failing, to keep up with his classmates must make the boy still more nervous and unhappy, but he had found that this was not so. Galo liked the Nunziatella and fitted in well enough. A friendly disposition and an eagerness to please went a long way, even in military circles, to atone for a lack of properly directed application. And anyway, as Beppo often thought with a commiserating shudder, almost anywhere would seem delightful by comparison with that grotesque Bourbon mansion out at Caserta, and almost any company charming set against its morose and eccentric inhabitants.

On weekends and Thursday evenings when the junior cadets were allowed out until half past nine, Galo invariably came around to the Vomero flat and spent the time with Mina and her father. They played Canasta or Monopoly or the local version of slapjack with the narrow, brightly colored Neapolitan cards, and later Mina would cook the supper and then they would squeeze three chairs onto the tiny balcony and watch the evening life of the Via Raffaele Morghen passing below them. And on these occasions, watching Galo relaxed and happy in the ordinary background of a petit-bourgeois apartment, Beppo would think that despite the Lords and Ladies, despite the *damnosa hereditas* of the Colavolpe blood, Galo might yet succeed in growing up to be a normal enough human being. He hoped that even though he was leaving his job at the Nunziatella, Galo would still be allowed to visit the Vomero flat. But the Colavolpes, as he knew, had entertained wild hopes of inheriting at least a part of Ercole's fortune and in their present disappointment and chagrin they were more than likely to sever all further connection with the remaining Sanbrenedettos.

As the hands of his wristwatch came together over the figure 12 Beppo, aware that he was doing this for the last time, closed his books and watched the class rustle their papers into orange-colored folders. He cleared his throat, settled his spectacles firmly and smiled down at the benches with a sudden shy warmth. "Well, I must now say good-bye to you all. I think you know that I—that owing to personal circumstances I am leaving the Nunziatella and that I shall not be teaching you again. I've enjoyed my time here very much. I've enjoyed teaching you. . . ." He paused a moment and then, embarrassed by the polite silence of the listening class, continued with a rush. "English is a difficult language to learn, I know. Particularly when you have so many other subjects to study as well. But you have all worked hard and I think we have made good progress—as I've told the Commandant. So now I must wish you the best of luck in the exams. I'm sure you will all do well." He paused again, wanting both to conclude his speech yet to put more warmth into it; to somehow make these rows of uniformed boys realize that he was fond of them and sincerely wanted them to succeed.

And in that pause two boys rose—Lecco, the head of the class and little Ricci, its youngest member—and approached his desk, smiling and carrying something wrapped in a cloth. "This is for you, *professore*—from all of us." And taking off the wrapping they displayed an early nineteenth-century print of a Nunziatella cadet in full parade uniform.

Beppo, glancing from it to their smiling faces and then back to the class, was aware of a sudden triumphant surge of pleasure, a feeling that he had at last succeeded in something, that these boys had liked him—had even, perhaps, profited by his instruction. Tears pricked his eyes, his heart seemed to expand painfully. "Thank you—thank you all. I—I shall keep this always. It will remind me of you."

And as the class queued carefully in the aisle between the benches to pass by and shake his hand—it was characteristic of the Nunziatella that even now no one broke ranks or pushed forward—Beppo was thinking, behind his happiness, behind the warmth of his sudden newfound sentiment, that this parting present to him would make an ideal replacement for Vittorio's portrait on the bedroom wall.

◄§ 4

LECCO and Della Rocca went quickly, cheerfully down the line of juniors ranged before their beds, checking buttons, brasses, belts and shoes. Lecco had a yellow duster and a clothes brush, Della Rocca a velvet polishing pad. Everybody was very smart and clean but they found occasional minor exceptions. "Balassone—cap strap. Corrodino—belt. Hurry up both of you; we all want to get away. Masiello—get your hair cut. Pavan—Pavan, what in God's name do you use your *spadino* for? Digging the garden? Listen, everyone! You keep your *spadini* in their scabbards, see? You don't take them out except to clean them. They're not toys—they're part of your parade uniform. And another thing. We're not covering up for anyone who gets back late anymore. Until you get your stars up you have to be in by nine-thirty. And that *means* nine-thirty and not twenty to ten or a quarter to ten. All right—off you go."

Saturday afternoon sunlight pouring through the wide windows, glinting on a vivid medley of white, brass-buttoned tunics, pale blue, carmine-striped trousers, gilt and enamel daggers. The juniors rattled, laughing and chattering, down the stone stairs, crossed an open, hexagonal courtyard and slowed and straightened as they neared the flag-draped, sword-hung ceremonial precincts of the front hall. The white-gaitered guards clicked and stamped and swung their right arms across their chests, hands edgeways against rigidly straight carbines, and were saluted in their turn with wooden precision. The atmosphere was rock-hard with reciprocal military compliments though, since there were no officers or seniors present; no one in the cavernous, banner-draped vestibule was yet sixteen years old.

Outside, in the hot sunlight of the Via Generale Parisi, Galo blinked, wishing that he was not in parade uniform so that he could wear his dark glasses. His overlarge eyes were sensitive to strong light and hurt him. There were three or four taxis at the bottom of the street but he had no money to hire one. He smiled at the thought and turning down the Monte di Dio made his way slowly through the hot June afternoon toward the Piazza Plebiscito and the long dusty walk up the Toledo.

The clash and hiss of trolley-buses and trams, the continual grind of gears, blare of horns and clatter of hoofs beat at him in a thundering surf of sound—the unending tidal roar of Naples. Galo had that type of sensuous nervousness upon which sights, smells and noises strike like bewildering blows—tiring, confusing, dazing. Before he had even reached the Piazza Dante his head was aching and he was feeling sick. What was more, he felt conspicuous and knew that as soon as he reached the Via Tribunali and turned off toward the *bassifondi* of San Lorenzo and the Porta Capuana he would feel still more so. Naples was accustomed to the sight of brightly uniformed Nunziatella cadets in the main streets but they were less common in the slums. Also Galo was frightened for his white tunic. He had only one—the one which was standard issue and paid for by the State—and if it became dirty he would be in trouble at home. They would be expecting him to wear his uniform at lunch tomorrow when De Santis came.

The passage along the narrow Via Tribunali was particularly trying; the arcades near the Piazzetta San Girolamo where the morning and evening fish markets were held had just been washed down and the street was a mass of puddles full of fishy water, scales and sardine heads. Galo had to retreat to the church steps to avoid being drenched every time one of the roaring little three-wheeled delivery trucks, which were the bane of the narrower streets, rocketed past in a splash of fishy spray. By the time he reached the Piazza Vittime Civili di Guerra he was exhausted and dusty, the shirt beneath his tight white tunic soaked with sweat.

Crocifissa, as usual, welcomed him with more than motherly warmth. "*Contino!* Come in—come in and sit down! *Poverino*—how tired you look! Why ever did you come here on foot? And at this time of the day! I'll get you some wine—or would you like brandy?"

"Just water, Crocifissa. And may I take off my coat?"

"Of course! Come into the kitchen. Gigi—get a glass of water for the *contino*. Run the tap until it's properly cold, mind!"

In the back room behind the shop Crocifissa helped to unbuckle his belt and to extricate him from his tunic; she pulled her own big wooden armchair up for him, ejected Otello from the seat and padded it with cushions. Under her fussing, in the cool dimness of the shuttered kitchen and sipping his water, Galo began to revive. "Did Quong's do my wreath?"

"Yes indeed, *caro mio!*" Crocifissa nodded fervently. "Gennaro did it himself on the morning of the funeral. It was a nice one, too. I told him, 'Now, Gennà, it must be something nice for the *contino*—something tasteful but not expensive because he's only a boy like you and can't be expected to pay a lot.' So Gennaro bought two dozen dark red carnations—they last

better than the white ones—and some pink stock which was going cheap, and the dealer let him have the tops of two paradise
flowers for nothing because he couldn't sell them since the stalks
were broken."

Galo said slowly, "I should have liked to have gone to the
funeral myself. I couldn't get away, though. I'd had to ask for
a special pass for tonight and tomorrow and they won't let you
out just as you like."

"Of course not."

"Did you go, Crocifissa?"

"No. I couldn't leave the shop. But I saw it set off. Gennaro
did it all himself. It was a nice funeral—small but nice. Signor
Giuseppe was there."

"I know. Mina told me."

"Of course it's sad about your great-uncle—Don Ercole, I
should say. I'd known him so long myself. Why, I was hardly
more than a girl when I went to work at his house—that was
when he was living in Pendino. I'd just got married and Dino
was born there." Both of them instinctively lifted their eyes to
the photograph that hung on the wall above the dresser and
under which a small electric lamp mounted on a gilt cross
glowed perpetually. Dino smiled down at them—smiled across
twenty years of grief and emptiness—wide-collared, sleek and
brushed; a little embarrassed by the photographer's light and
his own picturesque white uniform. Crocifissa sighed. "Yes, it
was a happy time. Don Ercole was a good *padrone*. He was
strict, of course. I remember how frightened your mother used
to be of him when she was a girl—and Signor Giuseppe, too. I
remember once . . ." She launched herself into a luxurious
sea of reminiscence while Galo sat sipping his water, feeling his
damp shirt drying coolly on his skin, the ache in his temples
and his eyes subsiding in the restful gloom.

Here he was always at peace—here and at Vomero. Here he
had planned—how often? A dozen times at least—to take refuge if things became too bad. And always he had put it off. "I'll
wait this time—just this once. But if they do it again I'll go. I'll
go straight to Crocifissa and tell her and say I want to stay. I'll
say I will work in the shop or for Quong's or anyone else who
will let me. I'll do anything—only I *won't* go back to Caserta!"

Why had he never done it? Because a voice told him inwardly that he had feared too deeply he would be taken back—screaming and kicking and biting if need be but still taken inexorably back—to a future in which there would no longer be even a hypothetical refuge. And then later there had been Beppo and Mina . . . a world beginning to widen and lighten, to show hints of coming day.

". . . left everything to him, it seems. Well, of course it was only to be expected, really. There had been some sort of quarrel once, I understand, but then Signor Giuseppe is the last of the family, isn't he? And, you know, I always think old Don Ercole put a lot of weight on that. I told Signor Giuseppe so when I congratulated him on his good fortune. He asked me if I'd seen you lately, too. I told him not for some weeks. 'Not since he came back from his last visit to your uncle, Signore Giuseppe,' I said. 'And that must have been at Easter. He always comes to see me after he's been staying with Don Ercole because there's generally some message and he knows I like to hear how Don Ercole has been keeping.' "

Galo said suddenly, "It was cold. I didn't think he used to feel it; there was hardly ever any heating in the house. But that time he wore his overcoat all day. He sent me into Pescara to buy one for myself. We walked along the beach." Long, long miles of flat sand flanked on one side by shallow, breaking waves, on the other by dismal marshes beyond the straight coast road: and wind . . . always the continual wind. . . . The two of them walking together in uncompanionable silence, their overcoats flapping round their knees. Sand and sea and the dreary, windy winter sky. . . . "And now he's dead."

"And at peace," added Crocifissa piously.

For a moment they sat in silence; then Galo rose. "I must go and pay Quong's for my wreath. How is the old man?"

"Much the same. No worse and no better."

"He's not going to—?"

Crocifissa sighed. "Well, *contino,* for some in such a state I'd say it would be a merciful release if they did. But Quong isn't like that. I don't think he's unhappy. And of course *when* it happens it will break poor Gennaro's heart."

ᴥᵹ 5

GENNARO was planing the bottom board of a
coffin, watched benignly by Quong who was perched doll-like
in a high-backed armchair opposite the carpenter's bench.
Galo's shadow in the doorway made them both look up.

"*Permesso?*"

"*Vien', vien'! Benvenuto!* No, my hands are covered in glue
—shake Quong's instead."

Quong's smile widened a little toward the left, the unpara-
lyzed, side of his face and his dark, almond eyes shone with a
pleasure he could no longer articulate. Galo smiled down at
him, holding the mutilated, birdlike yellow hand carefully in
his own. The third and fourth fingers were missing and for a
long time Galo had believed this to be the result of a carpenter-
ing accident until Gennaro had confided in him that the fingers
had been publicly cut off at a street court in Pekin when, as a
child of eight, Quong had been convicted of stealing two man-
goes from a stall. Gennaro's voice as he spoke of it had been
bitter with rage but the effect on Galo had been one of dumb
horror—it was something straight from the nightmare world
that mowed and gibbered too often at his own shoulder.

And yet despite this manual defect Quong had been a magnificent woodcarver right up to his paralytic stroke. Galo had
watched, with the same delighted admiration as Gennaro, while
Quong's thin steel gouges traced the most exact and delicate patterns on pale oak or pink mahogany. The big rosewood carving
of Kwang-Yin, the Goddess of Mercy, which stood against one
wall of the workshop, its gentle slim-eyed face bent forward in
calm, all-comprehending compassion, had been Quong's own
work. But now there would be no more.

Turning away Galo said "The wreath— Crocifissa told me it
was very nice."

"*Non c'era male.*" Gennaro's voice held the judicious modesty
of an artist who cannot actually praise his own work but would
very much like to. "And I got the flowers cheap in the Abate."

"How much?"

"A thousand will cover it. I can take the palm leaves back and use them again."

Galo pulled out his wallet and extricated one of the three thousand-lire notes he had stolen from a secret cache he had recently discovered in the lining of his grandmother's workbox. He had expected to be charged at least two thousand—and even that would have been cheap. "You can't make much profit out of wreaths."

"Oh, we do! But not from friends, of course." Gennaro bent quickly over his coffin board, blushing crimson. He was sure he had committed a grave error of taste but he had taken Galo's words as an unintentional slight upon his business ability—something concerning which he was acutely sensitive.

Galo colored in his turn and looked away. He should not have said that about profit. Gennaro must think him most ungrateful. Quong, watching them both, understanding precisely what each was thinking, was amused, touched, mildly contemptuous. How very much better two young Chinese would have managed the situation. How infinitely more adapted for the subtle exchange of every civility was the magnificent mandarin of his own people in comparison with this Latin-based Italian. How pitifully awkward Occidentals could be.

Gennaro's plane skidded as the wood beneath it moved. He clicked his tongue angrily, *"Mannaggia!"* and Galo grinned and stepping forward, held the end of the plank. "Don't you need an assistant now?"

"Sometimes. But I can't afford one. Later, when business is better, perhaps. At the moment there's a—a trade recession. Now the other end—that's right."

For an hour or more Galo worked happily in the coffin shop listening to Gennaro's constant chatter about funerals—Ercole's in particular—and putting off still further the time when he must take the train to Caserta. After all, he was only needed for tomorrow's lunch; nobody would care if he did not arrive home before this evening.

Gennaro, in his turn, was pleased to have some unpaid labor. There were certain operations in the construction of even the worst coffin which needed four hands. He made full use of Galo's willing presence. "Now just give that glue a stir while I bevel up the edges. . . . No—the *purple* lining. Widows like purple. We do a lot of widows because we're cheap. . . . Hold it tight. Pull it out straight—that's it! It's quite expensive so we don't want to waste any."

At four o'clock he called a halt. "I'm going around to pay some money to our wood merchant in the Vico dei Lepri." He eyed Galo carefully up and down. "Would you like to come?"

"All right."

"What about your coat—and dagger?"

"They're with Crocifissa—quite safe."

Gennaro nodded. He was a little disappointed for he would have liked to be seen walking across the *piazza* with a fully uniformed Nunziatella cadet whom later he could have described as "one of our clients." Signor Savoldi, too. . . .

Signor Savoldi sat behind his big desk covered in ledgers and rulers.

"*Beh!* You again, Gennaro! No more credit, boy! A little cash is what I want from *you*." He grasped Gennaro's extended hand and pretended to pull him off his feet. Behind, in the timber yard, the circular saw shrieked agonizingly as it tore through great planks of wood. Gennaro thought longingly, enviously, of all that wood—in his mind it was all destined for coffins. He owed Savoldi over sixty thousand lire.

Having failed to pull Gennaro off his feet Signor Savoldi patted his shoulder, rumpled his hair and playfully smacked his bottom with a long ruler. All these things were the usual accompaniments to making a deal with the wood merchant. Today, however, Savoldi's hands suddenly dropped and he stared over Gennaro's shoulder to where Galo stood behind him.

"*Corpo di Dio!* Who's your friend?"

"One of our clients."

"Nonsense! He's just as alive as I am—and a great deal handsomer! *Uno dei nostri dei cadetti.*" Signor Savoldi took in Galo's slender figure, the wide-eyed oval of his face, high cheekboned, smoothly biscuit-colored as if carried out in glazed china, with the frank admiration of a connoisseur.

"This is our wood merchant," said Gennaro, mentally willing Galo to come forward and shake hands. "We are old business friends."

"Yes, indeed." Signor Savoldi took Galo's hand in his and

held it for a long minute. "Well, well, this *is* a treat!" He began
to say something else but fortunately the circular saw lifted its
high scream and drowned his words. When at last it whined
down to a groan and ceased, Gennaro had his old wallet out.
"I've got a bit for you on account—fifteen." He laid the notes
on Signor Savoldi's desk and at last the wood merchant
dropped Galo's hand and turned, sighing, to business.

"Well done, Gennà! Business is looking up I hope?"

"A little, I think. I'd pay more if I could."

"I know you would, Gennà. How's your grandfather?"

"The same. I've got to get back now. I've left him alone in the
shop."

"So soon?" Savoldi looked regretfully at Galo, then down at
the money.

"Well, thank you for this, anyway. My compliments to Quong,
as usual. Oh! And here are five Australian stamps for you—off
letters from my brother in Perth. I nearly forgot them." He
smiled warmly at the two boys and then, taking a couple of cigarettes from a packet on the desk, pressed one into each of their
palms. "Bring your friend along another day, eh? We'll have a
chat and I'll send out for coffee."

"*Senz' altro.*" Gennaro, slipping the stamps into his overall
pocket, backed away grinning widely. "*Ciao!*"

"*Ciao.*"

Once more in the shop they found Quong just as they had left
him but now he made a small gesture with one hand and at once
Gennaro said, "He wants to write something." He picked up a
carpenter's pencil and a piece of scrap plywood and waited
while Quong laboriously wrote a sentence in words so cramped
and shaky that even Gennaro, who had much practice, found
difficulty in deciphering them. But at last his face broke into a
wide, delighted grin. "Wait a minute!" He left the shop and
Galo heard him running upstairs. When he came back he held
a small, dark wooden box of heavily carved and polished cedar
wood. "He wants to give you this. He used to make them often
until . . . This is one of his best."

Galo took it, coloring with pleasure, then suddenly slapped a
hand to his hip pocket. "But this is just what I need. *Vero!* I
have to leave something with Crocifissa and now I can put it
in this box. It's got a lock, too. And now—" he looked regret-

fully around the cluttered workshop—"I must get my things and go."

"You'll come back soon, eh?"

"Yes, yes." Galo suddenly smiled as if struck by a secret thought. "I'll come often. Why not? After all . . ." He broke off, laughing softly. "I'll come back all right."

Crocifissa was waiting for him in her kitchen. She had brushed the dust from his tunic and now she helped him dress. "Have you had a nice time, *caro mio?*"

"Very nice. Crocifissa—I've got something I want to leave here with you. Something I want you to keep safely for me. Will you?"

"Of course, *contino*. What is it?"

"This—" From his hip pocket Galo pulled a thick envelope, a little battered at the corners and sealed heavily with red wax. He placed it in the carved cedar box and locking it stood for a moment hesitating with the tiny gilt key in his hand. Then unbuttoning the front of his shirt he pulled out his gold crucifix on its thin gold chain and hung the little key beside it.

Crocifissa took the box and glanced around the room. "Now let me see—ah yes, in the top drawer of the dresser. It can go behind my account books. It will be quite safe there until you want it again."

And rebuttoning his shirt, watching the old woman stow the box carefully away in her cupboard, Galo was once more reading the contents of the envelope it contained, as he had read them last Easter, standing beside his great-uncle's chair in the Adriatic villa. . . . "*—do hereby revoke all previous wills and testamentary dispositions heretofore made by me . . . and give, devise and bequeath all my real and personal estate of whatsoever kind and wheresoever situated to my great-nephew Galeazzo Arconovaldo Maria Ignacio Colavolpe. . . .*"

For Ercole Sanbrenedetto was not a man to change his mind. He had said he was going to disinherit Beppo and he had disinherited him.

Lords and Ladies

1

THERE were seven small white eggs on the table. They lay wrapped in a piece of newspaper on a cracked dish.

"Seven— And how is one supposed to make a *zabaglione* for a party of ten people with seven eggs?" The man with the gloved wooden hand and the raw purple stain down the left side of his face glowered across the table. "Yesterday evening there were ten. Someone's taken three."

"Filippa took one for the old man."

"So— Well, where are the other two?"

"Tarquinio got up in the night. Maria Celeste met him in a passage."

"I was going out to defecate. I suppose I've a right to do that, haven't I? What was Maria Celeste doing, anyway?"

"Exactly what you *say* you were doing, Tarquinio. Though why any of us should ever need to, considering we get practically nothing to eat, I can't imagine."

"Considering you never do any work, why should you get anything to eat?"

"Concezio, that's not a nice thing to say; and we do a lot of work—considering our ages."

"*Fetiuk!* Let's stop considering things and find out where these eggs have got to. You, Galo! You took them, eh?"

"No," lied Galo sullenly. He stood by one of the tall windows wearing his "home" clothes—a castoff army shirt of his uncle's and a pair of old gray flannel shorts which he had grown out of a year ago at least and whose top buttons he could no longer fasten.

"What have you been doing since you got up?"

"Homework."

"In your room?"

"Yes."

"Anyone seen him about this morning?"

Galo glanced covertly at old Maria Fausta who sat nervously entwining her knobbly fingers. Concezio's frequent household courts-martial always upset her intensely. Galo knew she had seen him going down the backstairs an hour ago when he was getting rid of the eggshells. She probably would not say anything, though, unless she was directly accused herself.

Concezio glared around him. "Well, no one is leaving this room until I find out!"

"In that case," said Tarquinio comfortably, "one may assume that there will not only be no *zabaglione* but no lunch at all, either."

Concezio's scarred face flushed, his wide, well-shaped lips—the Colavolpes all had beautiful mouths, it was their most distinguishing feature—thinned ominously. He glanced with a contemptuous loathing from his old uncle to his still older aunts, and then to his young nephew. "Every one of you depends on me for every single thing you've got—and *still* you steal! You knew perfectly well why we needed those eggs for lunch. De Santis is bringing American friends. They must be properly entertained and given what they, at any rate, think of as typical Italian food. With the exception of spaghetti and pizza, *zabaglione* is probably the only one of our dishes of which they have ever heard."

"Well, since you've killed four of the remaining chickens for them there are not likely to be any eggs in future, anyway—at least until we get to the Sila."

Concezio said savagely, "I'd kill the goat, too, if I thought they'd eat it!"

"It isn't your goat, Concezio," quavered Maria Fausta from her seat beside an imitation alabaster pillar. "It belongs to the house—to us all."

"That wouldn't worry him," remarked Tarquino. "Like the boy's rabbit—remember?"

Concezio banged his wooden, leather-gloved hand on the table with a crash "Whatever does or does not belong to me, *nothing* whatever belongs to any of you! You live entirely off my pension, Speranza's dowry and a few odd lire from my mother." And now his remarkable memory began to play upon them like rapid cannon fire. "That suit, Tarquinio, was bought for you by me eight years ago. It cost seven thousand eight hundred lire. Your shirt—my mother paid for that—fifteen hundred. Your shoes—my money again—two thousand. Your underclothes, too—I think Speranza gave them to you as a Christmas present. *Dio!* Think of a *man*—if that's what you call yourself—of fifty-nine who can't even afford to buy his own underclothes!

"Maria Fausta—two years in hospital. Who paid? I and Speranza. Maria Celeste has to go into Naples twice a month for her arthritis. Who pays? I do. And—and you—" He turned to his nephew, trying to find some equally insulting taunts, but Galo had not been attacked by any expensive illnesses and his clothes could hardly be considered as anything save a reproach to those who had provided them. "I got you into the Nunziatella—you're too stupid and too lazy to pass the exams properly yourself. *I* pay for your haircuts and your soap and your toothpaste and—"

"What's the trouble *now?*" A big woman whose thick, red-gold hair glinted in the morning sun, entered the room walking quickly, heavily in heelless peasant slippers. "What is it, Concezio? Who's been worrying you?"

"Someone's stolen two eggs. My mother took one for the old man—against my express instructions—but we might have done with nine. Now someone's stolen two more. Probably your precious son, Speranza."

"Did you? Did you, Galo?"

"No!"

"Come here! I can generally tell. You were told not to touch anything on the table, weren't you—*weren't you?*"

"I didn't." Mother and son stared at each other with mutual hatred.

Speranza's eyes were a fierce, bright tawny gold. "You *did!* You little beast—little brute!" Suddenly she grasped him by the tattered collar of his shirt and hit him hard across the face. "Go on—admit it!"

Galo swallowed. High-voiced, shaky, he cried, "I did *not!* I didn't take them! Leave me alone! Anyway"—desperately he pulled back from her upraised hand, the buttons tearing from his shirtfront—"you stole my overcoat—the one Uncle Ercole gave me. And—"

Crack went her hand across the side of his head—*crack*—*crack*.

"Calling your mother a thief! It's you who are the thief! Liar! Thief! Wretched, mean little egg-stealer!"

Concezio watched for a moment with satisfaction. Then he grunted, "That's enough, Speranza. He's got to look present-able at lunch."

"He doesn't deserve any lunch!"

"*Basta!* He's got to be there because . . . Listen to me, Galo, and stop crying and shivering like a baby. *Dio!* You're nearly sixteen, though no one would think it. Speranza, you've made his face bleed. Can no one"—Concezio's voice rose to a sudden wolf-howl of frustrated rage—"*can no one do anything right at all this morning! Are you all mad*—" He stopped abruptly, bit-ing his lower lip. In the shocked silence the word "mad" seemed to rebound in ominous echoes up and down the room. It was the one term of abuse the Colavolpes never used in the unending, smoldering, sputtering fights which made up existence—no one could call it "life"—in the Caserta household.

Controlling himself with an effort Concezio said sharply, "Galo! Listen. Is your uniform clean and pressed?"

Swallowing, red-eyed, sniffing, Galo nodded.

"You get into it at midday—understand? And when they're here you behave—see? These are important people, not your friends in the San Lorenzo *bassifondi*. They'll ask about the Nunziatella. You can tell them about it. Later, they may want to see over this place—and the church, too. I expect they will. They may want you to show them over because they may feel embarrassed about me doing it with my leg. If so, you know what they can see and—much more important—what they can't. And remember what they say—anything they admire par-ticularly. You're supposed to be learning English from that idiotic cousin of your mother's, so you will probably understand even if they are not speaking Italian. I'll want to know all about it later— Are you listening?"

"Yes."

"Well, try—for God's sake—to remember what I've said. Your mother's quite right—you're a useless, lazy, lying, little lout. You couldn't even make old Ercole think enough of you to leave you a single lire—though, God knows, we sent you there often enough and wasted enough money. . . . But you're still not too big for us to deal with—I and your mother—if you let us down again. So be careful! Now get out. I don't want to see you or hear you again until midday."

ᴥᔮ 2

THE Colavolpes were aristocrats—a noble family; and, like the Sanbrenedettos, they came originally from Sicily, owing their transference to the mainland to the Spanish Bourbon King Ferdinand I rather than to Garibaldi.

In the intervals of hunting, which was his main passion, the King, at least in youth, had made frequent efforts to improve the government of his people but in these he was invariably unsuccessful since his guiding principle, when a serious difficulty had to be solved, was to leave the difficulty to solve itself. In 1798, jubilant at the British victory of the Nile, he attacked the Revolutionary French forces occupying Rome only to be at once driven back in headlong rout to Naples. Rescued by Nelson before the city fell, he and his family were taken to their second capital of Palermo to be guarded indefinitely by the British fleet while Naples became first the Partenopean Republic and then a kingdom again under Murat.

Ferdinand, safe in Sicily, hunted and played billiards; his queen fell in love with a young country squire and Nelson, watching the goings-on from the white, scrubbed quarterdeck of the *Vanguard* in Palermo roadstead, remarked acidly, "The Neapolitans have not lost much honor for—God knows—they had little enough to lose. But they have lost what they had."

Queen Maria Carolina's lover, Arconovaldo Colavolpe, was the sort of man upon whom any British admiral, historical or modern, would unhesitatingly have made such a comment, and perhaps because of this, he not only delighted his royal mistress but charmed the King. He hunted competently, he exhibited an exquisite skill at billiards and his liaison with the Queen was unlikely to worry a man who had said publicly of his wife on the morning after their wedding, "She sleeps as if she had been killed and she sweats like a pig."

When at last the war was over, when Napoleon was on his way to St. Helena and Murat had been deposed, driven out, captured and shot, the royal family returned bringing Arconovaldo, now Marchese Colavolpe, with them. As a reward for his prowess in bed and at the billiards table he received an estate at Caserta and sufficient additional Court sinecures to allow him to build his big baroque mansion, the Palazzo Colavolpe, and to live there in state. And there he died in 1844, a jovial, vulgar, lewd old man—and at once the Colavolpe fortunes began their long decline.

For in the same way that Arconovaldo had borne a strange affinity, a *simpaticezza speciale*, to Ferdinand I, his son Giulio had an odd spiritual, and in some respects even physical, resemblance to the king's heir, the dark, bigoted, savage "Bomba."

"The negation of God erected into a system of government," wrote the outraged Gladstone on a visit to Naples during the reign of Ferdinand II; but the orgiastic lusts and savageries of the Marchese Giulio Colavolpe went further than even Bomba was prepared to tolerate. The Court sinecures and pensions upon which Arconovaldo had relied for the greater part of his income were allowed to lapse without renewal, and when syphilis had added physical horror to his other degradations, Giulio Colavolpe was kept under what amounted to house arrest until the end of the reign. Bomba died. Francis II, "Bombino," ascended the Neapolitan throne. But far away in Turin, Cavour was saying ominously, "They have stopped me making Italy by diplomacy from the north; I will make it by revolution from the south."

That May they landed in Sicily, Garibaldi and the Thousand. . . . And four months later on a hot, blue September day the General, dusty and sunburned, rode into roaring Naples with his young, red-shirted orderly, Vittorio Sanbrenedetto, at his side. The Bourbon dynasty ended abruptly; but the Colavolpes lingered on.

The third Marchese Colavolpe, Arconovaldo Melchiorre, was born in 1868, inheriting the title at the age of five when his father, blind and insane for the last three years of his life, was accidentally poisoned by the negligence of a careless attendant. Unlike the grandfather after whom he was named, Arconovaldo Melchiorre was of a gloomy, morose and unstable nature. For a long time his family considered that he must be some sort of hermaphrodite for his high voice did not break, nor did his testicles descend, until he was in his late twenties. From the age of eighteen he slept with a holy relic—the front tooth of a saint —between his legs and when that, or the various cures prescribed by his doctors, or the working of a reluctant Nature brought his reproductive organs at last into working order, the Colavolpes scraped up enough money to build a small church on the rapidly diminishing estate near their palace. They had made a vow to do this if the saint's tooth was effective, and though they tried to evade it, pleading poverty and the excessive tardiness of the tooth's cure, the ecclesiastical authorities were in no mood for quibbling and the church was raised.

Both the expense of this building and the reason for its existence brought almost immediate financial disaster to the family; for the cost of the church exceeded the original estimate by over sixty percent, while Arconovaldo Melchiorre, fascinated by the physical sensations he was now able to enjoy for the first time, at once got married and fathered seven children in the shortest possible order. These four girls and three boys were reared in an atmosphere of genteel poverty which became less and less genteel as the years passed and more land was sold off to local peasants to pay debts which grew ever greater and more pressing. Since the Colavolpes were aristocrats they did not consider it right to earn their livings by their own efforts; since they were lazy they did not want to and since they were unintelligent, even by aristocratic standards, they did not in any case know how. The family income was derived exclusively from the Italian *mezzadria* system of sharecropping, and as the tired earth about their palace grew less and less productive it was only the most miserably poor and incapable peasant who would come to work it upon those terms.

None of Arconovaldo Melchiorre's daughters could marry, of course. Without dowries they would have found immense difficulty in acquiring husbands even if they had been superbly beautiful, which they were not. Such good looks as the family possessed seemed to be exclusively monopolized by the men, yet only one of these—the eldest, Antonio—was able to find a wife with a little money of her own whose parents were prepared, for the sake of the future inheritance of the estate and title, to sanction a marriage. But neither estate nor title ever passed to Antonio. For despite the reemergence in his blood of the inherited syphilis, old Arconovaldo Melchiorre showed an astonishing propensity to go on living. In 1915 he beame paralyzed from the waist down and ten years later he became blind like his father before him, the grim Marchese Giulio. But still he lived on, an old sightless cripple in a wheelchair who never left his two rooms in the second story, the *piano nobile,* of the baroque palace.

Then the infection—or perhaps the general environment in which they lived—began to take its toll of his children. The eldest daughter went into a mental asylum in 1928 and her brother, Eugenio, followed her five years later. Both events were a further drain on the expiring Colavolpe resources. The family was now headed for all practical purposes by Antonio, who already had children of his own—two boys, Arconovaldo Ignacio and Concezio—born in the early twenties. Had Antonio thrown in his lot with the Fascists he might have improved his family's condition but he refused to do this. The Colavolpes had been "noble" for over a hundred years by now and, as if they had not enough defects already, Antonio added that of family pride. A Colavolpe was an aristocrat, an Italian of high birth and blue blood. When once, at a local feast day, a kindly Caserta baker gave Arconovaldo Ignacio and Concezio some cakes the two small boys were severely chastised for accepting them and were in deep disgrace for days afterwards. The lesson went home: the Colavolpes might be poor but they *must* be "noble." Someone whose ancestor had played billiards with the Bourbons could not accept buns from a baker—even if he had no money to buy them for himself. Other boys might romp in black-shirted gangs along the Caserta roads but Colavolpe children could not be members of the Figli della Lupa or the Balilla or the Avanguardiste because such organizations were middle class, if not lower, and the Colavolpes were royalists—and Spanish Bourbon royalists at that.

Then came World War II. Antonio was too old to fight even if he had felt so inclined. Young Arconovaldo Ignacio was turned down on medical grounds; only Concezio was drafted. And then, for the first time since the days of King Ferdinand I, a Colavolpe demonstrated some ability. Concezio found his métier in the army. Brutal, loudmouthed, personally vain, he now found an outlet for those unbecoming emotions which others of his generation had discovered in the Fascist *squadristi*. He rose rapidly from the ranks, fought heroically in Russia and, hideously wounded, marked forever by frostbite, was carried home to receive Italy's highest award for valor and a pension which, if distinctly modest by the standards of most other countries, was a godsend to the penurious family at Caserta.

In the last years of the war, while Naples sprawled, battered and full of foreign troops, far behind the lines, Arconovaldo Ignacio married. His weak lungs and poor heart had kept him for some years under the care of a doctor—a humane and dedicated man—who knew of the Colavolpe family circumstances and charged his patient almost nothing. Not only this, but in order to ensure that the poor young man had at least the minimum nourishment, he was in the habit of frequently inviting him to dinners at which various black market foods, acquired from Allied sources, gave Arconovaldo Ignacio the only substantial meals he had ever had.

At one of these dinners he met a handsome, red-haired young woman chaperoned by her mother, and while Arconovaldo Ignacio hungrily ate bully beef and canned pilchards he found himself discreetly questioned about his position, family and circumstances. Since he saw no reason to hide these—after all, he was interested in what was on the table rather than the company around it—it was a surprise when the couple appeared again on his next visit to the hospitable doctor. This time they told him of their own circumstances. The elder woman was a widow, a Signora Sanbrenedetto whose husband had been long dead, and mother and daughter lived sometimes at their apartment in Bagnuoli but more often with various relations. It was quietly indicated that the girl, Speranza, was her father's sole

heir and also that the support of her mother would be undertaken by other relatives upon her marriage. This was the sort of
proposition which always interested a Colavolpe. Arconovaldo
Ignacio came more frequently to the doctor's house and shortly
the engagement and then the marriage date were announced.
The kindly doctor's wedding present included a whole crate of
bully beef.

But the combination of ill fortune and bad management
which dogged the Colavolpes had not deserted them even now.
Arconovaldo soon found that he had married a domineering,
harsh-tempered shrew who was not a virgin and who—safely
married at last—boasted that she had not been one since the age
of twelve. It was true that she possessed her father's portion of
Vittorio Sanbrenedetto's fortune, but he had been the youngest
son and had been left proportionately little. Most of it was
wretchedly invested in devalued stock and the tiny income it
brought in did not console Arconovaldo Ignacio for his wife's
evil temper and unrelenting sexual demands. After the birth of
their son Galeazzo, in the second year of their marriage, the
poor man began to show unmistakable signs of that dementia
which haunted the lives of all the family like a terrifying black
shadow. A few months after Galo's third birthday that darkness
finally closed over the mind of Arconovaldo Ignacio and he
was removed to what the family now euphemistically called
"hospital" to die unseen, almost unnoticed, a few years later.
For Speranza, taking the battered yet virile Concezio as her
lover—or bedmate, for there was nothing of love in the spasmodic couplings, fights and endless recriminations that made
up their liaison—had forgotten him long since.

So there, at last, they all were—a bestially poor, neurosis-
ridden family engaged in killing each other off in psychological warfare. Four old women, three of them completely penniless and only one of whom, Concezio's mother, had never been
married. A sly, drunken, equally penniless old man—Tarquinio;
the mutilated hero, his dead brother's sluttish wife, her wretched
little son and—high above them all, shut away in a single room
at the top of the house—an ancient, paralyzed, blind old creature whose face had long ago become so fearful with the ravages
of his disease that he habitually wore a cloth mask.

The Colavolpes—aristocrats; a noble family of blue blood and high birth.

⋅ॐ 3

THE Colavolpes had no servants. Their slavish poverty prevented them from paying wages and they were not the sort of people for whom even the most idle, drunken or dishonest of Caserta's unemployed would think of serving save for an adequate financial reward. Occasionally they managed to get a peasant woman to come and clean the few rooms in general use, but mostly they did the work themselves. Concezio, whose army training had given him a taste for rosters and lists, apportioned household duties and bullied and nagged the various members of the family into performing them. His old mother, Filippa, did the cooking. His oldest surviving aunt, Maria Valeria, looked after the senile and incontinent nonagenarian upstairs. The two other aunts, Maria Celeste and Maria Fausta, were supposed to do the housework while Tarquinio, who was incurably lazy but could sew and use a sewing machine, was browbeaten into coping with the endless mending and patching of clothes and bed linen. Galo, when at home, was made to work the half acre or so of vegetable garden and perform any of the more unpleasant jobs which other members of the family had managed to evade.

This morning he had been presented with a ball of string and told to repair the chicken-run and then transfer to it the four remaining fowls which were at present living in the vestry of the Church of the Holy Tooth. After this the vestry itself must be cleaned and the interior of the church dusted and made ready for an afternoon visit by De Santis and his Americans.

The chicken-run lay rotting away beside an ancient marble well, now used as a rubbish pit, among a grove of umbrella pines. It was a most unpleasant place; a patch of ground covered in a riot of nettles and backed by the wall of the church vestry which held a dozen rough immurement niches. Three Colavolpes already lay behind three cheap marble slabs and the other niches waited—forbidding, gray cement boxes full of chicken-dirt, blowflies and scraps of rubbish—for the rest of the family.

Galo, hesitating at the edge of this wilderness, thought for a moment of going back and asking to borrow an old pair of his uncle's trousers but realized at once that they would be refused. He waded with sullen stoicism into the nettles and soon his bare legs were blotched red and white with their stings.

If a childhood of constant neglect and abuse had done less damage to Galo than might otherwise have been expected it was because his physical standard was high. He had inherited all of his mother's robustly plebeian Sanbrenedetto constitution and although existence in the Palazzo Colavolpe had ruined his nervous system, that was something for which the full price would be exacted in later life; his body, at present, was unharmed. Had he been less sturdy he would by now have been an inmate of the same sort of "hospital" in which his father had died and where his great-aunt and great-uncle still lingered in the miserable limbo of the insane. For Concezio and Speranza, in their treatment of a small boy, had exhibited a flair for Grand Guignol which even the macabre Marchese Giulio could hardly have exceeded.

Once as a child of seven, one still, hot, twilit evening, Galo had penetrated into the upper regions of the house and wandering along a dim corridor had entered a room which at first had appeared to be empty except for junk and lumber. Then something had moved among a heap of ragged old blankets piled on a bed and, as Galo turned in fright from the window, two small crumpled hands had crawled above a tattered counterpane, clutched a bedpost and hauled a misshapen figure into view—a figure with a completely black, completely blank cloth face. Galo, rooted to the floor, had gasped in dumb, cold panic and then let out a small moan of terror. At this the figure had moved again and a fetid stench had risen from the bed, a stink that caught in the mouth and clogged the nostrils. Galo had been about to dash for the door when one wizened hand had moved slowly to the black mask and in a movement babylike in its weak and clumsy anger, had jerked it off. Galo had stared for a long second of frozen horror; then, pressing himself back into a corner, his screams had torn the still, evening silence of the house.When Speranza arrived on the scene he was three-quarters out of the window.

After that, on the many occasions when he displeased his mother or uncle, the invariable threat had been to lock him in alone with that thing upstairs. And sometimes they had actually managed between them to drag him screaming and biting to the very door behind which the horror lurked. Probably only the knowledge that the window was unbarred had prevented them from completing their work and saved Galo from suicide or "hospital."

Then there had been the rabbit—a large, soft, placid animal called Foufi—presented one day to Galo by a peasant woman who could ill afford the gift but was touched by the sight of the ragged little urchin who attempted to cultivate a weedy patch of vegetable garden near the great, wrought-iron gates of the old house and who was supposed to be "noble." Galo, who even at an early age had learned that if he wanted anything he must steal it and if he wished to retain it must hide it, had kept Foufi in the vestry of the Church of the Holy Tooth where the chickens now lived and which was seldom visited since Concezio's sexual organs functioned only too well while Tarquinio did not seem to have or to desire any.

Nonetheless it was Tarquinio who found the rabbit and brought it to the house. Everyone guessed to whom it belonged but they had had no meat for nearly a month and Foufi turned up, with tomatoes, onions and garlic, at the next meal. At first no one mentioned the origin of the contents of the big earthenware dish and this unusual squeamishness annoyed Concezio, who was sufficiently unsqueamish himself to have eaten human flesh had it been available. When Maria Celeste hopefully remarked, "What a good chicken!" Concezio had corrected her bluntly. For a moment Galo had glanced around, puzzled. Then—"You don't mean . . . ? This isn't . . . *It's Foufi!*" He had screamed his head off; not so much because Foufi was dead as because he had eaten some of her. He had actually put bits of Foufi—he saw her as still alive—*into his mouth and swallowed them.* He had vomited most of the night.

Damage of that sort was permanent and irreparable, and despite eighteen months in the calm and ordered routine of the

Nunziatella, Galo's inward nature was off-balance and slanted toward hysteria. Like an originally well-built house which has been subject to too many earth tremors he was now fundamentally unstable. Life in the Naples military academy was designed for adolescents; the discipline was decorative rather than rigid, paternal rather than harshly applied. Nonetheless one or two boys each year found it too much for them and ran away. "Where to?" Galo had asked. "Home, of course." *"Dio!"* had exclaimed Galo in amazement.

But of course he already knew well enough that all homes were not such as his own. Beppo's modest apartment at Vomero, for instance, appeared to him to exude peace, ease and comfort and even old Ercole's villa by the Adriatic had possessed a forlorn tranquillity. Since he was twelve and adjudged old enough to behave with discretion Galo had been sent at increasingly frequent intervals to his great-uncle's house. The excuse had been that, suffering from a mild form of the lung trouble which had attacked his father, he needed frequent changes of air, and for the first two or three visits Ercole had accepted this. Then, with strict instructions to say nothing to his uncle or his mother, the old man had taken Galo to a Pescara specialist who had said that there was nothing in the least wrong with the boy's lungs. "Who is your doctor in Naples?"

"I don't go to one."

"I mean," the specialist had asked patiently, "why do you think that there's something wrong with your chest?"

"I don't."

"Then why on earth—"

"It's quite all right, Doctor," Ercole had soothed, pulling out his checkbook. "Merely a—a suspicion of my own. I'm most grateful to you for your opinion."

And after that, though the visits continued, Ercole took a perverse delight in writing letters to Speranza, saying that he thought Galo's lung trouble was growing worse and that he would like to get in touch with the Neapolitan doctor who had diagnosed the illness. Speranza's involved and often contradictory evasions amused the old man considerably.

For of course Ercole knew what his niece was up to: he was no fool but a shrewd man and more suspicious than most. As the eldest of Vittorio's seven children he had inherited by far the greater part of his father's fortune whereas Speranza was the daughter of the youngest and he was well aware that her income was pitifully small—about a hundred and fifty thousand lire a year, he guessed, if not less. Yet Speranza herself must know perfectly well that she would never receive a legacy from him. Apart from the mutual animosity with which he and his niece had always regarded each other, Ercole had a contemptuous dislike for the Colavolpes, whom he considered effete and vain and out-of-date. Their consistent anti-Fascism alone would have been enough to damn them in his eyes, but to make matters worse they were—or said they were, for it was difficult to believe in such frivolity in the mid-twentieth century—Spanish Bourbon royalists; the supporters of a regime against which his beloved father had fought and triumphed. And anyway Ercole came of a generation of Italians which would never have dreamed of leaving money to a woman if there was any related male available to inherit it.

No—Speranza intended to use her son as a bait. The boy had Sanbrenedetto blood and, if one ruled out Beppo, he was the closest male heir. And, since the affair of his nephew's unwarrantable interference in the matter of the San Lorenzo property, Ercole *did* rule out Beppo. He had never liked his nephew in the least, judging him a fool and a failure and a wastrel and blaming him bitterly for having a daughter, rather than a son, to carry on the Sanbrenedetto name. Could one imagine Vittorio voluntarily being taken prisoner without a fight? Cleaning out his enemy's chicken-droppings during the day, learning their language at night and later making a profession of teaching it to his own countrymen? Beppo's ridiculous indiscretion came, on the whole, as a welcome excuse to disinherit him.

But, then—who? There was, it seemed, only this boy. Ercole was a man who had neither given nor inspired affection throughout his misogynistic life; he did not particularly like Galo and he assumed, rightly, that Galo did not like him. But he had a mildly contemptuous interest in the boy and had he been capable of pity would have pitied him. At last illness, and a sense that the end was not far off, had forced him to make up his mind. During the usual Easter visit, he had sent for Galo to his study and with the boy standing beside him had explained briefly the document which lay on his desk. "I am making you my sole

heir. You understand what that means? Good. Now listen carefully. In a minute I will explain exactly what will become yours
at my death, but first there is something more important. When
I die—and that may not be very long now—you will at once
become the owner of a considerable amount of money and valuable property, entirely irrespective of what age you may be at
the time. There are no conditions in my will. You get everything
and you get it at once. But I tell you that if you let this"—
Ercole tapped the paper on the desk before him—"get into the
hands of your mother or your precious uncle or any of your
other relatives at Caserta you won't see that money or that property again—ever."

Galo had nodded, standing beside the desk looking taller,
more adult than usual in his new overcoat. "I know. Tarquinio
stole my clock—the one I got from the soap people for the tops
of their packets. They always take my things if they can find
them."

Ercole had given a grunt of satisfaction. "Well, you understand *that,* at any rate. You'll need a lawyer. I'm not going to
recommend mine. I don't like him. You'll have to find a good
one. One you can trust not to let your relations interfere. That
may not be easy so be careful in your choice." He had abruptly
changed the subject. "How are you doing at school?"

"All right."

"When your great-grandfather dies—if he ever does, which
seems doubtful—you inherit the title and the *palazzo,* I assume.
The latter's almost certainly mortgaged and you'd be a fool not
to let it go. But you've got an army career open to you and you'll
have a title, which always helps, and on top of that—if you keep
your head—you'll have an adequate private fortune. Here." He
had been folding and sealing the will in a strong envelope and
now he thrust it almost savagely at Galo. "Remember what I've
said about this. Never let it into your relations' hands. Your
Cousin Beppo may think he's my heir, but he's not. I've not told
my own lawyer about this will—I don't trust him. There's another at his office, but this invalidates it."

"Inval—?"

"Look it up in a dictionary if you don't know it. And now"—
Ercole pulled a small file toward him—"I'm going to explain—
once and once only—exactly what will be yours after my

death; where it is, what it is, and, as far as possible, what it's worth. After that the matter is closed; I shan't refer to it again. You've heard me talk often of my father—your great-grandfather. He was a soldier on Garibaldi's staff when he was not much older than you are today. It was he who made most—I've added a little to it, but not much—of what is going to be yours one day soon. If *he* had been left this inheritance, even at your present age, it would have been safe with him. *He* wouldn't have let anyone take it from him, you can be sure of that. That is partly why I'm not putting it in trust for you and tying it up with lawyers and so forth and making it as safe as the Bank of Rome. The other reason—" But Ercole had stopped abruptly. For the other reason was to allow Beppo—for a few days or weeks or even months, perhaps—to believe that he had, after all, inherited the Sanbrenedetto fortune, and then to deliver, posthumously but very certainly, the biggest blow his nephew had ever suffered in his life.

⊷§ 4

CHRONIC unpunctuality was the least of the Colavolpes' multifarious defects, though like most of the others it appeared to be congenital. No Colavolpe in the family's recorded history had ever been on time for anything and as far as they were concerned, clocks and calendars might as well never have been invented. That the Nunziatella was particularly intolerant of this failing was something Galo had quickly learned, but then one always knew where one should be at the military academy, which rang with bells and bugles, whereas since Tarquino's theft and sale of the little clock for which Galo had saved so many soap-packet tops there was not a single working timepiece in the Colavolpe household.

When, polished, brushed and shining, though with his legs still stinging under his bright trousers, Galo descended the wide double-staircase sometime after midday, the rest of the family was still upstairs and he found De Santis and the Americans standing about in the hall—the Americans looking a little bored, De Santis more than a little angry. But Galo's appearance put them all into a better humor at once. He shook hands with De

Santis and De Santis's American wife and their daughter Toni, a big blond girl of sixteen, and was introduced to the friends, a couple from the NATO base at Naples.

"This is Galeazzo, the Marchese's great-grandson. As I've said, I don't suppose we'll meet the Marchese himself. He's very old indeed and seldom receives company these days. That's so, isn't it, Galo?"

"Come, Signor Commendatore?"

"Don't they teach you English at the Nunziatella?"

"They teach it," Galo admitted, remembering yesterday morning and with a sudden confused vision of Garibaldi and Colonel Malenchini racing each other on night-horses down the road to Bologna, "but I haven't learned it yet."

Everyone laughed and the Americans were delighted. "Gee, isn't he cute?" they said. And, "That certainly is a dandy outfit."

"Somewhat resembling the West Point uniform, would you not agree, Colonel Forth? Though not so smart of course."

De Santis had acquired an automatic habit of complimenting Americans on all occasions. In his mind they resembled a herd of huge, graceless cows who would consume any amount of flattery fed to them and give off gallons of golden milk as a result. It was a slightly outdated view but then Commendatore De Santis was an elderly, rich and powerful man; he did not change his views easily.

Colonel Forth eyed Galo cheerfully and winked. "Why no, Commendatore. If anything I'd say it was smarter." The colonel also made it a habit to compliment Italians whenever possible. "Compliments and coffee," he used to remark to his staff. "Plenty of both and I'll guarantee to have any wop this side of Hell eating out of my hand in next to no time." But the staff merely replied, "Yes, Colonel, if you say so, sir." They were not impressed. Colonel Forth prided himself on being all things to all men and had therefore, and far too early in his career, become nothing much to anybody.

"Well, well, doubtless such uniforms are a matter of military taste, upon which I would not presume to argue." De Santis's voice held a note of slightly testy irritation. He was not used to being contradicted—even in the most complimentary way.

There was a brief silence and Galo said, "Perhaps you would like to see over the house?"

De Santis assented at once though privately he had hoped to be offered a drink first and was sure that the Forths had hoped the same. However, it was unlikely that modern ideas of hospitality had yet penetrated to this backwoods family out at Caserta and anyway it admirably suited his purpose today to spend as much time as possible with young Galo and as little as politeness permitted with the other members of the family.

Some people considered the Palazzo Colavolpe very beautiful; others thought it an architectural horror. In fact it was both. It was exactly the sort of house which a poor, eighteenth-century Sicilian adventurer, ennobled and enriched by the Bourbons, might have been expected to build, and it had given its original owner a great deal of unsophisticated pleasure. Though it was large it seemed oddly cramped because of the shapes of its rooms. These were never rectangular but round, oval or hexagonal with high domed ceilings resembling, as they were intended to do, a series of small, intercommunicating ballrooms. The spaces between were therefore triangular with at least one convex wall and often no window—uncomfortable, dirty little cabins which had been the family bedrooms until, with the disappearance of all resident domestics, the Colavolpes had moved upstairs into the servants' quarters.

Everything had been built with this series of Bourbon *salons* —the *piano nobile*—in mind and without any attempt at domestic comfort, a concept which was totally unknown to southern Italians before the early years of the twentieth century and not very well understood even today. There were no fireplaces— they would have spoiled the geometrical curves—and no drains. In the first Marchese's time heating was supplied by Oriental brass containers filled with charcoal, carried in and replenished by servants throughout the day, while when he or his family wished to perform their bodily functions they did so outside in the open, indifferently beside their grooms and scullions. And because of the long years of somnambulistic poverty through which the family had sleepily stumbled ever since, the house, in these two respects at any rate, had remained unchanged. Galo's introduction to central heating had been at the Nunziatella and he had first used a water-closet at his great-uncle's seaside villa at the age of twelve.

The main interest of the *piano nobile* was the extraordinary effect produced by endless skillful and laborious attempts at imitation and deception. Walls painted to imitate marble that curved between fake alabaster pillars to sculpted ceilings of simulated gilt latticework. Bronze statues on corner pedestals, or suits of gilded armor in niches, which were discovered upon closer inspection to be high-relief plaster moldings—as were the spiky military trophies of swords and banners, breastplates, drums and trumpets, above the doors. Mock mirrors threw back counterfeit reflections of the opposite walls with a grotesque effect of optical illusion and even the stone floors, now rough and worn, had once been painted to represent involved mosaics.

More than a century and a quarter had passed since the house had been built and there had very seldom been any money for even the most necessary repairs, yet surprisingly the family had managed to keep the *piano nobile* in a reasonable state of preservation. Here and there patches of damp ruined part of a classical ceiling painting, sometimes gilding had flaked from a cornice or mice bored a hole in a wainscot, but the general effect— shoddy, ornate, grotesque yet somehow strangely charming— still remained.

Galo showed De Santis and his party all that was considered suitable for them to see. He brought them before the portrait of the first Marchese Colavolpe and the small, darker one of the second and took them on to the terrace to admire the view. Then he took them to the Church of the Holy Tooth and showed them the reliquary upon the altar. Colonel and Mrs. Forth spoke passably good Italian but they were not Catholics and the reliquary puzzled them. "I still don't see what it's *for*."

"For testicles," said Galo indifferently.

"For *what?*"

Commendatore De Santis broke in hurriedly. "For infertility, he means. It prevents infertility."

But Galo thought that "infertility" was a purely agrarian term. The Colavolpe estate was said to be the most infertile land around Caserta. Anyway he had been brought up on the legend of the Holy Tooth and often told that without its aid he himself would never have existed. It was oddly daunting, in a way, to think that without that small bit of blackened bone in its gilded, star-shaped glass case he would not be here now. "No, no. For *testicles*." He touched the front of his red-striped trousers. "Here. My great-grandfather had none when he was young, you understand, so he could not—could not—"

"Yes, yes, Galo. But I think—"

"Let him go on, Commendatore." Colonel Forth was highly amused. This was going to be one of his better stories when he got back to the States. But Galo did not know the correct words for what he wanted to say. Also he was becoming aware that this subject might not, after all, be suitable for discussion in front of a mixed audience, sincerely interesting—indeed miraculous—as it was. "Without the miracle of the Tooth none of us could have been born. It is very holy," he finished lamely, blushing despite himself.

The Commendatore breathed a sigh of relief and began to say, "Come, let us leave this church and—" But he was not to be let off so lightly. Colonel Forth refused to be cheated in that way.

"I don't understand, Galo," he said with an air of quizzical mystification. "Why couldn't you have been born?"

Equally surprised, Galo looked up at the immaculately uniformed American beside him. The colonel must be at least forty and he was married. Didn't he know . . . ? Galo himself had known ever since he could remember. Indeed nobody could live in the same house as Concezio without constantly being reminded of the facts of life in their most strident barrack-room interpretations. "If," he explained patiently, "one has no testicles one cannot do this—" He made a circle with the thumb and forefinger of his left hand and thrust the stiff index finger of his right one through it. "And if one cannot do this one cannot have babies—can one?"

Then suddenly a possible reason for the colonel's astonishing ignorance flashed upon him—*of course!* "Oh, I see. You would like to borrow the Tooth? I must warn you that it took my great-grandfather seven years to get *his;* but it might be quicker now. And of course you will have to build a small church if it works. But my uncle will arrange to lend it to you, I am sure."

⋅⋅§ 5

THE lunch was long, elaborate and messily served; the sort of meal to which the Colavolpes, in their dreams, sat down every day but which in reality they were only able to afford at Christmas and Easter and by no means always even then. With the exception of Galo, who for the last eighteen months had been receiving two good meals a day at the Nunziatella, they had all been looking forward to it for over a week and it had cost them a small watercolor study of the first Marchesa Colavolpe, the promise (later unredeemed) to a local peasant of the next kid their goat dropped, and Concezio's presentation silver cigarette case. They had even hired a girl from Caserta to wait at table and another to help Filippa, who had to stay in the kitchen and cook.

There was a large dish of hors-d'oeuvres; bean soup; *spaghetti alla napolitano;* a fish stew of octopus, onions and mussels; bacon and sausages—a compliment, this, to the Americans; fried chicken; cold roast veal with tuna fish sauce; tripe and trotters; *zabaglione* eked out with yoghurt from rather grimy paper cartons; and then sliced fennel and raw broad beans served in a dressing of peppered olive oil. Maria Celeste had forgotten to buy white rolls so there was only the long, flat loaf of hard *comune* bread—but this was angrily ordered off the table by Concezio and placed out of the way on a windowsill. In the Italian manner all the meat dishes were served unaccompanied by any vegetables and there were no condiments on the table.

It was a southern Italian meal, and by southern Italian standards a thoroughly good one—almost a banquet—King Bomba or Garibaldi would have sat down to it with pleasure. But Commendatore De Santis was a Milanese and accustomed to what the Colavolpes would have called "French" food, whereas his family and his two friends had transatlantic tastes of an altogether lighter and cooler variety. In coping with their lunch the guests went to still more trouble, discomfort and expense—of the spirit, at any rate—than their hosts had gone to in providing it.

The atmosphere, too, lacked geniality. Colonel Forth had not recovered from the misunderstanding in the church; he believed, wrongly, that De Santis had been highly amused and would repeat the story later, and it made him go hot and cold by turns to think of what would happen when it reached his army colleagues. Then the Colavolpes themselves had fallen out over various matters. There had been a fierce, rapid interchange between Galo and his uncle over whether or not the boy could take off his white tunic before sitting down to lunch. If the guests had known that it was his only one, and if they had seen the uninhibited and headlong way in which the Colavolpes normally devoured their food, they would have been more sympathetic; as it was they were uncomprehending and embarrassed.

Then as soon as they had sat down, the red-haired woman, whom the Forth's wrongly believed to be Major Colavolpe's wife, had become furious with one of the old ladies—the one with the huge, frizzed hair style that made her look like a frightened rat peering out of a ball of oakum—apparently over the bread, which, as Mrs. Forth later remarked, was the only wholesome thing served at that disgusting meal. And as if that was not enough, there was another scene about the tablecloth. It was old and there certainly was a large rent near the middle, but was that a reason for the major to bawl out that poor old man stuffing away happily in a corner near the window?

Then the Colavolpes did not appear to know anyone among the cosmopolitan set at the NATO base who largely made up the guests' selection of friends. The major belonged to the Union Club but he practically never went there. "They charge you eighty-five lire for a Campari soda!" he exclaimed indignantly. "And then there's the tip—another five!"

"Yes, yes, shocking!" agreed Colonel Forth sympathetically, although he paid twice as much for his own drinks and would no more have dared tip a Neapolitan waiter five lire than appear on parade in his pajamas.

"And if you're fool enough to order sandwiches—well, Signor Colonello, you might just as well go and eat at the Ambassadors and have done with it! Out here at Caserta it's better, of course. I get oil at a hundred and fifty lire the liter. Naturally one has to know where to go. . . ."

Like many Italian heads of families, Concezio was in charge of the commissariat and did the marketing himself, an ugly, battered figure with his scarred face and old black suit, stumping round the local stalls haggling for a kilo of cheese, a few ettos of cheap coffee, thrusting his purchases—at least until eighteen months ago—into the basket of his barefooted nephew who toiled along beside him. He liked to talk about his bargains, his saving of twenty lire here, thirty there, and Colonel Forth had to listen —but it was not the sort of conversation to which he was accustomed.

The wine alone was good, a harsh, red Camaldoli from the slopes of Vesuvius. Mrs. Forth took several glasses to help her cope with the greasy food, and being an inquisitive and meddlesome woman, and since she was sitting between Galo and the Commendatore's daughter, she began to investigate the former's relations with girls. When he told her that he knew none she was at first frankly unbelieving and then shocked. "But Galo—why ever not? I mean, back home boys of your age have been dating for years—sure they have! Why, a fellow your age is probably running at least a couple of girls—more, if he's got what it takes. Anyone who can't date a girl *at all*—why, I guess there's something wrong somewhere, isn't there, Toni?"

The De Santis girl giggled agreement but Galo went on eating stolidly. After all, unlike the guests, he knew there would be no more food in the Colavolpe household that day; his next meal would be tomorrow's lunch at the Nunziatella. Moreover he had no intention of discussing his personal affairs with a stranger and was, in fact, amazed that one should expect him to do so. By Neapolitan standards Mrs. Forth's remarks went beyond the limits of the worst taste—they were outrageous.

Galo's personal affections were largely centered upon Mina Sanbrenedetto. A relationship had slowly grown over the past year, based on his Thursday and Saturday afternoons at Beppo's Vomero apartment. It was a delicate and, at present, entirely platonic affair; a friendship with carefully modulated romantic overtones, carried on almost always in Beppo's presence with an easy warmth, a gracefully contented pleasure in each other's company that could not have been bettered by the most sophisticated pair of adults. It was benign, calm and extremely private— the antithesis of everything Mrs. Forth meant when she spoke of "dating."

There is a weighty and comprehensive American viewpoint unlike anything known in Europe, an imposing structure of be-

liefs ranging from the value of the "old" way of life to the nice-
ness of all children and the importance of salesmanship, into
which every American is born and through which he must fight
his way, cope with and master before he can come face to face
with the rest of the world. Failure in this respect can be meas-
ured fairly accurately when abroad by the amount of unintentional shocks both given and received. Having offended Galo,
Mrs. Forth proceeded to scandalize the rest of the family. "Say
George!" she called to her husband. "Just listen to this! Junior,
here, says he's never dated a girl!" She turned to Concezio.
"Major, I don't believe it. Galo tells me he never takes out girls.
I bet he does, doesn't he? Why, around his age George was running three! He certainly was! You were, weren't you, George?
You had that old convertible your dad gave you and not a night
went by, I declare, without you dating some girl and taking her
places!" Becoming aware of a strained silence she glanced round
the table and added defiantly, "And that's how it ought to be.
Boys and girls ought to have fun! They do at home."

Galo's face was as crimson as the broad stripes on his trousers.
Toni De Santis who, despite an American education, had
enough Italian social instincts to understand what the Colavolpes
were thinking, kept her eyes on her plate, while Maria Valeria,
Maria Celeste and Maria Fausta stared down their long scarlet
noses like three shocked and shabby old turkeys. As far as they
could understand it this American woman was suggesting that
Galo should spend his time with back-street harlots—in fact
suggesting that he probably did and wanting to know the details.
They had been brought up in the belief that no woman, certainly
no lady, ever mentioned anything remotely connected with sex
except in the tribal privacy of her own family—and even then
it was generally disgraceful to do so. A man might—and Concezio always did—boast about his own sexual prowess whenever
the mood took him, but for a woman to speak of the same subject was to proclaim herself a whore. Speranza admittedly said a
great deal more than she ought, but then Speranza *was* a whore,
unfortunately.

Concezio choked slightly into his wine, gave a weak grin at
De Santis and said, "Galo's still very young, signora. And of
course he has much homework to do in his spare time. In Italy
we expect . . . Hmm . . . well, we expect—"

The Commendatore cut in smoothly. "The Nunziatella keep their boys busy, Mrs. Forth. There are diversions, certainly, of a healthy sort and—"

"Well!" Mrs. Forth was by now thoroughly annoyed. When she considered what this boy had said in that dreadful church . . . And now, when she even mentioned something as normal and ordinary as dating a girl . . . "I wasn't suggesting anything *un*healthy, Commendatore!"

Colonel Forth broke into English. "Why, Ella, it's like I've often told you. In this country they have these ideas of arranged marriages and consequently their whole outlook—"

"Oh gosh, George, I wasn't talking about marriage. I was talking about boys and girls dating!"

"Then don't," said the colonel sensibly. "It's not a thing everybody understands about like at home." He turned resolutely to Concezio and began to speak about Italian politics, of which he knew a surprising amount.

Commendatore De Santis drank some wine and sighed with a mixture of relief that an awkward moment had passed and foreboding at the indigestion this heavy midday meal would soon inflict upon him. Perhaps it had been a mistake to bring the Forths here; they were the most cultivated Americans he knew and were extremely popular among their Italian neighbors and colleagues at Posillipo, but not unnaturally they had never before encountered a family like the Colavolpes.

For that matter he himself had only known the family some six months, having been introduced to Concezio shortly after last Christmas and during one of the major's rare visits to the Union Club. But Concezio, an unusual and, indeed, an improbable figure, had interested him, so he had bought his new acquaintance several drinks and a good lunch and listened to an involved account of the bloody retreat in Russia before returning to his office that afternoon.

Commendatore De Santis was a man of wide interests and considerable ability; he was also a skilled amateur sociologist. As a northern Italian from a wealthy Milanese family he was infinitely more European, cosmopolitan and modern in his outlook than any of his countrymen south of Rome. But then, like so many northerners, he did not really consider the people who

lived south of Rome to be his countrymen at all; they were—
one shrugged and smiled slightly as one said it—"Italians"; he
was a Milanese.

He had traveled fairly extensively in his youth and had spent
the war in America where he had married into an equally
wealthy Italo-American family. Like many of his kind he had
been instrumental in helping to put Italy on her feet again in the
postwar world, applying American business and industrial techniques, borrowing American money, using American contacts.
At present he was directing and expanding the Neapolitan
branch of the great ITOLGAS oil and methane industrial complex of which he was a senior and highly respected board
member. He was cultivated, rich and powerful; a leading Christian Democrat—politically speaking, for personally he was
neither the one nor the other—he had strong affiliations with
that group of men who decided his party's aims, in the rare moments when it had any, and his advice was often asked and sometimes even acted upon by government ministers.

Yet despite all these manifest advantages the Commendatore
had gone out of his way and spent much valuable time to take
up the Colavolpes. The fact was that they fascinated him. Like
a zoological collector who, to his surprised delight, finds and
tracks to its lair a living animal whose species he had supposed
extinct, the Commendatore discovered in the Colavolpes a family of genuine, early-nineteenth-century Spanish Bourbon royalists living in a uniquely baroque Bourbon palace in a manner
which, except for their grinding poverty, had hardly changed in
a century and a half.

For a sociologist they were an astonishing prize. Their Oriental squalor and arrogance captivated him equally; their past
—and he had managed to sort out the facts behind Concezio's
endless, boasting lies—was exactly in accord with what he felt
it ought to be; and their house was almost too good to be true.
The scientist in him would have liked to preserve them intact for
posterity—put some sort of high wire fence around their natural
habitat and warn off the public. The realist knew that this was
impossible; the Colavolpes would either have to demonstrate a
last-minute ability to conform with the mid-twentieth century or
else die out completely. For nearly six months the Commenda-

tore had kept them under scientific scrutiny, and he had already filled two large notebooks with their data, when he had a new idea.

Concezio himself had been equally delighted with his new friend. He borrowed money from him on their second, third and fourth meetings. Ten, twenty, fifteen thousand lire—tiny sums to the Commendatore but most substantial ones to Concezio, who was able to buy himself three new shirts, a summer suit and a tie, as well as paying off the grocer and the baker. He regarded De Santis with contempt, of course—for he had been taught so to regard everyone who was not of "noble" birth. But the Commendatore did not, like most other people, return it in full measure. And soon it struck Concezio that his new friend was after something. But what? There was only one thing the Colavolpes possessed which by the longest stretch of imagination could be termed desirable—their house. For even someone as unaesthetic as Concezio could see that there was a great deal of charm in this rambling old palace with its fantastic stucco-and-plaster imitations, its air of timeless, tideless vulgarity—of sunlit, amoral, innocent squalor where Southern Europe and the Levant seemed to hold each other in a flyblown embrace under the Neapolitan sky.

Concezio, like the rest of the family save Galo, was very fond of his home. Nor, since it did not belong to him, could he have sold it had he wished to. It was legally the possession of his ancient grandfather upstairs and would, when that indestructible old man died, become Galo's—though not until the boy reached his eighteenth birthday. In the meantime, however, there was no harm in hinting that some arrangement might be made, in disposing of a few bits of doubtful furniture or pictures of dubious origin for a suitably high price. Above all the new friendship seemed to hold out the possibility of a long series of small but most useful loans—loans which, even Concezio realized, their maker would never seriously expect to be repaid. For in a way Concezio had grasped more of what De Santis wanted than the Commendatore himself would have entirely approved of—though from a slightly different angle. As Concezio saw it the Colavolpes were, indeed, an interesting family and De Santis had every reason to find them so. Were they not old and noble? Did not he himself possess the Gold Medal? Where else could one find such blue-blooded valor inhabiting such a beautiful home? And if De Santis wanted to show off his new friends to various envious Americans—well, that was quite in order, too. Of course the Commendatore had better realize that entertainment of the sort he was receiving today was not cheap. It could not be done continually without sufficient subsidies. Sitting back in his chair at the head of the table, replete with fish and spaghetti and meat and wine, Concezio contemplated a future full of endless meals such as this, all paid for by someone else yet all held in his house and presided over by himself as host. And soon he would suggest another loan. Twenty-five—no, *thirty* thousand lire it should be this time.

The westering sun shone through the high open windows, laying patterns of gold across the cluttered table while Colonel Forth's voice intoned ". . . among the civilized nations of Europe with the support of the United States . . ." and Concezio became slowly aware that the long meal was over, the guests becoming a little restive.

"Yes, yes, we must unite; stand together in defense of our continent," he agreed vaguely.

"That," said Colonel Forth, who was enthusiastic for European federation, "is *exactly* what I'm always saying, Major. It could be done. It *should* be done."

But Mrs. Forth, who was hot and uncomfortably full, was not so sure. "It could, yes, if only you Europeans would combine to make it. If Europeans would only get together without all this eternal quarreling." She was displeased with Europeans today—especially this particular group. "If Europe would just behave like one big family, instead of—"

"It often seems to me," said the Commendatore dryly, glancing up and down the table, "that Europe generally *does* behave like one big family—that's the whole trouble." He rose as he spoke and the rest rose with him, Tarquinio slightly later than the others since he felt it necessary to slip a handful of biscuits into his pocket first.

The cars were at the door; the hired girl had found and brought the Commendatore's hat, and good-byes and thanks were being exchanged in the circular entrance hall when Mrs. Forth's need became no longer supportable. After all, she had drunk a lot of wine and then, feeling a little dizzy, still more water. The "major's wife," as she thought of Speranza, seemed to have vanished and she was most doubtful of making her meaning clear to any of the three old ladies who hovered and quivered in the background. Heaven alone knew what their personal habits were. No, it would have to be the boy again. "Galo," she said quickly, "can you show me the toilet, please?"

"The . . . the . . . ?"

"Yes, yes—the *toilet*."

Galo swallowed and stared helplessly about him. He had been given strict instructions as to what parts of the house might be shown, and equally strict ones as to what parts might not. Perhaps Concezio . . . He took a step toward his uncle and then thought better of it. Concezio had said that the one thing no one was ever to do was to interrupt a conversation between himself and De Santis. Galo took a deep breath and followed by Mrs. Forth, walked to a heavily molded door in one wall and opened it. "In here."

Mrs. Forth brushed thankfully past him—then halted abruptly. She was in a tiny, bare room lit by an unglazed, iron-grilled window. A room fizzing with flies over whose floor of cracked flagstones beetles scurried away into the shadows. Against one wall were ranged a battered enamel chamber pot, two rusty kerosene cans and a pile of torn newspapers. And the place stank to heaven.

It was, though she did not know this, used only by the family when the summer thunderbursts or the rare Neapolitan winter rainstorms made a retreat into the area around the chicken-run entirely impracticable. They did not like using it, even then; it was not natural to them—but there had to be somewhere.

For a moment Mrs. Forth stared unbelievingly around her; then, scarlet-faced, she turned and strode out past an equally scarlet-faced Galo, past the bowing old aunts, past the Commendatore, past her host and her husband to the waiting cars.

De Santis had seen, and had understood, what had occurred. Concezio's stained face flamed with rage and mortification, his hot eyes met Galo's, promising vengeance. But the Commendatore was obscurely delighted. Here it was again—as it had been earlier in the church; as it had been over the lunch table—the completely unintentional, sudden confrontation, the jarring shock as one culture collided with some previously unsuspected defect in another. Mr. Gladstone being shown over one of Bomba's prisons could hardly have managed a more outraged expression of disgust than Forth's wife.

With an effort Concezio returned to his attempt to induce the Commendatore to come upstairs and look over some books and furniture which had been hopefully arranged for his inspection. But De Santis shook his head impatiently. He had no time to waste in examining sham antiques. He smiled amusedly at the unhappy Galo and then, patting his host's shoulder, turned to the door. He had no intention of buying a few shabby books or worm-eaten chairs; for that matter he had no intention of buying the Palazzo Colavolpe. He intended instead, and in his own time and way, to buy Galo.

✍ঌ 6

". . . said so. Concezio was perfectly right, you're a little fool—*un' asino di prim' ordine.*" Tarquinio grumbled on as he sat beside his sewing-machine, stilled for the moment in the midst of repairs to the tablecloth, while he sewed the buttons back on the old shirt Speranza had torn that morning. Galo, naked to the waist, leaned morosely against the wall beside him. "Well, *per l'amor' di Dio!* What was I to do? She asked—"

"Like Concezio said—tell her it was out of order! 'I'm sorry, *signora,* but the toilet is temporarily out of order. The workmen are repairing it at this moment.' Easy, idiot, eh?"

"I didn't have time—"

"You didn't *think!*" Tarquinio finished the last button, snapped the thread in his fingers and threw the shirt to Galo. "There you are—simpleton! Concezio was quite right to make you clean that place out—teach you a lesson. Besides," added Tarquinio more practically, "it needed cleaning badly."

Buttoning the shirt, Galo came slowly nearer to the sewing table. He stopped beside his great-uncle, staring down malevolently. "Listen. In a few years I shall be the Marchese. This house will be mine. Then the first thing I'm going to do is to throw you all out—you particularly. I'll get the Carabinieri in and I'll say, 'Throw them all out of here—that old fat one first—right off my land.' " This was a threat he had used before on Tarquinio

—he had never yet dared to use it elsewhere—and it had its usual effect. The old man's face flushed a bright scarlet and he gobbled with a shrill mixture of indignation and fear.

"What do you mean! How dare you! Such words to me, your great-uncle! And you couldn't live a moment without us. You've got no *money*—none at all! You'd *starve* alone by yourself—and serve you right! You're *penniless!*"

"You think so? Just wait and see!" Galo ran from the room while the old man screamed after him, "I'll tell Concezio! I won't be insulted at my age! I'll tell him and he'll . . ."

But Galo, climbing the stone stairs to his own room, knew that Tarquinio would tell Concezio nothing for fear of the latter's increased derision under enough of which he writhed daily. And anyway he himself had just stolen Tarquinio's biscuits—the ones his great-uncle had abstracted from the lunch table. Tarquinio's coat had been hanging over the back of his chair and Galo had slid behind him and felt in its pockets. Now he took the biscuits out of his own and threw them from a window. He did not want them. Accustomed as he was to dirt, the cleaning out of the place Mrs. Forth called "the toilet" had turned even his hardened stomach.

The sun was nearly down now and the house was still with an evening calm. Reaching his own room Galo went to the cupboard in which his uniform hung and examined it anxiously. Maria Celeste had been sitting next to him at lunch and ever since she had broken her bottom plate . . . Sure enough, there were no less than three spots of grease on the left shoulder. A piece of yellow soap and a jar of water stood beside the windowsill and for a quarter of an hour Galo worked laboriously, but with little success, to repair the damage. Then he hung the damp tunic beside the open window and returned to the cupboard to clean his shoes, to be ready for tomorrow's journey back to school.

A month ago the cupboard had held his new overcoat—the one Ercole had sent him to buy in Pescara—but on his return to the Nunziatella, Speranza had taken it to the Caserta market and sold it, saying that by next winter he would have grown too big for it. But that wasn't true for he had taken trouble to buy one a size too large. Squatting on his heels on the cupboard floor Galo mourned his overcoat, the only brand-new garment save his State-provided uniforms which he had ever possessed. Before him in a corner lay a great pile of old newspapers—a material of which the Colavolpes made a wide variety of use—and from time to time, lacking a brush, he tore off sheets to rub the black leather to a glossy polish. Then suddenly he was looking at the front page of the *Corriere della Sera* for the 10th of June, 1940. WAR DECLARED AGAINST ENGLAND AND FRANCE—*From the Alps to the Shores of the Indian Ocean Rises One Cry of Faith and Passion, Duce!*"—and the leader was headed VIN-CEREMO!—We shall conquer!

Galo stared down, motionless, one polish-smeared hand holding his shoe, the other arrested over those great black head-lines flaring back their twenty-year-old news. Headlines which someone had once read in this very house; his father, perhaps, or his grandfather—shadows without substance even in his memory. Headlines which had meant catastrophe and slaughter, which had changed even his own unborn fate as they had changed the name of a *piazza* in Naples. Uncle Ercole must have read them, too. How? With Faith? With Passion? And in the end they had driven him out—an old man alone in a cold seaside villa, walking along the windy shore with the great-nephew for whom he had just bought an overcoat. And even that had been stolen and sold—a last unnecessary insult to the dead old man.

Galo, squatting on the floor of the cupboard, felt the sadness of life well up in a great tide of sorrow and engulf him. He cried silently, helplessly, his shoulders shaking, still holding his shoe in one hand; weeping for the folly and wickedness of the world, for himself, his overcoat, most of all, perhaps, for his loveless old great-uncle. He had begun the day in tears and in tears he ended it. They were the only ones ever shed for Ercole Sanbren-edetto.

Vomero

ᴥᶴ 1

BRIGHT and hot, June arched its clean blue sky over the city, over the gulf. Each morning the gray bulk of Vesuvius looming to the south lost its clear-cut outline earlier and earlier in an expanding, quivering haze of heat while in Vomero, the water carts trundled endlessly between the Piazza Medaglio d'Oro and the Vanvitelli, fanning their jets of spray across the hot *piperno* blocks.

From his balcony above the green heads of the plane trees in the Via Raffaele Morghen, Beppo watched them pass. In a light summer shirt and linen trousers he leaned for hours over the ornamental balustrade and pondered contentedly upon his future; at forty he considered that he had plenty of it and though he was undoubtedly past his first youth he felt that time was still very much on his side. Forty was a good age to inherit money; an age at which one knew its value and knew, too, what one wanted—or so it was commonly believed. Yet somewhat to his surprise, Beppo found that his wants were few. He intended to cease all work, of course; in fact he had already done so, for no Italian could think of work as a pleasure in itself—that was a purely Nordic concept.

But otherwise . . . a better apartment and new furniture, perhaps, though he had to admit that he was happy enough where he was. A car certainly he must have, and a holiday abroad with Mina. Both must wait until the will was proved and that might not be for some months; but then he would immediately buy a car and take Mina to England where he had spent those long, happy years to which he still looked back so wistfully.

He had possessed literally nothing then; neither liberty, money nor even a proper name—they had called him "Joe." Yet his fondest memories were all centered in the West English countryside. The bright elation of early summer mornings in the buttercup meadows; the mild, damp stillness of autumn woods smelling of mushrooms; the gleaming snow, the glittering icy stars of midwinter. And all the time, at every season, the big farmhouse which in moments of nostalgia he still thought of as "home," close at hand, always accessible. Today, twenty years later, his memories of that time were ringed and edged with the almost holy glow of childhood recollections—"Devon," he would say to himself and smile as at an inward, uncommunicable secret.

Meanwhile he and Mina lived in a limbo world suspended between the straitened circumstances of the past and the affluence of the future—a hypothetical, tantalizing, yet not unhappy world in which plans were continually made and amended and where window-shopping along the Toledo ceased to be a wistful make-believe and became a serious, practical occupation. . . . "Comparing prices," Beppo called it. A world of brochures and folders, explanatory leaflets and prospectuses.

For the bank had made no difficulty in advancing him money and though for the present Beppo had no intention of spectacularly raising his living standard he was able to indulge in the delight of undisturbed leisure. Only once before in his life had he been totally unemployed: a period of two months during which he had sat in a barbed-wire cage, supplied with slightly less than the minimum food necessary to keep a living man in normal health and waiting to be shipped to he knew not where. A time of boredom and despair and continual nagging hunger, overshadowed by the bloodstained memories of the desert march. Yet even then Devon and the Pinnigers' farm had only been just over Time's horizon and coming nearer with every passing minute. Now he lounged idly about the flat, made weekly calls upon the lawyer who was examining and bringing up to date the various records of Ercole's Naples property, and went shopping for daily household necessaries with Mina along the Via Alessandro Scarlatti.

To add to his pleasure there had not been any break with Galo. Beppo had known all about the boy's visits to the Adriatic villa and had found no difficulty in guessing their intent, but Speranza, rather than her son, had been the object of the anger and jealousy he had felt at that attempt to cheat him of what was truly his. For despite his unfortunate misunderstanding with his uncle, Beppo, as the last of the living male Sanbrenedettos, had never had any doubt concerning the justice of his claim to inherit the family fortune. After all, Vittorio was his grandfather just as much as he was Ercole's father. It had never seemed in the least important—in fact Beppo seldom remembered it—that Vittorio was also Galo's great-grandfather; after all, Galo was a Colavolpe. Still, it was a relief that despite Speranza's silly and unsuccessful attempt to defraud her cousin of his rightful inheritance Galo, at least, saw no reason for resentment. He continued to visit the Vomero flat on Thursdays and often Saturdays or Sundays as well, and Beppo welcomed him even more warmly than before.

Not that there could be many more such visits, for in less than a fortnight the academic year ended and the Nunziatella would close, not to reopen again until the autumn. "But I suppose you'll be going to the summer camp?" Beppo asked as one warm evening he adjusted his tie and put on his jacket before the sitting room mirror. He had received an invitation to discuss a possible offer for his San Lorenzo property with a firm named the Mergellina Construction & Development Company and was on his way to meet a director.

Galo nodded. "Oh yes. It's going to be somewhere up near Avezzano this year."

"You'll enjoy that. And then—down to the Sila?"

"I suppose so. They say they're going earlier this summer."

They, as Beppo knew, meant the Colavolpes. Galo, away from home, never said "my family" but always "they"—disassociating himself as far as possible from the Caserta household.

"I thought there was some talk of renting it to tourists for August or September?" Beppo knew the Colavolpes still possessed an old stone farmhouse down in Calabria to which they migrated each year for the traditional summer holiday. In lieu of an annual rental the family of peasants who tilled the few hectares of Colavolpe land fed "them" free of charge during this vacation.

Galo shook his head. "They wanted to rent it but there weren't any offers. Then they thought of renting the *palazzo* while they were away, but there weren't any offers for that either. Both places are much too far inland. Tourists want to be near the sea— Oh yes, and I'm to ask you if you know of anybody who might take it. You don't, do you?"

Beppo shook his head. "I'm sorry, Galo, I don't. I'm looking for a summer tenant myself for my—for Uncle Ercole's place on the Adriatic."

For some reason that Beppo could not understand, Galo's head lifted abruptly and his voice seemed almost to hold a note of indignation. "You are, are you?" Then he smiled "Yes, yes —well, it ought to be bringing in money instead of standing empty all the summer. You and Mina—you're not going there yourselves?"

Beppo, picking up his briefcase—it held nothing save a notebook but like so many Italians he carried it more as a mark of respectability than as a receptacle—shook his head. "There's too much to see to here. Since my uncle's death I've been very busy." Four or five visits to a lawyer's office could not, Beppo supposed, be called really busy, but even so the boy needn't stare at him so suspiciously.

"Busy? Doing what?"

"Oh *Dio,* all sorts of things, Galo!" Beppo grinned suddenly. "There's a lot to be done, you see. And then the old man's will has to be proved and that takes a long time."

"How long—about?"

"That depends." Beppo felt a little uncomfortable; he did not want to discuss Ercole's fortune with Galo even though the boy had been nothing but an innocent tool in the hands of his scheming mother. "I doubt, though, if it will be finally settled before the autumn. And now I must go! I've got to meet a businessman with a completely illegible name somewhere down in Mergellina. I shan't be back for supper. You'll stay and have it with Mina, though, won't you?"

"I think we're going to take something round to Nicola's—" Mina said."

Beppo grinned. "Performing good works? Here—" He pulled out his wallet and put a thousand-lire note into Galo's hand. "Get something nice, then."

"Grazie assai!"

Was there a tinge of mockery in the boy's voice? No, no. Galo had always been truly, humbly grateful for the few small gifts Beppo had occasionally made him. "Nothing, nothing. Have a good time, then—both of you!" He turned smiling at the door and then was gone.

Mina had been in the kitchen packing the supper and whistling, very loudly and beautifully and accurately, the theme from the *La Traviata* prelude. Now, entering the sitting room and carrying one of the miniature, brightly striped kit-bags which were so popular that year with all Italian students, she glanced across at Galo where he leaned against the balcony balustrade between the open windows. "Wait! Stay like that!" Galo remained motionless, as if frozen, while Mina put down her bag and viewed him from various angles and distances. Then she shook her head "No use *again*."

Galo pushed himself upright and came into the room. "No? What was wrong this time?"

"The light. Your face looked mauve."

Galo held out the thousand-lire note. "Your father gave me this and told me to get something nice to take to Nicola's. What shall it be?"

"Brandy. How delightful! He *will* be pleased!"

"But—isn't that bad for him?"

"It's not good for him—but that's not the same thing, is it? And the Maresciallo gives it to him, so why shouldn't we? He likes it. It cheers him up and helps him to sleep. Anyway, I've got everything else. We'll get a bottle in the Vanvitelli. I want to go that way because there's a new fish shop I'll show you. They've got tanks—all lit up—and you can buy live fish out of them, though only at the most horrifying prices."

Galo picked up the kit-bag. "You're not going to cook live fish in Nicola's place, are you? You know what the Maresciallo said that time you—"

"No, no. I just want you to see them swimming about."

"Are you going to paint them?"

"I might—the whole shopfront. It would mean sitting in the road, but that would be all right because they're starting work on a drain or something and the road is up. It's an opportunity— Galo, should you be carrying that?"

"Oh yes—when we're in khaki we can. It's only in parade uniform that we must not carry things."

They left the flat. Since the elevator was out of order they rattled down the bare concrete stairs which always smelled of cold cement and metal, and coming out together on to the wide, tree-lined street, turned up toward the Piazza Vanvitelli, merging quickly into the crowd.

৩১ 2

IF Galo Colavolpe believed that he owed his existence in the world to the miraculous powers of an old front tooth, Giacomina Sanbrenedetto knew that she owed hers to the irritable bad temper of a young officer in the British military police. For one day in 1945 this lieutenant had appeared, with two police corporals and a truck at the Pinnigers' Devonshire chicken farm and, abducting Beppo, had sent him back to Italy, to early marriage and immediate procreation.

Mr. Pinniger was over at Tiverton market at the time selling a pig, or it might all have been prevented. Mrs. Pinniger, covered in brown feathers for she was in the midst of plucking a Rhode Island Red, had met the three soldiers on the doorstep.

"I believe that you have P.O.W. 68951 resident here, have you not?"

"Have we? Oh, I suppose you mean Joe."

"I mean P.O.W. 68951. Let's see—yes, Sanbrenedetto G."

"That's Joe."

"Well, that's as may be. Anyway this is his lucky day—he's listed for repatriation."

"But—but he hasn't *done* anything! He's always been as good as—as butter," had exclaimed Mrs. Pinniger distractedly. "You can't do that to him now!"

"Lady, repatriation is not a form of punishment. It means he's going to be sent home—going to be set free."

"But he doesn't *want* to be set free! He wants to stay here. And we need him."

"I can't help that. He's listed for repatriation. You're to get a German in lieu."

"I don't *want* a German! I hate Germans!"

"Well, you'll have to have him all the same. Unless," said the lieutenant with heavy sarcasm, "we arrange another war so's you can pick your P.O.W.s especially to suit." He had turned to his men. "Go and get him."

"No! Wait! My husband's over at Tiverton. Wait till he comes back. We—if necessary we'll adopt Joe. Legally I mean. We can do that. We've no children of our own and—"

The corporals had tittered but their officer was not amused. He was very busy and had no time to waste. "I can't help what you want. And this is the army—not an orphanage. 68951 goes back to Italy on the next transport. Your new man"—the officer had glanced maliciously up from a notebook—"is a fellow called Schmundt. He's got *H.J* after his name which means he's been in the Hitler Youth. Why don't you try adopting *him?* And the best of British luck to you!"

Beppo was removed, dazed, white-faced and in tears; a small, shabby figure in red-dyed battle dress holding a basket of eggs on his lap, sitting in the jeep between two huge military policemen. As one said disgustedly to the other over his head, "You'd think he was *going* to prison rather than getting out!"

And though Mr. Pinniger, returned from Tiverton, spent futile hours on the telephone trying to contact various army organizations to retrieve Beppo, he was unsuccessful. The military police officer had taken offense at Mrs. Pinniger's manner and pushed Beppo's repatriation through with a purposefully efficient speed. Schmundt, a moronic lout who broke the eggs and kicked the chickens and was dirty in his personal habits, was thrust on the despairing Pinnigers and Beppo sailed red-eyed from his beloved England, an exile among a lot of gay and garrulous fellow countrymen.

Even though he felt much better by the time he landed in Naples, Beppo's first months in postwar Italy were lonely. His parents were dead, he lived with an old aunt, and with his small share of the Sanbrenedetto money he started the first of his unsuccessful business ventures—a wholesale cheese business. More to cure his loneliness than for love he had married a woman several years older than himself, a mild, kindhearted bourgeois girl who, despite her robust appearance, had born him only one child and died after ten years of blameless and uneventful family life. She had been a good though uninspiring wife and Beppo for his part a conscientious though erratic husband. Her death had saddened him deeply but, as he realized remorsefully at the time, nothing like as deeply as his parting from the Pinnigers, his exile from England—and he recovered far more quickly.

And so he was left with Mina. Mina was an exceptional child for such very unexceptional parents; unlike either of them she possessed intelligence, talent of a sort and a strong will. During her infancy she had suffered from continual illnesses, none serious but all of a long-drawn-out and debilitating kind. Beppo had believed that it was his fate to rear and care for a sickly invalid, but soon after her tenth birthday and less than a year before her mother's death Mina had suddenly, unexpectedly, blossomed into full health and since then had never known a day's sickness.

Dark, sallow with that clear pallor of the southern Latin, Mina was already as tall as her father and rose a further two inches above him when she wore stiletto heels. Yet, except for the large, black-framed spectacles they both wore for their short sight, father and daughter had nothing in common; for Mina had, at fifteen, an odd elegance, a fine-boned distinction of form—form without color—which, even without her glasses, her big flat portfolio and carefully faded blue jeans, made passersby look at her carefully, smile a little and guess correctly—art student.

Nonetheless, Mina had taken all the place in Beppo's life which her mother had left vacant; she gave him something to live for and made him at once a companion and a competent enough housekeeper. She ruled him—since she had a domineering nature and Beppo a submissive one she was bound to—but unfussily and unemotionally. She gave him good food, good advice and a certain amount of affection, though not as much as he would have liked for, though possessed by that type of compassion which sometimes verges upon *schadenfreude,* she had not an affectionate nature—none of the Sanbrenedettos, with the exception of Beppo, had ever had that.

Pity and painting were the two most important elements in Mina's life. For the first she took up friends like Galo and Nicola, for the other she attended a Vomero art school, and she was loved by the first and mildly disliked at the second.

✎§ 3

MINA'S fish shop gleamed so brightly that it could be seen halfway down the Via Scarlatti. Its name, *Il Gambero d'Oro,* flared in scarlet neon across its front below the gleaming sign of a golden prawn, and in its illuminated glass tanks all the edible sea life of the gulf swam or crawled among colored seaweed and piled rocks. Galo and Mina were entranced and wandered in and out of the doorway exclaiming over sinister, thorny crayfish and angry octopi until asked irritably whether they wanted to buy anything. Then, in a sudden access of embarrassment, they purchased half a kilo of winkles and, collecting the brandy at a small self-service store on the other side of the *piazza,* retraced their steps to the Via Michele Kerbaker and climbed to Nicola's seventh-floor apartment.

They rang and in a few seconds the door opened automatically, admitting them to a small vestibule, empty save for the gold-badged cap of a senior Carabinieri warrant officer hanging above an earthenware pot containing an insulted-looking cactus.

Nicola greeted them with excited nervous pleasure. A dark-haired, pallid youth who looked much younger than his twenty-one years, he lay propped up in a bed whose large expanse of flat surface—covered with a litter of books, a jointed Pinocchio doll and the scattered pieces of a jigsaw puzzle—showed that its occupant had lost both legs above the knee.

"Mina! I thought you weren't coming. You said seven—and it's nearly twenty past."

"I know, I know. It's my fault. I took Galo to see a lovely new fish shop in the Vanvitelli. All glass tanks and—" Mina broke off quickly, remembering Nicola's angry impatience at descriptions of things he could not see himself. "We bought some winkles. I'll just get them ready in the kitchen. You amuse Galo until I come back."

Nicola lifted a drawing board from beside his bed and held it out for Galo's inspection. "This week's work," he said.

Two raging cocks, all hackles, talons and beaks, confronted each other in stilled fury. The work was carried out with immense precision in colored inks—green, red, black and yellow; the effect was that of a freshly pulled early-nineteenth-century print. It was almost certainly a copy, or a near copy, of just such a picture, for Nicola, despite considerable skill, had only the ordinary Italian's attitude to art—he was painstaking, dexterous but unoriginal. Galo thought the picture extremely beautiful and praised it with a fervent sincerity which even Nicola found adequate, but Mina, returning from the kitchen, was slightly less complimentary. "It's beautifully done, Nico, but it's not your own idea. It could have come from a shop in the Toledo."

Nicola's handsome sallow face flushed slightly. "Well, that's all right then. If it's good enough for a window in the Toledo—"

"Oh it is. It is!" Galo said.

"Then it's Art. At least as far as I'm concerned."

But Mina, who was at present full of ideas concerning self-expression, the integrity of the artist to his personal vision and other excuses for the messier styles of modern painting, was not prepared to accept this, and the usual argument between them began over winkles and glasses of brandy. Nicola liked nothing better. He was extremely erudite in a dogmatic way, was as good an arguer as he was a draughtsman and, had he possessed legs, would have spent hours discussing painting at every pavement café in Naples. As it was he had to make the best of his chances during Mina's visits. Even so, Mina was one of the few people who could conduct an argument with Nicola without reducing him to final rage or tears; it was a delicate matter since it was necessary never to lose sight of a shut-in personality which took cognizance of a world largely seen from the viewpoint of someone lying on his back.

It would have been much better, Mina often thought sadly, if Nicola had been born legless; he would have suffered infinitely less both physically and mentally. For until he was eight years old Nicola had possessed ordinary, healthy limbs; then he had lost his legs and his mother in six seconds of exploding grenades and roaring bullets that had turned a small sitting room on the outskirts of Genoa into a blood-spattered slaughterhouse.

At that time his father had been a Brigadiere of Carabinieri whose ability as a criminal detective had earned him both quick promotion and the hatred of the great port's turbulent, postwar racketeers. They came for him one night as he sat at supper with his wife and small son. A door flung suddenly open, a hand grenade hurled amongst the splintering plates and glasses, a long burst of submachine-gun fire rocking the disintegrating room, then a second bomb. No one should have survived that small inferno of blast and ricocheting bullets. But the Brigadiere's wife seized the first grenade and clutching it to her breast rolled to the floor to be blown to fragments, and to save her son and husband. The Brigadiere himself, although hit in five places, drew his pistol and drove his assailants out before they could finish their work—aided in this by the second bomb which, exploding in the fireplace, brought down much of the roof. Nicola, his legs shattered by the bomb which had killed his mother and with a machine-gun bullet through one lung, lay bleeding and senseless under a smashed chair until the rescue squads arrived.

Father and son hung for days on the edge of death, lay for weeks in the hospital. The Brigadiere made an almost complete recovery but Nicola was ruined. One leg had been amputated as soon as he was brought in but it was thought possible to save the other, and for months which elongated themselves into years surgeons and doctors strove to do so. The pain Nicola suffered during those years was endless and terrible. He was growing, and while the reknit bones of his smashed leg expanded weakly and crookedly, the ruined nerves and tissue could not keep pace; even the amputated stump had to be continually reopened to shorten the ever-extending femur. Before he was ten Nicola was longing for death, demanding to be allowed to die, weeping bitterly every time he emerged alive from the long succession of operations. But while a man with one leg can lead an almost normal life, a man with neither is a hopeless cripple and therefore the doctors were adamant that, whatever the child's sufferings, they must be accepted as the price for retaining his leg. But in the weary end even that hope had to be abandoned; by Nicola's eleventh birthday the leg was so hopelessly deformed that it could never be of use to him and it was taken off.

Meanwhile the assassins had been hunted down, caught or killed. The Carabinieri were not a force to be squeamish in dealing with such an attack on one of their members and the first of the criminals to fall into their hands did not survive the methods used upon him during his interrogation. But before he died he gasped out enough information to incriminate two others, and a year before Nicola lost his remaining leg the last of the eight men responsible had been arrested. Of these eight, four died resisting the police or awaiting trial in the police barracks, three were subsequently imprisoned for life and only one, a boy still in his teens and thus too young for the full murder penalty, received a twenty-eight-year sentence instead. To Nicola's father the account was now closed.

But not to Nicola. To him, the chief sufferer, no vengeance or atonement could make any amends or give any satisfaction. He blamed his father as much as the criminals who had tried to kill him. No man, he felt and often said, had the right to undertake the sort of work his father performed while possessing such easy hostages as a wife and a child. Brigadiere Valdemarin should either have remained a bachelor or taken up normal Carabinieri duty—traffic control and patrolling the beat. In an attempt to gain quick promotion his father had negligently and willfully exposed his wife and child to the terrible disaster which had overtaken him. He was culpable.

The Brigadiere—now risen to the powerful position of Maresciallo-maggiore and *de facto* chief of a Naples homicide squad—also felt the weight of his moral guilt in this respect. A sad, sullen, immensely fat man, greatly esteemed by his colleagues, greatly feared by the criminal underworld, he waddled through his duties thinking only of Nicola and of ways to make him happier, his life more meaningful. A senior warrant officer of the Carabinieri receives a good salary, but there are ways of doubling and trebling it and Maresciallo Valdemarin knew and used them all. Every lira was spent on Nicola, mostly for doctors and specialists, new forms of treatment, new drugs. For the amputations had not ended Nicola's pain though they had greatly reduced it. But the nerves of his thighs and the lower part of his body had suffered too much outrage ever to be quiescent again and except under drugs he could seldom achieve anything but a fitful and broken sleep.

Mina had first met the young cripple a year ago when he had been enrolled as a sort of non-visiting member of her art school. It was the third school of this kind which Nicola had entered in a similar manner, for he disliked anything but praise of his work and since it is an art master's profession to criticize, however helpfully, his students' endeavors, Nicola and his instructors invariably fell out.

Mina had been asked, since she lived nearby, to take some portfolios of classical reproductions to the apartment on the Via Kerbaker, and her strong sense of pity had been so inflamed by the dark-haired, dark-eyed, legless boy alone in his small room that she had been a constant visitor ever since. And when it became apparent that Nicola would accept criticism from her that he would accept from no one else, the principal of the school had unashamedly used her as a go-between. "Tell him to soften his approach. Tell him—in your own words of course, Mina—not to use such excessively hard outlines. He's got a magnificent sense of design, but his coloring is so crude. . . ."

Mina did all these things very successfully. She talked art by the hour with Nicola and was delighted when she found that he was, like her, an atheist. Mina had considered Christianity a fraudulent faith for years and Nicola, with the aid of many books, proved to her that it was historically questionable, philosphically inconsistent and morally eccentric as well. Their lack of faith, in this most superstitiously religious of all Italian cities, bound them together with the same bonds that had held and strengthened the early Christians in the Roman catacombs and both would cheerfully have been martyred for their unbelief. Art and atheism made up their friendship.

To Nicola, waiting through the long days for Mina's visits, this friendship soon became the most important thing in his life —and also the most frustrating. For after a few months he knew that he was in love with her and realized also that it was a hopeless passion. In a year or eighteen months at the most Mina would be eligible for marriage, but even if Nicola had been a whole man in good health his chances would not have been of the best. The Sanbrenedettos were a bourgeois family whereas the Valdemarins were of working-class origin. Nicola himself had no money and little prospect of earning any. Even in the best of circumstances Mina's father would probably have refused his consent. But as it was . . .

The introduction to Galo, some six months ago, had been an additional bitterness. For to Nicola, Galo and Mina were so obviously—ostentatiously, even—suited to each other that it could be only a question of time before they realized it themselves, if indeed they did not do so already. Yet since Mina could never be his, Nicola began to find some vicarious satisfaction in knowing the boy who would one day be her husband. It permitted him, in a short time, to become much more intimate with Mina herself since she liked to discuss Galo, and it was not long before Nicola was listening, amused, shocked, but enthralled, to her descriptions of the Colavolpe household at Caserta. He would sit, propped upon his pillows, sipping brandy from his special, ornately gilded goblet, his dark eyes wide with wonder as Mina, who among her many gifts possessed that of an excellent raconteur, described the time Concezio had threatened to burn Maria Fausta alive as a witch and had actually thrown half a can of kerosene over her before being knocked down by Speranza with a garden spade; the day Eugenio—now locked up—had ridden a donkey, stark-naked, through Caserta on a marketday, proclaiming himself the risen Christ; the time Filippa had poisoned them all with a dish of toadstools and the suspicions which had lingered ever since; the time Tarquinio poisoned them all with homemade gin and the suspicions about that: the story of Speranza's fig trees . . . the story of the edible mice . . . the legend of the Holy Tooth. . . .

And soon Galo became to Nicola less an object of jealousy than a character from some fairy story; for Mina's accounts were biased and colored and designed to show off Galo in a good light. In Nicola's imagination he was forever playing Tom Sawyer-like tricks on his ogreish relations and slipping unscathed through their hands, a mocking Puck in a bright uniform. It came as a shock when Galo explained offhandedly one day that his fear and dislike of the sea were probably due to the time his uncle had pushed his head into a bucket of water and held it there until he was three-quarters drowned. Nicola began to realize that even the possession of legs did not necessarily guarantee a happy or normal life.

Tonight, perhaps because of Galo's unstinted praise lavished on his newest picture, perhaps because his two friends seemed even more attentive and agreeable than usual, or more probably because he had slept soundly for nearly three hours that afternoon, Nicola enjoyed himself to the full. They chattered and argued amicably, drank—both Galo and Mina liked brandy just as much as Nicola though they pretended otherwise—ate the winkles and the cold supper which Mina had provided and then played Canasta until it was time for Galo to leave.

They had hardly been gone ten minutes when Nicola heard the door of the flat open quietly, a ponderous tread on the carpeted floor of the vestibule outside and then the sigh and creak of a chair taking a heavy weight. Very carefully Nicola put down his brandy glass and then, silently turning out the light, he lay back in the darkness, his eyes shut. Soon he heard that step outside his door and the door itself opened a crack.

"Nicola?" softly.

Silence.

Still more softly. "Are you all right?"

"Yes."

"You've had your supper?"

"Of course."

"Mina brought it?"

"Like I told you."

"Did you—did you have a nice time?"

"As good as I ever can. Is there any more news?"

"They think he's probably gone to Genoa."

"So?"

"I shall write to colleagues there—Sante and old Belazzini and Coro. I'll tell them what I can—ask them to use all their efforts. They will do their best."

"Oh yes—their best!" Nicola's voice in the darkness was quiet and bitter.

"What else can I do? I can't ask for a transfer to Genoa and leave you here by yourself."

"I could come, too."

"We'd have to find a new apartment. That's not at all easy up there today. And it wouldn't be as good as this one. You'd lose your friends, too—Mina and the school and—"

"If you don't go he'll get away."

"No, no—not necessarily. Coro is a good man and—and—we *can't* go, Nicola. All that can be—" The voice in the doorway, at once self-exculpatory and pleading, was cut short by Nicola's own; steely cold, clear, very quiet.

"You've got to find him—and kill him, wherever he is. He only got twenty-eight years, remember. He's done thirteen. If he goes back it will only be for another fifteen—then he will be free. He's ruined me for life—if you can call it life that I lead—and still they would set him free! You must find him and kill him— or else I shall kill myself."

↭ 4

GALO and Mina sauntered slowly back down the Via Scarlatti under the trolley wires and the plane trees as the soft, warm evening deepened over Vomero and streetlamps gleamed golden down the long street. Tonight, exhilarated by the brandy and the sense of a newly arrived summer still fresh and unfaded by the greater heat to come, the city seemed made especially for them. As they turned into the Via Morghen and gazed down over the ramparts of Sant'Elmo across that great jumble of roofs and terraces that stretched out in a curving, twinkling arc toward the distant bulk of Vesuvius, they each thought contentedly, We are Neapolitans, both of us—this is our place.

And this feeling induced in both of them an odd, excited abandon, a heightened awareness of each other's physical presence which was as new as it was delightful. Instinctively and for the first time they went hand in hand as they strolled down the broad sidewalk of the crowded street. For at this hour, the hour of the *"passaggiata,"* the citizens of all Naples were taking their evening promenade—as family groups, married couples, or as lovers, arms entwined; as gangs of boys, linked lines of giggling girls, elderly business friends, cigars gesticulating as they discussed the market, or as purposeful priests and habited mendicant monks with jingling money-boxes. And everywhere—for Naples had always been a garrison city and was now an international base—could be seen the pale khaki shirts and trousers of soldiers, the gleaming white of the navy.

Here among this slow-moving kaleidoscopic crowd, caught up in the scented ambience of the southern night, Galo and Mina were alone and free and anonymous—a young soldier and his girl. They stopped at a kiosk hung with fruit and leaves and drank freshly pressed orange juice; they bought toasted melon seeds from a hawker and wandered on toward the station of the Funiculare Centrale, seeing how far they could spit the husks. The heat of the high stucco walls, baked day-long in the sun, the drifting, lingering smell of roasting coffee, the hiss and clang of the *filobuses* showering blue sparks from their high antennae, the chatter and music from the crowded cafés which spilled chairs and tables across the sidewalks—Vomero, cleanest and brightest of Neapolitan suburbs on any summer evening.

At the entrance to the funicular station they stopped under the naphtha flares of a shellfish stall so that Mina might demonstrate to Galo and several amused customers her newly acquired knowledge of how to open sea-dates. Eating, rather than drinking, together is the social custom in southern Italy where stomachs have a capacity and strength beyond the northern norm. Both Mina and Galo had already consumed a substantial meal that evening but when an elderly businessman, with his handkerchief tucked into his collar to serve as a napkin, bought them both large plates of mussels and clams, they had no difficulty in eating these, too.

Perhaps because they were, that evening, particularly pleased with themselves, there was a glinting, youthful radiance upon them which delighted the stall-holder and his customers so that for a brief moment of time they reigned here, became the admired center, the focus of the small crowd under the flares—a symbol of youth and all the bright beauty of Naples. *"Che belezza! Che bella, bella coppia!"* The exclamatory compliments, the soft pats and caresses of their momentary courtiers lifted them both to a peak of heightened awareness at once sensual, sensitive and arrogant, of which neither had previously suspected the existence. They had long been friends; they had long held each other in the dreamy, romantic fondness of childhood affection; tonight the crowd around the shellfish stall made them lovers by seeing them as such. For when Galo, glancing up at the station clock, saw that he must catch the next train, when they had accepted the well-wishes of their new friends, they knew that all eyes were upon them as they walked to the barrier. In the circumstances there was only one thing to do and they did it, being Neapolitans and therefore natural actors, as publicly and gracefully as possible. For a moment Galo stood looking down at Mina; she smiling up at him. Then they were in each other's arms in one long embrace—illegal, since such action was prohibited in public, but copied with great virtuosity from all the movies they had ever seen.

⊷§ 5

WHEN Mina, hot and a little breathless, entered the apartment she found her father sitting in his shirtsleeves beside the table upon which stood a bottle of expensive Scotch whisky.

"*Carissima mia*—aren't you a little late?"

"No, I don't think so. After Nicola's I went to see Galo off; then I walked home."

But Beppo was not interested in his daughter's evening; he was bursting to tell her about his own. "I went up and down the Via Mergellina looking for the number I'd been given and I couldn't find it anywhere. In the end I thought it must be a hoax. I nearly gave up and came home. However, I was near that restaurant we went to the other day, the O Sole Mio—in fact I'd passed it once or twice already—so I thought I would ask the doorman if he could help me. I showed him the letterhead and he was most amused. '*Signore,*' he said, 'that's us! I've watched you walking up and down and I wondered what you were after.' 'But,' I said, 'I want the Mergellina Construction and Development Company—an office, not a restaurant.' 'That's upstairs,' he said. 'I'll send someone with you to show you the way.' And he called a waiter and I was taken to an office above the restaurant, and there was that man who showed you how to open sea-dates—Signor Bighencomer—behind a desk."

Beppo paused, smiling, and helped himself to some whisky. "Well anyway, it turned out that he is the managing director of this construction company as well as the owner of the O Sole Mio. He seems to be a man of wide interests, born a Swiss but now a naturalized Italian. . . . And a man who does not waste many words, either. He wants to buy my San Lorenzo property. What is more, he seems to know a good deal more about it than I do. We did not talk long in the office but went into his private apartment which is on the same floor and sat in his lounge overlooking the sea. Then he—well, he more or less explained my position to *me*"—Beppo giggled—"and it appears to be complicated. The Municipality has decided that the San Lorenzo property must remain residential. Well, I suppose that is natural enough since they're always under pressure to provide more homes. But of course it is a nuisance for it may mean—in fact Bighencomer thinks it does—that any new building there will become subject to the rent laws. His firm is anxious to buy the site, clear it out and put up a block of cheap apartments of a standard type accepted by the authorities—'workers' apartments,' they call them. I suggested that if the rent laws were applied to such a project the profit to the owners would be extraordinarily small. He agreed but said that his company accepted that; they were not interested in a quick return for their outlay but on a steady long-term investment. My guess is that they would use the possession of such property as a means of off-loading income tax—perfectly legitimately, I have no doubt.

"But of course they will only pay a price for the site based on the income they expect to draw from it. As Bighencomer said, the price must be related to the use to which the site can be put. At the end of our talk he seemed to be offering something around sixty million, though nothing definite was said."

Mina crossed to the open window and stared down for a moment into the Via Morghen. The crowds were thinning now as people made for a late supper and television or the last house at the movies. "What about old Ercole's tenants—Crocifissa and the others?"

"Oh, I hadn't forgotten them. I told him that there were people living in the remaining building whom I was most anxious should be considered. He was in complete agreement I'm happy to say. He envisages a big modern block with shops on the ground floor. Crocifissa and the Quongs could each be given a shop and the apartment above it."

"Given?"

"Well, no—rented, of course. And I suppose they would

have to pay rather more than they've been paying up till now. But they wouldn't be turned out and—"

"What about the old cabman? And they would all have to go somewhere else while the place was being built."

"Yes, yes, of course—that's obvious. But something or other could be done for all of them even then, I've no doubt. Bighencomer is a most resourceful man. And I really have not had time to think it *all* out. As I was saying, they would be better off in the end with clean modern apartments and efficient business premises—as he said to me himself. No—it's the other poor young woman who is a weight on my mind now—that Signora Giansante I told you about. I don't think she would be able to pay more than whatever it is she gives Crocifissa now. . . . And anyway it is her husband she wants, not a cheap place to live." Beppo sighed, shook his head and rose. Standing by the table he picked up an open letter. "I had dinner at the restaurant, too—with Bighencomer! Oh, Mina, I wish you could have been there! All the time I was thinking, How I wish I'd brought Mina with me! We had a truly magnificent meal and most of it was cooked at the table by the headwaiter and served flaming with spirits. Oh yes, it was most grand! And the wine! But even so I made no firm promises. I kept"—Beppo giggled again—"my head, as they say; even when he gave me this whisky as a parting present. And a good thing, too, for the first thing I found when I got home was *this!*" He smacked the letter he held so that the stiff paper crackled.

"And that is—?"

"Another request to buy the site in San Lorenzo. From the ITOLGAS offices at Poggioreale!" Beppo laughed triumphantly. "So now we have two offers and we can weigh them both and take our time to decide. I will show this to the lawyers when I go there tomorrow, and tell them about Bighencomer's offer as well."

He looked so absurdly happy standing there in his shirtsleeves, flushed and gleaming with his spectacles slipping, as they always did, down his nearly bridgeless nose, that Mina laughed and kissed him. "That's what it is like to be rich. Free dinners and free bottles of whisky. But now surely you'd better go to bed. You can dream about the things the ITOLGAS people will give you."

Beppo clasped his daughter to him, grinning. "If there is going to be another free dinner you must be there, Mina."

"Oh yes, yes—I will!"

But later, in her own small bedroom whose window looked down from the hillside suburb over the myriad lights of the city, Mina stood for a long time staring at that immense panorama. Far below her the Castel dell' Ovo thrust its battered floodlit bulk into the dark waters of the gulf and behind it rose the lights of Pizzafalcone. Somewhere there, among that galaxy of twinkling lights and shadowed obscurity, Galo was lying in his room at the Nunziatella—not, as she, alone but surrounded by the rest of his platoon. Momentarily the thought of all those other unknown bodies so much physically closer to him than she filled her with a queerly wistful anger. Tonight, for the first time, she forgot that Galo was a schoolboy among schoolboys, thinking only that he was her lover, that he was not beside her and that with the summer vacation commencing in a few days it might be as much as three months before she saw him again.

In the Scirocco

⇜§ 1

THE sky was dull and low, a hot, dank, misty gray; the air lifeless and stirred only by occasional gusts of sultry wind that lifted the dust, grit and torn paper from the black flagstones, swinging them in sudden fierce whirls and dropping them again. The *scirocco* lay over Naples in a steamy cloud, vitiating all life, toning every color down to a drab, grimy gray and even turning the gulf into a leaden lake. *Scirocco*—it might last only a day or continue for a week and in its grip the city lay, at once feverish and low-spirited, angry and sullen.

Quong sat in his high-backed chair in the front of his shop, a small yellow-faced figure in white shirt and black trousers, as still as an image and gazing out at the *piazza* which lay blank and ugly under the diffused glare of the whitish sky. It was not a beautiful square at the best of times—though in the soft dusk of a summer evening it held a certain charm—and it was always dirty, but now under the dead and fishy stare of heaven it looked repellently squalid. The blotched, worn housefronts were sloughing their skin of stucco leprously in the sticky heat, the flagstones were scattered with torn paper and excrement, both animal and human, the public urinal, as so often, was blocked and surrounded by a viscous pool of spreading filth. Flies and children swirled in knots which broke apart, fanned out and came together again; many of the children wore nothing but tattered swimsuits and their bare feet were black and crusted with dirt. The girls nursed fretful, wailing babies, the boys played interminably noisy games of *vago* and *morra*, ran after vivid rubber footballs or gambled in doorways with the narrow Neapolitan playing cards.

Quong's shop had once been part of a livery stable and its doorway was flanked by stone hitching posts with hanging iron rings. These had been a continual source of trouble to the old undertaker, for the rival gangs of children which inhabited the square and its adjacent alleys used them as pillories to which to fasten captives. For years Quong had been forced to emerge from his shop at intervals during the day and night to untie some tearstained urchin—who occasionally turned out to be his own son—in the manner of a nineteenth-century African explorer liberating slaves along the banks of the Nile. The shop itself was small and cramped, allowing only room for the display of one magnificently carved coffin partly draped in the black, skull-bedecked velvet pall, a large wooden crucifix, a Chinese scroll whose improper message was fortunately undecipherable to the San Lorenzini, and Quong's own armchair.

Quong had landed in Naples in 1903, a very small sturdy Chinese of twenty-five who despite his mutilated hand was a carpenter skilled in carving. As industrious, thrifty and resilient as most of his race, Quong had prospered modestly, working ten years for others and another ten as an independent jobbing carpenter until at last, in 1923, he had gone into the undertaking business and opened his own funeral parlor. By then he had married an Italian girl, had a son by her and was, at least officially, a Roman Catholic. But the Chinese are not a religious people, cultivating only a vague and optimistic piety, a mixture of Shamanism and myth, Taoism and Confucianism, full of smiling deities and precepts for polite behavior. Quong attended High Mass with pleasure and then came home to perform the kowtow in front of the tablets of his ancestors. He burned candles before a three-foot plaster statue of the Madonna and josssticks before his personally carved wooden one of the goddess Kwang-Yin. Angels and *feng-shui* watched over him in benign accord and when the silver bust of San Gennaro was borne, palanquined and glittering, along the Corso, Quong genuflected and crossed himself and remembered the Feast of Lanterns jigging and glowing through the twisting Pekin alleys toward the dragon gates of the Forbidden City.

And the years had passed and Quong's son Fulvio had grown up like any other Neapolitan child to know first its own *piazza,* then the adjoining alleys, then the Quarter, and—bolder now and filled with the gay, rubbery resilience of the southern street-boy, all the other sections of the city as far as Posillipo to the north and Portici to the south—a true citizen of Naples, born and bred.

Quong had sometimes tried to interest his son with stories of that other, so distant town far across the world, had told him stories of his own boyhood in the little street of the Threshold of the Autumn Moon within the Tartar City where the woodcarvers plied their trade; for as he aged, as the accumulated years began to press more heavily upon him and to bow his shoulders, Pekin came back to him in vivid, jumbled flashes of remembrance. But Fulvio had never been interested: was in fact made uncomfortable by these exotic reminiscences. He was an Italian and a good Catholic and it was embarrassing enough to have a Chinese father without having to listen to tales of his barbarian and heathen youth.

For Fulvio had to make his way as the Neapolitan he was and both his surname and his slanting eyes were a source of inward shame to him, characteristics which, as he saw it, placed him at a disadvantage compared with all his black-shirted young compatriots who were forever being reminded of their Roman origins and being exhorted to live like lions. He seldom invited his friends home and spent as much time as possible away from the *piazza.* Quong felt this estrangement from his son deeply but understood its cause and sympathized. His wife had given him no more children after Fulvio and now he was glad of it for the sake of those unborn ones.

And then had come the war and Fulvio had been called to the colors in its second year. He had gone contentedly, even eagerly, seizing the opportunity to prove by his actions that despite his mixed blood he was a good Italian, determined to follow the inflammatory exhortations of his nation's leader and be as a lion. Old Quong, seeing his son for the first—and as it turned out for the last—time in gray-green uniform and steel helmet had realized completely and irrevocably the great gulf which separated them; had smiled and bowed with a breaking heart as Fulvio, grinning, hitched up his rifle, shouted *"Ciao, Papa!"* and clambered aboard the train with all the other shouting, grinning gray-green figures of this foreign army.

Quong had once been a soldier himself; for a short six months during his twenty-second year he had worn the fantastic uniform of an Imperial bannerman and paraded the streets of Pekin with flags and gongs and war-horns. But service under the Manchus had nothing in common with service under Mussolini; this European war was something he could not comprehend. Then far away on the frozen steppes Gariboldi's 8th Italian Army was overwhelmed and shattered to fragments by a tidal wave of Russian armor and Quong was told that his foreign son was never coming back to the city of his birth.

Four years later Quong's wife died, too, and he was left alone. He had married an Italian and fathered an Italian son—both were dead and it was as if they had never existed. Quong was again an immigrant Chinese living alone in a foreign land. He had his few friends of course, his neighbors in the *piazza*—Crocifissa, Biagio Bonitatibus, the Tenerinis—but they were aliens who neither knew nor cared about Pekin or could speak a word, much less paint a character, of Chinese. Soon, when at last the old man filled one of his own coffins—perhaps the beautiful one displayed in the window—there would be no one left to reverence the ancestral tablets, to think winged and kindly thoughts to the *feng-shui* or burn joss-sticks before the statue of Kwang-Yin, and all this had troubled old Quong and sometimes saddened him.

And then Gennaro had arrived. Unguessed at, unheralded, unexpected, there he had been in Crocifissa's shop when Quong had come back one winter night from a debt-collecting journey round the Porta Capuana. "This is your grandson—Fulvio's child." And all the gray, slow-gathering shadows of life's evening had vanished under the rising sun of a new dawn. For Quong and Gennaro had taken to each other with a passionate intensity which close familiarity had caused to grow rather than lessen. Each was everything the other wanted, each appeared perfect in the other's eyes; their mutual happiness filled the funeral parlor to such an extent that even the coffined corpses which sometimes passed the night before burial in a curtained alcove of the shop must have felt it.

Gennaro could never have enough of China. Quong had to repeat all the stories he had tried to tell Fulvio and a great many more; he had to draw from memory maps of Pekin from the Yung Ting Men to the Bridge of Heaven; to show his grandson how to paint Chinese characters and how to eat with chopsticks; to make him kites of bamboo and silk and delicate paper lanterns. Together in two small rooms in a Naples slum the old man and the boy recreated a China that had long ceased to be —the ancient Imperial China of Manchu and mandarin and mulberry, of blossom and bamboo and sampans on still lakes where great golden carp lay motionless under water-reflected willows.

Quong taught Gennaro his trade, or at least taught him adequate funeral carpentry for Gennaro, like most Occidentals, could never acquire the limitless patience to become a woodcarver in the Chinese manner. But in everything else he was an enthusiastic and intelligent pupil. Undertaking, at least on the small scale practiced by Quong, was not the sort of work which might have suited most adolescents, but it suited Gennaro; in fact he reveled in it. Quong could never decide whether the business was looked on as work or play by his grandson but whichever it was the boy threw himself wholeheartedly into it and in certain techniques—the more modern ones of salesmanship and advertising in particular—showed himself much more able than the old man.

But it was a very small business after all and had been adjusted to times when even the poorest class of Neapolitans would reduce themselves to bitter want in order to bury one of the family in a fitting manner—which meant with every macabre trapping and necrophilistic embellishment that their lire could buy. Today things were different: the Neapolitans' attitude to death had not changed but wages had risen and there was money to pay for more lavish funeral pomps than Quong's small shop could provide. Then, too, most of the great new industrial firms which postwar government grants had induced to erect plants in the city's suburbs ran their own insurance schemes which included funeral arrangements among their benefits. All these things drained custom steadily away from the undertaker in the Piazza Vittime Civili di Guerra.

A small business going downhill is a melancholy prospect,

yet had it not been for Gennaro, Quong would not have minded. He needed so little himself, had no desires of any kind, that the funeral parlor would have lasted long enough to see his time out. Had it not been for Gennaro he would have died at the time of his stroke, contentedly slipping out of life's stream, knowing that his little shop would die with him and leave only a fading legend in the memories of San Lorenzo's inhabitants. *"They say there was once an old Chinese who had a funeral parlor in the piazza. . . ."*

As it was he had struggled back to this half-life in order, if humanly possible, to see his grandson through the last few years into full manhood.

And yesterday he had sat in the police court and heard the dry, cold voice of the magistrate fine Gennaro one hundred thousand lire—the equivalent of the profit of at least eight funerals—threaten him with prison and delicense of the hearse for eighteen months— ". . . to put temptation out of your way until you are legally of age to drive the vehicle. And I want to make it plain that this Court will punish, and punish severely, any such infractions of the traffic laws which come before it. A large percentage of the deaths on the roads are due to the illegal use of vehicles by unlicensed, underage drivers. Had your conduct led to a traffic accident of any sort I should not have hesitated to send you to prison today. As it is, however . . ."

As it was, however, the magistrate had effectively destroyed the business—or at least delivered its death blow. Quong knew this but he also knew that Gennaro refused to accept it. Occidentals had no sense of resignation to even the most obvious dictates of Fate; it was at once the source of their immense strength and of their weakness. Quong had thought up a dozen Chinese proverbs of great antiquity, elegance of expression and obscenity of metaphor to explain the necessity of resignation to Gennaro, but he had not written them down since he knew it would be useless. Gennaro delighted in Chinese proverbs and often quoted them but his grandfather had never known him to act on their advice.

Meanwhile the old man sat and watched the *piazza* children playing in the dirt around the urinal, watched an almost empty *filobus* clang up and deposit two old women and a monk, while a knife-grinder trundled his machine out of the Via Buonuomini and his high howl, rising above the screams of the children, echoed flatly from the opposite housefronts. La Gobba slid, bent double over her mop and bucket, shuffled out of the dark archway beyond the Annunziata, traversing the gutters in her never-ending search for cigarette butts, and before that hideous moving mound of rags the children splayed out and fled in mock terror. Now a gang of boys in tattered jeans or grimy shorts and swimming trunks ran laughing and yelling from the entrance to the Vico dei Lepri, dragging one of their number, protesting shrilly, across the *piazza*. As Quong guessed, they were coming to hitch a prisoner to one of his posts. Since there was nothing he could do to prevent them he put his own precepts into practice and watched calmly from his chair while the captive's wrists were roped to a ring, his jeans pulled down to his ankles and handfuls of sticky mud, scooped from the gutter, rubbed over his face and genitals. Screams rent the air and suddenly Tenerini's big son came out of the tobacconist's shop and strode purposefully across the square, a magnificent figure with his great cartwheel hat tilting its sweeping mane of iridescent cocks' plumes to his left shoulder.

The half of Quong's mouth that could move smiled briefly. The military traditions of the Tenerinis had amused him for years and the tall Bersagliere crossing the square shrank suddenly to the little fair-haired boy of fifteen years ago playing with his wooden sword and tin drum—to Quong it seemed only yesterday.

At Raimondo's approach the gang scattered like mice, disappearing with shrieks of glee into the alley from which they had come. Unspeaking, unsmiling, the soldier untied the cursing, crying, filthy prisoner, delivered a sharp slap across his bare thighs and sent him stumbling off, sobbing and swearing and pulling up his trousers, into the Vico dei Lepri after his associates.

From his seat Quong tried to bow, tried to smile his thanks, and Raimondo entering the shop dropped his military manner and grinned widely, ceasing to be a soldier of Italy's most brilliant and beloved regiment and becoming the big, good-humored boy whom everyone in the *piazza* had known since his infancy. "*Quei maledetti scugnizzi! Buon' giorno, Signor Quong*. Gennaro is not at home, then?"

Quong shook his head and Raimondo, glancing around the small shop, rubbed his nose hesitantly. "*Allora*—when he comes back you ask him to come across? My father wants to see him. And for you— You are all right? There is nothing I can get you?"

Quong shook his head, trying to smile, and Raimondo patted one small yellow hand and left the shop.

⊷§ 2

GENNARO returned half an hour later, at noon. He had spent the morning in the Abate painting price cards. It was one of two secondary occupations he possessed—both quite unconnected with undertaking—and one he had acquired by chance when he was just twelve years old and which his acquisitively jackdaw nature had prevented him from ever entirely relinquishing. He had commenced it, like much else, with the help and encouragement of Crocifissa who years ago had, as it were, set him up in the business.

Before that Crocifissa, in common with most local shopkeepers, had bought her price cards from a small, grinning cripple who came around with pots of quick-drying poster paints, squatted on the floor of her shop and painted the cards in accordance with her instructions. Gennaro had watched him, fascinated by the man's freehand dexterity, and later had practiced himself on pieces of scrap cardboard. Crocifissa had praised his work and on her own initiative had bought him paints and brushes, and with this encouragement he had soon achieved a professional adeptness as great as the poor cripple's whose livelihood he had then proceeded to imperil. For much of Crocifissa's stock came in cardboard containers which could be cut neatly into deckled tickets and there was always a supply of wooden slats from the cheese boxes which could be whittled into the little stakes to which these tickets were attached by means of a tin staple. All these materials were free to Gennaro while the cripple had to buy his for cash which, as he had a family to support, he could ill afford.

When with Crocifissa's encouragement and carrying Crocifissa's urgent recommendations to certain stall-holders, Gennaro had first shyly plied his new trade in the Abate he had met with a limited response. The cards, after all, lasted for days in good weather and the cripple had been in full possession of the trade for years. But Gennaro painted tickets well and—far more important—his prices were considerably lower than those of the older man. Yet he might never have acquired the solid custom which was now his if one bright October morning the cripple, whose fear and anger had been smoldering for days, had not at last screwed up courage for a personal attack. After all, something had to be done; his sole means of livelihood was in danger and he was already a week behind with the rent of his hovel of a room.

He had found Gennaro working beside a fish-stall and then, carefully putting down his own worn box of materials, he had launched into a long, stuttering tirade of abuse, waving his arms, rolling his eyes, and calling for sympathy to God, the saints and all the passers-by. Gennaro, startled, embarrassed, had stared at him wide-eyed without replying and then, remembering that after all he had undertaken to paint these cards and they were wanted at once, had shrugged and continued his work, his flushed face bowed silently above his pots and brushes while the stream of abuse poured over him unanswered. This attitude and his own rhetoric had enraged the cripple to such a degree that suddenly, and with a howl of fury, he had run at Gennaro in a dreadful, dragging rush, knocked over his paints and seizing the newly finished cards, had flung them into the nearby eel-trough. To Gennaro, still in the black trousers of the Ferrara college, this was a first introduction to personal violence; he was shocked and frightened—and then furious. *His* cards, *his* paints—his own possessions had been destroyed and scattered. He let out a wail of anguish and charging the cripple received a blow on the head from the man's crutch which knocked him half-senseless to the cobbles. But it also unbalanced the cripple, who lost his footing and fell beside him. Gennaro had staggered dizzily to his feet and with tears and blood dripping down his face he was weakly trying to kick his opponent's head in when the police arrived to sort the matter out. There could be no doubt who was to blame. The cripple was severely admonished, made to pay for the spoiled cards and banished for the day while Gennaro, his bruised face washed by a motherly stall-holder, received more sympathy than was entirely his due and a considerable amount of custom.

Later, of course, the cripple came back but he was no longer prepared to join issue against the small, pugnacious child with the spiky black hair and the street was tacitly divided between them; Gennaro had the left side, the cripple the right. And since that day Gennaro had taken his paints to the Abate at least once a week and, when business was slack in the undertaking profession, sometimes twice or three times. It was not a very rewarding job, but like his other non-necrophilous occupation—skinning eels for Clemente's fish restaurant on Thursday nights—it all helped out.

The street of the Blessed Abate Antonio is the main thoroughfare of the poor in Naples, in the same way that the Toledo belongs to the rich and well-to-do. The long, twisting road is one great open-air market from its entrance off the Piazza Re Carlo III to its tremendous terminus in the roaring hurly-burly of the Porta Capuana. But the Abate is much more than a place in which to buy pig's-feet, shellfish and melons or to haggle over a pair of secondhand children's shoes. It is a place of employment for a great many more people than the few hundred stall-owners who scream their wares in shrill competition with each other up and down its length. No one knows how many of the semi-employed, semi-destitute inhabitants of Naples acquire a part of their subsistence by some form of endeavor in the Abate, but it must be a sizable proportion. There are so many errands to run and messages to deliver, so many overflowing shopping-bags to be carried, so many arrangements to be made concerning exchanges and discounts from other people's cousins on a commission basis—and, because of the state of the street, so many pairs of shoes to be cleaned at either end.

As a part-time pensioner of the Abate, Gennaro had contacts up and down the length of the street. Today he had begun as usual with the Roccatelli fish stall. A quick, wavy yellow band round the card's edge, the name of the fish in blue, the price in scarlet . . . *Cernia—800 chilo . . . Spigole—550 chilo . . . Calamari—690 chilo*. This last card had to be painted carefully, for the trick was in the middle figure. By making the nine look like a zero and then adding only the tiniest

flick of a tail the unwary housewife might be persuaded to buy
her cuttlefish under the mistaken belief that the cost was actually six hundred lire the kilo rather than practically seven hundred. But if she did not discover this until the fish were weighed
and wrapped she would often pay up, albeit grudgingly.

Frowning, tongue-tip between teeth, Gennaro used his brush
with the firm yet supple dexterity learned patiently from Quong
in many winter evenings spent copying Chinese characters. But
his thoughts were as gloomy and oppressive as the *scirocco*
weather lying over the city. That fine and the eighteen months'
endorsement of the hearse's license loomed like great barriers
between today and the future—barriers which somehow or
other he was determined to surmount. The temporary loss of
the hearse was the most formidable and the most difficult to
overcome. It might be possible to find another undertaker who
would rent his hearse and driver when necessary but of course
this would cut the profits of a single funeral by nearly fifty percent and it would be both difficult and vexatious to arrange.
Nonetheless it would enable Quong's to continue to function
after a fashion. The alternative was to allow the business to sink
to that of a mere coffinmaker's—and a cut-rate coffinmaker's
at that. No more wreaths, no more black crepe, funeral cards
and notices, layings-out or arrangements with priests and cemetery authorities. . . . One might just as well sell one's lavender
suit and become a jobbing carpenter. It would mean the end of
Quong's. No—that was not to be thought of; somehow the business must be pulled through the next eighteen months even if it
meant running up heavy debts with other, more fortunate, un-
dertakers.

Then the fine—the fine that must somehow be paid within
the next eight days. For if it was not, Gennaro would be faced
with a four-month prison sentence. Not that he would be sent
to a regular prison—his age and the comparative veniality of
his offense would prevent that—but to a *casa di correzione,*
which by all accounts was considerably worse since the emphasis
was on reform rather than punishment. And by what methods, Gennaro wondered bitterly, did the authorities reform
someone whose only crime was attempting to hold his business
together and keep his paralyzed grandfather out of an institu-

tion for incurables? For while he was on the island of Procida being reformed, Quong would have no one to look after him and would be taken away.

But of course the fine could be paid, and would have to be. Once again Gennaro listed mentally all the possessions he could sell to raise the money—his new electric iron, the small radio which was now Quong's sole source of interest, a few clothes, his bed, Quong's woodcarving tools and the last four carved wooden boxes. At the most they might raise sixty thousand. . . . And despairingly he knew at the back of his mind that it would have to be the white jade horse. The horse was worth at least two hundred thousand, probably much more, but its loss would be a blow of a size almost equal to losing the business. For it was the last, genuine link with China; to Gennaro it was many other things as well but that was the most obviously important. Quong had brought it with him across the world from Pekin more than half a century ago and Gennaro, laying his fingertips on that smooth polished jade, cold even in the height of summer, was in personal contact with his own—to him, entrancingly romantic—heredity. The horse was testamentary evidence to his peculiar pedigree. Standing in lieu of the birth certificate he did not possess, it stated more plainly than any words on paper that Gualtierra G.—wartime bastard of a half-caste Italian soldier though he might be—in actual fact had his origins in the street of the Threshold of the Autumn Moon near the Tung Chi gate within the Tartar City of Imperial Pekin. To lose it would be to lose a part of himself, to lose direct touch with all that colored background of curly-eaved temples, yellow silk palanquins, dragons and lanterns and water-willows which Quong had taught him to think of as "China."

The fish stall took six cards and on his way to the butcher's farther down the street Gennaro was stopped for a single one by a man selling slabs from a round cake of pig's blood mixed into a stiff paste with corn flour. The butcher ordered four and Gennaro sat out of the hot, gritty wind below a dangling bullock's forequarter and painted *Sottolingua—240 chilo . . . Pulmone di vitello—300 chilo . . . Trippa Assortita—10 il pezzo.* Around him the great throbbing arteries of Naples, driven from the city's heart at Porta Capuana, pulsed and thundered in an unending roar of shouting voices and laughter, of wild radio music from balconies, of angry hooters and grinding gears and of hoofs and iron wheels clattering over rough cobbles. It was deafening, that noise, until at last the ears became deadened so that much of it went unheeded, and because of this it was natural for the city-born to carry on conversations at the tops of their voices. Gennaro's own monk-trained voice carried nowhere and in the Abate he seldom spoke if he could help it, nodding to his instructions, signaling with his fingers the amount owed and smiling his thanks on payment.

After the butcher there were more than a dozen fruit and vegetable stalls to be visited and also some florists. These were often Gennaro's best customers, for as the summer swung up through its blazing blue orbit the country produce for sale in the Abate became ever more varied and luxuriant and erratic in price. Also, since these stalls and barrows were dismantled and trundled away at night, their owners inevitably lost some tickets and renewals were in constant demand. Yet even so, Gennaro had only painted some fifty cards by noon and because of the discount expected on his larger orders had made less than five hundred lire—about a quarter of the wage of a daily laborer. Dejectedly he washed his brushes, cleaned his paints and wandered back through the airless streets.

✥ 3

WHEN Gennaro entered Tenerini's shop he found Gigi holding the floor. He had run in ostensibly to get the time for Crocifissa from the big clock above the counter, the one reliable timepiece used by everyone in the *piazza,* but actually to ask if Raimondo would come for a walk with him. Raimondo was the little boy's chosen hero and Gigi's greatest pleasure was to walk hand in hand with the tall soldier through the streets, flaunting his friend before an admiring world.

Gigi's mother was enjoying a period of mild affluence due to the arrival at Naples of a Japanese aircraft carrier on a courtesy visit, and in a moment of absentminded generosity she had bought her son his first pair of long trousers—bright blue jeans ornamented with many zips and with a plastic dollar bill stitched to the hip pocket. Now these had to be correctly admired and business was at a standstill while Gigi demonstrated all his zips and preened himself in the long mirror which advertised Toscana cigars. No one thought of disregarding him for in Naples every child possessed that freedom of the city bestowed in other countries only upon the rich, the elderly and the eminent—so Raimondo and his father and old Biagio the cabdriver, listened, nodded and made the right rejoinders.

Once the Tenerinis had been as numerous as most other Neapolitan families but now only the old shopkeeper and his son remained—the rest were merely names on various war memorials scattered about the city. For the Tenerinis had military traditions of misfortune which stretched back into the last century in a long line of defeat, retreat, rout and sheer disaster. It was not for any of them to fight victoriously at Calatafimi or the Volturno, to be presented with swords by Garibaldi or to ride, red-shirted and triumphant, to hail Victor Emmanuel King of United Italy at Teano. Two of their ancestors had been shut up with "Bombino" and his troops at Gaeta but neither had survived the siege, one poisoning himself with shellfish, the other being blown to fragments when the cannon he was serving exploded on the ramparts.

And since that distant day at least one Tenerini had been painfully present at each of Italy's more spectacular military reverses. Tenerinis had died gruesomely under arms in Africa and in Greece, in Russia, Albania and upon their own frontiers. Ethiopian sabers had drunk their blood at Dogali, Arab matchlocks had blown their heads off at Kufra, Greek freedom fighters had garroted a Tenerini on sentry-go, French maquis had crept up to a sleeping Tenerini and slit his throat, the SS had hanged a Tenerini as a hostage while Communist partisans had dropped another, bound and weighted, into a well. They were not fortunate as soldiers and despite their martial sacrifices none had ever risen above the rank of sergeant in the field, though Raimondo's great-uncle, Giulio-Cesare Tenerini, had achieved this much the day before he surrendered with the remains of Albertone's brigade at Adowa—only to have his head hacked off the following afternoon.

Even so, the tobacconist himself, Napoleone Tenerini, had risen to the same rank after having taken part in seven of the eleven battles of the Isonzo and might have made sergeant major if he had not lost a leg during a vain attempt to storm a motor ambulance in the rout from Caporetto. But since the inhabitants of the *piazza* were an easygoing lot they gave him the benefit of his lost opportunity and invariably addressed him as "Maresciallo."

When at last Raimondo had led Gigi off to exhibit his new jeans round the Porta Capuana, Gennaro said, "Quong says you want to see me, Maresciallo?" Despite the notice saying No CREDIT, Gennaro owed for at least ten packs of cigarettes. Now that his catastrophe was common knowledge in the *piazza* he expected that most of those to whom he owed money would wish to foreclose their debts while there was anything to get. They need not have worried, though; with the white horse sold there would be plenty for everyone.

"Ah yes. Yes, Raimondo went across." Tenerini blinked through his spectacles and shifted his artificial leg which squeaked metallically at the knee; *scirocco* weather always made his stump ache and he amazed Gigi by claiming, justly, that he could feel the pain all the way down to his wood-and-metal ankle. "This is a bad business, Gennaro, isn't it? Crocifissa says that you're going to try to keep on, though. Is that so?"

Gennaro nodded.

"It won't be easy, boy—without your hearse. Do you think you can?"

"I'll have to—won't I?"

"You could close down. Get a job. You'd be better off. It's a pity you're not old enough for the army, though I suppose you might give a false age. Look at Raimondo—it's a good life; no worries or responsibilities and everything found." He paused and from the shadows below a rack of fading picture postcards old Biagio croaked, "It is today, certainly. Not when we were young, though." He himself had joined the army in 1910 to escape the blows and curses of the foreman in the brickworks at Barra where he had labored since the age of eight, but had only exchanged these for the harder blows and more obscene curses of his military superiors.

Gennaro's dark eyes slid from one to the other of the two old men. "I'm in business," he said slowly, "and I'm going to stay in business—at least until Quong is . . . While Quong is here."

"*Va bene, va bene!* Nobody's trying to stop you. I just wanted to know . . ." Maresciallo Tenerini took off his spectacles, wiped them and replaced them and at once became brisker as if suddenly achieving a clearer mental as well as physical vision. "About this fine. You'll have to raise the money. I'd talk to Quong myself if he was in good health, but as it is . . . Look, Gennaro, I'll lend you fifty thousand toward it on condition that you can raise the other fifty."

Gennaro stared at him in amazement which gave way to joyful gratitude. "Maresciallo!"

"*Niente, niente.* I've known your grandfather since—oh, long before *you* were ever born or thought of. Personally, Gennaro, I don't think you've got much chance of holding on, so my money is probably going to be wasted. That's why I can only afford to pay half. But I know you want to hold on if you can and I know Quong would want you to. Now about the other fifty. The people to apply to should be tradesmen with whom Quong's done business for years—people who owe you a good turn for your custom, you understand. What about your wood-merchant?"

"Savoldi?" Gennaro swallowed. Didn't Tenerini know about Savoldi?

"Yes—why not? Go along to him and explain what's happened and—"

"I owe him money as it is."

"Much?"

"Forty-five."

"Hmm—I see. Yes. Well"—Tenerini's leg mewed like a protesting cat as he moved on his stool—"you could still try. Those wood-merchants are always near millionaires. I wish I'd had the capital to start that way myself. *Mamma mia,* I'd have a proper leg from America today—not this old music-box! Yes, Gennaro, you run along to Savoldi and tell him you've got half the money promised from me if he'll let you have the other half—and see what he says."

Ten minutes later Gennaro approached the wood-merchant's premises scowling and shrugging his shoulders madly. He was telling himself that he did not mind what the wood-merchant wanted from him in exchange. Why should he mind? It did not matter in the least. He had once met another boy who had been invited to Savoldi's bachelor apartment and who came away

after a good dinner with three thousand lire in his pocket, as
happy as a cat with two tails— "But what did he *do?*" "He said
I smelled bad—well, I'd been working in the fish market all
day—so I had a bath." "Yes, but what—" "Oh, don't be so
ignorant! What do you suppose he did?" "I don't know—that's
why I'm asking." "Well, if you don't know, you don't. I'm not
telling you. *Sotto il nostro cielo non si naque i sciocci*—fools
aren't born here. But then you come from Ferrara, don't you?"
And Gennaro, though he now had a fairly accurate idea of what
happened to boys who went home with the wood-merchant, was
still quite unaware of the details of Signor Savoldi's routine.

Sex, guilt and anxiety—the three black demons of European
male adolescence—prey upon Italian youth less than upon that
of the more unfortunate northern nations, and upon Neapolitan
youth this burden is the least irksome of all. Sex—like food and
drink—is something to be sold if possible, embezzled if necessary, bought as a last resort; an appetite to be enjoyed personally or to be gainfully exploited in others. It is also a means of
demonstrating genuine affection—sometimes toward girls,
more often with each other, not infrequently with members of
their own families. The reason the city-born Neapolitan's mind
dwells so continuously upon sex is because he has such a wide
variety of uses for it.

But Gennaro was not a city-born Neapolitan and had spent
his first eleven years under conditions of blank chastity. Since
then, happy and busy, he had little time or thought to spare for
anything except death and money. He would have agreed with
the ordinary Neapolitan's financial attitude to sex, but only in
the sense that people must, presumably, be born before they
could die, and he acquired as much satisfaction from the contemplation of a corpse he was going to bury as other boys received from that of a girl they were going to seduce. Yet the continuous company of cadavers is not conducive to a respect for
the human body and Gennaro had no personal delicacy at all.
But he had an inordinate professional pride: he was an undertaker, and as such it was not his job to sell his body like one of
the boy-prostitutes of the Galleria. Besides, he did not want
three thousand lire and a free dinner; he wanted a business
loan. But he doubted if Signor Savoldi would see the matter in
that light.

He found the wood-merchant perched as usual at his high desk on its dais in his resin- and sawdust-scented office. Behind in the timber yard the buzz-saw shrieked and droned like a demented ghoul. Savoldi greeted him with all the usual heartiness. "Aha—Gennaro, again! How are you, Gennà, my boy? I've some more stamps for you—Brazil and British Honduras, this time; real beauties. And how's Quong?"

"The same as usual, Signor Savoldi. No better, no worse. I—I want to talk to you about something."

"You do, eh? Come up here, then." Savoldi stretched down a muscular hand and pulling Gennaro up onto the dais by the belt of his overalls, put an arm round his waist and said, "*Eccoci* —here we are, all nice and friendly— Now, what is it?"

Gennaro licked his lips, wishing desperately that he was thirty or forty years old instead of sixteen and a half. How easy it would be then to ask for what he wanted. But of course if he was that age he wouldn't need to ask at all since he would have had a proper license and would not have been fined. The adult world seemed to take a sadistic pleasure in making life as difficult as possible for minors and then studying their struggles with the ugly dispassion of people watching flies stuck in treacle. But this was not the time for analytical self-pity—standing here beside the desk with Savoldi's hand slipping down in exploratory maneuvers around his thighs. He said, "I need a loan. A loan on strictly business terms you understand, Signor Savoldi. It's to meet a—an emergency—a business emergency."

"Gennaro," said Savoldi as if he had not heard a word, "I think you need a bath."

Gennaro swallowed and looked away. "I always wash my hands after I've been touching corpses," he stammered quickly, and Savoldi let out a bellow of laughter and released him. "You do, do you? *Oh, Dio! Oh, per l'amor' di Dio!* He washes his hands after he's been touching corpses!" The wood-merchant rocked back and forth on his stool in a paroxysm of mirth. "And I should hope you did! Indeed I should! *Oh Mamma mia!* Gennaro, you'll be the death of me someday!" He shook his head, wiped his eyes and then, still chuckling, asked, "How much do you want, Gennà?"

"Fifty thousand. You see I—"

"For how long?"

"I don't know. I'll pay it back as soon as I possibly can. I know I—we—owe you forty-five already. I know that. Of course this is purely a business matter, you understand . . ."

Gravely Savoldi said, "Naturally it is. One businessman to another, eh?" and gratefully Gennaro answered, "Yes, that's what I mean. A reasonable percentage, of course—"

"Say two percent per annum?"

"That's very low. You mean—you really will?"

"I mean I really will." The wood-merchant drew a large bunch of keys from his pocket and unlocking a drawer of his desk pulled out a cashbox. As he opened it he said, "I needn't remind you that I'm in business myself, Gennaro, and that I don't make unsecured loans every day. And I'll tell you something else. I had intended to allow you credit for wood up to one hundred thousand. Instead, I'll lend you this money. But from now on— until it's repaid—you'll have to pay cash for all further purchases here—you understand?"

"Yes—of course."

"Very well. Here you are, then."

But as Gennaro buttoned the notes carefully into a shirt pocket beneath the bib of his overalls he felt Savoldi's hand clamp firmly on the front of his belt and when at last he looked up, Savoldi's big, hot eyes were staring into his own. For a long moment there was silence; even the buzz-saw was stilled. Gennaro felt again the blood heating his face under that probing, frightening scrutiny. Savoldi rocked him back and forth by his belt still staring at him—appraisingly, questioningly. At last he said, "You're getting a big boy, Gennà, now. But I can remember the first time you came here—just as if it was yesterday. You were eleven and dressed completely in black, and you began by saying *"Salve"* like a priest. You had a note from Quong and you said, "My grandfather has sent me to say he wants wood for half a coffin." You did, indeed! And when I asked you if your grandfather was intending to bury half a corpse you said that he hadn't told you but that you thought he must be. And so we had a long discussion about which half it was likely to be because—as I pointed out, and as you fully agreed—the legs would need more wood than the top half—you remember?"

Grinning, Gennaro nodded, and with a gentle push Savoldi

released his hold and turned him off the dais. "All right, Gennaro—off you go. My compliments to Quong, as usual."

"*Grazie assai, Signor Savoldi!* I won't forget your kindness."

"Just don't forget to pay back the cash, Gennà—that's all I ask!"

And then he was out in the hot, dank, airless street, but filled with such relief and happiness that the sky might have been its brightest, sun-filled blue, the air filled with birdsong of Perugia's strength and quality. The business and the white horse—both were rescued, secure and safe in his possession once more. For that moment Gennaro believed profoundly that all would be well. Somehow he would find a substitute hearse; business would unexpectedly improve; Quong would miraculously recover and they would live together happily ever after among their friends and neighbors, their fellow citizens—Neapolitans. Neapolitans. A kindly, superstitious, yet reasonable people. A people who, in the midst of savage social injustices and stupidities, still held each other's rights and day-to-day struggles and difficulties in complete, unthinking respect. A highly strung, intelligent people who, despite centuries of appalling misgovernment and corruption, still wore the glinting, grime-stained badges of a courageous, undespairing tenacity to life. A noisy, laughing people, naïvely impressed by material grandeur, yet whom neither vulgarity, nor squalor nor ostentation could ever blind to the unchanging, unalterable values of the human spirit.

❧ 4

THE *scirocco* held Naples panting in its gloomy thrall and daily the heat increased. Tourists, arriving in fast trains from Rome, left again immediately on the SPAN ferries for Capri, Ischia and Sorrento; only the most persistent sightseers remained in the city long enough for a quick visit to the Duomo and the Castelnuovo. The lifeless, sunless heat was bad enough along the wide, hotel-lined waterfront of Chiaia and Partenope, but in the jumbled hinterland, the stifling alleys and tiny squares of San Lorenzo and the Forcella, it was tropic; all the windows and doors gaped wide and no man could escape the sense of menace which comes with the too heavily felt pressure of other men. Everyone was in the streets, day and night; lounging on the sidewalks, jostling at corners, sitting on curbstones, sleeping fitfully in doorways—since the *bassi* of Naples contained more than forty thousand one-room basement apartments, each housing an average of five people, there was nowhere else for them to go.

On Monday morning Gennaro stood cramped beside Renato Paolantonio upon the crowded platform of a *filobus* bound for Poggioreale. Around them both other workmen, short, broadshouldered, unshaven, swayed and jolted, patiently gripping the roof bars in an atmosphere of sweat, cheap tobacco and the acrid, metallic odor of stained canvas overalls.

Monday was a day on which, unless particularly busy, Gennaro normally cleaned out the shop, checked his stock of materials and then, in his lavender suit bedecked with its black velvet rose, went out distributing his business cards and canvassing for custom—Quong's special representative. In the evenings he ironed yesterday's washing and then stuck into his album such stamps as had come his way during the previous week. But now he was on his way—rebelliously and with a great many inward reservations—to take up what might well be a full-time job.

The fault was Crocifissa's, and Gennaro looked upon it almost as a betrayal. When he had returned so happily from Savoldi's on Friday, he had found Crocifissa waiting for him and demanding that he come into the kitchen behind the shop for a little talk. And the talk had taken up most of the next twenty-four hours. For Crocifissa had become increasingly worried concerning Gennaro's position and had decided that for his own sake the time had come for some plain speaking before it was too late. "Now listen, *caro mio*. It really is no use thinking that just because you've borrowed the money to pay that fine you have nothing more to worry about. All it means is that you're a hundred thousand lire in debt—and I know you owe Savoldi for wood, as well. You owe me for three months' rent, too, though we'll forget about that for the present. But you must see, Gennarino, that you can't go on piling up debts. You haven't had any custom either, since you buried the *padrone*. And now you can't use your hearse—even if you get a commission."

"There's a business recession at present," had said Gennaro a little sulkily. "Everybody's hit by it."

"Nonsense!" Crocifissa was too worried to accept Gennaro's line of business-talk. "The fact is that no one's come to you—not even to buy a wreath—for weeks."

"The firm is going through a difficult period, I admit. I've been thinking that a reorganization of our sales campaign might—"

"Oh Gennaro, *do* try to be sensible! If Quong was in good health and working I'm sure he'd suggest that you took a proper job and earned a wage instead of—"

"He wouldn't suggest anything of the sort!" Gennaro had exclaimed, outraged. "Quong *taught* me the business!"

"Well, I don't know how else you'd both live, I'm sure." Crocifissa had rubbed her forehead distractedly "I know how much the business means to you, *caro mio,* but you'll have to do something. I don't want to upset you but you must remember that as tenant-in-chief here I've had three months' notice from Signor Giuseppe. He says it is only formal at present, but I'm sure he'll sell this place soon—and then what will you do?" Gennaro had licked his lips. "We shall have to find some new premises."

"You'll have to find some new money, first," Biagio had spoken up from the dark corner where he had been sitting silently screwing up his mouth and pursing his lips. "You ought to get a proper job, boy. At your age I—"

"I don't want a job. I've got a trade—a *profession.* Besides," added Gennaro a little shakily, for he was not used to being talked to like this and under the combined assault of Crocifissa and Biagio the myth-citadel of "Quong's" was tottering—"who would look after my grandfather if I wasn't there?"

But Crocifissa had been ready for him. "I've been talking to Signora Giansante. She's perfectly willing to stay with Quong and—"

"I couldn't pay her."

"She doesn't want paying. She said she would be grateful for something to do. She'll sit in the shop, see that Quong is all right, and take down any orders or commissions that come. She's an educated lady; I'm sure she would do it very well." Playing accurately on her knowledge of Gennaro's character, Crocifissa added, "It would be nice for Quong's to have its own lady-receptionist, wouldn't it? We could put my small table near the window with a vase of lilies or white carnations on it. She could sit there. Think how impressed customers would be."

"She can't make coffins or wreaths." But Gennaro's objection had been halfhearted. Crocifissa, with the natural psychological insight of the uneducated, had triumphed with the vase of white carnations. "She could easily learn to make wreaths, I'm sure. And you could make the coffins in the evenings or at weekends."

"But she couldn't arrange a whole funeral."

"I expect," grunted Biagio sourly, "that she could. If there ever are any to arrange."

Crocifissa had frowned him to silence. "No. You'd have to take the day off then, Gennaro, of course. You could always say next day that you were ill."

"Or that I'd had a pressing business appointment."

"Well . . ."

And though Gennaro had needed a great deal more persuasion, in the end he had acquiesced—angrily, sulkily and with a sense of personal loss which even Crocifissa could not comprehend fully—to make the experiment. He would try to get a job which would tide him over the year and a half until his eighteenth birthday and the legal use of his hearse. He made many stipulations. If business looked up he would return at once to full-time undertaking. He would return equally if Iole Giansante did not look after Quong properly or failed to show the expected competence in caring for his business interests. His new job, whatever it might be, must never be put before his true profession or allowed to interfere with the proper arrangements for a commissioned funeral. And on these conditions alone Gennaro had agreed to search for work. It had not been a long search, for Crocifissa had privately spoken to Renato Paolantonio and next day Gennaro was called into the old woman's shop to hear his offer.

"Look—if you like to come with me on Monday I might be able to get you taken on at ITOLGAS. It's hard work, of course, but it's well paid—as jobs go."

"When I was this boy's age," old Biagio, who was again present, had remarked, "I and my two brothers were doing ten hours a day in the brickworks—and the foreman used a stick on us if we didn't move fast enough."

"Oh Dio!" Renato had said, grinning. "If you had that fore-man on the box today behind Baldissera you might get a little more custom, eh? Well, Gennà—what about it?"

Gennaro had agreed, politely but without enthusiasm, and now they were both on their way to Poggioreale, rattling and swaying through the dull, windy morning.

Some of the men in the *filobus* knew Renato and exchanged brief greetings in the Neapolitan dialect which even after five years in the city was still largely a foreign language to Gennaro. They grinned and nodded and swung off the bus at intervals with quick, curt *ciao*'s; burly, compact men who more often than not wore the small red enamel badge of the Communists on their workshirts. Gennaro noticed several of them remove these badges before they left the bus.

He and Renato descended a hundred meters beyond the Jew-ish cemetery and turned into a narrow lane between high con-crete walls above which loomed the skeletal iron towers and domed silver tanks of the methane works. The air stank of gas and chemicals; their feet crunched on gritty cinders and eight meters above them an endless chain of iron tubs clattered and banged along a heavy cable. "The *teleferica*." Renato cocked an eye upward. "You might get put on that."

"What—riding in one of those?"

"No—filling them. Working one of the feeding chutes."

A gateway in a wire fence; a wooden hut with three guichets. Renato's air of preoccupation, which had lasted throughout the journey, dropped from him and was replaced by an apologetic, grinning deference. He approached one of the guichets through which a small, elderly man with steel-rimmed glasses was peer-ing suspiciously. "Signor Trulli, I've brought someone with me who might suit for work on the *teleferica*."

"Not on the *teleferica*. South excavation may take him. That him?"

"Yes—Gennaro Gualtierra."

"Name doesn't matter—not unless he's taken on." The little man stared beadily at Gennaro who smiled awkwardly back. "How old?"

"Eighteen."

"What's he been doing?"

"Carpenter's assistant."

"Let him say it, then. Hasn't he got a voice of his own? Oh, never mind. Take him along to Pietrini. Say I sent you."

"Many thanks, Signor Trulli. But, is it not possible—the *teleferica?*"

"I've told you—no! Pietrini wants men—he's the only one. Hurry along now."

As they threaded their way between the looming tanks and under the continually crisscrossing tangle of great pipes which curled and curved everywhere like the intestines of some eviscerated giant, Renato said lamely, "It's a pity about the *teleferica*. I'd hoped . . . Now you'll be shoveling most of the time. Still, you get more breaks that way and Pietrini's a good foreman. . . ."

The south excavation was a great gap in a low rock cliff of yellow shale. Four dozen men lounged before an assortment of earth-stained mechanical diggers, angle-dozers and dump-trucks. Renato, once more grinning deferentially, sought out Signor Pietrini, a tall, youngish, light-haired man who detached himself from a group beside a power-shovel, smiling a brief acknowledgment of Renato's respectful greeting.

Renato repeated much of what he had said at the gate and Pietrini listened, nodding and glancing from him to Gennaro and back again. "Very well, your friend can come on trial for today." He looked appraisingly at Gennaro. "It's heavy work, you know—not like carpentry."

Renato nodded. "I hoped they would have a place for him on the *teleferica* but they didn't."

"Who said so?"

"Trulli."

Pietrini smiled, rubbing a finger and thumb together and Renato nodded somberly. "How much?"

"Ten. He might take eight. It's good work, after all."

"We haven't got that sort of money." A sudden thought struck him. "Signor Pietrini, tomorrow—that is, if he suits you . . ."

"Two, comrade. But he needn't hand it over until the end of the week."

"*Si—va bene.* Very well, then, Gennà. I'll see you later." Renato grinned and turned away and as he did so a hooter blasted its long admonitory note to the low sky.

Immediately the men around the machines came to life and

Pietrini took Gennaro over to six of them who stood around the squat, silent bulk of a skip-loader. "That thing's out of action. You'll be on shoveling today, Gualtierra—filling the skips. Watch the others and do it like them. And for the sake of God and His Mother keep out from under when the skips move off. You're not insured like the rest, remember. If you get hurt you won't get any compensation from the Company—not until you're properly engaged."

The mechanical diggers were chuntering away at the cliff face and the first line of skips ground slowly along their miniature railway line behind them. Gennaro found himself one of a gang who were filling them and pushing them down the slow gradient to the trucks. The long-handled, narrow-headed Italian shovels swung rhythmically and broken stones and dry yellow earth rattled into the iron tubs. It was Gennaro's first taste of heavy manual labor and to begin with he enjoyed it. The feel of the shovel, once he had accustomed himself to its balance, was comfortably reassuring; he fell into the automatic silent rhythm of his companions, his muscles moving firmly, elastically, his breathing steady and even. A stoop and a thrust under the stony shale, a heave and then a turn bringing the loaded shovel swinging up and around over the lip of the tub, a twist of the wrists and the spoil cascading, drumming to the iron bottom—and then a quick, careful turn with the shovel held high to avoid that of the man on his right.

But within an hour his arms were beginning to ache, his hands to feel stiff and cramped. He felt the sweat sticky on his shoulders and copying some of the other men, he dropped out of the gang, took off his shirt and hung it on one of the gleaming hydraulic booms of the silent skip-loader. As he was returning to the line Pietrini strolled up and spoke to him in dialect.

"*Come?*"

"I said 'How's it going, comrade?' Aren't you a Neapolitan, then?"

"Yes—now. But I came from Ferrara."

"So?" The foreman nodded and passed on.

And now the shovel began to feel less reassuring and much less comfortable. Gennaro became aware of an ache in his arms and thighs, a constricted tightness across his shoulders. He had not until now been troubled by the noise and fumes of the various machines but slowly these made themselves felt as a jarring background continually increasing his growing physical discomfort.

They knocked off for ten minutes an hour later and stiff and sore, Gennaro followed the others to the gravel-stained side of the skip-loader; it appeared to be the exclusive retreat of his particular gang and he noticed other groups clustered in the same way around other man-dwarfing machines. There was a pail of water and a tin mug and one by one, each patiently waiting his turn, they drank. The oldest of the gang, a man of about fifty named Mario who seemed to hold the unofficial position of charge-hand, smiled at Gennaro from out of a mask of yellow dust and offered him a crumpled cigarette. "Smoking is permitted here on the excavation—but nowhere else, of course. It is the one advantage of this job. Where are you from, *figliolo?*"

"I live in San Lorenzo near the Porta Capuana."

"You like this work?"

Gennaro's shoulders lifted. "I have never done it before."

"Is that true?" Mario glanced at him sharply, approached and putting out one hand as hard and hairy as a bear's paw, gripped Gennaro's arm midway between shoulder and elbow. Gennaro gave a quick gasp of pain at the pressure on his strained biceps and Mario shook his head commiseratingly. "It gets you there to start with." He took Gennaro's left hand in his and glancing at the open palm shook his head again, and for the first time Gennaro saw that the flesh at the base of his fingers and on the cushion of his thumb was puffy and crimson.

For the next hour Gennaro, working stolidly beside the skips, was aware of Mario's eye continually upon him. It was embarrassing to be watched like that and it had the effect of preventing him from relaxing even for the few seconds when the filled skips were trundled away. He knew what Mario was thinking—that he was not capable of the work—and the knowledge was at once a goad and a fear. For by now the truth was beginning to dawn on Gennaro that shoveling earth was not unskilled work and that heavy manual labor was a great deal more unpleasant than he had ever supposed.

Once, years ago in Ferrara, some workmen had come to the Collegio di San Francesco to lay a new water main under the courtyard and Gennaro, at his desk beside the classroom window, had watched them with envy. How pleasantly informal and easy it had all appeared from the other side of the glass. How contented and complacent those overalled workmen had seemed, out in the sun with bare, bronzed arms gleaming as spadeful after spadeful of earth was thrown rhythmically to the trench top—while he himself sat hot and bored and Father Benedicto droned on and on about rainfall in India. But now— an hour, two hours of listening to Father Benedicto on rainfall, or even struggling with algebra under Father Celestino, would have been bliss. Just to sit at a desk with a pen in one's hand. . . . By the time the hooter went at midday his legs were trembling with exhaustion, his whole body was one dull ache.

They took their shirts from the skip-loader and under that gray, hot sky straggled off down the slope to the works canteen, an elaborate hall gleaming with chromium and ornamented with vivid, modernistic mosaics above the polished oak doors. There was a washroom adjoining the hall, a place almost equally large and full of porcelain basins and shower recesses, but there was no water—according to Mario there had not been any for months. Gennaro, in common with the others, was given a metal bowl of boiled rice topped with a spoonful of tomato pulp, but he was too tired to eat more than a quarter of it. He kept looking for Renato but could not see him among the great crowd of milling men, overalled or in canvas trousers or old jeans, who thronged the metal tables and the alleyways between.

After ten minutes the flood of music which poured from amplifiers high up in every wall was abruptly cut off and a sudden silence fell. At the canteen doorway had appeared a group of people; men in smart suits and women in bright summer costumes. Led by a tall, white-haired director they came slowly down the central alleyway of the canteen and as they did so the sitting men rose respectfully from their benches and despite the affable and deprecatory waves of the tall director, remained standing.

"Commendatore De Santis—*il capo*—the boss," Mario said softly to Gennaro and added gently, as an afterthought, "May he burn forever in Hell with his own methane."

From time to time the group stopped at a table while the Commendatore spoke a few cheerful words to a random selection of workers who grinned and bowed and murmured, *"Grazie, Eccellenza, grazie."*

As he came abreast of the table at which Gennaro sat the director saw Mario and beamed. "Well, here's my old friend Martino!" he said jovially. "How are you, Martino? How's your wife? How are the children?"

"All very well, thank you, *Eccellenza.*"

"Good, good—yes. And who is your young friend?"

Without any hesitation Mario said, "Giovanni, Excellency —Giovanni Rossi."

"Ah. New here, I think?"

"Yes, Excellency. He started today."

The Commendatore smiled widely and held out a hand. "I'm glad—very glad indeed—to welcome you personally, Giovanni!"

Gennaro glanced down at his own grimy, earth-stained hands with embarrassment. *"Scusi, signore—"*

"Nonsense!" The director seized Gennaro's blistered right hand in a grip that made him wince with the sudden hot pain. "One can't work hard without getting dirty. Why shouldn't we shake hands? Your work is just as important as mine. After all, it is people like you and Martino who keep this place going. In a real sense we are all equals here—all members of the same family." He turned and spoke to a tall American colonel in an immaculate summer uniform who stood beside him. "We start them young, as you see. Old Martino here will look after and instruct this boy and very soon we will have a worker who will, as we say, identify with ITOLGAS. And the firm assists in this process by a wide variety of interlocked welfare and benefit schemes. Besides our graded pension scheme—which I can safely say is the only one of its kind at present operating in this country to be fully based on the most modern theories of industrial psychology—there are, in all, some fifteen other schemes, ranging from our Dental scheme for Dependents to our Young Workers' Overseas Holiday Exchange scheme.

"When this boy who starts today has been with us for certain qualifying periods he is automatically enrolled on these schemes. For the first year he undergoes a medical checkup every three weeks to see that he is physically conforming to our high standard and after his first six months his appendix and tonsils are

emoved in our ITOLCLINIC—this guards against unnecessary disruption in the plant's efficiency at a later date, of course.
When one day he marries—and we encourage our young workers of both sexes to mix freely—it will be with an ITOLGAS
marriage grant. Should he marry one of our own girl workers
the marriage grant is, of course, doubled. His children will be
born in our special ITOLGAS birth clinic and attend an ITOL-
GAS school staffed by excellent state-diplomaed teachers. The
little family, as it grows, will be watched over by ITOLGAS welfare officers at all times and will live in an apartment on the new
ITOLGAS housing estate—ITOLVILLAGGIO—and buy its
food and clothing at our special ITOL Stores.

"From now onward this boy will be ours—all his life. Playing in our football teams, for we take a great interest in sport—
in fact some form of sport is compulsory for all workers under
twenty-five—having his eyes tested by our oculists, his teeth
drilled by our dentists, attending Sunday mass said by our
priests. And when at last he dies—after a pleasant period, we
hope, spent in our Old People's Home—he will be buried in
our own cemetery—ITOLSEPPOLTO." The Commendatore
beamed and putting a theatrically fatherly hand on Gennaro's
shoulder, turned once more to the group of smiling, approving
visitors. "Colonel Forth and Madam. I was recently in England
studying that most interesting experiment in applied sociology,
the Welfare State. I admit I was impressed, although I myself
believe that social welfare is best undertaken on the smaller
and therefore more concentrated scope of the individual firm.
The English have a saying—'Welfare from the Cradle to the
Grave.' We have not, it is true, had young Giovanni here from
the cradle—but we shall have him to the grave!"

With a final paternal pat to Gennaro's shoulder the director
passed on, leading his group down the canteen toward the
gleaming, waterless washrooms. Their lack of water—though
the Commendatore was not intending to explain this to his
guests—was largely an experiment of his own. By checking the
number and urgency of the complaints received he hoped to acquire what he termed a "statistical picture" of Neapolitan attitudes toward personal hygiene. Up to date, no complaints of
any sort had been brought to his notice.

"All equals," said old Mario dryly as he sat down to the remains of his rice. "All equals, you and I and the Commendatore —that's nice, isn't it, Giovanni?"

"Why did you call me that?"

"I didn't know your name, son, so I had to invent one. Don't worry—that *figlio di puttana* will have forgotten it by now. He likes to pretend he knows all our names, so we have to answer to any he gives us. Today I was Martino—but I've been Claudio, Alberto, Carlo, Franco and Vincenzo in my time. So will you be."

If the morning had seemed long, the afternoon was endless. Gennaro's hands were now so sore that the pressure of the weighted shovel upon them was a constant fierce pain. His shoulders and back seemed to be made of rusty metal, without any joints fitting properly, and his knees of loose rubber. Every shovelful of earth he shifted made him grunt and gasp and, heedless now of Mario's watchful eye, his pace grew slower and slower. From time to time he tried to keep up with the steady, unflagging rhythm of the others but long before the hooter blasted its dismissal to the drab sky he was working in a sullen haze of pain and exhaustion, throwing one spadeful into the skip for every three thrown by Mario. And sometimes his shovel, sticky with the water from the broken blisters on his palms, slipped and allowed its load to cascade uselessly to the ground below the skip. An older man, or someone without an institutional background, would have downed tools and walked out, but Gennaro did not even think of this. In the Ferrara college one automatically remained at a task until it was officially time to cease; one never dreamt of questioning the despotism of the clock; and later in business and save for his sole, disastrous lapse on the occasion of the transfer of Ercole Sanbrenedetto's body to Naples, Gennaro had been punctual and precise in all his arrangements. Besides, without Renato he did not know his way out of this mechanical maze of tanks and tall chimneys, great iron buildings and clattering *teleferice*.

When, at five o'clock, work ended and he limped back to the skip-loader for his shirt, he found Pietrini waiting for him. The foreman smiled but shook his head. *"Niente da fare*—no good I'm afraid, little comrade. I'm sorry—but you are not strong enough. It's not your fault." He eyed Gennaro's grimy figure and pale, strained face. "Tell me—truly, now—what is your age?" "Sixteen."

Pietrini nodded. "Yes, I thought so. And this work is for grown men." He shrugged. "Well, there it is. I am sorry. Signor Trulli will give you a day's pay at the gate; I will phone him. Look—here comes your friend."

Walking slowly together toward the gate Renato said, "What happened?" and Gennaro shrugged wordlessly. He had not wanted the job in the first place, had only gone because of Crocifissa's prompting—but now, what with the pain in his torn hands, his sick exhaustion and the degrading sense of failure, he was closer to tears than he remembered being for a long time. His feeling for the whole firm of ITOLGAS and everyone connected with it—Commendatore De Santis, Pietrini, Mario and the other, unknown members of his work gang—was one of loathing and fear. Inwardly he blamed Renato bitterly for bringing him here. Renato had been responsible for a day's torture ending with humiliating rejection, and though he had been moved by the best of motives Gennaro found it hard to forgive.

Renato sensed his mood and saying nothing, put a sympathetic hand on his shoulder. The gesture was reminiscent to Gennaro of the director's and he shook it off impatiently. At the gate Renato approached the spectacled Trulli behind his guichet. "No good, I'm afraid, Signor Trulli." He smiled apologetically. "So—could my friend have his money, please?"

Trulli's eyes narrowed at once behind his glasses "Money—what for?"

"For his work. He has worked one full day."

"He was only on trial—not employed. I told you both that." "Even so—"

"And you told me he was eighteen! But he is *sixteen*. He—and you, too—have imposed upon the firm—lied!"

Renato flushed. Politely but stubbornly he said, "He has done a man's work all day. He is entitled to two thousand lire."

"He's entitled to nothing! If you had told the truth I would not have sent him to the south excavation. If there had been a boy's job available I would have sent him to that—and he would have earned at the correct rate. But as it is—"

Gennaro tugged at Renato's arm. He had no thought for anything now except to get away from this terrible place as quickly as possible; this place where men labored like old-time convicts in a modern hell of drumming noise and throat-searing fumes. "Come on! It doesn't matter. I don't want it. Come on—let's go."

But to Renato, used to a day's work at least as hard as that which Gennaro had just undergone, it did matter. One did not sweat and pant and strain over a full eight hours for nothing. "He's *earned* his money!" he shouted angrily at Trulli's tight, lined face. "He's earned it more than you have—sitting there on a stool all day reading the paper! If you don't give it to him I'll—I'll—"

"You won't do anything!" Trulli's voice was coldly menacing and before his gleaming, spectacled stare Renato's eyes dropped. "You'll do nothing at all and you'll be careful how you speak to me. I'm not a Neapolitan, remember. I came down with the firm from the north. It wouldn't be at all difficult for me to have you fired. And I could get a hundred men to take your job at any moment I like. Don't forget that. As for this boy—" Picking up a silver five-hundred-lire piece he dropped it contemptuously into a small brown envelope and thrust it at Gennaro. "Here you are—and you can think yourself lucky! Now get along out of here, both of you!"

⋄§ 5

AND in the night the wind came. It came from the great crests of the Apennines, blowing from the northeast— cool and fresh and clean. First as a soft stir in the humid breathlessness which encompassed the city, a light puff of air dying out almost before it had commenced; then as a period of quickly increasing gusts, and by midnight as a steady, strong breeze blowing out to sea all the lifeless fetor that had lain over the city for the past week. At dawn, its work accomplished, it dropped and Naples shone out in full summer sunlight across its gulf, again a glittering blue shield studded with the gleaming jewels of its islands. The *scirocco* had gone.

A Prison by the Sea

❧ 1

BEPPO had a deep and long-standing distaste for soldiers and all things military which his time as an English teacher at the Nunziatella had done nothing to abate. Like the upper classes of Imperial China he relegated the warrior to one of the lowest grades of society, somewhere between a mountain brigand and a hired assassin, and the peculiar, and in some cases grotesque, schemes which his countrymen so often thought up to avoid their highly unpopular draft service invariably met with his sympathetic approval. He was therefore naturally inclined to think that of all the lodgers in his San Lorenzo property, Iole Giansante was the one who stood most in need of help. The others—Crocifissa, the two Quongs and old Bonitatibus— fought a long, grueling struggle with poverty, yet that was the lot of the majority of their fellow citizens in Naples—a city which held extremes of destitution unknown in any other western European metropolis. An entire government aid program was needed and was, in a dilatory fashion, under way in order to help them.

But Iole's case was different. Crocifissa and the others suffered only from a set of largely historical circumstances for which no one living was to blame and which, present-day society was generally agreed, must be alleviated. Iole's life had been wrecked by that same present-day society, acting deliberately and with wanton stupidity against two innocent people. For to Beppo the girl's husband was completely innocent. An unstable and insecure nature had been thwarted, frustrated and exasperated beyond endurance; it had then broken loose and damaged one of its tormentors. Present-day society had no one to blame but itself. One could not wave red capes at bulls—let alone stick colored darts into them—without expecting to get charged and possibly gored. Beppo's sympathies were fully aroused, and urged on by Mina he decided to take the matter up. If enough people were made aware of this injustice, if enough fuss was made about it, surely public pressure would secure the release of the poor girl's husband or a large remission of his sentence. Like so many people who have survived savage and searching experiences, Beppo had a sanguine nature.

The first thing to do was to get in touch with the military authorities—informally, if possible. Beppo composed a polite, somewhat ambiguous letter to General Lecco, the father of his ex-pupil, stating that he would be in Rome on the third of July and would like to call upon him. To his pleasure, though also to his surprise, he received an invitation to lunch.

When, at a quarter to one, he rang the bell of the Lecco apartment on the Piazza Melozzo da Forli the door was opened by Galo. Beppo stared at him in astonishment. "*Benedetto Dio!* What are you doing here?"

Galo said "I'm on a visit. But the servants walked out this morning because the general spoke to them in a—a military manner. So I and Pietro are taking their places."

The general turned out to be a tall, plump man not much older than his guest, with sparse hair and deep-set eyes beneath the thickest, wiriest gray eyebrows Beppo had ever seen. Though he himself was in civilian clothes, both his son and Galo wore their pale summer khakis. "You've heard about the servants, Professor? Shocking! When I think of what I pay them and their short hours of work and the time off which they get . . . Well, there it is. You can't do anything with the lower classes these days, can you? I'm entitled to a soldier of course, but if I have him here he upsets the civilians. Pietro and his friend have volunteered to stand in for the present so I've no idea what we'll be getting for lunch."

But in fact they had a good one. Most Italians have an instinctive knowledge of simple cookery, and in any case its rudiments were taught at the Nunziatella. The air of improvisation and restrained hilarity produced by the two boys' efforts and their continual bustling in and out of the kitchen lent an informal air to the meal which improved Beppo's view of his host while allowing him ample opportunity to praise his ex-pupils. "Don't you go to camp next week?" he asked Lecco.

"Yes, Professor. It starts on Monday. That's why Galo has to go back tomorrow to get his things ready."

By the time lunch was over and Beppo was taken into the general's study for coffee and a glass of cognac, he felt that the time and place were as propitious as could reasonably be expected for the request he wished to make. He told the story of the Giansantes, as he had heard it from Iole, with the care and pedantic accuracy with which he had been wont to explain English grammatical constructions to his class.

The general nodded and sipped his brandy, his eyebrows lifting and falling as if each led an independent life of its own. "I see," he said at last. "I see. Of course I know of this case. I imagine the whole army does. It was—hmm—particularly spectacular." He paused. "Now tell me, frankly please, Professor, what you would do if, in a class of students, you had one who was continually unruly and insulting, who disregarded every reproof and rebuke and who eventually attacked you and injured you severely in an alley outside the school?"

Beppo sighed inwardly. "As an analogy, General, I don't think this is going to get us far. But in fact, of course, I would do two things. I would strongly recommend that this hypothetical student was examined by a psychiatrist and I would equally strongly suggest that he was unfitted for cooperative study. In effect I would say that he possessed an abnormal aversion to being educated and that therefore his education had better cease. There are a wide variety of valuable tasks which may be undertaken by uneducated men, and—if you'll excuse the liberty—there are a great many more uses for mankind in general than that of bearing arms."

"Doubtless. Yet our laws say that every able-bodied Italian, unencumbered by certain family responsibilities, must learn to bear arms."

"Evaldo Giansante is not able-bodied, though. That is to say, he is mentally unfit."

"Our doctors do not agree."

"But he was not examined by a psychiatrical specialist."

General Lecco offered a silver box of cigarettes to Beppo and took one himself. For a moment he was silent, his eyebrows drawn together into one Cyclopean line. Then he said, "The difficulty about psychiatric diagnoses, Professor, is their vagueness. I understand that by the standards of a qualified psychologist none of us—not one—is entirely sane. We are all mentally adrift somewhere."

"Yes," assented Beppo, to whom the idea was not unattractive, "I expect we are."

"Which in effect means that if we insisted on a mental as well as a physical examination for the draft service we would get no soldiers at all, of course."

"Oh come, General, I hardly think so!"

The general smiled. "No, no—I was joking. But what I mean is that there would be far too many young men in the marginal class who would have to be excused. Boys who had a stammer or perhaps an overactive thyroid gland or who were generally nervous and highly strung. And on top of that think of the malingering! You know, I suppose, that any parent who can pay a doctor a million lire or more can invariably get his son excused from military service on a trumped-up physical defect? It's done all the time. If we allowed psychiatric defects to be taken into account the position would become chaotic. And in my opinion—you'll excuse me, I hope—the whole thing is dubious at best and probably nonsense from a military point of view. Our army fought a long and bitter war from nineteen-fifteen to nineteen-eighteen and won it, on a system of national conscription which had never even heard the word 'psychology.' "

"Today, however, I like to think we are more civilized."

"Today, Professor, we are largely in the hands of America. They supply us with most of our arms and, as you know, they guarantee our defense. What they ask in return is an army of a size we can only achieve by retaining the draft."

"And which," said Beppo, a little surprised at his own audacity and wondering if it was due to righteous indignation or merely to the general's brandy, "sweeps into its net and trains a very large quantity of young Communists. It can't do anything else—can it?"

"Are you suggesting," asked the general with a hint of stiffness in his voice, "that they would not fight for Italy—in the last resort?"

"Oh, they would fight for Italy—certainly. Only it would be for the Italy *they* wanted. And since Communists have this peculiarly tortuous way of thinking, they would find nothing in the least improper in joining with an enemy to fight with sincere patriotism for a Communist Italy. About one quarter of the army is my guess," said Beppo boldly. "Perhaps a little more."

But instead of anger the general's face showed only a resigned, perhaps rueful, amusement. "I think that figure is far too high. But it is one of our problems, I admit. As I said to an American colleague recently, 'Our soldiers will fight when the time comes—but who, or what, they'll fight *for* is another matter altogether.'" He shook his head and pulled himself up in his chair. "But this is all something of a digression. The facts of the matter are these. We have to keep the draft. We have too many malingerers escaping it under our present medical rules without adding to them by instituting psychiatric tests— You're not, I take it, claiming that his man Giansante is actually insane in the normally accepted meaning of the word? Because if so he would not be locked up for twelve years but for life."

"No, no. I don't call him insane in that sense—not at all. Merely—"

"And we don't call him insane, either. Very well. In that case he is genuinely guilty of desertion, resisting arrest and striking—actually attempting to murder—a superior officer. I'm just as sorry for his wife as you are, but that does not alter the gravity of his offense or the justice of his punishment."

"Twelve years? For someone just twenty years old?"

"In some other armies he would have been shot. No, Professor. I know what you want; you want to get permission to send a psychiatrist—first, of course, briefed by yourself—to see this man and subsequently to put in a technical report to the effect that he was not responsible for his actions at the time, is unfitted for the army and should be freed unconditionally. Well, as I've said, it won't do. There are military, and therefore State, reasons for refusing to allow it."

"Then—you can't help me at all?"

The general sighed. "I'd like to, Professor. Among other

things, Pietro has always spoken so highly of you. You appear to have been one of the most popular teachers at the Nunziatella."

Beppo beamed. "Really? I certainly never thought—"

"Oh yes, I assure you. And do you know why? They liked you because—in Pietro's words 'we could see he liked us.' But all I can do is to make a suggestion. If I remember rightly, one of the things which told heavily against Giansante at his court-martial was his unrepentant attitude. He took the same view of his actions as you appear to do—that is to say, he saw himself as the victim of a great injustice. Naturally no one else saw it in that light."

"Naturally," echoed Beppo dryly and received a dubious glance from his host.

"But if he could be persuaded to change his attitude even now, it might help. If he would put in a *domanda* to the authorities fully admitting his guilt and expressing sorrow and contrition; well, with that and his family circumstances—you say the wife's having a baby? Good. Well then, taking all that into account, I think a substantial reduction of his sentence would certainly be a possibility."

"By how much?"

The general shrugged. "I can't say. Three or four—perhaps even five years if he was lucky."

Beppo's shoulders lifted in a sad shrug. "And that really is all—all that can be done?"

"Yes, Professor, I'm afraid so. I can only do one more thing for you. I can arrange that you see Giansante personally. At least you'll be able to explain about the *domanda*. And now," the general rose stiffly, "I think we ought to see what those boys have been up to in the kitchen and then I have an appointment. . . ."

✍§ 2

WITH an hour to wait for his train Beppo sauntered under the trees in the Borghese Gardens. It was quiet here for the Romans had not yet completed their lengthy luncheons or the siesta which followed them. Only a few mothers and nursemaids taking small children for an afternoon airing strolled along the tree-shaded, statue-lined paths.

Beppo was dissatisfied with the outcome of his visit to the capital though he had to admit that General Lecco had been patient, reasonable and as helpful as it apparently lay within his power to be. And yet—what was a reduction of three or four years to the prisoner in the Gaeta castle, or to his wife in the Piazza Vittime Civili di Guerra? Both were young enough to look upon four years as near-eternity and there seemed little chance of the sentence being reduced to less than eight. Beppo sighed, asking himself, not for the first time, why this case meant so much to him. Yet he knew the answer. It was not Iole Giansante herself, much as her plight moved him. It was not the still unknown Evaldo. It was his own deep, complex need for some sort of—of exorcism really, he supposed, to cast out the memories of what had happened in North Africa twenty years ago. Justice—at least as the world knew it—was not involved, any more than it had been at those far-off sunset murders. An act of redemption—of compassion—was called for from him who had survived in the name of those other poor, exhausted, frightened conscripts who had died. That those ghosts might no longer haunt his dreams Evaldo Giansante must be brought out of his prison and restored to his wife. If only . . . Sunk in thought, Beppo had not heard the footsteps approaching from behind him, felt only a gentle touch on his arm and looked up with a mild start into the long, smiling, spectacled face of Signor Bighencomer. "Good afternoon, Professor. You also are taking a stroll in these delightful gardens?"

"Yes. As a matter of fact I've been putting in time until my train leaves." Beppo glanced at his wristwatch. "But I think I shall have to go now—at least if I'm to secure a good seat."

"You're returning to Naples?"

"Yes. And you—do you stay long in Rome?"

The restaurant owner shook his head. "No, no. I hope to go back tomorrow. I'm here on someone else's business—not my own. I'm trying to help a young friend of mine to emigrate to America. He's a promising youth whose talents have been—hmm —somewhat confined in Italy. I think he'll do very well in the States, though—if I can get him there."

Beppo's heart warmed at once toward this intelligent, rich and very busy man who could yet find time to come to Rome in order to help a young protégé. He would have liked to explain his own somewhat similar role in the capital but felt the comparison between Evaldo Giansante, a military prisoner, with Signor Bighencomer's talented and probably most respectable young friend might be thought invidious. Instead he shook Bighencomer warmly by the hand. "Let me wish you the best of luck, then. I hope we'll meet again very shortly."

"Indeed, I hope so, Professor. You have to go now? Then, good-bye—until our next meeting."

ᜒᢩ 3

POVERTY is not only degrading but also complicated; few, except members of those religious orders for whom it is a part of their triple vow, ever come to a comfortable accommodation with it, and its degradations and complications rise in direct ratio to the social standing of the indigent. Yet the Colavolpes had been so poor for so long that despite their Bourbon-bestowed title they should have eased themselves somehow into their impecuniousness in the way a hardened old beggar shuffles and burrows himself into his bed of rags and straw. But only Galo, the last and youngest of the line, had succeeded in this— probably because the poverty in which he had been reared had been more dire, more complete, than anything the others had known in early life.

Tarquinio and the great-aunts could remember a time when there were still two or three serf-servants in the *palazzo* to cook and wait and carry. Concezio had known the life of an officers' mess and Speranza, before her marriage, had taken for granted the bourgeois background of the Sanbrenedettos. But Galo had no memories of this sort, at all. To him it was quite normal to be hungry, to wear third- or fourth-hand clothes bought at open-air market stalls, to be cold throughout the short but fireless winter and to go to bed in the dark for want of lamp oil. And the necessary responses to these things he accepted equally unthinkingly; he stole food or money or anything he could find which might be turned into either and, at least until he went to the Nunziatella, he very seldom washed himself and never washed his clothes.

During his early years in the elementary school at Caserta he had been indistinguishable from the children of the poorer *conta-dini*, and if his family had been less bestial and eccentric he would have been as grubbily happy as they.

But the elder Colavolpes had never, of course, accepted poverty as their permanent state. With no rational prospects of alleviating their lot by their own efforts they still kept their gaze fixed upon a mirage of future wealth which glowed and flickered dimly through a rosy fog of wishful "ifs." *If* Concezio could handle the family's only pen with a little more dexterity he might write a magnificent book about his fabulous experiences in the Russian campaign, receive a government literary prize and become a best-selling author overnight. *If* an American film company wanted to make an historical movie about early-nineteenth-century Naples and rented the *palazzo* for a huge sum. . . . *If* Maria Fausta's frequent prophetic visions ceased to deal in picturesque details of the damnation of her relatives' souls and instead foretold the winning numbers in the State lottery. . . . *If*—even —the family goat gave birth to a kid with two heads or six legs. . . .

But for some time past all these fascinating but improbable hypotheses had been swallowed up in the much more relevant and promising one—"*if* old Ercole Sanbrenedetto can be induced to make Galo his heir." And the family had gone to what was, for them, considerable trouble and lavish outlay to bring this about. To start with, Galo had been cleaned up. He had been taken to a barber, he had been bought his first toothbrush, the sores on his lips—due as much to lack of protein as to the unwashed things he ate—had been cured with expensive medicine. And later, dressed in a clean and well-pressed secondhand suit and some almost new shoes, equipped with a handkerchief and replete with threatening instructions about his behavior, he had been sent off by motorbus on the first of his series of visits to his great-uncle. The first visit had nearly been the last since the Colavolpes had neglected to explain what a water-closet was and Galo had scandalized Ercole's servants by using the open beach outside the kitchen window. Also, his table manners had not been regulated and his habit of eating the things most people left on their plates—fish-heads, chicken bones, apple cores —had annoyed his great-uncle. But somehow he had induced enough interest in Ercole to be grudgingly accepted for a second visit and after that his trips had become a routine. Shortly the family, satisfied with the progress of their scheme and seeking to impress Ercole's nationalistic and military mind, had inserted Galo into the Nunziatella—using the lever of Concezio's Gold Medal and with considerable recourse to Concezio's formidable wooden hand during the long hours of home study while Galo prepared for an examination beyond his natural ability.

The apparent failure of the scheme into which they had put so much effort and cost—let alone upon which they had pinned their hopes for several years—had enraged them all and since Ercole's death their behavior toward Galo had become worse than ever. This was particularly the case with Speranza, who had a genuine and instinctive loathing for her son—a loathing which he fully reciprocated. On the day after the contents of the old man's will were known, she had ransacked the boy's room and taken everything, even the bed-sheets, to Caserta market and sold them for what they could fetch. In discordant chorus the family had abused him for a whole weekend in long, spiteful sessions of exasperated disappointment which had invariably ended in blows, curses and tears.

To start with they had laid a complete ban on further visits to Beppo and his daughter, but this was hastily rescinded when Tarquinio pointed out that there was no reason why, once the will was proved, they should not approach Beppo for a "loan." But Galo was in disgrace and it was only grudgingly that they had agreed to let him visit his friend Lecco in Rome, and then only after he had explained that his hosts would pay his fare both ways. This was not true since he had himself stolen the necessary money and a little more from his grandmother's work-box cache but it—and the fact that he would be fed at some else's expense for three days—had ultimately turned the scales and permission had been given.

Yet on his return Galo, expecting to find his unpopularity undiminished, was surprised to note a subtle change in the family's attitude. They exuded an air of covertly malign geniality, impatient yet gloating. Maria Celeste, staring at him from her large, slightly mad, hare's eyes, even quavered an inquiry as to whether he had enjoyed himself in Rome. Galo glanced at her blankly without replying—since no one had ever asked him such a question before, he did not know how to answer.

In the evening, he was called into the main bedroom where Concezio and Speranza—who had long since ceased to pretend to anything but their true relationship—slept together in tousled sin. Now both of them sat on chairs by the window with their backs to the evening light. Beside the sagging bed was a smart suitcase and upon it were laid out some clothes. Pointing to these with his wooden hand and with his battered mouth twisted into a conciliatory grin Concezio said, "Those are all for you, Galo. We got them as a surprise for you while you were away. You'd better try them. If they need altering, Tarquinio's ready to do it at once."

Galo, looking down at three new shirts, a lightweight suit, ties, striped T-shirts, blue jeans, felt a quick stab of panic. He knew perfectly well that this sudden unlooked-for largesse contained a trap somewhere. He picked up the clothes with the extreme care of one who expected to find a nest of hissing vipers beneath them. From the window Speranza said, "What's wrong? Don't you like them? They cost enough."

Galo said nothing but slowly changed first into one set of clothes, then into another. Speranza, or more probably Concezio, had an accurate eye and everything fitted satisfactorily except one shirt whose sleeves were too long and which was set aside for Tarquinio's attention. Under the last shirt Galo found a pair of scarlet swimming trunks. He held them up, mystified. "I don't want these. I *never* go in the sea."

"You don't have to go in the sea—they've got a swimming pool."

"Who have?"

"De Santis. He's invited you to spend the weekend at his villa in Posillipo. We thought it would be a nice change for you, before you go to camp."

✒ 4

COMMENDATORE De Santis had bought the Villa Sanfelice some four years ago on his appointment as managing director of the new ITOLGAS plant: a big, white house, all pillars and arcades and bougainvillea-bedizened loggias, constructed like most of the large Posillipo houses in an excavation in the cliff-face directly above the sea. The house had been built some seventy years before by a wealthy Yorkshire mill owner—built correctly in the "rich foreigners' quarter" and named the Villa Myerscough after its owner. In those days it had been flanked by two equally large houses, the Villa Van Meers and the Villa Patterson. Though both these latter names were just possible for the Italian tongue, no native of Posillipo or of Naples itself had been able to even commence to pronounce "Myerscough" or to copy it correctly on any document. Very few visitors and practically no mail had been successfully delivered to the villa while it had been in foreign hands and it was a relief, as well as something of a triumph, when the name was changed to an Italian one which foreigners often mispronounced in their turn.

In common with all the other large houses which since the war had found their way into the hands of rich Italian businessmen, the Villa Sanfelice had been modernized and improved. The plumbing, the water supply and the lighting had all been renovated along up-to-date lines, central heating and air conditioning had been installed, there was parking space for six cars on the road-level roof, a swimming pool and—newest of all—a rumpus room in what had once been part of the great wine cellar. De Santis was very proud of the rumpus room which he had fitted out with table tennis, billiards, a jukebox and a home movie apparatus as well as various other youthful amenities. It had been designed for his daughter, Toni, and she obligingly made a rumpus in it whenever it was possible to acquire the company of any of the rumpus-minded young from the American-staffed NATO base.

During the first evening of Galo's visit she had done her best to initiate him into American playtime habits but with only limited success for, unlike the founder of the short-lived Colavolpe fortunes, he was not playful by nature—not even at billiards. But it was not only at billiards that the first Marchese Arconovaldo Colavolpe had shown skill and it was upon the prominent, but until now dormant, side of Galo's unbecoming heredity that Toni De Santis was to have her real effect. She was an unattractive girl in whom adolescence, aided by an unsettled

environment, had produced its worst effects. Short, with an over-
developed figure, too high a color and dun-shaded hair, she
had neither the staid decorum of the well-brought-up young
Italian nor the carefully calculated camaraderie of her American counterpart. Falling between these two stools she sat, as it
were, splayed on her broad bottom and laughed with a determined vivacity which she had been taught would atone in the
eyes of many men for a lack of beauty but which only rendered
her more hoydenish. She had been attracted by Galo from the
first, knew her father had some sort of plan for him, and was
piqued at his apparent lack of interest either in her or her
possessions. After all, when you considered the slum the boy
habitually lived in . . .

But, had she known it, Galo was deeply impressed by the
Villa Sanfelice. In the usual Italian way he spent his time silently
reckoning up the cost of everything when, as was generally the
case, he felt it impolite to inquire openly. He had soon worked
out that even by using every lira of his inheritance from Ercole
he would be unable to afford to live in a replica of the Villa Sanfelice. But still he was learning, and learning avidly, what money
could accomplish in terms of living style and standards and the
continuing lesson, as well as his innate fear of some sort of a
trap, kept him preoccupied and reserved. Toni alone was a nuisance—particularly as her mother was in Rome and he had
to bear her undivided company. He wished she had gone to
Rome, too, so that he could have spent the weekend alone with
De Santis for, with his experience of Ercole to call upon, he felt
no embarrassment nor difficulty in the undiluted company of old
men. In his experience they demanded little except an audience
for their reminiscences and an obedient deference to their household habits. Besides, alone with De Santis he might have found
out what this invitation augured for the future.

On the second morning of his visit Toni insisted that they
should "play" in the swimming pool, so Galo unwillingly got
into his new red trunks and wandered about the tiled edge, staring suspiciously at the vivid mosaics beneath the calm, transparent water.

"Come on *in!*" called Toni, splashing him from a plastic raft
a few feet from the pool's edge. "Come on in—it's lovely!"

Galo hesitated; his fear of drowning—of water in large quantities—warring with a halfhearted desire to actually enter a swimming pool for the first time. He could not make up his mind and Toni, tiring of his indecision, paddled to the side and clambering up, seized his sunglasses and threw them far out into the gleaming water. "Now you'll *have* to go in—to get them!" She tried to push him over the edge and for a moment they struggled, locked together upon the verge. But Galo was the stronger and when they fell it was not into the pool but onto the grass beside it. Their hands on each other's bare flesh, their legs entangled, they rolled over together and fell apart. It was a brief enough contact, but like a spark to dry straw it was enough; when Galo sat up, panting a little, smiling and pushing the hair back from his forehead, he looked at Toni with new eyes—with the X-ray eyes of the ordinary Neapolitan who sees only the naked female body beneath the clothes. It was a look which the girl beside him knew and approved of. She put a hand gently on his thigh. "Tell me, Galo, why won't you come in? Can't you swim?"

A few minutes ago Galo would probably have refused to admit this but now he agreed calmly enough. "No—I've never tried. Anyway I'm not interested. I'm going to be a soldier, not a sailor."

"But it's so nice! And all boys should be able to swim. Look —I'll teach you. The pool is shallow at the other end—you can't drown."

For the next half-hour Galo floundered and splashed about in four feet of water. He took little notice of Toni's instructions but every opportunity to touch her or be touched by her. In the end they had both reached a state of laughing, excited anticipation, of tacitly reckless eroticism, expressed by their hands rather than their tongues, which was jarred to a halt by the appearance of Toni's father between the cypresses at the pool's side, accompanied as so often by Colonel and Mrs. Forth.

The adults stood beside the pool and the boy and the girl in the water stood decorously apart, smiling up at them. "They certainly do make a lovely picture," said Mrs. Forth with the automatic complaisance of one who never lets slip the opportunity for a banality. "Sure," muttered the colonel uneasily, wriggling his shoulders under his tunic. He had sharper eyes than the others and had been trained to use them; he had seen a little of what was going on in the pool before Galo or Toni had noticed the approach of their elders.

"Well"—Commendatore De Santis's voice was briskly genial as he glanced down at the rippling water—"it is nearly time for lunch so you two had better come out and get dressed."

Walking back to the house, leaving wet footprints that dried rapidly on the hot stones of the stepped terraces, Toni said quietly, "I'll give you another swimming lesson later, if you like."

"Yes—when?"

"Tonight. After dinner."

"It—won't it be dark?"

"The pool's got underwater lighting—but we won't need it because there's a moon. I often swim at night; then I don't have to wear a swimsuit—if there's no one else there, of course."

Galo glanced over his shoulder. The Commendatore and his guests were ten yards behind, talking animatedly. "And—if there is?"

"That depends—"

"Then we won't."

"All right."

◆§ 5

BUT after dinner that night the Commendatore dismissed a flushed and sulky Toni and putting a hand on Galo's arm led him down a long marble corridor to a surprisingly workmanlike business office. Opening a wall cupboard he poured himself a drink, fleetingly considered offering one to his young guest, decided against it, and sitting down behind his desk motioned Galo to take the chair opposite.

For a moment there was silence and Galo glanced uncomfortably, nervously, at the Commendatore's white head bowed over his balloon goblet of Armagnac which gleamed golden in the bright fluorescence of a central light-strip. The urgent, tingling excitement which had filled him all through the magnificent dinner he had just eaten had vanished, giving place to a wary, frightened anticipation. Something was going to happen now. The trap into which he had been made to walk was about to be sprung. He drew in, closing up on himself like an apprehensive tortoise.

Then De Santis said, "You're off to camp on Monday, aren't you?"

"Yes."

"Are you looking forward to it?"

"Yes."

"You enjoy that sort of thing?"

"Yes."

"How about the exams in October?"

"How——?"

"I mean—you think you'll pass them?"

Silently, sullenly, Galo gave a slight shrug.

"I understand," pursued De Santis, "that classwork in the traditional subjects is not exactly your strong point?"

Galo shrugged again and the Commendatore sat back and gazed into his brandy. He realized that he was not getting very far and decided to risk a firm question. "Galo, are you sure— quite certain—that you really want to be a soldier?"

If Galo had been two or three years older or younger he would probably have answered "Yes" again. But he was at the center of that period of metamorphosis when nothing at all is absolutely certain, when everything is doubtful and continually being proved so. If the Commendatore had asked him in the same grave tone whether he was sure—quite certain—that water was wet, he would have hesitated equally to give a firm answer. "I—suppose so," he said at last.

"Because, you know, it's such a competitive profession, isn't it? Naturally everything is competitive these days but in most cases at least the competition is unrestricted. But in the army there are posts for only a limited number of—say, colonels; and a still more limited number of generals—and of course there can only be one commander-in-chief. Somebody," said the Commendatore with what he hoped was delicacy, "who is not absolutely sure he is going to achieve a top post might waste his whole career struggling along in the lower ranks and eventually become pensioned off—probably most inadequately pensioned off—as a mere major."

Galo's ambitions had never risen higher than becoming a

mere major—and to someone who in the past had been hungry
enough to boil snails in an old tomato can for his supper, a major's pension was not likely to appear inadequate. He nodded
uncomprehending assent.

"And then the life," pursued the Commendatore, encouraged
by what he took to be Galo's reasoned agreement. "I mean, even
now you must find it sometimes a little irksome, eh? I know I
should. All the parading and the orders and implicit obedience
to an entirely mechanical routine. Never being allowed to
think for oneself or to make any decisions of a personal nature,
eh?" He waited once more for Galo's assent but instead the boy
merely stared at him stupidly. For Galo did not find life at the
Nunziatella in the least irksome—in general he found it reassuring and comfortable and he guessed, accurately for once, that
beyond it life as a regular army officer would be still more reassuring, still more comfortable.

"Well," said the Commendatore a little irritably, "I daresay
there are compensations. You have your friends and your smart
uniforms and so forth—yes. But one must consider the future.
Now, if you were *my* son—do you know what I'd suggest?"

"No," said Galo, though with the forlorn percipience of youth
he guessed that it would be something unpleasant.

"I'd suggest a change. I'd agree wholeheartedly that a year or
so in the military academy was a good thing. Discipline," said
the Commendatore vaguely. "Obedience. Smartness. *Esprit-de-
corps*. All very satisfactory in themselves if not carried too far.
But in the end there's nothing to match a sound commercial
education."

"A—what?"

"I said 'a commercial education.' I meant a period spent
studying such things as business technique, financial law, salesmanship and industrial psychology. All immensely useful and
interesting subjects."

"Are they?"

"Certainly. You can't get far without them today. And the
people who understand them best are the Americans. If," said
the Commendatore carefully and with a significance which was
not lost upon Galo, "I had a son I would send him to a really
good business training college in America for a year or two and
then"—De Santis's voice became heavily, deliberately, meas-

ured—"I would bring him back and start him off as a junior executive in ITOLGAS where he could work under my personal supervision. By the time he was twenty-four or -five he could easily be a director. Do you know what sort of salary an ITOLGAS director—even a junior one—receives? Well—it's approximately two and a half times the stipend of a General of Division in the Italian Army."

Fear, stabbing swiftly across the desk before him, as sharp as the thin steel paperknife which glittered in the strong overhead light, drove Galo's habitual wary caution aside. "You've explained—told all this—to my mother and my uncle. And—and they agree?"

The Commendatore was shaken in his turn. "Not so fast! Not so fast! What do you mean, Galo? I was talking about a mere hypothesis; about what I would do with a son of my own if I had one—which I haven't."

"No," said Galo flatly. "You were talking about me."

The Commendatore's old, lined face flushed a little. This was not the way he had expected the interview to go and like all elderly persons he was put out when other people did not behave in the way he had hopefully expected. After all, there had been no difficulty with the boy's dreadful mother or his fantastic uncle. Both had been delighted though they had made an attempt to disguise it. Of course they had tried to raise the price—openly bargaining as if in a market. "Two million *only?* I'm not sure, Commendatore . . . I mean, we all know how cheap the Galleria prices were just after the war, but times were very different then—and in any case it was for babies or small children. We've had all the trouble and expense of rearing him up to practically sixteen. He's big for his age, too, and in excellent health. You can take him to any doctor you like and you'll find that's completely true! They'll tell you he's just what we say. *And* he's intelligent. He passed into the Nunziatella, didn't he? You know their standards are the highest in Italy. For only *two million . . .*"

De Santis had felt compelled to expostulate. "My dear Major, I'm not trying to *buy* the boy from you."

"No?"

"Certainly not! Other considerations apart, it would be completely illegal and I'm not in the habit of breaking the law. I'm merely suggesting that for his sake—and, yes, I admit for my own interest and pleasure—I would very much like to *unofficially* adopt him; to become, as it were, his guardian and provider for the rest of his minority. The—hmm—the title *and* the *palazzo* are likely to become his well before he becomes of age to inherit. When is that, by the way?"

"Eighteen," Concezio had replied glumly. "It always has been. It's in the entail. We've tried to get it put back at least to twenty-one but we can't. Perhaps with a good lawyer—"

"Well, if you do let him come to me I'll guarantee you the continued possession of the *palazzo* until he's of age. Afterwards —well that's up to him. But with a secure position in ITOLGAS and a good salary he might easily feel inclined to make some provision for his family."

"I doubt it. He's an ungrateful little bastard," Concezio had said morosely and then quickly corrected himself. "I mean he's got a great many good qualities, but the young are—careless about that sort of thing." He had paused. "I suppose you'll arrange for him to marry your girl—once he's old enough and has the title?"

Despite himself the Commendatore had flushed slightly. He enjoyed the Colavolpes immensely—so much so that he wanted to buy a young specimen, largely for study under controlled conditions—but their brutal Bourbon bluntness still came as an occasional shock. "Not necessarily," he had replied a little stiffly, "not necessarily at all." And he had at once received a sidelong leer and a poke in the ribs from Concezio. "Oho! Then I suppose you want him for yourself, eh? Well, he's a very good-looking boy, Commendatore—a real beauty. You don't see many like that today. I can't say my own taste lies that way but if you saw him without his clothes on you'd agree that two million was hardly . . ."

No—the Colavolpes were unbelievable. Dream people living in a dream world. In the end he had raised his offer to three million, mainly in order to forestall further devastating speculations on his reason for wanting Galo, and it had been rapidly accepted. "But," he had added cautiously, "it must be dependent on his consent—naturally. He may not want to fall in with my plans for him."

"Not *want* to? What has that got to do with it?"

"Well, we can hardly make him—can we?"

For the first time in their acquaintanceship Concezio Colavolpe had stared at the Commendatore with something very like open contempt. "Of course we can, if necessary! He's got no money—nothing—and he's not even sixteen yet."

And now—and not for the first time—the Commendatore asked himself if he was not being a fool; was not allowing himself to stray into that old man's habit of trying to gratify the most unlikely and irrational of whims. And yet he had given the matter a great deal of careful thought and planning; basically he knew his scheme to be anything but irrational. For despite what he had said to Concezio Colavolpe he would, under certain circumstances, have no objection at all to a liaison between the future Marchese Colavolpe and his daughter. An engagement in, say four years, when the boy returned from America, and subsequent marriage as soon as he had proved his ability in the ITOLGAS offices. De Santis belonged to a generation which still held an instinctive regard for a title of almost any sort, but he had no intention of subsidizing a young army son-in-law whose profession would effectively place him beyond control. And—since the one thing which Concezio had succeeded in keeping from the older man was the black stain of lunacy in the Colavolpe blood—the plan appeared to the Commendatore to be extremely altruistic. Everyone would gain all round. He himself would be able to continue, with still wider scope, his studies of the Colavolpe family both here in Naples and during his constant trips to America. In a few years he would have transformed Galo from a superstitious, ignorant, unhygienic Neapolitan into a modern, efficient, American-schooled executive who might then be brought back, imbued with his own ideas and trained for high position. If Galo then chose to marry Toni—and he foresaw that otherwise the poor girl's chances of a suitable marriage were not of the brightest—he would make the young man his heir. And the Colavolpes would get their three million now and, as they were well aware, further judicious but sufficient assistance as the need arose.

But the boy stood to benefit more than anyone else. De Santis had spoken no more than the truth when he had said he would do the same for the son he regrettably did not possess. Galo had no money at all and no real prospects in the army. De Santis guessed that he would pass out of the Nunziatella very low on the list, if indeed he succeeded in passing out at all, and would end at best as a half-pay major in some thirty years' time. Whereas if he fell in with the present plans for his future . . . The Commendatore glanced at the suspicious, sulky young face at the other side of his broad desk, drained his brandy and said, "Very well, Galo. We *were* discussing the possibility of a future for you in my firm. You were away in Rome or else, I've no doubt, you would have been asked for your comments earlier."

Knowing this last remark for the nonsense it was, Galo brushed it aside. "What are *they* getting out of it?"

De Santis leaned forward and carefully shifted two paper-weights and a cigarette box. Really, the boy was as bad as his uncle! "Nobody has decided anything at all yet," he said carefully. "The whole thing is just an idea—just a notion we talked of—nothing more at all. But all the same, I'd like your comments on it."

"I don't want to."

"Why not?"

"I like it where I am."

"But you'd like to see America? *Everybody* wants to see America. And everybody ought to, I think."

"Not me."

"Well—well, I'm a little disappointed, Galo. I'd hoped you would be more enthusiastic. But it has been sprung on you as a surprise, I know. I think that when you've thought it over by yourself you may see it all in a more favorable light." De Santis's voice was as kindly as a pardonable irritation would permit. He had expected—had hoped for—a shy but warming enthusiasm; he had been prepared for a certain awed hesitance—but not for a blank, curt refusal. What was more, he knew privately that he was not going to accept that refusal. If Galo was still too young, or merely too obstinate and stupid, to know where his own best interests lay he must expect to have the decision taken for him. And taken it would be—but not by De Santis himself of course, that would never do. Concezio and the boy's mother could undertake the necessary forceful coercion—and later bear whatever odium might derive from it. He himself would stand ready to soothe and smooth down Galo's ruffled feathers after the brawl was over.

And yet, looking across the desk the Commendatore felt his mouth thinning with controlled exasperation. At present he felt less like smoothing down and soothing Galo than picking up his round ebony ruler and knocking a little common sense into the boy's stupid head. He reminded himself in time that one could not—and certainly should not—expect common, or any other sort of sense from a Colavolpe, and smiled instead. "Well, we won't talk about it anymore just yet then, eh?" He glanced at his watch. "It's a little late, but I expect Toni is still up. Do you want to go and find her?"

But Galo shook his head. The trap had been sprung now and for the moment its implications absorbed him to the exclusion of all else. "I'll go to bed, I think. I have to leave early tomorrow."

·§ 6

FOR the last twenty minutes of the journey it kept appearing and disappearing behind the patches of umbrella pine and the hedges of prickly pear and aloe that lined the coast road from Naples—beautiful and misshapen and grotesque across the sparkling summer sea, like a great round-headed dolphin pushing out a raft with the tip of its blunt nose. As one drew closer one could make out a ridiculously small pillbox hat perched on the crown of the dolphin's head. This view, seen through the varied patches of semitropical shrubbery, was one of exotic beauty, even for Italy—and yet it was one which had sent a cold shudder down the spines of generations of southern Italians and today its sinister reputation was known and feared as far north as the Alps. For that was Gaeta shining there, beautiful and peculiar across its gulf—Angevin castle, Spanish stronghold, Bourbon fortress, but always, throughout the centuries, a prison. And no ordinary State penitentiary but something far grimmer—a political prison and Italy's main military detention center. Even today when the Angevin multiple gallows, the viceregal wheels and pulleys and blocks, and even Bomba's notorious galleys were only gruesome historical memories the place, despite its beauty, struck the beholder with something more than fascination—it looked, somehow, improper.

Sitting behind the wheel of the hired car, sweating a little in the heat, Beppo felt that enough evil had been perpetrated on that extraordinary site to cloak it forever with an impalpable but very definite atmosphere of distress which must affect even someone totally ignorant of its horrible history. It was said that some Neapolitan businessmen had formed a company to make the place into a holiday resort—a peculiarly inept idea, even for Neapolitan businessmen. Beppo did not think they would succeed.

In the briefcase on the seat beside him lay the documents, signed and stamped by the Defense Ministry—and one of which bore the signature of the Minister himself—which would soon open all the ponderous gates of the fortress for his entry. With them, disguised in a business envelope, was a letter from Iole Giansante to her husband and the long and carefully worded petition which it was Beppo's task to induce the young man to sign.

"It won't be easy," Iole had said two days ago when they had talked in Quong's Funeral Parlor where the poor girl appeared to be working as a receptionist. "He's worse than any mule when he doesn't want to do something."

"I suppose so," Beppo had answered sadly. "That's been the whole trouble from the start, hasn't it?" And Iole had looked up at him wonderingly and asked suddenly, "Tell me—why do you want to help us?" She had colored a little and gone on quickly. "I mean, everyone has always said that he is guilty and that it serves him right. And he did do all they say he did. I hope you have not got the idea that he is really innocent and that the whole thing is some sort of sinister conspiracy—like the Dreyfus case. He did what they say. I know him and I know that—that he does that sort of thing."

"Oh yes, I fully realize the position. I know he is legally guilty without the slightest doubt."

"Then it is really because you are sorry for me?"

Beppo had frowned and resettled his spectacles. Could no woman ever consider any tangle of human affairs without wanting to plant herself firmly in the middle? "No," he had answered a little tartly, "I'm sorry for *him*. I'm sorry for you, too, of course

—but you don't happen to be in prison. As to this talk of guilt or innocence—it's the system, and still more the circumstances under which on this occasion it unfortunately worked, which bears the main responsibility. Anyway, retribution for a refusal to obey the State is seldom synonymous with justice and in this case it is the reverse."

"That's just what Evaldo thinks."

"Good."

"No, it isn't at all good. Because while he thinks like that he won't sign this *domanda* you talk about. If only they would let us send a psychiatrist . . ."

"They won't. They know what would happen. They would have to let your husband go free and it would get into the papers and then everyone else who doesn't like the draft would try the same thing and so shortly the draft would have to go and the Americans would be angry and a very great deal of trouble and confusion would be caused. It's better to keep Evaldo locked up for twelve years—and very much cheaper, too. I can see their point. After all," said Beppo with an unusual depth of cynicism, "they're helping to defend the Free World, aren't they?"

It was nearly midday when Beppo reached the object of his journey. Document after document must be studied, gate after gate opened. As Beppo penetrated ever deeper into the heart of the great prison his spirit descended into even deeper abysses of gloom. He saw very few military prisoners, perhaps most of them were at work or still in their cells; those he did see wore summer fatigue uniforms—khaki shirts and shorts—not unlike the guards except that they had no hats or belts.

The formalities were slow rather than complicated, the prison guards polite and genial. Eventually one of a row of red steel doors in a newly whitewashed corridor was unlocked and swung open. "Just call through the grill when you want to come out." "All right, Corporal. How long have I got?" "As long as you like, as far as I know. You can stay the weekend if you want to." The corporal grinned, the steel door clashed to behind him, and Beppo stood just inside the doorway, holding his briefcase, feeling somehow intrusive and a little foolish and staring across the cell at Evaldo Giansante.

So this was he—the object of so much speculation and preoccupation—that girl's husband; the man who had somehow become a sad symbol of modern injustice and whose forlorn fate seemed linked in a strange way with men—men whose names Beppo had mercifully forgotten—who had died before he was born.

Rather short but heavy for his height. A strange face that looked intelligent, easy-smiling, somehow well-mannered—until one noticed the black, simian eyes. It suddenly struck Beppo that despite all his talk of psychiatrists and his sincere belief that their intervention would free the prisoner, he had never seriously considered that there might be something much more the matter with Evaldo Giansante than an inflammable temper reacting in furious disappointment upon the harshly destructive circumstances in which it found itself trapped. Now, looking at those animal eyes, he knew that he had been wrong. A psychiatrist would certainly free this man from a military prison—but equally, he might not see his way to allowing him full freedom in a civilized society. Beppo thought for a second of what Captain Santorelli must have seen on that lonely street in the moment before he was struck down—and he shuddered.

Carefully he introduced himself and explained the reason for his visit. Evaldo offered him the single wooden chair which the cell contained and himself sat on the bed, rocking gently back and forth with his interlocked hands clasping one bare knee. When Beppo ceased talking he said, "It's very kind of you to take all this trouble. I don't see why you should, though." His voice was slow and distinct as if he was listening to it himself and controlling it consciously.

Beppo said, "Well, apart from knowing your wife and wanting to help her, I've been a military prisoner myself."

"Here?"

"No, no. In the war. I was taken prisoner."

"You were in a concentration camp?"

"No," said Beppo grinning, "a chicken farm." Evaldo looked blank, uninterested. Beppo went on quickly. "I know—up to a point, anyhow—what it feels like."

"Do you?"

"I—I think so."

"I should have liked to have been in the war. It must have been interesting."

"It was horrible."

"You found killing people horrible? Or them trying to kill you? Or both?"

"I didn't kill anyone and nobody tried—directly, at any rate—to kill me."

Evaldo nodded. "I see—yes." He was staring all the time at some point over Beppo's left shoulder, but when Beppo glanced instinctively around there was nothing to see—merely the blank stone wall.

Beppo felt that the time had come to get down to the reasons for his visit. "Listen—I've been into your case with a general I know." He explained about his visit to General Lecco and gave a summary of that officer's advice. "So I have had this *domanda* drawn up very carefully by my lawyer and if you'll sign it I will have it properly presented to the Defense Ministry as soon as I get back." He handed it to Evaldo, who read it carefully and then, placing it gently on the bare wooden table, sat back and continued his rocking on the bed. Beppo had a sudden feeling that he probably sat like this, one knee clasped in his hands and rocking regularly like a metronome, for hours on end.

"It's very damning," Evaldo said at last in the same careful, distinct voice.

"It only admits what you did."

"And states that I'm full of deep remorse and contrition for it."

"Well," said Beppo sensibly, "you must be sorry that you did it—considering where it's placed you."

"Yes," said Evaldo thoughtfully. "Yes."

"And possibly you regret injuring that unfortunate captain. He is being invalided out of the service, I understand, so his career's over and he'll have to keep his wife and children on his pension."

"No," remarked Evaldo in the same judiciously impartial tone, "I don't regret that part at all. It's lucky for Santorelli that I did not have a knife at the time."

"And lucky for you, too!" said Beppo, blinking angrily behind his glasses. "Do you *like* doing things like that to people?"

"If they've done things to me—yes, I like it very much."

"He believed he was only doing his duty—in punishing you, I mean."

Evaldo smiled gently. "There are two men in here for life—

German SS officers—who believed the same when they shot three hundred hostages during the war."

"But—" began Beppo, and then broke off quickly. How was it that he came to be arguing the case against this man when he had expressly taken on the task of arguing it for him? And yet—how on earth could an ordinary reasonable girl like Iole have married someone like this; someone with such gentle good manners who looked at one from the hard, stony black eyes of a wild animal—savage, remote, merciless. With an effort he said, "But all the same, if you will sign this we may get four, or perhaps even five, years removed from your sentence."

"That still leaves seven or eight—so it would be no use."

"How do you mean 'no use'? I should have thought—"

"If I can't get out fairly soon—within a year at the most—I shall die."

Evaldo had not ceased his rocking nor had his voice changed from its ordinary tone. He had only stated something which to him was a known fact and which Beppo, after a momentary desire to protest, accepted also as the ineluctable truth. For he realized with a bleak certainty which even in the cool depths of the castle brought a slight sweat to his forehead that Evaldo was someone who could not tolerate imprisonment. Everything in his past went to prove it—the restlessness which had driven him from Calabria to Rome and would have taken him across the world in search of ever wider freedom, ever greater space; the fury with which he had fought against the constrictions of army life; the frustrated dash to the border. And here now, with all vestiges of liberty removed, caged in with iron, blocked in with stone, he could not be still. That ceaseless, timeless rocking was the exact equivalent of the endless prowl of a wild animal up and down its zoo bars. Yes—if he was not freed within twelve months he would be dead; possibly by his own hand but more probably from the extinction of his will to go on living. The latter would be termed "death from natural causes" and for once that ambiguous term would be used most precisely.

"If," said Beppo with an effort, "you will sign this *domanda* we can use it as a lever to try and get you a psychiatric examination. It may not succeed. In fact I doubt if it will. But one thing is certain—if you don't sign we cannot get you any remission or any help at all."

"In effect the army says I must be guilty before I can be mad —is that it?"

"In a manner of speaking—yes," answered Beppo uneasily. "If you admit your guilt they may be prepared to admit extenuating circumstances—as a sort of quid pro quo. And it cannot do you any harm—only good. We must have something to go on; something material that we can take around and show to people to gain their support and help. Without it we are empty-handed."

"I suppose Iole wants me to sign?"

"Of course—or I wouldn't be here. You've had your permitted letter from her this month or she would have written again."

Evaldo released his knee, put his feet to the ground and rose. "Very well, Signor Sanbrenedetto." He took the pen Beppo offered and signed his name in small, neat, regular writing. "That signature is the only thing I have left to give her, so she had better have it. Now"—he put down the ballpoint pen—"I've got nothing left at all."

Beppo took the paper in hands that shook a little and put it carefully in his briefcase. Then he took out Iole's letter, holding it so that his body shielded it from anyone looking through the door grill. Evaldo, his eyes on the grill, took it without a word and slipped it inside his shirt. Beppo zipped up his case. "And now I'd better go. There's nothing I can do for you outside? Any messages or—or anything?"

Silently, standing in front of him, Evaldo opened his hands in negation. It was a gesture so mutely despairing that Beppo felt his breath catch in his throat. He turned away quickly to the door, shouted, "Corporal! I'm ready" and was almost immediately let out into the whitewashed corridor. As they climbed the first flight of echoing stone stairs at the end of the long passage the corporal confirmed Beppo's suspicion that he had been listening close outside the cell door throughout the visit by saying, "He was much better today than I thought he would be. Better than he has been for a long time."

"Oh? Better in what way?"

"Well, he has his bad days and his good ones, of course. But more bad than good."

"And then—?"

"Then he is face down on his bed all the time. He won't move or speak. To begin with he would not eat, either. We could not allow that, of course. The doctor told him what would have to be done if he wouldn't take some food in the ordinary way. But he didn't listen. So then I tried. I sat beside him for an hour telling him very slowly again and again that it was no good behaving in that way. I told him that teeth often got broken when we had to use the forcible feeding appliance—and sometimes a jaw, too. In the end he heard me and it was all right. He seems to go into a trance of some sort when he's bad. He gets rigid all over and sweats—cold sweat."

"But—but does the doctor know?" Beppo's voice was urgent. "I mean, he's ill—really ill! Not pretending."

Opening the last door the guard nodded somberly. "Yes—he is ill all right—here." He tapped his forehead with a finger. "Yes, of course the doctor knows. But what can *we* do about it?"

Beppo stopped at Formia for a late lunch and ate it on the terrace of a cheap *trattoria* overlooking the Gulf of Gaeta. Across the sparkling afternoon sea the great porpoise of Mont' Orlando, ludicrously crowned with the mausoleum of Lucius Marius Planco, Roman proconsul and founder of Basle, nudged out to sea the great castle and the little fishing village which crouched at its foot. Gaeta—fortress, dungeon, gallows and galley-port; the haven to which Pio Nono had fled during the days of Mazzini's Roman Republic and to which Francis II had retired in a vain attempt to retain his throne as absolute monarch of the Two Sicilies. Gaeta—throughout its bloodstained history a symbol of the tyrant and a refuge for the reactionary.

Wearily, for he had started early that morning from Naples and now the heat was intense and the light blindingly bright, Beppo pondered on what the next move should be. Of course they would press for a heavy remission—if they could halve the sentence Evaldo would be out in little more than five years. But even to Beppo at forty, five years seemed an enormous stretch of time. He realized at once that to someone half his age it would seem an eternity.

Then because he was tired and his head was aching he thought vaguely and rather wildly of going to Rome and demanding an audience of the President of the Republic or the Supreme Court. Since the war, Italy's rulers had invariably been elderly lawyers; civilians, worldly-wise, cosmopolitan by nature, intelligent and unendingly tolerant. Under their discreet and patient competence this difficult, troublesome and often silly nation had been lifted from an abyss of want and degradation to a new prosperity. Surely they—wise, old and civilized— would understand that the peculiar judicial murder which was progressing over there across the shining waters of the gulf must be halted—the whole, dreadful, impersonal horror stopped before it was too late. But no—they would not. Or rather, they *could* not. They had neither the power nor the right to override the imposing pyramidal complex of laws that safeguarded and governed a modern democratic republic. Twenty-five years ago such an appeal would have had a good chance of success. The Duce would have listened, understood, whisked Evaldo out of prison with a single scrawled "M" and sent him back to complete his military service with strict injunctions to behave himself in the future. Or else, if the news from Africa had been unsatisfactory that day, he might have had him summarily shot in the castle courtyard. But it would have been a risk well worth taking. And of course Mussolini's desk could have been reached easily enough by using Ercole's influence.

Beppo, calling for his check and counting his money onto the tablecloth before him, smiled wryly at the irony of his reflections. Then he entered his car and drove away through the still, hot afternoon. Yet ever and again as the car swung out on the curves of the coast road the crowned porpoise, nosing its raft out to sea, appeared, small and bright between the trees and hedges. And every time it did so Beppo had a quick vision of a stone cell and a figure rocking itself on a narrow bed, rocking to and fro silently, rocking on and on and on . . .

"O Sole Mio"

✍ 1

DESPITE the fact that Gennaro's job at Poggia-
reale had lasted but one day, Iole had remained as receptionist
of Quong's Funeral Parlor. She sat at a small table draped
with the black, silver-embroidered funeral pall which so much
resembled the Jolly Roger and at her elbow there was invariably
a vase of white flowers—carnations a little tarnished at the
edges or a couple of yellowing arum lilies. Twice in one week
she took orders for wreaths, and once a red-eyed woman came
to arrange for the burial of her small son but left again with
nothing settled—put off, perhaps, by the overcheerful grins of
the pall's sequin skulls.

Gennaro was extravagantly pleased with the new arrangement and when trade looked up he promised Iole a salary;
meanwhile he bought her little presents whenever he managed
to scrape a few hundred lire together—small packs of chocolate, cartons of ice cream, and once a packet of soap of a brand
that was advertising itself by affixing an imitation pearl neck-
lace to every tablet. And with her new position and these small
attentions Iole became less unhappy than she had believed possible since that cold dawn at Domodossola when the Carabinieri had closed ominously around the compartment in which
she and Evaldo had sat, white-faced and drained of hope.

Beppo had not told her much, had kept to himself his impressions of Gaeta and the prisoner he had found there, but the
domanda had been signed and a lawyer had sent it, with the nec-

essary covering documents, to Rome. Somewhere in the laby-
rinthine offices of the Defense Ministry those papers were moving inexorably upward, carrying Iole's hopes and prayers, toward some faceless deity who might be sufficiently placated to
restore Evaldo to the light of common day. Nothing more, it
seemed, could be done at present and Iole, controlling her impatience, sat behind her funereal desk and watched the summer
life of the *piazza* or read the back numbers of the women's magazines which Crocifissa bought in bulk for wrapping paper and
which Gennaro was forever purloining from her shop.

It was perhaps through these magazines even more than the
little presents he made her or the constant talk of what he would
do when business looked up, that Gennaro endeared himself
to Iole. She discovered in him an avid if erratic interest in do-
mesticity which more than matched her own. Though they both
enjoyed the photo-serials, and ransacked Crocifissa's stock of
wrapping paper to find missing installments, it was the making of discoveries among the home hints and the advertisements which afforded them the greater pleasure. . . . "A little
warm grapefruit juice (lemon is too acidulous) together with
the merest pinch of salt and a teaspoon of ordinary soda will
bring up the most tarnished chromium plating and make it as
good as new," Gennaro would read aloud from the doorway of
the coffin shop. "I've got two sets of chromium corners, but they
aren't tarnished. If they get tarnished I'll try that." Or—"To
preserve your olive oil from becoming rancid once it is opened
add a teaspoonful of sugar to every two liters." Iole would ponder, eyebrows raised. "I don't like the idea, I must say. Oh, listen, Gennaro!—To keep buttons neatly, lay them flat on a strip
of sticky transparent tape and cover them with another strip—
when you need a button you simply cut it off its section of
tape. One day I must try that." Most of the hints were ear-
marked for use "one day"—and all the advertisements. "One
day I'll buy a glass pepper mill," or "an electric spaghetti machine," or "a clockwork hat brush"—for they vied with each
other in coveting the ludicrous and the unnecessary. But they
were equally happy discussing the vaunted merits of various
brands of soap, cooking oil or tomato paste.

Iole knew that Gennaro had done all his own and Quong's
washing and ironing for several years and now, as a friend and

an honorary member of the firm, she was allowed something
which she had often thought of asking for in the past but never
quite dared—the loan of his electric iron. Gennaro's electric
iron—which made its own steam, had thermostatic adjust-
ment and a red light to show when it was running out of water
—was something everyone in the *piazza* knew about. It was
quite possibly the only one of its sort in the whole Quarter,
since none of the inhabitants of San Lorenzo were the sort of
people to spend eight thousand lire on such an unnecessary
luxury when a solid, secondhand flatiron could be picked up in
the Abate for a hundred and fifty. It had been Quong's present
to Gennaro on his fifteenth birthday and the old man had considered it and saved the money for it over a full three months.
He could not have thought of a more acceptable gift. Gennaro was delighted and ironed everything in the place he could
set his hands on. When he had finished all his own and Quong's
and Crocifissa's ironable possessions, he took the iron over to
Tenerini's for due exhibition and praise, and for nearly a fortnight ironed anything that anyone would bring him. The *piazza*
took full advantage of this and Gennaro, who was not easily
bored with a new toy, did not tire until, as old Biagio remarked, there was nothing left unironed and unstarched except
Baldissera's nosebag. . . . "And he'd do that if I let him," he
had added, spitting out of the tobacconist's doorway. "He's a
strange one, our Gennaro." "Chinese blood coming out in him,"
had explained Maresciallo Tenerini sagely as he creaked around
his postcard rack with a feather duster. "All Chinese are natural laundrymen."

But though Gennaro would still press up the occasional garment if it was brought to him, and though he had a tacit arrangement with Raimondo whereby he pressed the soldier's
summer uniforms in return for packets of cheap cigarettes, he
did not like allowing the iron out of his own hands and generally
lent it only to Crocifissa. It was thus a great compliment and a
firm cementing of their friendship when he at once agreed to
Iole's suggestion that she might borrow it occasionally for her
own use.

Renato's wife, Rosalba, also took to visiting the funeral parlor. Her baby was due in September some weeks before Iole's,
and though her visits were ostensibly to borrow the purloined

magazines she really came to talk of childbirth and babies in general. Since babycraft was, with knitting and dressmaking, one of the magazines' subjects which held no appeal for Gennaro, he became slightly jealous over these visits and retiring to the coffin shop banged about with his tools until Rosalba departed.

But if Iole, befriended and assisted by Beppo, consoled insofar as possible by her neighbors, was more hopeful and happier than she had been since her marriage, Crocifissa was less content. Iole sat in Quong's not in order that Gennaro might gossip with her about household hints but that he might go to work. Crocifissa, better than anyone else, knew the state of the Quongs' finances and that Gennaro was getting deeper into debt every day. She guessed too, with the prescience born of her love for him, that he was still more worried about this than she herself but that the fear of losing the business outweighed all other considerations in his curiously devious mind. It was ridiculous to see a boy of sixteen breaking his heart over the retention of an old hearse which he might not use, and a little jumble of wood, decorative religious metal fitments and the rows of frames for wreaths which no one wanted—ridiculous but tragic, too. He was saving on food, she more than half suspected. Probably the only times he ate well were on the occasions he took a meal in her kitchen or on Thursdays when he skinned eels for Clemente in the Piazza San Francesco and received a free fish dinner as part of his wages. His face already seemed thinner, the high, slightly flattened cheekbones were more prominent and the lavender suit seemed looser when he went out on Mondays and Thursdays with his rapidly diminishing supply of black-edged business cards.

Then suddenly, and with an abruptness which startled Crocifissa almost as much as it pleased her, Gennaro came home one day and announced that he had got his second job. "I didn't even know that you'd been looking for one, *caro!* I thought you were just doing your ordinary rounds with the cards."

"I was." Gennaro grinned with an uneasy, dubious triumph. "I was going down the Vico dei Lepri when—when Savoldi saw me and called me across. He said he had heard I was looking for work and he knew of a job which he thought would suit me. I told him I couldn't take anything that interfered with the business"—Crocifissa shook her head and clucked her tongue disapprovingly and Gennaro frowned and shrugged— "but I don't think he listened to me. Anyway, we'll have to see. If it does get in the way— And of course it is only for eighteen months—less, now, really."

"Yes, yes—but what is it, Gennà?"

"I'm telling you. One of Savoldi's friends, a young waiter, had told him there was a vacancy in a restaurant—a new tourist place called the O Sole Mio out at Mergellina. This boy worked there and he said they needed someone in a hurry. He was still in Savoldi's office when I was there—he's called Andrea. So Savoldi said would I take it and I said I'd never done any waiting and this boy said it didn't matter because the job was for an apprentice waiter—a beginner. And so I said I'd have to think about it and Savoldi and the boy said I'd better think quickly because it would be gone in about an hour. So I—I said very well then, I'd take it if I could get it and Savoldi told Andrea to go with me at once and make certain I did get it. He told Andrea that if I *didn't* get it he would—" Gennaro stopped abruptly and reddened; the genial threats with which Savoldi interlarded his conversation with his young friends were of an entirely unrepeatable nature. "So I went there at once—in a taxi."

"In a *taxi!*"

"Yes. Savoldi paid. And we saw the assistant manager and—and I start tomorrow."

"Oh, *caro mio!*" Crocifissa grasped him to her and kissed him and tried as so often before to smooth down his springy hair. "How glad I am! How good Signor Savoldi is to you! I know they say things about him and perhaps in a way some of them—" She stopped quickly, blushing in her turn. "But he's a good man, nonetheless," she added firmly.

"You've got to be careful," grunted old Biagio from his seat beside the counter, "careful of men like that. I remember, in the army—"

"Why careful?" demanded Gigi from behind the big enamel basin where he was soaking stockfish in preparation for tomorrow's Friday customers.

Biagio swiveled a bleary eye in his direction. "You'll know about men like Savoldi when you're older."

"I know *now*," said Gigi contemptuously. "I just don't see what—"

"Savoldi and I"—Gennaro's voice was almost savage—"are business friends. It is quite natural that we should help each other when we can!"

"Yes, yes, yes," soothed Crocifissa. "Of course it is. You know, Gennaro, you're very fortunate—you really are. To get a chance like that. Generally it's only the friends of *padroni* or headwaiters who get taken on—truly! And even they have to pay large amounts." She nodded her head with portentous satisfaction and made a mental note to burn three hundred lire's worth of candles at the altars of the various saints connected in one way or another with the food and catering trades.

"It's not as if I'm going to make a *profession* out of it," began Gennaro hurriedly, but no one listened.

"Oh Gennà, you'll love it—I know! And you'll look so—"

"If I'd had that sort of luck when I was a boy," Biagio grumbled as he began sorting through a box of mixed garbage in search of pieces of edible material for his horse, "I'd have been a rich man today."

Only Gigi, filled with tricolors and trumpet fanfares and military glory, was scornful. It was incredible to him that anyone who was almost old enough to join the Bersaglieri could possibly want to do anything else. "Can you think of Raimondo as a waiter!"

"No," grunted Biagio vindictively, "I can't. There wouldn't be an unbroken plate or a table on its legs within a couple of hours."

✺§ 2

THE O Sole Mio, even from some distance away, did not look its best at ten o'clock in the morning. It was designed to be seen at night and the tubular iron frames holding the great neon-lit name and the electrically rocked fishing-boat sign lifted, complicated and skeletal, above paintwork which less than three months after the restaurant's opening was beginning to flake and crack.

Gennaro, arriving punctually on time, was taken to the dining-room by an assistant manager and handed over to the head-waiter, a tall saturnine man whose first demand was to see his hands. These were not approved of, for the work in the coffin shop had roughened them and stained and blunted the finger-nails. "Manual worker!" the headwaiter had exclaimed angrily. "What will they send me next? Well—what was it?"

"Carpenter's assistant, *signore*." Gennaro had been advised to say nothing about undertaking—some people thought it un-lucky.

"*Gesù!*—Well, when you get home tonight you clean them, see? Soak them in hot water and lye, use pumice or something, but get those nails clean and polished. I'll check them again tomorrow and if they're not right I'll knock a thousand off your week's wages. Now go down to the linen room and get Maria to rig you out properly. You know where the linen room is?"

"No, *signore*."

"Then find it!"

Perplexedly Gennaro descended the stairs from the dining room to a long corridor now deserted save for a short, dark man in an expensively cut lightweight suit who stood outside one of the assistant manager's offices smoking a cigarette in an amber holder. He looked at Gennaro and grinned amiably. "Well, brother, how goes it?"

"I'm looking for the linen room. Do you—"

At the sound of Gennaro's voice the short man gave a quick start and then approaching closely, stared him up and down. He grinned slowly, wonderingly. "Well, well, *well!*" Then, as if suddenly aware of Gennaro's astonished glance, he shook him-self like a dog and said, "Up this passage, turn left and it's the second door. Come with me, I'll show you."

They walked together up the passage and Gennaro explained that he was starting work today. "I've never done it before, of course. I'll have to learn a lot. Do you work here, too?"

"In a way. I have business here with Ferenc—with Signor Bighencomer. I have a contract for the kitchen refuse—among other things. You'll see me about a good deal, particularly in the evenings. I'm Signor Domenichelli—if anyone asks for me you'll know who they mean."

At the linen room they found an old woman and two girls

sorting hundreds of table napkins into piles. "New waiter, Maria
—wants fitting out."

Domenichelli turned, grinning, seemingly laughing to himself, his little eyes sparkling. Suddenly he slapped Gennaro's
shoulder "*Ciao,* boy—and good luck!" Then he sauntered back
along the passage, a heavy-lidded, elegant little tough, with his
cigarette holder cocked arrogantly from the side of his mouth.

Maria beckoned Gennaro to follow her and silently led him
to a shelf piled with the red shirts and blue, tan-patched trousers
that lent the waiters at the O Sole Mio their spurious air of
fishermen. She was, as Gennaro found out later, both deaf and
dumb, but by eye alone she rigged him out at once with two
sets of clothes which fitted accurately and when, ten minutes
later, he once again presented himself to the headwaiter, he met
with a better reception. "That's more like it. Yes, that's not at
all bad. Not that I approve of those clothes, for I don't. A
waiter is a waiter and should dress like one. The *padrone* actually suggested that I and Signor Croce, the wine waiter,
should wear them, too. But we absolutely refused. Nor would he
find any persons of our position who would demean themselves so, I think. You have two sets?"

"Yes."

"You must try to keep them clean. Aprons are forbidden because it would destroy the effect, apparently. *Gesù!* Who ever
heard of a restaurant waiter without an apron? Does the *padrone* really imagine that the clients think that you have all just
returned from the open sea with netfuls of sardines? *Non fa
niente!* Now come with me."

For the rest of the day and far into the night Gennaro, a red-
shirted acolyte, followed a few respectful paces behind the headwaiter whence, from time to time, he was sent with a scribbled
message to the kitchen or to a manager's office. He was seldom
spoken to and he only learned his new master's name, Achille
Dru, by reading it on a list pinned to the cashier's desk behind
the main foyer.

Gennaro had never before been into a restaurant dining room
—not even into the rough bench-filled room of Clemente's place
—and his first impressions were ones of pleasure and interest
and a suppressed impatience to be allowed to do something

more than run messages for Dru. The sun shone, the sea was a
bright blue lake beyond the jetty, and the striped umbrellas cast
a colored shade upon the gleaming glass and cutlery of the
tables below. For the first hour, until the restaurant began to
fill up, the red-shirted waiters talked among themselves or,
more deferentially, with early customers, and Gennaro even
had a few words with Andrea, who was a junior wine waiter and
thus came under a different set of rules. But by one o'clock,
and with nearly every table filled, the atmosphere changed rapidly through brisk attentiveness to taut, frenetic speed. No
longer did the waiters, sliding swiftly between the tables, laugh
or talk; the tight-lipped, brief, mandatory smiles they gave the
customers were meaningless and perfunctory while the customers themselves were different—impatient, irritable at any delay,
and often querulous. The *ping* of forks knocked against glasses
to attract attention and the waiters' jerked response of *"Vengo
subito!"* took the place of the good-humored chatter which had
greeted the first-comers.

Gennaro was now made properly aware for the first time of
the difficulties inherent in his probationary position—for those
diners in need of attention and who saw a waiter apparently
doing nothing called out to him, beckoned or caught his sleeve
as he passed their tables. Dru had firmly forbidden him to
serve anybody with anything and he shortly received a lesson
which taught him the reason for this. He was standing the correct two paces behind the headwaiter when he felt a tap on the
arm and turned to look down at a florid, elderly customer, one
of a group of six businessmen at a round table, who was mo-
tioning toward the ornate conch shell filled with a high spray of
flowers which formed the centerpiece. "Take that forest away,
boy. I can't talk through a damned jungle!" The man laughed
genially and Gennaro, smiling back, carefully lifted the heavy
shell and carried it back to the row of serving tables beside the
wall. As he did so another waiter not much older than himself,
a pallid black-haired youth with hot dark eyes who was sliding
eel-like between the crowded tables with a row of plates balanced along one arm, shot him a silent glare of astonished fury.
Gennaro had no idea in what way he had offended but on his
next errand beyond the dining room the waiter followed him,
and as soon as they were out of sight or sound of the customers

grabbed his arm and swung him around. "Here—you! What in God's name do you think you're doing?"

"Me?" Gennaro stared back, amazed at the other's vibrant anger. "How?"

"Interfering with my table like that! Who told you that you could touch my flowers?"

"The customer—one of the clients—wanted it removed. He asked—"

"*Al diavolo con i clienti!* You keep your dirty paws off my table, see?"

"I had to take it! I can't refuse to do something like that. They'd call the manager!"

The older waiter's hot eyes widened; he swallowed, seemed about to say something, but instead seized a half-finished plate of fish soup that lay on a nearby counter and flung the contents over Gennaro. "That will teach you!" He leapt back, his fists clenched. "And if you touch either of my tables again you'll be sorry!"

Then Dru was suddenly in the doorway. He took in the whole scene with the immediacy of one who had been a waiter ever since he was tall enough to lay a table. "Ilario—that's cost you two thousand lire."

"Signor Dru! He interfered with—"

"*Zitto!* You're a Sicilian, aren't you, Ilario? All Sicilians are barbarous scum. I'll have you out in the street if you open that ugly mouth of yours just once more. Get out! As for you, Gualtierra—I told you not to touch anything except upon my orders, didn't I?"

"Yes—but—"

"Then it will cost *you* two thousand lire for disobeying me. Go and change your clothes. If you can't just do *nothing* when you're told to I can't even imagine what sort of infernal nuisance you'll be when you have to *work!*"

It was Gennaro's first initiation into the complex social relationships, rigid laws and taboos of the restaurant world. A caste system as fierce and as savagely enforced as that of any feudal despotism governed this world, one to which everybody was in thrall and in which everybody had his proper place, duties and privileges delimited, jealously guarded and hallowed by tradition. In the same way that the crew of a ship divides itself automatically into "the engine room" and "the deck," so the staff of a restaurant is self-segregated into "the kitchen" and "the dining room." And as on a liner the only authority to wield power over both sections is the captain, so in a restaurant it is the manager or the owner. Signor Bighencomer, through two assistant managers, ruled over the O Sole Mio with the unsmiling efficiency of a mechanical robot. Below the managers, but equally in awe of the owner, Signor Fonseca, the chef, and Signor Dru, the headwaiter, controlled their own departments in tacit but traditional hostility to one another. The cooks, who were highly proficient men, despised the waiters for their comparatively unskilled work while the waiters, who prided themselves upon their appearance and suavity, held the cooks in contempt for their uncouthness amid the dirt and fury of the kitchen. Both groups existed under a perpetual nerve-fraying strain and both took their exasperation out on their immediate subordinates—the *guatteri*—scullery-hands— in the case of the kitchen staff, the apprentice waiters in that of the dining room. Since the waiters were, as a class, vain, jealous and spiteful, their underlings came in for treatment that if less brutal was perhaps more unpleasant than the tyranny under which the half-naked *guatteri* drudged in the fetid regions of the kitchen quarters.

The waiters not only abused the apprentices but quarreled constantly among themselves—a thing the cooks had neither the incentive nor the leisure to do. These quarrels were invariably centered around regular customers. It was common practice for the waiters to "make friends" with the regulars, learning their names, studying their idiosyncrasies and, if possible, supplying some special individual service which demonstrated personal regard. In return for this treatment the waiters invariably received tips which were much larger than those from casual diners and which often grew greater while never decreasing. Since the restaurant had only been open for three months, there were as yet few regular customers and these were hotly competed for. Waiters, given the smallest opportunity, would poach each other's regular clients, hanging around the entrance to the dining room, bowing, smiling, leading the way to their own rather than their rivals' tables. If the client was strong-minded or sincerely preferred one waiter to another, he might insist on sitting at one of his favorite's tables, but such clients were not common and it was generally easy enough to capture the others if one happened to be at the dining room entrance at the right time.

Ilario, the young Sicilian, had managed to acquire a family of five Belgian tourists who had been coming to lunch at the restaurant nearly every day for more than a week. As regulars they were not a particularly fine prize, for though they ate like hogs, consuming huge quantities of food and wine, they never left more than three or four hundred lire on the table at the end of their meal. But Ilario, despite the airs he gave himself, was still only a junior waiter and the Belgians were the only regulars he had. He used to prepare a table especially for them and surreptitiously took flowers from other tables' conch shells and vases to decorate it.

Gennaro, watching him from behind the *batterie de cuisine flambé* which it had become his duty to wheel out for Dru whenever it was needed, noticed that his whole manner, even his appearance, changed when the Belgians entered the restaurant. The irritable, bad-tempered strain which marked his general demeanor disappeared at once and was replaced by a smiling welcome which lit up his whole face and seemed so genuine that Gennaro could only conclude that he sincerely liked this dull, gross family as much at least for themselves as for the few hundred lire they would leave him. He hung around the table adjusting a knife here, an ashtray there, grinning his pleasure at any remark made to him, delighted to advise with the menu, find lighter cutlery for the younger children and tie napkins around their necks. And in fact Gennaro had hit upon the truth. Ilario's affection for the Belgians was quite sincere. Since all the waiters were on permanently bad terms with each other and with the cooks, the only friendly words they ever heard were from the customers and therefore they had a natural tendency to overvalue these. Far from deceiving the Belgians with his sudden access of warm friendliness, Ilario was deceiving himself with the belief that their own reciprocal affability meant as genuine a fondness for him.

Dru, checking the lamps and salvers on the trolley, must have seen the direction of Gennaro's gaze—he was a man who missed practically nothing, as omnipresent in the dining room as Signor Fonseca was in his kitchen—for he said in his low, toneless voice, "See that? That's all right so long as you know how far to go. Customers will often come back just because they like a waiter. But never talk to a customer if another one is waiting. When you are at one of your tables you must constantly be thinking about the others. Very well—come on." And together, priest and acolyte, they moved slowly, religiously away behind the softly gliding *batterie*.

Next day an older waiter, a French-Italian from Switzerland named Laroc, was at the doors when the Belgians appeared. He bowed, smiled, addressed them in their own language and led them away to one of his own tables by the edge of the jetty. A couple of minutes later Ilario came up from the kitchen carrying two plates of *calamaretti Livornese*. From the threshold of the serving-door he saw Laroc standing beside his stolen Belgians, a napkin over one arm, taking their orders, and his lips whitened with rage. He took a deep breath and went off to serve his table with jaw muscles standing out like knots under his darkly pallid skin. As soon as Laroc left the restaurant with the Belgians' order Ilario tried to follow him, but one of his own customers was demanding attention and he did not succeed in getting away until Laroc was halfway back from the kitchen with the great dish of *risotto di frutti di mare* with which the Belgians invariably began their heavy meal.

"Out of my way, Sicilian whore-pig," said Laroc genially enough. He was twice Ilario's size and had been a waiter for eight years as against the other's two. Silently Ilario stood aside but as Laroc passed he punched him under his lifted right arm and when he drew back his fist a short wet knife blade protruded from it. Laroc took two more paces forward, dropped the *risotto* with a shattering crash and sat down amongst the ruins trying clumsily and ineffectually to get his left hand inside his shirt.

"*Sacrament!* You—you've killed me!" His hand came away covered in blood and at the sight his voice rose to a scream. "Help! Quick! Help! *Sono assassinato!*"

And then the passage was full of waiters and *guatteri* and Laroc was lifted, still screaming in a way which showed considerable vivacity from one who supposed he was dying, while Ilario was seized and bundled unresisting into a manager's office. Later the Carabinieri arrived and took him away. Gennaro saw him leave, handcuffed between the two red-faced, khaki-clad policemen. He looked calm and a little remote and held himself with an arrogant erectness as if he had managed to assassinate a bloodthirsty tyrant rather than to knife a man as poor and hardworking as himself over a futile dispute as to which of them should serve lunch to a family of middle-class foreigners.

"Typical Sicilian," said Dru later. "I won't have another in my dining room—not if he has testimonials from the President of the Republic himself."

Gennaro's first few days in the O Sole Mio were passed in what, by comparison with his slave-labor on the south excavation of the ITOLGAS plant, was almost complete idleness. His duties, though continually increasing, were limited to the simplest things and even these had to be first explained. If two ordinary wineglasses were wanted for a certain table it was of no use to go to the big glassware counter and take a couple. First a salver must be collected from the silver table. Then a clean colored cloth depicting the restaurant's fishing-boat sign must be arranged over it. On this must be placed a folded table napkin and lastly the two glasses, carefully checked and polished, must be set upside down upon the napkin. Then the salver was carried to the correct table where the waiter in attendance would lift each glass to the light, polish it, lift it to the light again and only then set it before the customer and nod Gennaro's dismissal. A knife, a fork or a spoon must be accorded the same reverent ritual. Gennaro began to realize why it was that even on his second day he had only been allowed to deliver ashtrays, the sole objects in the dining room which might be carried unceremoniously by hand.

And if it took several days to learn how to handle cutlery and glass it would take—according to Dru—months to learn how to serve a meal, and years, decades perhaps, to acquire professional skill with the *batterie de cuisine flambé*. Of all the things Gennaro saw at the O Sole Mio the most impressive was the headwaiter's display of esoteric skill with the lamps and brilliant silver cooking utensils of the *batterie*. On a sign from Dru, Gennaro would carefully wheel the trolley toward a table and on this occasion, and this occasion only, he had priority of passage and the other waiters, however busy and burdened with dishes, must make immediate way for him; the *batterie* was sacred, the restaurant's Ark of the Covenant. And once at the client's table, Dru would take charge. With a grave, nonchalant competence, without haste yet without a single wasted movement, he would deftly prepare a variety of dishes—*oeufs mollet Florentine; steak Diane; tornedos Casanova;* and his own special variations on the theme of *crêpes Suzette*—each one of which was completed and served in the flickering, transparent blue flames of burning spirits. This expertise impressed Gennaro as deeply as it did the customers who, since *flambé* dishes were by far the most expensive on the menu, were invariably rich foreigners or Milanese businessmen or special guests dining with the *padrone* himself.

Until the end of his first week, Dru gave Gennaro no hint as to whether or not he was proving satisfactory, but on Saturday morning before the lunch hour rush began and while Gennaro was carefully cleaning the trolley—he was not allowed to touch the actual lamps or cooking apparatus—Dru said, "I'm going to keep you on this work for the time being, and in a week or two you may be able to hand me things when I want them."

He paused expectantly and Gennaro said, "*Si, signore.*"

"Don't imagine it's because I think any more of you than of any other fool of an apprentice," grunted the headwaiter as if disappointed with Gennaro's response. "It's merely because you seem able to stand still. That's a thing which practically no one of your age ever seems able to do. I will not have someone fidgeting about while I'm working—and you don't." And Gennaro realized that in his new position this was as much of a compliment as he was ever likely to be paid.

That evening Gennaro drew his week's wages, the three thousand lire which was all that was left after Dru had deducted two thousand as he had threatened. Three thousand. . . . Jolting home on a late tram along the Chiaia, Gennaro stared dully at his reflection in the shiny blackness of the opposite window. In good times he and Quong had made four or five times as much in a week, yet now—after six days during which he had worked from ten-thirty in the morning to twelve-thirty at night—he was returning with only three thousand lire in his pocket. It was true that he was only a beginner and that unless he made more culpable mistakes he would bring five thousand back next week. It was true that he and Quong could just manage to live on five thousand a week and that within a month he would be qualified to take a share of the fifteen percent service charge which, according to Andrea, would add another two thousand a week to his earnings—later, too, when he had a table of his own there would be tips. But tonight, tired-out and dirty, he thought only of his three thousand lire and that he had spent the week not, as was his wont, among friendly neighbors, but among hostile strangers who jostled and abused him at the slightest excuse; that his legs ached, his head was ringing with fatigue and that what he wanted more than anything else was to be in his bed above the coffin shop and there, guarded by the white jade horse on the windowsill, to sleep and sleep and sleep again.

⊷§ 3

        GENNARO spent Sunday at home. Iole had cleaned the shop and done all his own and Quong's washing and ironing as well. So beyond setting two saws and honing the blade of a jack-plane in the workroom, Gennaro could find nothing to do. He sat for much of the morning in a chair beside his grandfather, but for the first time in his life he found it difficult to talk to him. The world he now inhabited was a mean-spirited, vicious place of fear and strain and never-ending hurry; a place quite foreign to Quong's calm Oriental gentleness. Somehow he did not want Quong to know about it. And perhaps Quong understood this, for he wrote no questions on his slate but sat quietly smiling and at last took Gennaro's hand gently in his own small wrinkled yellow one as he had done so often in the past on the various occasions that he had sensed the onset of one of the dark emotional upsets which threw this odd grandson of his into moods of despairing gloom.

        But that afternoon there was actually an order for two wreaths, and in the breathless joyful hurry of choosing and buying the cheap flowers and preparing the dusty frames, Gennaro forgot all about the O Sole Mio. But he remembered in time to overcharge his client by fifty percent and thus, by taking a profit of two thousand lire, to make up for the money deducted from his week's wages.

By Monday morning Dru appeared to have forgotten his intention of keeping Gennaro on the trolley and instead used him almost exclusively as a messenger to the kitchen, so that Gennaro spent much of the time on the stairs or passages or at one end or another of the service lifts—the hurrying, scurrying limbo between the smooth and gleaming dining room and Signor Fonseca's tartarean domain.

Owing to the excessive cramping of the service quarters these low, sloping passages were never free from piles of crates and sacks, garbage bins, gas cylinders and stacks of bottles. *Guatteri* squatted in them doing jobs for which there was no room in the kitchen, scaling fish, sharpening knives, unpacking crockery and inevitably getting in the way of the constant cursing stream of waiters. Though the O Sole Mio was supposed to specialize in fish, it also hoped to attain a reputation for its game and poultry, and since Signor Bighencomer had found a way of buying local chickens more cheaply than birds already plucked and cleaned from the broilers, there were generally two or three scullery-hands somewhere along the corridors immersed in blowing feathers. These feathers got into the food and onto the waiter's hair and clothes and caused more loss of temper and waste of time than any of the other manifold inconveniences under which the staff labored. They were also a cause of friction between the headwaiter, who kept demanding that the plucking should be done in the kitchen, and the chef, who insisted on using the passages. Since the passages were no-man's-land, the matter was referred to Signor Bighencomer, who lifted his head from his accounts for barely ten seconds to snap out the intelligent answer that the chickens were to be soaked in water and plucked on wet burlap.

Once Gennaro found a *guattero* in a dark hole by a kitchen larder clumsily attempting to skin latitudinally one of a basket of eels. He offered to show him the correct way and skinned half a dozen with the rapid dexterity he had learned from Clemente in the Piazza San Francesco. As he finished the last, a huge hand fell on his shoulder and he looked up to see the chef looming portentously over him. "Well, well—so you want to help in the kitchen, do you? You haven't got enough work of your own, have you?" The huge man rocked him to and fro like a doll. "If I *want* one of Dru's little red-shirted rats down here *I'll* ask. Now—get out of here and *stay* out!" He swung Gennaro around and booted him into the passage with a kick which jarred his spine and rattled his teeth, and then, seizing a skinned eel, wrapped it round the *guattero's* neck and pulled it tight, swearing horribly between his teeth, his vast red face glowering into that of the strangling scullion.

Limping down to the kitchen with an amended order half an hour later, Gennaro was accosted with a great bellow of "Hi, *uaglio!*— You eel-skinner—come here!" and saw Fonseca beckoning to him through the steam and smoke and lurid lighting. "Did I hurt you, eel-skinner?"

"Si."

" *'Si, Signor Capo!' Dio!* you waiters! Never any respect. Well —that's because I'm strong. *Strong*—see? Not a miserable specimen like you. You'll never amount to anything. No waiter ever does."

Still staring down at Gennaro he swung a hand quickly behind his back and clouted one of his grill stokers, who had been watching the scene with delight, heavily across the face "Get on with your work, *topolino!* Well, let me inform you, eel-skinner, that your mother was a diseased hermaphrodite unnaturally made pregnant by a male prostitute from the Galleria. And you yourself— No, words fail me! Here—take this!" A sizzling slice of liver was thrust out at Gennaro on a long fork. "Quick! Before I ram it up your rear end!"

The accolade of the liver was, as Gennaro found out later, tantamount to official recognition in the kitchen quarters. Under the soubriquet of "Eel-skinner" he was now raised from the common herd of waiters who had no such nicknames and were habitually addressed by Signor Fonseca—collectively or individually as "Dog's Excrement."

But so carefully circumscribed were the territories of kitchen and dining room, so hedged about with rigid traditional jealousies and suspicions, that the eel-skinning episode was by no means closed by the chef's official forgiveness. For it was not, after all, Signor Fonseca but Signor Dru who had been truly outraged. It was nearing the busiest hour of the day—twelve-thirty—when the story reached him, but he immediately left the dining room and five minutes later Gennaro was summoned to the underground office of one of the assistant managers. Dru was standing by the desk, his face seeming still more darkly sallow in the harsh illumination of the overhead neon lighting.

The interview was short. "You have been interfering in the kitchen, it seems?"

"Me? *No, signore.* I only showed someone how to skin an eel. You see, he was doing it wrong and I know how to do it properly because—"

"Don't you know that as a member of the dining room staff you have no right ever to touch any unprepared food?"

"No."

The manager knocked the ash from his cigarette and slid his eyes to Dru. "You don't want him, then?"

"No."

"You've been training him on the *batterie?*"

"There are plenty of others I can train. I'm not having him in the dining room again, though—not after this."

"He didn't know."

"I'm still not having him."

The manager shrugged. *"Va bene."* He paused, staring Gennaro up and down. "Well—there you are, Gualtierra. You're through as a waiter. You're lucky, though, because Signor Fonseca says he'll take you in the kitchen. You can start right away. Hand in your waiter's clothes to the linen room and go and report to the chef."

The kitchen of the O Sole Mio was a long, narrow concrete cave largely, though not entirely, underground, for a row of narrow frosted windows just below the ceiling let in enough daylight for work in all except the most distant corners. Nevertheless, the main illumination was from bar after bar of fluorescent lighting which flung its blue-white glare over what to Gennaro, entering it for the first time as a member of its staff, seemed an infernal cross between a riot in a madhouse and a crowded pit in Hell.

The heat was the first thing that struck him and it did so physically like a blow in the face. Outside in the hot summer noon the temperature might have stood at eighty-five degrees; here it was perhaps one hundred and fifteen. It was so hot that most of the metalwork, except the actual cooking stoves, had to be wrapped in insulating layers of cloth. The stoves themselves were ranged in a long double bank down the center of the cavern and they were fired by great cylinders of bottled industrial gas—the bulbous, bright orange cylinders of ITOLGAS which Gennaro had seen piled on heavy trailer-trucks lurching out of the factory gates at Poggiareale. Only at the far end of the line of stoves was any other fuel used, for there lay the great charcoal grill, a six-foot by three-foot bed of glowing coal whose shimmering, eye-searing maw was continually fed and tended by two dripping scullions armed with thin antennalike pokers and shovels. Along the left side of the kitchen were the work tables and along the right lay the counters, stacked with towers of clean plates, while beyond them and at the farthest end of the tunnel the washing troughs stood in a perpetual cloud of steam. Around the stoves, around the work tables and counters, cooks, assistant cooks and *guatteri* jostled, swore and shouted, crashing pots and saucepans from stove to concrete floor, clanging open oven doors and the lids of *bains-marie* until the kitchen thundered with oaths and the clash of metal on metal and metal on stone. At the end of the line of stoves, gigantic and crimson-faced and draped in white, Signor Fonseca towered over the scene, roaring out an indiscriminate mixture of orders, threats and curses.

Gennaro waited until the chef had suspiciously examined a tray of raw veal fillets and then said, "*Scusi, signore*. I have been sent to work for you—the manager says."

Fonseca lifted his bull-like head and stared for a moment in silence. "Oh, it's you, is it—young Eel-skinner. Yes. Dru threw you out, eh? I thought he would. Yes, I told them I would add you to my menagerie. You want to be a *guattero*, eh?"

Gennaro nodded. "*Si*."

Very slowly the head cook put out a huge red hand and brought it close to Gennaro's face. Very slowly he opened his thumb and forefinger.

Gennaro stood mesmerised. Suddenly the slow-motion became snakelike action. Gennaro's left ear was seized and twisted with a savage jerk.

"*Si, Signor Capo! Si, signore! Si, Eccellenza! Si, Altessa,* if you like! But *never* just '*si*'—understand?"

"*Si, signore,*" gasped Gennaro, his eyes watering.

"*Va bene.* Well, at least you can skin eels and that's something, I suppose. And though you're a puny little bastard compared to a real *man* like me, you're not quite such a misbegotten scarecrow as these two little rats here!" Signor Fonseca stretched out gorilla arms, grabbed the two grill stokers who had stopped work to listen and banged their heads together. He threw one of the dazed pair back with such force that he only saved himself from falling into the blazing grill by cannoning off a furious assistant cook—and thrust the other at Gennaro. "This rat is Giona. Giona, take Eel-skinner to the changing room and show him where to put his things. Then bring him back here. Hurry!"

The changing room was a narrow crowded alleyway hung with the cheap smart suits of the cooks and assistant cooks and the shabbier shirts and jeans of the scullions. Giona, a thin, monkey-faced, crop-headed youth wearing only a pair of greasy blue shorts which sagged below his navel, stood feeling his head tentatively with two fingers as Gennaro took off his shirt and hung it from an empty hook. "You'll ruin those trousers," he said at last. "Haven't you got anything else?"

"No. Anyway they are only old ones."

"As you like, then. You can wear what you please in the kitchen except for swimming trunks—the *capo* won't allow those." He paused. "You mustn't worry about him doing that— twisting your ear. It doesn't mean anything. He'll threaten to murder you at least a dozen times a day. But if you answer him back—*Caro Gesù!* I saw him throw a whole half-cooked omelette in a *guattero's* face for that—and of course the fool was fired at the same time. But he is not bad really. He lets us eat well; meat twice a day—as much as we like, too. And once when I had toothache he gave me money to go to a dentist—*Vero!* No, he is a good man, the *capo.* But you have to be careful."

From one o'clock until four, Gennaro worked in the kitchen, worked in a daze of searing heat and deafening noise, of screamed orders and counterorders, of bellowed curses and the banging and rattling of a myriad cooking pots as the infernal bedlam of lunch hour swung to its peak and the whole complex machine of a modern restaurant was raced at full throttle for over two and a half hours.

It was to be several days before Gennaro could even begin to understand what was happening around him; could comprehend even the barest essentials of the manner in which the O Sole Mio and dozens of other places of the same sort were run. As a *guattero* he learned that speed, intelligence and adaptability were just as important as untiring physical endurance. He had not only one task but several and he was expected to be able to understand accurately in which order they must be performed. As a scullery-hand the washing of a never-ending succession of plates and cutlery was his main occupation, but it must be dropped at any moment when a cook wished a saucepan cleaned for further use, when a great gas cylinder must be manhandled into place and connected to one of the stoves, or when a side of meat, a basket of fish or a crate of wine needed to be brought from the icehouse or one of the larders. And always everything must be done at top speed. The kitchen, the store-cellars and larders and the passages connecting them became, for three hours at midday and four and a half hours at night, a pandemonium that surpassed anything in the *Inferno*. Raging cooks, swearing porters, dripping, half-naked scullions, yelled and struggled in the stifling ill-lit dusk of the narrow passages and the steamy glare of the kitchen, charging and jostling in the confined spaces with crates and trays of food and blocks of ice, fighting out furious, bitter little quarrels like hysterical rats in an overcharged electric maze.

The substance of the matter was that during these hours some two hundred or more people were simultaneously demanding four, five, and sometimes six different dishes apiece from a staff of thirty-five whose job it was to cook them. Speed—hectic, furious, delirious speed—was essential if they were not to be kept waiting with growing impatience for their food. It was the waiters who bore the brunt of the clients' annoyance at any undue delay and they came down and yelled at the cooks, who in turn screamed at the scullions. Within an hour of the first rush everyone was dizzy with heat and fatigue but somehow the meals always did get cooked and away in time.

This was almost entirely due to Signor Fonseca; in fact it was his reliability and punctuality, rather than his skill as a culinary artist, for which he was paid the high wage of two hundred thousand lire a month. He was a man of phenomenal memory who never forgot an order and who knew exactly when each one was due. Despite his strings of bellowed oaths he never really lost his temper and he seldom—at least during the rush hours—moved far from his place at the head of the long line of stoves. He cooked nothing himself but all main dishes—*secondi,* as they were called—had to be brought to him for inspection before they were served, as did any other cooked dish which would be charged for at over five hundred lire. In effect this meant that he supervised everything except the *pasta* dishes— the piled plates of spaghetti, vermicelli, ravioli and lasagne— with which all Italian and many foreign clients began their meals. He knew exactly what was being prepared on each of the stoves and exactly when it should be ready. Looming, vast and white among the steam of the *bains-marie* and the blue fumes of bubbling oil, he would boom, *"Pronto un lingua con salsa verde!"* . . . *"Pronto un sogliole alla Parmegiana!"* . . . . *"Pronto due piccioni coi piselli, e un rognoni trifolati!"*—and the various dishes would be brought up for his scrutiny and rushed to the impatient waiters jostling before the counters. He was admired and, since he was ruthless in dismissing anyone who did not come up to his exacting standards, deeply feared by cooks and *guatteri* alike.

If he showed discrimination in his dealings with any of his minions it was toward the two grill stokers, Giona and Mauro, his *topolini*—little rats—as he called them; but it was a discrimination Gennaro was glad he did not share. The grill was close to the *capo's* chosen position at the far end of the line of stoves and the two stokers were perpetually under his eye. In theory their job—in any case not an easy one—was to keep the great grill at a fierce but even temperature throughout its length and breadth. Nonetheless they were made to take considerable responsibility for the various cuts of meat and splayed-out, spatchcocked birds sizzling and searing on the bars. These were extremely expensive dishes, particularly the great Florentine steaks selling at over two thousand lire apiece, and their timing, in accordance with a customer's demands, was an exacting ritual. Once, by the clumsy use of his long iron tongs, Giona allowed a steak to slip between the bars into the furnace. The chef let out a bellow that must surely have been heard in the restaurant above and seizing the appalled stoker by the neck administered a terrific beating with a heavy wooden spoon. Half an hour later Gennaro passed Giona weeping with pain among old bread crusts and decayed cabbage leaves in a filthy cluttered corner near the icehouse. "So much for your friend the *capo,* eh?"

"He didn't *mean* it," Giona had protested between sobs. "He didn't mean to hurt me so much. He doesn't realize how strong he is." And later in the day Gennaro saw him being fed a huge piece of fried liver by the chef.

Signor Fonseca had an uncanny ability to judge within a very few degrees the heat of any given stove at any time and at least once in Gennaro's memory he put this gift to frightening use. Mauro, Giona's mate, had mistakenly given a waiter a nearly raw steak instead of a properly cooked one and the customer had sliced it open—ruining it in the process—and angrily sent it back by the same abusive waiter. The chef had stared at the steak for a full half-minute and then beckoned the wretched Mauro with that hypnotic, slow-motion action which always meant trouble. Mauro was even smaller and thinner than Giona —almost a pigmy. It was difficult, seeing him standing in his filthy cotton shorts before the huge chef, to believe that they could possibly belong to the same species. "A well-cooked steak, Mauro?" The chef's voice was terrible in its controlled calm. "A *well-cooked* steak, is it?"

The *guattero* shook his head, dumb with terror and the *capo* gripped one skinny shoulder and dragging Mauro with him strode down the line of stoves. "I'll show you what well-cooked means—Jesus Mary, I will!" And suddenly he swung the shivering Mauro off his feet, lifted him high in the air and banged him down in a sitting position on top of a hot stove. Mauro's scream tore the kitchen and he leapt off into the arms of Signor Fonseca, who promptly set him back again. Another animal howl and the tiny Mauro was on the floor groveling around the chef's feet. "Are you well-cooked, Mauro? Good! Now you know what well-cooked means, I think."

Gennaro, passing the stove a minute later, touched it surreptitiously. It was nearly, but not quite, hot enough to sear the flesh on contact. Mauro had been severely scorched but his sweat-soaked pants had prevented his flesh from being actually burnt. Later he, too, was consoled with fried liver.

They really were like little kitchen rats—the two stokers. Signor Fonseca's tame pet rodents, to be abused or stuffed with meat as the mood took him but, unlike anyone else in the kitchen, quite safe from the unspoken but ever-present threat of instant dismissal.

For Gennaro the kitchen and its terrifying master held a fearful fascination overshadowing and, despite the exacting labor, certainly preferable to the suavely tense and feline undercurrents of spite and jealousy which permeated Dru's dining room. In this infernal workshop he saw the making of all those dishes over which the waiters bowed and smiled at the side of snowy tables gleaming with silver and glass. He saw, too, that the beautiful service was a sham, a ritualistic deception to induce the customer to believe he was purchasing choice delicacies cooked with loving care and skill when in fact he was buying inferior food prepared with a rough, dirty but very rapid efficiency. Gennaro had never seen food treated as it was in the restaurant's kitchen. When he or Crocifissa bought meat, fish and vegetables in the Abate they selected the best they could afford and used it with care and thoughtful economy, while even the plain and simple meals at the Collegio di San Francesco at Ferrara had been prepared and cooked in immaculately clean kitchens under the supervision of thrifty but painstaking monks. The cooks of the O Sole Mio treated their materials as if they hated them—as indeed they probably did. Meat and fish were flung into pans; vegetables and fruit left lying indiscriminately in buckets of dirty water upon whose scummy surfaces spent matches and cigarette butts often floated; hacked loaves of bread lay in confused piles on the stone floor to be seized when wanted, kicked aside when in the way. All food that could be precooked was precooked. The famous *fritto misto* was merely a soggy pile of half-fried, batter-covered prawns, cuttlefish and small red mullet which, upon demand, was thrown by the handful into wire baskets of bubbling oil for forty seconds before serving; while an order for roast veal or lamb meant that three thin slices of meat were taken off cold boiled joints, placed on a hot plate in a high-temperature oven for three minutes, covered with boiling gravy and sent up steaming. Everything was handled continually since it was quicker for a cook or a *guattero* to use his fingers than the kitchen instruments.

Sometimes the cooks washed their hands in the water in which the plates were being rinsed but they generally contented themselves with licking their fingers between arranging the various foods on the dishes. No practice was too filthy if time could be saved, and food which fell on the floor was invariably wiped with a dishcloth and sent away damaged side downward and garnished with sprigs of parsley or frilly slices of lemon.

Anything left uneaten upon a customer's plate that could be reused was scraped off and thrown back into a saucepan to be served up again and once, for a bet of five hundred lire, one of the cooks urinated into a cauldron of vegetable soup which was served and sold without complaint, as he had known it would be, later in the evening.

The only completely clean food served at the O Sole Mio was that prepared before the eyes of the customers by Dru at the *batterie*—which was, doubtless, why the *padrone* and his guests always had the trolley wheeled to their table.

↩§ 4

GENNARO's pay as a *guattero* was nine thousand lire a week and, as Giona had informed him, he received two good meals a day. Signor Fonseca too, once he discovered that Gennaro was the sole support of a paralyzed grandfather, presented him from time to time with food to take home. The chef's idea of what a very old, very small, very ill man could eat was as outsize as his own vast body. Gennaro found himself carrying home three kilos of rump steak, two complete sets of veal kidneys or a whole sheep's liver. But if Quong, who had long existed upon thin vegetable soup and a little rice, could not benefit by Signor Fonseca's kindness, Iole and Crocifissa and Gigi could, and during the three weeks Gennaro worked in the O Sole Mio kitchen they were all fed to repletion on an un-Italian diet of every sort of meat.

Gennaro saw much less of the *padrone*, Signor Bighencomer, now that he worked in the kitchen, for the owner seldom appeared there until late at night and then only for the briefest of moments and a few quick words with the *capo*. On these occasions, following at his heels like a little grinning pug dog, he seemed invariably to trail the garbage contractor, Domenichelli; and for some reason Domenichelli's small, dark, restless eyes invariably searched out Gennaro among the steam and fumes and tumult. Gennaro asked Giona about him but Giona knew nothing. "He has a sort of business connection with the *padrone*, I think. He contracts for our garbage but I think he has other work as well. Anyway he is practically never about during the day. I wish I was a contractor—that's the thing to be! One takes percentages all the time. Think of living off percentages!" said Giona wonderingly as if percentages were some particularly exotic sort of food, still more desirable than his own diet of fried liver.

Domenichelli's garbage collection took place each night as soon as the restaurant was closed. He backed a three-wheeled "Ape" up to a concrete loading-ramp at the end of the main corridor and great burlap sacks of cabbage stalks, bones, chickens' heads and bread crusts were loaded onto it and driven away into the dark. "They get sold to pig farmers out beyond Bagnuoli," Giona explained knowledgeably.

Sometimes Domenichelli brought a man with him to carry the sacks from the kitchen but often he came alone and then a sulky *guattero* was ordered to stay behind and perform the work. Since this task was placed upon one of the last to leave the premises there was generally a hasty scramble in the changing-room as each scullery-hand tried hard to be away before his fellows.

On his third Saturday night in the kitchen Gennaro, struggling into his shirt, felt a hand on his shoulder and turned to see one of the assistant managers at his side. "You'd better take that off again. You're on the garbage job tonight."

Angrily Gennaro hung his shirt back on its hook. There had been three deaths in the San Lorenzo Quarter last night and he had been filled all day with the premonition that at least one of them would result in custom for Quong's. If so, Iole would have booked the details and be waiting up for him. Muttering crossly, shrugging his shoulders, he went back to the kitchen while his colleagues, tired and irritable after the long hours of work, set out for home.

It was surprising how quickly the working quarters emptied and how different they appeared when they had done so. Now the whole place, so strident and crowded all day, fell into a silent, ghostly repose. The lights were either out or dimmed, the passages silent save for the last hurrying echoes of departing waiters and cooks. Everywhere lay signs of violent movement suddenly, temporarily, suspended or abandoned: half a dozen unwashed plates lying beside a half-plucked chicken on a crate of empty wine bottles, a great pile of crumpled napkins at a passage corner and the flutter and rustle of torn paper caught in a draft from an open window; a couple of Mergellina cats prowling unmolested toward the larders and the sudden dark appearance of Maria, draped in her home-going widow's black, from the linen room. It was an exhausted, unnatural silence broken only by the spasmodic tap and click of a typewriter behind the glowing glass door of a managerial office, the whir of late cars along the Via Mergellina and, if one listened carefully, the soft ripple and slap of seawater against the wooden jetty.

When Gennaro arrived at the loading ramp with the first great sack of garbage on his shoulders the "Ape" was already in place and Domenichelli, with his jacket off and his amber cigarette holder cocked from one corner of his undershot mouth, was lowering the last of four large cardboard cartons on to the truck's floor. When he saw Gennaro he rose, dusting his hands. "Ah—my young friend from the kitchen. You've been sent to load the garbage? Good. You're a useful boy, Gennaro—always on hand when one needs a little help."

Gennaro was surprised and somehow a little uneasy that Domenichelli should have learned his name. He recalled the continual flickering gaze that invariably sought him out amongst the hurly-burly of the kitchen and somewhere in the back of his mind he had an odd idea that he had once seen Domenichelli before—long ago in some distant time.

"Yes, put the sacks on top of those boxes—gently though." Domenichelli, putting on his jacket, turned to Gennaro saying casually, "Tell me—before you came here what were you doing?"

"Carpenter's assistant."

"So? Making what?"

"Well"—Gennaro shrugged uneasily—"coffins, mostly."

"Working for an undertaker, perhaps?"

"My grandfather—yes."

Domenichelli nodded, grinning widely, but this time his heavy lids were lowered so that Gennaro did not see his eyes. "All right then. Get the sacks on board. I'm going up to the bar, if it's still open."

"It will be." Gennaro nodded affirmation. "They always stay open half an hour longer than the rest." He turned away wondering, not for the first time, what there was about the small garbage contractor that disturbed him. Domenichelli had always been friendly, always had a grin or a cheerful word to say if they met in the course of an evening—and yet Gennaro could not get it out of his head that there was something oddly repellent, a little frightening, about him. Probably it was due to a dream he had had a few nights back, a dream in which Domenichelli had somehow acquired—not exactly illegally but nevertheless by a subtle trick—the white jade horse. But the horse had been alive and in the dream Gennaro had known that he must get it back or else Domenichelli would kill it. A stupid sort of dream; but it had been an immense relief to wake in the dawn and see the horse still there, rearing up from its rosewood pedestal on the window-sill against the first cool light of day.

When he returned, panting a little, with the fifth sack of refuse he found the *padrone* himself standing by the loading ramp staring down at the "Ape." Gennaro lowered the sack to the ground and said deferentially, *"Buona sera, signore"* and the tall man with the cropped hair and the rimless pince-nez turned abruptly. "What's your name, boy?"

"Gualtierra, *signore*."

"How long have you been working here?"

"In the kitchen—three weeks."

"And have you loaded—" But Domenichelli's quick tread sounded suddenly on the stairs leading up to the ramp and Signor Bighencomer broke off. It was only then that Gennaro, noting the pale face and compressed lips, realized that he was in a deep, cold rage.

"Ah, Fer—Francesco! Having a little gossip with young Gennaro, is it?"

There was a touch of contemptuous banter in the tone which surprised Gennaro. After all, Domenichelli was only the garbage contractor, yet he spoke to the *padrone* as an equal. Signor Bighencomer took no notice of this at all. Instead he turned to Gennaro. "Take those sacks out."

"Out of the truck?"

"Of course, out of the truck!"

Shrugging, Gennaro obeyed and when he had done so Bighencomer stooped from the ramp and opened one and then another of the cardboard boxes. Bottles of wine gleamed darkly in the strong light, flasks of brandy, whisky, liqueurs. . . . "Garbage," he said dryly, lifting his face to Domenichelli. "You call this 'garbage,' do you?"

"*Dio!* Not I! I call it drink. But I didn't put it there, Francesco. It's no use blaming me."

"If you didn't—then who did?"

Domenichelli shrugged. His grin was fixed like a crooked bar across his face but his eyes, dark and filled with menace, were on the owner's. "Why don't you ask Gennaro? He's been loading the truck."

Gennaro stared at him with incredulity. "But—but these boxes were already there when I came! You told me to put the sacks on top of them!"

Domenichelli shook his head "What a little liar you are. Dio! Who'd have believed it? No, Francesco. I'm afraid that this boy has—"

"Don't be ridiculous!" Bighencomer's voice was cold and sharp as steel. "He had nothing to do with it. At least unless you made him put the stuff on board. No—this time you've—"

And then suddenly Domenichelli moved. He took four quick dancer's steps and was pressing close up to the bigger man as though he would embrace him. "You don't believe me, Ferenc? I think you'd better do so. . . . I said *I think you'd better do so!*"

Bighencomer took a step back. His mouth was a grim line under his long, clean-shaven upper lip. "We'll talk about this in my office."

"Certainly we will!"

"Come, then."

Domenichelli grinned triumphantly. "*Subito, signore!*" Then paused and cocked an eye at Gennaro, standing uncomprehendingly by, his empty hands at his sides. "What about the—the thief himself?"

"I'm not! I didn't—"

Bighencomer held up a hand with a quick, threatening demand for silence. "Gualtierra—I'm not going to press this affair as far as you're concerned. I imagine that you've had something to do with it, but— No! I don't want argument. I tell you I'm not going to press it."

"No," agreed Domenichelli gratuitiously, "I shouldn't press it."

With an effort Bighencomer disregarded him. "But I won't need you here anymore after this evening. You've been paid for this week?"

"Yes, but—"

The owner took out his wallet. "Nine thousand, isn't it?"

"Yes. Listen, Signor Bighencomer. I don't understand why you—"

"*Basta!* Here is eighteen thousand. One week's pay in lieu of notice and a further week's because—because I think you have been led into this affair without entirely understanding what you were conniving at."

Gennaro, finding the notes thrust into his hand, took them in a daze. He shook his head, his shoulders hunched. "*Signori*"— he turned from the pale Bighencomer to the grinning Domenichelli—"I don't understand! I haven't done anything, and—"

"And no one's going to do anything to you. Take your money. Go and get your clothes. And then go home. I don't want you here any longer."

"Go back to your coffins, Gennaro," added Domenichelli genially and Bighencomer suddenly jerked around as if he had been sharply struck. He stared down at Domenichelli, his pale eyes wide behind the pince-nez.

"Is this . . . Is this the . . ."

Domenichelli grinned back blandly. "Yes, it is."

"You—*you mad fool!*" The owner swung back to Gennaro and his voice was no longer coldly matter-of-fact but harsh and frightening. "Gualtierra, you've been involved in robbing this restaurant of valuable stock. You were found by me placing sacks of garbage over cases of spirits in order to disguise them and smuggle them out of the premises. If I liked to call in the police you'd be in serious trouble. I've said I'm not going to do that, and I won't. But remember that I *could!* Now get out of here and stay right away in future— Quick!"

For a moment Gennaro thought of holding his ground and protesting his innocence—but only for a moment. There was too much he did not understand and the expression on the owner's face made it obvious that he was not going to be enlightened. Also it was now clear that if the police were to be called in, both the owner and his domineering garbage contractor would be giving evidence on the same side. So strong was the atmosphere of menace in this deserted underground loading dock that Gennaro began to believe that he really had been involved, unwittingly but criminally, in theft. It had not been his fault—but would that matter? Would the police see it that way? He looked down. He had eighteen thousand lire in his hand and another nine thousand in his hip pocket, and at home there might be an order for a funeral. Home—Iole waiting up for him. Quong—his own place. At the thought of home he forgot everything but his desire to be there. Casting one frightened look from the grim-faced Bighencomer to the grinning Domenichelli he nodded a quick assent and turning, ran back down the passage to retrieve his shirt and to be away and out into the warm, free night as soon as possible.

✑§ 5

ONCE upstairs in his office Bighencomer shut the door and striding over to a cupboard, poured himself a drink. Without turning around he said, "You've learned nothing, Duilio —nothing at all. You tried to cheat me at least once before— and you're still trying, it seems."

"No, no. Just keeping my hand in."

"Do you expect me to go on helping you, in the circumstances?"

"Yes, Ferenc—I do."

Bighencomer drew a deep breath and let it out again. "There's a point beyond which even I—"

"Perhaps there is. But we haven't reached it yet."

"You'd better be very certain."

"I am. What is sixty thousand lire's worth of spirits to you, in any case?"

"Enough! And why didn't you, for God's sake, ask me for the money instead of—"

"Because you probably wouldn't have given it to me. You are mean with money, Ferenc. You always have been."

"And that boy! You knew he was the one you told me about and you never said anything!"

"Why should I? He never even saw me. He has no more idea of what happened than you had until I told you."

"How can you tell? How can you ever be sure? Supposing a dog or something—some accident—finds that body. They'll trace the affair straight back to him. They'll check the dates. They'll immediately suspect something and they'll question him. They'll show him your photograph and then—then they'll come straight around here. Don't you ever *think*, Duilio?"

"We were always told to leave the thinking to you—remember?"

Bighencomer swung around so abruptly that the drink slopped from his glass. "Very well. Then leave me to do the thinking now."

"So long as it doesn't get me where it did last time. But it won't. I'm taking good care of that."

Bighencomer took no notice. "Well, anyway you can't stay here—not any longer. Not after tonight. If that boy's parents like to make trouble and—"

"He hasn't got any. Only an old grandfather."

"*Will* you listen to me! I'm not having you around here any longer. It's not safe. Until I can fix your journey to America you'll have to stay away from this place."

"I'll need money."

"I'll give you what's necessary. For God's sake, Duilio, just lay up somewhere and keep quiet." Bighencomer's voice seemed, for the first time that evening, to hold a note of despair—almost of panic. "I'm doing everything I can to get you away, but—"

"But you do wish so much that the blowtorch had been alight when I went headfirst into the prison incinerator—don't you?"

"By God I do—yes!" For a moment—a fleeting second —some small spark of mutual understanding flickered between them and they laughed. Then Domenichelli's face darkened abruptly.

"Well, it wasn't. It wasn't, see, Ferenc? So we'll just go on from where we are now—understand?"

The Red Room

GALO lay in the pup-tent he shared with Pavan, staring up at the spots of gleaming light where the sun shone through the lace holes along the ridgepole. The ridgepole was an ash sapling which he and Panan, in common with the rest of their classmates, had cut—strictly against orders—on the first day of the camp. But the yearly pleas of the Forestry Department were invariably disregarded and wood was cut and fires were lit when and where the cadets felt inclined. And anyway, it was only the officer instructors who got into trouble, as Lieutenant Tollis, fat and friendly and perspiring freely in the thin mountain air, complained. "It's all very well you boys hacking down young trees—but it's *I* who get the telling-off afterward from the Commandant when the Forestry people complain. You don't want that, do you?"

"Yes!" the cadets had sung out happily and Tollis's face had flushed a deeper red and his grin had gone lopsided and weak. "I know you don't mean that." But he had an uncomfortable feeling that they did—and he was right.

"Tollis!" Pavan had complained to Galo when they had found that their officer at this year's camp was to be the mathematics instructor. "Why have we got to have *that* creature? Everyone knows he wanted to be a priest, really."

"Why didn't he, then?"

"In the end he found he hadn't got a vocation—so he joined the army instead."

"Well, at least we can do as we like. You wouldn't want Berluti or Lorenzini or one of the other drill men, would you?"

"Tollis is a virgin," had said Pavan damningly if inconsequentially.

"How do you know?"

"Well—it's obvious."

"You can't tell."

"Anyway he's from Piedmont—a northerner. Not one of us."

The dubious sexual potency of Lieutenant Tollis became a subject of ribald controversy. Various efforts were made to find out more about it. One day the cadets discovered a mountain pool and stripping off their light summer uniforms leapt into it and splashed about shouting for their officer to join them. But Tollis only sat grinning on a rock and shook his head. "Just like your great-grandfather," Pavan said to Galo. "No balls. Poor man! But still, they shouldn't send him to us as an instructor —it's an insult."

"Or the reason they sent him," suggested Lecco significantly. "There was once a captain called Vedanias—a Sardinian. It was before your time and—"

"We all know about that."

"Then don't complain about Tollis. You can't have it both ways."

"*Dio!* I only want it *one* way."

During their route marches, which were more in the nature of hikes than military exercises, the cadets sang the lewd old song about the unnatural goings-on at various imaginary taverns:

"All' osteria numero mille
Il mio cazzo fa scintille
Fa scintille, scintelline
Per le belle signorine!"

And, since the mathematics instructor was alleged to be religious:

"All' osteria del Vaticano
E successo un fatto strano.
Due guardie Papalini
S'inculavano i gallini!"

The lieutenant's uncertain grin faded and he scowled. "That's enough of—"

But Pavan and Galo took up the next verse, their voices high, jeering and jaunty:

> *"Al cancello d'un cimitero*
> *E successo un fatto vero.*
> *Due morti putrefatti*
> *S'inculavano come matti!"*

"Halt!" shouted Tollis, his voice breaking with rage. "You two—yes, and you, Lecco, you're supposed to be a senior and responsible—fall out and come here!"

Reluctantly, yet suppressing their laughter with difficulty, the three boys broke ranks and approached their furious instructor. "How dare you! How dare you disobey me when I give you an order and—"

"*Scusi, Signor Tenente,*" said Lecco, his eyebrows raised. "But I didn't hear any order. Otherwise, of course I would have—"

"I said 'That's enough,' didn't I?"

"But I didn't understand. Enough of what? It didn't sound like an order to me."

"Or me," added Pavan.

Tollis swallowed with difficulty. He was never able to adopt the proper ruthlessness which he knew to be the only way of dealing with the cadets during their occasional, inevitable lapses into childish, arrogant perversity. "You know perfectly well what I meant—all of you! Enough of that filth!"

"That song?"

"Of course, that song!"

"But all the troops sing it. It's an ordinary soldier's song."

"That's as may be. But you're not soldiers yet. You're just dirty-minded little boys *playing* at soldiers!"

"*I'm* a soldier," said Lecco sulkily, touching the silver stars on his collar.

"*You'll* be in the guard tent if I have another word out of you! And you two others—you're both Neapolitans, aren't you? I thought as much! You shouldn't even know that song. You're—you're just *bambini!* Just you wait till you get to Modena—that's all!"

"My uncle sings that song all the time," said Galo suddenly. "He taught it to me before I was seven years old."

Tollis stared. "Your uncle—Major Colavolpe?"

"*Si, signore.* And I know a lot more verses, too. There is the one about the Russian women soldiers and the Polar bears; and what happened to the German general who had his orderly model him a full-scale woman out of snow. And—"

"*Basta!*" Tollis's voice broke against a roar of laughter from the halted cadets. "That's quite enough! What you do at home is your own affair, but what you do while I'm in charge is mine. And I'm not having you polluting the mountain air just so that you can show off your scatological mentality to your comrades! All right—fall in! And try to behave a little more like adults in future!"

Everyone agreed that Galo had won on points. "Tollis is a wretched creature," Pavan had said disgustedly. "He ought to be in the Boy Scouts, not the army."

"He's not good enough even for them!"

"I'd like to lock him in a brothel with twenty huge prostitutes all armed with rubber hoses, and then— No, I wouldn't. I'd like to take him to the Galleria and—"

"The trouble is," Galo had said gloomily, "that I'm going to get really terrible class marks next year."

But now, lying on his back and staring up at the ten lace holes in the sloping roof of the pup-tent, Galo wondered uneasily if there would be a next year for him. After that talk in De Santis's study he was certain that his family planned to hand him over— presumably to sell him—to the old man. He wondered distractedly why De Santis wanted him. It was true that you could always buy a baby or a small child in Naples; in fact there were always far more on the market than could ever find buyers. But who would ever want to buy a fifteen-and-a-half-year-old—and a Nunziatella cadet, at that? There was rumored to be a dark and silent trade in adolescents of both sexes who were taken, half-drugged, from the depths of the *bassi* and shipped rapidly to Egypt or the Levant. He shuddered. Could De Santis be some sort of kidnapper? But no—surely he could not be. And anyway, to abduct someone of his age from the military academy was unthinkable. De Santis would never risk the scandal and disgrace, let alone the huge prison sentence, merely for financial profit. Yet De Santis's own explanation, which seemed to indicate a sort of adoption in place of the son he had not got, was something which Galo dismissed almost immediately from his mind. For who, in his right senses, would adopt a Colavolpe? Did not De Santis know—had he not found out about—about those members of the family who were in the "hospital"? Even in the heat of the small pup-tent Galo felt himself shiver coldly. Maria Fausta had recently been two years in the "hospital" and might go in again any day by the look of things. And how could he himself know that one day that black shadow might not wrap its stifling folds around his own head . . . That, in a way, was one reason he wanted so badly to stay in the army. The continual company of ordinary cheerful people carrying out routine communal tasks—everything plain, clear, laid-down, completely comprehensible—was the best antidote he knew for the gloomy melancholy which so often fell upon him at home and which he fearfully guessed hinted at something worse to come.

But De Santis wanted to take him away and send him to a strange land to study, in a foreign language, subjects of which he had never even heard and whose names meant nothing to him. To take him away from his friends Lecco and Pavan and Ricci and Corrodino, with whom he had expected to go on to the senior academy at Modena. . . .

Well, he would not allow it. Whatever happened back at the *palazzo*—whatever "they" did—he wouldn't go. He would burn all those new clothes they had given him; he would write to De Santis explaining all about those members of the family in the "hospital" and why they were there. But of course that wouldn't stop "them" from taking him away from the Nunziatella. Nothing he could do would prevent that. And they'd do it, he knew. If he wouldn't fall in with their plans they'd bring him home merely for spite and in order to work the vegetable patch. He could not prevent them—he was still too young.

Then—what about the will? Old Ercole's will? His brows drew together in sudden thought. Perhaps he could use his still secret inheritance as a bargaining counter. Ercole's estate against a promise of noninterference with his military career. It was certainly a possibility, but the trouble was that he couldn't trust "them." The old man's voice rang once more in his ears: *"If you let this get into the hands of your mother or your precious uncle or any of your other relatives at Caserta . . .*" "They" might even seize everything and still hand him over to De Santis—he could even see that, in the circumstances, it would be very convenient for them to do so.

Of course if only the ancient ghoul in the top of the *palazzo* would die things would be made easier almost at once. The house would be his in less than three years and he could use that as a bribe—or better, as a threat. He had always intended to turn "them" out into the road that edged the estate on the morning of his eighteenth birthday. The details of the eviction had been planned for years and it was a painful effort to think of giving them up now. . . . The early-morning walk to the Carabinieri station at Caserta, the careful explanations, the return with a squad of policemen (somehow he was always commanding them and wearing the uniform of a lieutenant), the rushing from room to room pulling Concezio, Speranza, the three Marias and Filippa out of their beds and bundling them, just as they were, out of the *palazzo,* out of the grounds, and slamming the great iron gates in their faces. Then back to a curiously silent house with all the danger, all the fear and horror gone for good. . . .

Yes, but the thing in the top of the house might not die; why should it when it had lived so long already that it appeared quite beyond the natural law of human mortality? In which case . . . He shook his head wearily over the complexity of his future possessions, the things that were his and yet still out of his hands, which he needed and wanted yet knew not how to grasp. His inheritance—Ercole had estimated it to be worth, all told, about one hundred and fifty million . . . His *palazzo* . . . His title . . . His army career. . . . Somehow they all had to be balanced and chosen and worked out and he was old enough to realize, almost too clearly, that mistakes made by him, or forced upon him, now would be bitterly regretted for years afterwards. And he must manage the business himself. It never occurred to him that there were many people who could, and certainly would, have helped him—from Lieutenant Tollis to the Commandant himself. And he was not to blame for this since in his experience all adults were tricky, in league one with another and each concerned solely with attaining his own ends.

He sighed again and rubbed his eyes, turning his head im-

patiently to avoid the tiny piercing shafts of sunlight from the
lace holes. It was very hot in the pup-tent. Soon he slept.

⋖§ 2

WHEN he awoke it was to find Pavan kneeling at
the entrance, struggling out of his sticky shirt. "Berluti's come
up. He's taken over from Tollis, who goes on leave this afternoon. Tollis gave us a very bad report and Berluti has told
Lecco that if there is any further indiscipline he'll give us two
hours' drill in full equipment every morning for the rest of our
time here." Pavan bundled up his shirt, threw it onto his blankets
and crawled into the pup-tent wearing only his khaki shorts. "I'm
not staying here if it's going to be like that!" His voice was dis-
gusted. "I'll tell Berluti that my family has changed its holiday
plans and that I've got to leave early."

"Will he let you go?"

"He can't keep me. This camp is supposed to be voluntary,
isn't it? Why should we volunteer to be pushed around by a great
ox like Berluti?"

Galo stretched and yawned. He had been dreaming about
the De Santis swimming pool and that morning two weeks ago
when he and Toni . . . He smiled sleepily at Pavan with a mild
amusement. His friend's presence, which was generally an acute
irritation to other people, had a calming effect upon him. He
remembered that Pavan had told Lecco and himself—had,
indeed, told everybody who would listen—of a peculiar affair
between himself and a swimming instructress last summer.
"Will you tell Berluti that you've got to take some more swimming lessons at Positano, Paolo?"

Pavan giggled. It was the first time that Galo had ever called
him by his Christian name and he glanced across at him with a
glint of surprise. "Oh *Gesù!* That would be a good line to take,
wouldn't it? *She* might be there—the *Svedesa* who taught us last
year. *Santo Gesù!*"

"Tell me about it—I mean last year."

Pavan giggled again and rolled over on his blankets. "I told
you—the same time I told Lecco. I can't go on telling it." He

lifted a hand, staring at the spots of sunlight which patterned it through the lace holes above. "She was huge. She smelled of salt and seaweed like—like a mermaid. It was evening and we were in her room alone. She made me feel all her muscles. 'You could have muscles like these, Pavan,' she said—she always called us by our surnames unless our parents were around. 'If only you weren't so lazy and did the exercises I've shown you all, you'd have muscles like these. All you Italians are lazy. If it wasn't for me you'd sunbathe all day and only go into the water to cool off.' That was right enough, too!"

"Yes, yes—but what about—"

"I'm *telling* you, aren't I? So then she started to show me jujitsu or yoga or something like that—I don't know. I had to hold her left wrist and try to pull her over and then suddenly I was upside down and she was holding my feet in the air. Then I had to run at her and try to kick her in the stomach. . . ."

"But—"

"Well, after a bit we ended up on the bed—with me underneath. So she started to feel *my* muscles. 'Not much there, Pavan,' she said. 'Let's see what else you've got. Lift up!' And she undid my belt and pulled my pants down and started to kiss me all over the stomach. She had a great, wet, sticky mouth and after a bit she started *chewing* me."

"*Gesù!*—Why?"

"She knew why all right!" Pavan gave a half-hysterical giggle. "Then she said, 'That's not too bad, Pavan—considering your age. *Va bene,* we're ready to start now. Change places—quick!' So"—Pavan's voice had an odd breathless quality—"so we did. And everything went off fine."

"*Vero?* It was your first time?"

"It was my first time. And it went off fine. Of course she knew how to make it. *Dio!*" Pavan shuddered. "I can still feel her fingers between my legs! Anyway"—his voice returned to its normal tone—"she was very pleased, very complimentary—for the first time, I may say. 'Pavan,' she said, 'you're a rotten swimmer and you're a lazy little beast and as cheeky as they come. And I'll tell you that until today nothing would have given me greater pleasure than to see someone lay into you with a dog-whip.' '*Grazie, signorina!*' I said—I'd got up off her by this time and was standing by the bed cleaning the lipstick off my stomach with her eau-de-cologne. '*Grazie assai!*' 'But with this,' she said, putting out a hand and lifting it up, 'you're definitely going to be good. It's going to give a lot of girls a lot of fun—this little devil.' "

"She did?" Galo glanced at his friend admiringly.

"She did," echoed Pavan, then added more modestly, "Still, she had every other boy in the class as well and she probably said much the same to them for all I know. Anyway, later on she found herself a Carabiniere officer—a swimming champion coaching an army team—and lost interest in us."

"And—since then?"

"*Niente!* Nothing. Not once! Ah, how I want to do it again! But there's never been an opportunity. Not for us. Can you imagine me going to the Commandant and clicking my heels and saying '*Signor Colonello, permesso!* I need a woman'? He's a Piedmontese, like Tollis. They don't understand us. He'd just say I was a dirty-minded Neapolitan and hand me over to this great ox-face Berluti for a lot of extra drill or something. They don't *understand* us!" Glancing across at him Galo saw his face was flushed, his eyes bright with frustrated tears. After a little he said sulkily, "You shouldn't make me tell it; it only makes it worse for me."

At mail call that evening Galo was given a letter with a Naples postmark and sealed, for no very comprehensible reason, with a large amount of emerald green sealing wax. He sat between two gray boulders under the fretted shade of a mountain ash and opened it.

CARISSIMO GALO:

How are you, and are you having a nice time? I saw a picture of your camp in the paper yesterday, with quite a lot of boys and a rather fat officer, only I couldn't see you—at least I don't think so. There was one who might have been you but it was too blurry to be certain. It is very hot down here and I wish I was in the mountains, too. Last year we had a fortnight at Scanno and it was very nice except that you can't swim in the lake because it is dangerous. But this year we've got to stay at home because of the inheritance. I don't think we will have a holiday until the autumn and then we will probably go to England. Well, I painted the fish shop in the Vanvitelli. I took my stool and easel and asked the roadmen if I could sit near their hole and they said yes, certainly I could, and it took three days though I only worked in the mornings. I think it is very good and the grit that blew onto it from the hole gives the surface an attractive patina—at least I think so though Nicola doesn't like it at all. All the workmen kept stopping work to get out of the hole and see how I was progressing and in the end the foreman told me that because of my picture the hole—or whatever was in it that was being done—would take an extra day to complete. I told him I was sorry, but that was a price the world owed to Art.

Nicola has done his cocks again. This time the fight is over and one of them is dead (in a *very* symmetrical pool of blood) and the other is crowing and waving its wings. I tell him that it is not Art but he still says that if it is good enough for the Toledo it *must* be.

The porter's cat has had its kittens—one ginger, two brindle and one black-and-white. I am trying to find homes for them or else they will be drowned. Would any of your friends like one? How about the fat officer? He looked the sort of man who is kind to cats. The black-and-white one is reserved for Nicola.

Are you coming back to Caserta before you go down to the Sila? If you are, do try to come to lunch or supper here. We can either have it at home or go round to Nicola—just as you like. I do miss you, my pet, and think of you daily—sometimes hourly. Come, therefore, and gladden the empty heart of

your MINA

P.S. You could then see the kittens.

P.P.S. I have been given a gold signet ring—the first fruits of the inheritance—and now I seal all my letters with it. You will see the seal on this one. I hope you will approve.

Within five minutes of reading this letter Galo had determined to emulate Pavan's experience of twelve months before—but with Mina in place of the Swedish swimming instructress. He wondered why he had not thought of it before. He and Pavan were almost precisely the same age, which meant that Pavan had had his first woman at slightly more than fourteen and a half—and a year had passed since then. And if it was so pleasant with a great cow of a Swede, how incomparably delightful it must be with someone of one's own age with whom one was—in love. Was he in love with Mina? He did not really know, but he had often thought he was, certainly. She was not just a friend—his feelings for her had nothing in common with those he had for

Pavan or Lecco. He had often thought of marrying her and had once designed a house for them both on the back of his musketry manual.

But anyway love had nothing to do with it; it would be just enjoyment for both of them—as much for her as for him and perhaps even more. What had the Swede said to Pavan, *'It's going to give a lot of girls a lot of fun—this little devil.'* Would she have said the same about him? Probably—just as she probably had with all the other boys in her swimming class. Anyway he knew that he was not like his great-grandfather and he could burn a candle to the Holy Tooth and pray for its benevolent assistance.

Reassured, he buttoned the letter into his shirt pocket and rose. He must write to Mina and suggest, not that he go to Vomero, but that she come to Caserta. Now that he knew what he wanted to do he found himself planning with astonishing speed and completeness. He was to spend one night at home before going down to the dilapidated Calabrian farmhouse. The *palazzo* would be empty save for the ancient creature in the top story and the ever-attendant Maria Valeria. Yet even so the *palazzo* was not where—where he wanted it to happen. He loathed the *palazzo* and everything to do with it. But half a kilometer away and set in the middle of a small pine copse was the Dorrucci villa and at this time of the year old Signor Dorrucci was invariably at Aix-en-Provence where he went every year to visit his daughter and son-in-law. The villa would be shuttered and empty, but though Galo had never been inside he had long since abstracted the key to a door of the walled garden and often prowled around the grounds during the owner's frequent absences. He had caught—and later cooked and eaten—three big goldfish from the ornamental pool and had once stolen an umbrella from the porch and sold it in Caserta for five hundred lire. And for years he had unsuccessfully tried to snare the tame wild ducks which Signor Dorrucci kept in a small, fenced-off lake and which, dressed in full hunting paraphernalia, he massacred meticulously once or twice a year at point-blank range with an automatic shotgun.

Hands in pockets, Galo strolled slowly back to the camp and after supper he borrowed a sheet of paper and an envelope from Lecco and, sitting under a hissing kerosene lamp in the communal mess tent, composed an urgent yet guarded letter to Mina.

The camp lasted a week longer in a state of simmering but suppressed indignation. Lieutenant Berluti had as much contempt for Lieutenant Tollis as most of the cadets but he understood well enough that, whatever their personal likes or dislikes, the officers must stand together in the matter of discipline. Berluti was young and only three years out of Modena where he had been cadet captain; he was not fatherly nor amiable and stood no nonsense from anyone. "This," he said ominously on his first day, "is supposed to be a military camp—not a Boy Scouts' jamboree." And he had proceeded to make it so. All the tents had been rigidly realigned, the firebreaks redug and widened, the refuse pits deepened. The route marches had ceased to be hikes and become military endurance tests undertaken in full equipment and steel helmets, while the guard had turned out at the double with white gloves and polished boots.

Lecco and three senior cadets, pushed on by the rest, had complained. After all, the camp was a traditionally easygoing affair, more holiday than work. "The camp," Berluti had snapped, "is what the officer in charge makes it!"

"But it's voluntary, after all, Signor Tenente," Lecco had reminded him politely. "And if we can't enjoy ourselves I don't suppose we'd want to come again. Next year—"

"Next year," Berluti had interrupted, "you'll be going to Modena, Lecco."

He had smiled thinly. "And then you'll find out what military discipline really is. If you think I'm hard on you here—well, I assure you that you have a very unpleasant surprise awaiting you in the future!"

"I don't know," said Pavan that afternoon as he buckled on his equipment for a last twelve-kilometer route march, "why I ever thought of joining the army. It would have been easier to become a priest. One has a good time in this world and a better one in the next."

"No women, though," said Galo.

"Oh no? Priests have plenty of women all right—at least the ones who prefer them to boys."

"Let this," said Lecco, who with the peculiarly cynical changeability of adolescence, had swung over to side with Berluti against his fellow cadets, "be a lesson to you not to torment Tollis."

❧ 3

NEXT day they broke up and Galo went back to Caserta. He arrived at three in the afternoon, trudging up the dusty, poplar-lined side road from the bus-stop, wrinkling his eyes behind his big dark sunglasses. The *palazzo* lay dozing in a sleepy dream of pink and white rococo ornamentations among its straggling oleanders and spire-pointed cypresses in the heat-still silence of midafternoon. Somewhere beside the immurement wall behind the vestry of the Church of the Holy Tooth a cicada charged the tinder-dry air with its high-tension electric drone.

Galo went up to his room, threw his equipment into the cupboard among the old newspapers and lay down on his bed. But he did not sleep. He had received no answer to his letter though this did not perturb him since the dispatch and delivery of mail at the mountain camp was an uncertain and eccentric process at best. This evening at seven Mina would be descending at the same bus-stop at which he had so recently alighted. He had asked her to bring some supper so that they could eat outside —it looked more normal—and in any case he could not ask Maria Valeria for food to take out, even supposing that there was anything in the house which was improbable.

Mina, in less than four hours—in hardly more than three. What would she say? Would she agree? How would he explain? He swallowed dryly, filled for the first time with misgiving. Supposing she did not want to? But why should she not want to? Toni De Santis had wanted to—badly; he realized that now. If only De Santis himself had not captured him and taken him to his study that evening he would have gone to the pool. . . . Toni's naked body, warm in the cool water against his own, and then out on the soft grass under the great golden moon. . . . He gave a shuddering sigh, feeling the sweat dripping from his hot face, and rubbed an unwashed hand across his tired eyes.

At half past five he rose and dressed in his "home" clothes, his overtight shorts and Concezio's old shirt: he must not give Maria Valeria the impression that there was anything unusual afoot, that he was going out. But first the church. . . .

Inside the Church of the Holy Tooth it was already dusky and smelled of old incense and mice and decaying plaster and fowls. A chicken crooned to itself from the vestry and the evening sun fell through a stained-glass window above the altar, luridly lighting the purgatorial flames in which souls struggled lamentably upward toward a pitying but placid Madonna. Galo went quickly, carefully around the Stations of the Cross, his bare feet moving soundlessly over the colored tiles, crossing himself, genuflecting and clicking off the beads of his rosary as he prayed, fast, fervently and with great sincerity. At the statue of the Virgin in the west corner he knelt with arms stretched wide. "*Ava Maria piena di grazia. Il signore è teco e benedetto è il frutto del ventre tuo, Gesù. . . .*" Then he rose, crossed himself thrice, kissing his thumb between each completed sign—and reverently, humbly, approached the Holy Tooth.

The Roman Catholic faith, at least in southern Italy, has many obvious advantages over the heresies practiced by other Christian sects. Among these can be counted its extreme attraction for the young. It goes out of its vulgar, stately way to make things pleasant for them with a kaleidoscopic mixture of drama and ritual and colored patterns of interwoven superstitions healthily satisfying to the juvenile hunger for the magical and the miraculous. God—insofar as He comes into the picture at all—is much more closely akin to the smiling, tolerant, obese Buddha of Asia than to the stern, bigoted and boring deity of the various Anglo-Saxon and Scandinavian churches. And this Italian God and His family and His host of saints and martyrs and dependents are perpetually doing things—granting wishes, curing incurable afflictions, making dramatic personal appearances in visions and, of course, holding a crowded, yearlong succession of open birthday parties invariably terminated with firework displays.

Galo, though he had not received the religious upbringing of Gennaro among the Ferrara monks, was equally devout. He had known several experiences of a supernatural and beneficent nature, generally culminating in unexpected gifts of food, and he had a talent for extempore prayer. For many years indeed, attracted by the hellish gleam of sunlight through the altar window, he had prayed fervently for the fiery damnation of his mother and his uncle until the practice had been discovered and stopped by a scandalized parish priest. Galo had repented obediently and supplicated forgiveness, yet he often felt that his early prayers, even if theoretically improper, must at least have drawn attention to the behavior of Speranza and Concezio—in which case, presumably, nothing further need be done.

But the Tooth was something else again. Though of course extremely holy, it was fraught by now with the full significance of the most potent pagan fertility symbol, inspiring the same feelings of awe, fear, excitement and abasement as those darker bestowers or withholders of procreated human life. The Tooth was very strong magic indeed.

Galo approached the altar slowly, inching forward on his bare knees, praying fervently, rapidly: *"Santo Dento! Santo Dento! Santo Dento! Aiutemi stasera e per sempre! Anima di fiamma! Espressione dell'eternità! Benedemi e aiutemi!"* For a long moment he knelt rigidly upright, his hands crossed against his chest, his eyes wide, slightly glazed, staring fixedly at the blackened little object in the reliquary. Then, leaning forward he took it, holding it with immense care, kissed the glass panel three times, opened his shirt and held it to his heart, unbuttoned his shorts and held it to his genitals and at last, with a long, shuddering sigh, replaced it upon the altar.

Only then, trembling and exhausted with the nervous strain of his invocation, did he rise to his feet, extract the promised candle from the torn pocket of his shirt and spike and light it upon the metal plate before the altar. He turned once at the door of the church, glancing up the short aisle to where the pointed flame lifted its golden flower in the dusk and gleamed upon the glass of the reliquary. And he smiled suddenly, widely back at the Tooth—his silent forebear—knowing now that everything was going to be all right.

~§ 4

MARIA Valeria gave him his supper, a wide, thick slice of *comune* bread with two spoonfuls of olive oil poured onto it. She was a gaunt, silent woman who, unbeknown to the others, had fought a long terrifying inward battle against insanity and had eventually won it at the cost of a largely atrophied mind. Like her two sisters she was very religious and served the ancient nonagenarian upstairs as a satisfying earthly mortification for which she confidently expected a heavenly crown of considerably more splendor than would be bestowed upon the majority of her contemporaries.

Galo slowly climbed to his room eating his bread and, as soon as it was finished, he changed rapidly into his new blue jeans and a striped T-shirt, took his shoes in his hand and slipped quickly down the back stairs and out of the house.

Ten minutes later the bus rolled to a halt beside the lamppost at the end of the lane and Galo's heart jolted with delight as Mina descended into the soft, warm dusk of the country evening. Their last parting had been in a dramatically public embrace before the brightly lit entrance to the *Funicular Centrale* on Vomero and now they both felt that this reunion should be marked in the same way. And yet so much more acute had the intervening time rendered their feelings for each other that somehow this was now impossible. Instead they stood together as the bus rolled away into the early summer night, drinking in each other's presence with their eyes, saying only "Mina!" and "Galo!"

And when they spoke after that first greeting it was with an odd, shy restraint as if both were laboring under some heavy, secret, bad news which must sooner or later be broken but which for the present necessitated an awkward guard on the tongue. Walking together along the soft dust of the lane which branched off to the Dorrucci villa, asking the conventional questions about Beppo, Nicola, the porter's kittens, Galo had a growing conviction that Mina knew why she was here, what this evening portended for them both. This belief was at once a source of exultation and doubt and, surprisingly, of extreme unease. Now that Mina was here in the flesh at his side he was no longer certain that he wanted her. Their earlier relationship, easy, amused, fondly appreciative with its shared allusions and small, important interests and discoveries, was changing with every step along this dark lane. If it had been Toni De Santis beside him in the dusk this would not have been the case and would not have mattered—because she did not matter. But with Mina . . . He shook his head impatiently. He loved Mina—not Toni—and this, or so he had always understood, was something which, ideally, you did with someone you loved.

". . . so I said I might be late back and not to wait up. Of course he *might* phone Nicola, but I don't think so because he might get the Maresciallo instead and he doesn't like that, he finds it embarrassing, I think. Where are we going?"

"To—to a place I know." Galo's voice was a little breathless as if he was carrying something much heavier than Mina's picnic basket. "There's an old villa near here and the owner is away. But he's got a proper garden—all terraces and roses and fountains. I thought we'd have supper there."

"It sounds nice." But Mina's voice held a dubiety which belied her words. "Galo, you do think of odd things. Is it much farther?"

"No, we're nearly there. Look, you can see the pine trees."

The night pressed down hot and black and very still, a sultry, breathless night with a hint of thunder. Galo and Mina, small furtive figures in their dark, close-fitting jeans, slid along a high old garden wall and soon came to a wrought-iron gate, heavy, ornate and guarded by thick ilexes. "This is it." Despite his knowledge of the house's desertion Galo found himself whispering. He took a heavy key from his hip pocket and thrust it into the lock. But he had not entered this way for more than a year and the villa's owner invariably used the great double gates which opened upon the carriage drive. Tonight the wards of the lock, jammed with rust and time, would not yield. Galo twisted the key this way and that with all his might and paused, panting. Again. Still the stiff lock would not budge. And now a fierce pang of furious disappointment stabbed through him. All his doubts, all his hesitations were swept away in the knowledge that he had come here with a girl of his own for one purpose and that purpose, whatever he might have thought just now in the lane, held firm and hard and cold and resolute—not to be balked. With jaws clenched and tears of frustration already pricking behind his eyelids Galo threw his whole weight on the key, exerting a frantic, desperate strength born of despair. And then with a grating rasp the heavy wedges inched back into their sockets and he was leaning against the wall, heart pounding, sweat popping all over him, but with the gate open. And now everything seemed resolved and simple and easy. The Dorrucci garden was beautiful with that tamed but extravagant splendor which only money and patience, a disregard for nature and a

team of skilled gardeners can among them achieve. Even in this
dark night lit only by the stars its beauty was apparent in the
fine gravel of the walks, the velvet of the small lawns decorated
with statues, urns and fountains, the pergolas and terraces and
parterres—above all the heavy scent of roses and tuberoses and
flowering shrubs.

Near the dark and silent house, at a stone table under a bower
of vines, they lit two candles and unpacked the picnic basket. At
their feet goldfish a foot long gleamed in a great marble basin
and came, gasping and interested, to the surface to goggle at the
candle flames. Galo, with a sudden return to the boyhood he was
so rapidly leaving behind him, suggested catching two and cooking them but Mina vetoed the idea immediately. They were far
too pretty and tame for such a sordid end—and anyway a fire
would be a messy business in this immaculate garden and might
lead to discovery. Galo, a little ashamed of his naïveté, assented
at once and together, with glasses of brandy from the small flask
Mina had included in her basket, they sat on the marble edge of
the basin and soon made the delightful discovery that the goldfish would take bits of bread from their fingers.

And it was now, sitting on the basin edge and in some danger
of falling into the pool, that they put down their glasses and suddenly, mutually, kissed for the first time as lovers, their mouths,
soft and warm with brandy, pressed exultantly together, their
arms about each other's bodies. Holding her triumphantly, Galo
unbuttoned Mina's pale blue shirt to the waist and stroked her
small, firm, pointed breasts. *"Carissima Mina! Tu sai bella—
bella! Io te voglio."* But he would not look up at her, waiting
—half hoping, half doubting—that she had misunderstood him.
Stealthily he dropped a hand to the belt of her jeans but she
caught it in her own, pulled it up and kissed the palm lightly.

"Not now. *Basta cosi. Oh, Dio!* We haven't eaten yet, even!"
And as Galo looked up a little sulkily she brushed aside the curtain of hair that had fallen across his forehead, and shivering
with excited laughter, caught him by both ears and kissed him
on the bridge of his nose. "That's how the old Romans kissed
their children— Did you know that? They always held them
steady by the ears first."

"How do you know?"

"Nicola told me."

"How does *he* know?"

"Oh, he read it I expect. He reads a lot—*poveretto!*"

"Mina—when we've eaten—"

"Yes, yes—I expect so."

"You *knew,* then. You—"

"I guessed. Have some ham. Or there's fish paste in these. I don't know whether it's very *nice* fish paste. I got it at STANDA yesterday. It just said 'Fish Paste' on the bottle—not what sort of fish. I asked the girl. She said she didn't know. I said, 'You *ought* to know—after all, you're selling it, aren't you?' Tell me, Galo—do you know what to do?"

"Yes, of course."

"Why 'of course'? Have you done it before?"

"No."

"Then *how* do you know?"

"I—I've known always, I think."

"Or just from what your friends say? Have some tomatoes, for goodness' sake! What do you suppose I brought all this food for? *Mannaggia!* Something's got inside my shirt and bitten me!"

"I'll find it."

"You eat your supper. Oh, Galo, it's lovely out here, isn't it? You were clever to find this place. The tuberoses—how they smell! Still, I don't suppose you've ever seen a naked girl—and, at least, I've seen a naked boy."

"How? Who?"

"Nicola. He upset his colored inks all over himself and I changed his pajamas."

Galo was horrified. "Mina, you *shouldn't!*"—and then sulky —"I wanted to be the first. I wanted you to see me first."

"Poor Galo!" Mina was suddenly contrite, and grasping his ears kissed him firmly on the nose again. "But it was quite different, I promise you. I didn't think of him at all like that. And anyway I don't think—" She stopped abruptly.

"What?"

"Poor Nicola. He is our dear friend. But we needn't think of him tonight. Only you must never say that you know—about me changing his pajamas. Only I couldn't do anything else, could I? I couldn't leave him smothered in green and yellow ink. He didn't want me to, though. He kept shutting his eyes. He cried a little afterwards, too."

"He—he must look terrible."

"He does. That's what he cried for. Galo," Mina's voice was strained, "talk about something else. Tell me about the camp. Have a peach—or some cherries?"

"I don't want to eat any more. As for the camp—we annoyed the fat officer so much that—"

"The cat-lover? How wrong of you!"

"He's not a cat-lover—as far as I know. Anyway, he threw in his hand and we got Berluti instead and he made things very unpleasant for everyone."

"So you didn't have a nice time—*povero te!* Come and kiss me!"

"*Subito!* But I can't hold you by the ears. I'm frightened your glasses would fall off."

"They only held the boys by the ears anyway. The girls didn't resist so gravely. Oh, Galo! How beautifully you kiss—you really do! And I can feel your lovely ribs under this striped affair— each one. And *don't* spit cherry stones into the pool! Supposing the goldfish ate them?"

"I don't suppose they'd be harmed. I can feel your ribs, too."

"Of course they would! They'd die. Do you know what happens inside you when you swallow a cherry stone? There's a diagram in our encyclopaedia—"

Galo rose and pulled Mina to her feet. "Let's go into the house. We can probably get in if we try."

"We'd be burglars."

"Not if we didn't take anything. Come on."

They entered the house with less difficulty than Galo had expected. The very first window they tried was unlocked and moved inward at a light push. But it was higher in the wall than either could easily climb and they had to fetch a large stone from the border of a rose bed to use as a mounting-block. Mina split her jeans; it distressed her extremely.

Once inside, the sinister stillness, the odd, slightly musty, indefinable smell of a house recently abandoned reached out and encompassed them. Mina edged closer to Galo and her bare forearm touched his so that the candle he held shuddered and danced on the gleaming marble of the corridor in which they stood. "Have you ever been here before?" she whispered nervously.

"No. He—old Signor Dorrucci—he's been here about thirty years or more, I think. He bought it from some people called Tourville who built it at the beginning of the century or thereabouts. He lives here for only about half the year. He's very rich. He doesn't know us, of course. At least he does in a way because Concezio shot his dog when it came and chased our chickens and he sued us. It was his fault because the dog was on our land and after our fowls but he had money for a good lawyer and we hadn't, so naturally . . . Anyway, Concezio had to sell his gun and our cow to pay the fine because the dog was a prize spaniel. So then we didn't have any milk— Come on, we'd better explore a bit."

Passages, doors, mysterious alcoves full of looming shadows. A dining room crowded with hideous gilt and marble furniture, a wide, pillared hall in which tall, dim old mirrors in baroque frames glinted winking eyes of light back from Galo's candle. Something—a cat? a rat?—scurried into the deeper darkness of a vast marquetry console and they both caught their breath in quick gasps, jerked rigid and still.

"It's nothing—come on." Galo lifted a heavy curtain and suddenly they were in a small, high, semicircular room, carpeted, upholstered, and papered in deep crimson—all velvet and quilted plush, a style at once Victorian and Oriental and common among the richer Neapolitans in the early years of the century. Galo let the curtain fall behind them with a soft rustle and held his candle high, its light bulging and expanding, then steadying to an even glow. Everything heavy, dark red and edged with tarnished, dusty gilding; everything costly and thick and redolent of old age; the great brocade curtains broadly fringed and hanging in impenetrable folds from swagged, braided pelmets, the somberly magnificent Turkish rugs scattered over the thick carpet, the ebony and ivory coffee tables, the tall Chinese vases and the lacquered cabinets. Against one wall a pedestaled bronze reproduction of the Cellini "Perseus" lifted Medusa's snake-tangled face high above her trampled body while from beside the doorway Verrocchio's curious, simpering "David" thumbed his sword blade and Goliath's severed head lay sightless at his feet. Decapitation, ornate and exotic, seemed a strangely suitable motif for this blood-colored velvet grotto.

Galo placed a candle at the feet of each of the statues and

turned to Mina. "Well . . ." For a moment they stood, avoid-
ing each other's eyes, in the muffling, waiting silence of the
empty house. Now that the time was upon them they were suddenly timid, standing wonderingly, doubtfully on the threshold
of a new experience of awe-inspiring dimensions. Inward dubiety,
the inevitable desire to retreat while there was still time, fought
with the instinctive adolescent belief that all progress forward,
the whole complex, painful business of growing up, lay in ex-
periencing every physical adult attribute as soon as possible.
Every achievement in this direction was another barrier swept
away between themselves and the expanding future. They were
drawn forward, now, at least as much by a serious sense of ex-
ploration and research as by any desire for an as yet unknown
sensual gratification.

"Well . . ." Galo swallowed and with fingers that shook
a little unbuckled his belt and pulled down his jeans. Mina did
the same. There was no reason for speech; they knew why they
were here and to both of them it seemed as if this room knew it,
too; as if it had been specially built and furnished for this one
act and had waited patiently, heavy, dark and unfading,
through the long slow years, waited for the light tread of their
rubber-soled feet outside in the dark, the soft, awed lifting of the
great curtain—and then their entrance.

Only when they were both completely naked, as bare as they
had been born, did they raise their eyes, and then Mina said
shakily, "Galo—how brown you've got. You—you're parti-
colored—like a Belgian rabbit!"

And at once the spell of this red room, so respectable and
sinister and savage, loosened. Grinning awkwardly, Galo
moved a hesitant step toward her. "It will be much more when I
come back from the Sila."

"Will it? Can you go about naked down there?"

"No—I mean my top half."

"What a pity. I wish you were brown all over. Then I'd paint
you like that—with a lovely little fig-leaf like the statues have in
the Chiaia."

"I don't think that would be at all a good idea. Anyway I
thought you always wanted to paint me in parade uniform."

"I did. But now I've seen you like this I think differently."

Galo, realizing that she was trying to talk normally, to accustom herself to their mutual nudity, perhaps to put off for a few more moments something which she was not at all sure, now, that she desired, sought desperately for words to reassure her. He would have liked to tell her that she was beautiful, perhaps to have compared her with some Renaissance masterpiece of the sort whose reproductions lined so many corridors of the De Santis home and which he had studied with interest—believing, until informed otherwise, that they were originals and of immense value. But he could not remember the names of the pictures and, now that he studied her, he found Mina obscurely disappointing. She was far too slender, too thin for a taste which, after all, was a southern one and thought in terms of the heavily voluptuous curves, the great breasts and wide thighs of the typical Calabrian peasant girl. Mina's breasts were small and immature, her waist tiny, her thighs narrow and her legs as long and slender as his own. Altogether she bore, in her light bony physique, a dismaying resemblance to the adolescent bodies of the boys he had left so recently at the mountain camp. But at all costs he must not let her perceive this. He walked firmly across to her and took her in his arms. And at the feel of her flesh against his own all the hesitations and doubts of the last minute disappeared in a rush of purely sensual pleasure. They were together, as he had planned for them to be, alone and naked in this sealed and silent room.

And now animal instinct came to the aid of their immature knowledge; they kissed open-lipped and lingeringly, holding each other in a tight embrace, breasts, bellies and thighs in glowing contact. When, breathless, they at last loosed each other to stand panting, flushed and gleaming with excited pleasure, they no longer remembered their earlier doubts—could think of nothing but present delight.

Galo turned and seizing some cushions from the ugly furniture threw them onto the carpet. "Look—this will do."

"What—on the floor? And—oh, Galo!"

"What—?"

Mina pointed. "You—I mean is that going to . . . ?"

Grinning, abashed despite himself, Galo nodded yes.

"But it won't. It *can't!*"

"It will. Come on—lie down."

Then they were on the floor amongst the velvet cushions,

under the gaze of the statues whose dark, immobile bronze faces seemed, in the still glow of the candlelight, to express derisive encouragement.

It was encouragement which was lost upon Mina. Galo was hurting her hideously and she struggled to throw him off. "No, no! You're not doing it right! It *hurts!* I told you it wouldn't—"

"No—wait a moment. It will be all right," Galo muttered. His face was strained and damp and raised slightly from her own; his teeth clenched in concentrated effort. He thrust forward with his hips and Mina let out a smothered scream. *"Galo! Oh, Dio! Galo, get off!"*

But Galo took no notice. He had forced an entry now and if he had used unnecessary strength it had been only through inexperience—he had hurt himself slightly in the process, too. Now he muttered indistinctly, "It'll be all right. It's there now—right in. It won't hurt anymore." And as Mina, sobbing with the fierce, splitting pain, struggled below him, he felt a surging swell of triumph rising to such a crescendo of physical delight that he could only dimly, through a singing fog, hear Mina's further cry of pain as his belly seemed to fill with flames and with a shuddering moan of ecstasy he felt his seed shoot from him in a series of uncontrollable convulsions which ebbed away on a tide of relief, leaving him panting weakly for breath. And then slowly, as if each listless limb was a dragging weight, he rolled off Mina and lay back upon the velvet cushions staring up unseeingly at the high, dark shadows of the ceiling, amazed, incredulous.

When at last he turned his eyes to Mina she was sitting up, her legs wide, staring down wet-eyed and with trembling mouth at her parted thighs. "Look—blood! Look what you've done!" Sobbing, she gazed down at him, accusing, childish, tearstained —wide-eyed with grief and pain.

"Didn't you—didn't you *like* it?" he asked stupidly, his mind still lost in the remembrance of those astonishing sensations of which his body was apparently capable.

"I *hated* it! It's horrible! How *could* you!"

"No, no." He grinned weakly. "It—it's magnificent!"

"It isn't—And I *told* you to stop!"

"It is."

"And you went on—when I *told* you to stop. You must have

done it wrong. You've hurt me so badly! I'm never, never, *never* going to do it again!"

Moaning to herself Mina rose painfully to her feet and, limping over to her clothes lying on a chair, began tiredly to dress. Galo watched her for a moment and then rose sulkily to join her. He had experienced something tonight which had opened a totally new dimension to him; he could not understand why it should not have done the same for Mina. Yet it had not—and for that he could not help but criticize her. If only—if only he could have done it with a proper woman, with a proper woman's body below his own urging him on rather than drawing back— instead of with a little girl which, from his newly found vantage point, was how he now regarded Mina. Mina was not good at it: that was disappointingly obvious. She was not good at it just as he was not good at certain things—English and fencing, for example. It was presumably something you either had a natural aptitude for, or hadn't. And he had—after tonight he was sure of that.

Mina, sore and sorry and waiting for him to finish dressing, was unhappily aware that she had failed him in some way. And yet what it was she had expected in place of that searing pain between her thighs she hardly knew. Caresses, kisses, the satisfaction of intimate fleshly contact with a part of Galo which was soft, delicate and pliable; she had not realized nor been prepared for the hard physical change in him as soon as their bodies embraced. And perhaps she had spoilt it for him. She felt guilty yet somehow aggrieved—above all, lost. She and Galo had tried to enter a world from which they were supposed to be debarred by reason of their ages. Galo had apparently succeeded while she had not. She was left outside, a failure and alone, while he passed inward and onward. She guessed with a miserably instinctive accuracy that he was even now wondering with whom he could do it next—and leaving her out of account.

Painfully she bent and helped him replace the cushions on their various red plush chairs. Then for a moment they glanced around to see that everything was as they had found it, no telltale object out of place. And in that moment the room seemed to close in upon them with silent, implacable finality—dark and still with its heavy plush, tarnished gilt and dusty bronzes, the apotheosis of age and judgment and doom.

"We'd better go." Galo glanced with a last, odd, shy fear at the two sword-bearing statues. They had watched; they had seen; they knew. Even when the curtain had dropped behind them, when they had traversed the long corridor, climbed through the window and were back beside the goldfish pool, that room seemed to be with them yet, surrounding them with its malign silence.

As they packed the picnic basket a flash of summer lightning flickered across the dark sky and far off beyond Vesuvius thunder growled, low and ominous. Galo said flatly, "Tomorrow I go down to the Sila."

"I know."

"We'll meet again in the autumn—when I'm back."

"Yes, of course."

"Yes. You—you'll remember me to Nicola?"

"All right."

For the first time both were anxious, rather than reluctant, to part. Galo wanted to get away and think: Mina to rest, to sleep and only later to try to sort out her jumbled emotions. For both knew that their relationship had been entirely changed tonight: both guessed darkly that it had been irreparably damaged. The old happiness of those afternoons in the Vomero flat, the evening walks up to the Vanvitelli under the lamplit plane trees of the Via Raffaele Morghen and the parties at Nicola's bedside discussing art and the pregnancy of the porter's cat were all over now—bits of a vanished past, unrepeatable and slipping slowly away, illuminated bubbles on the long black wake of Time. They could never make the journey back—back through that still, red room which had separated them—to the last, bright romance of childhood.

As they walked silently along the soft gravel toward the garden wall the thunder grunted again in the distance and Galo had an odd, tingling fear that Perseus and David would be waiting for them among the ilexes—waiting for them with drawn swords, smiling coldly. But at the gate there was no one—only silence, only darkness and the glimmering lane beyond. Mina stood back, patient, pale-faced in the shadows and Galo, heaving the heavy gate open, heard its unoiled hinges rasping loudly in the still night as if it ground its teeth to let them pass.

August

~§ 1

AUGUST—and the city lay stinking and bubbling in the heat-zenith of the year under a sky drained almost white, beside a sea whose blueness had the hard unreality of cheap dye. In San Lorenzo, in the Forcella—Spaccanapoli—the lines of tattered washing dried almost as soon as they were hung out and the women went ceaselessly to the iron fountains with jugs and buckets, pushing aside the hordes of dirty children who played perpetually in the puddles under the spouts.

From the open windows and the gaping doorways of dark, cavernous dwellings a ceaseless flood of radio music and television patter added its stridency to the perennial harsh clangor of Neapolitan life. The clogged and pullulating city, boxed by mass media—hungry, taut, tense and tearful—plunged headlong through its summer at once exhausted and yet tireless—always moving, never still for an instant.

The rich and middle-rich had long since departed for their mountain villas or their vacations abroad: the schools and the university had long since concluded the academic year and closed doors which would not reopen until the autumn. Only the poor stayed on—the poor and the police.

August was always a bad month for Crocifissa; a time of dust and flies and of baking hot weeks when the *piazza* was an oven by day, a stifling catacomb by night; when her legs swelled, her feet throbbed and ached and the slightest exertion brought her out in profuse sweat.

And the stock went bad. She had never been able to afford a refrigerator so that from May until October the wastage among her perishable goods often swallowed as much as a quarter of her profits. Two years ago, after a satisfactorily lethal epidemic of diphtheria, Gennaro had persuaded his grandfather to install a large zinc icebox in the back of the funeral parlor, and for a trifling sum Crocifissa had been able to keep her ciccòli, mortadella and salami alongside the cooling corpses of her neighbors. But the cost of the ice had worried the old Chinese; after less than a year he had ceased to use the box and now the great cylindrical sausages sweated their grease over the meat slab and soon gave off a faint but discernible smell of putrefaction. Crocifissa never sold bad goods if she could help it, but she was not always able to detect the first signs of decay and recently a new hygiene inspector—a young man with a State diploma, quite unlike tolerant old Inspector Mateis who had been recently retired after a disabling attack of food poisoning—had confiscated twelve kilos of cooked meats and reported her as well. The fine had not been light and in order to pay it Crocifissa had been forced to sell her wedding ring, her carved ivory crucifix and, worst of all, a small mosaic ikon which Dino had brought back from his first voyage to Greece.

The distress and worry caused by this affair had reduced the old woman to an unusual, voluble querulousness, a flustered, nervous defiance which, together with the heat of high summer, had brought on a mild heart attack. For all of one painful night she had lain in gasping, twitching fever and for three days afterward had been prostrated. The doctor had taken her blood pressure, listened to her jerky heartbeat and shaken his head. "You must rest and you *must* take things more calmly. At your age . . ."

She had known what he meant, had smiled and nodded weakly. Redeemed from pain by his drugs she had lain somnolently in the small, hot cave of her bedroom with Otello curled up on the floor beside her while she listened to Gennaro and Gigi moving about in the kitchen and the shop and thought of her next meeting with Dino. It was something that could not be far off now—a few years at the most—and was coming nearer every day. What would he look like? What would he be wearing? And for some reason the eighteen-year-old sailor in his white uniform gave place slowly to the eight-year-old child in his white, first-communion suit who looked down at her with solemn, wide-eyed gravity from the peeling wall at the foot of her bed. She particularly remembered one distant spring day when, only recently widowed, she had taken him out of the city into the hills behind Pozzuoli and they had collected great bunches of wild narcissi to bring back that evening. A still, bright day and Dino running excitedly among the gray rocks and low, twisted carob trees and then at last rushing to her, his arms full of the white and gold flowers. That was how it would be when they met again. She had sighed and slept under the buzzing flies, and two days later she was sufficiently recovered to return to the shop.

◆§ 2

DOWN below, in the dank, dark cave of his room behind Baldissera's stable, old Biagio was passing the torrid weeks of high summer in fear; fluttery little periods of panic during which he muttered to himself and rubbed his knobbly old hands together and clasped them between his knees. Then he would stand up, pull the collarless shirt and thick gray vest he wore, even in the height of summer, from his trousers and press experimentally at a lump which lay under the flesh high up between the 'V' of his ribs. Sometimes the lump responded with a sharp stab of pain; sometimes nothing happened at all. How long had it been there, that irregular, egg-shaped thing within him? A few weeks? Or more? Or less? And was it growing? Was it a *tumore?* Would it kill him?

Biagio had two other lumps—one in the calf of his left leg and one low down near the base of his throat—and he took much comfort in these since he had had them for longer than he could remember and if they had once been painful they had ceased to hurt somewhere back in the hazy past. If this new lump was of the same sort he had nothing to fear. And for several days at a time he pushed fear to the back of his mind—only to have it brought sharply back into bright focus by a burning stab, a sudden twisting spiral of pain within him on some occasion when he least expected it.

Once, far back in his distant, barefooted childhood, he had wandered by himself in a little wood out in the country looking for late blackberries on a warm September morning. There had been a gentleman in the wood—a proper *signore* taking his pleasure, in the hunting dress of the period: cutaway green coat, buckskin breeches, high boots—and with a falcon perched on one heavy leather gauntlet. Biagio had never seen such a bird before and had stared round-eyed, his berry-stained mouth open in wonder, at the hooded hawk. And the gentleman had smiled down and said something to him and then—Biagio could not remember the details clearly—had let him take the falcon on his own wrist, while retaining careful hold of the jess. Biagio could still remember his frightened shock as those cold claws had hesitated for a moment on his forearm and then circled it confidently—and gripped. Gripped with a fearful, steely, viselike contraction, inhumanly, unbelievably powerful. He had winced and gasped, too frightened to do more than hiss *"Signore! Signore!"* And the gentleman had smiled again and removed the hawk without difficulty— When the pain gripped and wrenched him between the ribs it reminded him of the grasp of those metal talons.

Despite appearances to the contrary Biagio received immense satisfaction from being alive; not from any positive aspect of life but from the negative position of not being dead. By a lucky chance he had escaped death before the rifles of Cadorna's execution squads and since this was the most important as well as the most terrifying event in his life he had begun, as the years passed, to take credit for it upon himself. It was difficult to do this publicly since facts were facts, and during the barbaric decimations ordered by the savage old general to assuage the blow to his military vanity, the position of number nine in the line was as safe as that of number one; but in his own mind he had come to believe that he had somehow cheated death and had anyone troubled to ask him—and practically nobody ever did—"What did you do in the First War, Biagio?" he might well have triumphantly echoed the Abbé Sieyès—"I survived."

And after all, when he came to think of it, to have been born was in itself a triumph amongst all that waste of sperm. To have been born into a Naples haunted by the twin terrors of cholera and the *cammorra;* to have endured a childhood of dirt, poverty

and hunger and an adolescence as a little slave working eleven
or twelve hours a day in the brickworks—and all these long
before he was herded off to assist, with rapidly diminishing
enthusiasm, the "completion of the Risorgimento" upon the
Isonzo and the Piave. And then there had been the Fascists and
later still the Germans and afterward the Americans—and
he himself, a more or less silent but ever-present witness, watching them come and go as the wheel of Time threw them from its
rim while he sat, sucking his teeth ruminatively in the still center.
He was a survivor.

He put thirty lire into the collecting boxes of various street-
corner monks, receiving in exchange little pictures of St. Joseph,
St. Anna and St. Luke the Physician. These he pasted over his
ribs with St. Luke in the center and felt very much better for
several days.

ৰ৯ 3

        "THOU art Peter and upon this rock I will build
my Church, and the gates of Hell shall never prevail against it
for to thee I have given the keys of the Kingdom of Heaven.
. . ." But Iole, in the back rows of the old church and listening
to the triumphant surge of the *"Tu es Petrus"* could only think
of the keys of the fortress of Gaeta.

There had been no answer, no faintest response to the
domanda forwarded through the correct channels to the Defense Ministry more than a month ago. Of course, as she well
knew, everything in Rome ground to a halt in August; but even
so, surely something might have come through—some acknowledgment, some indication that the petition had at least passed
the earlier stages of its journey. But as yet—nothing. And meanwhile the last of her money was nearly gone and within less than
three months now her baby should be born. Sometimes she felt
desperately that it would have been best to have terminated her
pregnancy months ago. But in the spring she had still been too
shocked, too angry to think of abandoning hope for Evaldo's
quick release. It had seemed then, with so many sources un-
tapped, so many friends untried, that perseverance and effort
would soon amend a lamentable miscarriage of justice and re-

store her husband to her in time for the birth of his child. Only now, as time had calmed and hardened her, did she accept the knowledge of how unlikely this was. The worst blow had been the recent invaliding from the service of Captain Santorelli. It had brought home to her for the first time exactly what Evaldo had done. With an immense effort she had tried to put herself in the place of the captain's wife—a woman quite as innocent as herself—whose husband's eyesight had been permanently damaged and his whole professional career destroyed. Someone whose hopes and plans, whose whole way of life, must now be radically altered because one night in a dark alley a murderous maniac had . . . But she could not go on.

Yet that was not only how it must appear to Signora Santorelli —but also to the military authorities. Insubordination and desertion were one thing; the destruction of a regular army officer's career was quite another. If the *domanda* was still unanswered it might well be because it had come up against a phalanx of now implacable military men who, since they could not put Evaldo before a firing squad as they would probably have wished, were determined that he should serve every day of his twelve-year sentence.

There seemed little to do, now, save to follow Crocifissa's incessantly repeated advice and put her whole trust in God, the Blessed Madonna and some dozen assorted saints. But Iole, an educated, well-read bourgeois girl from a skeptical and cosmopolitan Roman background, was unable to throw herself with the necessary luxurious abandon into the bosom of the Almighty. Everybody in Naples—at least everyone of the sort Iole now met —believed in heavenly miraculous power as unself-consciously and rather more firmly than they believed in electricity—one could not actually see either in operation but their end products were equally obvious and convincing, save that the electric current, being man-made, was fallible and quite often broke down. If Evaldo had landed from a chariot of golden cloud in the *piazza* at midday neither Crocifissa nor Gennaro nor any of the neighbors would have been unduly surprised; it was the sort of occurrence for which they were always in readiness with a few hundred lire's worth of candles, some incense and a phial of holy water.

And knowing this cut Iole off from what might have been at

least a small source of comfort—rational discussion with her neighbors. You could not expect logical help from people whose idea of assistance was to recommend pilgrimages to the more potent holy relics in various old city churches. Even so, in her extremity Iole did make these journeys and today she had piously kissed the glass front of a box containing a few minute gray threads said to be part of the shroud of St. Anna, mother of the Madonna. But leaving the church, removing her black lace scarf on the sun-scorched steps, Iole felt only a futile, helpless despair.

Back in the *piazza* she found Gennaro carefully polishing four small, dark, intricately carved wooden boxes. He glanced up at her as she came in and said briefly, "Quong's—the last he made. I'm going down to the Galleria to see if I can sell them at one of the shops." —And Iole knew that at last the "bad" time had come. For weeks now the funeral parlor had done practically no business. There had been only one proper funeral— that on the day after Gennaro had left his job at the Mergellina restaurant—and since then only the sale of a baby's white-painted coffin and less than half a dozen wreaths. It was due, of course, to the lack of a hearse. People now knew that Quong's could only arrange a full funeral by renting another undertaker's vehicle and they suspected, with some justice, that at least a part of the extra cost involved might be passed on to the client. It was easier, probably cheaper and certainly more advisable to make arrangements with a firm which operated its own transport. To Iole, whose own plight had widened and sharpened her sense of justice, it was bitterly unfair that Gennaro should be so penalized, should, in fact, be forced closer and closer to ruin upon a technical offense due entirely to his age. But the law, as she knew now, was not interested in justice but only in the enforcement of its own regulations.

"If things get bad," Gennaro had often said, "I'll have to sell the boxes, that's all." Iole had never inquired the nature of the mysterious boxes and now that she saw them for the first time she was more than ever aware of the feeling of amused pity which so many of Gennaro's words and doings aroused in her. For by her own standards, which were certainly those of the better shops dealing in *objets d'art,* the boxes were hideous. Small, ornate and carved with that massy, entangled, Oriental detail which produces its own inextricable inlay of dust and dirt, they belonged unequivocally to the bric-à-brac of a late-nineteenth-century bourgeois drawing room. One expected to find them stuffed with old holiday letters from spinster cousins, or worthless keepsakes—a broken cigar-piercer, a souvenir program for a charity ball of 1890, an embroidered needle case. But being the last boxes Quong had made they were, to Gennaro, objects of great beauty and value.

"Do you think," she asked gently, "that the Galleria is the best place to sell them? There are shops in the Piazza Municipio, down by the docks which—"

Gennaro looked up puzzled. "But those places only sell trashy tourist things. These are *Chinese* boxes."

"I don't suppose the Galleria shops will give you what they're worth."

"Nor do I," said Gennaro realistically. "But if I can get even a third of their value I'll have to be content." He paused, looking down at the shining wood. "They *are* beautiful, aren't they? Quong used to do them in the evenings after the shop was shut. Each one took weeks and weeks and they all have stories —legends. He used to tell me them while he was working." Raising his eyes suddenly he asked, "Did you see the Holy Shroud?"

"Oh yes—yes, I did. If you're going now, Gennaro, I'll take over the shop."

◦§ 4

THE Galleria Umberto I, a vast, cavernous, glass-roofed cross made up of four wide arcades and a central hall and lined with shops selling the more expensive merchandise— antiques, jewelry and furs—was the conventional trysting place for Neapolitans engaged on business deals both legal and otherwise. Once contact had been made, the various cafés with their rows of small tables offered ideal sites at which to get down to preliminary discussions. For this reason the inevitable tiny cup of black coffee—the statutory price for a table—cost more than twice as much as anywhere else in the city. Yet since one could arrange to buy or sell anything in the Galleria from an army contract to twin babies this was by no means exorbitant.

Nonetheless it was not a place which Gennaro would normally

have entered and despite his newly pressed lavender suit he felt
ill at ease and conspicuous among the sauntering crowd of doe-
eyed boys in tight jeans and bright shirts and the better-class
prostitutes who moved indifferently among them, their handsome, plump faces empty of all expression under the heavy
makeup. This was a very different world from that of the San
Lorenzo Quarter as was demonstrated by the two Carabinieri in
the central hall who, slimly elegant in their full-dress uniforms,
leaned white-gloved hands on shining silver swords and surveyed
the passing crowd with that peculiar air, at once grave, arrogant
but not ungracious, which is the hallmark of the more privileged
sections of the Italian police.

The first shop Gennaro tried was a large silversmith's, but
one which also dealt in antique swords and firearms and a few
choice pieces of furniture. There were no customers within its
tranquil, carpeted interior and at Gennaro's request the two
assistants, handsome, gray-haired and as polished as their own
silver, brought the manager from his unseen office. Despite the
fact that Gennaro was attempting to sell rather than buy, all
three treated him with the greatest courtesy, addressed him as
signore and went through all the motions of carefully examining
his boxes.

"All done by hand. By a *Chinese*," explained Gennaro, desir-
ing, but modestly refraining from adding, that the Chinese was
his grandfather.

"Ah yes? Most interesting work. Unfortunately we don't
handle objects of this sort. We really only deal in silver and
some specialized types of antiques."

"You don't want them?"

"I fear not—no. As I said, we don't deal in this type of thing.
Perhaps you would care to try the shop on the corner of the arcade opposite?"

The next shop was owned by a family of Jews—genial, jovial
and knowing.

"What's this? Boxes? Chinese carving? Umm—yes. What
dynasty?"

"What *what?*"

"Dynasty—*dynasty*. You know—what historical period?"

"They were carved by a Chinese."

"Yes, yes. But *when?*"

"Mostly about three years ago. I watched him doing it."

For a moment the Jewish father and his two sons stared unbelievingly at Gennaro. Then they stared at each other. Then they broke out into roars of laughter which made even the passersby stop and stare through the plate-glass window. At last the father, wiping his eyes and still spluttering, patted Gennaro's shoulder with mirthful apology. "Don't worry, boy, don't worry. No offense meant at all! It's just—well, we deal in historical objects here, you see. Naturally we believed that you were offering us genuine antiques. A misunderstanding on our part. No harm done, boy. Don't worry."

"You—can't take them?"

"No, no—out of the question."

"I see. Well—" Unhappily Gennaro began to wrap the boxes up once more. Then he stopped. "Tell me, is it important that things like these—genuine Chinese things—should have a—a what you said?"

"And what did I say?"

"A dyn—something."

"Oh yes—a dynasty. Well, if they're genuine it's a good idea." The father and sons were smiling at him amusedly now.

"And these boxes have not got it?"

"Well—" The old man examined one again carefully, opened it, shut it, turned it over. "Yes—yes, I should say they had, upon the whole. Yes, they've certainly got one."

"What is it?"

"I would say they were of the Junk dynasty myself." The sons spluttered but the father frowned them into shaking silence. "Yes. You can safely tell anyone who is interested that they are remarkably fine examples of that—hmm—very modern period."

The next shop he tried practically threw Gennaro out into the arcade. "*Fine examples of the very modern Junk dynasty!* —If you're being funny we'll call the police! If you're being serious we ought to telephone a lunatic asylum!"

"I'm trying to sell these boxes—that's all!"

"*Dio!* Why try here, then? We don't deal in tourist trash in the Galleria. Go and stand on the docks and hawk them to Americans off a liner!"

"They're not trash! They're *genuine*! They were made by a *Chinese!*"

"They're trash and nothing but trash! If they were made by the Pope himself with his very own holy hands they'd *still* be

trash and I'd tell him so! Now get out of here before you get into
real trouble!"

Savagely Gennaro seized his boxes and stormed out. He was
furiously angry and on the verge of tears. They were beautiful
boxes! They were Quong's boxes—the last he would ever
make. It was impossible—quite impossible—that they could
have no value. He slumped down at a café table and with
shaking hands set the boxes on the checked cloth before him.
Iole had suggested trying the tourist shops in the Piazza Municipio, but that had been merely an error on her part, he had not
been affronted. After all, Iole had not seen Quong at work, she
could not realize the hours of infinitely careful manipulation, the
fantastically precise skill, which had gone into each one of the
dark, convoluted squares of wood that lay now on this café
table. But it was quite another thing when shopkeepers whose
business it was to understand such work made the same suggestion. Gennaro had never been so deeply wounded or insulted
in the whole of his life. And—more practically—he had hoped
to sell each box for at least twenty thousand lire. They were,
the four of them, to have kept Quong and himself right around
the curve of the year and into the first of the winter. Without
that money there was only the white horse left. Of course he
would not part with the white horse unless he and Quong were
actually starving to death, but—panic flickered suddenly within
him—supposing everyone said that the white horse was trash,
too?

"Che freggatura!" He shook his head and sucked in air with
a deep, exasperated sigh. He wished he had not come to the
Galleria. Now he was sitting at a table he would have to
order a cup of coffee at a hundred lire—with ten, at least, for
the tip. A waiter behind him was already tapping his shoulder
to call his attention. He turned his head and looked up into the
pug-dog grin, the cocked cigarette holder, of Domenichelli.

◆§ 5

FIFTEEN minutes later Domenichelli stubbed out
his cigarette in the saucer of his coffee cup and carefully fitted
a fresh one into his holder. He glanced across the table at Gennaro, who sat indecisively tracing with his forefinger a con-

voluted dragon on one of the box lids. "So you see, he would never have kept you on afterwards in any case. Once you'd seen how easy it was to smuggle stuff out of the place he would have been frightened that you'd start something on your own or put ideas into the heads of some of the others. Anyway, it wasn't much of a job, was it? I wouldn't be a *guattero* for half a million a week, myself. Besides—aren't you meant to be a—a coffinmaker?"

"I'm an undertaker. Only business is bad at the moment."

"How is that? Don't people die any longer?"

"They don't get sent to me for burial. I have not got a hearse on the road any longer. And one must have that. You see, last May I had a commission which took me right across the peninsula to a place on the coast well below Pescara. I was driving the hearse myself—" Gennaro launched into the story of his disastrous trip to the Adriatic and opposite him Domenichelli listened, nodded and gave small occasional grunts indicative, so at least Gennaro presumed, of comprehension and sympathy. It was a long story and Gennaro embellished it here and there, particularly in the matter of several neatly sarcastic remarks with which he might, perhaps, have answered the traffic policemen if he had thought of them in time. These seemed to give Domenichelli much pleasure.

"You said *that*, did you? Quite right, too!" . . . "That must have put them in their places!" . . . "Well done!" . . . "But of course you couldn't just stand there looking guilty and admitting things, could you?"

"No," said Gennaro a little hurriedly. "No, of course not." Domenichelli's presence held for him the same vaguely disturbing sensations that he had noticed when working in the O Sole Mio. In some curious way he knew that Domenichelli was strangely drawn toward him, had a genuine interest in him of a sort which might have been normal enough in a friend of some years but which in the present case was inexplicable. Gennaro was flattered and in his turn a little fascinated. He no longer thought of Domenichelli as the fraudulent contractor responsible for the loss of his last job but as someone who might be confided in—at least to the extent of asking how best to sell Quong's boxes. It was just possible, too, that the small, grinning, determined man might think of some way to assist him in his present difficulties.

When he had finished, Domenichelli sat back smoking in silence and watching one of the Galleria boys who stood beside a nearby pillar earnestly talking with an elderly, heavily built foreigner, his hand laid caressingly upon the man's arm. Disappointed, Gennaro shuffled his feet irritably. He had hoped for advice or at least encouragement. Then Domenichelli said, "What about a horse?"

"A what?"

"A horse-drawn hearse. They couldn't stop you driving one of those."

Gennaro shrugged impatiently. "I can't drive a horse. And anyway it costs just as much to hire one of those as a motor. It comes to the same thing."

"Like you do it, yes—by the day. But if you hired one for— well, until you were eighteen, anyway, and kept it where you keep your motor . . . But"—Domenichelli shook his head— "there's the horse too, of course. That's not so easy."

Gennaro said glumly, "The horse is the easiest part. I could always borrow Baldissera. But—"

"Who's Baldissera?"

"A horse I know. But to hire a good hearse without a horse or driver—and for sixteen months—I'd have to put down a huge deposit for a start."

"How much?"

"A hundred to a hundred and fifty, probably." A wild hope sprang suddenly in Gennaro's heart. "You—you couldn't lend me a hundred and fifty thousand? On a good percentage, of course. On a *good* percentage—say ten—no, fifteen! And with our motor hearse as security! Your money would be quite safe. Listen!" He leaned forward, eyes wide, boxes forgotten, across the table. "Look—I can't get customers because I've no hearse. But a horse-drawn one would do just as well as a motor one —for city funerals, anyway. Many people prefer it. They think it's more dignified. And I wouldn't even have to drive it myself. There's an old *carròzza* driver living in the same building. He'd put his own horse in the shafts and drive it for—oh, six or seven hundred lire, I expect. He's a surly old man, but he and his horse—they do look sad. People like sadness at funerals, you see. Look—if I could borrow that money I could do that; hire a hearse for sixteen months. Then we could carry on. Everything would be fine!"

A waiter, seeing an obvious deal being made, came up, looked meaningly at the empty coffee cups and coughed. "Two more," said Gennaro quickly, then turned to Domenichelli. "Would you like a brandy? Or a liqueur? Or an ice cream?"

Domenichelli shook his head, grinning, and as soon as the waiter had gone he said, "I can't lend you anything—anything like that. I haven't got it myself."

"Oh." Gennaro sank back in his seat, his bright dream fading.

"But I might help you earn it."

"Find me a job? But what's the good? To earn that money— or at least to save it—would take sixteen months anyway."

"No it wouldn't. It would take"—Domenichelli consulted his black-faced wristwatch—"about twenty minutes. And only ten of those would be real work. You'd be working for me, too."

"A hundred and fifty thousand in *ten minutes!*"

"A little more, probably—money, not time. Something like two hundred thousand. I was looking for someone else to help me when I saw you." Domenichelli stared across at Gennaro thoughtfully. "I'm not sure I'm wise to offer you the job, anyway. You're too young and I wanted someone stronger."

"I am strong! I'm much stronger than I look."

"You haven't got the muscles I need. I've seen you without your clothes, so I know."

"You've seen *me* like that? Where?"

Domenichelli looked suddenly put out. "Where? Where? Oh, in the kitchen changing room at the restaurant."

"But—"

"Anyway I *am* offering it to you, so what I've seen or where I've seen it doesn't matter, does it?"

"No—no of course not. But"—Gennaro hesitated, licking his lips—"what are you—we, I mean—going to do?" Instinctively he had lowered his voice as if he knew already that whatever it might be there was little question of its legality.

"Remove some goods from one place to another."

"Steal them?"

"You could put it like that, I suppose."

"Not—not jewels?" Gennaro looked apprehensively at the nearby floodlit windows full of necklaces and rings while Domenichelli, following his glance, gave a yelp of laughter. "No

—not jewels! Who wants jewels, anyway? With all the difficulty and the cost of selling them afterwards . . . No. Motor horns. Imported German motor horns." He saw Gennaro's incomprehension and nodded slowly. "Musical motor horns. You've heard them sometimes in the street. They play the first bars of the 'Marseillaise' or something well-known like that. They're a new idea—here in Italy at any rate, and they're only fitted to expensive sports cars; naturally, because they cost a great deal. I know where I can collect about thirty or forty—and I know where I can sell them. I just need someone to help me. And since I think I owe you a good turn it might as well be you. You want it?"

Gennaro hesitated for a long moment. He was sincerely frightened both by Domenichelli's proposal and, at last and more strangely, by Domenichelli himself. Those dark eyes, now that the little man across the table was not grinning, seemed almost to glare with a watching, baleful venom as if daring him equally to accept or refuse. Yet with a panicky sense of dread Gennaro knew that he was going to accept. He might try to make conditions and reservations; he would certainly want to know exactly what his own part was to be, but in the end—with another hearse in view—he would accept. There was nothing else he could do. Swallowing, he nodded dumbly and through a ringing in his ears heard Domenichelli say, "All right, then. Come with me now and we'll find somewhere quiet to talk."

◆§ 6

FOUR nights later, at half-past ten, Gennaro stood in the tiny, three-sided Piazza Ruggiero Bonghi off the Via De Pretis, a small, inconspicuous figure in dark workshirt and belted overalls lounging against the plinth of the Bonghi statue and trying to concentrate on the account of a recent bicycle race in the *Corriere dello Sport*. He was tired, nervous and overexcited. The last days had been almost hectically busy with three funerals to arrange and no less than twelve wreaths to make. Since he'd only had one coffin in stock he had been forced to contract for two from outside makers, and since the last of the palm leaves for the wreath frames were so rusty as to be no longer presentable, he had had to buy three dozen more—one could not buy wholesale for less than three dozen—at two hundred lire apiece. Iole had helped him with the wreaths and Gigi, for a hundred lire, had run errands to the printers, the florists, the photographers, the local demographic office and—by tram—to the Capodichino Cemetery. For three days and nights Gennaro had almost been able to forget this appointment in the dark and had, in fact, tried to forget it. But he had remembered it soon enough when this morning he had seen his profits slashed almost in half by the heavy outlay for the hired hearses. The three funerals had put a clear profit of only twelve thousand eight hundred lire into his pocket when, six months ago, it would have been over twenty.

And two of the clients had grumbled when they could not be shown the hearse in advance. What was the good of an undertaker who was unable to show them the actual car which was to carry their dead in state upon this last journey? They might have changed firms there and then had the weather not been so hot that delay was unwise. Gennaro had hurriedly knocked two thousand off his original price and the bargain had been clinched, but amidst dubious head-shakings.

Yet tonight, trying but failing to read of champion cyclists by the white neon light of Di Biase's towering sign, he could not but feel that in a curious way Domenichelli brought him luck— or at least funerals, which came to the same thing. And now— He shivered slightly despite the heat of the summer evening. Domenichelli had told him the details of tonight's work and it seemed a very ordinary affair of breaking and entering a wholesaler's warehouse; the sort of thing which made minor headlines in the *Corriere di Napoli* almost every day of the week. Gennaro was no more honest or law-abiding than the rest of his fellow citizens. As a matter of course he altered his accounts, evaded his taxes, cheated his clients and sometimes absentmindedly added things to his shopping bag—a tin of shoe polish, a bar of chocolate, a packet of soap—which he failed to pay for. But serious, premeditated crime had so far been outside his scope. Nor, under more favorable circumstances, would anything have induced him to attempt it; not through any principle on his part, for he firmly believed that the richest and most famous of his contemporary countrymen were thieves on an enormous scale, but because it was too dangerous.

Tonight he was cramped with the same sort of fear a soldier feels on entering battle for the first time and it needed all his determination to remain standing in this small, lamplit square waiting for Domenichelli, rather than to slide away among the throng of passersby and run quickly home to Quong's calm presence in the room above the coffin shop. Only by keeping his mind on the ostrich-feathered glories of a horse-drawn hearse could he keep his feet on the lava flagstones of the Piazza Ruggiero Bonghi.

And, as if this was not enough, Domenichelli was late. He had told Gennaro that he would be in the *piazza* between a quarter and half-past ten and now, by the big, illuminated clock across the road, it was twenty to eleven. While the clock's long black minute-hand moved upwards in slow jerks toward a quarter to, and then ten to, eleven Gennaro's hopes alternately soared and sank as his passionate desire for a hearse and his equally passionate desire to be safe at home fought fiercely within him. But by five to eleven, when it seemed almost certain that Domenichelli had changed his plan or found another and better assistant, the hearse won. Then, with fear banished, disappointment took its place and Gennaro could have wept with frustration and despair. All he could think of was that half an hour ago he had been in a position to redeem his cherished business from approaching ruin, and now that was no longer so. From the pages of the *Corriere dello Spòrt* the smudgy features of the champion bicyclists grinned back at him idiotically. He crumpled the paper and threw it viciously into the gutter and as he did so Domenichelli came at last, bumping a battered, dirty little "Ape" right into the curb so that the single front wheel crushed the pink newspaper into the dirt of the street. Then the door was pushed open and in the shadowy interior Gennaro caught the gleam of the undershot, pug-dog grin. "Get in—quick!"

In a moment he was crouched uncomfortably in the tiny cab and the "Ape" turned with a shattering roar of its broken, unmuffled exhaust and rocketed away down the Via De Pretis among the grinding trams and flashing lights of the night traffic—a grubby blunt-nosed beetle among a lot of dinosaurs.

When he had overcome his first hot surge of relief Gennaro shouted, "You're late! I thought you weren't coming."

Domenichelli swung into a quiet side street before the Piazza Nicola Amore and pulled up. He stared irritably up and down the narrow sidewalks. "I haven't got something I want. I forgot it and now I've got to find it."

"What?"

For the first time Domenichelli slewed his dark eyes toward Gennaro.

"Garbage," he said and grinned from ear to ear. "I need something—anything—to put in the back. We'll have to cover the boxes with it. I thought there would be a tarpaulin or at least a couple of old sacks— There generally is. I picked this truck up out at San Giovanni. I've been keeping an eye on it for some days and I don't think the owner will miss it until tomorrow morning. But we must have something to put in the back."

"I see. Look—would some old wreaths do?"

"Wreaths?"

"*Corone*—funeral wreaths. Old flowers and bits of palm leaf."

"They'd do very well. You've got some?"

"Yes. At my place. You know the Piazza Vittime Civili di Guerra—near the Capuana?"

"No."

"San Lorenzo. I'll tell you the way. It's not far."

Four minutes later the battered "Ape" crawled slowly into the *piazza* and came to a halt in the last pool of shadow before the turning into the Via Buonuomini. Gennaro got out and sliding quickly into the dark bomb ruins behind Crocifissa's shop, approached his own premises from the rear. There was a light in the room above the coffin shop; Quong was probably reading the paper—perhaps with Iole for company. Gennaro walked quickly, silently into the workroom and opening the front door carried in the remains of the wreaths which he had collected that afternoon for the sake of their frames from Capodichino and which now awaited the municipal scavengers, piled untidily against the stone hitching posts. Twice he made the journey with the prickly bunches of faded flowers and dusty palm leaves and then, with the "Ape's" small truck full of wilted vegetation, Domenichelli let in the clutch and they stuttered slowly away in the direction of the Via Tribunali.

Suddenly Gennaro snapped his fingers. *"Mannaggia*—we must go back!"

Domenichelli drew quickly into the curb. "What is it?"

"I forgot to turn off the light—in the workshop."

"Does that matter?"

"Well—electric light costs money."

"Porco Dio!" swore Domenichelli angrily, wrenching the "Ape" onto the road again. "You're on the way to earn two hundred thousand lire, and you worry about wasting electric light! Now just stay quiet and do what you're told—see?"

Abashed, Gennaro nodded and then gripped his seat as Domenichelli began to drive with a fierce ruthlessness which hurled the little three-wheeler in quick darting rushes beween the traffic, stopping and starting with bone-jarring abruptness as they weaved through the crowded street and then turned into a complex of narrow alleys behind the Duomo. They crossed the Corso at the Church of Sant'Agostino, and Gennaro had the impression that the bright lights annoyed Domenichelli and that he would have avoided them had it been possible. Despite the heat of the night the windows of the "Ape" were closed, although they were so dirty that it would have been impossible to see into the cab in broad daylight. Then they were in the Porto Quarter and suddenly Domenichelli swung the "Ape" out of the comparatively well-lit Via Savarese into a narrow arched alley, swung from that into a courtyard so shallow as to be hardly more than a deep recess in the side of a warehouse, and jammed on the brakes with the little vehicle's blunt front nuzzling the brickwork of a high blank wall. *"Va bene*— Get out."

There was a weak lamp suspended from a hook high up in the wall and by its light Gennaro saw that what he had at first taken to be a dark shadow in one corner was a passage, a slot barely half a meter wide between one warehouse and the next.

"Down here." Domenichelli, a squat figure, black-shirted and jeaned, edged sideways into the slot and Gennaro followed him. Crabwise they moved along for some fifteen meters and then emerged into a curving cobbled alley, a cul-de-sac filled with the pounding rattle and thud of printing presses in action behind a long set of grills low in one wall. A tin plate clamped to the stucco bore the name VICOLO CIEGO DI POMODORI.

"It's down here." And followed by Gennaro, Domenichelli

led the way around the curve of the alley and stopped at a heavy iron shutter let into the right-hand wall. "We've got to get this up—and I don't suppose it has been lifted for years."

Gennaro saw that the reticulated metal door was thick with grime and rust, its flanged bottom buried in ten or more centimeters of weed-grown dirt. "Is it fixed down?" he asked and Domenichelli, dropping to his knees and taking a small department-store hacksaw from inside his shirt, grunted. "A bar and two old locks. One's broken. I'm cutting the other now. You'd better clear the earth off the edge— Here!" He pulled a short tire lever from his hip pocket. "Use this. And be quick."

Side by side in the half-dark they worked together, the grate of the saw and the chink of the tire lever drowned by the noise of the printing presses further up the alley. In three minutes the lock was cut and the accumulated filth of years scraped from the flange. The long bar between the locks was rusted stiffly into one socket and they could not remove it until Domenichelli, cursing the delay, had cut it in half; then they drew it, rasping and reluctant, from its hasps and the shutter was—in theory, at any rate—free.

"Inside," asked Gennaro, panting a little from the struggle with the bar, "is it loose?" He knew from experience that the ceiling rollers of these shutters became easily jammed, particularly if they were left ungreased for any length of time, and if that was the case with this one . . .

Domenichelli said, "It looked loose when I saw it last Friday. There's nothing piled up against it, anyway. We'll have to try. Ready?"

"Yes."

They each grasped a handle and bent, straining upward. With a rumbling, protesting creak the stiff slats of the door moved up a quarter of a meter and stopped. "Again!" Ten more centimeters. They stood back panting and then bent in taut unison once more. But this time there was no further movement and Domenichelli, scowling at Gennaro, grunted "*Porco Dio!* Why didn't I get a proper man on the job? Well—come on. And *pull* this time, see?" Once again they heaved at the handles, exerting their utmost strength, pouring with sweat, the breath rasping in their throats. Then very slowly, centimeter by grating centimeter, the shutter lifted another half meter from the ground and then stopped with a solidity which both of them recognized instinctively to be final.

"*Va bene*. That will have to do." Domenichelli turned, wiping the sweat from his face with the back of one gloved hand. "All you have to do now is just to keep it up in this position. Get under it and get it set on your back. I'll hold it until you're under—but be quick!"

Gennaro slid quickly onto his knees below the shutter and raised himself until it was pressing, hard and heavy, across his shoulders. Its weight was much greater than he had imagined and for a quick moment of panic he wondered if he was to be trapped here, kneeling immovably on the stones, held down by the massive metal door. But Domenichelli had already slipped eel-like into the interior blackness behind him and he was alone, panting and gasping, a criminal caryatid burdened grimly beneath an allegorical doom.

Then Domenichelli was back, clutching a pile of five cardboard boxes. Muttering, "Stay where you are. I'll be as quick as I can," he ran swiftly back up the curve of the alley and disappeared into the slotted cleft in the wall. In less than two minutes he was back. "That's the first lot. There'll be about six more. You think you can hold it?"

"I'll try." But by the time Domenichelli had returned from depositing his second load in the "Ape" the flanged edge of the shutter was cutting painfully into Gennaro's shoulders, and by the third his face was pale and taut with pain. "Be quick! I can't manage much longer."

"You must. I'm being as quick as I can. If we leave now I can only pay you half what I said."

Once more Domenichelli disappeared and Gennaro shut his eyes, trying to force his mind away from his burning shoulder muscles and breaking back by the thought of tomorrow and the new hearse.

He must hold out somehow. Only another six minutes—perhaps five. As the pain increased and the sweat trickled in rivulets down his face he began to count the seconds in short, gasping hisses between clenched teeth ". . . five . . . six . . . seven . . . eight . . . nine . . ." Domenichelli was back for the fifth load, shooting him a rapid glance from those dark, bright eyes and then wriggling under the shutter and scurrying into the darkness beyond. Lights began to circle and swirl in front of Gennaro's eyes and, still desperately counting, he thought, "If I faint I'll fall forward and the shutter will come down on top of me and break my back . . . fifty-one . . . fifty-two . . . fifty-three . . . Domenichelli will be trapped and everything will be over . . . sixty . . . I mustn't faint . . . one . . . two . . . three. Only one more load . . . five . . . six."

He opened his eyes and there, rounding the curve of the alley some ten meters away, came a man. A man in the dark uniform of the Urban night patrol. The sword-thrust of terror which Gennaro felt then dispersed his physical agony as if it had never existed. He moved convulsively and the shutter rattled down six centimeters to slide off his shoulders and scrape the skin from his back. "Domenichelli!" He fell on hands and knees and the patrolman saw him, stared a moment, and shouted, "Hi—you! What—?" Then with a quick wriggle Domenichelli was out below the crushing edge of the shutter, a box tumbling from his arms. Gennaro gasped, "Police!" and heaved himself sideways onto the stones as the shutter thundered to the ground behind him.

He scrambled to his feet to see Domenichelli backing quickly away down the alley, his boxes scattered on the cobbles. They could still get away—there were two of them, after all. Then he remembered with a sick shock that this was a cul-de-sac and the patrolman blocked the only exit. The guard must have realized this at about the same time, for instead of running at them he stayed where he was, booted feet planted firmly on the stones, and drew his revolver. "All right. Come on out of it. Both of you!" His other hand fumbled for the whistle in his breast pocket, but before he reached it there was a sudden movement from Domenichelli and the flash and bang of a pistol that was not the guard's. Gennaro stared unbelievingly as the patrolman swayed a moment and then fell clumsily to his knees.

And while he stood in a shocked daze, Domenichelli was away. A short, demonic figure, pistol clutched in one hand, he leapt past the fallen policeman and raced toward the slotted cleft. But before he reached it the patrolman managed to lift his gun and fire two random shots. Domenichelli's head jerked back, he seemed to bounce from one wall to the other and then with a scream of pain he disappeared into the narrow cleft.

The policeman was on hands and knees now, blood dripping from his mouth over his fallen revolver which lay beneath his hanging head. As Gennaro passed him, his elbows were slowly buckling outward into collapse. Then Gennaro was again in that claustrophobic slot and almost screaming aloud with horror, for his legs, numbed by minutes of cramped circulation, would only respond at half their normal speed to his frantic desire to escape. For some reason, perhaps connected to the motor of the printing presses, the slot was now filled with acrid fumes which tore at the lungs and seared the eyes and throat. Caught in a choking nightmare, Gennaro reeled and bumped down the brick-sided chasm after the moving blot at the farther end which was Domenichelli. He could think of nothing but flight. Flight from this dark place of unbreathable air where, behind him, a crumpled man lay face downward on rough stones amid blood and scattered cardboard boxes.

At last he reached the end of the passage and saw the truck under the weak wall lamp. Even as he emerged he heard the slam of the door and saw the "Ape" shake under Domenichelli's sudden weight. He stumbled across the flagstones toward his own side of the cab and as he did so a dark, humped shadow lifted slowly from beside the pile of broken wreaths which spilled over the truck's sides. A grotesque form turned toward him, a filthy paw stretched out in cringing supplication, and for a moment he was looking into the crumpled, grime-encrusted face of La Gobba, wry-necked and peering upward—inquisitive, malicious, mad. In one hand she grasped four faded roses pulled from one of the partially decayed wreaths.

"*Dieci!*" she mumbled "*Dieci lire!*" and the claw extended further.

Gennaro shouted "*Va!*" and thrusting a splayed hand into her face—aware, even through his panic fear, of a shudder of revulsion at the physical contact—pushed her back as Domenichelli let in the clutch and reversed the "Ape" with a roar.

Then Gennaro was on the other side and wrenching open the door. One foot was on the shaking floor of the cab, one hand gripping the back of the seat, before he saw Domenichelli's face and the red glare of murder plain upon it. A flash, a stunning bang, something ripping the shirt under his armpit and then the door was torn from his grasp, throwing him rolling on the stones as the "Ape" leapt forward and swinging round in a tight circle, shot out into the Via Savarese and disappeared in the direction of the Porta Nolana.

✥ 7

TWELVE minutes later Gennaro, breathless and trembling, edged carefully from the shadows at the mouth of the Via Buonuomini and glanced swiftly across the *piazza* to where the dusty window of his workshop next to the funeral parlor glowed in the darkness. From where he stood, on the other side of the narrow square, he seemed to see the silhouette of someone within and his stomach turned over with nauseous fear at the thought that it might be Domenichelli. But he must get home at all costs. Home—peace—safety, were all bound up in his mind with the cracked old walls of the bombed building in which he had lived so long. Home, shut-inness, the security of bricks and mortar between himself and a world turned suddenly implacably hostile and vengeful. He was a small, hunted animal, breathless from the chase through the forest, whimpering a little with a mixture of panic and relief as at last it neared its burrow.

Still keeping in the shadows he turned into the deserted courtyard behind the Annunziata and by climbing, as he had not done for three years or more, to the stone wellhead and then to the broken wall behind the church, made his way in the manner of the *piazza's* childish gangs to the rear of the bombed buildings and quietly let himself in at his own back door. Silence. Stillness. He approached the workshop on tiptoes and looked in. Then, for the first time that evening, he almost laughed with relief. On a low stool by the workbench, with her pedestal half covered in sawdust, the Goddess of Mercy, Kwang-Yin, bent her gentle, carved face over the rough table—where he had moved her yesterday morning in order to shift the new coffin into the funeral parlor.

And now at last Gennaro became calmer. He could not—or would not—yet think of what had happened or of his own part in it. Perhaps, in a way it had not happened at all—perhaps it had been some sort of dream. One part of his mind accepted this view eagerly, seized upon it and began rapidly inventing a new evening in which he had been nowhere near the Piazza Ruggiero Bonghi or the Via Savarese, but instead had stayed at home cleaning and sharpening his tools. This part of his mind even made him take up a chisel and draw it a few careful times across his oilstone. But a deeper, inward mechanism was working in a small clarity of its own and this part of his mind accepted coldly everything that had happened and was interested only in negating its future consequences. This part of his mind made him put down the chisel, shift Kwang-Yin noisily out of the way, clatter open the door of the workshop, emerge whistling onto the piazza and walk with admirable firmness across the *piperno* to the tobacconist's.

"Hullo, Gennaro. You've been working late." Old Maresciallo Tenerini looked up from his evening paper and smiled over his glasses. "Cleaning up after all that work, eh?"

"Yes, Maresciallo." Gennaro's voice sounded oddly high and unsteady in his own ears; he tried to modulate it. "There's been a lot to do. And then I had to sharpen all my tools."

"Ready for more, eh?"

"I—well, trade does seem to be looking up a little."

"For your sake I'm glad—though it sounds callous to say so."

Gennaro tried to laugh and putting twenty lire on the counter took two cigarettes from the glass bowl—quickly, so that the shaking of his hand should not be noticed.

Then Gigi ran in. "Crocifissa said she saw you in the workshop an hour ago. I told her I'd come and help you clear up and she said no, I wasn't to, as I'd get in the way. But I wouldn't have been in the way, would I?"

Gennaro, breathing as much as he could remember of a Chinese prayer to Kwang-Yin, said, "You would have been—when I'm cleaning tools. I always have to see you don't cut your hands off." He shuddered suddenly.

"*Dio,* it's hot tonight!"

"You've been sweating"—Gigi looked at his soaked shirt— "like an ox."

"So would you, if you'd been working in this heat." Putting a ten-lire piece on the counter, Gennaro pointed to the three jars of sweets lined up beside the postcard rack and gratefully Gigi selected one and unwrapped it. Then he said, "You've torn your shirt—under the arm."

"I know. I caught it on a nail."

"Crocifissa will mend it for you." Gigi's voice came contentedly complacent through the sweet in his mouth. "She mends all mine."

Suddenly Maresciallo said, "Gennaro—are you all right? You're an odd color—and you're shivering!"

Gennaro tried to grin, rubbed a shaky hand through his thick, black hair and, aware that he was trembling all over and that his whole body was one exhausted ache, said, "I'm just tired, that's all." He moved away from the direct light and pausing at the door turned for a second, smiling weakly. *"Buona notte, Maresciallo. Ciao, Gigi!"*

Then he was out into the shadow pools and golden lamplight of the *piazza,* knowing now that by a most unusual combination of good fortune and sheer, self-preserving instinct, he had secured his own safety and plunged back from the abyss which, such a short time ago, had gaped below his feet. And now that first part of his mind which had assured him that the last hour had been a dream, a nightmare hallucination, took over full control and banished the small, cold, warning voice in a flood of warm self-congratulation and warmer self-pity. Now, stumbling with tiredness, he recrossed the square, let himself in to the funeral parlor and climbed the rickety stairs to his room. But one last prompting from that almost soundless voice made itself heard and was obeyed. Before he fell face-downwards on his bed he locked and double-locked his door and jammed a chair under the handle.

Valdemarin

~§ 1

FOR such a fat man, Maresciallo Valdemarin moved very quietly. He had trained himself in this over many years in order to avoid waking Nicola when he came home late or rose early or was called out on a police emergency during the night. This had been particularly necessary during the long, agonizing years while the doctors were trying to save Nicola's leg and the pain of the protracted and eventually useless operations made sleep at best a matter of shallow dream-filled dozes and long, restless periods of drugged semiconsciousness. Since the amputation Nicola had slept better but, denied all the exercise his maimed but growing body had needed and with his nerves continually strained to a fretful tautness, he was easily wakened. And then—then followed the usual restless demands for whichever new drug or medicine was being presently tried out, for coffee . . . a sandwich . . . a half-completed jig-saw puzzle . . . yesterday's paper . . .

Though Valdemarin guessed that most of these requests were made purposely to plague him, he tried to make himself believe that the boy was lonely and only wanted company. But deep within him struggled the uncomfortable belief that they were, in fact, merely further manifestations of Nicola's bitter resentment of his father and his father's profession.

On these occasions he would reluctantly remember things best forgotten; smoke signals from the dull, glowing fire of Nicola's implacable anger which shot in sudden acrid spurts from cracks in his martyr's façade. Nicola at eleven, parading and massing his lead soldiers by the hour on a board across his bed and once breaking the legs off an entire new box of Carabinieri. Nicola at fifteen, writing his autobiography—a book secretly hidden away but which the Maresciallo had found and which contained five long descriptions of his son's mutilation, each differing widely in detail and in each of which his own role varied from collusion with the criminals to the organizer and originator of the whole outrage. Nicola at eighteen, attempting suicide and sending what was intended to be a posthumous letter to *Il Messaggero*—thank God it had been retrieved unopened . . . Nicola, through all the long, sad, widowed years.

Asleep he was happiest. He himself knew that, too, and was therefore irascible if he should be accidentally wakened. The Maresciallo held his breath and stole soundlessly past Nicola's door on his way to the bathroom. When he had shaved he went into the tiny kitchen and prepared Nicola's breakfast. A tray containing two small thermos jugs, one of hot coffee, one of milk; a cake from the café bar across the street, still in its plastic envelope; a banana. Carefully the Maresciallo arranged these and added a paper napkin, the last of a packet of twelve—he must remember to buy some more at the STANDA department store on his way home this evening. Then came the trickiest part, the opening of Nicola's door and the placing of the tray beside his bed without waking him. It could not always be done and then, in the half-darkness, would come that light, exhausted whisper, *"Oh, Dio!"*, from the bed. But this morning he managed it, backed gingerly from the room and softly closed the door. Dressed in his second best summer suit—like the rest of the Homicide Squad he very seldom wore anything but plainclothes—he left the apartment, hesitated in the passageway and returned. Tiptoeing once again to the kitchen he opened the door at the side of the stove, felt for the knurled wheel on the top of the gas cylinder and turned it to the OFF position with all the strength of his fingers until it jammed tight. Then once more he went out.

Jolting slowly down Montesanto in the funicular he wondered tiredly whether psychotherapy could help. Psychiatrists were very few in Italy—it was said that there were only two even in Rome and that for lack of patients they often passed the time analyzing each other—but there must be some doctors in Naples who had a smattering of this art. Of course the Church disapproved strongly—though that would not worry Nicola, who had been an atheist for years now—and the expense would be great. But expenses in connection with Nicola always had been great. Not that Valdemarin grudged spending all he earned and made on Nicola, but even so he was sometimes forced into debt and this disturbed him deeply.

He sighed, very aware of the heat and of his weight which made that heat so much less endurable to him than to others of a more normal build. There were cures for gross overweight, too, but they cost money and it had long since ceased to occur to him that he should spend money upon himself. Even now, leaving the funicular station, he did not consider taking a taxi from the rank in the Piazza Dante, but stood patiently in a queue for the *filobus*: a gross, sweating man in a creased suit who possessed the power to imprison; under certain circumstances—not too closely defined—to kill, and under others to torture; but not to arrive at his own office in modest comfort.

◆§ 2

HALF an hour later Brigadiere Calvanese, personal assistant to the de facto chief of the Homicide Squad, stood respectfully beside his superior's desk waiting for that thick, hairy hand to finish its crablike crawl over the weekly Vehicle Report, waiting for those small, sullen eyes to lift to his in silent permission to speak. When this happened he said, "Elena Steno. Widow of Erasmo Erasmini—laborer. She died on the twenty-fifth of natural causes—old age, chronic phlebitis, probably hastened by malnutrition. She lived in a single room in the Via Duchesca IX where she received minor help from the local priest. She was buried on the twenty-sixth by an undertaker named Quong with a place in the Piazza Vittime Civili di Guerra—formerly the Piazza Giovanni Nicòtera—in San Lorenzo." He paused for a moment, received an almost imperceptible nod, and went on more confidently. "I've been round to have a look. I took Fabrizi with me. The position is this—the business is nominally owned by an old immigrant Chinese who, in fact, is paralyzed after a stroke and can do nothing. All business, such as it is, is performed by his grandson, a boy not yet seventeen, with the unpaid help of a young married woman whose husband is doing twelve years in Gaeta for attempted desertion and striking a superior officer while doing national draft service. The boy himself is illegitimate—the result of a wartime affair between old Quong's son, who was later killed on the Russian front, and a peasant woman at Ferrara—and was in trouble with the Public Security police last May when he was found driving his grandfather's hearse without a license. He was fined and the license for the hearse suspended. Since then the undertaking business has been going downhill rapidly."

"Debts?"

"I think so, Signor Maresciallo. Mainly to pay the fine. Most of the information is from the P.S. They could hardly keep it back in the circumstances, of course."

"They didn't let you see the file?"

"No."

"Naturally. Well—bring in the boy. Take an ordinary taxi, not a squad car, and do it quietly—no fuss. I'll see him downstairs in the *camera di sicurezza*."

"*Si, signore!*" As Calvanese was in plain clothes he could not salute, but by clicking his heels and bowing sharply from the waist he managed to give his departure from the office a military air.

When he had gone, Valdemarin pushed aside the Vehicle Report—it was practically a palimpsest by now—and taking a small, dirty pipe from his wire letter tray, clamped it in the side of his mouth and lit it. Slumped in his specially strengthened desk chair he considered various ways of keeping the rival force —the Public Security police—out of the present business until at least he had completed the first investigations and assumed a strong measure of personal control over the later ones. There was the question of keeping Lieutenant Giacobelli out of the affair, too—that presented greater difficulties.

It had been a two-man Carabinieri patrol which had been first beside the dying Vigile Notturno and had heard his last, gasping description of the crime, and it was they who had found the broken piece of funeral wreath with the name STENO picked out in golden paper letters on the tattered purple ribbon. It was

they, too, who had pulled in that old creature known as La
Gobba, whom they had found crouching under a nearby wall
clasping her bucket and mop and four withered roses. Only later
had the P.S. turned up and by then the patrolman was unconscious, the ribbon buttoned safely into a Carabiniere's pocket,
and La Gobba on the way to this station house from which she
had only been released after an exhaustive, exhausting and
largely futile examination. Largely futile—but not quite, since
she made a connecting link between the dead man's half-inco-
herent mention of an "Ape" filled with wreaths and the escape
in that vehicle of at least one, perhaps both, of the criminals involved.

The P.S. had naturally begun their own inquiries into the affair—inquiries which in theory were being carried out "in close
cooperation with the Carabinieri" while in practice both forces
kept their investigations jealously secret from each other. The
Maresciallo doubted if his rivals, denied all early information,
were making much progress—even so, he would have given a
lot to look at their criminal files which were much more ex-
tensive than those at his own disposal.

A double knock on the office door was immediately followed
by the entrance of Lieutenant Giacobelli. Valdemarin removed
his pipe, lifted his bulk some two centimeters from his office chair
and slumped back again. Both he and Giacobelli paid each
other only the most perfunctory marks of military respect in private—in public of course they were somewhat more formal—for
Valdemarin's long service, not to speak of his reputation,
canceled out the difference between senior noncommissioned
and junior commissioned rank. Besides, all the real power lay
with the Maresciallo—or it should, and indeed would, have
done had not Giacobelli been a national swimming champion
and consequently a petted favorite of the Corps. The Maresciallo
had never had sporting or athletic interests and the view that a
police force's reputation was enhanced by the prowess of its
members at games irritated him considerably. But it was a view
which was increasingly taken in Italy and star athletes in the
Carabinieri held privileged positions. Lieutenant Giacobelli had
only had to indicate his desire to join the Homicide Bureau to
be posted immediately with a position as nominal head of Valdemarin's squad. It had to be merely nominal since, as the

Maresciallo had said sarcastically to his personal assistant, Giacobelli knew precisely as much about homicide investigation as he himself knew about swimming—which was nothing at all, save what he read in the papers.

"Well, well—and how is everything, Ugo?" Giacobelli, who as an officer was compelled to wear uniform rather than plain clothes when on duty, took off his cap and threw it on a filing cabinet, then he took out a cigarette case of scarlet enamel embossed with the flaming grenade of the Corps. He was a man of twenty-eight years, tall, muscular and handsome in a dark, ruddy-faced way, though with jowls that were already becoming a trifle heavy, a waistline already losing its youthful slimness. Sometimes Valdemarin contemplated with pleasure the not-so-distant future when Giacobelli would be almost as fat as himself.

"Everything is—in order." The Maresciallo would have liked to have added an emphatic "Signor Tenente!" just to show Giacobelli that he objected to an assumption of friendly Christian-name terms on the part of someone who wore only two stars; but since he hoped to sidetrack his nominal superior he felt that an indirect snub of that sort might be out of place. "Everything," he repeated with a resigned shrug of his shapeless shoulders, "except our Vehicle Report, of course."

The response was immediate and satisfactory. Giacobelli's sunburned face creased at once into ridges of weary annoyance; his voice when he spoke held an angry exasperation. "Mannaggia! Not again!"

"I'm afraid so."

"But why? Why? When I gave him such careful instruction last time! Two hours I had him in my own office! Like a father—like a—a university professor, I was with him!"

"When Lorens comes out of hospital, I'm sure—"

"No, no! It won't do, Maresciallo. It won't do. Very well, Teobaldi shan't get his promotion. You advised against it and you were quite right. A man who can't profit by two hours of clear and simple instruction is certainly not a man to make up to vice-brigadiere."

Valdemarin nodded slowly. "Theobaldi's an adequate mechanic—but that's as far as it goes."

"Yes, yes. You're quite right as usual." Giacobelli seized his hat from the filing cabinet, rubbed out his half-smoked cigarette in a broken coffee saucer on the windowsill and turned toward the door. "Just send the report up to me with all the relevant papers. I'll have it completed by this evening, even if it means staying here all the afternoon."

"Very well, Tenente." Valdemarin found himself almost liking his superior for a moment. After all, there must be a lot of good in a man who was prepared to do a hard and dull day's work to rectify the mistakes of an inefficient subordinate. He thought with pleasure of Giacobelli, self-imprisoned all day in his upstairs office, calling for endless cups of black coffee, while he himself began the careful collecting and checking of evidence in what looked like being one of his most interesting homicide cases.

Valdemarin was not a particularly ambitious man and certainly not a vain one but, at least within the Corps, he had a reputation for tracking down murderers. Today sixteen men and three women were serving life sentences in maximum security prisons owing almost entirely to his efforts. During the war he had sent four Allied—and—after Italy's *volte-face*—eleven German agents to straddle chairs before military firing squads and he had subsequently helped hunt down the last of the Fascists with a ferocity which few who knew him would have believed possible. But he liked to work by himself; to take no one into his confidence, to keep everyone in the dark until at least he had built up a set of reasonable premises and tested the most important. The opinions and suggestions of others—and he had not met the policeman who could resist producing these over a murder case—only confused and irritated him. In the present instance Giacobelli's interference would have been intolerable, but now—thanks to Teobaldi's inefficiency—this had been avoided; at least for the important beginning. He smiled at the lieutenant and rose as much as five centimeters from his seat in respectful farewell.

But before Giacobelli could reach the door, it was flung open after a quick knock and Calvanese stood in the entrance. Seeing the lieutenant he hesitated a moment, then bowed, turned toward the desk and bowed again and announced, "I have him here, Signor Maresciallo. The boy for questioning over the murder off the Via Savarese."

Valdemarin gave Calvanese a look which made the Brigadiere turn dark red with mortification and then rubbed one pudgy hand across a face which, behind the splayed fingers, became for a moment a mask of fury and exasperated disappointment. Sagging back in his chair he heard Giacobelli's crisp voice. "Aha! We're on to something already, are we? Excellent! Calvanese—is this your work?"

"The Maresciallo's, *signore*."

"So! Ugo—you old devil!" Giacobelli strode across the room grinning broadly. "Why didn't you tell me you were on to something? You want to keep everything exciting to yourself, don't you?"

"Signor Tenente, this is merely routine, I assure—"

"Not what *I* call routine. The Vehicle Report is what I call routine. I didn't get myself posted to the Homicide Squad to do the Vehicle Report when there's a—"

"Tenente. I tell you that I had no intention of hiding anything." Valdemarin strove to achieve a tone of geniality he was far from feeling. "I merely wanted to get a few facts straight before bothering you. At present we have very little to work on—"

"You've got a suspect, it seems."

The Maresciallo groaned inwardly in the spirit. "Not a *suspect*. Merely a person who may—or may not—be able to help us with information."

"Isn't that"—Giacobelli laughed—"generally the same thing?"

Valdemarin sighed deeply and rose without answering. He placed some notes, and the purple ribbon still attached to a piece of broken palm-leaf, in a cardboard box-file and turned to the door. "I think we'd better go down to the *camera di sicurezza*."

The lieutenant let out a joyful yelp of laughter. "And you say this fellow's not a suspect!"

Valdemarin regarded him with a blandness which disguised despair. Slowly and entirely untruthfully he said, "Some men are coming to this office in ten minutes to repair the shutters. The *camera di sicurezza* is the only private place left to me."

3

THE *camera di sicurezza* was not, as its name implied, the strong room where the police kept their archives; nor was it a maximum-security cell for recalcitrant prisoners. It was a medium-sized basement room containing a few pieces of dull furniture: a desk, two heavy old-fashioned wooden armchairs, a large plain kitchen table, a tall cupboard and, in one corner, a big zinc laundry tub under a single tap. There was one unshaded electric lamp hanging from the ceiling in which—but whitewashed so that they hardly showed—were two or three hooks. Rooms of the same sort existed in police stations throughout the civilized world; generally in the basement, always without windows, invariable in their innocuous furnishings. If these rooms held any secrets they were presumably in the cupboards —but the cupboards were always locked.

The only strange thing about these dull-looking rooms was that though they were so much alike they had widely differing and often facetious names. "The goldfish bowl," "The butler's pantry," "Le passage au tabac"—unless they had no name at all and were referred to as "downstairs." To the person entering for the first time there is nothing either interesting or sinister in these rooms—but it is different at the second visit, for then he knows himself to be standing in the hygienic modern equivalent of the medieval torture-chamber.

Gennaro, entering the *camera di sicurezza* between Calvanese and his fellow detective, Fabrizi, had no idea where he was. He was very frightened but surprisingly controlled. After all, he had not been arrested but merely asked to "help" with a little information, and though the appearance in the funeral parlor of two polite men who said they were police officers had sent a jagged stroke of electric terror through his whole body, he had said nothing but followed them dumbly to the taxi and been driven silently, swiftly, to the station house. Of one thing at least he was now certain; Domenichelli had not been captured —for if this had happened he himself would have been arrested and taken away handcuffed in a police van in the normal way. And if Domenichelli was not in the hands of the police, there

was no one else to connect him with what had happened last
night in the alley off the Via Savarese. Unless—a cold hand had
touched his heart—that old creature, La Gobba . . . But she
did not know him, had never looked at him, much less spoken
to him, before—and anyway she was *toccatta*—a mental defective whose word could never be used against him after Gigi
and Crocifissa had sworn they had seen him in the workshop.
The optical illusion performed for his benefit by the Goddess of
Mercy must exonerate him completely. He had only to keep
calm, refuse to budge an inch form his own version of his
whereabouts last night. But then how—and why—had the police come for him so quickly? He had shivered apprehensively,
sitting between the two plainclothesmen in the hot taxi. But perhaps it would turn out to be something quite different; something
to do with Quong's business license or his arrears of tax or the
trouble with the hearse last May or . . . or—A dozen different
small offenses passed comfortingly across his mind.

But they did not comfort him for long and his mouth was dry
and his throat felt swollen and closed as he entered this underground room to see a very fat man in a crumpled suit sitting
at a desk with, at his side, a florid Carabiniere lieutenant in summer khaki.

He stood silently before the desk, between his escorts, and so
quiet was it down here away from the traffic roar and street
noise which filled the rest of the station that he could distinctly
hear someone's watch ticking. For a long minute no one moved
or spoke. The fat man was reading a typed paper before him and
only the lieutenant stared up silently from behind the desk, his
hot, dark eyes searching and hostile. Gennaro met his gaze for
a moment and then looked sullenly down at his own dirty shoes.

"Gualtierra, Gennaro. Born in Ferrara the twenty-eighth of
October nineteen forty-three; illegitimate son of Fulvio Quong
and Emilia Maria Gualtierra?" The fat man looked up and
Gennaro nodded yes. "You work as an undertaker's assistant in
your grandfather's funeral parlor at Number thirty-one, Piazza
Vittime Civili di Guerra, Quarter of San Lorenzo?" Another nod.

"When the Maresciallo asks you a question"—the lieutenant
was speaking for the first time—"you answer it orally. You also
say '*signore*.'"

The fat man sighed gently and turned over his paper. Again

there was silence save for the hasty tick-tick-tick of that watch.

"You've been living with your grandfather for how long—five years?"

Gennaro nodded again, received an angry look from the lieutenant and muttered hoarsely "*Si, signore*—five years."

"Or five and a half years?"

"Yes—five and a half."

"You must try to be precise when I ask you questions. Before that you were at a church college in Ferrara?"

"*Si, signore.*"

"You must have been"—the Maresciallo was slow and almost sleepy—"about eleven years and six months old when you ran away, then?"

Gennaro swallowed. "*Si.*"

"You didn't like Ferrara? Or was it the school you didn't like?"

"The school—in a way."

"You were unhappy there?"

The lieutenant fidgeted and cleared his throat, but slowly, gently rapping a pencil against the desk-edge, the Maresciallo repeated the question, his small eyes fixed on Gennaro's face. "You didn't like it there?"

"No."

"No '*signore*'!" snapped the lieutenant, and at his voice the fat man's shoulders twitched and sagged.

"*Scusi, signore,*" muttered Gennaro red-faced.

"*Non fa niente.* Your education ceased when you were eleven and a half. Hmm. Yes. And since then you've been acting as assistant to your grandfather?"

"*Si, signore.*"

"What actual work do you do?"

"Everything. I make coffins, wreaths, arrange funerals."

"Make coffins, wreaths, arrange funerals," murmured the Maresciallo sleepily. "Which do you do most of?"

"Well—I suppose I make more wreaths than anything else. People want to buy them more often."

The lieutenant shifted his chair impatiently and said, "Maresciallo, I don't know what—" And then was waved into sulky silence.

"You have to work late hours sometimes, I suppose?"

"*Si, signore*—often halfway through the night."

"Yes—yes probably. Yes, I imagine so. Hmm. Your grandfather taught you the trade?"

"*Si, signore*. I learned everything from him."

"Maresciallo! Really, I can't imagine what—"

"*Pazienza, pazienza, Tenente*." The Maresciallo frowned down at his paper. Then with a bored shrug he said, "Take him outside a minute" and Gennaro felt the plainclothesman on his right touch his arm.

As soon as the door closed, Giacobelli turned on Valdemarin. "Really, Ugo! What are you doing? Are you investigating a murder case or"—he grinned but there was impatient anger in his eyes—"carrying on some sort of social science survey?"

"Probably both," grunted the Maresciallo morosely. "They often go together."

"Well, you're not getting anywhere, are you?"

"You don't think so?"

"No, I don't!"

The Maresciallo sighed deeply and sat back. "Well, what *do* you think, then?"

"About this boy? He's got a bad record. Ran away from school"—Giacobelli picked up the typed paper—"has a previous police conviction, consorts with the wife of a military prisoner. Then he's of mixed blood and illegitimate at that. And his grandfather's business is failing, it seems. Probably the old man gives him hardly any money and the woman badgers him for it. And he belongs to that age when they want money more than anything else. In the circumstances I should feel very suspicious."

"He's not a big boy by any means—for his age."

"What of that?"

"Two things. He's not been hit by a pistol bullet within the last twenty-four hours. You'll agree to *that*, perhaps?"

"Maresciallo, I don't think there's any reason to use that tone!"

"I beg your pardon, Tenente. But the patrolman said, before he died—it's on that paper you've got there—that of the two men involved, the one whom he wounded came out with the boxes. Thus the second, unwounded, man was the one who held up that shutter. Considering the quantity of boxes stolen and the distance from the place of theft to the 'Ape' one can work out approximately the time needed to support that very heavy shutter. This boy couldn't have done it. He's not strong enough."

"One can't be sure."

"One can seldom be sure in these sort of investigations, certainly. Does anything else about him strike you?"

Giacobelli looked sullen. "He's the right age for this sort of thing. Irresponsible—obviously unstable—needs money. Is that what you mean?"

"No, Tenente. And let me, if I may"—the Maresciallo sighed and rubbed an eyebrow with one forefinger—"point out that psychological guesswork, however interesting in itself, is not the same thing as criminal investigation. Equally, I don't agree with you. I have a son of my own. I don't take the view that everyone is basically criminal at a certain age. I don't think I was. I doubt if you were. Why should he be?"

Giacobelli mumbled something about youth being different these days, but the Maresciallo was not listening. "No. What interests me about Gualtierra is—quite simply—that neither in here nor when he was picked up by Calvanese has he asked what all this is about. Not once—and I've given him plenty of opportunities—has he wanted to know why he's been pulled in. You'd think, wouldn't you—"

"Yes! By God, Ugo, that's something!"

The Maresciallo shook his head ponderously. "*No, scusi, Tenente.* It is very little. There is a large class of people—the poor and particularly the young poor—who invariably keep their mouths shut in the presence of the police. And all the more so if they have ever been in trouble before—as this boy has over a driving offense. No. It's interesting as a point to note, that's all. It probably means nothing at all."

"So—what are you going to do?"

"Oh, let him go, of course. What else?"

Giacobelli sat forward urgently. "But that bit of wreath. What about that?"

"Stolen from Capodichino, I expect. La Gobba said the back of that truck was full of wreaths. It was," said the Maresciallo gloomily, "almost the only piece of information we got out of her."

"But she saw the two men. She might recognize this boy—
you think?"

"Perhaps—perhaps not. Her word would not be any good in
a law court, though. No, Tenente. Gobba's been given a couple
of thousand lire and told to keep a lookout for the man she saw
—or whom we assume she may have seen—if indeed it was not
some hallucination of her own. If she can find him and *then*
tell us—well, that's a different matter. But to pull her in and
get her to identify someone here—No, no. Any lawyer would
have that thrown out of evidence at once. Also, it would damage
Corps prestige even to try it. And anyway," added the Maresciallo more practically, "she's done one of her disappearances
again. Nobody can find her this morning."

Giacobelli jumped to his feet. "Maresciallo!" His voice held
a note of almost hysterical frustration. "A policeman was shot
and killed last night! I must say I think you're taking this matter extraordinarily calmly—frivolously, almost!"

Valdemarin's face darkened slowly. "Tenente, do you really
think that someone with my history would take the killing of a
policeman frivolously?"

"Certainly he shouldn't—that's true enough!" Giacobelli's
voice was sullen. He felt his last remark had gone too far, but
owing to his higher rank he did not know how to retreat.

Slowly the Maresciallo put the typed paper back in the box-
file at his elbow. Slowly, very slowly, he tied the tapes. Then,
still silently, he picked up the file, rose and handed it to Giacobelli. "Perhaps, since the lieutenant is not satisfied with the way
I am conducting the investigation of this case, he would prefer
to undertake the entire matter himself?"

Giacobelli swallowed. His face flushed a dark red and his
lips thinned. No one had spoken to him like that for years—not,
at any rate, since he had won his Olympic medal. Savagely he
said, "Very well! Yes, Maresciallo, I will do just that! I will take
over the entire case and handle it my own way and we'll see
who—But please sit down."

"You would not rather that I went upstairs and got on with
the Vehicle Report?"

"I'd rather you *sat down!*"

Giacobelli strode to the door, jerked it open and snapped,
"All right. Bring him back!"

Reentering the room, Gennaro noticed that the two men at the desk had changed places. The lieutenant sat at the center with the box-file before him; the fat Maresciallo, looking flushed and angry, sat to one side. Almost before Gennaro had reached the desk Giacobelli snapped, "Gualtierra, where were you last night?"

"At home."

"At your—your grandfather's place?"

"*Si, signore.*"

"All night?"

"Yes. I was cleaning up the workshop and sharpening some tools."

"When did you go to bed?"

"About midnight."

"Before that you were at home—all the evening?"

"*Si, signore.*"

Giacobelli wrenched open the box-file and pulling something out, thrust it at Gennaro. "Ever seen this before?"

With a grunt of anguished exasperation, Maresciallo Valdemarin lifted a splayed hand across his face to hide the emotions he was otherwise incapable of disguising. Did Giacobelli really know nothing, *nothing at all*, after all these months? Could he not understand that the proper way to interrogate anyone— but particularly someone young and nervous like Gualtierra— was to commence very slowly, very easily, with scores of simple, irrelevant questions until the suspect was lured into giving unthought-out answers. Then a few, still apparently easy, questions—but ones with important implications—were slipped in. And only after that—after the suspect had gone back, tried to cover up, contradicted himself—only then must the tempo suddenly increase with fast, hard, brutal questions interspersed with shouted threats and slaps. But as for this—theatrical, dramatic, ridiculous . . . Oh Holy Mother of God, why, in his retiring years, should he be plagued with a vain, ignorant idiot of a swimming champion as a superior officer?

But Giacobelli was looking at Gennaro's face, and across it had passed such an expression of shocked fear as confirmed at once all the lieutenant's vague and unfounded suspicions. This boy might, or might not, have been the "second man"—the unwounded accomplice who held up the shutter—but he *knew* about it. Giacobelli turned quickly, triumphantly, to the Maresciallo—surely that picture of guilt and terror had not been lost upon him—only to see that the old fool had his hand across his face and with his eyes shut to everything was nodding his exasperation down at the desk.

The lieutenant swung back to Gennaro. "Well—come on! Have you seen this before?"

"No—I mean I don't know. Is it—is it something of ours?"

"It's yours all right!"

"St—Steno?"

"Steno."

"We buried her on the twenty-sixth."

"You supplied the wreaths?"

"Yes."

"And afterwards"—it was an inspired guess—"you went back to the cemetery and collected them?"

Gennaro's face was dull red. "The frames are ours. It's not stealing. If we did not do that we would have to charge for the frames, too. The frames cost much more than the flowers. The clients pay for the flowers, not the frames."

"So you *do* collect the wreaths later?"

"Yes."

"And bring them back to your shop and demolish them?"

Gennaro nodded.

"And what do you do with the flowers and ribbons and so forth?"

"Throw them away."

Giacobelli leaned forward across the desk, his eyes narrow and accusing. "Or put them in the back of an 'Ape' and go off to steal motor horns and incidentally murder a night patrolman? Yes—he died!"

This time Gennaro stared at him wide-eyed, his mouth partly open. The expression on his face could have been horror or, equally, immense surprise. Valdemarin assumed it was the latter, shook his head and gave a gusty sigh. *"Really!"*

Giacobelli realized it was the former. "Quick!"

"I don't know what you mean!"

"Say '*signore*' when you address me!"

"Signore—si."

Once more Valdemarin wiped his face with his hand. Not content with bungling this interrogation in a manner which would have sent any other detective officer back to traffic duty, Giacobelli apparently wanted to play soldiers. . . .

"You don't know what I mean?" The lieutenant's voice was filled with menace. "I think you do. Now—are you going to tell me where you were last night?"

"I've told you! I was in my workshop cleaning my tools."

"That's a lie!"

"No."

Giacobelli rose abruptly from behind the desk. He was furiously aware that his interrogation had been ridiculously clumsy, had brought him quickly to the undignified impasse of assertion countered by contradiction, and that not only Valdemarin, but Calvanese and Fabrizi, were inwardly ridiculing him for it. In their eyes he was showing himself an incompetent fool. Very well! But none of them had seen the expression on Gualtierra's face when he first saw that ribbon and bit of palm leaf—Valdemarin because he had his eyes shut, the two others because they were on each side of Gualtierra and looking in the same direction.

Giacobelli, like many athletes, had always believed in instinct, and he had a great contempt for routine procedure. He would show Valdemarin and these others just how right he was —and how wrong they were. It was true that there was only one method of doing this now, and it was a method which it would be highly irregular to use at this stage; but he was not a man to draw back from anything when his personal prestige was at stake. He took a small key from a drawer and striding across to the tall cupboard, unlocked and opened it.

Valdemarin shot to his feet with an alacrity which, for a man of his size, was alarming. "*Tenente!* What are you doing?"

"You'll see." Giacobelli threw a pair of handcuffs to Calvanese. "Behind his back. Take his shirt off first." Then he pulled out three black rubber aprons, a block and tackle with hooks and ropes, a rickety stepladder, and lastly a heavy piece of canvas reinforced with steel bars—something between a large surgical splint and a folding hospital stretcher.

In a despairing voice Valdemarin said, "Tenente—you've got

nothing to go on yet. You haven't even checked Gualtierra's statement of where he was last night! There may have been people who visited him or saw him at the time."

"There were! There were!" Gennaro was struggling in the powerful arms of Fabrizi while Calvanese unbuttoned his shirt and pulled it from his jeans. "There *were* people who saw me!"

"Tenente, please think what you're doing. Police regulations state strictly that—"

"Damn police regulations! Lay him down, you two—strap him in."

Giacobelli slipped a black rubber apron over his head and turned on the tap above the zinc tub. Then he climbed the stepladder with the block and tackle and hung it from a hook in the ceiling.

When he got down, Gennaro was lying on the floor strapped into the steel-and-canvas cocoon which held him rigidly motionless from his feet to his first ribs. His eyes wide with panic, he was gasping out, "I *was* at home! I *was!* I *was!* Gigi will tell you! Crocifissa saw me . . . the Maresciallo. . . . I was in his shop!"

No one took any notice. Valdemarin sat hunched in his chair staring down at the desk and blowing out his huge cheeks. Calvanese and Fabrizi, poker-faced, slipped on black aprons, took Gennaro's feet and hauling him across the concrete floor like a bundle of firewood, slipped a hook from the hanging tackle into a big metal ring at the bottom of the canvas stretcher. Then they heaved on the ropes and in a moment Gennaro was hanging upside-down by his heels over the zinc tub, now almost full of water.

"Gualtierra—for the last time—where were you last night at eleven o'clock?"

"At home! At home!"

Giacobelli nodded to his two assistants, the ropes whirred gently through the sheaves of the block and Gennaro's head and shoulders disappeared below the surface of the water in the zinc tub.

A sudden silence filled the interrogation room. Giacobelli had his shirt-cuff turned back and his eyes fixed on the long second-hand of his watch. Through thin lips he said, "Don't worry,

Maresciallo, I know all about drowning. I've sometimes nearly done it myself."

"This isn't the same." There was a quiet desperation in Valdemarin's voice. "You haven't even had his heart checked!"

"He's all right."

A sudden hissing shower of bubbles broke the water-surface of the tub.

"He'll be dead in another"—the Maresciallo consulted his own watch—"twenty-five seconds. Don't you know what happens when they're upside-down like that?"

"Yes—they generally tell the truth afterwards. All right—pull him up."

Calvanese and Fabrizi heaved on the rope, the canvas cocoon lifted toward the ceiling and Gennaro's livid face rose dripping from the tub. His eyes were half closed, water drooled from his slack lips, he made no sound. Then, with a rasping shudder, the contents of his stomach poured from his gaping mouth, and as a vessel in his nose broke under the strain, bright scarlet blood jetted over his inverted face and ran into his eyes and through his soaking hair.

"Where were you at eleven o'clock last night? *Where*? *Where*?"

Giacobelli's face swam upside-down in a flaring red mist before Gennaro's eyes. Through nauseating pain, consciousness flickered dimly, a small candle flame swaying in the howling darkness. He moaned feebly and vomit jerked from his lips and dripped over his clogged nose and pulsing eyeballs.

"Where were you? *Where were you*? Do you want to go in again? All right, then! Down you go!" Giacobelli signed to Calvanese, but the Maresciallo was between them. "Stop!" You'll kill him, Tenente! For God's sake—for your *own* sake, stop this! Do you want to ruin yourself?"

"*Basta!*" Giacobelli was fast losing control both of the situation and himself. He had not realized that the effects of inverted immersion were so much quicker and more lethal than the slower process of drowning the right way up. He knew only one thing —that Gualtierra would tell the truth very soon now, perhaps even before his head was underwater again. "Lower him slowly —slowly."

The ropes creaked in the block and Gennaro felt himself

descending once more. Swaying on the verge of black oblivion, his water-seared lungs tugging and straining to draw even a tiny quantity of air through his clogged throat into their inflamed and swollen tissues, his heart bouncing and thundering within his fiery chest, he knew at last that it was no good. He would have to tell them about last night. Even when they knew the full story there was nothing as terrifying or agonizing that they could do with him as what they had just done and were now preparing to do again. He tried to speak, but at the first attempt he only retched and threw out bloody water. He *must* speak! The top of his head was already cold on the water-surface—in two or three more seconds it would be too late. He moaned and then in a barely audible whisper gasped, "Last night—I was there. In the Via Savarese. I'll tell you everything—everything."

But no one was paying attention to him for the rope had jammed in the block hanging from the ceiling and Giacobelli in exasperated anger was shouting, *"Per l'amore di Dio, Calvanese!* Can't you do *anything* right!" It was a relief to take at least some of his anger out on his subordinates, and although he knew little of interrogation procedure, at least he knew that a victim of third-degree methods must never be given any unplanned respite; that the pressure, once commenced, must never be relaxed for a single instant until the confession has been extracted. "Get up on the ladder and—no! *Oh, Dio!* I'll do it myself." Giacobelli leapt up the stepladder and began furiously tugging at the jammed tackle. But the whole weight of Gennaro's suspended body held the twisted rope out of place and the lieutenant soon saw that the entire tackle would have to be taken down and untangled on the floor. Caught up in a spurt of raging frustration, he gave one immense tug at the jammed rope and in that instant two things happened. Gennaro found his voice with a sudden wail of *"San Gennaro! San Gennaro, aiutemi!"*—and the stepladder broke.

Giacobelli fell heavily and clumsily with one leg caught in the broken rungs of the ladder. He cannoned off Calvanese in his fall and landed on his left shoulder and the left side of his head. Valdemarin had once watched a man hanged and had heard the gristly snap of breaking vertebrae, so when he heard it again he recognized it for what it was immediately.

4

TWO hours later Gennaro, pale and still weak but cleaned up and restored to a recognizable semblance of humanity by the liberal use of brandy, was ushered into the Maresciallo's upstairs office—this time by only one uniformed policeman, who then left the room.

Frog-faced, his chin and neck sunk in immense rolls of fat, Valdemarin stared up from small, sullen eyes and silently, with a gesture of the pencil he held, indicated a chair on the other side of the desk. Under that stare, searching and, it seemed, doubtful, Gennaro sat down. He was curiously calm now, emptied of both fear and guilt—of all emotion—by the events of the morning. In his extremity he had demanded aid from his patron saint and that aid had been swift and certain. With such supernatural backing there was no longer reason to be afraid of mortal men. The long dead martyr-bishop whose great presence guarded Naples was no gentle Francis of Assisi but one of the more ruthless saints and Gennaro felt that the dead lieutenant's two black-aproned assistants had been fortunate to come out of the affair unscathed themselves. So, in fact, did they, and privately each had determined to visit the Duomo as soon as he was off duty to burn a conciliatory candle before the Silver shrine. They hoped sincerely that they would not suffer the embarrassment of meeting each other while in the sacred precincts.

Maresciallo Valdemarin, who was a northerner and therefore more skeptical, was less impressed—perhaps because as an opponent of the business in the *camera di sicurezza* he had no superstitious fears for himself. He told himself firmly that Gualtierra's anguished cry for heavenly help and the immediate breaking of the stepladder were nothing but an ordinary coincidence of totally unrelated events. But if not—and since it would be equally impractical and impious to indict the Patron of Naples for homicide—he himself would be inclined to burn a candle of thanksgiving for the abrupt removal of his intolerable superior officer. Anyway, the case of the murdered patrolman was now back in his hands and the box-file lay before him on his desk.

For a long moment they looked at each other—the sallow, spiky-haired boy in the shabby jeans and open shirt, the mountainously fat, grayhaired man in the crumpled linen suit. Then Valdemarin sighed deeply, pushed some papers to one side and said, "This has been a bad business." Gennaro nodded wordlessly and the Maresciallo continued. "It was a mistake on the part of the lieutenant. We've checked your statement concerning where you were last night—checked it very discreetly so that you've nothing to worry about in that direction. It was quite in order. You were seen in your workshop, as you told us." He paused. "Yes, it was a mistake. We don't often make mistakes of that sort. And we don't like them being talked about when we do." He stared significantly at Gennaro and received a nod of comprehension. "So—you were never in the *camera di sicurezza*. Nothing happened to you. You were brought to this office and you spent the morning here. You know nothing of Lieutenant Giacobelli's death. You understand?"

"Yes."

"Then repeat it."

Tonelessly Gennaro said, "I spent the morning here in this office. Nothing happened to me. I know nothing of Lieutenant Giacobelli's death."

"Good. Because if you did not understand that you would find yourself involved over the inquiry into this—ah—accident. And that would seriously annoy the police. You don't want to annoy the police, do you?"

"No, Signor Maresciallo."

"No—naturally. Then remember what I've said. Very well, you can go. No—wait a moment!" Puffing with the effort, Valdemarin bent down, unlocked a drawer in his desk and fumbled within. When he held out a pudgy hand to Gennaro it contained two red ten-thousand lire notes. "Take these—and keep your mouth shut."

Yet once the boy had left his office, Valdemarin stared down at his desk, moody and thoughtful. Somehow—somewhere— he was vaguely unsatisfied. What had made Giacobelli so suddenly sure of Gualtierra's guilt? And Gualtierra himself—his attitude, his whole behavior—had lacked any of that explosive protestation of innocence which one might have expected in the circumstances. His alibi appeared, at least from a brief investigation, to be perfectly sound. But alibis did not always stand up to careful probing. . . . And what had caused that heavy, bruised graze down his bare back which the Maresciallo had noted when he helped Calvanese to unstrap him from the stretcher? It had not been done in the interrogation room, certainly.

Valdemarin sighed again, sitting slumped at his desk, staring at the door through which the boy had gone minutes ago, and tapping a pencil thoughtfully against his thick underlip.

Bighencomer

⮞ 1

THE plane trees along the Via Raffaele Morghen were flecked and spotted with rusty gold and one by one the shuttered apartments in the high blocks of flats were reopening as family after family came back from the mountains or the wide, bright Adriatic beaches. In little more than three weeks the new academic year would commence, but until then it was officially summer and the families of the Vomero commuters still wore their bright holiday clothes, greeted each other's reappearance with cries of delighted surprise and sat together by the hour at the shaded sidewalk cafés on the Vanvitelli, comparing their vacation experiences and costs, their suntan, the growth of their children and the performance of their cars.

These, the flat-dwellers in the many-tiered dovecotes of the clean, green hillside suburb, were newcomers upon the Italian —and particularly the Neapolitan—scene; the last beneficiaries of the *miracolo economico*, that lighthouse in Milan whose beam illuminated the peninsula as far as this—but no farther. Prefabricated by newly acquired executive skills and a sharp rise in living standards; preconditioned by an American-slanted outlook which, nonetheless, decisively abandoned New World idealism for Old World skepticism; and prepacked with the widest range of desires and ambitions which could be inculcated by glossy magazines and commercialized television—these people were at home in mid-twentieth-century Europe as were few others. Since they had not existed in the past, the past hardly existed for them; they felt for it neither the debilitating nostalgia of the British and French nor the paranoic guilt or the Germans.

The future was theirs in any case, and meanwhile the present was satisfactory enough. They were hygienic, unpatriotic, intelligent, and anticlerical and very well-mannered. They coped with their lives—business, social and sex—with a day-to-day competence at once cynical, self-assured and kindly. One day soon, when the last few faded hangovers from the bad old days had been swept into history's ashcan—tarnished monarchies, threadbare aristocracies, preposterous old generals clanking the ghostly spurs of nineteenth-century nationalism—these people would form the basis of the new Europe which was already, and with ever-growing fidelity, reflecting back at them their own attitudes, standards and values.

Despite the fact that Beppo had lived in Vomero for nearly four years he had never succeeded in merging socially with his neighbors. There was no good reason for this. It was true that until recently his economic position had been among the lower brackets, but it was well compensated for by his occupational status and his courtesy title of "Professor" teaching at the Nunziatella. It was true that he had no car—the most important of all Italian status symbols—but his family was correctly small, his apartment correctly furnished and unvisited by priests or nuns.

But he was some four or five years older than the majority of his male neighbors, and those years were of ominous significance for they placed him firmly in the wartime generation. And to make matters worse he had worn the black shirt of the Militia. Vomero, with its slick, new, drip-dry internationalism, might perhaps have overlooked a year or so of forced military service as an unwilling boy-conscript—but it would not easily forgive someone who had carried the gilt fasces on his collar instead of silver State stars. Beppo was understood to belong to the generation of racist destroyers, while his neighbors considered themselves a generation of cosmopolitan builders. If many of them had suffered in a childhood they very seldom spoke of today, that suffering was laid at the door of the men who had fought in the war and who were suspected, particularly if they had worn the black shirt, of having wanted it and condoned it. Beppo's fellow commuters were always polite, but the gap that separated him from them—those few years when they had been entering their teens and Beppo had been emerging from his— formed an unbridgeable gulf between them.

And Beppo realized this and accepted it without resentment. His neighbors were, in the main, better than he at the art of living; more successful in their work, more self-assured, competent and secure. It was not his fault but it was so. One does not improve a human being by beating him, starving him and frightening the wits out of him, before sending him to an indefinite period of forced labor in exile to recuperate. Beppo was damaged goods before he had properly left the assembly line; the others had rolled off it new and shining and in proper working order.

Nonetheless, it was in Vomero that he lived and intended to remain. And he was well aware that his newly acquired wealth would, in the eyes of his neighbors, fully make up for his unfortunate youth. He would demonstrate his altered circumstances carefully but unmistakably. To start, with a car—not the invariable Fiat 600 but a long, sleek Alfa-Romeo costing four times as much. In a few months he would move to a larger apartment with a garden and a wide view over the gulf rather than into the classroom of the medical school. And next summer he would add the final touch—a motor-boat down at Mergellina.

Though he would undoubtedly enjoy his new affluence to the full, all these things would be done mainly for Mina. She, of course, had always been accepted by the neighbors as equal with their own children, though she had made few friends amongst them. In the future Beppo saw her, in his imagination, as the leading light on the Vomero scene.

Mina was not looking well—paler and with a most unusual listlessness. She went about her housework with what sometimes seemed a weary exasperation, an impatient boredom. Beppo had meant to take her away for the whole of August—right away for a proper vacation somewhere high up in the Alto Adige among the mountain pastures and the mountain lakes. In other years and by dint of much saving for months in advance, they had generally managed to pass a fortnight of August in a cheap *pensione* at Roccaraso or Scanno; not far enough away to strain their limited finances yet sufficiently high to let them breathe

the cool air of the hills and to be, if only for a few days, *in villag-giatura*. But his schemes for a proper holiday this summer, a holiday that was to be so much longer and better than any they had ever had before, a luxurious introduction to a new, freer, wealthier life, had been postponed once, then again, and at last reluctantly laid aside.

Every sort of difficulty that could conceivably have arisen over both the will and the property of old Ercole Sanbrenedetto seemed, to his nephew, to have drifted up like a storm of threatening clouds during the past months. There was a horrible tangle of leasehold and freehold tenures enmeshing the entire Pendino section of his inheritance. The Adriatic villa was—heaven alone knew why—mortgaged in some obscure fashion to a Greek contractor at present in Buenos Aires. Two of Beppo's aunts had sunk long-standing feuds to join in contesting that part of the will which dealt with Vittorio's Risorgimento relics, and there was an odious young ex-manservant who hinted at peculiar irregularities between himself and the dead old man and wanted to be bought off with a lump sum—or at least a sports car.

Then, to complete the picture, the municipal authorities had been behaving very oddly over the bombed buildings in San Lorenzo. They had dug up a fifteen-year-old demand for war damage compensation from Uncle Ercole and were busy contesting the sum involved even though Beppo had told them that he had no intention of pressing the claim or rebuilding the houses. He had been in and out of the Municipio throughout July without achieving anything save constant references to various officials who referred him to others and, eventually, a frightening demand for a large sum in unpaid city rates. The urban police were complaining that some of the ruins were used for illicit gambling by gangs of unemployed and demanding that they should be wired off; a local priest complained that the darker parts were used for illicit love-making and demanded that they should be fully illuminated; the Sanitary Department said they were being used as a rubbish dump and an open-air latrine and wanted them pulled down while the Survey Department said that they were a public danger in their present condition and insisted that they be shored up. When Beppo explained that he intended to sell them he was told that some, or perhaps all, of these things must be done first and referred to a city plan which he could not understand and a host of regulations dating from 1870, liberally amended by the Fascist regime and re-amended by postwar authorities until they ground to a deadlock of impossible contradictions.

Beppo had spent still more time in his lawyer's office than he had in the Municipio, but the results had been almost equally disappointing. July and August were notoriously the worst months of the year in which to transact any serious business; everyone was too hot, too tired, too anxious to get away on his summer vacation to press forward with the unraveling of complex testamentary and property legalities. Sometimes it had entered Beppo's head to call on Signor Bighencomer to assist him in his difficulties but such a request, he realized, would be tantamount to an agreement to sell the San Lorenzo property at the last price—sixty-five million—which the restaurant owner had offered, and this was something which Beppo hesitated to do. He had hoped for a larger sum and for some time had toyed with the idea of pursuing the inquiry he had received in June from ITOLGAS.

But he had got no further than the making of a single telephone call. Since the Piazza Vittime Civili di Guerra—he no longer thought of it as "the Nicòtera" now—was clearly marked on the municipal plans as a residential area, he had originally assumed that the great oil company was intending to erect some sort of apartment accommodation for their own workers—the autocratic paternalism of the firm was a byword in Naples— and perhaps an arrangement might be made whereby Crocifissa and her tenants could be included. So he had telephoned to find out the ITOLGAS intention—an unwise thing to do for the call had been relayed from department to department and taken twenty minutes to arrive at its right destination—only to be told that the site was wanted for an auto service station. It didn't make sense. Someone must be making a mistake somewhere. In any case Beppo was no businessman, as his past had adequately proved, and though he had boasted of the contrary to Mina, the thought of trying to play a man like Bighencomer and a firm like ITOLGAS against one another had filled him with fright. He was sure he would get the worst of such a stratagem himself and—as he had often to remind himself these days —the will was not yet proved.

But now, with the year waning into early autumn, official Naples had begun to yawn and stretch and emerge slowly, little by little, from its lethargic summer trance. Within the last week Beppo had more or less cleared up the Pendino property tangle, had frustrated the two litigious aunts and even rented the Adriatic villa to a family from Turin at a profitable figure. The Bank had come forward, at last, with a reasonable advance of money and his lawyer had returned to the long formalities of proving old Ercole's will with something which almost amounted to zest.

Even the San Lorenzo property was untangling itself at last. On Beppo's most recent visit to the Municipio he had managed to see the head of the Town Planning Office, a friendly, middle-aged man just back from Madonna di Campiglio and with the healthy effects of the mountain air still visible on his cheeks. For once Beppo had received some clear answers to his questions, some sympathy for his difficulties. Yes, it was true that the municipality intended that the property in the Piazza Vittime Civili di Guerra should remain residential—"Industrial development of every sort must take place outside the city." The director had explained clearly, briefly, that what the Municipality wanted in place of Beppo's broken buildings was a block of small, cheap apartments. "And I understand, Signor Sanbrenedetto, that you feel the same way?"

Beppo had agreed. He had gone back mentally to Crocifissa's little box of a kitchen on that afternoon three months ago when he had attended Ercole's funeral, and then had visualized the old woman properly lodged in a clean new flat, able to end her days in a little comfort at last. . . . "What about shops? I mean on the ground floor."

The director seemed to take his point at once. "Yes. Small individual ones, certainly. Nothing in the way of a large store, of course. In fact"—a plan had been taken from a folder and spread across the desk—"this is the sort of thing we had in mind. It is something that was put up in the Avvocata Quarter last year." Beppo had looked down at the design for a tall, multi-windowed block whose bottom story was set with the glass fronts of a chain of small shops. "This sort of thing, as you can see, Signor Sanbrenedetto, is an asset to a poor community."

"I know someone who is anxious to buy the site and put up something exactly like this."

"You do?" The town planning chief had raised his eyebrows in pleased surprise. "And—if it is not an improper question at this stage—are you intending to sell your property to him?"

"It depends." Beppo had stalled at answering something so direct. "We are not agreed on the price yet. And there are so many difficulties. The Municipality wants so many things straightened out first. There are back taxes and all this business of war damage and they say I must not complete a sale until—"

"I don't think you need worry too much about that. Once we have an assurance—a firm assurance—that the sort of building we want is going to be constructed I don't think you'll find that there will be any difficulty raised on our side."

"I've been here so often—A dozen times at least since June. And everything has become more difficult rather than less." Beppo's voice had been mournful.

"I wish you had come straight to me, then. All these other departments—they get in each other's way. Continually niggling over things which don't matter in the least. No, no—settle your price, Signor Sanbrenedetto, and then come to me and I'll guarantee that you'll have permission to sell within a week."

Beppo's face lit up. He wanted only two things now. To get the San Lorenzo property off his hands and to ensure, for his conscience' sake, that old Crocifissa and her lodgers should not be turned out into the street. The friendly helpfulness of the man across the wide desk, a man whose big, comfortable office was adequate proof of his power to implement his promises, made him suddenly bold. "Tell me. Signor Direttore, from your own experience what would you consider that property worth?"

The director had laughed with a show of embarrassment. "My dear sir, that is hardly for me to say. I really don't think I can—"

"Your *personal* opinion," Beppo had persisted. "Just between you and me."

"Well—well, let me see. Hmm . . . Roughly I suppose one

might say something about fifty-five to sixty million, I suppose. Approximately that figure, anyhow."

Beppo's face had fallen. "Fifty-five to sixty? No more than that?" A shrug and a smile had answered him better than words. "But I've been offered more—considerably more, I assure you."

"Then, if I might advise you, I should certainly take it."

And Beppo had come away with the feeling that perhaps, after all, he was not such a bad businessman himself. Had he not pushed up Bighencomer's price from sixty to sixty-five million merely by being noncommittal? To press an extra five million out of a man like Bighencomer, when the head of the Town Planning Office believed ten million less to be a reasonable price, surely demonstrated a certain financial acumen. Perhaps after all there was something of his grandfather in him, unrecognized as it had been in his youth.

And it was true, thought Beppo, that ITOLGAS had not, despite their originally courteous letter, contacted him again. They, too, must have found out that the site was to be restricted to residential building only. He and Mina had discussed the matter for two more days and in the end they had agreed upon a simple plan. Beppo must see Bighencomer again —better, perhaps, to telephone him, since the man's overpowering presence was less oppressive at two kilometers' distance—and suggest a selling price of seventy-five million. They would argue a little. Bighencomer would come up to seventy and Beppo would descend to that figure—an amicable splitting of the difference on both sides.

And once the decision had been made, Beppo had sighed with relief and fetched a bottle of cognac from the kitchen cupboard. Standing beside Mina, pouring the brandy into the small glasses, he had been filled with an immense sensation of lightness as if a burden he had borne for too long had been lifted from his shoulders. He was aware of an exuberance which he had hardly known since the end of May when the news of his inheritance had first reached him. Now at last, and with the ending of summer, his difficulties, too, were ending; and in October, with them all behind him—with everything settled —he would be in Devon, taking Mina for their long-delayed vacation. October was a good month, perhaps the best, in West England. Looking down at the golden cognac he recalled the golden woods, the leaf-scattered lanes, the autumn stillness of a country drowsy with harvest and now turning to rest.

❧ 2

THE next day was his birthday. Waking in the early dawn Beppo remembered that today he was forty-one, healthy, content and—by his standards, at any rate—rich. There was nothing more to worry about at all.

At breakfast he found a card from the Pinnigers; they never forgot and year by year a card of the most florid sort—for the Pinnigers, despite their erudition, had execrable artistic taste (but then Beppo's was no better)—arrived on the seventh of September. The only other letter he received was further reminder from the Municipality of the tax owing on the San Lorenzo property, and despite his recent friendly talk with the planning director it was written in a threatening, indeed a menacing, manner, demanding payment of the full sum within a week.

This so upset Beppo that he could only with an effort bring his mind back to the important business of opening his birthday presents. Since, for the last four years, Beppo and Mina had had no one but each other with whom to exchange presents at Christmas and birthdays, and since they felt this to be a sad pointer to their lack of family or acceptable relations, they had taken to sending each other presents purporting to come from others. Thus Mina was in the habit of receiving pieces of costume jewelry with a note of fulsome flattery from the President of the Republic, cosmetics and blessings from the Pope and minor items of artist's equipment from European royalty, regnant, deposed or currently and scandalously in the news. Beppo's presents were generally from local and less exalted sources. This year they included two ties from the proprietors of the new fish shop in the Piazza Vanvitelli, wrapped in an unpaid account for mullet, sole and cuttlefish supplied over the past month, one of the porter's cat's kittens with a kind note from its mother and a new sort of patent toothbrush from Mina's

Vittorio—"so that your smile may be as bright as mine."
"Only," said Mina a little sadly, for she disapproved of the
occasional dismemberment of the skeleton, "they took away his
lower jaw yesterday so it's only half a smile at present."

Beppo rose and kissed her warmly and their spectacles clashed
in happy unison. But throughout the rest of the meal, with
the blue-eyed kitten wandering gingerly about the table ex-
ploring milk jug and marmalade, teapot and toast, his mind
dwelt on the San Lorenzo property. It was obvious, now, that
he must sell it at once; there was nothing else he could do. Despite the fact that Ercole's will remained unproved the sale could
be effected with the help of a lawyer. He must contact Bighencomer without delay and clinch the deal.

After breakfast he went to the telephone to call the restaurant owner but was told that it was too early and that Signor
Bighencomer was not yet available. . . . "Ring again after
ten o'clock—or better, after ten-thirty," said someone at the
other end brusquely and clicked down the receiver.

Mina went off with her shopping-bag and Beppo settled
down with the morning paper—or what remained of it after
Mina had cut out a cooking recipe, an art critique and used the
middle page to clear up the first of the kitten's indiscretions.

Mina had been gone less than half an hour when the doorbell rang and Beppo put down a description of the latest government scandal and went to answer it. At the door stood a tall,
sallow saturnine man, thin-lipped, poker-faced and dressed
in severe black. Beppo had a vague feeling of having seen him
on some previous occasion but could not think when or where.
Wrinkling his forehead, his glasses slipping down his bridgeless
nose, he said, "I believe we've met before but . . ."

"Not formally, Signor Sanbrenedetto." The visitor gave a
small, thin smile, his black eyes peering over Beppo's shoulder
into the flat, noting the smart, cheap "modern" mass-produced
furniture, the plastic flowers and the enlarged and tinted photograph of Beppo's dead wife. "But I have seen you at the O Sole
Mio Restaurant at Mergellina. Until recently I was headwaiter
there. My name is Dru—Achille Dru."

"Oh—oh, yes. Now I remember you. I know the proprietor,
you see."

Dru bowed slightly. "I am aware of that. Can I come in?"

"Yes, certainly." Beppo turned from the door and showed his visitor into the sitting room. "It's a nice place, the O Sole Mio," he said conversationally and wondering what Bighencomer's ex-headwaiter could possibly want with him.

"One of the worst I ever came across," said Dru calmly, "and I've been in the trade all my life. If Signor Bighencomer had not got influential friends in the Public Health Office that place would be shut down for contravening every single one of the hygiene laws. . . . But I've come to see you about something else; something which affects you much more closely, I think."

"Yes? Please sit down, then."

"Thank you. I have some information concerning property of yours. Information which should be of value to you. Which will, I think, save you several million lire at the least." Dru paused and stared at Beppo closely from eyes as black as his suit—for a second Beppo found himself wondering, irrelevantly, if he had chosen the material for that reason.

There was silence for a minute and then Dru gave the slight sigh of one who has hoped and waited for a response that has not been forthcoming. "If I'm right, Signor Sanbrenedetto, and that will be for you to judge, I should expect a certain reward for my help in effecting this saving."

Beppo nodded cautiously." I see. How much?"

"I shall certainly be helping you to avoid a heavy loss—so shall we say two hundred and fifty thousand?"

"That's a lot of money."

"You stand to lose very much more at present. But I will leave it to you to decide. I understand that my late employer Francesco Bighencomer—or the Mergellina Construction and Development Company, which is the official name he gives himself on these occasions—is attempting to buy some old property of yours in the San Lorenzo Quarter?"

Beppo nodded. He did not ask how Dru knew this; in his experience of Naples everyone always seemed to know everything.

"And he is intending to pull it down and put up a block of cheap apartments on the site?"

"Yes, with shops underneath. That is what has to be done. The Municipality has ruled that it must remain residential."

"Then you will doubtless be surprised to hear that Signor

Bighencomer intends to put up a block of offices." Dru smiled coldly. "It is a trick he has done very successfully once before —at Salerno, to be precise. He bought a site in the town center after its owner had been officially informed that it could be used for residential purposes only—and a year later there was a tall block of offices in that place.

"It is really extremely simple—though ingenious, of course. Bighencomer sees the local planning office whose members are easily induced to cooperate in the matter for suitable financial reward. Since there is no question of breaking the law they have nothing to lose by such cooperation. Once the owner of the property knows he may only put up apartments he is generally prepared to sell at a low figure because of the rent laws and the extremely small return on capital outlay that they ensure—not to speak of the cost and difficulty of repairs and troublesome tenants and so forth. So Bighencomer buys him out. And then it is found that the place is not, *at present*, suitable for the construction of apartments owing to the inadequacy of the water supply.

"You may not know it, but before building a new residence of any sort at Naples or as far down the coast as Salerno, you must acquire special permission from the authorities of the Office of Reservoirs and Aqueducts—the water-supply people. That is because the supply is already inadequate in most places and the authorities understandably cannot allow uncontrolled building and uncontrolled demands for water. Bighencomer, however, carefully neglects to ask permission until his foundations and skeleton are up. Then he suddenly remembers. He hurries around to the water office and an obliging official, who will later receive a handsome gift, is then insolent to him in front of as many people as possible and refuses permission to build on half a dozen technical points. Bighencomer does all he can; he apologizes, he pleads, he explains over and over again that it has all been a mistake. The official is colder and more contemptuous and repeats his refusal emphatically. There is no chance of an adequate water supply for the new building until the mains have been enlarged. This is to happen one day of course—but until then . . . No.

"What can poor Signor Bighencomer do? He has made a mistake. He is, needless to say, too honest to even think of bribery in such a case. He returns, wringing his hands, to the Municipal Planning Office and explains what has happened. Can they help him? No, they cannot. The Public Health Office states—politely this time, but very firmly—that unless a full water supply is guaranteed, the Municipality must withdraw its permission and no residential building may be erected. So what can this poor man, who has only made one little slip, do with his building and his site? 'Well,' says a senior official in the Planning Office, "what about using the building—temporarily only, of course—for commercial offices? When, one day, the enlarged water mains are laid, the building must be put to its prearranged use, certainly, but until then . . .' There is a great demand for office space today and if centrally situated it is roughly fifty to two hundred times more valuable than living space, since the rent laws do not apply to it—and all that is necessary, of course, is a very modest supply of water. So the Planning Office suggest that Signor Bighencomer goes around again to the water authorities and asks humbly if he might, perhaps, be allowed the very small supply of water necessary for an office block."

Dru, who appeared to be extracting a certain dry enjoyment from his narrative, paused. "You will hardly be surprised to hear that the brusque official at the water offices relents and brusquely grants Signor Bighencomer's modest request. The office block is then built on a set of plans which, surprisingly enough, fit the skeleton just as easily as the original plans for the apartments which were submitted to, and accepted by, the municipal authorities in the first place. So—since, of course, the new water mains are a nice dream which will not materialize before the end of the century or Judgment Day, whichever is the sooner—everything turns out all right in the end and everyone is happy—except, one assumes, the original owner of the site who now realizes that he has sold it at less than half its true value." Dru looked long and meaningly at Beppo's shocked face. "That is how he did it at Salerno—and it is how he intends to do it here."

"But—how do you know?"

"I have several sources of information. And remember that until recently I was headwaiter at his restaurant. He entertained there constantly and every time he did so I cooked and served the food at his table from my *batterie de cuisine*—for reasons which, had you seen our kitchen, would be obvious to you. This process naturally took some time and I was able— indeed, forced—to hear all that was said between him and his guests. I have a good memory; it is something which is most important in my profession—and I forget nothing. I well remember his conversation with you. He has also entertained an official from the Town Planning Office, and one from the water authorities. I expect I shall be calling on them both in due course. Well, have I done what I promised—saved you several million lire?"

"Yes—yes I suppose so." Beppo rubbed one hand across his forehead. He was more startled than indignant. Like most Neapolitans he admired a clever trick even when it was aimed at himself—though only if he was able to frustrate it in time. He might have become angry at the way in which Bighencomer would have cheated poor old Crocifissa out of the new home and shop he so much wanted for her had not a greater question suddenly loomed up, overshadowing all else. If he did not sell to Bighencomer almost immediately he could not meet the Municipality's seven-day ultimatum for payment of taxes. And now it came to him that this morning's threatening letter, far from being a mistake, as he had thought, had been carefully composed and timed to give him the ultimate necessary incentive to close the deal with Bighencomer. Bighencomer knew all about that letter and had arranged for it to be sent. At this moment Bighencomer was, in all probability, waiting for the response he never doubted would come; waiting to hear Beppo's voice on the telephone. "Signor Bighencomer? I've thought about your proposition and I'd like to . . ."

But what could he do, even now that he knew of what Bighencomer had intended? He could not expose him since nothing technically illegal had been planned, far less done—or, at least, there neither was nor would be the slightest shred of evidence to the contrary. He could not sell the site to any other purchaser who wanted to build apartments since none other than Bighencomer had come forward, and Beppo saw bleakly enough now, that none would—it was a poor sort of investment and he had often wondered why Bighencomer should be prepared to accept it. And as for developing the site himself—that was quite out of the question. Meanwhile, not only must he pay over three and a half million lire in retroactive tax within seven days— money which, in fact, he had not got—but every department in the Municipio's great pile of offices, not to speak of the police and the church, were looming over him with demands to do something about the present state of the property. He guessed with panicky despair that a refusal to sell to Bighencomer would bring the majority of these demands crashing down upon him with small delay—and he turned abruptly to the sallow, impassive man sitting in Mina's armchair.

"Look—you may be right about what you've told me. I'm sure you are. But it doesn't help. I'll still have to sell to Bighencomer."

Dru took a leather cigarette case from his pocket and without offering it to Beppo lit a cigarette. "Why?"

"Because I can't do anything else. Listen . . ." Beppo took a deep breath and came out with the whole story. He explained about Uncle Ercole; about his own frustrated attempt to assist in the sale of the site while his uncle was still alive; about his inheritance, his feelings for Crocifissa, the meeting with Bighencomer and, ruefully, the offer from ITOLGAS.

Dru nodded and nodded and at last, when Beppo ended his story with raised shoulders and widespread hands, said, "Yes, yes. I see. He's a clever one—that Bighencomer. If you had taken the oil firm's offer at once you would have done better, because undoubtedly they would have arranged something satisfactory with the Municipio. As it is—well, you didn't and Bighencomer got in first. And since the municipal officials have taken his money they cannot back down." He frowned thoughtfully down at his cigarette. "If they tried to do so they would place themselves in Bighencomer's power for the rest of their lives—their careers would be in his hands. No, no—they are not such fools. Even if ITOLGAS were to approach them with a good proposition—no." He shook his head and then asked curiously, "And Signor Sanbrenedetto—all this, this difficulty, has been because you were sorry for your old nurse? Otherwise you might have investigated the ITOLGAS proposition? But could you not have helped her in some other way—given her money or a pension for instance?"

"Yes—I suppose so." Beppo's shoulders were slumped and

he stared down at his hands hanging loosely between his knees. "It must seem stupidly sentimental to you. You see it is not only she herself—though to me she is naturally the most important —but some other people also. People who live in the building too, as her lodgers. They are all poor—as poor as she is— and unfortunate in various ways; persons whom the English proverb would term lame dogs who need helping over stiles. They have lived together in the Piazza Vittime Civili di Guerra for many years and they are happy there. So is she, Crocifissa. She belongs there in that *piazza* with her friends. And then she is old and has had a hard life. I felt that if somehow I could make sure that she could remain—and even, perhaps, her poor lodgers, too . . ." He paused, staring down at his hands. "Once—long ago—I, too, learned what it was like to be—to be one of the dispossessed. To have everything taken away and to be left with nothing at all—no future—nothing."

Dru nodded with brief but complete understanding. Like the vast majority of Europeans of his generation—that generation from which Beppo's comparative youth had so nearly, but not quite, excluded him—Dru knew about dispossession. But there would always be the old and the poor; it did not do to become sentimental about them. Suddenly he said, "Have you got a copy of the municipal planning regulations here?"

"*Oh Benedetto Dio!*" Beppo gave a wan smile and thrust a hand through his thinning hair. "I've got a whole sackful!"

"I mean the one which deals specifically with the residential building orders. I'd like to see it."

Beppo got up, opened a drawer of his desk and threw a sheaf of papers upon the table. "It's one of those—a yellow one, I think."

"Hmm . . ." Dru's long, immaculately clean fingers leafed rapidly through the pile, flicked aside two large yellow forms and then carefully withdrew a third partially covered with the smallest possible print. For five minutes he was silent, his head bent, his brows drawn together in a frown of concentration. Then he took a thin, old-fashioned silver pencil from his pocket and carefully underlined a few words. "Listen to this, Signor Sanbrenedetto . . . 'no permanent buildings save for residential habitation' . . . And then we get an asterisk and there is a footnote listing every sort of residential building imaginable."

"Well—?"

"ITOLGAS—what sort of building do they want to put up?" Beppo shrugged. "A service station, I think. Why?"

"Because that is not—or need not be—a building. A concrete parking place, a raised concrete platform about ten centimeters high as a base for half a dozen pumps—and a kiosk. The pumps are not buildings, of course, nor are the underground tanks which supply them. And the kiosk—well, they're generally movable plastic things on wheels. Even if it could be called a building it certainly isn't permanent, since one must take permanent to mean 'constructed on a fixed foundation.' No, I imagine that—"

"But the Municipio—"

"Oh, they'll be happy enough. Why should they not be?" But looking up, Dru saw that his mind had been far outpacing Beppo's slower one and he retraced his steps. "Listen. ITOLGAS have been expanding their gasoline interests in this area for months. Among other things they need central sites for competitive filling stations. That place of yours could be worth a lot to them. Why they did not follow up their first letter I can't imagine, but one must suppose that it was one of those clerical slips which occur even in the biggest and best organized firms. What you should do is to get on to them immediately, quote their letter and ask for an offer. When it comes, demand half as much again and at the same time indicate that you are open to reasonable negotiation."

"I've only got a week. I've told you that."

"ITOLGAS is a Milan firm and the Milanese don't take a week to fix a deal—they're not like Neapolitans. They'll send someone over from Poggioreale within twenty-four hours if they are really interested. When they do, tell him the position and let him go around to the Municipio with this—" Dru held up the yellow, closely printed form. "The planning officials will undoubtedly agree with him since he will have instructions to make it well worth their while to do so."

"I thought you said that they couldn't back down on Bighencomer?"

Dru gave the slightest of sighs. "That was before I read this form. This"—he tapped the paper—"lets them out of that difficulty. They can merely quote it to Bighencomer and explain that you have found a legal loophole of which neither he nor they were previously aware. Then they are not going back on anything. It's merely that you have outsmarted Bighencomer."

Beppo grinned widely. "*You* have, you mean. I think I owe you much more than two hundred and fifty thousand."

"I think so—now."

Beppo nodded; a new thought had suddenly struck him. "But rather than close the matter with a cash payment I would much prefer it if you would conclude the whole affair for me as my agent—on a satisfactory commission basis, of course," he added hurriedly.

For the first time since he had entered the room a faint look of pleasure appeared on Dru's narrow, sallow, face. "I think— if I may say so—that your suggestion is a wise one. Yes, I'll willingly do so." He suddenly glanced at his watch and rose. "I have an appointment in fifteen minutes, Signor Sanbrenedetto. If it is convenient I'll return here at six o'clock this evening? Good. Until then—"

"Until then, very many thanks!" Beppo grasped the strong, carefully manicured hand and, shaking it fervently, led Dru to the door and showed him out.

Turning back to the sitting room he chuckled to himself and wriggled his shoulders under his shirt with a new feeling of freedom. He found no difficulty in believing every word of Dru's story; there had always been something about Bighencomer, a suavely catlike flexibility oddly contradicted by cold gleams of shrewd self-assurance from behind the pince-nez, which he had deeply distrusted and feared. He had accepted the fact that Bighencomer intended, in some way he did not understand, to make a profit out of what appeared, on the face of it, to be an unprofitable venture. He had vaguely guessed that it might have something to do with tax evasion measures, but he had never dreamed that he was to be the main victim himself.

But—an auto service station in place of the old buildings . . . If that turned out to be the oil firm's intention he would have to make sure that Crocifissa and her lodgers were compensated in some way. This man Dru would have to see to it since he was taking charge of the affair now; but Beppo wondered a little uneasily if Dru could be relied upon to do much. Even as the thought crossed his mind he heard the quick double ring with which the porter announced the arrival of the midday mail and went out to be handed a single letter—a letter in a long, stiff, legal envelope. He ripped it open, unfolded it and, as he read it, his shoulders sagged and for a moment he looked much older than his forty-one years—a small, lonely defeated man in an ugly room with plastic flowers on the table. The Giansante petition had been rejected at the highest quarter. Nothing had been accorded it save the single word *Respinto* and the scrawled ministerial signature. And Beppo was once more in that cell in the prison fortress, hearing again that voice: *"If I can't get out fairly soon—within a year at the most—I shall die."*

↭ 3

NEXT evening, in his office above the restaurant, Signor Bighencomer reread for the fourth time the letter with the Vomero postmark which had arrived *espresso*—by the hand of special postman—an hour before. It was a short letter stating firmly yet with an irony which was not lost on its recipient that the San Lorenzo property deal was over. After the first angry, unbelieving shock, Bighencomer had sat down to puzzle it out. There was no doubt that in some way Sanbrenedetto had discovered his plan and that was surprising enough in itself, for who would have expected that the spectacled little English-teacher would have had even the background knowledge of building regulations to have become suspicious.

No—someone had got at him; someone who knew much more than was comfortable to think about; someone with prior knowledge of the Salerno affair. One possible source of information which loomed largely in Bighencomer's speculative mind was ITOLGAS. De Santis, on the instructions of Milan, was after auto service sites for the new gasoline and there was no doubt at all that a central city possibility such as the Sanbrendetto property would not have escaped him. On finding that the owner was already negotiating with a potential buyer it would seem quite normal to him to investigate that buyer's background in the hope of finding something to upset the deal. Alternatively, there were certain officials in the Municipio and others in the

Reservoirs and Aqueducts Office who knew—who had to know
—a certain amount. But none of them, or so Bighencomer believed, knew about Salerno.

Then an employee of his own? He himself kept no secretary;
he never had. He drafted, typed and filed his own correspondence
and preferred to do so. Nor, as far as he was aware, did any of
his employees or ex-employees bear him especial malice. From
time to time a waiter or a *guattero* was dismissed but unless it
was a case of open theft they were given reasonable notice or
equivalent wages. The most recent employee to leave him, and
by far the most important, had been his headwaiter—but that
had not been by dismissal so much as resignation. An appalling—even Bighencomer, who was not easily appalled, could
only use that word—fight with the chef had at last flared up in
the running battle between the kitchen and the dining room.
Things had been alleged and said and shouted and screamed—
things had even been thrown—that could not possibly be overlooked. It had come to a choice—both contestants were agreed
upon this point—between parting with the chef or the headwaiter and reluctantly, for Dru as well as being amazingly efficient was a real artist with the *batterie de cuisine,* Bighencomer
had decided to retain Fonseca. There had been little real choice.
The restaurant could get along after a fashion until a new headwaiter was found, but without that vast, crimson-faced presence
in the kitchen it would grind to a jarring stop. Fonseca had
stayed. Dru, supplied with excellent references, had gone. But
Dru, in any case, could know nothing of the transactions of the
Mergellina Construction and Development Company.

Then—who? And as if that question needed a tangible, visible answer, there came a knock on the door and as it opened a
familiar voice said, "Good evening, Ferenc. Can I come in a
minute?"

From behind his desk Bighencomer, as expressionless as ever,
looked up at Domenichelli and noted a surprising change.
Domenichelli looked ill. The flesh of his face had fallen away,
his eyes were sunken and had a feverish glitter and he carried
himself oddly, awkwardly, with his left hand in his jacket pocket,
his left arm held close and stiff to his side.

"Well?" Bighencomer's voice was cold but impassive. If
Domenichelli had found out about Salerno and betrayed his

scheme it was a matter which might have to be dealt with in what Bighencomer preferred to think of as "the old way." And he thought of it with a certain grim despair. For more than twelve years now he had put such things behind him. There had been a time in the past, a period of chaos, when it had been necessary to adapt oneself to jungle law in order to survive and though Bighencomer had done this better than most he did not look back upon it with nostalgia, as many did, but preferred to forget it and remember only that he was now a successful businessman living in a successful business country within the law as that law was interpreted. Domenichelli was a hateful reminder of the past, but he must not be allowed to tamper with the present.

"What's happened to you?"

"An accident, Ferenc." Domenichelli's grin was almost skull-like now—a snarl of small broken teeth.

"Where have you been?"

"In bed, mostly."

"So? You've been getting the money I sent?"

"Oh yes. I got up for that."

"And for other things, I've no doubt?"

"Perhaps." Without asking, Domenichelli went to the small cupboard-bar and helped himself to a strong brandy. Bighencomer noted that he did everything with his right hand, his left remained immobile in his jacket pocket.

Carefully he said, "Your passport and papers will be ready by next week. I've provisionally booked a single cabin on the *Vulcania*."

Over his glass Domenichelli shook his head. "That's what I've come to see you about. I can't go that way. Or to the United States, for that matter."

"What do you mean—*can't?* It's practically all arrranged and paid for."

"I'd have to go through police barriers and customs at both ends—and with all the usual immigration and emigration formalities, wouldn't I?"

"Of course. But"—Bighencomer's voice held a wearily irritated impatience—"the whole reason that this affair has taken so long is, as you well know, in order that you shall have nothing to fear from the police. All the papers you will have will be in precise order—every one, and there are a lot. You are going to America as a legal Italian immigrant and no one can stop you at either end."

"Still—I can't risk it."

"There *is* no risk."

"There is now. Listen, Ferenc. I want to get away. I want to get away quickly—understand? But not to America. It's too dangerous. They are too inquisitive at the other end. No, I want to go to Egypt or Israel or the Lebanon. Lebanon would be best. Don't worry about passports and papers. Just find a small ship and give the captain or someone a few hundred thousand—"

Bighencomer's face had flushed darkly and his voice when he spoke was almost a bark. "What, in the name of God, are you talking about! Have you gone even madder than usual? Do you seriously think that I'm going to involve myself in criminal collusion any further for you? You are going to do what *I* say and go to America on legal papers."

"No." Domenichelli shook his head. "I can't."

"And why not?"

For a moment Domenichelli grinned over his brandy, malicious, uncertain, wary. "This." Putting down his glass carefully he tapped his left shoulder. "I've got something here I don't want the Customs to find at either end—a police bullet."

"Where? How?"

"The Via Savarese—last month."

"It was—*you!*" Bighencomer jumped to his feet. "You killed that patrolman?"

"Poor man!" Domenichelli's voice was openly jeering. "Yes. So I'm a murderer. Isn't that dreadful, Ferenc? Doesn't it shock you? Make your blood run cold? But it couldn't be much colder than it was twenty years ago when a certain person in charge of an antipartisan *sondercommando,* whose name, I think, was—"

Bighencomer leaped around the desk, seized the half-empty brandy glass and flung it in Domenichelli's face. It smashed on his low forehead and blood, sliding in thin streaks from the ensuing lacerations, trickled over Domenichelli's upper lip and across his fixed grin. But this time it was he, rather than Bighencomer, who retained his self-control. "You keep forgetting, Ferenc—because you want to forget—that I know it all. I realize

I was not supposed to; that you imagined your faithful Sollier would never tell anyone. But he told me—No!" His right hand whipped quickly inside his jacket as Bighencomer, white-faced, his mouth a thin, hard line, took a step toward him. "You keep your distance, Ferenc. Unless you'd rather I did the job instead of the Jugoslavs. Because, when they get you back there they will do it, of course. At night, by electric light on a prison gallows with army officers and newspaper correspondents there to watch. All this talk of amnesty!" Domenichelli's voice was a harsh jeer and he spat on the thick carpet. "Amnesty for *you!*"

But he had gone too far. Bighencomer had had enough. With an immense effort he turned back to the desk and in a voice that shook only slightly, said, "Very well. We'll see. But you'll find that you're quite wrong. I'm an Italian national today. Italy also had troops in that country and engaged in the same work. They will never hand me over. But *you*—after this no one could help you, and I certainly shall not. You forget—you murderous imbecile—that what happens in war is considered entirely differently from what happens in peacetime. You confuse the two—as you did in Genoa. Here—!" He pulled a handkerchief from his pocket and flung it at Domenichelli's feet. "Wipe your face and get out! That's the last thing I'm giving you."

"You're giving me that money!"

"What money?"

"To get out of Italy"

"I'm not giving you a single lira!"

"Then—"

Bighencomer went toward a bell-push on the wall. "I'll let you have twenty seconds to get out. If you don't, I'll have you kept here until the police arrive. You can say exactly what you like to them—after I've told them what you've just told me. They don't like police-killers here. You'll have a very unpleasant night before they take you back to prison—forever."

For a moment they stared at each other—hatred so intense as to be almost visible crackling in the air between them. Then Bighencomer said, "Anyway, I imagine Sanbrenedetto was very grateful to you financially. You don't need money from me."

"You're mad! I don't know what you mean." Domenichelli's voice was a breathless hiss as he turned to the door. "I'll go now.

But I'm not finished with you, Ferenc. I'll never be finished with you as long as I live!"

And then Bighencomer was alone in the quiet, softly lit office, breathing quickly, deeply, looking down at a wet stain and pieces of broken glass in the middle of the carpet. For a long time he stood there and from below, the music of the restaurant band—four itinerant musicians whom he had picked up in a café on the Via Foria and who now strummed Piedigrotta songs almost as inaccurately as if they really were the fishermen they were dressed to represent—floated up to him with every hesitation and false note magnified by the amplifiers around the jetty.

But Signor Bighencomer was not seeing broken glass and brandy stains as he stood in the middle of his office but faces from the past; he was not hearing the music of his infelicitously chosen instrumentalists but only a voice, harsh with exultant hatred . . . *"at night, by electric light, on a prison gallows with army officers and newspaper correspondents there to watch."* . . . And he was sweating heavily and shivering a little at the same time. For several of the faces that now shone so clearly in his memory had died in just that way. Men he had known and had worked for, or who had worked for him. But . . . "I'm a national now. They can't extradite me—not for things which happened so long ago. Not now—not now!"

The Last of Summer

⚜ 1

THE Colavolpes returned from their yearly holiday on the Sila in a battered condition. They came, as usual, by hard-seated third-class carriage and as they spilled out, unshaven, dirty, clutching half-empty wine flasks and greasy packets of half-eaten food, on the platform of Caserta station old Signor Dorrucci, awaiting the *rapido di lusso* for Rome with his immaculate pigskin luggage under the eye of his immaculate manservant a few paces behind him, thought they looked like a rabble of gypsies back from a quarrelsome funeral.

That was the notorious Major—that one with the false leg and the missing hand and wearing the old black suit—who had shot his prize spaniel, a dog far better bred and infinitely better fed than its assassin. Indeed Signor Dorrucci, who was a malicious old man, had put it about afterwards that the Colavolpes had shot his spaniel in the hope of eating it undetected. There was the old uncle, bleary-eyed and red-nosed, his shirt stained with rough Calabrian wine, his fly-buttons mostly missing or undone. Then came the red-haired woman in a torn dress, the three old creatures in dusty, peasant black and, of course, the boy, dragging out an ancient suitcase, two sacks and four limp hens tied together by the legs.

But—what had they been doing? The Major's face was puffy and bore a deep red scratch across the violet frostbite stain, there was a large piece of adhesive tape across the old uncle's bulbous nose, and one of the drab old women had her arm in a sling. And as for the boy—Signor Dorrucci was shocked at the sight of him. His face was as bruised and cut and swollen as if he had fallen down an elevator shaft onto a pile of stones, his bare legs—under the usual Colavolpe coating of dirt—were covered in abrasions and he was limping. The whole lot of them, thought Signor Dorrucci disgustedly, looked as though they had been engaged in a free fight.

The fight had taken place nearly a week before and, even by Colavolpe standards, it had been unusually ferocious. Before it was over, most of the furniture was broken and a corner of the farmhouse in flames. As always it was about money—this time Filippa's small secret hoard which she kept in the lining of her workbasket and from which Galo had occasionally extracted minor sums.

But down on the Sila, among the Calabrian pastures, he had found that he needed more than at any time before. One of the first things he had done on his arrival at the family's farmhouse was to scout the district for suitable and available women. He knew quite enough about southern Italian customs to leave any respectable girl severely alone—he had no intention of having his head blown off by an irate father's blast of heavy buckshot—but there must be some *puttane* in the district. In fact there were two; elderly, competent and venal. They enjoyed Galo almost as much as he enjoyed them, showing him a dozen new tricks, giving him all and more than all he should have wanted. But the Colavolpe inheritance or the Holy Tooth, or both, had made Galo insatiable. He spent much of the day and all the night with one *puttana* or the other and physically it seemed to do him nothing but good. He ate like a pig—though all the Colavolpes did this when they were being fed gratis on their vacation—slept like a log and filled out, muscular and brown-skinned, until he was bursting out of his shabby shirt and shorts. The rest of the family, sunk in a daze of *polenta* and milk, butter, eggs, homemade *pasta* and strong rough wine, took no notice of him save to discuss, during his long absences, the De Santis proposition with cupidity and satisfaction. Concezio, looking with anticipatory approval at his handsome nephew, had said, "Get plenty of sun, Galo—it improves you."

"It makes him look like a peasant," had sniffed Maria Celeste, who retained the old-fashioned notion that gentlefolk, let alone aristocrats, should have delicate complexions and white skins.

"Some people like peasant boys," Concezio had answered cryptically. He still considered it probable that De Santis had immoral intentions toward Galo.

Then the two *puttane* began to make financial demands. They sincerely liked Galo; his smooth brown body was a delightful change from those of the coarse old widowers, skinny and wizened or flabby and bulbous, who were their main clientele. But they were professionals and it was not in their nature to give their services free. What was more, they realized that Galo was now incapable of doing without the delights they offered. "You'll have to pay, *figliolo*." "But—I haven't got any money," said Galo truthfully. "Then you'll have to get some, won't you?" "I can't," lied Galo, who had every intention, if pressed, of resorting to his grandmother's workbasket. "Then you won't be able to come here, will you? You'll have to be like the other boys who use each other or the goats." "I couldn't use a goat— not after you," Galo had replied, and added more practically, "Anyway, they're not our goats. And I certainly won't use another boy."

"Quite right, dear," had said the *puttana* approvingly. She had quoted a little jingle:

> "D'inculare non e un cosa bella,
> Porta, invece, la fica dell'tua sorella. . .

But since you haven't got a sister I'd advise you to find some money."

So Galo went to the workbasket and for three days he extracted a thousand lire a day and gave five hundred to each *puttana*. They were charmed. "You're a good boy—a really *good* boy!" had said one of them, stroking his hair and kissing him. "And so beautiful," had added the other, "and so *strong!*" The old widowers very seldom paid more than three hundred and fifty and often demanded half of it back if they were unable to achieve an orgasm.

Then, on the fourth day, Filippa caught Galo red-handed at the workbasket. She screamed the house down and everybody rushed in from outside and the battle commenced. The other Colavolpes were, in fact, almost more furious with Filippa for concealing money from them than with Galo for stealing it. That the poor old woman, who was only a Colavolpe by marriage, had been saving long and carefully to have her body taken back for burial to her parents' decent grave in Campobasso, rather than thrust into one of the gruesomely gaping niches behind the vestry of the Church of the Holy Tooth, made no difference at all.

To the genuinely poor, money is almost sacred since, more than anything else, it mitigates the greatest of all ills—physical pain. Hunger, of course, is the most common of these, but there are so many others. That money of Filippa's could have bought the drugs which lulled the dull ache in Concezio's stumps and which he generally had to do without. It could have bought the medicine for Tarquinio's chronic liver trouble or further treatment for Maria Celeste's arthritis. To save it merely for the disposal of one's own dead body—particularly when there was a perfectly adequate tomb already at hand—seemed, understandably enough, a piece of crass selfishness.

But Filippa could be dealt with later. First there was Galo. And what had Galo wanted the money for? There was no cinema or place of amusement within miles and he had all the food he could possibly eat. There was only one answer. When the family realized what it was, their fury redoubled—illogically, since there could be no rational objection to a fifteen-year-old Italian having sexual intercourse with women. In fact fifteen was a little backward—particularly by Neapolitan standards. Concezio had had his first woman just before his twelfth birthday—but of course she had been a peasant woman from the Colavolpe land at Caserta and he had not paid her.

Speranza was, for some reason, the most enraged—filled with a peculiar venomous jealousy which had very little to do with Filippa's secret hoard. It was she who first understood, with an immediate instinctive accuracy, the reason for which Galo had taken the money and she threw herself at him like a charge of cavalry. Fortunately for Galo she fell over one of the farmhouse cats and he had time to get behind the kitchen table before the rest were upon him. Then he fought with all the mindless ferocity his uncle had displayed on the Russian steppes some twenty odd years before. The table was overturned, dishes went flying into splinters across the stone floor, pots and pans—

some full of cooked or cooking food—clattered and rolled among broken chairs and writhing figures. Concezio, striking out with his wooden hand, broke Tarquinio's nose and then broke the hand itself across Galo's head. Galo, bleeding and breathless, landed a savage kick on Concezio's single knee and sending him to the floor bellowing Russian curses, made a leap for the doorway. He might have escaped had not Filippa caught him around the waist and, burying her head in his chest to avoid the blows of his fists, fastened her few remaining teeth in the flesh below his right armpit. Galo screamed with pain and wrenched her arms away, dislocating one of her elbows, but by then Speranza was upon him again—an infuriated ginger tigress. Galo got a hand under her chin—a trick he and Pavan had practiced together, wrestling in the Nunziatella gymnasium— and forcing her head back was about to drive his fist into her stomach when Speranza, demonstrating an instinctive knowledge of infighting, brought her knee up sharply between her son's legs and the fight ended abruptly. For after that Galo was finished. He staggered, ashen-faced, retching and reeling, about the smashed kitchen and, eventually collapsing on hands and knees, vomited weakly over the flagstones. Speranza, looking around for a weapon, seized a broomstick and beat him with all the force of her strong arms about the legs and thighs and back. Galo felt none of it, his whole being caught up in the agonizing, nauseating pain between his legs. Shortly, under the flailing blows, his arms gave way and he fell flat on his face.

Meanwhile the rest of the family picked themselves up and gathered breathlessly around. Filippa, her old face streaked with tears, moaning and clutching her disjointed elbow, aimed a few feeble kicks at her grandson's head. Tarquinio, one hand holding his bleeding nose, sought and found another broomstick and was about to join Speranza when Concezio, at last on his feet, limped up and grasping his sister-in-law's ginger hair yanked her away from the groaning figure of her prostrate son. "Imbecile! Whore! *Sai pazzo?*" The well-known wolf-howl drowned her scream of pain. "D'you want to kill him? Kill three million lire? *Come si fa andare avanti cosi!*" Then he turned on his mother. "And you—you old ratbag! Stop kicking his head! You're as bad as he is! By God, I won't have you buried at all after this, I swear it on the tits of the Blessed Mary! I'll have your moldy carcass thrown on the Caserta rubbish dump, where it should have been years ago by rights! And as for *you*"— with difficulty he bent down and grasped Galo by the back of his belt—"I'll teach you to kick me! I'll give you such a—"

It was then that Tarquinio informed the rest of his relations that the house was on fire.

৺৯ 2

THE battle had several immediate and lasting after effects. First and foremost it shifted Galo's status in the family group upwards in a sharp ascent. Before it occurred, the other Colavolpes had still regarded Galo as a child, someone whose views or wishes need never be considered, much less consulted. In the continual dogfight for existence at Caserta his position had been generally upon the periphery. A fracas might start over something he had done but before many minutes he had been pushed to the side in favor of an adult protagonist. Since he could, on the occasions of his misdemeanors, fancied or real, be slapped or cuffed or knocked down with impunity, he existed as something which it might be worth quarreling about but seldom worth quarreling with. On the rare occasions on which he had a defender it was either Maria Fausta, of whom no one took any notice or, if his offense had been against Tarquinio, Concezio, who still held the real power in the household by reason of his temper, his wooden hand and, most of all, his pension.

As Galo had grown older it had been Speranza who had increasingly become his real enemy. Speranza belonged to that class of women who, while they often enjoy babies and small children and are deeply attracted to fully adult men, have a peculiar aversion to all adolescents, regarding them as neither the one thing nor the other—an unnatural obscenity. And in Speranza's case this feeling was continually heightened by jealousy of Galo's good looks and the knowledge that soon he was going to be far more successful with women—women much younger and more attractive than herself—than she had ever been with men. Like many highly oversexed people Speranza was capable of insensate and furious jealousy over fantasies. For the last year she had been Galo's implacable foe and his recent behavior had confirmed her hatred once and for all.

But the others, with the exception of Concezio, were now thoroughly frightened of him. He had very nearly won that fight against their combined force and had demonstrated a fierce physical strength which they themselves could not match. In the estimation of Maria Celeste, Maria Fausta, and even Filippa, Galo had risen to second place in the family after Concezio— for none of them ever counted Tarquinio as a proper male. When, that evening, they sat around their shored-up table on boxes or partially mended chairs to consume their huge supper, Maria Celeste almost unconsciously served Galo after Concezio and not, as was customary, after everyone else. Speranza took the plate away at once but Concezio, glowering at the head of the table, was not slow to realize the implications of Maria Celeste's involuntary action. He stared balefully at the bruised and swollen face of his sullen nephew, noted the broadening shoulders under the torn shirt, the strong arms below the short sleeves, and understood at once that something must be done— and done quickly. Galo had knocked him down without much difficulty today. In another year Galo, at sixteen and a half, would do it with ease. At any moment the old Marchese back at Caserta might die and Galo would have the title with all the inevitable prestige that it conferred. A big sixteen-year-old calling himself Marchese Galeazzo Colavolpe—even if he was still a Nunziatella cadet—would be almost, if not quite, beyond the effective control of a middle-aged cripple. And then, at eighteen . . . No, Galo must be got rid of—sold to De Santis and bundled off to America or wherever that rich but otherwise undesirable old man wanted to take him.

But when they got back to Caserta it was only to find that Commendatore De Santis himself was on holiday. Concezio wrote; Concezio even stumped into Caserta and telephoned; but the fact remained that De Santis had gone to Milan and from there to the Côte d'Azure and was not expected back for a fortnight at the least.

Since he could not go forward with the actual transaction, Concezio did his best to covertly interest Galo in the matter. It would be far better if Galo went to De Santis enthusiastically and of his own accord rather than unwillingly and by force.

Concezio started by disparaging the army. "I wish to God I'd managed to avoid it. Look what it's done to me! Used me, wrecked me, crippled me for life and thrown me out with a pittance a beggar wouldn't thank you for! I don't know what we're doing, pushing you into the army, Galo. We must have been mad, I think now."

"No one's pushing me. I like it."

"You don't know the half of it yet. You don't know what happens at Modena, for instance."

"Yes we do. They tell us."

"Only a little. They wouldn't dare tell you everything or none of you would go. It's a concentration camp—that place. Nothing but drill and parades and punishments from morning to night. They wake you up in the middle of the night if they find that your uniform has not been hung up exactly in line with the next one."

"I don't mind waking up in the middle of the night. I can always go to sleep again."

"They don't," went on Concezio, whose genius for prurient invention was unending—"let you touch a woman while you're there—not for the whole two years! If they think you've been with a woman they make you run around the parade ground until you fall flat from exhaustion. If you do it again they give you an injection which stops you wanting to. It's very painful and sometimes its effects last for years. That's why so many young officers are unmarried—the injection they got at Modena hasn't worn off. It's made from a serum taken from goats, you see, and sometimes it does dreadful things. I knew an officer whose skin had gone quite green because of it. We used to call him Major Verdigris, but he suffered terribly, poor fellow—and of course he was quite impotent. Luckily he died in Russia. No —the army's no life for anyone. Now if I had my time over again I'd go into business. I'd try to get a sound commercial background first, of course. I'd go to a business training college if I could find the money. The best are in America, I'm told. . . ."

Galo listened, sullen, expressionless, as his uncle paraphrased De Santis's monologue in the Villa Sanfelice last June. He said nothing, but later in his room, pacing restlessly up and down the bare boards, he realized that something must be done. Done, if it was ever going to be done—done now and done by *him*. The summer was nearly over and for him it had been a climacteric; one of those peculiar times of painful stress when the chrysalis breaks and splits and a new animal, still blinking and unsure but much closer to adult stature, emerges from one of the multiple yet fragile shells of childhood. Galo was moving forward far more quickly than even his family realized. Things which were hardly, or only partially, understood before were now becoming evident. The peculiar, reflecting, refracting vision of childhood was giving way to clear sight, and though he would still, for a few years, have trouble in focusing correctly, he was out of the hall of mirrors at last. Gennaro had passed the same milestones a year before, moving more easily along a smoother road as the colored mists of his dear Quong's China thinned and blew wispily from the path ahead.

Like most boys Galo had always been naturally self-absorbed, too busy coping with half-understood experiences—mostly unpleasant—to look further than tomorrow, next week or at the most next month. His involvement, his interest in the rest of mankind, had been instinctively minimal wherever he himself was not touched. But in the last months two people—Pavan and Mina—had impinged with enough force upon that self-absorption to break it open and to free him into a wider world. And in that world he intended to get his own way.

The time had come to claim his inheritance. He had shied away from doing this throughout the summer, continually remembering old Ercole's reiterated warnings of the complexities and difficulties ahead and as dubious as his great-uncle of his own ability to keep either money or property from the grasping hands of his adult relatives. But he was much less dubious now that his newly found sexual maturity had added a measure to his own self-esteem—something which he realized was not lost on his relations. They might—they certainly would—try to trick him out of his fortune, but they would no longer be able to brush him easily aside and grasp it for themselves.

But adult help he must have and he was despairingly aware how little was available. In another eventuality he would have turned to Beppo, but in the present circumstances that was out of the question. Until Ercole's death last May, Galo had regarded Beppo as his only adult friend. He had even felt it safe, regardless of his great-uncle's words, to leave the sealed will at the Vomero apartment. But since that date the continued complacent acceptance by Beppo of the fortune that was really his own had changed and cooled his feelings toward his cousin. Beppo, if not an enemy, could only be termed a dubious neutral today.

Yet who else was there—friend or neighbor? Crocifissa was only a kind old woman—Quong, even if in good health, an ignorant carpenter. For a time he played with the idea of taking Gennaro into his confidence. Gennaro was able and quick and clever—but only in the petty dealings of Neapolitan slum life; someone who could haggle successfully over the price of a piece of fish or a bunch of flowers in the market and who spent half an hour of argument to save twenty lire. If only, thought Galo wearily, he had made a friend of old Signor Dorrucci instead of catching his goldfish and stealing his umbrella. But Signor Dorrucci was certainly not the man to make friends with a ragged boy from a family as notoriously eccentric as the Colavolpes.

And then Galo thought of General Lecco. Of course! Why not his friend's father? After all, he knew the general and had been invited to the Lecco apartment. It would mean going to Rome and it would mean a long and embarrassing explanation, for Galo had kept the worst enormities of his family carefully secret from his Nunziatella friends. But once the general knew the full story he would undoubtedly help him—Galo was certain of that. He would find a sound firm of Roman lawyers and make sure that the whole affair was securely in their hands, as safe and solid as the Bank of Rome.

✔️ 3

WHEN Crocifissa had read the letter twice she folded it and slid it under the marble meat slab and then automatically checked the scales to see that Gigi, measuring half a kilo of sugar for a customer, was giving fair weight. Gigi had recently acquired the bad habit of trying to hold back a few grammes on most orders and thus, or so he believed, save his employer money. Crocifissa had spoken to him sharply about this. "Don't you see, Gigi, that quite apart from being wrong it will give the shop a bad name? It will make everyone dislike us and buy elsewhere. You don't want that, do you?" But she had apparently failed to convince him, for the habit persisted. Now she took the little plastic scoop, shook sugar from it until the needle of the scales was well past the five-hundred-gram mark, then firmly closed the paper bag and handed it to the young girl on the customer's side of the counter. *"E poi?"* she asked automatically.

"Niente, signora, grazie."

"Then that will be ninety-five lire. Gigi—get out some more dried figs. About eight kilos should do. You know where they are." And now the shop was empty again and she could let the import of that letter come flooding back once more.

So it had happened—just as she had first believed it would. All through the summer she had awaited a blow which did not fall and then slowly, as the burning, airless days succeeded each other, the doom which had seemed so blackly imminent on that late May evening when Gennaro had returned from the Adriatic with the old *padrone's* body had faded into a remote threat in the background. There had been so many other things; her frightening brush with the Public Health authorities followed by her illness—an illness from which she privately doubted that she had completely recovered. The heat, too, was surely worse than ever this year; an extra burden which perhaps, with prices rising all the summer, helped account for the simmering discontent growing ominously not only in the *bassifondi* of the workless and work-shy but among the ordinary laborers and artisans who made up most of her clients. There was poor Biagio's illness —only today and after much persuasion, Tenerini had induced his old friend to go, in his company, to the Cardinale Ascalasi Hospital in the Forcella. And, more worrying still, the white-faced, silent despair which had fallen upon Iole Giansante with the news of the rejection of her husband's petition. Her baby was due toward the end of next month and it was terrible to think that it would be a child of eleven before it could hope to see its own father. Rosalba's baby had been born ten days ago and already she and Renato walked proudly with it around the *piazza* at the time of the evening *passaggiata*. But with the instinctive delicacy of the working-class they kept away from the west side of the square and Crocifissa had even had to visit their one-room apartment to get her first glimpse of the child.

And Gennaro, her dear Gennaro, was not well. Perhaps it was the heat but more probably his failing business coupled with his apparent inability to find or hold a steady job. He was thinner than she liked, his cheekbones, more prominent than before, in a face whose olive coloring had turned imperceptibly to the dull, unhealthy yellow of the airless slums. Crocifissa had reminded herself that Gennaro was still growing and was under far more strain and pressure than was proper for someone of his age. But even so . . . And there were other, more disquieting changes, too. He was silent now, he rarely smiled and his eyes were dark-circled and held a haunted, almost a hunted, look. He had given up reading the women's magazines from the stock of wrapping paper, was becoming entirely careless of his personal appearance, and his manner of walking, which had once had the precise, slightly sinuous character of the priest, had degenerated into the sag-shouldered slouch of the Neapolitan loiterers. There had been plenty to think about, enough to sadden and worry her without the sudden fulfillment of her dark prophecy of spring: *"They'll sell this place as a building site."* And that was what they had done. That was what the letter told her. The old house and the ruins on either side had been disposed of not, as she had once believed, in order to make way for apartments in which she, and perhaps the others, would be rehoused—that had been a ridiculously fanciful dream, she saw now—but to an oil company. And the sale, if not actually completed, was under way for the letter, polite but curt, was signed not by Signor Giuseppe but by someone named Dru.

While Gigi came back, staggering under the big box of dried figs, she took the letter from under the meat slab and read it for the third time:

> . . . you will recall the notice of the expiry of your tenancy within three months which was forwarded to you on the 1st June last. Your tenancy expired, therefore, on the 31st August. It is understood, however, that you are still resident in the above-mentioned property and on behalf both of the present and future owners I am requested to make it plain that you and your sub-tenants must vacate the said property, completely and absolutely, before midnight of the 30th September. I must point

out plainly that, while you have been illegally occupying the premises since the 1st of the present month, and while it has been decided that no rental will be requested or required of you or your above-mentioned sub-tenants for your occupation since that date, that the time limit of your removal as stated above admits of no extension whatever and will, if necessary, be physically enforced, for the commencement of the demolition of the standing property has been fixed for October the 1st and cannot under any circumstances be retarded. . . .

Today was the sixteenth—that left fourteen more days. Crocifissa shook her head as she tried to grasp that within such a short time she would no longer be here—even the counter against which she now leaned would no longer be here. She remembered, vividly, the day that it had been installed nearly thirty years ago. Dino—younger, then, than Gigi was now—skipping excitedly around the workmen; herself in her still-new widow's black. Opposite, on the other side of the *piazza,* had been a great line of posters figuring the enlarged scowling face of Mussolini. DUCE! YOU ARE ALL OF US!

The counter was old and cracked now, the warped wood chipped by a million rattled coins, the skirting-board bruised and dented by more than a generation of scuffling feet—the sandaled feet of children which had become the booted feet of adults who now sent their own children for half a kilo of sugar or two hundred grams of coffee. Those thirty years slid irrevocably into the past and there were only fourteen days left.

Half an hour later Galo came into the shop. He was not in uniform but dressed like a local boy in T-shirt and jeans so that for a moment Crocifissa did not recognize him. He was tired and dusty, for he had been up before dawn in order silently to remove from their roosts two of the sleeping hens brought back from the Sila. These he had taken to Caserta and sold in the marketplace, standing in line with black-shawled peasant women holding sacks of beans, eggs, rabbits and more chickens. To the amusement of the peasants, Galo had sold his hens at little more than half their real value—but it did not matter, for all he wanted was the money for a third-class fare into Naples and a thirty-lire stamp for the letter to Lecco which he carried in his pocket. With any luck no one would count the hens

for a day or two—after all, they were his responsibility—and by
then he would be in Rome.

Now he submitted as usual to Crocifissa's flood of delighted
greetings, her pats and caresses, as she led him into the kitchen,
shouting orders to Gigi over her shoulder. "*Contino*—you've
grown! *Benedetto Dio*—how you've shot up! It wasn't only your
clothes, it was your size which stopped me recognizing you. But
—your face! Have you hurt yourself?"

"I—I fell down."

Crocifissa said nothing. She had always had a shrewd notion
of the sort of existence Galo led at Caserta, which was why she
was always so fond of him and the reason, too, why she never
asked after his family. "Did you have a nice holiday?"

"Yes," said Galo truthfully. "The best I've ever had.
Crocifissa, I have to go to Rome soon—in two or three days, I
hope—and—and I haven't the money for the fare." He colored slightly, smiling. "Could you lend me five thousand for
about a month?"

"Of course, *caro!* Wait a minute and I'll get it from the till.
Just sit down and rest. You look tired."

When the old woman returned Galo buttoned the notes into
a back pocket of his jeans and said, "There's one more thing,
Crocifissa." His eyes slid to the old dresser above which Dino's
big photograph gleamed in the perpetual glow of the votive
lamp. "That box—you remember? The one I asked you to look
after for me early last June?"

"It's still here—in the drawer where I put it. Do you want it?"

"Yes, I'll need it in Rome."

"I'll get it for you now." But Galo stopped her quickly. "No,
no, Crocifissa. I don't want it now. I can't—can't take it home.
No—I want you to send it to me in Rome. Look—" He took a
small piece of paper from his pocket. "This is where I'll be staying there. I'll send you a telegram from Rome and when you receive it you must send the box to me at once. Send it registered
and *espresso*—understand?"

"Of course, *contino*. Just as you say."

Galo took her wrinkled old hand in his. "This is very important to me," he said seriously. "It must reach me, that box—
safely and when I want it."

"It will, *contino*. I promise you."

Galo rose. "Well then, I'd better be going. Once more, many thanks, Crocifissa. You cannot know how much you are helping me!"

"It is nothing—nothing at all! But don't you want to stay and see Quong and Gennaro before you leave?"

"I can't now. I must get home. I'll see them next month when I'm back at the Nunziatella."

To Galo's dismay, Crocifissa shook her head sorrowfully. "I doubt it, *caro mio*. We'll all be gone by then. This place is being sold. Signor Giuseppe is selling it and they are going to pull it down."

"Pull it down!" Galo stared at her aghast. "Pull down your shop, and Quong's place and— But it doesn't *belong* to them— whoever 'they' are."

"Not yet, but it soon will. As soon as Signor Giuseppe has sold it."

"It doesn't *belong* to Signor—" Galo cut himself short abruptly. "No, no, they can't do that. It can't be allowed." His face flushed darkly with anger that Beppo should try to sell *his* property like this. Very well—very well, then! He had been thinking of making Beppo a present of part of the Ercole legacy to make up, partially, for his forthcoming disappointment. The Adriatic villa had been in his mind. But after this—this treach- ery—no! Beppo should have every lira wrenched from him and get nothing at all. And he himself would see that no one touched the San Lorenzo property. It would remain forever the home of Crocifissa and the Quongs and old Biagio. He could not under- stand why Beppo should have thought of doing such a brutal thing. Was there not ample money from the industrial shares, the Pendino property and the rent of the seaside villa? But adults were like that when it came to money; they were insatia- ble.

Crocifissa was touched at his obvious distress. "You mustn't worry about it, *caro contino*. It's not your fault—and it can't be helped." She sighed. "I had thought that Signor Giu- seppe would probably do something to help us. But—we can't do anything about it."

"Can't we?" Galo grinned angrily. "You'll see!"

◆§ 4

WHITENESS and bright light; a light brighter even than the sun on snow. Biagio lay on a white table under great arc lights in a white-painted room somewhere in the depths of the huge hospital. He wore nothing but his trousers and he shivered and trembled in the dry, antiseptic, conditioned air. Two men in white coats rolled a great machine silently above him and one grunted, "Lie still! Lie perfectly still. Don't jerk about like that."

Biagio swallowed but could say nothing. His mouth was dry with fear and he longed, with a passion he had not felt for decades, to be out of this evil white catacomb and back on his box with Baldissera drooping before him in the dusty cab-rank. He blamed Napoleone Tenerini bitterly for bringing him here. Napoleone was sitting uncomfortably on a bench somewhere far away along what seemed miles of intricate corridors and anterooms. Half an hour ago he himself had been sitting there, too; nervously rolling up the brim of his old hat and staring with dislike at the worn faces of the other patients upon the benches opposite. Then he had been led away by a young nurse—had cast one fear-filled, silent appeal for company to Napoleone and received only a weak, lopsided smile before entering the maze of red-tiled alleys which had led only to further waiting on benches, followed by interviews, questions, form-fillings innumerable. "Biagio Bonitatibus. Age 74. Unmarried. Cabdriver."

Then the first examination with testy doctors prodding him between the ribs. "Does that hurt? Well, does *that* hurt? Ah! Again, now—take a deep breath. Does *that* hurt? Here?—And here? Right. Go over there." And more forms. "Biagio Bonitatibus. Age 74. Unmarried. Cabdriver." "How long have you been aware of this? When does it hurt? When did it begin hurting? Has the pain increased? Come over here. Lie down. Take a deep breath. . . ."

He had tried to explain about his other lumps "Signor Dottore, look at this—and this" "*Santo Cielo!* The old man's got *three* of

them! How long—? *Years!* Then don't waste our time. It's the
one that hurts that we want to know about. . . ."

And at last this room and the table and the great photo-
graphic machine. Silence and cool dryness—and fear. The doctors were going to peer inside him and in a minute they would
know if he was going to die. This was the anteroom to death. It
was worse than that day, a week after Caporetto, when they
had been disarmed—those who still retained their arms—
stripped of their equipment and marched between files of battle
police to that grim, walled courtyard of the farm beside the Tag-
liamento to be lined up and counted off in tens . . . Because
this time there would be no mistake.

"Lie still—quite still. If you move it will spoil everything."

Whiteness and bright light. Biagio shut his eyes, remembering that march along the muddy road nearly half a century before. It had begun to snow a little, even though it was only early
November. Thin, wet flakes had drifted down sparsely from a
low, yellow-gray sky, touching the olive-green backs of that
abject column, every tenth man of which must die, melting at
once upon the churned mud. And the remembrance of that thin
snow brought back an earlier memory of the day he and Anna
had seen proper snow for the first time.

Anna had been his elder sister, sent away at twelve years of
age to some cousins, peasants who lived up in the mountains
near Castel d'Ieri beyond Avezzano, and he had been allowed
to go with her for a day. They had been put on the cheap night
train, had changed to the *diligenza* at Avezzano, and had arrived at dawn to see something they had never seen before—
snow. The snow had lain thickly over the old stone village, burying it in mounds of pure, glittering whiteness under a sky as blue
as the Virgin's robes. For two hours, before the *diligenza* had
returned to take him back to Avezzano, they had played in the
snow; running, plunging, shouting and forgetting their heart-
ache at the approaching parting in childhood's rapture at early
morning and winter snow. Plumes of smoking breath in the icy
air and cries that echoed thinly in the glassy stillness of the
frozen mountains.

A few months later they had told him that Anna was dead,
but he had not believed it. She had been too much a part of him,

they had been too close to one another, for her to die without him knowing of it instantly—long before the news could come from the mountains in the shaky scrawl of a peasant's laborious letter. No, she was still there in the high hills, waiting for him in a limitless, sun-filled world of white—a small, vivid Madonna of the Snows.

"All right, you can get up now." Biagio opened his eyes and then shut them quickly, for the great X-ray camera had been rolled away and he was staring up into powerful arc lights. With the same immense effort, dry-tongued and breathless, with which, nearly fifty years ago, he had stammered, "Capitano! I—I'm number *nine!*" he asked, "Dottore—Signor Dottore. What did you see?"

"What do you mean—'What did I see'? I've seen nothing yet."

"But—didn't you look inside me?"

"We took photographs. We'll know more about you when they've been developed."

"When?"

"About a week—maybe a little less. We'll let you know. Now hurry up and dress. There are several others waiting outside."

His fingers shook so much that he could hardly button his shirt, and his lined old face with its silver-gray unshaven stubble trembled like an idiot's. A whole week—five or six days at any rate! Dreadful days, poised on a knife-edge of fear and hope. The army had only taken some seven seconds to decide his fate. Suddenly, over all the immense gulf of years, Biagio longed with an intensity which brought the tears to his eyes for his sister. To have Anna with him at this moment, to hear her say, "Don't cry, Bo-bo. It will be all right." But she had been twelve then and now he was seventy-four—*Biagio Bonitatibus. Age 74. Unmarried. Cabdriver.* And then he was struck by an astonishing idea, an idea so surprising that he stopped buttoning his shabby waistcoat and stared for a long moment at the impersonal, antiseptic white wall. He would not drive his cab today—or tomorrow—or the next day. . . . He would go instead to Castel d'Ieri, find Anna and hear her say, "Don't cry, Bo-bo. It will be all right."

⨀ 5

THE next morning Maresciallo Valdemarin arrived late at his office. He had been up most of the night with Nicola, who had been suffering one of his periodic bouts of nervous fever. Sitting beside the bed, stroking that small, hot hand and looking sorrowfully at the taut face, the fever-bright eyes, Valdemarin had felt, not for the first time, that it would be a merciful release for Nicola if only the boy could die. He hated the thought and was ashamed of it—but when he entered his headquarters at nine-thirty he received a piece of news that drove it entirely from his mind.

The vehicle used in last month's murder off the Via Savarese, and which despite the most careful investigation had remained undiscovered, was now in the hands of the Carabinieri. Brigadiere Calvanese reported the matter as soon as the Maresciallo had crossed the threshold. "Four hours ago, *signore,* at dawn. We didn't ring you because of your instructions about telephoning you at night, but—"

"Yes, yes—you were correct. A delay of four hours can hardly make much difference now. Well—?"

"Out beyond the Campi Flegrei. It was just a lucky chance. One of our patrols was coming down a small side road. Just two men on normal *servizio.* One of them wanted to relieve himself and moved into the bushes—"

"How hygienic of him."

Calvanese permitted himself a grin. "Only the P.S. actually do it in the road, of course. Well, he saw something in the bushes and went in farther—and there was this abandoned 'Ape.' "

"Did he touch anything?" The Maresciallo's voice was sharp, his eyes narrowed with anticipatory anger.

"No, *signore.* At least he says he did not. He took the number and checked it and recognized at once what he had found. He stood guard over it while his colleague went to telephone us."

"Good."

"There's a squad car waiting."

"Well done, Calvanese. Right—let's go."

Fifteen minutes later Valdemarin, with Calvanese and a

fingerprint technician a respectful two paces behind him, nodded to the salute of a khaki-uniformed Carabiniere at the border of a country road and pushed his way through some thick bushes of broom whose pods hung brown and curled among the higher branches. And there it was, just as it must have been left on the night of the killing, a small, battered three-wheeler with a faded transfer of a naked girl peeling from the front and a thin strip of red paper with the words VOTA COMMUNISTA already soaked by rain from the door and lying in the grass below.

While the fingerprint officer went gingerly to work with his equipment, Valdemarin and Calvanese moved carefully around the "Ape," peering into the rusty truck bed and through the grimy windows into the cab. In the former they found ample evidence of the use to which the "Ape" had been put. Twenty cardboard boxes, the top ones rotting, half-dissolved by rain and sun and disclosing the stolen German motor horns, lay among brown and withered palm leaves and the ghostly remnants of roses and carnations. A forlorn piece of purple ribbon bore the words *Cara Elena da*—. When the fingerprint tests were concluded they examined the interior of the cab. The back of the seat was heavily smeared with brown, dried blood and there were blood smears on the left handlebar. A small hacksaw and a tire lever lay on the floor. An empty package which had once contained cheap cigarettes was crumpled below the steering column and above the windshield hung the inevitable red plastic horn—charm against the *gettatori*. Nothing else. No telltale personal clues to indicate who had sat here for the last time in the hot darkness of that August night, roaring out of Naples, bleeding from a deep bullet wound, sweating with fear and anger—perhaps despair.

Carefully the two policemen turned up the seat and stared at dust and a small spider crawling into a metal crevice from which a frayed piece of paper showed its grimy edge. Valdemarin extracted it between his thumb and forefinger. It was the end of an envelope of that coarse, thick paper used by commercial firms to contain a worker's weekly pay: OLGAS DI NAPOLI.

"Might have been there for months," muttered Calvanese.

"Still, we'll check up. It won't be much use. If we'd had the other end there would have been a serial number—*that* might have helped." Valdemarin stared down morosely at the dirty scrap in his hand. "The owner of this truck never worked for ITOLGAS as far as I know. But he might easily have given a lift to someone who did—or of course this might have blown in through a window. Still, we'll check. It's all we have."

"Unless the fingerprints help."

"They'll have to go to the P.S." Valdemarin's voice was bitter. "*They've* got a suspect—or so they *say*."

But later in the morning when, back in his office, he grudgingly telephoned the Public Security inspector engaged on the rival inquiry, he received some news which, at least from the Carabinieri viewpoint, was consoling. Putting down the phone he said to Calvanese, "They say it's almost certain that they've been on the wrong track. Their suspect seems to have been with his sister in Portici that night. But they'd still like to see the prints."

"There aren't any—the report's just come through. There's a lot of mess but nothing of any value. They say it looks as if whoever it was wore gloves."

"Sensible fellow," said the Maresciallo complacently and dialled the P.S. number. He held his hand over the mouthpiece and lifted his eyes to Calvanese. "One thing. Just check whether that boy we had here when Giacobelli killed himself has ever been in ITOLGAS employ. I doubt it very much but we'd better find out. And say—" But there was a buzzing behind his palm and a muted tinny voice demanded insistently who was calling. "*Si—si, Valdemarin. Allora, Ispettore, mi dispiace ma . . .*"

A Sword for Galo

ᕽᔦ 1

"*BUT while they seem to me most amiable for their gentleness of tone, and for their freedom from sullenness and pride, they are, I must say, admirable in their powers of patient endurance, and for the elasticity and buoyance, with which in them the spirit lives under a weight that would crush minds of a more masculine and tougher texture, but gifted with less power of reactive play*—That was a nice thing to say about us."

"Us? I thought you were a Genovese."

Nicola's smile turned at once to a frown. "No, no, certainly I'm not. And I've been here long enough to feel I belong—if I belong anywhere." He waited expectantly for Mina's comforting assurance that of course he belonged somewhere—was as much a Neapolitan as herself. It did not come and the frown darkened. He shut his Italian translation of Gladstone's *Letters to Lord Aberdeen* with an angry snap. "You seem to lack elasticity and buoyance tonight, Mina."

Mina put down the black and white kitten which she had been stroking. "The heat," she said uncertainly, "and no holiday or anything."

"*I* never have a holiday."

Mina might have retorted that he also lacked elasticity and buoyance and had few powers of patient endurance, but no one said things like that to Nicola. "I know. I wish the Maresciallo could arrange to take you away somewhere for a week or so."

"*I* don't," said Nicola tightly. "If I did, we'd go."

"But it would do you so much good."

"And have everyone looking at me and pitying me and being shocked?"

"But you often see people who got hurt in the war. No one looks shocked."

"War's different. Soldiers who fire on other soldiers are taking a deliberate risk. If they get hurt—well, they deserve to because they've been trying to do just the same to soldiers on the other side. Those," quoted Nicola, with a fine disregard for his own disapproval of Holy Writ, "who live by the sword shall perish by the sword."

"My father—"

"Blackshirt" said Nicola briefly, damningly.

"Nico! You know he didn't want to be! He—he was pushed into it against his will by old Ercole."

Nicola considered this a moment, bringing to bear a judgment at once intelligent and penetrating yet warped by the four high, narrow walls of his shut-in existence. "If he had joined of his own accord it would have been better. He would have been making a bad personal and political mistake, certainly, but people do that all the time—most of them. But to be *pushed in* merely shows weakness of character. I can't see how one can look at it in any other light."

"He was very young—younger than you—at the time."

"That is not a very good excuse. He wasn't a child, after all."

"He was a boy. And boys," said Mina shakily, "do stupid things."

"So do girls!" Nicola snapped, wrongly sensing a possible criticism.

But the result of this retort was so remarkable that for a moment he could hardly believe his eyes.

For Mina was crying. Tears welled up behind her great black-rimmed glasses and trickled down her face. Nicola had never seen her cry before and had believed that she never did. Now he was shocked and annoyed. Tears he had always considered to be his personal prerogative. He often wept himself—with pain or frustration or self-pity—but he could not understand why anyone with a strong, healthy, complete body should need to do so. It would be a lamentable weakness of character. Mina had taken off her glasses and was fumbling for her handkerchief;

her thin body was shaken with sobs. The kitten had scrambled back onto her lap and in her myopic despair she grasped it and lifted it to her face.

"*Not* with the cat," said Nicola disapprovingly. "It has its uses, but that is not one of them. Your handkerchief's on the floor."

Mina's tears redoubled and Nicola stared at her with concerned deprecation. He fidgeted with the pieces of his current jigsaw puzzle. "You are overwrought, Mina," he said at last. "I think you are right; you need a vacation."

"We were . . ." Mina's voice was broken and muffled behind her handkerchief. ". . . were going to—to Devon."

"The English western province?"

"Yes."

"But—something has prevented it?"

Mina took a great gulp of air, wiped her eyes and said in almost her normal tone, "I think Galo has. I think he's given me a baby."

Nicola's whole legless body jerked in a sudden spasm and the jigsaw pieces scattered over the bed. "You—you mean you have—"

"Yes. Nearly six weeks ago—no, almost seven. Before—before he went down to the Sila. But only one time . . . only once."

"But"—Nicola's voice was appalled—"you weren't even *engaged!* And he's only a *schoolboy!*"

Mina nodded dumbly, the tears still trickling from her swollen eyelids.

"How could you be so—so"—Nicola cast wildly around for a suitable epithet and found a most unsatisfactory one—"so lost to shame!"

"It wasn't shameful." Even through her tears Mina smiled weakly. "It was horribly painful, though."

"Did you *want* to?"

"I don't know! I don't remember! He wanted to and—so I suppose I agreed. In a way I suppose I wanted to. But I didn't know what it would be like. I hated it. It hurt!"

"Did it hurt him?"

"No, no—not at all." Mina's voice was bitter. "He loved it."

"Well!" said Nicola, lost for words. "*Well!*"

"So now I'm going to have a baby—it's horrible!"

Nicola leaned over and removed the kitten which, though fascinated, was becoming dampened with tears. "Have some brandy," he suggested. "We'll both have some."

Shakily Mina got up and filled the glasses. "You—you're not too terribly shocked are you, Nico?"

"Yes I am. Could you expect anything else?"

"It's much worse for me."

"What does Galo say?"

"I haven't told him."

"You'll have to. He won't like it. But it was partly his fault."

"It was *all* his fault!" Mina was indignant.

"It was weak of you to allow it. And you just said that you wanted to—in a way."

"You're not being any help!"

"Well, I can't prevent you doing these things, can I? Anyway I always thought that you and Galo would get married one day. Now you'll have to. It will look very silly—marrying a boy not yet sixteen, I mean. And everyone will guess why, of course. I suppose Galo will have to leave the Nunziatella, but—"

"Galo—I don't think he would marry me even if . . . I—I'm sure he wouldn't. I don't think he was ever in love with me —not properly. And since he went away I've heard nothing from him, not even a postcard. And he's back now—and still nothing."

Nicola stared over the rim of his golden goblet at her white, strained, tear-streaked face. From below came the rumble of traffic along the Via Michele Kerbaker borne up to the open window on the warm evening air. "But he *must* marry you. What else can be done? If you were both older—"

"If we were both older"—Mina's voice was clearer now but more tired than Nicola had ever believed it could be—"everything would be different. Probably we'd have been engaged before we did—what we did. But as it was . . . And don't you see, Nico—I can't marry Galo. You are quite right when you say he's a schoolboy. He's not sixteen. And he's got no money—not a single lira. It would mean him leaving the Nunziatella and never getting into the army and—oh, terrible trouble for all of us. I don't suppose I could even make him marry me at his age

—legally, I mean. And even if I could, he would hate me for it
—if it meant spoiling his career."

"You haven't told him what's happened yet. You can't tell
what he'll do until—"

"I can," said Mina wearily and with an intuition beyond her
years. "I can. He will be very frightened. He'll be frightened of
what he's done and of what I may do. And so he will begin to
hate me almost at once. He'll probably run away from home and
disappear. He's often nearly done it before—he once told me so.
The only reason he hasn't is because he likes the Nunziatella."

Nicola held his goblet in both hands, yet even so it shook
slightly and the imitation glass jewels with which it was encrusted
glittered in the electric light. His face was flushed and his breathing quicker than normal. When he spoke his voice was low.
"But Mina, if you don't marry him what are you going to do?"

"I don't know. I don't know at all!"

"I mean, in the old days people who got into this sort of trouble entered convents. You'd hardly do that, would you?"

Mina began to cry again with a quiet hopelessness and Nicola
put down his goblet and reached out to take one of her hands in
his. "Mina," he said shakily, "would you like to . . . to marry
me?"

Mina was so surprised that her tears ceased at once as
if turned off from a tap. "Me marry *you*, Nico?"

"Only if you want to. You see it would make everything all
right. I mean," Nicola hurried on, stammering in his urgency,
"I'm twenty-one, not fifteen. No one could possibly suspect anything irregular. There'd be no difficulties or trouble, like there'd
be with Galo."

"But"—Mina stared at him, blinked, and put on her glasses;
sobered into speculation by this sudden proposal—"do you *want*
to marry me, Nico?"

"Of course. I've always wanted to."

"You never"—Mina's voice sounded almost reproving—
"said anything about it before."

"Of course not." Nicola gestured briefly at the flat, empty expanse of bed where his legs should have been but where, instead,
the Pinocchio doll stared back in sharp-nosed angularity. "Why
should you want to marry me?"

"But—but I never thought . . . Oh, Nico—I never even imagined! How most extraordinary!" For a moment Mina was lost in wonder. Then she shook her head. "No, no, Nico. It is so kind of you that it almost breaks my heart. Truly! But it would only be to get me out of trouble. You wouldn't do it otherwise— not with Galo's baby coming, I mean."

Carefully Nicola said, "Yes—it is partly because of that." Mina sighed. "I thought so."

"But not in the way you mean." Nicola opened one hand that lay on the bed before him and stared at it intently; the soft, pink palm glittered with sweat. "The baby would be our baby— mine as much as yours. And—you see—it would be the only one we would have."

"I don't understand."

"Then try," said Nicola with a sudden return to his normal impatience. "You remember the time I spilt my inks and you changed my pajamas?"

"Yes."

"Well then—did I look like Galo, when you and he—"

"You mean—?"

"*Oh, Santo Cielo!* Mina, you are not demonstrating any intelligence at all!" Nicola took a deep breath and, staring down at his open hand, said slowly, "I could, perhaps, have asked you to marry me even though I have no legs. But I obviously could not ask you if I could not do what Galo did. Well—I can't."

"But I never want to do that again!" Mina's voice was suddenly joyful. "Oh Nico, I *am* glad!"

Nicola's voice was breaking with a mixture of tears and almost hysterical laughter. "Mina! But you see now—with a baby —we'd be all right. Without a baby we could have had no family at all. Now we can get married and live together with our baby—just like everyone else."

Mina would have liked to have flung herself upon him in a rapturous embrace but Nicola could only be touched very carefully, so she leaned over and turned his head toward her and kissed him gently and their tears mingled, dripping, this time unnoticed, over the kitten. "Nico, everything's going to be lovely now. Everything's going to be all right."

◆§ 2

"EVERYTHING is *not* all right!" Beppo stood trembling with rage in the shaft of morning sunlight which fell through the kitchen window while his English breakfast of bacon and eggs lay half-eaten and disregarded on the table before him. Crimson-faced he glared at his daughter. "You can't marry that man! It's monstrous! Absolutely monstrous and completely out of the question! Mina—I can't believe all this, even now! Tell me—for God's sake—that it's all a joke."

Mina stared up at him amazed from behind the teapot. She had never seen her father in such a state before and could not account for it now. She, herself, had just passed her first good night of unbroken sleep for weeks and, restored and contented by what she took to be the resolution of her difficulties, she had informed Beppo of her engagement as soon as he sat down to his breakfast. "I have some interesting news for you. Dear Nicola has asked me to marry him."

Beppo had started by being amused. There was nothing very wrong in the poor crippled boy indulging in such fantasies, though indeed it was pathetic—tragic, even—if he was really serious. But he could not be, of course. For fully five minutes Beppo believed sincerely that his daughter was merely evolving one of the complex and fantastic absurdities in which she specialized—only last April she had spoken, apparently in full seriousness, of abstracting the skeletal Vittorio from the anatomy classroom opposite and taking him for "a healthy day's outing" to Ischia or Capri. And now it dawned upon him only slowly that Mina was serious, that Nicola was serious, that they were both in earnest.

Then he had become increasingly angry. The whole thing was ridiculous, but not, as he became uneasily aware, so ridiculous as to be a stupid joke. It was true for instance, as Mina said, that she and Nicola had much in common. They had their Art—Beppo knew that they often disagreed over its interpretation, but that was hardly important. They had their mutual interest in certain sorts of literary exoticism and their common atheism. Painting, books, ungodliness—it was an impressive trinity. Beppo had started to become distinctly worried. "Mina, you had no right to lead this poor boy on. It's a—"

"I didn't lead him on. I've told you—he has asked me."

"Then *he* had no right to do so. Even less right! He's older and should know better. Either he is completely unscrupulous or else he's a fool. I'm inclined to think the latter. I hope I'm right. Because obviously you can't marry someone like that. I mean, *think,* Mina—just think! You'd be tied all your life to a complete cripple. It would be horribly unfair to you. A dreadful handicap forever. I'm sorry for the boy, of course. And I know you are—even more so. But to be sorry and to help him is one thing. To marry him—to tie yourself irrevocably to him—that's quite another. And even though I've only met him two or three times I should not say that he was an easy person to get on with."

"No, not for most people," had agreed Mina placidly. "But he's always been sweet with me."

"That may not last indefinitely. And there's something much more important. What about money? Nicola earns none at all and, poor boy, I don't see how he ever can. You've got to live, after all."

"Nico has more chance of making money with his pictures than I have. His work is the sort that could easily be sold—in the Toledo."

Beppo had sniffed. "Perhaps. But even so that's most unreliable." He had paused a moment feeling thwarted and angry. Here was Mina's first proposal and he was behaving like an outraged parent in the first years of the century. Old Vittorio could hardly have shown more petulant vexation. In a moment, he guessed, Mina would be telling him this. She had always been patient with him—but only up to a point.

Then—"I had thought"—his voice had been gentle and hesitant—"that perhaps you were—were fond of Galo. I mean, you always seemed to be. Of course it would have been several years yet—six or seven at least—but it did seem as if—What's wrong? What have I said?"

For Mina's face had become crimson, her eyes behind her glasses blinking rapidly. But she did not reply and Beppo had been too interested in his own attempt to persuade her away

from this, to him disastrous, alliance with a permanently bedridden cripple to press the question. "Yes, I had thought that
perhaps you and Galo would become engaged one day. Despite
the Lords and Ladies, Galo is a good boy. And look—I don't
want to seem salacious, but—well, married couples share the
same bed and so forth. Don't forget that. What is more to the
point, it is very probable, from what I've heard of poor Nicola's
injuries, that he could never be a father. In other words, you
and he would be childless. Surely if any argument was needed
to show how completely—"

And at that point Mina had done something which she had
promised Nicola that she would not do—had come out brutally,
bluntly, with the full story. And—"No!" Beppo had shouted at
the end. "Everything is *not* all right!"

The strongest influence on Beppo's life had been his years in
Devon. With the exception of Mina, the two persons for whom
he bore the deepest affection were the Pinnigers. But life on the
chicken-farm had been, of necessity, too shut away from the
rest of England to broaden his views to any perceptible degree.
He had learned English but not the cool Anglo-Saxon pragma-
tism which he admired but did not comprehend. He was, as he
had always been, a southern Italian at heart. And now he reacted to Mina's story with the full fury of his race. Galo became
at once a treacherous monster in hardly human form—an un-
forgivable enemy and betrayer. What had happened was, by
Neapolitan standards, completely natural and at the same time
completely, utterly, infamous. By Neapolitan standards Galo's
virility was enhanced triumphantly, Mina was ruined for life and
Beppo himself turned to a contemptible laughingstock.

For ten minutes Beppo stormed at his white-faced, trembling
daughter—raged and shouted as he himself had never believed
he could. Deep within him lay the knowledge that sooner or later
he would have to accept this thing; have to look at it with calm
—or at least calmer—eyes and have to deal with it. But not yet
—not yet! For the present he allowed himself to be caught up
and swept away in the full flood-rip of his fury.

The first thing was to get even with Galo. Galo for whom he
had so often been sorry; to whom he had given better marks than
he deserved and nursed through heaven-knew-how-many Eng-

lish lessons at the military academy. Galo who had come to this
flat, eaten his food, accepted his small gifts of money, and then
. . . and then . . . Beppo rushed to the telephone before remembering with boiling frustration that the Palazzo Colavolpe
did not, and probably never would, possess such an instrument.
He could not reach Galo—or Galo's uncle and mother—immediately. Very well—very well, then! A letter, sent *espresso*,
would arrive at Caserta that evening. Beppo left Mina slumped
and crying behind the breakfast table in the kitchen and breathing heavily, his brain coining one furious phrase after another,
sat down at his desk and seized his pen.

The letter he wrote was the most venomous, insulting and,
indeed, mendacious document that he knew how to compose.
He described, for its recipients' benefit, the more glaring defects
of all the Colavolpes, dead and alive. He enlarged upon their
lunacy, jeered at their degeneracy and taunted them with their
wretched poverty, their antisocial uselessness to mankind and
the well-known relationship between Speranza and Concezio.
He informed them that he knew perfectly well that they had
conspired in an attempt to defraud him of his inheritance—he
gloated that they had failed. Nonetheless, he stated that he had
intended, as soon as the will was proved, to make them a handsome gift to alleviate their disastrous penury. He had, he said,
intended to hand over ten million lire to them on the day Ercole
Sanbrenedetto's money came legally under his full disposition.
Then he called Galo every ugly name he could bring to mind;
swore that he would make his abominable behavior a public
scandal, sue for heavy damages and have him thrown out of the
military academy.

It was in many respects the letter of a madman, and even as
his racing pen scrawled his threats Beppo knew, somewhere
deep within him, that he would never put them into effect. But
as he wrote them they seemed real enough and for the moment
that was all that counted. Then, breathing heavily, his face
suffused, he slammed out of the flat to mail the letter at the
post office down the road near the funicular station.

Once that was done he felt better; almost as if, in some way
he could not understand, he had partly rectified the whole sorry
business already. Empty now, feeling faint and a little sick after

his emotional storm, he dropped into a small bar and ordered a black coffee and a glass of water. It was while waiting beside the hissing Espresso machine, running a finger around the inside of his damp collar, that the idea suddenly came to him that it would be as well to take Mina to a doctor.

⋘ 3

EVENING sunlight, falling through one of the four small circular windows which lit the bedroom, shone upon Concezio's bare chest, glinting on the mat of hair already beginning to turn gray, as he eased himself into a sitting position and looked down at Speranza. In only his belted old black trousers he yet displayed a handsome figure, flat-stomached, narrow-waisted, strong-shouldered. His wooden hand was still with a carpenter at Caserta being mended and for the present he had to make what use he could of his stump. It was remarkable how much he was able to perform with it.

As usual he was arguing with his sister-in-law. "And I say that's nonsense! Let him go by all means. Two or three days in Rome—what does it matter? It should at least show him what money can buy. When he comes back I'll talk about that. He's reaching the stage when money means a lot to him. Very well— let him see what can be done with it. When he comes back I can point out the difference between what he'll get as one of De Santis's people compared with army pay. In fact I don't think he's really as keen on the army as he pretends. He's just got used to the Nunziatella and doesn't want to make a fresh start somewhere else. When he realizes— Yes, what is it?" Concezio turned from the bed as Maria Fausta scurried across the room, her wooden-soled peasant's slippers clattering on the tiles.

"A letter for you, Concezio. A local one from Naples—*espresso,* too."

"*Fetiuk!* Give it here. And don't look at me as if I'd won the State lottery! It will be a bill of some sort—they always are." He shot Maria Fausta a quick, suspicious look. "Have you been buying things on credit again? Has Tarquinio?"

From the bed Speranza gave a grunting sigh of impatience.

"Of course they haven't—nor have I! Your precious pension's safe—what there is of it."

"It had better be!" said Concezio dourly. "Since it's all we've got to live on" and he ripped open the envelope.

⋑ 4

UPSTAIRS Galo was packing. His uniforms, summer and winter, were strewn about the bed and on the table by the window lay a pile of textbooks and notes—last year's work upon which he would shortly have to take an examination. The uniforms were mostly too tight or too short and must be altered, and this he hoped to have done in Rome. The books and papers he wished to discuss with Lecco, who had often helped him with his classwork in the past and would probably do so again.

Lecco's requested letter of invitation had arrived that morning and after the inevitably acrimonious discussion with "them" he had received grudging permission for the visit. His mother had been flatly against it but Concezio still retained a certain nostalgia for the army and an ill-defined idea that it might still find some way of using his services.

"Does this general ever talk about me?"

"Sometimes."

"Was he in Russia?"

"No—Africa."

"*Beh!* They had it easy enough there. Well anyway, you try to get him interested, see? Tell him some of the things I've told you. Let him know I'm still available for a desk job if there's one going."

"All right."

Except in the most uncomplimentary manner, and in regard to the difficulties of retaining his inheritance, Galo had no intention whatever of bringing Concezio's name to the general's notice. The older he grew the more he detested his uncle and his other relatives—and the more he became ashamed of them. Far from having any family pride Galo had for some years felt a growing conviction that to be born a Colavolpe was the most shameful and humiliating fate that could befall anyone—almost as bad as being born a leper—except that it was easier for a Colavolpe to take refuge in the anonymity of military uniform.

He had grown fast in the last months and the only clothes that seemed to fit him were the pale blue, crimson-striped trousers of his parade uniform. Perhaps these could remain unaltered. He tried them on for the second time and, deciding that they would do for the next few months at least, sighed and wandered over to the window, absently polishing his ornate, gilt-and-ivory-hilted *spadino* with an old handkerchief.

An evening calm enveloped the house. Thirty meters away the sun-baked cupola of the Church of the Holy Tooth shone out amongst its cluster of dark umbrella pines and from its vestry a chicken lifted its voice in the triumph of egg production. Galo hoped Tarquinio would not hear it and, going out, discover the missing hens. The old man had the habit of furtively stealing the occasional new-laid egg—which was why Galo, rather than he, had charge of the hens. Speranza always swore that she could tell when Galo had been eating the eggs but her gift of divination in this respect failed with her uncle-in-law.

But soon now—very soon—there would be no further question of looking after the chickens or of doing any other menial chores. Once in full command of his inheritance Galo had determined that "they" were going to wait on him. He would dole out money carefully and only after repeated requests. They would have to come to him for every sum, however small. And very soon they would be made to realize that if they displeased him those sums would not be forthcoming. He would buy three cows, but they would be *his* cows and the milk they produced would be *his* milk. In the coming winter there would be new gas-heaters, but the gas would come in containers from Caserta and be strictly rationed by himself. For the old days, the long, long years of childhood, were over at last, were falling quickly away behind him like ugly ruined houses passed in a train. A new day was dawning. . . .

Somewhere at the other end of the house a door banged open and someone called out loudly. The sounds were muffled and he hardly heard them, staring from the window, lost in a dream, absently polishing his silver dagger. Then there were footsteps, heavy and fast in the passage outside; his uncle's uncertain, thudding limp and the quick clatter of women's slippers. Suddenly his own door was flung open with a crash that shook the whole room. And framed in the doorway stood Concezio—or what, at first, appeared to be a distorted caricature of Concezio —so empurpled, so twisted and shaken with rage that for a moment Galo believed he must be staggering in the throes of some cerebral or cardiac stroke and seeking desperately for help. Through Galo's mind passed the sudden thought that his uncle was going to die and a thrill of exultation swept over him like a quick wind-ruffle across the face of a pond. But behind that panting figure in the doorway pressed Speranza, and behind her was something black and bobbing which must be one of the great-aunts. Even Tarquinio's face, crimson-nosed, bulging-eyed, appeared for a moment beyond the doorpost.

And now Concezio had got his breath back and at once spewed it out again in a flood of acrid military blasphemy and abuse, shouting the wild obscenities and insults of the frozen Russian trenches and the barrack-rooms of the old army. Only when his uncle had exhausted his great fund of profanity and lurched back into semicomprehensible idiom did Galo receive an idea of what had happened.

". . . of all the mad, idiotic, senseless things to do! At the very time when I was fixing things with De Santis for you! Yes— for your advantage, you filthy little lecher! You were going to get a proper training, a proper position, a future! Do you think he'll look at you now—you shop-soiled punk! And once I thought—*Porco Dio!*—that you had some sense! You—you— you . . . *Oh, Gesù!*" With a shuddering effort Concezio controlled himself, gritted his teeth and thudded into the room while behind him, like flotsam flooding through a suddenly unblocked sluice, poured the others.

"Yes—she's going to have a child—Sanbrenedetto's girl. *Your* child!" Sweat glittered on Concezio's stained face and at the base of his sloping forehead a heavy blue vein throbbed and pulsed. "She's ruined, of course—finished for good. Not that I care for that. But—but he was going to—*Oh, Dio!*—he was going to *let us have ten million of Ercole's money!* And now! It's lucky for you this isn't the old days and that she has no brothers. Otherwise you wouldn't be able to leave this house and get back alive! But nowadays people don't take the law into their own hands in these parts. It's left to the State. A boy who dishonors a girl goes to the *casa di correzione*. Sanbrenedetto's going to prosecute you so that's where you'll go. You'll be locked up! You won't be wearing *that* uniform any longer. You'll be in prison stripes out at Procida. That's where you'll be. That's going to be your new home, you filthy fornicating puppy!"

Concezio's voice had risen to a howl of frenzy and Galo backed away, his face pale as paper, his hands trembling. He understood at last what had occurred and he was so appalled, so frightened, that he looked idiotic, his mouth hanging open, his eyes wide. He had never dreamed, he had never once considered, that what he had done to Mina was likely to impregnate her. Lecco, as he knew, went nearly once every week to a woman in the Porto Quarter and even Pavan, at the end of retelling his peculiar, involuntary experience with the Swedish swimmer, had said, ". . . she had every boy in the class . . ." While he and Mina— Of course he knew vaguely that there were precautions, but he hardly knew what they were and in any case had no idea of their proper use. And now . . . Words failed him and for a moment he stood gasping, white, trapped, his eyes flickering over the furious, vicious, vengeful faces which were closing ominously in upon him.

Then, suddenly, Concezio was convulsed into an outburst of berserk action. Galo's uniforms were lying on the bed and he lurched to them and hurled them to the floor. He seized the full-dress tunic and grasping it with his teeth and his one hand savagely tore off the collar and ripped away one sleeve and a handful of gilt buttons before trampling that, too, with his feet. Behind him, Speranza caught the infection of destruction and jerking the two glazed and framed groups of her son's military classes from the wall, kicked them into a shower of splinters across the tiles. "*There!* And *there!* And *there!* Then, together with Concezio, who moved with astonishing speed for a cripple, she turned to the table covered in books and disagrams and seizing the first of them ripped it apart and apart again. Concezio followed suit; paper fragments fluttered to the floor and then, suddenly, Galo came to life. Those books were important; many of them were his own notebooks filled with detailed and meticulously drawn designs and tracings, the patient, irreplaceable productions of a whole year's classwork and study. They must at all costs be saved from this orgy of destruction.

He ran forward and seized them. "No, no! These are *mine!* You can't—" Furious in his turn, disregarding the vicious blows Speranza struck at his face, he struggled to hold on to his cherished notebooks, tugging a handful away from Concezio and trying futilely to anchor the others on the table with the point of his *spadino.*

For a moment uncle, mother and son grunted, gasped and panted across the disordered pile of colored papers. Then Concezio leaned forward and, tearing the *spadino* from Galo's grasp, made a grab at the remaining notebooks. His wooden foot slipped upon the broken glass below and losing his balance, his arms flailing wildly, he cannoned off Galo, seized Speranza and crashed with her to the floor among a mass of fluttering papers.

Speranza was below her lover and her head hit the tiled floor with sufficient force to effectively stun her; but Concezio fell on the thigh of his amputated leg and the agonizing flame that seared him brought a scarlet shutter of pain flapping darkly across the day. He swayed on the verge of consciousness, gasping through clenched teeth in a whistling hiss; but despite the torture and the shattering shock of his fall he was aware that something was wrong with Galo, and with a nearly intolerable effort he rose, groaning, on one elbow and looked up.

Above him, swaying, holding on to the table, Galo stared stupidly at the rest of them—Tarquinio, Maria Celeste, Maria Valeria, Filippa, Maria Fausta—huddled together in the doorway, their faces wide-eyed with dawning horror, and Concezio saw that from his nephew's chest, pressed tightly against his darkening shirt just below the breastbone, the hilt of the *spadino* stood out gleaming in gilt and enamel like some exotic military decoration.

For a moment Galo reeled on his feet, his mouth open wide in the rigor of dumb, breathless anguish, the square-lipped howl on the mask of classic tragedy. Then his legs gave way and he crumpled limply, soundlessly, to the floor to lie on his back among his torn clothes and scattered papers. He looked very small like that; very young. Very neat in his pale blue, crimson-striped trousers—very still among the wreckage of what had been his life.

Liquefaction

1

   *PROTEGGICI le nostre famiglie—Benedeci i no-
stri bambini—Sorridi ai nostri malattie.* The colored posters,
half demand, half supplication, glowed from the walls and everywhere throughout Naples, but particularly in the poorer dis-
tricts, the flag-decked arches had gone up and bright blue poles
supported convoluted sprays of colored bulbs which this evening would blaze through the alleys and the squares from the
Via Foria to the sea.

   It was his saint's day and later he would be going, with a complacent Crocifissa and an excited Gigi, to the Duomo to witness
the yearly miracle; but now, lying on his bed, watching Perugia
peck at a wilted leaf of lettuce while the sunlight moved
in golden bars across the floor, he felt none of the usual happy
elation but only a cold emptiness, an oddly painful vacuum driving out the rubbery resilience with which he normally confronted
the day-to-day struggle with life.

   More than two hours ago the sun had fired the white jade
horse into an icy heart of flame but still Gennaro lay on the bed,
motionless, staring up at the stained, cracked ceiling. For the
first time he could remember there was no reason to rise—nothing to do up here or down in the funeral parlor or the workshop.
In the little cupboard of a closet next door Quong was either
asleep or in that silent, seemingly half-conscious state of suspended animation which had increasingly taken the place of his
waking hours. Quong was slowly sinking now, as Crocifissa

said; slipping gently and by almost imperceptible gradations out of his calm life into a still deeper and serener calm. He no longer used his slate, which lay dustily on the shelf by his bed, and sometimes he hardly appeared to recognize Gennaro, his wrinkled almond eyes fixed and blank in his immobile face. Gennaro spent more time with him than ever; sitting by his side talking softly, holding one small, cool yellow claw and trying, somehow, to blow to a flicker the fading embers of Quong's spirit.

Had there been any work below he would have been unable to spend so long with his grandfather. But there was none. Everything downstairs was in immaculate order; the tools in the workshop sharp and oiled, the floor painfully clean of sawdust, while in the funeral parlor the sequin skulls grinned genially from the velvet pall below a vase which no longer held flowers. For Iole seldom sat there now. Since the failure of her husband's petition she had withdrawn more and more into herself and spent most of the day in her own room, the pretense of "working" for Quong's tacitly abandoned.

And yesterday for the first time Gennaro had been forced to refuse a commission—if one could call a request for a simple coffin a commission which, a few months ago, he most certainly would not have done. The fact was that he had no more wood. Gennaro, like many carpenters, had a special feeling about wood; the sort of sensuous affection farmers are said to experience when gazing over a field of ripening grain. It was the basic material of his profession and despite the fact that he himself seldom fashioned it into anything except cheap coffins, Kwang-Yin stood at his elbow to remind him constantly of its magnificent plasticity in the hands of an expert. Sometimes in the past he had dreamed of running out of wood—generally in the most embarrassing circumstances with a pile of commissioned but un-coffined cadavers at his door, and hearses, priests and angry mourners impatiently waiting in the street outside. But real-life situations are fortunately more prosaic. Yesterday he had merely expressed his regrets that "owing to illness" Quong's Funerals was temporarily unable to accept further work. It had caused him much less pain than he would have believed. As soon as his would-be client had gone he had shut the door and stood for a moment in the empty funeral parlor, glancing through at the neat, empty workshop and surrounded by silence and a thin coating of dust.

He could not buy more wood until he had paid off the loan from Savoldi and so far he had not paid back a single lira. Of course there were other wood merchants, but in the present state of the business it was certain that none would give him credit. So, for the present, coffin-making was over. But he still had twenty-four wreath frames and a bucket in which stood eighteen tall palm leaves only a little rusty at the edges. Quong's wasn't dead while wreaths could be made and sold.

Not yet dead—but what was to happen in less than a fortnight when, according to Crocifissa, they would all have to leave the old building? During the last months Gennaro had sometimes questioned Crocifissa about this and she had generally put him off with the assurance that "Signor Giuseppe will do something —make some arrangements for us." If pressed she would say that she expected Signor Giuseppe to assist them all in finding new premises; she was sure of it—he had always been so good, so kind. And with this Gennaro had been very willing to remain content—he had plenty of other worries of his own without adding future homelessness to them.

But today, with less than a fortnight to go before the threatened demolition began, he could not help but worry. There was the hearse—silent in its garage for nearly five months now—the workshop with all his tools, his small store of purple ribbon and gold paper letters, his frames and palm leaves. Above all there was Quong. To explain to Quong—and would he comprehend, even then, what was happening?—was going to be very difficult in any case. Gennaro dreaded the effect of a sudden move to strange surroundings upon his grandfather. Iole would help of course, and if only they could know sufficiently early where they were to go the old man might be moved carefully and gently in advance. Yes, it was certainly more than time that Signor Giuseppe, despite his personal preoccupations, came to the *piazza* and made his intentions known.

Yet dominating all these somber speculations, eclipsing even the knowledge that the total sum of money between himself and destitution was now exactly eight thousand, six hundred and forty-five lire, lay a dark shadow, the shadow of a small man with an undershot jaw and a fixed, snarling grin.

Gennaro possessed the ostrichlike capacity of youth to shut off unpleasant facts, a capacity now beginning to fail in the cold light of adult reasoning but upon which he was still able to call, albeit with a continually increasing mental effort. What had happened that night in the Vicolo Ciego di Pomodori had, in one sense, not happened at all—that is to say that it was no longer real, or that it existed in a different dimension, on much the same plane as the dreams of uncoffined corpses with funeral processions waiting angrily at the door. Even under the water-treatment in the *camera di sicurezza* Gennaro had not believed in the reality of his presence on the scene of the crime, nor would he have believed in his own confession once it had been extorted from him. After all, San Gennaro had made it more than plain that his namesake and protégé was guiltless in the eyes of Heaven. And of course he *was* guiltless: he had been involved in nothing more than a vain attempt to raise the money for a horse-drawn hearse.

But below this knowledge lay a hot, dark, troubled confusion of fear and doubt with Domenichelli grinning at its center. Domenichelli had tried to kill him, and despite all his shuttings-off and mental conjuring tricks with time and space, Gennaro knew perfectly well why. The patrolman had fired two shots before collapsing under the effect of Domenichelli's own bullet. If Gennaro's dead body, with the assassin's revolver conveniently beside it, had been found at the end of that slotlike gulley between the warehouse walls, Domenichelli's chances of escape would have seemed infinitely greater. For Domenichelli had not seen La Gobba and believed that the only possible witness to testify against him was Gennaro. And that in the hands of the police Gennaro would so testify—either readily or under the pressures of which he himself had ample knowledge—Domenichelli rightly believed. Quick-thinking and completely ruthless, he had seen what he must do, had tried to do it and had failed by some four centimeters off aim.

Yet if Gennaro alive was a threat to Domenichelli, Domenichelli himself was an equal threat to Gennaro. In the back of Gennaro's mind a cold voice sometimes said that in the hands of the police Domenichelli and La Gobba between them might send him to prison for a period of time which did not bear contemplation. That small piece of purple ribbon and palm leaf in its box-file could damningly connect the two in testimony against him.

But—as he told himself hurriedly upon these occasions—there was no reason at all to worry. For he had *not* been in the Vicolo Ciego di Pomodori that night. He had been in his workshop sharpening his tools. Gigi and Crocifissa had seen him there and Gigi had talked with him in Tenerini's immediately afterward. Reality consisted not only in seeing things as they were but as they appeared to other people. Yet Domenichelli still grinned—down there in the shadowy dark.

An hour later when Gennaro had at last risen, looked in on the still-sleeping Quong, and tidied the room—he had not made himself his usual cup of coffee since, thrifty as ever, he was hoarding his last few grams—Gigi ran in. A Gigi brushed and washed and dressed in a clean white shirt, his face flushed with the excitement of a prospective outing.

"Gennaro—why aren't you ready? You know we're going with Crocifissa. She said to tell you to come down quickly. If we are late we won't find places. . . ."

◆§ 2

BUT in the end they found places—or rather Gigi found them—beside one of the pillars under the third Station of the Cross. Three hard wooden stools cramped together at the edge of a worn strip of coconut matting and upon which they climbed to peer over the heads and between the shoulders of the jostling, shifting crowd which packed the side aisles and eddied in and out of the chapel of the Silver Treasure.

Today the interior of the Duomo resembled a fair rather than the inside of a cathedral. The whole place blazed with light, resounded to the clang of bells and the cries of hawkers selling amulets, medals, illuminated prayers and brightly colored pictures of the Patron Saint himself, while the great silver bust, coped and mitered in gold, gleamed among the hundred candle-bearing sconces on the high altar. A dozen or so doves, which had prematurely escaped from the cages in the roof, flew, frenzied by the noise, half doped by the incense, in erratic circles, or swooped distractedly over the heads of the sweating, shouting crowd already working itself into fever-pitch excitement at the expectation of the annual miracle. Soon, very soon now, the fortunes of the next twelve months must be made known: the safety of Naples or its jeopardy; the happiness and success in business, love, childbirth and even, in a somewhat complex manner, in death of all its citizens from Mayor Achille Lauro—the "Commandante"—to the most destitute and verminous *scugnizzo* of the slum alleys— And even more, perhaps, the annual destinies of those one-in-every-fifteen males of the city who had been christened for the saint and bore his name.

At a lower level than the bust and well to one side of the altar the life-size figure of a woman in a flowing red dress stood upon a gilded pedestal. This was Eusebia, the saint's wet nurse, and though the figure was not exactly holy it was nonetheless more than a decoration. There were a few tattered five-hundred-lire notes pinned to its skirts by persons who had erroneously taken it for the Madonna and a photograph of some children in first communion dress lay askew at its feet. The priests would remove all these in due course, but at the moment they were too busy and too hindered by the doves to do so. For they were preparing the miracle. Somewhere among that coven of them beside the high altar was the reliquary, the heavy circular glass box set in gem-embossed gold which was the heart—the very essence—of this whole huge church. Within the reliquary, but clearly seen through the glass, two small, bulb-shaped phials were half full of a dry, murky gum—specimens of the saint's blood collected by Eusebia at his decapitation sixteen hundred years ago. Three times a year, but most particularly at noon on the nineteenth of September, this blood must become red, liquid, and alive before the eyes of all who thronged the cathedral. In this way, firmly and categorically and as if the silver bust had spoken aloud from the high altar, the saint renewed his annual promise to his city and his people—*"Proteggerò la mia Napoli."*

Gennaro had seen the miracle five times—every year since he had come to Naples. Yet despite the fact that he was standing in the presence of his patron saint, the Duomo was a church which disturbed and vaguely depressed him with its lack of form or symmetry—so unlike the great, high-vaulted churches of his Ferrara childhood with their immaculate arched and decorated Venetian marbles. Today, however, there was a gay barbarity about the Duomo which could not but excite him. If the Ferrara churches—the Cathedral, San Francesco, San Giorgio and San Domenico—were at their most impressive when filled with ordered rows of chanting monks and nuns lifting the Kyrie Eleison to the lofty painted roofs, then surely here, in this southern sea-city, the Duomo needed its throngs of shouting, impatient townsfolk passionately eager for the miracle to be made manifest in order to secure themselves and their families for another year.

They stood on their stools, the three of them: a shock-haired boy in a shabby lavender suit, a white-shirted child and an old woman in black, and each began to feel the hot, tingling excitement, the mounting tension as the time of the miracle drew close. Gigi—in common, had he known it, with some three-quarters of the congregation—had his small, red, plastic cow's horn clutched firmly in his hand. This one sure periapt against the casually malicious, doom-laden glance of the *gettatore* must be with him, gripped warm in living human flesh, at the time of the miracle to be charged like an electric battery with full protective powers for another year.

Crocifissa had three holy medals, a crucifix and five religious picture-postcards which she, in her turn, wished impregnated by the miraculous influence. She held them in one hand at shoulder-level and considerably to the detriment of her balance on the stool. The postcards were the most difficult to manage since they must not be held in a firm pack but spread out fanwise to catch the invisible rays from the altar. This was most important, for every year she dispatched them, with notes explaining their particular merit, to friends in various religious orders. Correctly, she believed that they were deeply appreciated and treasured by their recipients.

Gennaro alone had neither cow's horn nor postcards. The possession of the former was perhaps the only misdemeanor which the Ferrara monks had punished with anything approaching severity, while he knew no one to whom to send the latter. Below the collar of his mauve shirt his gold crucifix lay against his skin and in one trouser pocket was the medal of cheap alloy he had bought on the steps of the Duomo at his first visit. Now he took this out and held it up as Crocifissa held her own sacred knick-knacks. *"San Gennaro, proteggimi e guidami in ogni momento!"* Amongst the increasing tumult of the last moments before the miracle he prayed with fervent confidence for help in all his many difficulties. "San Gennaro—give me a sign. Great bishop, sacred martyr, holy one—show me that all will yet be well! Remember me, pity me, help me, save me here in this, your city. Show me a sign, great saint of Napoli!" But it must not be the miracle—that was for Naples. For him there must be something more—a personal message. And standing motionless on his stool, his medal displayed at shoulder-level, his eyes fixed on the gleaming, arrogant silver face upon the altar, he was quite certain that he would receive one. Had not San Gennaro, himself thrown into a furnace unhurt, into a pit of wild beasts unscathed, rescued him from torture three weeks ago? Had not San Gennaro, who although himself beheaded had condemned his executioner to die hideously that same day, promptly struck dead the police officer who had hurt his protégé?

Noise, noise—the swelling roar of the congregation drunk with excitement, stupefied with the clouds of incense. Somewhere near the front the dozen or so families who called themselves the "relations of San Gennaro"—though by this was meant only the hazardous belief that they were all descended from his wet nurse—had begun to shout cries of affectionate raillery and ritually genial abuse with which the saint was urged to hurry. "San Gennà, fai il miracolo! Facci la grazia di fare il miracolo!" Behind them the crowd took up the theme, using the local patois, demanding, cajoling: "Iesci e fance grazia, Santo bello Santone nuoste! San Gennà tienece mente! Faccia 'ingialluta! Schiarisce 'sta faccia e nun la tene' verde, Santone bello! San' Gennà fa' priesto! . . ."

And then, quite suddenly, it was accomplished. A scarlet-robed, gold-aproned priest swung abruptly from the altar lifting high the reliquary while behind him an acolyte raised an electric candle. The light, shining through the glass container, glowed on a ruby spot of liquid red. It was exactly noon. In the city where all else was unpunctual the saint alone was chronometrically exact.

A great roar of satisfaction thundered through the church and by a complex mechanical contrivance of wires and pulleys the cages concealed in the roof were opened and scores of doves rose circling among the clash of bells into the sky. Now all of Naples knew that the liquefaction had taken place and every belfry in the city let loose its brazen clangor while the steamy boom of ships' sirens and the thunder of cannon from the Arsenal swelled the diapason of exultant joy. The yearly promise had been renewed. "I will protect my Naples. . . ." Protection from great Vesuvius looming to the south over Torre and Portici; from earthquakes in the heat of summer and tempests in the winter—from cholera and plague and interference, well-meant or otherwise, from the government in Rome. Protection for rich and for poor—though, of course, rather more for the rich—against almost everything save each other. The saint had spoken.

But he had not spoken to Gennaro. No sign, no smallest indication, had crossed the smoky, purple, sun-shafted air from the high altar. And it was too late now. Already the reliquary was being exhibited at close quarters to the "relations of San Gennaro" who knelt and kissed the glass, weeping with joy; already the bland silver bust was being manhandled somewhat roughly from its podium to its gilded palanquin in preparation for the procession through the streets. No—the moment had passed. Expressionlessly Gennaro climbed down from his stool and helped Crocifissa descend from hers. The old woman was delighted and uplifted by the glowing riot of color and the dramatic tension of the last few minutes and their successful outcome—an outcome of which one could be almost, but never quite, certain. Her eyes were wet with emotion at the saint's goodness. She shuffled the irradiated postcards into a flat pack and put them, together with the medals, into her old black handbag. She smiled with misty benevolence at Gennaro and Gigi; they looked so clean and good in their best clothes. They, too, had been irradiated and were under the great saint's protection for the next twelve months. "It's no use waiting now to kiss the reliquary. The Relations take up at least half an hour and we are too far to the back. But we can return this evening. I'll shut the shop for an hour and we'll come then. I—" But the bells broke out again in a deafening crash directly overhead; the palanquin was swaying down the aisle on the shoulders of a dozen scarlet-aproned priests and as the doors of the church were flung open the three of them were caught up in the crowd and carried with it out into the sunlit tumult of the jubilant streets.

⋖§ 3

"THIS is all very unusual."

"No doubt."

"I mean, as a condition of sale. It's unbusinesslike for one thing and—at least so I would have thought—quite unnecessary. It's putting us to a lot of trouble." ITOLGAS's legal representative was a small, fattish man in his late fifties, a lawyer from Milan. He sat beside Dru in the back of a company car, his briefcase on his knees, staring disapprovingly out through thick spectacles at the teeming, festering streets, hung with shabby washing and paved with the unevenly worn *piperno* which made such an uncomfortable surface over which to drive. "If I had been able to meet your principal—but I suppose in the circumstances . . ."

"In the circumstances," Dru coughed, "he has—hmm—considerable preoccupations of a personal nature, as you are aware."

The lawyer muttered something in which Dru seemed to catch the words "distressingly scandalous" and "deplorable from every aspect" and then, raising his voice, returned doggedly to what he had in mind. "As I say, if I had been able to meet him I might have been able to suggest something else."

"Such as?"

"Oh, a monetary compensation of course. I mean this other arrangement is so troublesome. Time is money, you know, Signor Dru—at least in the north."

"Quite right. But tell me; what sum would you have suggested to Signor Sanbrenedetto?"

The lawyer wriggled his shoulders irritably in the stuffy heat of the closed car but he would not lower the window; the dust and the flies and the smells would be far worse than the heat. "Well," he said caustically, "I'd have made it more than generous if it would have saved me this journey." He glanced sideways at his companion, wondering whether perhaps there was still time, calculating quickly. . . . "Say two hundred thousand for the old woman, a hundred thousand for the undertaker and the same for the cabdriver. The last case is difficult, of course. Fifty thousand, perhaps. Say about half a million in all."

"Not a very generous sum."

"On the contrary, Signor Dru!" The lawyer's voice was sharp with offended propriety. "I consider it a *very* generous sum in the circumstances. What have these people done for my company that—"

"No, no, you mistake me," Dru soothed quickly. "I meant that as against the time and trouble—the difficulties and inconvenience this clause must inevitably cause you and your company—against all *that* the sum seems small."

"Hmm. Well, personally speaking, I'd certainly pay more to have that clause retracted—but there it is. What sum would you have thought . . ."

"Double."

For a moment their eyes met and read quick mutual understanding. The lawyer said uncertainly, "If you could change your principal's mind . . . naturally a gratuity . . . the difference . . . saying it could be done."

"It," Dru spoke carefully, "may not be necessary to change Signor Sanbrenedetto's mind, exactly. In the present circumstances he appears to have lost interest in the entire matter."

"Yes, yes. I can understand that."

"But I think, perhaps, that if I was left to make these various offers in my own way—they might be unacceptable. If so, that would save your company all the trouble of putting them into effect. The clause, if you will recall it, states only that the offers are to be made; there is no mention of any compensatory alternative, financial or otherwise, if they are not accepted."

The lawyer looked at Dru with new respect. "Yes, that is so, of course. Yes, but I would have to be there, too."

"Naturally. I am merely suggesting that you allow me to make at least the more troublesome offers in my own fashion."

They drew up in the *piazza* and picked their way, two well-dressed, middle-aged men, across the dirty flagstones under the raw gaze of a score of shabby children, to the little shop. Crocifissa, still suffused with the religious emotions of the morning, received them amiably and set Gigi to make coffee. "I knew Signor Giuseppe would do something for us." She removed Otello from her armchair and drew it up to the table.

"In fact," the lawyer from Milan remarked with dry politeness, "it is my firm which is making these offers and who will be responsible for their fulfillment. But since Signor Sanbrenedetto made such help a clause in the contract of sale you can of course, if you wish, rightly consider him responsible. I'm sure I do, myself."

"He was always such a kind man."

The lawyer nodded in dubious assent and Dru said, "Signora Buonafede, I think you should understand that Signor Sanbrenedetto was most anxious to help you—all of you—to carry on with your lives, as far as that was possible, with the minimum of disruption. Therefore we examined each of your several cases individually to see in what way we could mitigate the effects of your removal from this building. What Signor Sanbrenedetto, through the ITOLGAS company, wants to do is to resettle you where that is feasible and help you in some other way where it is not. In your case and that of Signor Bonitatibus I think we have succeeded best in finding how to do this. The other cases are somewhat more difficult. Can we—that is to say, can Signor Quong and Signor Bonitatibus and Signora Giansante come to us here?"

Crocifissa shook her head. "Biagio's gone off to somewhere near Avezzano for a few days and Quong is very ill." She turned to Gigi. "Run off and find Gennaro and Signora. Tell them to come here as soon as they can."

"Meanwhile . . ." Dru paused, sitting at the table in the place which had long ago been Dino's and had since been so often occupied by Gennaro, an open file spread under his hands while the lawyer beside him frowned and examined his fingernails. "Meanwhile, for yourself we are offering a shop at Portici. That is to say, we are offering to pay the entrance deposit of a hundred thousand lire and also two months' rent in anticipation, as well as bear the cost of removal."

"But I don't know Portici." Struck by a sudden hope for Gennaro and Quong, Crocifissa asked, "How many rooms are there —behind the shop, I mean?"

"None. It's a lock-up. Just the shop. The rent is twenty-five thousand a month. As I say—we will pay the first two months."

"Twenty-five *thousand!* I could never make enough to pay that. My rent here has always been four thousand—and I've had two rooms, as well. If this place at Portici has no rooms behind it how—where could I live?"

"You would have to find yourself accommodation—obviously."

"No, no. No, *signori*. I can't do that." Flushed, dismayed, Crocifissa shook her head obstinately. "I'm old. I have to live behind my shop. And twenty-five thousand! No—it's out of the question."

Dru nodded noncommittally. The rent of the shop was, in fact, fifteen thousand and though there was no living accommodation included, there were two reasonable storerooms which could have been used as such with only the minimum of alteration. But he saw no reason to explain this. "Very well. These are only offers, please remember. No one is in any way forcing you to accept them. The choice is entirely yours. Now we come to Signor Bonitatibus— You say he's gone away?"

"Only for a few days."

"I see. Well, then when he returns please tell him this. We—that is Signor Sanbrenedetto for whom I'm acting and the company which has purchased this site—represented by this gentleman here—realize that considerable inconvenience will regrettably be caused to Signor Bonitatibus, as well as yourself. We cannot, of course, search Naples for stabling in order to set him up elsewhere. But what we are willing to do—and I think it is distinctly generous—is to exchange his horse and cab for a taxi. This taxi, though certainly not new, will be in adequate condition and fully licensed. In fact he will obviously be better off as a result because—"

"He—Biagio!" Despite herself Crocifissa laughed. "Biagio couldn't drive a taxi! Not now. He's seventy-four. And he'd never part with Baldissera—that's his horse. No, no—I'm afraid you're wasting your time. Biagio—a taxi!" She shook her head unbelievingly.

The lawyer sighed gently, staring across the small, hot room, glancing at the enlarged portrait of the sailor—dead, presumably, in view of the little votive lamp—above the dresser. Despite the importance of this deal to his firm's Neapolitan interests he wished that it had failed. All this nonsense of shops and secondhand taxis! The only sensible offer was the one they were to make to the undertaker's grandson. . . . He thought of the long, hot journey which had brought him down here from his comfortable, well-ordered Milan office—brought him, incongruously dressed and bilious from the smells and heat, to this squalid back kitchen in a southern slum. It was quite true, the old saying that "Africa begins south of Rome." He took off his glasses, cleaned them with a small piece of chamois leather and sighed once more.

Then there were voices in the shop beyond the bead curtain and a young woman, pale-faced, haggard, obviously far gone in pregnancy, entered the kitchen followed by a boy in the sort of suit, at once ostentatious and poorly cut, which one would expect a Neapolitan to wear.

The old woman had begun to say "Signora Iole, these are . . ." when the boy suddenly exclaimed, "Signor Dru!"

"Gualtierra! But—what are you doing here?"

"What are *you* doing?" The boy's voice was suspicious, accusing, hostile.

The lawyer looked from one to the other. "You—you know each other, then?"

Dru had recovered himself rapidly. "Gualtierra worked under me for a week last summer—not for long."

"His name—surely his name's *Quong?* If he's the undertaker's grandson—"

"His name—well the one he told *me*—is Gualtierra."

The lawyer gave a quick grunt of exasperation. "It will mean changing all sorts of documents."

"Well—that's your job, isn't it?"

Gennaro said coldly, "My name's Gualtierra, but my grandfather's name is Quong—and he's an undertaker. . . . And so am I."

"It's all very irregular—"

"What is?"

Dru said quickly, "I think we should start with the lady." He turned to Iole. "Signora Giansante?"

"Yes."

"I'm representing Signor Sanbrenedetto, the recent owner of this building, and this gentleman represents the firm of ITOLGAS, the present owners. As you know, this building is due to be demolished at the end of the month. On the instructions of the owners, past and present, we are here to make certain offers of help by way of offsetting, as far as possible, the inconvenience you will all be caused by the loss of your accommodation."

Iole said flatly, "I can probably find another room if I have to. Though it will have to be very cheap."

"Your case is rather special—according to Signor Sanbrenedetto."

"He's done all he can for me. I will always be grateful to him."

"He has done something more now," put in the lawyer, "for he has asked our managing director in Naples, Commendatore De Santis himself, to—ah—interest himself in procuring, if at all possible, some mitigation of your husband's sentence."

"The *domanda* was refused by the Minister of Defense."

"I know. We realize that. Signor Sanbrenedetto put us in full possession of the facts of the case. Nothing more can be done *officially*. But Commendatore De Santis has certain unofficial contacts at his disposal. He's a very important man who knows a lot of people in Rome. . . ."

Iole's eyes brightened hopefully. "And he really can do something?"

"He can *try*. He can *see* if anything can be done."

"Will he?"

"He has undertaken"—the lawyer looked primly down at his clean, clasped hands—"to look into the matter."

"I see," said Iole, deflated. She no longer really believed in help for Evaldo shut away in his prison up the coast. Then she said urgently, "If he—this Commendatore—could somehow get me permission to visit my husband sometimes. You see, he needs—"

The lawyer looked up sharply. "Visit a *military* prisoner? Most unlikely. Quite against regulations. Your husband is—ah —where he is not for a civil crime committed against an individual or individuals in a private capacity but for the much more serious offense of a crime against the State. No, no, I think you mistake me, *signora*. Commendatore De Santis has said no more than that he will look into the case to see if anything can be done."

"You've said that already. But what does it mean?"

"Exactly what the words imply!" The lawyer's voice was

sharp. "Commendatore De Santis is a very busy man. It is extremely generous of him to do this much—yes." He shuffled his papers irritably. A timid man of a vaguely benign but cautious disposition he disliked the Giansante case more than any of the others. This girl's husband undoubtedly deserved to serve a full twelve years—and he almost certainly would. To interfere—unofficially, too—in the course of military justice was most repugnant to his legal mind; but apparently this particular case was the one in which Giuseppe Sanbrenedetto took the greatest interest. Not, thought the lawyer approvingly, that Commendatore De Santis was in the least likely to do anything about it, despite his words.

And now he turned with relief to what he considered to be the most generous, farsighted and sensible of all these irritating compensatory offers. But Dru, speaking to Gualtierra, forestalled him. "Have you got another job yet?"

Gennaro flushed. He hated, as he ever had, this talk of jobs—seeing it always as a contemptuous setting-aside of his true profession. Not that Dru could know of that, of course, but even so his voice was rough, as he replied, "I'm all right."

"You mean that you don't need any help?"

"Not from—"

"Oh, he does!" Crocifissa's voice was almost a wail. "Of course he does! We all need help but Gennaro needs it most because—because Quong's so ill and they can't use the hearse and business is so bad and they have no money!"

Gennaro's face was bright red now. Every word had been a saber-hack at his carefully preserved *amour-propre,* a humiliation of his self-esteem. In all his trials and difficulties he had kept up a fiercely preserved front of independence. It was his last, most cherished possession and he was not going to relinquish it. Crocifissa's words were achingly true but they were also a betrayal; they should never have been uttered. Gennaro had never heard of Cambronne's obscenely terse reply on being called upon to surrender his broken remnant of the Old Guard after Waterloo, but he would unhesitatingly have approved it.

Dru said, "If he doesn't want to be helped—"

But despite his agreement to leave the making of the material offers to his present colleague, the ITOLGAS lawyer now plunged in with all the blundering fervour of misplaced philanthropy. "One minute—one minute, *please.* I don't think this young man understands what we mean. When he does so I've no doubt at all that he will quickly change his mind. Because"— he looked over his glasses at Gennaro with an owl-like earnest- ness—"in your case our offer is a particularly valuable one, you see."

"A—a horse-drawn hearse?" Wild hope leapt for a second in Gennaro's heart and then collapsed as the lawyer shook his head irritably.

"I'm not talking about undertaking. We understand that your grandfather's business has more or less failed in any case. No, I'm talking about *you.* What someone of your age needs is a proper start in life; a good, specialist-type, artisan training; the assurance of a job with a secure future. We are offering you something we only normally offer to properly educated boys from good, solid home backgrounds—a position as an appren- tice at one of our plants at Rho, outside Milan. You'll be given a sound industrial training *and* paid a wage at the same time. You'll live in comfortable quarters with the other appren- tices and receive all the benefits of a full-time ITOLGAS em- ployee—industrial insurance, free medical and dental care and so forth. There are"—the lawyer was warming to his theme now for, like many tidy-minded northern Italians, the thought of tidying up even a tiny corner of Naples—that exasperatingly un- tidy city—lent him a glow of righteous benevolence—"dozens of different ways in which you will benefit greatly. For instance, we provide facilities for further education—night classes, study groups, libraries. We have playing fields and sports tracks and" —incongruously, though without any conscious intention of be- ing sardonic, but because Naples both frightened and depressed him, the lawyer added—"plenty of hot and cold water and free soap. Also we will do something else which I think demonstrates —if, indeed, demonstration is necessary—the humanity and concern for individuals as people which is the hallmark of to- day's great industrial firms. We will"—the lawyer paused im- pressively—"take your grandfather into one of our ITOLGAS homes for the elderly and incurable and in—in due course we will undertake his interment in our own cemetery— ITOLSEPPOLTO."

If Gennaro's face had been red before, it was fiery now. For a moment he stared in almost unbelieving hatred at the two middle-aged faces on the other side of Crocifissa's kitchen table —one bored and expressionless, the other filled with a fatuous, unctuous enthusiasm. Then in one quick movement he turned to the stove, seized the great pot of beans, the *fagioli cotti* for the evening customers simmering gently in oil, and flung its contents over Dru and his companion.

For a single second there was an appalled silence. Then the lawyer leapt to his feet with a shrill scream of fury, his face and clothes dripping yellow beans and viscous scummy oil, while Dru let out a bellow of rage and lunged round the table after Gennaro.

At once the kitchen was a scene of chaos, Crocifissa screaming, Gigi yelling, Gennaro and Dru rolling on the floor among the torn-down strings of the bead curtain, oil, beans, broken glass and smashed pottery. The table and chairs went over and the Milanese lawyer, who had lost his glasses and was almost blind without them, stumbled frightened and pleading as further plates and pictures crashed, calling out, "Please—please mind where you walk! My spectacles are somewhere on the floor. Please pay attention! A little patience! A little *consideration!* A little *respect!*" adding his thin, anguished lament to the screams of Gigi and the women and Dru's breathless, gasping curses.

Then suddenly Renato Paolantonio and Raimondo Tenerini were in the shop, in the kitchen. Dru was hauled off Gennaro, and the lawyer, knocked down by Raimondo in the not entirely mistaken belief that he was somehow responsible for all this, was picked up and pushed into a kitchen chair where he sat gasping, panting and demanding his spectacles. He could not fully believe what had happened. To have a great pan of beans thrown full in his face! To sprawl amongst dirt and spilt food upon the floor of a slum kitchen! No—it was impossible. Somebody thrust his glasses into his hand and though one lens was cracked across he was again able to see the world in focus. To see grinning, jeering men's faces and hysterical women's faces and a little boy doubled up with gleeful laughter. To see this man Dru, who had brought him here, panting and sucking his skinned knuckles like a tramp! The whole thing was mad—

nightmarish—Neapolitan. He said breathlessly, "None of the ⟨ fers I have made are any longer open! That matter is closed no and for good. I—I shall report your attitudes to my firm and they may very probably take punitive legal measures—yes! And as for you—"

He turned to Dru but the ex-headwaiter cut him short. "Let's get out of here for God's sake! I'll tell Sanbrenedetto the whole thing and he won't lift another finger for them. Come on . . ." And seizing the lawyer by one arm he hurried him out through the shop and into the street.

In the kitchen, amongst the exclamations and explanations, the shrillness and chatter and shouting, Gennaro sank down on the chair vacated by the lawyer and stared numbly around the room—at the broken crockery, the ruins of the bead curtain, the spilled food. A feeling he could not understand, a desolation which he had never known in his life before, constricted his heart and tightened his throat, so that he gave one sudden convulsive gulp of agony and then folded up, his face bowed in his hands, his shoulders heaving and shaking.

The others were struck to sudden silence. Somehow none of them had ever conceived of Gennaro crying and now it shocked them as deeply as anything they had ever known. Looking down at that crouched, sobbing figure, bowed and hopeless in the torn, oil-smeared ruins of its lavender suit, they knew that its tears were not the facile emotional release of so many Italians but the outward manifestation of some heavy disaster of the spirit which they could not comprehend.

Then Crocifissa was beside him, holding him tightly to her, stroking his rough hair, clucking, soothing. "What is it, *carissimo?* What is it, then? That man—did he hurt you? What happened? Why?"

But Gennaro hardly heard her. Alone in the darkness which enveloped him he wept for the lost, the impossible, dream of personal freedom, of individual dignity and of a rightful place in the world. Wept for all the weary, uncomprehending struggle that was life day-by-day, year-by-year—wept, most of all, for a lost innocence which only now, after such a long, vain battle, surrendered to acceptance and resignation.

4

LATER, much later that evening—hours after the mess in the kitchen had all been cleared up, after the shop had been shut and Gigi had gone home with his great slab of *ciccioli* and bread—Crocifissa had sat with Gennaro at the table under the bare electric bulb—for the pink glass shade had been smashed—and she had been worried and sadder than he had ever known her while he himself, exhausted and still a little red-eyed, had been filled with a lethargic, dull emptiness, a midnight of the spirit, lost and lonely.

"*Caro mio,* you are too young. You can't manage any longer by yourself. I had hoped that something—I don't know what, exactly—might have helped us all. I suppose I thought Signor Giuseppe would do something. And he did—I suppose he did. But with this other dreadful business of his daughter and that poor boy"—she had shaken her head—"one can't expect him to have time for all of us as well."

He had nodded and Crocifissa, staring up at Dino's smiling picture still unharmed on the wall, had continued, "So we'll have to go. I—I don't know where, myself, yet. But I'm only an old woman and it's you I'm thinking of now." Again she had paused. "You're too young, *Gennarino caro,* to have to do all that you've been doing—running the business and looking after Quong and everything. If you'd been older and had had a proper job . . ."

Gennaro's shoulders had lifted in a slight, hopeless shrug. He knew now that much of what Crocifissa had urged during the summer had been at least partly true. To her a position, however lowly, in a proper firm offered a security which atoned for the defects to which, in any case, she would have been indifferent. It was toward such a position that she would undoubtedly have urged Dino. The poor, Gennaro saw now, had status ratings graded to their measure of personal security. A skilled or semi-skilled worker in a large firm had a standing out of all proportion to his weekly wage, gaining both in financial credit and immunity from minor persecution in direct relation to his firm's influence and power. The police would never have dared treat him as they had done if, instead of being the grandson of a small-time slum undertaker, he had been a mechanic in the employ of Commendatore De Santis's great organization. Even a waiter at the O Sole Mio would probably have been interrogated without physical force.

But those of the poor who worked for themselves or each other were totally vulnerable; objects for the casual cruelty of anyone possessing a little more power or money than they. Their position was analogous to those mediaeval peasants who lived too far from the village which clustered closely round the protecting walls of the baronial castle—any brigand might beat or rape or steal from them with impunity. Crocifissa had known this, known it for so long—known it ever since five years ago he had come blinking in out of the night, a small boy in black clothes clutching his yellow canary. Quong, too—Quong, he now realized, had known this as well. Yet both had seen what he wanted, both had done all that could be done to help him achieve that life of independence and individuality for which he longed so deeply—both happy when he was happy, sad when he was sad. Both had, for his sake, kept up until this bitter end the fiction of "Quong's."

So softly she spoke it seemed to Gennaro that her words came from a great distance. "Gennà . . . Gennà—would you go back?"

"Back?" Yet he guessed what she meant before she said "To Ferrara—the monks."

"There's Quong."

"He would want it. He would want you safe. You're not a *scugnizzo* to sleep on gratings and eat scraps from gutters. And Quong—won't be with us much longer, you see."

"I know."

"And they'd like to have you. You know that. Things are much easier there. You could go on with your education, too. You'd soon pick up where you left off. An educated man is different—much more free. One day, *caro*, you might have your own firm—again. Gennaro—Gennaro, my dear, you should go back."

She had paused a long moment as if expecting an answer, but he had not looked up, his dark head bowed over his arms folded before him on the table. He could go back, it was true. It would be simple since he need take nothing, reentering Ferrara as empty-handed as he had left it. A long journey—Avezzano, L'Aquila, Siena . . . farther and farther north with Naples fading away behind him, growing ever smaller in the distance— Perugia, Assisi, Modena . . . the flat, empty Po valley. Ferrara at last and the Corso della Giovecca . . . and then the familiar buildings, the front door.

They would be delighted to see him, he knew that. There would be neither recriminations nor reproaches from Father Damiano the Rector or his colleagues. They would treat him with nothing but solicitude, and with that astonishingly delicate consideration of which they were always capable they would ease him gently back into that quiet world of prayers and lessons and peace within their sheltering walls. And for a moment it seemed to him that he was already there. He was back again and Father Damiano and the others were beaming at him, clustering around him, taking his hand, making their mild exclamations of joy, their thanks to Heaven. He saw again their faces. Father Anselmo's—long, lantern-jawed, ascetic; Father Ubaldo's— bearded and rubicund; Father Celestino's—with its wide, gold-toothed grin . . . Father Benedicto . . . Father Gregorio . . . He would be with them again, and there would be no more doubt or difficulty or danger.

Tears filled his eyes. They wanted him back and now, suddenly, he realized with a rueful surprise how much a part of him wanted to go. All at once he longed for the quiet, undisturbed peace, the clean, calm routine of a life which was not a perpetual struggle against increasingly uneven odds. And yet to leave Naples would be to tear himself in half—to kill his heart. For however dark it seemed now, his life in this city had once shone for him with a radiant splendor such as neither he, nor, he suspected, the monks of Ferrara, had ever believed possible.

Mutely he sat staring at his sunburnt arms resting on the bare, scrubbed wood before him, and at last Crocifissa had sighed and risen and gone out. Passing behind him she had laid a hand softly on his shoulder as if in remorse for her words, which were yet true and had to be spoken.

⋖§ 5

THEY were packing their bags in the flat up at Vomero on the Via Raffaele Morghen. Or at least Beppo was packing, for Mina spent most of the time sitting mute in her room pretending to read but in fact doing nothing but stare out of the window.

Beppo worked in something approaching a frenzy; his tie off, his shirtsleeves rolled up, his spectacles forever slipping down his nose and having to be thrust back with splayed thumb and forefinger. Tomorrow they would leave for Rome and the next morning they would be in London—that same evening in Devon. He must get Mina to Devon—and as soon as possible. Nothing else mattered. The lawyers could look after the final stages of the will-proving; Dru could arrange the last details of the sale of the San Lorenzo property to ITOLGAS—his own job was to get Mina away from Naples to that quiet, damp, green English county with its red earth and soft winds where she could rest and recover and where he would try, painfully but perseveringly, to restore something of their shattered relationship.

Throughout his life Beppo had been told at various times that he was a fool. People had told him this in different ways which often meant different things—different sorts of folly. None had thought him defective mentally; few had considered him really unintelligent; but practically all had included in the meaning of their condemnation, rashness, ill-judgment and stupidity. And surely none had ever voiced that opinion with the depth of feeling Mina had used when she had said *"Oh Dio*—look what you've done! *You really are a complete fool!"*

For of course he should never have written that letter to the Colavolpes. Anyone who knew the family at all would have understood that to write in that way—and in particular to mention a large sum of money which could have been, but no longer was to be, theirs—was the equivalent of throwing a bag of gunpowder into an open furnace.

"You killed Galo with that letter," Mina had told him with a sort of icy despair. "And for no reason." For Mina was not going to have a child. The symptoms, as the doctor had explained to Beppo, were brought about by the strength and roughness with which she had been—"one would say 'raped,' Signor Sanbrenedetto, if she herself had not told one that—that—"

"She was seduced—one could say that."

"Exactly. One could. And the symptoms of false pregnancy, the failure of the monthly period, the sickness and so forth, stem directly from the emotional shock and distress so caused. Luckily there is nothing to worry about and though, of course, she is no longer *virgo intacta,* no permanent damage has been done— physically. Psychologically, I fear she may find considerable difficulty in overcoming a future repugnance for the sexual act which would naturally lead to marital complications later."

As soon as Beppo had heard the doctor's opinion he had sent another letter to the Colavolpes stating, coldly enough, the information he had just been given and withdrawing his threat to prosecute Galo. But since it was mailed in the late afternoon it could not arrive at Caserta before the following morning. And by that time the Colavolpe household had started on its headlong career to self-destruction.

For if Galo's death was the most terrible result of Beppo's letter, it was by no means the last. The Colavolpes, being what they were, had naturally made the very worst of the business. Firstly, they had not called in the police until the following morning, by which time Concezio and Speranza between them had invented a complicated story in which Galo, on hearing the news about Mina, had killed himself before their eyes. Unfortunately for them the police surgeon had stated firmly that the dead boy could not possibly have inflicted the great wound in his chest by his own hand. On this the police returned to the *palazzo,* and Concezio and Speranza were closely questioned for two hours. In the end they came out with something approaching the truth though both said the other had actually struck the death blow. The police, local Carabinieri from Caserta headquarters, became more and more dubious. But since they were military personnel they had a certain reluctance to take any immediate drastic measures which would disgrace an ex-major who held the Gold Medal for Military Valor. They wrote a detailed and elaborate report of the whole matter and dispatched it to the chief of the Carabinieri Homicide Squad in Naples and meanwhile kept a discreet watch on the *palazzo* to make sure that its inhabitants remained upon the premises.

But either the watch was too discreet or perhaps the men undertaking it mistook the shabby, red-nosed old man who wandered down the road for a local peasant; for Tarquinio left the *palazzo* that evening, posted a letter in Caserta and returned unobserved.

Next morning he was found by Maria Fausta hanging by his belt in the vestry of the Church of the Holy Tooth, his still feet in their old slippers only some fifteen centimeters above the sleepy line of roosting fowls.

At about the same time, a letter was being opened by an Inspector of Public Security Police in the Questura at Naples. And when he had read it a police van with an escort of four motorcycles roared off to Caserta, and Concezio, Speranza, Maria Valeria, Maria Celeste, Maria Fausta and Filippa were all summarily arrested and brought back to the city. Only the old nonagenarian upstairs was left, in the care of a peasant woman, to remain, unknowing, unseeing—the last Colavolpe in the *palazzo*.

Tarquinio's letter was not, strictly speaking, a legal document since he had not possessed the two hundred lire necessary to buy the stamped paper—the *carta bollata*—upon which all communications to the State services must be written. But in the circumstances, that was hardly noticed. For Tarquinio had written a confession in which he alleged that, together with the other members of the family, he had conspired to murder his great-nephew in order to prevent his accession to the title and the estate. Overcome immediately afterward by remorse at what he had done he intended to hang himself, but first he wanted to atone by confessing his crime publicly and by bringing the other malefactors to justice. The confession was long and rambling and contained some odd discrepancies. Tarquinio stated, for instance, that Concezio and Speranza had "repeatedly plunged" the *spadino* into the boy's body while Maria Celeste had stood by with a bowl "to catch the blood." As an apparent afterthought he had accused Concezio of selling military secrets to the Americans; had accused Filippa of fraudulent conversion of currency and Maria Valeria of simony—alleging that she had sold the genuine Holy Tooth to an Armenian merchant and replaced it with the filed-down incisor from a pig's jawbone.

Under other circumstances the officers in the Questura on the Via Armando Diaz might have been more critical of such a document, but the lies and evasions of the Colavolpes were far too sinister not to lend Tarquinio's fabrications an ominous ring of truth—and anyway, they naturally wanted to get the case out of the hands of the Carabinieri and into their own. So Concezio and Speranza were formally indicted for murder and conspiracy to murder, Maria Valeria, Maria Celeste and Filippa for conspiracy, while Maria Fausta, who had not recovered from the sight of Tarquinio's purple face suspended in the gloom of the vestry above the sleeping fowls, was considered unfit to be indicted for anything. She was taken away to what the Colavolpes had always called "hospital"—for good, as it turned out—while the others were imprisoned and the ponderously slow and complex preliminaries for an Italian murder trial were set in motion.

Meanwhile the press had got on to the story and their own investigations, if less accurate, were much faster and more exciting than those of the police. NUNZIATELLA CADET MURDERED BY MOTHER IN MIDST OF FAMILY! shouted the headlines. CASERTA HOUSEHOLD KILLS CADET!—HORRIFYING CRIME IN ANCIENT PALACE!, followed by MURDERED BOY'S GREAT-UNCLE SUICIDES ON HOLY PREMISES and, at last, CADET'S SEDUCTION OF ART STUDENT COUSIN LEADS TO MURDER. For in the end, that came out too—as it was bound to do. And the journalists and photographers who had clustered around the Palazzo Colavolpe leapt into their cars and drove to Naples, to Vomero—to the Via Raffaele Morghen.

"You *fool!*" Mina had said, ashen-faced, shivering, tear-stained as the doorbell rang and rang, and outside the high apartment-house police had to move on the interested crowds drawn by the camera-clicking, note-scribbling journalists.

Beppo had slammed down the shutters—though not in time to prevent a cameraman in the anatomy classroom opposite from taking telescopic pictures of the interior of his sitting room and bedroom—and poured whisky down his throat in great gulps. "How was I to know that Tarquinio Colavolpe would kill himself? Tell me that!"

"You know what they're like! They do *anything!*"

"They're all mad!"

"Galo wasn't mad. You maddened them—the others—until they killed him."

"Galo! Galo! Galo!—He deserved it, anyway."

"You—" For the first time in his experience Mina used one of the most abusive insults of the *bassifondi: "L'anima di chi tè muort'!* You *know* he didn't!"

"He ruined you."

"We—we ruined each other. No, we didn't! We would have been all right if you had let us alone. *You* ruined us both with that crazy letter! I told you I was going to marry Nicola. Everything would have been all right. Can't you *see* that I and Nicola together had put things right—until you came in and destroyed everything?"

Beppo swallowed. "I—I didn't want you to have to marry a cripple!" He almost shouted the words and then remembered that several newspapermen were quite possibly listening at the apartment's front door and lowered his voice. "Nicola is bad-tempered, selfish, completely egoistical. Why should you be chained to him for life? And you don't love him."

"What do you mean! How can you know?"

"Because," had said Beppo with the sudden flashing percipience of the normally frivolous man, "you loved Galo."

Mina had stared at him appalled and then collapsed into hysterical tears which it had seemed would never cease. But they had ceased at last, leaving her limp and weak and ready to agree numbly to almost anything. In this condition Beppo had acquired from her a promise not to decide anything about Nicola for at least another month. "What would be the good, anyway?" Mina had said hopelessly. "He wouldn't want to marry me now —how could he?" And she had agreed to leave for England immediately.

Tomorrow they would leave for Rome; the next morning they would be in London and that same evening in Devon.

ৰ্জ 6

BIAGIO had come home. Unobtrusively in the dusk of the evening he had returned to the *piazza* and without calling on Napoleone Tenerini or even dropping in to Crocifissa's shop had gone silently round to Baldissera's stable and then to his room.

He had left Naples on a sudden impulse, intending to visit Anna's grave and to come back at once. Instead, he had stayed five days at Castel d'Ieri, lodging cheaply in a small, stone-built room behind a peasants' tavern. But he had barely noticed material things—his room or his food or the company in which he ate it—for from the first day, from the moment he left the dusty provincial bus in the marketplace, time had rushed backward like a film reel rewound at full speed and he had been a child again with Anna, suddenly reborn and alive, beside him. She had come to him so vividly in that distant village of gray rocks among the mountain peaks that the people with whom he was forced to speak at times, the tavern owner and his wife and the local priest, had seemed an almost transparent species by comparison. Anna alone was real—the others were shadows.

She had no grave now. Under the usual customs of immurement a wall-niche was rented for ten, twenty-five, or fifty years—though few of the poor ever took up wall-space for more than the minimum period. Then the body was removed and buried in a numbered lot, the coffin broken up and burned. And after a further four years the bones were exhumed and piled in the communal ossuary.

Biagio gave the sexton fifty lire and was allowed into the ossuary. It was a chill, damp vault with an earthen floor. On one side skulls were piled neatly in long rows eight or nine high, on the other a great wall of leg and arm bones held back a chaotic jumble of vertebrae, broken pelvises and shoulder blades. Somewhere among this quiet refuse lay all that remained of Anna, hopelessly lost, forever entangled with generation after generation of bygone Abruzzi peasants. A part of the wall had collapsed at one end and bones and skulls lay among lichened stones in the sunlight. Weeds sprouted between them and the small, vivid wildflowers of the mountain slopes. Biagio hoped that Anna's were among the remains to have escaped thus from the dark charnel house into the bright day.

It was in the ossuary that his pain, which had been nagging away below his breastbone like a small, smouldering fire, suddenly caught him, twisted him in its fierce grip and brought him to his knees upon the powdery floor. The sexton had helped him out, brought him a cup of wine from the mortuary where he kept a flagon with his spades, and let him rest awhile on the monument to three partisans executed nearly twenty years before by the retreating Germans.

And later he had wandered slowly about the alleys and stairways of the little stone village that sprawled down the mountainside, and Naples seemed to exist only very far away as a distant memory. Peculiar things were happening in his mind; experience after experience sloughed away like layers of dead gray skin, and the faded pictures of the distant past became ever clearer. Faces and voices he had forgotten for more than half a century came back so plainly that their long-dead owners might have been with him yesterday. He was young again and the world was bright and new. Passing a shop window he saw within a bent old man, haggard and ill, and he sauntered on without realizing that it was his own reflection.

It was pain, eventually, that drove him back to Naples. It came blindingly on the fourth night; an attack which left him bathed in sweat and barely more than half-conscious. It brought him back to himself and to the realization that he must return at once. But something was missing. For a long time he lay weakly pondering over what it could be. The pain had surely been the same—fiercer, more lasting than before, but the same pain and in the same place. Then he realized, wonderingly, that he was no longer frightened.

On the evening of his return to the *piazza* Biagio went once more to the hospital. They were ready for him and he was treated with much more solicitude than at the time of his first visit. One of the nurses even addressed him as Signor Bonitatibus as she called him to the doctors' office. Three interested doctors were examining the X-ray photographs. They looked up as he came in and Biagio read his death sentence in their eyes. The impersonal glances he had met on the earlier visit were changed for looks of curiosity; the inevitable inquisitiveness of men looking upon a living man whom they knew would live but little longer. "Well—how's the pain now?"

"Worse," growled Biagio. "Much worse." He was not frightened but he was jealous of the doctors who were going to go on living after he was dead—in the same way that he had been jealous of his richer customers for having possessions he lacked.

"Mmmm—yes, I suppose so. Well—you'll have to come in here as soon as we've got a spare bed. Next week at the latest."

"Will I have to have an operation?"

"No, no—nothing like that. It will be just treatment. Injections and medicine. Nothing at all unpleasant. And we'll stop the pain."

Biagio nodded dourly; he was not deceived.

They gave him a bottle of pills with careful injunctions when and how to take them and then let him go. He sensed somehow that they knew he had guessed what they had not told him and that they felt both relieved and guilty because of this.

Yet as he left the hospital and went slowly back to the *piazza* through the humid, jostling heart of the city, fear once more caught him by the throat in a quick, strangling grasp. Here was Naples, alive and roaring with passionate vitality all around him. If he had stayed in the empty peace of Castel d'Ieri among the rocks and the mountains and the great expanses of sky he would have felt nothing. That landscape was eternal and made his own mortality insignificant by comparison. Death meant nothing there; one became merely a part of the high hills, integrated with the earth and grass and stones like the old bones among the rocks and weeds and slanting sunlight of the broken ossuary. But here, in this city by the sea, life was what counted— life vivid and real and intense and clothed in warm, bronzed flesh that was never still. He wished he had stayed in the mountains but knew it to have been impossible; his money would have run out in another week and besides, there was his horse and his cab with only Gigi to look after them.

Baldissera and the *carròzza;* he would have to dispose of them now and he wondered confusedly how to set about it. They were not worth much, certainly, but . . . A sudden thought struck him and he halted—an old man standing still and lost in a daze among the cries and shouts of the hawkers and the roar of the traffic. He was trying to sum up the value of all his possessions; not only the horse and cab but his bed and his table, his two chairs, his blankets, the cooking stove, the corn-bin, the spare harness. . . . Yes, there should be enough. But he must not go into that hospital; in the circumstances he could not afford to. For although the *comune* would pay for his bed and treatment it would also, when he died, distrain on his possessions to reimburse itself. And then he would receive only the ordinary pauper's funeral at municipal expense—an ultimate degradation.

He made the decision there among the crowd in the Via Colletta, and as he did so a young man in dark blue overalls, a mechanic from some auto service station probably, passed him, hands in pockets, whistling shrilly. He looked so like Francesco Dozzi that for a second Biagio half lifted a hand to hail him—before remembering that Francesco had been the correct number ten and had died straddling a chair nearly half a century ago.

Biagio wandered slowly home, and stopping at a small vegetable stall at the corner of the Via Buonuomini, he bought a kilo of carrots and half a kilo of apples. They were to be his last gift, his good-bye present to his horse.

It was all much simpler, much easier than he could ever have hoped. Even the grating pain within him seemed abated. He went first to his room and, lighting a candle, wrote a letter. Thunder boomed dully outside as he licked his pencil for the last scrawling signature—*Biagio Bonitatibus*. Then he rose and went into Baldissera's stable, and was recognized and greeted with an asthmatic snuffle. For a moment, as he filled the old horse's nosebag with the carrots and the apples, Biagio's resolution wilted. He was leaving somebody behind him; somebody who had worked patiently for him over long years, who in a silent, surly, taciturn way relied upon him, knew him, accepted him as the senior partner in the weary daily struggle for a livelihood. "Baldissera," he muttered, and again, "Baldissera." He stroked the thin, veined neck, wanting to do much more; to say things for which—even if Baldissera understood them—he could not have found the words. But Baldissera shook his head impatiently, intent upon his carrots and apples, and Biagio turned at last and went back to his candlelit room.

He swallowed all the pills in the bottle he had been given, helping them down with wine. Then he sat, lost in a reverie, on one of the two chairs and, as soon as he felt drowsy, blew out the candle and lay down on the bed. He was very calm—not in the least distressed. "This is death," he said to himself; but the word "death" brought back a mental picture of the chairs and the Carabinieri firing squad of long ago. He frowned in the darkness. No, no, that wasn't death; that had been merely panic—man-made terror—something quite different. He forgot it, sliding further back to the brickworks at Barra on a cold winter day—the foreman, in a sudden, unusual access of generosity, buying him a few centesimi's worth of roast chestnuts from an old woman on the street. *"Grazie, signore! Grazie assai!"* He felt them warm in his cold young hands, in his empty stomach.

Back and further back. He sloughed off all the aging years at last and was no longer an old man but a little boy again. The sky was a bright winter blue and he and Anna were seeing snow for the first time as the *diligenza* from Avezzano slowly climbed the road up to Castel d'Ieri. He felt the sun on his face, the pure, stinging cold of the mountain air on his round cheeks. The little town came into view around the bend—snow-covered, enchantingly beautiful—the Castle of Yesterday. Beside him, her voice laughing with excitement, Anna said, "Bo-bo! Bo-bo, look!"

A Light in a Tunnel

1

SEPTEMBER was ending in a sudden resurgence of heat as if the past summer, lingering with one foot in the doorway of the closing year, was making a sudden, unseasonable effort to return. In these last days of the month, when the waters of the gulf reflected the deeper blue of the sky, when great sunsets, each flaring like a tropical aurora borealis, turned the evenings into chiaroscuros of gold and pink and violet light, the temperature began once more to rise. The cool seasonal breezes which stirred the palms along the Riviera di Chiaia and rippled the sea to glistening, molten silver faded to nothing and Naples seemed back again in the stifling swelter of high summer.

It could not last, and the weatherwise glanced continually to the west and the south, to the long loom of Vesuvius and the distant, jagged outline of Calvano around which the inevitable storm clouds must surely soon gather. Meanwhile Naples groaned and sweated; foreheads were mopped, tempers became still more quickly exasperated, nerves unnaturally frayed.

It was in this atmosphere of tired and irritable vexation that Maresciallo Valdemarin rose wearily one evening to answer the door of his apartment on the Via Michele Kerbaker and to accept a letter from the late postman. He hated the heat which seemed to add a further dragging burden to the weight of his gross body, prevented his sleeping properly and dulled the edge of his otherwise sharp mind. His work was suffering as a consequence and even the faithful Brigadiere Calvanese had looked askance at him when a plain case of knifing in the Anticaglia had collapsed into a court acquittal through inferior police preparation and, a day later, the Public Security had picked up a poisoner for whom the Carabinieri had been searching half the summer. No further advance had been made in the matter of the shooting in the Vicolo Ciego di Pomodori and, much worse than that to the other members of the Homicide Squad, the rival police force had stepped in and taken the whole case of the Caserta killing out of Carabinieri hands. Merely because a suicide's highly dubious confession had come to them rather than to the Carabinieri they had arrested and indicted five prisoners and then audaciously called for copies of the original Carabinieri investigations and interrogatory reports.

Only a few months ago Valdemarin, far from handing over such documents, would have demanded that the confession be handed over to him. As it was he had submitted tamely to the Questura's application, and the most bizarre and complex case of the year was centering the salaciously scandalized attention of the entire country around the big white building in the Via Armando Diaz. Among the members of the Naples Carabinieri it was said that Maresciallo Valdemarin was slipping downhill. Too old, too fat—it was time he retired before he lost the remains of his once formidable reputation.

Valdemarin was well aware of the criticisms of his colleagues but he did not resent them for they were largely true. His time for retirement was nearly at hand and he had seen too many old officers slow down physically and mentally as their pensions drew near not to know that this fate had now overtaken himself—as it would one day inevitably overtake his critics also. He would be pleased to go—would have been pleased to go a year or two earlier but for Nicola. For when he did at last retire his income would be drastically reduced. Not only would his pension be merely a third of his present salary but the various perquisites of his position would dry up as suddenly as a summer stream. And then—? Somehow he would have to find other work, if he could. The costs of Nicola, his continually changing treatments, his demands for new and expensive books, new discs for his record-player, brandy, and all the various toys and games with which he whiled away the endless hours of his bedridden life, would have to be met somehow. Whatever happened, whatever work he might have to do—even if it meant using certain information he possessed to extract money from persons anxious for his continued silence—Valdemarin was determined that Nicola must not suffer; had he not suffered more than any human being should be called upon to suffer, already?

Unless—and for the last few days Valdemarin's heart had fluttered with an anguished hope which reflected his son's— unless Mina Sanbrenedetto really was going to marry him. If only she would. If only—even now—she would!

Valdemarin had never blinded himself to Nicola's defects, even though he humbly forgave them all; and when Nicola had told him with joyful triumph that he and Mina were engaged, the older man had been dumb with astonishment. Could anyone, particularly a handsome, gifted girl, heir to a rich father, be anxious to take on the burden which he had assumed must be his until the end of his days? Could Mina—like himself—disregard Nicola's neurotic upsets and spiteful rages in pleasure at his bright intelligence and twists of sardonic humor? If she could, then a new life would open for Nicola in which, though his body could never be cured, his spirit might be healed at last. That first night he had dared to believe it all, because Nicola was so sure.

And the next day Mina had not come to the apartment and Nicola's face had been puzzled and a little worried. And then had come the news of the Colavolpe murder and Nicola, white and shivering, had admitted that Mina was to have borne the dead boy's child. It was then that the dream began to fade for the Maresciallo; to die completely when it became known that no child was, after all, to be born. The Sanbrenedetto girl had panicked herself into finding an escape route from a nonexistent difficulty. His poor, crippled son had provided it, but now neither it nor he were necessary. He did not tell Nicola this, since Nicola doggedly refused to accept the slightest doubt as to Mina's sincerity. They were in love—baby or no baby, they would get married. Of course Mina could not come to him at present. Of course she was quite right to keep away. The last thing he or she wanted was public prying into their affairs. The whole Colavolpe débâcle was horrible, but when it died down, Mina would come back and they would be married. "Four or five weeks—two months, perhaps. If there's one thing I've learned in my life," said Nicola untruthfully, "it's patience."

But Valdemarin had known better. He had done his best to keep Nicola's mind off the Colavolpe case and had privately been most relieved to pass it over to the Questura. He had, too, bought a new and extremely expensive wheelchair which, by a complex arrangement of springs and straps, kept Nicola more or less upright yet in one of the few positions which were tolerable to him, and now the boy moved with increasing dexterity about the small apartment. "I must practice. I must be able to show Mina how easily I can get about. We'll have a flat of our own. It must be on the ground floor and I'll be able to go in and out—into the garden, too, when I like. I'll be able to do all sorts of things. I won't be at all the—the difficulty that she probably thinks."

And now had come this letter. The Maresciallo looked at it, his heart sinking, a queer dryness filling his throat. An English stamp, a postmark reading *Tiverton—Devon*. Yes, that was where they had gone; he had found that out from their porter.

From the sitting room Nicola called, "For me? Something for me?"

"Yes." Valdemarin, trying to make his voice casually noncommittal, walked as slowly as he dared back to the small, brightly lit lounge whose wide French windows, a great square of darkness patterned by lights in the buildings opposite, looked over the busy street below. "Here you are."

Nicola seized the envelope, studied it for a second with a face from which the blood was draining, and ripped it open with shaking fingers. "From him," he said briefly, "not her."

For the space of time it took Nicola to read the letter, Valdemarin remained motionless, unconsciously holding his breath. He watched the muscles of his son's face slowly tauten, his lips whiten and compress; then with a hand that trembled like an old man's Nicola held out the single sheet of paper and in a voice as thin and dry as dust in a deserted attic whispered, "Read it."

Short—polite—not unfeeling so much as unkind. Above all firm.

DEAR NICOLA,

I am writing to you at Mina's request because she is still not well enough to do so herself. As you can well imagine the recent death of Galeazzo, of whom she was extremely fond, has upset her severely. The whole terrible affair has been an immense shock to her—and hardly less so to me. In the last days before we left Naples I understand that you and Nina spoke of marriage and in terms which, in view of Mina's age, I think you must agree were extremely premature. I think I ought to tell you definitely—as I have told her—that I could not possibly give my consent to such a thing; and, as you know, without that consent any attempt at marriage would be illegal. Please believe me when I say that this in no way reflects upon you or my personal opinion of you. It is just that Mina is far too young for marriage as yet. She is not quite fifteen and a half. She must wait at least another eighteen months—preferably two or three years—before thinking of marriage or any form of engagement to anyone. But after that the matter will of course be entirely in her own hands—for I do not intend to interfere in her choice when she is of an age to choose wisely. Because of what has happened I have asked Mina—and she has agreed— not to communicate with you while we are in England, where we shall remain until at least next spring. I am sorry if this letter causes you distress, but I can only say that in proposing to Mina when, and in the terms, you did, you seem to me to have tried to take a most improper advantage both of her extreme youth and the unhappy position in which she believed herself to be at the time. Sincerely yours,

GIUSEPPE SANBRENEDETTO

The Maresciallo slowly handed the letter back. It was just what he had feared and the raging bitterness in his heart against the writer could not smother the knowledge that much of what he had to say was true. Much—but surely not all. Why write of "taking an improper advantage" of the girl's "unhappy position"? Her position would have been very much more unhappy if she really had been pregnant—particularly as she had been sure young Colavolpe would not have married her. In point of fact, thought the Maresciallo with sullen rage, it was she who had taken advantage of Nicola and of *his* unhappy position.

But—"Nico," he said gently. "She *is* too young at present. Her father's right there. No one marries at fifteen today."

"Peasants do—down in Calabria and Sicily."

"Yes. But we're not peasants, though, and neither are the Sanbrenedettos. You can't expect—"

"I can't expect anything! I never could and I never shall be able to! I know that—you don't have to tell me!"

"Nico, it's not as if it's all over. They'll be back next summer. She'll be sixteen then. There's nothing her father can do to prevent an informal engagement—an understanding between you both."

"*Oh, Porco Dio,* don't you see!" Nicola's voice came from his throat in a strangled hissing wail. "He'll have done it by then. He took her away to do it. He's doing it now! *'Mina, you can't marry someone with no legs. You're throwing yourself away. He'll make your life a dreadful burden. You'll be terribly sorry later! All your life you'll have to play the nursemaid. Think of it! Mina, you simply can't marry someone with no money—with no legs—with no—'* " He choked to anguished silence and the Maresciallo tried to do something which he knew was never allowed—to touch Nicola in order to caress him. Nicola jerked his chair away swiftly. When he spoke again his voice was fast and low. "All right. All right, then! It's all over. I've never had much, God knows! Now I've got nothing. Now it's all over and finished. I'm not a Christian. I'm not frightened of death. I ought to have died years ago—in Genoa, that night. The doctors kept me alive for their own obscene satisfaction—to see how much a human body could stand and still live. But *you* could have let me die! You've always prevented me—made me go on and on with nothing to hope for or live for. But now—"

While he had been talking he had been maneuvering his chair carefully, imperceptibly, until it was opposite the dark square of the open windows. There was nothing, now, between him and a plunge to the lamplit street five stories below save only a cement curb of some four centimeters which the chair's rubber wheels, under sufficient propulsion, would easily surmount. The Maresciallo saw in a flash what he was about to do and took a half pace forward. Then, though he had always been as brave as he was ruthless—and he could be very ruthless—he performed the bravest act of his life. He stood back again and, with the sweat popping on his forehead, closed his eyes and waited. For Nicola had a right to go. He saw that clearly now. Nicola was twenty-one and intelligent, with a full, bleak awareness of what the rest of his life would be like. It was true what he said— he should have been allowed to die long ago in Genoa. Any animal so shattered would have been given a quick release but Nicola, a human being, had been dragged back from death's crowded but unpersecuted ranks and tortured for weary, terrible years. No. If now an adult and in full possession of his senses, he wanted so badly to die, he must be allowed his choice. It was the last, and perhaps the best, thing his father could do for him.

The Maresciallo gritted his teeth and heard the soft rush of rubber wheels over the floor. In a moment there would be the bump at the curb—yes, Oh God, it came! And now Nicola would be dropping, hurtling down. . . . Even in that agonizing second Valdemarin had time to hope that no one below would be hurt. . . . Then there came a faint, small noise. No crash, no shouts, no screams. Painfully, as if they were weighted and glued, the Maresciallo opened his eyes. Nicola, his arms stretched wide as if in some caricatured crucifixion, was still in his chair in the window-bay, and with each hand Nicola was grasping the lintels of the window to arrest his fall.

And through the ringing in his ears Valdemarin heard again that small faint noise and realized it was Nicola crying. Unsure, unsteady on his feet, he lumbered across the room and pulled the chair back to safety. Then he was on his knees beside it, clasping Nicola—shaking, shivering, sobbing brokenly—to his huge chest—and he, too, was weeping.

It was then that the telephone rang urgently out in the hall.

⊷ 2

FOR the first time in his long career Maresciallo Valdemarin, who never ceased to urge the necessity of immediate preliminary investigations on his juniors, was deliberately late on the scene of a crime. He had sworn briefly but frighteningly at Calvanese over the telephone, threatening, for no reason whatever, to have him demoted and returned to uniformed street patrol, and then gone back to spend another half hour with Nicola—a Nicola whom he had never been so loath to leave as he was tonight.

Consequently, when he eventually left the apartment and lurched into the squad car which had been waiting outside for twenty-five minutes, he was in a furious temper. Neither the driver nor the two junior detective officers dared open their mouths but sat carefully still in their places, hoping thus to avoid attention.

But after sitting in sullen, glowering silence for a couple of minutes while they were jammed among a late traffic block in the Piazza Vanvitelli, the Maresciallo growled, "Well?"

"Signore?"

"What's it all about? *Porco Dio!* Do I have to interrogate *you* like some half-witted bag-snatcher from the Abate?—You're Brancati, aren't you?"

"Si, signore."

"Allora! When I say 'Well,' Brancati, it means you give me the facts of whatever case is on hand. If you don't know them, then you're useless to me and had better get back on traffic duty. If you know them but can't explain them clearly, then you're useless to the whole Corps and had better transfer to the municipal scavenging service and empty ashcans for a living."

"Signore," said Brancati swallowing, "this is a case of shooting in a restaurant at Mergellina. The proprietor was shot dead in his office an hour ago by an ex-employee."

"Why?"

"It appears the man was trying to extort money. Two of the staff, who were waiting to see their employer outside his office, heard the sounds of quarreling and the demands for money. Then they heard shots. They opened the door and saw the assassin standing over his victim and firing shots into his head. Then, when he saw them, the killer ran at them and they—"

"Ran away."

"Exactly, *signore.* And so did everyone else who was on or near the scene, it appears. The man held them off with his gun and got clear away."

"Are the P.S. interested?"

"A junior inspector arrived but the Brigadiere turned him off."

At this Maresciallo Valdemarin merely grunted.

There were two squad cars outside the O Sole Mio and the foyer was filled with uniformed police. Scowling, disregarding the salutes which greeted his arrival, Valdemarin strode past them and was led by Brancati upstairs to a quiet carpeted cor-

ridor and a brightly lit office. Calvanese rose at once from behind the big desk. "*Buona sera,* Signor Maresciallo!"

"You disturbed me. My son is ill."

"A thousand pardons, *signore!* I had no idea. I only followed ordinary instructions. Truly, I apologize deeply."

Valdemarin nodded at a blanket-covered object sprawled beside a small overturned table. "That him?"

"*Si, signore.*"

"Who did it?"

"A man named Duilio Domenichelli. He had been employed
here—or, rather, he was a garbage contractor who, up till some
six weeks ago, collected the kitchen refuse and sold it to pig
farmers in the usual way. Then he seems to have ceased work
here. No one knows why. One can only assume that they quarreled over their costs."

Valdemarin glanced around the office, noting its furnishing;
efficient, sensible but expensive. Desk, typing-table, leather-
covered armchairs, cocktail cabinet. The room of a modern,
progressive and—"northern" was the word that came at once to
his mind—executive. "I've known people killed for a lot of
things," he said dourly, "but this is the first time I've heard of it
being done for garbage. It had to take Naples to show me *that.*"

"It does seem a little unlikely." Calvanese came from Leg-
horn.

"Nothing's unlikely in this city. Well—go on."

"It appears that this man Domenichelli was, or had been,
some sort of friend or acquaintance of—him." Calvanese
nodded at the shrouded corpse. "Members of the staff say that
they had always seemed on unusually friendly terms since
Domenichelli started contracting here in early June. It was never
explained why he ceased work here. He just suddenly stopped
coming and a new man took his place. He was seen here once
again on a visit to the proprietor about the end of last month.
He always came straight up here to the office—as he seems to
have done tonight. But this evening the assistant headwaiter and
the wine waiter had some query for the proprietor and came
up to see him while Domenichelli was in the office. They heard
angry voices and an undoubted demand for money. 'I must have
two hundred thousand and I must have it now—tonight!' were
the words they say they heard."

"Blackmail of some sort, presumably."

"Presumably, *signore,* yes. Because there was also something about 'what Soliman, or Suliman, told me about you' from Domenichelli. After that there was whispering and then suddenly one yell of *Ferenc!* from Domenichelli—very loud, almost a scream, they say—and then the shots began."

"And they looked in?"

"Yes—to see Domenichelli firing a gun at the figure of their boss lying on the floor. Then he saw them and leapt at them and they ran. He dashed out and ran downstairs, threatened an assistant cook and three waiters with his gun and made off through a side door. No one seems to have felt like running after him."

"Quite rightly. One corpse an evening is enough. You've got his description circulated and the alert out, of course? Yes, yes, don't look so hurt. I was only checking." The Maresciallo strode across the room, pulled the blanket from the body and gazed dispassionately at the blood-covered face. "What's his name?"

"Francesco Bighencomer. A naturalized citizen of Swiss-Hungarian parentage. He—" But Calvanese stopped abruptly for the Maresciallo was no longer listening but staring down intensely at the corpse, his whole body seeming suddenly one vast, quivering question mark. Then he lifted his head and said quietly, "Get someone to clean him up—wash all this blood away. Quick!"

"Subito, signore!"

A couple of plainclothesmen were called in and while they completed their unpleasant task Calvanese saw that his chief was standing quite still, his back to the corpse, his gaze fixed on a piece of perfectly blank wall. At last he said "Ready?"

"Si, signore."

"All right." The Maresciallo turned, walked quickly to the dead man and stared down at the face now clean but for three blue-ringed bullet holes. Then he gave an odd, whistling sigh and throwing the blanket back again, nodded dismissal to the plainclothes officers and turned, hands thrust in pockets, to his assistant. "This Domenichelli—he shouted what, exactly—before he fired?"

" 'Ferenc'—they say."

"And Domenichelli's first name was—?"

"Duilio."

"What's he look like?"

"Small, dark. Young. And he appears to have a broken jaw, badly set so that—"

"The underjaw protrudes and his bottom teeth close over his front incisors?"

"Yes—yes, *signore!* How—"

"And that other name—the name of someone who told him something?"

"Soliman—or Suliman. They weren't sure."

"Or Sollier? I think it was Sollier." Valdemarin rubbed his heavy jowls with one hand, nodding his ponderous head. "Yes—yes." As if speaking to himself he murmured, "We'll have to send up to Genoa. But even so—" He turned once more to his assistant but he did not look at him as he spoke. "Calvanese, you remember that at the end of May a prisoner escaped from the jail beyond Vasto. A prisoner in whom I had once had a particular interest?"

"D'Ambri?"

"Yes. Duilio D'Ambri."

"*Santo Cielo!* And this is—Domenichelli?"

"I think so. I'm almost certain. It's just a matter of making quite sure who *this* is." Valdemarin, hands still in jacket pockets, nodded at the partially blanket-covered body. "Genoa may help us there. I'll ring Maresciallo Coro from the office later. My own opinion is that this man's original name was Ferenc Kovas. I saw him last in court—as a witness only—some thirteen years ago. At the trial of some of the men who had tried to kill me and who—destroyed my family. D'Ambri and three others were in the dock." The Maresciallo moved across the room and stared out of the window. "They're still eating down there," he said inconsequentially, "despite all the fuss. Neapolitans!"

"I thought it best not to—"

"Quite right, Calvanese. Quite so."

"And—Kovas?" prompted Calvanese politely after a minute had ticked away in silence.

"Kovas—yes. A postwar racketeer. Black market. American

goods. Food—tires—gasoline. One of many. We were after him
—not very successfully—at the time of that attempt to kill me."
"He was behind it?"
"I don't think so. At least, not directly; and there was no evidence to implicate him. My own opinion is that he knew nothing
much about it until afterwards. In fact, I think he was—horrified. It's an odd thing, Calvanese"—the Maresciallo edged his
great buttocks onto the edge of the desk which creaked ominously—"but there is often a certain, almost trade-union, feeling among policemen. Not perhaps fraternal exactly, no—but
a sort of wary understanding. Kovas had been a policeman; a
senior warrant officer—a maresciallo, you might say—of the
German military security corps—the S.D. He had been engaged
in antipartisan activities in Jugoslavia. And he had done well.
He has an Iron Cross first class and also our Silver Medal."
"So?"
"Oh yes. But you can't perform antipartisan work effectively
without being very firm—often, very rough. Prisoners must be
made to speak; reprisals must be taken. Kovas was wanted by
the Jugoslavs. They did not know where he was at the time, but
it came out later. We did not want to hand him over—after all,
he held our medal—but the Allies were pressing. It was a time
when they—particularly the British—were trying to show how
clean their own hands were by demonstrating how dirty were
those of everyone else. It was then that Kovas disappeared from
Genoa. No one ever heard of him after that." The Maresciallo
grunted and shifted his weight on the desk top. "But that took
place more than a year after the attempt on my life and some
months after D'Ambri's trial. Before that Kovas was just a Hun-
garian refugee trying to make a living as a real estate agent. Or
that was the front he put up to cover his black-marketeering. He
was too clever to be a real criminal, I think— By the way, if
there's something to drink in that cabinet I'll have a glass. Just
look and see."

Calvanese busied himself with glasses and bottles while from
his position, half sitting, half leaning on the desk, the Maresciallo continued. "In those days—well, practically everyone was
involved. You're too young to remember, Calvanese—Whisky,
not brandy. And bring the bottle over here—but black-marketeering of some sort was almost a way of life then. And if it

was that way in Genoa, God alone knows what it must have been like down here! No—Kovas was more an unscrupulous businessman than a criminal. All he wanted was to make capital quickly. He was doing well, too. Even though we were after him we never got enough evidence to justify an arrest.

"But he had some unpleasant contacts—operators. Young fools of self-demobilized fascists—Black Brigade boys who had learned how to shoot and stab but nothing else. D'Ambri is a fine example. All the black-marketeers had their own bands in those days—to protect themselves from rivals more than from the police. But the Kovas lot was largely under the control of a man named Rosmon Sollier, a Croat of sorts from Istria who had been a corporal under Kovas in the army and who clung to him afterwards. He was a real savage. He—he led the attempt against me, and later I killed him myself. I had been temporarily transferred from Homicide to help close down the black market. I was being too successful. I ought to have known someone would try. And it was Sollier and his gang who did. At first it was believed that Kovas had directed them—even though from what we knew of his methods it seemed unlikely on the face of it. But when we picked up the first of them—the man I'd wounded —he told us that it was Sollier's plan. At the most, Kovas may have known something about it, though of course he swore he did not. When the last three—including D'Ambri—were put on trial they probably hoped Kovas could save them by producing the usual well-organized alibis. Black-market bosses were always doing that for their men. But he did not. He must have known that if he had tried I would have been after him later. At all events his testimony, of which they hoped so much, was entirely noncommittal. Consequently they were found guilty."

The Maresciallo rose and put down his glass. "You can work the rest out easily enough for yourself, Calvanese. Why D'Ambri should come here on his escape from jail and what his feelings for his ex-chief were likely to be. I've given you the full background. You will use it with discretion."

"Of course, Signor Maresciallo."

"I don't talk about what happened in Genoa. I don't like remembering it more than I have to."

"No—naturally."

"But now"—and there was such cold menace in the Maresciallo's voice that his assistant felt a tingle down his spine—"we've got D'Ambri in Naples. He can't know the city well because the farthest south he has ever been before was when they took him to prison. It should not be too difficult to find him. But I want you to understand clearly that there can be no question of trying to take D'Ambri alive. When we find him we must shoot him at once—or there will be some dead Carabinieri around. There may well be some in any case, and since," said the Maresciallo dryly, getting up from the desk, "I make a very large target, it is necessary for you to know all that I've told you."

◄§ 3

AN hour later Maresciallo Valdemarin ascended heavily to his apartment on the Via Michele Kerbaker. Very carefully he opened the door and slipping off his shoes, tiptoed to Nicola's room and listened intently outside. He could hear nothing: perhaps the boy was asleep. But with the news he had to tell, the Maresciallo was, for once, prepared to wake him.

"Nico" he said softly "Nico?"

"Yes?"

Valdemarin opened the door gently and light from the hall, entering with him, showed Nicola's small white face, worn and curiously older, against the high pillows. "What is it?" His voice was quieter than usual, holding no trace of hostility—only a deep tiredness.

"Nico, I've got some news for you." Very carefully the Maresciallo lowered himself to the bedside chair and gently, with his heart thudding, felt for his son's hand. He had never dared do such a thing before, but this time there was no brusque rejection, the thin fingers lay passively in his own. "D'Ambri. He's here in Naples. He murdered again tonight, trying to get money —for escape, obviously. He got away. But I'll find him. I'll find him if I have to take this city apart brick by brick. He won't escape me, I promise!"

Nicola was silent for a moment. "It doesn't matter much now," he said at last, "one way or the other. I can't kill myself. I thought I could, but I can't. So I've got to go on living whatever happens. After tonight—after that letter—nothing matters very much anymore."

"It matters to me, though," said Valdemarin softly. "Just because of that letter. It matters to me more than ever now."

⚜ 4

EVALDO Giansante's escape from the military prison hospital had much in common with the escape which had originally brought him to the Gaeta fortress; it was unplanned and violent. It took place in the early afternoon of the fourth day after his admission.

Since the refusal of his *domanda* had been made known to him, Evaldo had stopped eating. He had also failed to perform his normal bodily functions. He had not refused food or made any overt attempt at a hunger strike; he had merely eaten less and less and eventually begun to bring up the little he managed to consume under the coaxing of the guards. There could be no question of forcible feeding in the circumstances; the authorities had to agree that the prisoner was ill and automatically he was moved to the hospital on the south side of Mont' Orlando. With more air and more space, with, above all, more light—for the prison ward, through heavily barred windows, looked out to the chief medical officer's semitropical garden and thence to the rising, pine-covered hillside of Orlando—Evaldo began to improve. "He's not malingering," said one of the doctors approvingly to the medical corpsman in charge of the ward. "It is merely that he's been suffering from a nervous disorder of the stomach and bowels. If he goes on improving we can cut out the sedation—by tomorrow evening, probably."

This was duly done with the result that Evaldo emerged from the wispy fog in which he seemed to have spent eons of unnatural time and slept not at all on his third night in the hospital.

The morning of the fourth day was vividly bright. Dawn broke in superb beauty over the rugged cliffs of the promontory, watched by Evaldo who left his cot and hauled himself into the window embrasure to sit clinging to the bars, breathing in the clean, salty air. Far above him the umbrella pines began to glow in the rising sun, their trunks becoming flames of bright orange, their boughs of dusky copper still holding the shadows of night within their evergreen depths. Then the banana trees and hibiscus bushes in the chief medical officer's garden brightened into vivid green and stars of red and yellow. Someone whistled from beyond the gateway; a dog barked on the hillside, chasing a bird. It was day. It was—Evaldo consulted the figures which lay in the front of his mind as if cast in great leaden molds—the one hundred and fifty-fifth day. There were some four thousand, two hundred and twenty more to come.

He was still sitting crouched in the window when the guard came around with the coffee an hour later. "Come on—get down. And get into bed. There's nothing much wrong with *you* —I can see that. We'll be getting rid of you tomorrow or the next day."

Throughout the morning Evaldo lay in bed staring out of the window—not thinking, or thinking only as vaguely and slowly as the two or three small white clouds which passed high across the huge, shining sky; the sky which, tomorrow or the next day, would once more become invisible to him.

On his rounds the doctor said the same thing while tapping Evaldo's knees with his rubber hammer. "Fine, fine. We'll have you out of here tomorrow or the next day." But he anticipated them and went out that afternoon.

At half-past two Evaldo wandered down the corridor toward the washroom. The door at the end was unlocked and the guard, his club lying on a windowsill behind him, sat reading a brightly colored comic. His back was turned to Evaldo, whose bare feet made no sound on the cement floor—but the noise as the club struck the back of the guard's head seemed frighteningly loud.

Out, now—and down some red-tiled stairs. A door which opened easily—and Evaldo was in the chief medical officer's garden. How beautiful it was at this hour, so cool and green and sparkling with water-drops. Water—Evaldo, the gravel prickly beneath his bare soles, turned a corner beside some oleanders and came upon a young soldier in gumboots wielding a hose.

"Hi! Where are you going? What—?"

The man put out an arm to bar his way and Evaldo immediately struck it down with his club. He heard the crack of breaking bone, heard the scream—then he was running through the wet flower beds to the low garden wall, was scrambling over it and dropping to the steeply rising, bush-covered hillside beyond. He was out—out and free. This was open land. For the first time in six months Evaldo was at large—out in the world of free men and women beneath the free sky.

But the afternoon was no longer still or tranquil or sleepy. As he started up the hillside, shouts and cries echoed behind him. A glance over his shoulder showed soldiers running, pale khaki figures across the bright shrubs of the garden; the chief medical officer, napkin in hand—he must still have been eating his lunch —staring from his veranda; faces at windows. Evaldo thrust quickly on and upward. Thorns embedded themselves in the soles of his feet, thorny bushes tore his thin striped prison pajamas and dragged their spines across the flesh beneath. A rifle banged out and Evaldo heard the thud as the bullet struck the trunk of an umbrella pine.

Up, up, up—some rocks loomed before him and he ducked in among them as further shots cracked out. He was panting now, sweating heavily; his feet were on fire with thorns and his pajamas already hung in tatters about his blood-marked body. But between the rocks a narrow, twisting track zigzagged out of bushes of shining ilex and tall wiry broom higher than he. Undercover, he raced on upward past a hillock of pines, past an old stone wall, until at a sudden turning in the track the whole Gulf of Gaeta shone out, a great lake of blue below him. There, jutting into the placid sea, was the fortress, the huge castle in whose depths he had been locked since May. Somewhere down there was his cell, the stone box where Signor Sanbrenedetto had visited him, talked him into signing that *domanda* and given him, as a reward, an illegal letter from Iole. Down there they intended to take him soon—tomorrow or the next day—to shut him away from the light and the air for four thousand, two hundred and twenty more slow circles of the earth turning its worn face to the fiery radiance of an unseen sun. And—look! Far away beyond that distant headland, south of the last faint scarps of the cliff fading into the horizon, lay Naples—where Iole was. He was closer to her now than he had been for months. Nothing but bright sea air lay between them at this moment.

A bell clonked nearby and a cow came swaying down the track followed by two boys. Evaldo darted past them and ran on.

Shouts, laughter, and the scamper of feet behind him; the boys were running after him. Stooping as he ran, Evaldo picked up a stone, stopped and swung around. The boys stopped too; panting, waiting to duck. Evaldo flung the stone, turned and ran. It had been a foolish move, for now the two boys took him for a personal enemy when they might otherwise have helped him. They were following, calling out at the tops of their voices, "He's here! He's here! This way! Quickly!"

Evaldo's bare feet were now so torn and broken and thorn-filled as to be almost numb. Also he had by no means recovered the strength lost by days of half or total fasting. The boys could catch him easily if they dared come close enough, but for the present they preferred to keep their distance and shout. Plunging through a dense acacia thicket, Evaldo left the remnants of his pajamas on its steely hooks and, wearing nothing but the wet red garment of his own blood, staggered out into a small clearing and saw before him the dark, stone-faced mouth of a tunnel.

It might be a cul-de-sac, a trap, but at least it offered immediate refuge from the two boys who, balked by the acacia thicket, were screaming and shouting beyond its encircling hedge. Within seconds Evaldo was lost in its cool gloom, stumbling at first over fallen stones and then running on and on in ever deepening darkness over a smooth, slimy stone floor. Ahead of him, far in the distance, there was a glimmer of light. When at last he reached it he found that it was an airshaft in the roof—a funnel some five meters in height, ending in a heavy iron grill. There was the sky again—blue and cut into eight square segments. Evaldo paused and listened. Silence—absolute and still. Only the echoes of his own harsh breathing came back to him from the stone walls.

Where was he? Somewhere under Mont'Orlando. But how? And in what fashion? Then he remembered once hearing his guards talking about the promontory—the huge, dolphin-shaped rock above the castle crowned by the Roman mausoleum—and, or so they said, honeycombed with underground military fortifications. Gallery after gallery, tunnel, reservoir and storeroom, leading in a spidery pattern of dark stone passages and stairs to the old gun emplacements which pitted Orlando's seaward cliffsides. He was somewhere in the deserted depths of the underground Bourbon fortress, hewed out more than a century ago by Bomba's chained, red-dressed gangs of political prisoners.

And for the moment, at any rate, he was safe. He was free and he was safe. If he could wait here for night to fall he might yet escape from the promontory. Before him, lit wanly by the airshaft, was a domed circular space into which five tunnels converged. He could just make out that one of them seemed to be filled, or partly filled, with a rubble of stone—perhaps the roof had fallen in; the others showed gaping black mouths and from somewhere in the stillness he heard the soft dripping of water. And suddenly water was what he wanted most—even more than freedom. He traced the sound to the third tunnel from the left and after twenty yards, found his feet paddling in an inch or two of thin slime. The water rose slowly as he advanced and soon he stood submerged to his thighs. He bent and drank and it tasted cold and sulphurous and metallic. Then he lay down in it, shivering but grateful for its soothing coolness on his torn flesh. A few minutes later he pulled himself out once more and, hobbling back to the domed room lit palely by the air-vent, he crouched down in a corner and almost immediately went to sleep.

⋐ 5

"WE ought," said Colonel Forth morosely, "to have hired a proper speedboat. Like this, we're getting nowhere fast!" He rested on his oars, gazing reproachfully at his wife who sat in the stern of the small rowboat.

"You always said you could row, George! Why, I guess I've heard you say ever so often that there was nothing like a good workout with a pair of oars. And then"—Mrs. Forth gestured from the towering cliffs of Mont'Orlando two hundred yards on the boat's port beam to the far horizon of the gulf fading away in a great curve beyond Mondragone—"you can't enjoy this in a speedboat."

The Forths had been on a trip to France, combining business with pleasure. The "business" had been Colonel Forth's attendance at a fifth-form sort of NATO briefing with bored French majors hoisting placards explaining "Mission" and "Infrastructure" onto easels while the American contingent, bursting with good intentions, if apt to forget the traditional terminus of the route paved with them, struggled with ever-decreasing bonhomie through the miasma of xenophobic conservatism and painstaking obsession with trivialities exuded by their European allies.

The "pleasure" had been a visit to the De Santis family at their rented St. Tropez villa, and that had been spoiled because Toni De Santis had contracted German measles just before they arrived and Mrs. Forth had a terror of infectious diseases. On the whole they were pleased to cut short their stay and make it up in their beloved Italy with a few days at Serapo, the beach resort separated from Gaeta only by the looming jut of Mont'Orlando. They felt much more at home in Italy where they spoke the language, liked the natives and had friends. In France—as Mrs. Forth remarked indignantly—the people were so malevolent when they were not having the political advantage; they cheated her in the shops. "In which case, Ella," her husband had replied with dry irony, "they certainly shouldn't have cheated you for a very, very long time."

France and Italy. . . . And one day soon West Germany or Turkey or Greece or Spain. New languages, new customs—neither very well comprehended, and very seldom approved of. New outfits, new "Mission," new "Infrastructure"—the continental *Herald Tribune* printed in Paris and out-of-date weeklies from the States. Homesick Americans, bowed beneath a weight which only history would one day recognize, admired and ridiculed, envied and laughed at—seldom understood, always begged from.

But this evening they were just a handsome, well-dressed couple in early middle-age, rocking gently in a hired boat on the calm summer sea. "The trouble is," the colonel was saying irritably, "these people don't row like us. They row standing up and facing the stem. Now that's a goddam inefficient way to propel a rowboat. Firstly, there's no proper purchase for the feet, and secondly—Hi! What's that?"

From the cliffs above them came a dull echoing bang. Then two more and then a wailing echo—a muted baying.

"Rifle shots!" said the colonel wonderingly, lying back on his oars. "And dogs!"

⊷§ 6

FOUR patrols of four men each with four police dogs and their handlers had gone into the subterranean galleries at a quarter to five. They could not have entered earlier since there was only one old map of the mazy complex of underground tunnels, and four tracings of this had to be made in order to supply each party with a copy. Without these they would certainly have become lost, perhaps for hours—or even dangerously hurt by falling into known cannonball chutes or reservoirs.

As it was, they progressed with extreme care and great noise, their boots and voices echoing and reechoing among the stone vaulting, their flashlights showing nothing but dank walls, slimy floors and sudden black turnings and openings.

Evaldo heard them from a great distance. He woke so cold, so stiff and sore that he could hardly move. For a minute he crouched huddled and shivering against the wall near the airvent, collecting his never-very-quick wits. Then, unmistakably, he heard the bark of a dog. It roared along the tunnel like the magnified bay of a pack of wolves. Dogs! And he must have left a trail of blood behind him. Then he remembered the tunnel of water, and hobbling back to it, began to wade into its blackness. He thought fearfully that perhaps soon it would be filled to roof level and he would be trapped. Deeper and deeper he waded; his belly, his chest, his armpits were submerged in turn. Now he was swimming. Then once more his feet touched bottom on what appeared to be a flight of steps. He rose rapidly out of the water and again saw a glimmer of pale light in the distance. He approached it at a crouching run but before he was halfway down the long stone passage he heard once more the muted boom of voices, and then a white electric beam struck transversely across the passage twenty yards ahead of him. They were coming down a gallery on the left. Evaldo flattened himself against a dank wall and waited, breath held.

Noises, boots, approaching down a side passage. If they turned their flashlights along this tunnel in which he crouched they were sure to see him—but it was much too late to run back and take refuge in the water at the far end.

Despite—because of—the colossally magnified volume of the voices, it was impossible to make out individual words, he only heard the booming echoes falling fast upon one another as one wave overtakes and subdues its predecessor upon the shoreline surf. Then they were in the tunnel and the light swept away from him, swept back—struck him—turned away a moment to show an ascending stairway almost opposite to where he crouched, and then swung back abruptly and steadied. The shouts exploded like cannon shells. Naked and blinded in the white glare of the spotlight, Evaldo made a dash across the tunnel and gained the stairway before shots, stunning and drowning every other noise in their immensity, tore down the tunnel behind him.

Evaldo leaped upward for perhaps twenty steps which curved to the right; then his feet were jarred and stubbed on blocks of stone and rubble. The ceiling had come down. With heart beating wildly he struggled upwards over the shale until his head cracked against the rugged roof. Then he went down on all fours and wriggled forward across the fallen stones and earth, wriggled with the top of his head always bumping the roof, always being pressed lower and lower in a midnight blackness of dank, sunless earth which smelled of the grave. And again he emerged —into what, he could not see, but into some black space in which he could stand upright once more. He paused, gasping for breath, and as hearing began to return to his gun-deafened ears, he realized that something was following him and he tensed once more for flight. But flight to where? In which direction? In the total blackness which enveloped him he could run straight into a stone wall—fall into a pit. He was lost, utterly and hopelessly, in the black bowels of these midnight galleries. Fear, mounting rapidly within him, touched off near hysteria. In the blackness, useless eyes wide, mouth gaping, he stood and waited with hands outstretched for whatever was approaching.

It was a dog. The eager whining, the scratching and scuffling, told of a police dog forcing its way across the almost roof-high rubble over which he had dragged his own bleeding body moments before. Evaldo pictured the dog—a great police Alsatian, savage and strong as a wolf. And with an instinctive realization that he must kill it or be killed by it, he searched rapidly at his feet and picked up a heavy stone. Then he climbed back up the pile of rubble until his groping hand showed that he was close to the narrow hole through which the dog must come, and stood waiting and taut and blind.

The dog sensed his presence well before it emerged. It gave a long rumbling growl, then a series of sharp, snarling barks and then—it must have crouched and gathered itself together in a space in which even Evaldo had been almost prone on his belly —it launched itself through the air with one long, baying howl.

As blind as its quarry, relying entirely on its accurate sense of smell, it missed Evaldo by so little that its bristling fur brushed his bare body like a caress as it shot past. Evaldo heard it thud to earth beyond him and flung the stone with all his might. The dog screamed and, as Evaldo felt for another stone and grasped one, it flung itself upon him. They rolled down the rubble pile with the dog's teeth buried deeply in the man's left thigh. Evaldo was screaming now, as raw flesh was wrenched and torn from his leg by those terrible jaws. He brought his stone down and down again, trying to break the dog's back, but its heavy pelt protected it and as they struggled on the slimy stone bottom it unhooked its dripping teeth from the lacerated leg and, snorting blood from its nostrils, fastened them in Evaldo's left breast. The next move would be higher still—to tear out his throat.

Shots from above and behind—then the sudden reflected gleam of a flashlight far back in the rubble. Evaldo crashed his stone onto the side of the dog's narrow skull and heard a crunch of breaking bone. But still it held on. Its great claws were tearing frantically down his belly, ripping bloody ribbons of flesh from breastbone to groin. A second, third, fourth blow with the stone—and then a gurgling whine in the dog's throat. Something gushed over Evaldo's mangled chest and the dog twitched and writhed. He dropped the stone, sticky now and slippery in his fingers, and with weakening hands tore the animals jaws apart and was free.

Free and agonized—mad with pain. The torn-out pectoral muscles of his chest had largely disabled his left arm, but with his right he flung another stone at the glaring flashlight as at last it topped the rubble pile. There was a crash, a shout and the unextinguished light rolled down the broken shale to rest at his feet. Evaldo bent to grasp it, a bullet ripped over his head and then he was away, the light in one hand, down a sloping staircase and into a great, empty, vaulted storeroom.

He was dizzy now from pain and loss of blood; weakening so rapidly that the torch swayed in his hand, flickering over arch and pillar and curved buttress. The storeroom seemed to have innumerable gaping tunnels opening from it. Evaldo staggered to one of them and stared down it to see—still far away, but approaching—a bobbing flashlight. He lurched to a second—to hear the sound of running feet and voices. A third—another flashlight, much nearer, and the sudden triumphant bay of a dog. It was hopeless. He was trapped—trapped completely, and the next dog would kill him. Down the passages the voices and thudding boots boomed ever louder; another dog bayed and then was answered from a further tunnel.

Noise, noise, noise—maddening, brain-battering, growing ever louder in a roaring multiplicity of echoes which seemed to burst in flashes of light within his reeling head. Evaldo ran lurching and terror-stricken from tunnel to tunnel but the echoes in each were so loud, so menacing, that they drove him back; he could no longer tell which were filled with approaching death and which might be empty. He stumbled over a fallen stone at the entrance to one sloping passageway and his flashlight, cracking upon the stone floor, broke and left him abruptly embedded in the cavernous, resounding black drum of the vaulted storeroom.

And now, on his knees, hands clasped to head, Evaldo's brain snapped and he joined in the howls, lifting his voice in scream upon terrible scream until the echoes roared back in hideous mockery of his pursuers. No longer a human being but a maddened animal he staggered screaming to his feet and screaming thrust into the blackness of the tunnel mouth beside him. With bursting lungs he shrieked his way for forty steps, and then was flung forward on his face, pitched into a nearly vertical chute of smooth stone to slither, to roll, to rush with gathering momentum through a blackness which ceased to be black, which became gray, pale, bright—and suddenly clear, vivid day.

◆§ 7

FAR below, in their rowboat, the Forths had listened with growing wonder to the din which seemed to boom and echo in—if that was possible—the muffled depths of Mont'Orlando. Rocking gently on the calm evening sea they were staring up at the cliff-face when the screaming began—inhuman, agonized, unforgettable in its animal terror.

With faces turned to the cliffs they sat unspeaking, staring upward, until the ghastly shrieks stopped as abruptly as they began and something shot suddenly out of a small black hole four hundred feet above them. Something that splayed out in full fall and was caught and illuminated brilliantly in the bright evening sunlight—the horribly mutilated body of a naked man.

So slowly did it seem to fall, so widespread were its arms and legs, so unreal appeared that death-flight from the high cliff, that for a moment neither of the two in the boat below could believe that the whole thing was not some pretense—somewhere, surely, there were teams with movie cameras recording this mock horror upon reels of film. Yet the smashing thud the body made when it hit a wave-lapped rock platform at the cliff's foot was grimly realistic. Colonel Forth bent to his oars and began to pull fast, if clumsily, for the place.

"George! George, you can't! It's a movie. You'll ruin everything!"

Undecided, the colonel hesitated, turning the boat quickly. "I guess it's not a movie, Ella. That guy looked real enough to me. I can't see him now, though. . . ."

"It's only a stuffed dummy!" Mrs. Forth was pale, but at all costs determined to stick to her cinematic theory. Nothing so horrible could, she felt, occur in real life. In real life people suicided, if not in their right minds, at least in their right clothes. It was only on the screen that people jumped, stark naked and covered in blood, from high cliffs over the open sea.

Colonel Forth had also been reared on the Hollywood epic and had a proper respect for that astonishing industry created almost entirely by his own nation. Yet he had seen war and had

seen plenty of ripped and gory bodies. And that particular one
. . . He hesitated and swung the boat around again. "I guess
I'd better make sure, Ella. It could be a—a genuine thing. There
might be something I could do."

But to Mrs. Forth this attitude was highly unacceptable. She
in her turn was beginning to entertain unpleasant doubts concerning the theatrical staging of what she had seen and the arti-
ficiality of that falling body. Yet if, by some terrible chance, it
was real—why, that was a better reason than any for keeping
away. At the thought of what might, perhaps, lie hidden on the
far side of that rocky platform her stomach turned over.
"George! George, do as I say! Turn the boat at once! George, it
is a film stunt. Why sure, you know how the Italians do all their
stunts on open location! Just you turn the boat this instant,
George Forth, before you ruin everything!"

Once more Colonel Forth backed water with one oar while
pulling on the other. Once more the boat came around. "But
Ella, I guess it's my duty to find out . . ." he began worriedly.

"It's not your duty to make us a laughingstock in Naples!"

"But it could be the real thing, I tell you! It looked goddam
like it to me and—"

"It was *not!* I tell you, it's just a stunt. Do you want to ruin
God knows how many feet of film? Why, they'd certainly make
us pay for it! Do you want that?"

The colonel backed water again. It always took him a long
time to make up his mind when arguing with his wife, but at last
he had done so. "Listen, Ella honey," he said firmly. "I guess
that was a genuine fall. I don't know why or how, but until I'm
certain it's a dummy—and I sure to God hope you're right—I
guess I *gotta* investigate."

Mrs. Forth, realizing that her husband was in earnest, rose
to her feet. "George—you turn this boat! You turn the boat this
instant or I'll jump into the sea!"

But she never had to carry out her threat for at that moment
a fast, gray Italian naval launch roared round the point from
Gaeta, cut its engine and slid in a subsiding bow wave toward
the cliff foot. It had left Gaeta jetty four and a half minutes ago,
during which time the Forths, in their rowboat, had performed
three slow but neatly complete circles.

The Jungle and the Barracks

◆§ 1

THE funeral of Biagio Bonitatibus started it. Before that the approaching eviction of Crocifissa and her sub-tenants from the old Sanbrenedetto property had stirred only a local, grumbling indignation and resentment among their immediate neighbors in the *piazza*, the Via Buonuomini, the Vico dei Lepri and the little alleys behind the Annunziata. But the death of the old cabman whose gaunt, swaybacked horse and dilapidated *carròzza* had been known from the Via Foria to the Carmine had the effect of propagating and hardening an angry bitterness throughout the whole of San Lorenzo.

Biagio's last letter had been addressed to Crocifissa, although its content had been meant for Gennaro. But at seventy-four, and with the full prejudice of his generation against the frivolity and fickleness of modern youth, Biagio had probably felt it unseemly to take his farewell of the world in words addressed to a sixteen-year-old boy: besides, he had known Crocifissa very much longer.

In his letter, a document surprisingly brief and simple for a Neapolitan, Biagio had said that he believed himself to be upon the point of death and doubted if he would see the sun rise again. In this way he had avoided any mention of hastening his own demise which, since the aim of the letter was to secure Christian burial, might well have defeated his purpose. But he had gone on to say that with the coming eviction and the impossibility of finding another room and stable at a price he could afford, he was not sorry to go—and it was this particular remark, quoted continually in tones of rising indignation and bandied from mouth to mouth among his neighbors, that was to inflame the San Lorenzini.

He had not specified his illness—he had always been prudish with regard to the functions and malfunctions of the human body—but turned at once to the manner of his burial. What he wanted most of all was to have his body taken to the cemetery of Castel d'Ieri in the Abruzzi Apennines where his sister had been buried more than half a century before. In order to defray the cost of this he left all his possessions to the firm of *L.P. Quong—Pompe Funebre* with the request that, for old times' sake, they would dispose of them and use the money to carry out his last wishes.

Crocifissa, even while crying liberally over the letter, had shaken her head. "Poor Biagio! But how typical of him to be so difficult—and at this of all times! But we must do what we can. He was an old friend."

She had called in Gennaro, glum and somber and with an air of brooding bitterness which nothing now seemed to dispel— not even the chance to organize another funeral. "Can you manage it, *caro mio?*"

"I don't see how we can possibly sell the cab and Baldissera in time. Who would want to buy them, anyway?"

"There are his other things. We—we ought to do our best to help. I'll try to do what I can."

"Yes. But"—Gennaro had stared at the ground for a moment, then shrugged his shoulders—"there's only the window coffin. He can have that."

Crocifissa had given him a look of watery gratitude and Gennaro had flushed a slow crimson. It was the first time he could remember when their roles had been genuinely reversed. So often before she had thanked him for small services; but they had been the indulgent thanks of someone pleased, perhaps touched, but who knew that it lay within her power to do the things herself or to have them done elsewhere. This was different. For the first time a feeling he could not comprehend touched Gennaro with a hint of something more to come.

Tentatively Crocifissa said, "The window coffin? But would Quong like that? And shouldn't you keep it for—for—"

"Quong wouldn't mind. He used to laugh at Biagio, but he liked him. Besides"—Gennaro struggled to put into his own words some of the things Quong had said to him; those complex and generally enigmatic remarks which he himself had guessed to be literal translations from the Chinese— *"I also, for all my magic of Age, am brought to the Black Hill of Death, to wear at last the Garment of the turning Globe."*

But it was too difficult. Crocifissa would not understand, for to her Quong had always been merely a friendly old foreigner who smiled and bowed and spoke bad Italian. Lamely he said, "Quong is not a real Christian, you know. Things that seem important to us seem different to him." And indeed Gennaro could not now think of anything that had ever seemed very important to Quong. "He has a book called *All Men Are Brothers* by a Chinese named Lin Yutang. He often read bits to me— when he wasn't quoting poems."

"But he didn't look on Biagio as a *brother?*"

"Oh, no. No more than everyone else. But he'd like Biagio to have the window coffin if it would have pleased him. I can ask him first, of course, but . . ."

So Biagio had the beautifully carved window coffin and Quong's lost its last professional appurtenance. The old man's possessions, other than his horse and cab, were sold for five thousand lire, most of which went on the various official forms and tax stamps which the Demographic Office required before they could allow his body to be shifted from Naples. So there was none left for the main funeral expenses. Crocifissa could only afford four thousand lire but, as usual, Maresciallo Tenerini came to the financial rescue. "Biagio was a very trying old man on occasions," he growled, "a very trying old man indeed. And he was entirely wrong about the crossing of the Anhovo in 'seventeen. He wasn't there and I was. But he was an old friend. One must do what one can. How much will it be, Gennà?"

"Twenty thousand for the hearse—that's including tax. Ten for the niche. Five for the local priest and another five for local taxes. Eight for the slab—if we just have his name and dates— and two for the mason. One for the sexton and—say five hundred for a couple of bottles of wine for the assistants—at least that's usual. Fifty-three should do it."

"Pòrca misèria!"

"That's what comes of being buried so far away. The last time we did this sort of thing was in May—old Signor Sanbrenedetto. That cost eighty-eight. But I'm not taking any profit this time, of course."

"You've got to—" began the tobacconist, but then cut himself short. He would have liked to make Gennaro take a reasonable profit but realized that the suggestion would have insulted him. One had to be so careful in dealing with someone as far down the slippery slope of professional bankruptcy as Quong's grandson.

"All right, Gennà. If you'll arrange it, I'll pay. What about flowers?"

"I can manage the wreath frames and the palm leaves. I can get the flowers themselves cheap at Porta Capuana."

And in the end Biagio's funeral was the most imposing that Quong's had ever undertaken. The hearse, with Gennaro beside the driver, was followed by Baldissera and the carròzza covered with wreaths and by no less than three other cabs all equally full. Biagio had never believed he had any friends in life, but in death there seemed innumerable people to mourn the passing of the dour old man who had sat, winter and summer, on the box of his cab, mumbling to himself, flicking his whip at small boys who came too close—a shabby but indomitable inhabitant of the Quarter.

The procession was followed all the way to the station on the Piazza Garibaldi by a crowd which numbered about fifty at the start from the piazza but, swelling rapidly during the slow journey through the Via Buonuomini and along the Via Alessandro Poerio, must have risen to almost four times as many when at last the great railway terminus was reached. At its head, behind the fourth carròzza, marched Renato Paolantonio and three other artisans; grim-faced, solid men in working clothes, they each wore the hammer-and-sickle badge prominently displayed on their shirts and carried an opulent wreath of bright scarlet salvia. The few followers who had known the dead man well enough to discuss politics with him found this odd, since Biagio had always expressed a contemptuous distrust of Communism.

At the station all the wreaths, except Maresciallo Tenerini's which remained on top of the coffin, were loaded into the luggage van of the Avezzano train which was also to transport the chief mourners—the Maresciallo himself and Crocifissa accompanied, inevitably, by Gigi. Respectful crowds, guided and guarded by saluting policemen, watched as hearse and mourners parted company for the journey, and the Avezzano train was actually delayed ten minutes so that the wreaths might be carefully arranged for their transport to the mountains. Altogether it was an astonishing farewell for the old man who had been born seventy-four years ago in the overcrowded filth and poverty of the San Lorenzo *fondachi*—and it was to have astonishing consequences.

For when Gennaro and the mourners returned to Naples, tired and dusty, at midnight they found themselves as much in the public eye as they had been when they set out. There had been a spontaneous meeting in the *piazza* that evening; one of those quickly gathering crowds which seem suddenly to spring from the black *piperno* of the Neapolitan streets and to gather around anyone who has the time or the wit to harangue them upon almost any subject.

This evening the first speaker had been Renato Paolantonio, his chosen stand the conventional one on the low concrete step of the public urinal and his subject the coming eviction of Crocifissa and the Quongs from their ruinous home. Renato possessed the full histrionic ability for which his fellow citizens were famous; he also had a loud voice, a handsome appearance, a truculent manner and a ready-made ideology. All he needed was a cause, and in the plight of the tenants of the old Sanbrenedetto property he found a most satisfactory one.

He began by reminding his hearers that many of them had, that very morning, attended the funeral of an old man whom most of them, like himself, had known all their lives. Why had Biagio died? Simply through despair at the thought of a homelessness as inevitable as the coming winter. He had said as much in his last letter. Did they know that he was to have been thrown out of his home now—in the autumn—with no compensation, no other accommodation, no way to continue to earn his living? Turned out to die in the streets. And he was seventy-four years old and had fought in at least seven of the battles of the Isonzo and on the Piave as well. This was not the way Italians treated their old soldiers—but it was the way the Naples municipality did. And who were the Naples municipality who did this thing? Renato, now surrounded by some eighty or ninety people, launched a flood of fiery invective at the entire staff of the Municipio, which soon doubled his audience and brought loud laughter and cheers of agreement. "These *signori*—" he screamed venomously, then waited a second and spat wetly into the urinal—"These *signori* who sit all day on their fat arses with nothing to do save draw their salaries and play indecently with themselves or each other to pass the time . . . These shameless ones, I say, *murdered* Biagio Bonitatibus! They murdered him and they haven't finished—oh, no! There are other people to destroy in that building over there. Over there is another old man—paralyzed this time, so he can't even write a last letter about it—they're going to kill him too! Just as soon as they can take time off from robbing their fellow citizens and from unnatural fornication they're going to turn him out into the street to die! Just as they were going to turn out old Biagio—the brigands, the vagabonds, the users-of-their-own-sisters!"

The crowd roared and stamped and under the high, swan-necked streetlamp, Renato wiped the sweat from his forehead with one bare forearm and grinned and lifted his voice in further furious polemics.

When at last he had finished someone else took over; a taller, older man, blond-haired, with a voice less loud but harder, more staccato than Renato's; a man whom some members of the crowd remembered having seen, wearing the hammer-and-sickle on his chest, beside Renato at the funeral. "Comrades! Workers! San Lorenzini! You do not know me—or perhaps only a few of you like my young comrade here. My name is Pietrini and, like Paolantonio, I am an employee of ITOLGAS—the firm which has bought the property from which it soon intends to throw your neighbors into the street. Despite the fact that I work for this firm I am not afraid of telling you my opinion of their behavior in this matter. No—I'm not afraid of them. Perhaps they may be"—Pietrini smiled briefly, without humor—"a little afraid of me. Comrades! Workers! San Lorenzini! Listen to me and then act with me to prevent a criminal piece of inhumanity and wrongdoing motivated by the most cynical avarice and a wanton disregard for social justice and the rights of the poor! Listen . . ."

And the crowd in the *piazza* listened with rising anger and indignation as old wrongs, old injustices were brought up and hurled one after another at the conventional targets of the Italian Communist Party—big business, the Church, the Christian Democrats. The Christian Democrats—big business—the Church. Again and again and again. Pietrini was a less emotional speaker than Renato, and he was not a local man like his predecessor on the urinal step, but he was a carefully trained and practiced demagogue with a full understanding of all the tricks of an accomplished mob orator. His jeers and taunts, if less brutal, were far more pointed than Renato's; his allusions and insinuations far more barbed. When, after half an hour, the police moved tentatively in upon the shouting, snarling crowd they would have met with still more than the usual hostility— perhaps even with violence—if Pietrini had not prevented it. But as soon as he saw the white belts of the Carabinieri glimmering beyond the fringes of his audience he brought his tirade to a close, slipped down from the urinal step and disappeared in the crowd. Yet far more than Renato he left his words behind him; smoldering barbs planted in the hearts of San Lorenzo's highly inflammable citizens.

⋅⋅§ 2

THE room was bright and hot with day when Gennaro awoke. He stretched and blinked, turned on his side and saw by the golden sunlight far advanced across the floor that it was late in the morning. He shivered once from the effects of some fading, ill-omened dream and recalled yesterday. The long, looping journey into the mountains, the little village of Castel d'Ieri where, leaving the hearse at the cemetery gates, he had waited an hour for the mourners off the Avezzano bus, eyed curiously by peasant children in heavy, square-toed boots. And he had understood then why Biagio had wanted to be buried here in this remote place among the silent sheep pastures and the towering hills. It was peaceful enough here to sleep forever. He had never known such peace—except once before. Only once in his whole life—the day he had left the hearse in the roadside bamboos and had swum far out into the slow-heaving expanse of the empty, shining Adriatic. It was only four months ago, he told himself incredulously, but it seemed an age—an age of blue memory.

He lay for a moment longer gazing around this room which he must leave no later than the day after tomorrow, and then swung his legs to the floor. Quong's had undertaken their last funeral. It was over. Today the old life must be dismantled—taken apart and disposed of. Soon it would be nothing but a memory and an ache in the heart.

Rising, he went quickly to look at Quong; aware that he would do this once again, and once only. Quong lay very still with eyes shut, and for a moment the fear which had touched Gennaro nearly every morning for the past six months—the fear that Quong had died—sprang up within him. But this time it was not really fear at all—it was hope.

But a touch on the yellow, two-fingered hand brought the wrinkled slit-eyes slowly open, brought a slight movement of the head. Gennaro smiled down at that pale yellow fleshless face and was about to lift Quong higher on the pillows from which he had slipped when someone began knocking at the shop door below. Someone who must have borrowed the spare key from Crocifissa, for as soon as the knocking stopped Gennaro heard the door open and footsteps on the stairs. Then Renato's voice —"Gennà! Are you *still* asleep?"

"Come in! No, I'm up now. What time is it?"

Gennaro turned from Quong's door as Renato, followed by someone else, entered the farther room. "What time? Past ten o'clock. But you were all late back last night, Crocifissa says. We've waited an hour in my place. Gennà—you remember Signor Pietrini? The day you worked at ITOLGAS?"

And Gennaro found himself shaking hands with the tall, blond foreman under whose charge he had spent that exhausting June day at the "south excavation" and who had, even in that short time, impressed him with his air of unhurried, masterful assurance. Pietrini grinned down at him. "Young Ferrara, again. How goes it with you, little comrade? None too well, I'm told."

Gennaro smiled and shrugged. "Renato's told you about—that we have to go from here?"

"Yes. Yes, indeed he has. We want to help you, if we can."
Pietrini glanced quickly round the room and Renato, as if used
to anticipating the foreman's desires, at once brought up a
chair. Pietrini sat down and crossed his legs, still smiling at
Gennaro; somehow, perhaps because of Renato's obvious deference, perhaps because of his own personality, he had taken
complete charge of everything. The room seemed smaller,
Renato insignificant, Gennaro himself younger and more uncertain.

"Tell me, *figliolo*—what are your plans? Have you decided
what you're going to do?"

Gennaro sat down on his rumpled bed. "More or less.
Crocifissa knows." "We haven't asked her." Pietrini's voice was
gentle but carried an unspoken rebuke.

"I am going back to Ferrara—the day after tomorrow." Said
like that, Gennaro could not really believe it. Someone else, not
himself, had spoken.

"And—your grandfather?"

"He—he will go into a home for sick old people tomorrow."
Suddenly Gennaro said in a rush, "Savoldi, the wood-merchant
in the Vico Lepri will take the hearse and sell it. I owe him
money, but he's agreed to take what he can get for the hearse
instead. Then there's only the tools below and the furniture and
—and Baldissera and the cab—they're mine now. Maresciallo
Tenerini will sell those. I owe him money but he won't take it.
He says he'll put what he gets for everything in the bank for
me."

Pietrini nodded. "You've made all your arrangements, then?
Disposed of everything?"

"Yes." Gennaro's voice was fast but toneless. "Yes; everything. I'll take only that—" He pointed to the white jade horse
on the windowsill. "They'll let me keep it in Ferrara." The white
horse would be the sole relic of his five and a half years
in Naples. It would hold—hold easily within its cold opaque
depths—every memory, every face and voice, thought and word
and gesture of those years.

Pietrini was turning, eyebrows raised, to Renato. "I thought
—You hadn't explained—"

"Tell him."

"But—"

"He doesn't *want* to go, Comrade Pietrini. *Tell him.*"

"All right." Pietrini sucked in his lower lip for a second and then said, "If it could be arranged for you to stay here—you'd want that? You'd want to stay?"

"How do you mean?"

"If the decision to demolish this place was—reversed. If, rather than allow ITOLGAS to pull it down, the Municipio withdrew their permission and instead allowed you to remain here as you are—you and your grandfather and Signora Buona-fede—you'd stay?"

Gennaro stared at the floor. "I don't see how I could—now. All the money's gone—and the window coffin. And I left my frames at Castel d'Ieri yesterday. I don't see how I could."

Renato said urgently, "But in only a little more than a year you'll be eighteen, Gennà. Then you can use the hearse again. And"—he swung round to Pietrini—"we could do something, couldn't we? I mean if—"

"Oh yes. I think we'd have to."

"A contribution from Party funds would—"

"A subscription," said Pietrini slowly and coldly, "organized among the friends and neighbors of these people and with a con-tribution—perhaps—from our funds."

Renato looked abashed for a moment, then turned again to Gennaro. "It's perfectly possible—like Signor Pietrini says. And I'll organize a subscription for you. We'll see you through the winter and until you can use the hearse. Then you'll be able to carry on by yourself."

Gennaro had sat silently, glancing from one to the other. A tiny flame of hope flickered in his heart but he would not allow it to grow. He had tried too many times, and too often in vain, to believe any longer in saving Quong's—to believe any longer in hope. "How could we stay on here, in any case? We're supposed to be out by Wednesday."

Pietrini nodded. "I know. But that gives us time to make the Municipio change its mind. We started"—he smiled briefly at Renato—"last night, before you came home. And we can carry on from there."

"But—"

"Listen. This house is outside the scope of the rent laws, so that in theory you can be evicted at any time after a reasonable notice and without the offer of alternative accommodation. But to put that eviction into practice could be something very different—very much more difficult. The housing position in this city is causing enough scandal as it is without pulling down a place in which people are living in order to make way for a gas station. That could cause real trouble—trouble enough, if properly handled, to lose the next city election for the present crew in the Municipio. At the moment they think that it can be done without any fuss—after all, it is only turning out one old woman and a boy and his paralyzed grandfather—oh, and an expectant mother, too, we mustn't forget her. And none of you are organized workers. So the Municipio people think they can get away with it. But if we show them that they can't—if we make it plain that there'll be trouble for them—then you'll see that they will change their minds at once. You'll be left where you are. They'll say, of course, that it is only temporary; that it is only until they find you new accommodation. But you needn't think of that. They haven't got any new accommodation to offer. No—you'll be here indefinitely."

"But—" Gennaro had followed his argument with interest and had gone even further—"this place belongs to ITOLGAS, now. They would only have to raise our rents to get rid of us. They'd do that—obviously."

"Oh, no, they would not!" contradicted Pietrini grimly. "Firstly, because I and the other P.C.I. foreman would call a strike if they did. We can bring the whole plant to a standstill over something like that—and they know it. They're doing everything they can to improve labor relations out at Poggioreale. They're not going to spoil all their work and lose millions of lire's worth of production in order to hurt you. And secondly, since the Municipio could not go back on its own order they would merely be left with this place as it is—which is no good to them. Then thirdly, their public image in Naples, which is something De Santis is extremely sensitive about, would be badly damaged. No, no—it's just a question of making a firm stand now."

"It will work, Gennaro!" Renato's voice was jubilant with triumph. "It will work all right—you'll see."

"They'll see," said Pietrini dryly, "if they'll help. Not otherwise."

Gennaro was still staring at the floor, but more to disguise his pounding, flooding emotion than through any sense of doubt. Pietrini's words, spoken with such calm authority, had come to him as a revelation, as something entirely new yet very simple, a sudden light dispersing the darkness and making everything clear and easy. That there might be disadvantages in the plan he did not consider; that was not for him. That Pietrini might have other, more obscure motives he could not at present guess. All he knew was that here was a determined, experienced and powerful man who offered, with every apparent sign of sincerity, to save him. To save him from losing his life in Naples and the business which supported it. To save him from a return— which at best could only be a humiliating admission of failure —to the monks at Ferrara; most of all to save him from tomorrow's parting from Quong. For Renato, only a few years older than himself, he had no particular respect but Pietrini, albeit in a different way, had worked the same magic upon him as upon last night's shouting crowd around the *piazza* urinal. But—

"What do you mean, 'help'? What can *we* do? Me and Crocifissa and the Signora?"

"You can be firm," said Pietrini promptly. "You can stop behaving like three frightened sheep and start trying to think of yourselves as human beings with equal rights—the same rights as everyone else." For a moment he eyed Gennaro with a look of contempt. "The other two are women but you're nearly a man —nearly seventeen. Do you have to run off back to school because some fools in the Municipio—who've got no more right to a roof over their heads than you have—decide to push you out of your home?"

"But what else . . . I mean, we *have* to go . . . if we're made to."

"No you don't. You don't 'have' to do anything. You merely *think* you have to."

Renato said, "Comrade Pietrini, he doesn't understand. There'll be time—later."

"Yes. I hope so." Pietrini's voice returned to its former friendly calm. "Listen, Gennaro. All we ask of you in return for our help is that you refuse to go voluntarily. That you stay here in this house and refuse to be evicted."

"But wouldn't we be breaking the law?"

"Only the law of trespass. And I assure you it is one for which neither ITOLGAS nor the Municipio would think of taking you to court. You can be certain of that."

"Then the police would come and put us out."

"On whose instructions? They could only act on the Municipio's orders, and I tell you that we're going to make the Municipio—and also ITOLGAS—understand that they'll lose much more than they'll gain by pressing this eviction."

"Can you really do that?"

"Yes."

"But only if we stay here—refuse to go?"

"Only if you refuse to go. Of course."

"Very well. I'll stay. I don't know about the others. Have you asked Crocifissa?"

Pietrini got up at once. "Not yet. We'll see her now. All right, Gennaro, just remember, then. On Wednesday you stay in this house. You lock your door and you refuse to let anyone in or to come out yourself—understand?"

⪧ 3

SINCE it was Sunday the shop was closed. Renato knocked at the side door, knocked and waited, then whistled and called out, "Crocifissa, Crocifissa! *Dove sei?*" Turning apologetically to Pietrini he said, "She's nearly always in at this hour. She goes to church early and then she comes back here."

"It will be awkward if we can't see her. We have not too much time as it is."

"I know." On a sudden impulse Renato turned to the older man, his voice low and hurried. "Listen, *capo*—they won't get hurt, will they? I mean, if this doesn't work out as it should . . ."

"How can one say? I don't think so."

"I—I mean if the police go into action. What we told Gennaro was—well, more what we hope will happen than what we are sure of."

Briefly Pietrini said, "We're giving them a chance, aren't we? Something they wouldn't have otherwise. If we fail, they get thrown out and perhaps a dinner plate or two will get broken in the process. If we succeed they stay. In either event the Party gains a propaganda success—so it will be a victory for us whatever happens."

"But you yourself," Renato persisted. "You think it will work out all right?"

"Yes, yes, yes. I think so. Now knock again—and harder this time."

And in the end they heard heavy steps within, the door opened and Crocifissa, red-faced, flushed and obviously deeply upset, stared at them angrily. "What is it? What is it? Renato—what do you mean by coming here at this of all times and banging and calling out like a street-boy! Have you no respect?"

Renato blushed, opened his hands, lifted his shoulders. "But it's nearly eleven, Signora Crocifissa. And on a Sunday. That's surely not too early to visit you? Especially as I and my friend here have something most important to say."

"It's not the time. I don't mean that at all! Haven't you seen the papers? Don't you know that Iole Giansante's husband was killed yesterday afternoon at Gaeta?"

"No!" Renato's eyes widened in horror. "But—how?"

"He escaped and they chased him and—and he jumped over a cliff."

"*Oh Dio!* So now . . ."

"I've got to be with her, haven't I?" Crocifissa was breathing heavily and she threw a quick look over her shoulder. "She's very calm at present. I don't think that's a good sign. I don't want to leave her alone in case she does something foolish. Now go away, Renato, like a good boy, and don't bother me. If you've something important to say it will just have to wait until tomorrow." She was about to shut the door when Pietrini put one foot in it.

"What we have to say won't wait until tomorrow, Signora Buonafede. It's extremely urgent. I had wanted to see Signora Giansante as well as you, although I suppose that in the circumstances that is now impossible. But you I must see—and this morning."

"I don't understand!" From the sagging doorway Crocifissa stared at him with a mixture of fear and indignation. "I don't

understand at all! Who are you? What can you want with me?—
Who is he, Renato? *Benedetto Dio!* As if I haven't got enough to
think of, without—"

Renato said, "He is Signor Pietrini and he works for
ITOLGAS and—"

"We had two men from them. They came last week—you remember. No"—Crocifissa put her hand to her head distractedly
—"it must have been the week before. Anyway, they upset Gennaro. But you remember, Renato—you were there. I don't want
any—"

"Signor Pietrini has not come on the firm's business. Really,
I think you must listen to him. What he has to say can be very
important to you."

"Well—well, if I must." Grudgingly Crocifissa led them into
the kitchen behind the shop and, with her mind obviously still
on the stricken woman upstairs, said "*Allora*—please be quick.
I have to go back to her."

Pietrini sighed. This was certainly no way to explain his plan
persuasively—and to an old and ignorant woman at that. He
doubted even before he began whether he could acquire her
agreement to cooperate. By the time he had finished, and he
was as brief as possible, he was certain of this and Crocifissa's
first words only confirmed it.

"What an idea! I've never heard of such a thing! I don't know
who you are, *signore,* but you'll certainly come to a bad end if
you go around putting such schemes into other people's heads!
Don't you understand that we have no right to be here
any longer? This place is not ours. It belongs to Signor Sanbrenedetto."

"In fact," said Pietrini gently, "it belongs to ITOLGAS now.
As for not having a right to be here—I don't agree at all. I think
you've got a perfect right. It's your home, isn't it?"

"But that's got nothing to do with it!"

"Don't you think so?"

"Of course I don't! It belongs to other people, and they've a
right to do as they like with it. I've no time for Renato's silly
Communist ideas! If he had his way none of us would have anything to call our own."

Renato, his face tomato-red with mortification, said, "If you agree with us you can probably stay here—not be turned out. And that means Quong and Gennaro, too. We've seen Gennaro. *He* agrees."

"He—he does?" For a moment Crocifissa looked trapped, uncertain. Her eyes sought the picture of Dino above the dresser as if for guidance. "But Gennaro's only a boy. He doesn't understand about these things."

"But *I'm* not a boy." Pietrini's voice was firm. "And I *do* understand about them. I understand, considerably more than you do, *signora*. And I repeat what Renato's said. If you agree with us you will be able to remain here—you and Gennaro and his grandfather and the unfortunate lady upstairs. I realize I can't ask her now, but I expect that she would agree if—"

From the open door behind them Iole said, "I do agree—completely."

The others swung around to stand staring, momentarily speechless. Iole stood in the doorway white-faced, dry-eyed, her swollen belly large under her loose cotton housecoat. She seemed shockingly composed and through the minds of the others—even through that of Pietrini—passed the thought that this was no Christian way for a wife to behave on receiving the news of her husband's violent death.

But to Iole, the final murder of Evaldo—which was how she saw yesterday's Gaeta man-hunt—had come as a relief. A shock, certainly—but also the end of an intolerable tension. She had known perfectly well, once the petition had been rejected, that Evaldo would die in prison. It had only been a question of how long he would take in dying. Now it was over, much more quickly than she had envisaged, and though she guessed that the manner of his death had been considerably more terrible than that recounted in the few gruesome details so far released to the press, it had, at least, not occurred in the dungeons of that macabre castle. He was gone—and at peace, if such a fiercely turbulent spirit could know peace. She had mourned him for six months while he was still alive and while she was trying to rescue him; somehow both the sorrow and the striving had become entangled together so that now that he was past help he was also past grieving for. Later, she told herself, she would think about him, remember him, pray for him, but for the present—for the next few days, or perhaps weeks—she wanted, not so much to

forget, as to rest from him. Once that little space of rest w
past she would have to start living again—with his child and his
ghost. It would be a life in Naples, here among the only people
who had helped her and sympathized with her. She would never
go back to Rome where lived her father and all the other men
responsible for what had occurred yesterday; they were her
enemies and would remain so until death.

She looked with approval at the red enamel badges on the
shirts of Renato and his tall blond friend. She had always disliked and feared Communism as much as the rest of the Italian
bourgeoisie, though with more discernment than most since at
one stage in her search for minor cultural eminence she had
studied politics and economics. And since she was fully aware
of the contrast between the utopian dedication of most Italian
Communists to the welfare of the working masses in the abstract,
and their Spartan unconcern for the present wellbeing of the individuals who composed those masses, she looked on them in
general as either dupes or dupers. No intelligent, rational, or
humane person could either accede to or desire their sterile,
ant-heap vision of life; only minds dark with ignorance or
warped by failure or hatred—or revenge—could accept it. But
today she did accept it. Today she wanted, more than anything else, to harm the society which had murdered her husband, and here in Crocifissa's shabby little room stood two men
whose badges proclaimed them as the relentless, sworn enemies
of that society. Today they were her allies. "I do agree—completely." Her eyes met Pietrini's in a quick glance of understanding and the tall foreman smiled with genuine relief; this
part of his mission, at least, would be accomplished successfully.

◆§ 4

NEXT evening Gennaro was ironing his own and
Quong's laundry. He had always given Monday evenings to
this task—though since the advent of his electric iron it could
more truthfully be termed a pleasure—and even now the unthinking respect for routine, instilled into him by the Ferrara
monks until it became a natural instinct, held him in its formal
bonds. He would have liked to be out at Porta Capuana listen-

ing to Renato haranguing the crowd on the subject of the coming eviction, but had he gone he would have felt depressed and ill at ease—guilty with the knowledge of yesterday's washing lying crumpled and unironed in the zinc tub under the table.

Yet now, as the heavy chrome iron slid smoothly across one of Quong's white shirts, he was glad that he had remained at home. He had time to think at last. There had been so little time to think since Biagio's death, and all too much to ponder upon. Before that—and why, he wondered, should the death of an old man who had always been taciturn and generally surly seem such a climacteric in the events of the past months?—he had come to what he had believed to be terms with Fate. Worn down by continual adverse circumstances he had at last accepted the fact that he could not go on—Quong's was finished. And almost immediately afterward had come Renato and Pietrini and a sudden rekindling of his dead hope. And they had done more than give him hope; they had returned to him a measure of the self-respect which had been taken from him on the day he had listened to the dry, matter-of-fact voice of the ITOLGAS lawyer from Milan demolishing him and everything he hoped and lived for—relegating Quong to a charity home and himself to the intolerable anonymity of an apprentice school in the distant north.

For to take Quong's from him was to take away much more than a bankrupt business, an old hearse and a few tools; it was to remove a large part of his personality—a psychological amputation of the gravest sort. He had never explained this to anyone, since he had no clear conception of how to do so and he had doubted if there was anyone who would have understood. But now he thought Pietrini understood.

Gennaro, like most small businessmen, had no time for Communism, but—also like most small businessmen—he would have readily turned to Satan himself for help when in financial difficulties. For as he now realized, one had to choose—life forced the choice upon one—between the jungle and the barracks. And if one chose the jungle one had to fight with everything one had and with any ally one could find. He had chosen the jungle—had made the original choice more than five years ago and had since confirmed it over and over again. Renato and Pietrini, on the other hand, had chosen the safe, ordered life of the barracks. They liked working for ITOLGAS, being part of a huge industrial mechanism of great power and prestige, and if they ever got their way they would change nothing but the ownership of the firm. A few signatures on a paper, the addition of a somewhat more complex bureaucracy, and ITOLGAS could pass tranquilly from private to State ownership—probably under Comrade rather than Commendatore De Santis—for De Santis, Gennaro guessed now, was as much a natural barrack-man as Pietrini. There would still be the "south excavation," still the great canteen, still—in all probability—no water in the washrooms. Communism triumphant certainly meant bigger barracks—but not necessarily better ones.

And then, since the people of the barracks were tidy-minded, they would set to work trying to clear up the jungle. They would certainly succeed, too, for the jungle people—himself, Crocifissa, Maresciallo Tenerini, Signor Savoldi—were pygmies, and thoroughly disorganized pygmies at that. One day they would succeed—but not yet. While the barracks-minded fought each other over abstract and largely meaningless issues the little people of the jungle were still safe to hunt or starve in untidy freedom.

The iron slid and hissed gently across the cloth and the room grew darker. Gennaro's mind drifted lazily in time with the soporific motion of his right arm and he began, as so often before, to tell himself a long and complicated story about China. Shadows gathered in the corners of the cracked and sagging ceiling and the window became a gray-blue square. At last Gennaro finished and in the half-dark unclipped the iron's long electric cord from the single light-socket and replaced the bulb. He was sweating both with the heat of the sultry night and that reflected from his iron and now he went and leaned from the windowsill, staring across the *piazza* at the same scene which had presented itself to him daily for more than five years.

The Annunziata, shabby and peeling; Tenerini's, brightly lit by its red neon sign—TABACCHI—above the doorway; the newsvendor's stall; the swan-necked lamps glowing on the tattered wall posters advertising *Gold Leaf* margarine, or urging one to *Join the Navy and Learn a Trade* or to go and see *The Seven Plagues of Egypt* at the local cinema. The *piazza* was unchanging. Five years ago he, too, had kicked a rubber football at a

goal-post chalked on the iron side of the urinal as the boys below were doing tonight. He, too, had played *vago* with flat stones
across the uneven *piperno* below the Annunziata steps and been
shouted at to desist by Don Ambrosio. He had bought his first
cigarette at Tenerini's; had tried to smoke one of Quong's thin,
knotty, Tuscan cigars beside the newspaper stall and been violently sick, doubled up in that very gutter below the advertise-
ment for *Gold Leaf* margarine.

And yet last week he had been prepared to give it all up—
his past which was as much a part of him as his hands or feet—
at the bidding of Crocifissa. Why had he thought Crocifissa knew
best? Because she was so much older? Or, perhaps, because of
Quong's so-often-quoted proverb from Po Chü-i: *"In the affairs
of others even fools are wise. In their own business even sages
err."* But now Gennaro thought that certainly Quong, and probably the long-dead poet as well, were being ambiguously sardonic.

Yesterday morning Crocifissa had changed her mind again
and again. One minute agreeing with himself, Pietrini, Iole
Giansante; the next minute obstinate over some doubt, declining
over some half-understood scruple to accept their plan. It had
taken an hour to persuade her and it was really Iole who had
accomplished it. Gennaro could never have done it himself, still
less Pietrini, to whom the old woman had taken an immediate
and unreasoning dislike. But Iole, with her Roman background
and her air of worldly intelligence—above all, perhaps, her position as at least an ex-member of that bourgeoisie up to whom
Crocifissa had always looked as her natural superiors—had succeeded. "If the Signora really thinks it's all right . . . If she's
certain it's quite all right . . . Then I suppose it must be. But
I don't like it. I don't like it at all."

Yet later Pietrini had pressed a five-thousand-lire note into
his hand—not into Iole's. "You did very well, Gennaro. She
would not have agreed except for you."

"No. It was because of the Signora."

"Because of Signora Giansante, certainly—but *for* you."

Gennaro had shrugged uncomfortably. He did not, even
though he believed faithfully in Pietrini's plan, like the thought
of having been the cause of Crocifissa going against her own
inclinations. But he had taken the money readily enough. He

needed it for Quong, who now existed largely on orange juice—an expensive commodity in September when the main orange harvest was still more than two months away.

Gennaro turned from the window. He must go to the Porta Capuana and buy more oranges—there were only a couple left in his cupboard. Perhaps, too, he would see Renato and learn what had taken place since this morning when they had all gone in a body to the Municipio to sign, before official witnesses, their formal *domanda* requesting a stay of the eviction order served on them by ITOLGAS last week. Pietrini had taken the day off from work, as well. He had not been at the Municipio but, according to Renato, either at the printer's preparing handbills and posters or at the local offices of *Unità,* the Communist daily, giving the staff facts for the angry headlines and editorials with which it was proposed to back the scheme.

Gennaro went quickly down the unlit stairs and through the dark workshop on his way to the street. Halfway across the room he paused a second, sniffing an oddly unpleasant odor—almost of putrefaction—as if, as sometimes happened, a rat had died in an obscure corner. Dimly the carved face of Kwang-Yin loomed by the workbench and he put out a hand to caress her in passing. But instead of the smooth, gentle, coolness of her cheek his fingers touched coarse, hot, stubbly flesh and a voice —a voice he recognized in a flame of inward terror—whispered hoarsely, "Stay still, you! Don't move!" And as he froze with a shuddering hiss of breath something moved up his body and prodded, hard and cold and metallic against the sweating flesh under the angle of his jaw.

⋅⊰ 5

"FOOD," Domenichelli had said, "first I must have food. Then we'll talk. Where do you keep your food?" He had been holding Gennaro firmly by the belt, his pistol cocked upwards under Gennaro's chin.

"Up—upstairs. Not here. There's no food here."

"Come on!" Domenichelli had pushed Gennaro in front of him. "And don't think this isn't loaded—because it is."

Upstairs Gennaro, sweating and trembling, had pulled the

tattered curtains across the window, then opened his small cupboard. The two oranges, a thick slice of grayish bread, a can
of cheap sardines, an egg, a little oil in a broken cup and three
and a half tomatoes on an enamel plate.

"Put them on the table—open the sardines. Now stand against
that wall where I can see you. Put your hands in your pockets
and don't take them out." Domenichelli laid the pistol on the
table before him and then thrust tomatoes, sardines and oil-
soaked bread into his mouth as if he had not eaten for a month
while Gennaro, dry-mouthed and with heart thudding, watched
him from against the wall.

Domenichelli had changed—changed horribly since that
morning in the restaurant service-passage when they had met
for the first time. Then he had been a small, compact, over-ele-
gant figure; dark, grinning, heavy-lidded but not unattractive
with his swagger and his assured bonhomie. Now he was almost
as fleshless as Quong, lying close behind Gennaro's shoulders in
the next room; his cheeks and eyes equally sunken, his neck a
scrawny bunch of veined cords and tendons. His face—what
could be seen of it under the black stubble of several days' beard-
growth—was hot and dry-looking and from the dark pits above
his knobbed cheekbones his eyes gleamed redly from behind lids
no longer half lowered but seemingly disappeared, eaten up in
the furnace that had dried and burned him. It was a face devoid
of all traces of humanity—the face of a savage animal or of a
delinquent imbecile snarling and gibbering at bay in a corner—
and he was, Gennaro now recognized, the source of that sourly
fetid smell that had hung in the air of the workshop below—
a smell of illness, fever, decay.

And yet now, when he spoke at last, his words were as rational as ever. "I know what you're thinking—but don't! I'm
not well—but I'm still much stronger than you. And I've got
this. And you know well enough that I'll use it if necessary."

"I wasn't thinking anything." Gennaro's voice was hollow
and shaky. He was in the presence of a man who had murdered
twice and had tried to kill him with that very gun. A man who
would certainly try again if he was not obeyed unhesitatingly—
and perhaps even if he was. "What else do—do you want?
There's no more food—but I've got a little money. Five thousand
lire—not quite, but near enough."

"What's through that door?"

"Nothing! Only my grandfather. He's ill. He's had a stroke. No—"

For Domenichelli had picked up his gun and rising to his feet moved towards the door. Even in his panic fear for Quong, Gennaro noticed that Domenichelli's left shoulder sagged below his right, that his left arm was held crookedly and close to his body.

Then the door was open and they were both in the tiny room staring down at Quong, who stared back with eyes mutely surprised, questioning.

"Lie down beside him—go on."

"Why? No! What are you—"

"Go on!" The pistol was jabbed savagely into Gennaro's stomach, so that he gasped with pain. Domenichelli's voice was low and fast and brutal. "Quick! Do what I tell you!"

And then Gennaro found himself on the bed and shivering uncontrollably beside Quong while Domenichelli stood above them both, the pistol in his hand. "You—you'll frighten him! I tell you—he's *ill!*"

Domenichelli kept the pistol pointed at Gennaro's head but now, for the first time, brought his left hand slowly forward until its wide, crooked fingers cast a spider-shadow over Quong's face. Then he felt, frowning thoughtfully, under Quong's chin, grasped the thin throat and squeezed. Quong gave a short, coughing hiss and Gennaro tried to struggle up but the gun jabbed him in the face, pushing him back on the pillow. Quong's breath came out in a queer stifled whistle and then caught again in abrupt silence as Domenichelli's grip tightened once more. And now Gennaro was weeping, hysterical with anguish. *"No, no, no!* Leave him *alone!* I'll do anything you want! Leave him, *leave him!* I'll help you any way you want, I'll do *anything* for you if you'll *leave him alone!"*

Slewing his eyes from the old man's popping ones, Domenichelli said, "Why shouldn't I kill him? What could you do if I did? Even if I didn't kill you, too, you couldn't do anything. The police want you as well as me—don't forget that for one moment. All right, all right." He relaxed his grip and as Quong's breath hissed into his expanding lungs he jabbed Gennaro with the pistol. "Get up and go into the next room."

Choking with fear and misery Gennaro clambered off the bed and gazed down at Quong. The old man's face was no longer pale but dark and reddish, he was breathing with difficulty in short, sharp spasms. "You *have* killed him!" Gennaro's voice, no longer under control, was a wail of agony. "You *have!*"

Domenichelli quickly reversed the gun in his hand, swung it once and brought it down on Gennaro's head. It was a blow not quite hard enough to stun, and as Gennaro reeled from the bed, his knees buckling, Domenichelli caught him, dragged him dazed into the next room and thrust him into the single chair before the mess of oil, broken bread, eggshell and orange rinds on the table.

"Now listen! You know why I'm here, don't you? I don't have to tell you, because you read it in the papers, didn't you? I killed him because he wouldn't help me. But you've got to help me—and you're *going* to help me! If you give me any trouble or don't do what I say I'll kill that—that thing next door. You couldn't stop me. And it wouldn't make any difference to me, even if I was caught later. I'll get life in any case—even if I've killed a dozen people in the meantime. If you think you can call the police you'd better think again. At present they only know that I killed Ko—Bighencomer. They don't know about that other business. But if you bring them in I'll tell them—I swear to you! Because it won't make any difference to me. But it will mean that *you* get twenty-eight years. Yes—twenty-eight! That's what I got for being an accessory to murder when I was your age—so I know." Domenichelli paused a moment, his undershot jaw thrust forward. "They might knock off ten for your help in catching me—or they might not. But you'd get eighteen at the least. That's longer than you've been alive already, isn't it? And I'd have killed your grandfather, too. Your grandfather dead and you in jail for eighteen years. And a single year in prison feels like eighteen outside."

Gennaro was crying again now; sobbing and choking, the tears streaming down his white face. Domenichelli slapped him hard across the mouth. "Shut that noise!"

Swallowing, Gennaro moaned weakly, wiped his lips and, looking at the blood on his fingers as if it was not his own, stammered, "Why—why are you d-doing this? I never did you any harm! I was—was only helping you and—and then you tried to kill me! And now—"

"Listen—if you do what I say I shall be gone—gone soon. Gone for good. Gone out of Italy. You'll never see me or hear of me again. The police won't, either, so you'll be quite safe— won't you? With me gone, who's to know about what happened that night?" Domenichelli bent over Gennaro and forced his head up, using the pistol barrel as a lever under his chin. "You want that, don't you—*don't you?*"

"Yes—yes, I do!" And staring up into that hot, gaunt, black-stubbled face whose pitted eyes glared into his, Gennaro knew that he wanted it more than anything else on earth. For he was completely trapped between Domenichelli on the one hand and the police on the other. No one could save him since there was no one to whom to appeal. He was horribly, horrifyingly alone not only in a room, but in a world, which contained only Domenichelli and himself—and Quong.

But nothing more was done that night. Gennaro was forced downstairs again behind Domenichelli's gun to rummage tearfully for bits of rope and cord. Once more upstairs, he was firmly bound to the wooden chair and the chair itself tied to the table. Despite Gennaro's protests and pleas, Domenichelli went into Quong's room and bound him as well.

"He'll *die* if you do that!"

"I don't suppose so. Anyway, I'm taking no chances."

"And he hasn't had his oranges. He needs—"

"*Basta!* He's all right." Domenichelli turned out the light and lay down on Gennaro's bed, his gun still in his hand. Outside from the *piazza* the usual noises lifted to the window on the hot night air: the laughter of children and the quick scutter of their feet on the flagstones, the hiss and rattle of a *filobus,* the sudden metallic clatter as Maresciallo Tenerini let fall his reticulated shutter across the front of his shop. And voices—most of them recognizable to Gennaro. The wailing shout of the newsvendor calling a late edition of the *Corriere di Napoli*—Gigi's voice raised in a screech of blasphemy as some other urchin tried to snatch his *ciccióli* sandwich—Crocifissa calling out sharply to them. . . . And at last, from directly below the window, Renato's voice: "Gennaro! Gennaro, come down a minute, I want to talk to you!"

"Don't answer!" Domenichelli hissed, low and hoarse from the darkness of the bed. "Don't make a sound!"

"Gennaro!" And then Crocifissa's voice, "He's out, I think." "So? Oh well, I can tell him tomorrow. . . ." Footsteps receding, and then once more the patter of children's feet, their shouts and laughter. Noises from a sane and friendly world penetrating a nightmare one and by doing so making it still more nightmarish.

⋅⁓§ 6

THE night was endless to Gennaro and he doubted, from the restless movements coming from the bed, if Domenichelli was sleeping, either. As to Quong . . . His thoughts circled the old man behind that closed door, whom he could neither reach nor help nor comfort, like weary birds wheeling above a tossing sea, unable to find any place to settle. Slowly, in the hours before dawn, the noises of the city grew less as the murmurous, muted roar of traffic abated. A cat howled and screamed nearby, a cart rattled somewhere up the Vico dei Lepri and a cock crowed. As the first faint light showed the edges of the curtained window, Gennaro's head sank exhaustedly to his chest and he slept. He was wakened an hour later by Domenichelli's hands as they untied him. And then for a couple of minutes he was so stiff and so numb that he groaned with pain every time he tried to move. But as soon as he could stand he staggered toward Quong's room with Domenichelli after him.

Quong, too, had spent a restless night. His pillow was on the floor and his head twisted uncomfortably sideways. He was twitching, half lost in a feverish doze. "Look what you've done! And he was quite well up till yesterday!"

But Domenichelli merely grunted. Then he said, "You can untie him. Then come back into the other room. We have to talk."

When Gennaro returned, Domenichelli was sitting on the table nursing his gun in the dim light of the curtained room. "I'll need at least two hundred thousand. More, if possible."

"I told you—I've only got five. Not quite that."

"Then you'll have to borrow the rest. You've got your hearse still. That's some security, anyway. But I don't suppose it's enough."

Gennaro was silent for a long minute. At last he said slowly, "If I find you that money—will you go away?"

"Of course. You don't suppose I *want* to stay here, do you?"

"When will you go?"

"Tonight—as soon as it's dark enough."

"All right." Gennaro walked over to the window and drew the curtains. The sun flooding in lit the white jade horse to vivid icy flame. For the last time. Tomorrow—forever after—the window-sill would be bare, the Chinese horse, the horse of the Tartar steppes gone, vanished—taking with it the last physical contact with the China of Quong, the China of lanterns and willows and great golden carp asleep in the lotus-studded lakes. But Domenichelli would be gone, too. A bright light, a dark shadow—canceling each other out in their common disappearance.

"I'll have to take this to the Galleria."

"What? That? Is it valuable?"

"I think so. No—don't touch it! You—you might break it."

"You think you can get two hundred thousand for it?"

"Yes."

"Or more?"

"I don't know."

Domenichelli stared down at the horse and blinked as if the vividly reflected sunlight hurt his eyes. "You bring back a receipt, then—see? I want to know just what you get for it. You're not going to cheat me. And just remember while you're outside that I'm in here"—Domenichelli jerked his head at Quong's closed door—"with him."

⊸§ 7

GENNARO had no difficulty in the Galleria this time. He was there well before most of the expensive art shops had opened and he hung around clutching the heavy jade horse in its wrapping of newspaper until the police on duty regarded him so suspiciously that he thought it best to enter one of the cafés. Here he drank coffee laced with brandy and ate two large stale cakes. But instead of doing him good the food and drink only made him feel sick and sleepy. He sat dully at the café table trying to reassure himself about Quong and comfort himself over the approaching loss of the horse. For a few minutes he toyed lightheadedly with the idea of enlisting Renato's help to kill Domenichelli. But he could see no way of doing this and, even if successful, no possibility of getting rid of the body.

Then suppose he went up to those two policemen and said, "I have a murderer hiding in my house." What would they do? Surround the place and call on Domenichelli to surrender? And after strangling Quong, Domenichelli would come out grinning with his hands up, and as the police snapped on the handcuffs he would nod to Gennaro and say, "You'd better put them on him, too."

At last the shops began to open for the day's business and the Galleria echoed to the rattle and rumble of rolling shutters. One of the first to open was the big silversmith's where Gennaro had been so courteously treated on the day he had tried to sell his boxes. They, at least, had not made fun of him then and perhaps they would not try to cheat him now.

The same two assistants, elegant, gray-haired, splendidly dressed, were behind the glass-topped show counter as Gennaro entered, and with them was the manager—a man, if possible, still more polished and urbane. But this time their expressions showed such surprised distaste that he nearly hastened out again. For on the previous occasion he had been in his lavender suit with collar and tie, whereas today he wore only the shabby overalls in which he had been forced to sleep. Hesitantly he crossed the thick carpet and with dirty fingers which shook a little unwrapped the horse. But once it stood, white and bright, savagely handsome rearing from its rosewood pedestal upon the counter, he knew that his physical appearance was no longer of interest to the shopmen. All together they stood in silent admiration of the horse and when the manager put out a hand to lift it he did so with the careful assurance of a connoisseur.

"Hmm. Yes. Well, it's a fine piece, certainly. How much do you want for it?"

In the usual Neapolitan way Gennaro doubled the sum he really required. "Four hundred thousand."

And in the same way the shopman, knowing immediately his bottom price, followed the normal practice and split the difference. "Three hundred thousand?"

"All right."

"I'm afraid that we must have your name and address."

"And I must have a receipt."

"Certainly."

It was all over as quickly as that. Gennaro, with thirty ten-thousand-lire notes in the pockets of his overalls and a stamped receipt in his hand, was out of the shop before he quite realized it. Stopping on the threshold he cast one look back. The white horse, glowing in the light of a great gold and crystal chandelier, stood on the glass showcase counter, pawing the air, tossing its mane. For the first time it was surrounded by other objects worthy to be its companions—ornate and splendid pieces of gold and silverware, jewel-encrusted chalices and salvers, chased and inlaid sixteenth-century armor, collectors' pieces, tamed over years of soft and careful handling, docketed and noted and catalogued. And now all these things would happen to the wild white Tartar horse which until today had known only the shabby precincts of the poor—the Street of the Threshold of the Autumn Moon in Pekin, the Piazza Vittime Civili di Guerra in Naples. And for a moment Gennaro felt that he was parting from a live horse and that it would miss him in its new surroundings of un-accustomed luxury and wealth, mourn for him and pine for his return, reciprocating all those feelings which he would feel for it.

◄§ 8

"THREE hundred thousand—that will do. And you've got five as well."

"I'll need some of that. I've got to buy oranges for—"

"*Basta!* Now listen to me carefully." Domenichelli picked one of the firm's black-edged funeral envelopes from the table. "This is a letter I've written to someone who can arrange a passage for me quickly. You must take this down to Porto—I'll give you directions in a minute. You'll ask for 'Giorgio' and hand this in. Then you'll wait for a reply and bring it back here. Tonight, as soon as it's dark, I'll be able to go. And then—then you've nothing whatever more to do save keep your mouth shut."

But it did not work out like that. When at noon Gennaro returned, weary and hungry from his errand, he was forced to tell Domenichelli of his failure. "He can't do it. I saw him and gave him your letter. Then he made me wait in another room for nearly an hour. When he came back he said it was impossible. He said—he said that it was too dangerous; that they've got plainclothes police all over the docks and that they're looking for you. And he said I was to tell you this, particularly—they know who you are."

For the first time he saw fear pass vividly over Domenichelli's face. The undershot jaw sagged, the taut skin whitened beneath its coating of dirt and stubble. "They know—*that?*" Then with a deep breath, a visible effort at self-control, he asked roughly, "What else? What more did he say?"

"Only that nothing was safe for you this side of Salerno. He said, 'Tell him that he should get much further south—Reggio or even Palermo. He'll be all right then.' "

Domenichelli shook his head with a fierce exasperation. In the heat of early afternoon his grimy blue shirt showed dark lines of sweat and the smell, the hot, feverish, sickly smell which Gennaro had noticed on his arrival, was stronger than ever—permeating the small room like the feral taint of an ill and caged wild animal. "Reggio or Palermo! And how does he imagine . . ." He shrugged his shoulders—or his right one, for the left remained motionless. "Well, I can't leave tonight. That's certain. I'll be here several more days yet. I'll just have to let things cool off."

"But"—Gennaro's voice had something of the wailing entreaty of a disappointed child—"you promised you'd go tonight! How can I hide you for days? People come in here. And anyway" —sudden hope gleamed before him—"we're being evicted tomorrow."

"*What!*" Domenichelli had him by his shirtfront and was shaking him; glaring into his face from wide, trapped eyes. "What's that you said?"

"Tomorrow—we've notice to get out—all of us—out of this house."

And disjointedly, bit by ragged bit, Domenichelli forced from him the story of the sale of the old building, the hopes and fears of the past months, the final demand to quit; everything except the involvement of Renato and Pietrini and their friends—that, Gennaro kept back.

"Then—then why aren't you packing? If this is all true, why aren't you getting ready to go?"

"Because we've nowhere to go to. Yesterday we—I and the others—put in a *domanda* at the Municipio asking to be allowed to stay."

Domenichelli gave an angry snort. "And what good do you think that will do? Against ITOLGAS? *Per l'amor' di Dio!*"

Gennaro swallowed, feeling hope rise again within him. "We're going to make them *put* us out. We're not going voluntarily."

"And they will!" Domenichelli's voice was grim. "They will, all right!" He turned, rasping one hand distractedly across his blackened jaw; breathing deeply.

Gennaro waited a moment, then said hesitantly, "You'd better go—tonight."

But Domenichelli was not listening to him; instead he was staring at the wall, lost in thought. Then slowly a grin widened across his haggard face and he nodded gently. "I'll go—yes. But not tonight. I'll go in"—he paused—"about two hours—perhaps three."

"In the middle of the afternoon? I thought you wanted to wait until dark?"

"Not now." Still grinning, Domenichelli raised himself onto the table. "And I'll tell you why, Gennaro." His manner had entirely changed in the last few seconds, had become almost jocular. Gennaro watched him with a growing sense of foreboding and alarm. "Yes, I'll tell you why—though you already know. It's because you cannot transport bodies at night."

"How?"

"I'll leave Naples in your hearse. In a coffin. Listen carefully. You lost the use of your hearse last May for driving it while under age, didn't you? And the day that happened—the day you were caught—I was in that hearse of yours in that coffin you thought held the old man. . . ." Domenichelli's grin was skull-wide now. "Yes, it's true what I say. You stopped in that clump of bamboos, didn't you? To go swimming. I was there, hiding from the police, and while you were fooling in the sea I got the old man out of the coffin, hid him in a hole and got in the coffin myself. And you took me back to Naples. And then, when the hearse was down below in this place, I got out and found a pair of old overalls and—just walked off! I passed you talking in the old woman's shop down below."

Gennaro whispered, "Yes—yes! I remember now. We—heard a noise. We thought some—some wood or something had fallen down in the workshop. Yes! And then a man passed the shop and—and he had stolen Quong's old overalls. It—was you!"

"It was me."

"But—next day we took the coffin to the family mausoleum—"

"Filled with stones and broken bricks."

"*Oh Dio!*" Numbly Gennaro stared at Domenichelli, perched on the table, swinging his legs, and in a voice hollow with defeat and surrender said, "So I brought you here. And everything that has happened—it's all because of that. And—yes, I remember now—they said at the villa that a prisoner had escaped. The cook told me. And—that was you, too?"

"It was me." Domenichelli rubbed his bristly chin with the muzzle of his ever-present pistol. "Now you know. All right. You brought me here and you can take me out again—the same way."

"I can't! I can't drive the hearse. You know that!"

"I know. But you can hire a driver, can't you? There are plenty of unemployed who can drive and who will take a job at a moment's notice, aren't there? Look—we'll set off with you beside the driver at—say three o'clock. We'll go through Salerno to Battipaglia. There you'll pay off the driver, then you'll take me on yourself. No one knows you out there and the police never stop hearses. I want to get to Agropoli just before dark. I'll leave you there. Then—listen, because I don't want you in the hands of the police for obvious reasons. You'll do this. You'll find somewhere to get rid of that coffin. Somewhere off the road —somewhere safe where it's not likely to be found. Then you'll drive back to Salerno. There you'll stop and find another driver. You can say you've suddenly been taken ill, or sprained a wrist or something. You can get back to Naples that way without any interference. Since the hearse will be empty you won't be breaking the law and no one will stop you even though it will be dark by then. And if they do—well, you've been to Salerno to deliver wreaths—some story like that would do. And so— What's the matter? Why are you looking like that?"

"I—haven't got a coffin. There's no coffin here."

"*Porco Dio!*" Domenichelli's triumphant grin changed to a screwed-up scowl of furious exasperation and he slammed the pistol-butt down on the table. "Well! Well—you can go out and buy one, then!"

"And have it delivered here? In broad daylight with everybody watching and asking who it was for and—"

"No—*no!*"

Gennaro said, "I can make one. I can get the wood on a handcart—bring it in the back way. No one will know."

"How long will it take?"

"That depends. . . . But it won't be ready before dark."

"*Gesù!* Then I'll have to wait twenty-four hours. And—what about tomorrow?"

Gennaro hesitated. He was, he realized, almost as disappointed as Domenichelli at the delay of the plan, for he longed above everything else to be free of this terrible black-faced incubus with its queer stink of the grave. And now he must endure its grisly presence for a further twenty-four hours—an eon of time. But—if Domenichelli was somehow to be driven into going now, and if because of this he fell into the hands of the police . . . Gennaro groaned with frustration; it was clearly almost as much in his interest to achieve Domenichelli's safe escape as it was in that of Domenichelli himself. "Tomorrow may be all right. We have put in our *domanda* and—and we have friends helping us."

Domenichelli grunted dubiously, frowning, staring at the wall. "In any case you could get the hearse away. If you were moving everything else you could put in some tools and spare wood as well, and people seeing the coffin would think that it was an empty one. After all, if you had a spare coffin that is how you'd take it away. . . ." He seemed suddenly to come to a decision. "All right. That is what must be done. Here—how much do you need for wood?"

"Six thousand will cover it."

Domenichelli pulled the bundled notes Gennaro had given him from his pocket and peeled off two five-thousand ones. "Get some food, too. But bring back the change. I'm going to need every lira from now on."

⋅⋐ 9

THE night was black and sultry. In his workshop Gennaro bent over the boards he had bought that afternoon from Savoldi. Though, curiously, he no longer felt tired he was nervously exhausted from the strain of the last twenty-four hours and his hands were unusually clumsy as he planed and shaped the wood. The workshop door was locked and Domenichelli sat in the shadows away from the one, low-powered bulb, watching, saying nothing, as the coffin which tomorrow would take him to safety was slowly fashioned on the scarred old workbench.

Gennaro's original fear of Domenichelli had grown slowly ever greater throughout the day. That the gun would be used in an emergency he did not doubt. That under certain circumstances Quong would be strangled and he himself betrayed to the police was still strongly probable. But there was something more—something which forced him into an unreal dimension of horror so that he stood outside himself, wondering and appalled, staring at a Gennaro he did not know, a physical presence which walked and worked under the somnambulistic compulsion of another's dark will. For tomorrow—what would happen tomorrow evening when the time came for Domenichelli to leave the hearse on the outskirts of Agropoli? Would he think —on that lonely road in the gathering dusk—that Gennaro dead was safer for him than Gennaro alive—as he had thought once before in the Vico Ciego di Pomodori?

The plane hissed up a long, thin shaving of white wood and Gennaro shivered. Yet try as he might he could not dispel the curious numbness, the dull ache in his head, which prevented the formation of any sort of plan for self-preservation. This time tomorrow he might well be dead, with a bullet hole behind his ear and his body stuffed into some country culvert among the stones and weeds. . . .

Spreading the glue, clamping the side-pieces into position,

Gennaro tried without success to free his mind from this new fear. After all, so far things had gone well enough. He had met Renato and learned that tomorrow there would be a full-scale demonstration in the *piazza* and later a march on the Municipio with banners and placards. His own role had not changed; it was still, like those of Crocifissa and Iole, to lock himself in the house and refuse to leave. Renato believed that the *domanda* would be given immediate provisional acceptance. "They can't do anything else. You'll get a stay of another month, or perhaps two. Probably we'll get that when the procession reaches the Municipio. Someone will come out and give it to us—in order to get us to disperse quietly. At least, Pietrini says so. By midday it will all be over. After that it will be a question of agitation in *Unità* and other papers. And of course the stay of eviction can be renewed indefinitely."

Savoldi, too, seemed to know all about it. "So you're fighting them after all are you, Gennà? Good boy! That's what I like to see! And you've got a job on hand, too. Excellent! It will all come right for you yet, I do believe."

But on the way back along the Vico dei Lepri, with his newly bought white planks piled upon the old handcart, Gennaro had doubted it. He lay under a far heavier and darker burden than either Renato or Savoldi could realize. For him, at least, nothing would be over by midday tomorrow; and he might never see the next day's dawn. Evening was falling and over the pantiled roofs, far to the south in the direction of Vesuvius, the sky was dark and low and misty. A sultry, still heat enveloped the cobbled alley over which the handcart jolted with its load; and atmosphere that bore a certain resemblance to the oncome of the *scirocco,* except that the *scirocco* was dead and flat—an empty, lethargic humidity—whereas tonight held the heavy, electric tension of an oncoming storm. Despite what he knew awaited him upstairs—the presence which, on every egress from the house, he must leave alone with the helpless Quong—he had been glad to be home and out of the close and sullen menace of the streets.

And now—the sides and end-pieces were fixed and Gennaro turned his attention to the lid. With bit and brace he cut three airholes in that section which would be directly above Domenichelli's face. And over these he carefully screwed the last of his hollow tin crucifixes, bought two years ago from a Swiss whole-saler. Dully he thought that however many coffinmakers were plying their trade throughout the city on this last, dark, hot night of September, none were constructing a coffin such as this—a coffin for a live man whose watchful eyes gleamed back from a shadowed corner of the same room.

In the Piazza

❧ 1

IT was a menacing sky at dawn: rags and banners of red cloud hung flaring and fading above the echoing streets and lit the faces of early risers with an angry flame; the high shouts of the newsvendors and itinerant hawkers rang out like cries of danger, warnings called forth by that wild light.

October the first, and despite the sultry heat summer was over. The weather must soon break and in a few weeks the long winter rains would be sweeping in dismally from the gray gulf and the humid, lifeless cold, the dank dreariness of the Neapolitan winter would penetrate the stone alleys of the *bassifondi,* seeping into the cavelike depths of *fondachi* where crowded families huddled disconsolately together to cough and spit and quarrel away the desolate days over insufficient food, inferior wine and packs of narrow, dirty playing cards.

The Piazza Vittime Civile di Guerra woke soon after dawn. The cracked bell sounded for early mass from the Annunziata, summoning the usual black-shawled old women to shuffle over its worn marble floor; children wandered in small groups to the baker's at the corner of the Vico dei Lepri to buy *pizze* and bread; workmen on the early shift, sleepy and unshaven, clambered noisily aboard the *filobus* for Poggiareale and Barra; Maresciallo Tenerini rattled up his iron shutter and Gigi whistled shrilly and proudly, filling Baldissera's water bucket at the standpipe among the broken stones beside the stable.

Only Crocifissa's shop, usually so prompt to open for its ear-

liest customers, remained dark and closed behind barred doors.
Quong's Pompe Funebre was also shut, but then it never had
opened early and in recent weeks it had often been difficult to
know whether it was open at all.

And soon the red dawnlight faded from clouds heavy with
unshed rain, and the San Lorenzini went fretfully, a little fearfully, about their daily business, casting quick, uncertain glances
at the strips of threatening sky above the narrow streets and
alleys, wondering when the storm would break and where it
might find them when it did.

Pietrini, entering the *piazza* at nine with a few friends, found
Renato and a dozen young local Communists clustered sulkily
around the urinal, smoking, spitting and kicking their heavy
boots against the concrete curb. They looked bored and dis-
pirited and their first words confirmed this impression. "Have
you seen the posters?"

"Yes." Pietrini's voice was grim. "Why weren't any of you
around at the time?"

For a moment only sullen silence answered him. Then Renato
said, "We didn't put them up until well after two o'clock—and
you told us all to be here early. We need some sleep—like everyone else."

"*Someone* could have been around, surely?"

"How were we to know—?"

Pietrini sighed. "It's been done before—and it will be done
again." He shook his head. "Two hundred posters calling for
popular participation and giving the time we wanted to start
from here—and now every one is covered with an advertise-
ment for ITOLGAS products."

"So what happens now—do we call it off?"

"No, we don't! We've still got the handbills."

"What about the weather?"

Pietrini lifted his face to the lowering sky. "With any luck it
will hold off until noon." He motioned Renato to follow him inside the urinal and there, in the acrid half-light, asked softly,
"The tenants—they're still all right?"

Renato nodded a little dubiously. "Yes. Crocifissa spends her
time saying that it's all foolishness and all wrong and can't
work. She was on about that for hours to my wife last night.
But she's going to do what we've told her. Of course it's the

Signora who keeps her to it. She was out with us putting up the posters last night." Renato, recalling that the posters were a sore point, hurriedly changed the subject. "I'm not sure about Gennaro—"

"What—young Ferrara?" Pietrini's voice was surprised. "He seemed enthusiastic enough earlier."

"Not now. He hasn't said anything against the scheme but he seems to have lost interest. I think his grandfather's got worse again. And he's been out a lot."

"Looking for another place, you mean?"

"Probably. One can't blame him. But he's still here and so I suppose he hasn't found one."

Pietrini shrugged uneasily. "The sooner we get started the better, then."

But before he left the urinal Renato caught his arm and swung him around. "Listen—about those posters. Someone's going to do something."

"De Santis, you mean?"

"I don't know. Only"—Renato's voice was perplexed, a little frightened—"it's not going to be like we thought—like we hoped."

But Pietrini shrugged him off brusquely. "I don't know what you thought or what you hoped."

The demonstration was not a success. Pietrini's handbills, scattered throughout the Porta Capuana and the Piazza San Francesco, thrust into the hands of every passerby at the corners of the Abate and the steps of the local churches, brought hardly more than a hundred unemployed loafers into the *piazza* by eleven o'clock. The threatening weather was largely to blame for this inadequate response but also, and to a greater degree, the lack of all opposition, of any sign or move to put into practice the eviction of the people who lived in that unprepossessing ruin of a building on the west side of the square.

Even Pietrini's oratory had less effect than usual, doubling but not quadrupling his audience, and failing to raise them from their taciturn lethargy. Pietrini was angry but unsurprised. He understood as well as anyone the mercurial element in the Neapolitan group personality. For reasons far too vague and irrational to be properly termed reasons, that fiery spirit of the city which could flame as fiercely as Vesuvius could also sink into a miasma of morose indifference, as stagnant and dull as an oil-filled puddle. Yet like a puddle of oil it could be set alight if the right incendiary material was at hand and no extinguisher available.

If only a demolition truck and a few officious police officers had appeared while he was speaking; if only the gloomy, threatening weather had not replaced the ordinary bright, sun-filled sky. . . . In the end they marched, behind their banners, to the Municipio. Barely a hundred started out from the *piazza* and less than sixty were in the ranks when, guided by a couple of bored municipal policemen, they arrived. They were kept waiting twenty minutes—too short a time to erect their folding podium and make any significant speeches yet long enough to become bored and irritable. And the answer, when it came at last, was a blunt "no." Flatly, finally, the Municipio stated that the *domanda* was refused. They gave no reasons that might be torn to public shreds; they made no equivocations that might be held up, jeered at and exposed for timid vacillation—they said "no" and refused to discuss the matter.

Under other, more favorable, circumstances such a refusal might not have been unwelcome to Pietrini and his friends, who could have made good capital out of it. But today's circumstances were not favorable; the municipal authorities, far from being defeated, had inflicted a defeat upon their enemies. That at least was how Renato saw it. He turned at once to Pietrini almost, it seemed, with a certain hangdog relief. "Well—we did all we could. Now I'll just have to tell them—that's all."

"Tell who what?"

Renato stared at him. "Why—Crocifissa and the other two. Tell them that we can't help them; that they'll have to go. I expect they'll be given an extra twenty-four hours if—"

Pietrini put a hand on Renato's broad chest and fingered his scarlet hammer-and-sickle badge. "You want to go on wearing this?"

"Of course!"

"Then do as I say—instead of telling *me* what to do. We are not finished yet, by any means."

"But—"

"We'll go back to the *piazza* and wait." He shot a malign

look up at the office windows above them. "They've waited for us. Very well—we'll wait for them."

There were hardly thirty following the red banners by the time they regained the *piazza* with but one sardonic policeman accompanying them—shepherding them like schoolchildren over busy crossroads, leading them with amused condescension along the gutters of the main thoroughfares, scorning to keep them from the indifferent eyes of the hurrying public by taking them on a detour through the quieter streets. Yet this treatment, which reduced Renato and his younger colleagues to sullen, red-faced mortification, had no discernible effect on Pietrini. He even chatted amicably with the policeman and offered him cigarettes. Then, turning unperturbed to his morose followers, he said gently, "Just wait—it will happen. Nothing's happened yet—but it will."

Their return to the *piazza* was as anticlimactic as their departure. Crocifissa had defiantly opened her shop and the attention of the usual loafers was entirely diverted by Gigi who, on the pretext of exercising Baldissera, was riding the old horse bareback around the urinal to the clamorous delight and envy of the other local children. Few noticed the dejected little procession which wended its way under its red banners from the mouth of the Via Buonuomini. Yet it had hardly crossed the square when a small orange van passed it—a van bearing in yellow letters the name ITOLGAS across its sides—and pulled up before the shop in the crumbling façade of the old building.

Automatically Renato hastened his step but Pietrini caught him by the arm and with a raised hand halted his other followers. "Wait. There is no hurry."

Urgently Renato said, "I ought to be there. I started all this. I can't just stand aside now—"

"Wait! Let them talk. We can find out what they have said later." Pietrini's quick eyes had seen Iole Giansante in the shop and he guessed correctly that it would be she, rather than Crocifissa, who would answer the two ITOLGAS officials whom the van had brought. He also guessed what that answer would be and when, barely a couple of minutes after their arrival, the two men, unsmiling and angry, left the shop and climbed back into their van, he turned to Renato. "It will start now," he said calmly. "Now or soon. If only it doesn't rain first."

◆§ 2

". . . if only it rains first." Commendatore De Santis strolled to one of the great plate-glass windows of his seventh-story office in the Poggioreale works, then turned back to the three men—his secretary, an assistant manager and a visiting director from Milan—sitting beside his desk. "That's what we are really waiting for. But we cannot wait indefinitely, I fear."

"If you were a modern American," remarked the visiting director dryly, "you could send an airplane over to—what do they call it?—to seed the clouds."

"Of if," answered De Santis mildly, "I was an ancient Roman I could make a sacrifice to Jupiter Pluvius. However, neither method would seem satisfactory today. It either rains or it doesn't. Since we're Italians we should be fatalists."

The director chuckled. "So? You're becoming a Neapolitan, my friend."

"Oh yes." De Santis nodded his handsome white head. "Quite possibly I am. I've had some very illuminating experiences while I've been here—and met some most extraordinary people! I like the Neapolitans—much more than I like their city."

"Not all of them, I hope."

"Our Signor Pietrini, you mean? An excellent man. Prompt. Reliable. Efficient. You would never take him for a Neapolitan. He's exactly like a northerner. Yes indeed, I have the warmest feelings toward Pietrini."

De Santis's secretary smiled approvingly in his turn. "We are thinking of giving him a somewhat better position soon, are we not, Commendatore?"

"Yes indeed."

"I don't understand!" The Milanese director's face was flushed with irritation. "I know you've got all these new theories, De Santis, but I'd like to see the old blacklist method used here. And it would work. These people have the mentality of slaves; it's only a question of removing their ringleaders."

The Commendatore laughed silently and thrust his hands deep into his trouser pockets. "My theories, as you call them, are not new at all; basically they are as old as history itself. As for slaves—you have undoubtedly failed to notice the most interesting thing about slaves, which is that they never really want freedom—what they crave above all else is dominion over other slaves of their own. And you're wrong about the Neapolitans, too. They are, in reality, much less slavish than our Milanese workers. They can appear more servile than anyone else when it happens to suit their ends, but when it comes to accepting modern slavery—becoming reliable, punctual cogs in an industrial machine—they don't take to it at all kindly, I can assure you. I'm doing all I'm able to make them into satisfactory slaves, though. And I think I'm succeeding."

"You're getting astonishingly good results from the point of view of labor relations, certainly. But I don't know why you have to talk of slaves."

"It was you who used the term first, not myself. But it is applicable enough in any case. Don't we go about recruiting our workers in the way a shrewd Roman would have purchased slaves two thousand years ago? The only difference is that when a potential worker comes to us he comes to sell himself—not to be sold by another. But in every other respect . . . he's got to be young; he's got to be strong; he's got to pass a fairly severe physical examination and various psychotechnical tests designed to find out his capacities. What is that but the modern equivalent of the running and jumping and lifting of weights and so forth which went on in the ancient markets when slaves were tested out by possible buyers?

"And if we decide to buy him—our prospective slave—how do we do it? We simply offer him security in exchange for his freedom. Fifty, even twenty, years ago this process was hardly understood. A man was taken on with no prior examination and offered only the minimum wages he would accept to perform a certain job—a job which seldom had any security of tenure at all. He might be dismissed at any moment for any or no reason —which of course meant equally that he might walk out at any moment for any or no reason. A thoroughly inefficient system which would never do today. It would mean permanent chaos in a plant such as this.

"No—when, after our examinations and tests, we take on a worker we are, in reality, buying a slave. You can't do that with a weekly pay envelope alone." De Santis paused, flexed his knees like an old-fashioned cavalryman and continued. "Security—that is the basic answer, of course. That is what modern man wants today above all else—or is taught to believe he wants. We offer security in exchange for freedom. And the more security we offer, the more freedom we expect to be laid down. We give our worker security against everything—against every sort of misfortune. We will care for him and his family with all the solicitude which a good slave-owner would show to a good slave—and for exactly the same reason; we have a valuable investment to protect. And we do protect it—for it is ours.

"For example, take a man of, say, twenty-five who has been with us for five years. Let us assume that his record is of the best. That not only is he a diligent and punctual worker but that he has shown the correct willingness to identify with the firm—has joined sufficient of our clubs and sports teams and discussion groups and so forth. We may assume too—though of course this cannot always, regrettably, be the case—that he has married one of our female staff of equal industry and fidelity—an ITALGIRL as I intend they shall shortly be known. Our worker will have been given an apartment at ITALVILLAGGIO at a very low rent. He will have been given a marriage grant on long-term interest. His children will have been born in our clinic and—well, well, you know the rest. . . . But how, my friend, can you call such a man free? He cannot leave us without losing infinitely more than his weekly pay envelope—without losing his home, his furniture, his car—all of which are still ours and will remain so for years. And that is by no means all, for he would lose many sorts of insurance against many forms of misfortune as well as a considerable quantity of money placed in our various pension funds and so forth.

"In theory he is as free as you or I. In practice he is as much a slave as any eighteenth-century Negro on a cotton plantation. For, after all, slavery does not necessarily mean whips and chains. It means, quite simply, the removal of freedom—freedom to choose to alter, if one so wishes, one's way of life. Pietrini understands that. He's a Communist; consequently he realizes that freedom, at least for the masses, is neither important nor desirable—not to be compared with security or material well-being."

De Santis paused again meditatively. "I'll tell you something.

X   A few months ago I decided to make a small psychological experiment of my own in order to ascertain how far our Neapolitans were progressing along the lines I have laid down. I did something which even in Milan has never been attempted. I issued an instruction that some form of sport was in future to be compulsory for all our workers under twenty-five years old. That for one hour a week *after* work they must either play football on our playing-fields or ride bicycles on our tracks or indulge in some such thing—for health reasons, I said. I awaited their reactions with interest. Several immediately complained. I called a committee of workers, including Pietrini, to discuss the matter and Pietrini easily won them all over to acceptance of the order. Of course he has his own reasons. He believes that the more disciplined and obedient our workers become the more easily he will be able to take them over to Communism. But"—Commendatore De Santis turned once more to the window—"I happen to have decided to take over Pietrini and some of his friends first."

"But this present business?"

"Oh, this affair in San Lorenzo. That's nothing. Merely what American college authorities term an 'extramural activity.' Pietrini's not trying to harm *us*—please remember that. As far as he's concerned it is entirely political."

"Even so—"

"And I shall win in any case." The Commendatore smiled to himself. "I won the first trick at four o'clock this morning. The only question now is when it will rain. And that is more important than it might appear. We can't allow ourselves to be balked —obviously. But we do not want the sort of demonstration which might harm our otherwise very satisfactory public image. These people in the building we now own—we've got to try to remove them without too much publicity or fuss. If there is a large public demonstration against it—well, our task could, under certain circumstances, become so difficult as to be no longer worthwhile. One can sacrifice too much, even for a valuable central site for a new gas station—at least I think so. But when it rains as heavily as it very soon will, there can be no possibility of a successful demonstration from Neapolitans. Like cats they have an intense dislike of water. We'll have those people in the building all out and the place empty before the sun appears again."

The Milanese director had been becoming more and more obviously impatient as De Santis had talked. Now he glanced at his watch and said curtly, "Commendatore, it is almost one o'clock. I must tell you that Head Office refuses to tolerate a twenty-four-hour delay. I'm interested in your theories, of course, and we all admire the good work you've done here. But the fact is that the firm's too big to have its schedule adjusted to—to—"

"To suit my theories?"

"Well—yes. Yes, if you put it like that."

"So?"

"So I'm afraid that rain or no rain, I must insist, as a deputy from Headquarters, that the business is dealt with today— and the sooner the better. Don't think that we in Milan do not see this as a test case—we do. But that's just why we're determined to win it."

"The hard way, if necessary?"

"The hard way if necessary—yes."

The Commendatore smiled. "How very Milanese!" He walked over to the telephone. "Very well. How long will you give me?"

"The place must be completely vacated and at least some symbolic demolition performed by nightfall. Let us be precise and say six P.M."

~§ 3

MARESCIALLO Valdemarin sat tieless and sweating at his desk before a small electric fan whose rubber blades whirred like an imprisoned blowfly barely a meter from his damp face. No replacement had as yet been sent to take the position of Lieutenant Giacobelli and Valdemarin was running the Homicide Squad entirely by himself. It was very pleasant to order things in his own way and without interference from above, but it meant more work.

It was because of this, because of the afternoon heat and because the fan had several times disorganized his papers and blown some of them to the floor, that the Maresciallo did not come across Fabrizi's summary of secondary evidence on the Mergellina restaurant shooting until he was about to go home for a late lunch at half past two. Even when he saw what it was, he was of two minds whether to read it now or leave it until his return to the office at five or six that evening. But in the end he read it. D'Ambri was still at large and though summaries of secondary evidence—the ideas and remarks and hallucinations of persons who had not actually witnessed the murder but had been on or about the premises at the time—were most unlikely to be of much value in a case where the identity of the killer was no longer in doubt, Valdemarin's personal preoccupation with every aspect of the affair overcame his tiredness, his irritable discomfort and his perennial anxiety to get home to Nicola.

So he drank a little of the water which an hour ago had been iced but was now almost lukewarm, and spreading the summary over his blotter and holding it down against the fan's draft, ran his eye quickly over the various inconsequential garrulities common to those who have, to their chagrin, missed seeing a murder committed at close quarters. . . .

"I had been down in the service quarters to acquire clean tablecloths from the head of the linen-room staff, Maria Zampichelli (born March 14th 1911 at San Giovanni to Giacomo Zampichelli and Assunta Buccino) when I heard a noise of shouts and running feet from above . . ."—"I was coming up the service stairs with a tray containing three plates of *lasagne al forno,* one of *risotto di frutta di mare* and two of *gnocchi Napolitani,* when I heard what appeared to be a motorcycle backfiring rapidly some distance to my right . . ." The Maresciallo skimmed rapidly on through page after page of neatly typed, self-important vapidities, letting the sentences reel out across his mind like ribbon from a tape recorder.

And then, suddenly, the recorder halted abruptly; the ribbon —motionless now—showing only the one name staring up at him—"Gennaro Gualtierra." Where had that name . . . *Giacobelli falling from the ladder . . . "San Gennaro aiutemi!" . . . a bit of ribbon and palm-leaf . . . the killing in the Vicolo Ciego di Pomodori in August . . . Gualtierra.* Carefully the Maresciallo went back several lines and began again: "I, Giona Cesarini, born December 8th 1941 at Portici to Antonio Cesarini, laborer, and his wife Silvia (Esposito), a *guattero* in the employ of the restaurant O Sole Mio . . . seen the man known as Duilio Domenichelli on several occasions . . . in the kitchen . . . to Signor Fonseca, the head cook under whom I worked as a grill-stoker. . . . Domenichelli was often about the premises late at night. I remember that the last time I saw him was on the evening of July 20th when he swore at me because a sack of charcoal I was carrying happened to brush against his suit. I remember the date exactly because the next morning a *guattero* named Gennaro Gualtierra failed to report for work and I had to undertake some of his duties until another was found. . . ."

July the 20th. That was the date after which it was generally agreed that D'Ambri had left his garbage-contracting due, probably, to some sort of quarrel with Kovas. July the 20th. And Gualtierra had left, apparently, on the same date. Valdemarin sat back in his chair and gazed up at the ceiling. There were, as he well knew, quantities of other possible explanations and there was much that was obscure and not a little that was contradictory, but—but there was a possibility—and even as he thought the word it changed to "probability"—that D'Ambri had been involved in the killing of the night patrolman in the Vico Ciego di Pomodori off the Via Savarese. Gualtierra was the link. But he himself had always considered Gualtierra innocent—or had he? Giacobelli had not thought so. And Gualtierra himself? That heavy, grazed bruise across his back which could have been caused by that shutter falling on him. . . . But Gualtierra —could he have held up that shutter at all? Perhaps . . . And if so—*if* so—D'Ambri could have been the man with the gun, the man who had collected those motor horns. And D'Ambri would shoot without scruple if surprised by a policeman. If D'Ambri had known Gualtierra in the restaurant . . . If, for some reason, they had left together . . .

Well, the police possessed the bullet that had killed the patrolman and the bullets which had killed Kovas. As soon as they were checked against each other by a ballistics expert it would be known if they had been fired from the same gun. That would be the first and most important test to make. Then, suddenly, the Maresciallo quivered all over like a huge jelly. It had been said in the evidence of those who had seen D'Ambri on the night of the Mergellina murder that his left hand was in his pocket and that he carried his left arm close to his body *"as if it had been recently hurt"*—one of the witnesses had added that. And that blood in the abandoned "Ape" out beyond Campi Flegrei—

that blood had been mainly on the *left* handlebar and on the left side of the seatback. So the patrolman's bullet had found its mark somewhere in D'Ambri's left arm or shoulder.

The Maresciallo, aware that he was now sweating intensely, drank the rest of his water and began methodically to go over the facts, as opposed to the suppositions, that might or might not support his new hypothesis. These were few and uncertain and must all be checked. First the bullets. Then the check to find out whether the Gennaro Gualtierra who had worked for the O Sole Mio last July was the same person as the young undertaker with the Chinese grandfather in San Lorenzo. And there was the riddle of the ITOLGAS envelope, too. The Maresciallo pressed his bell and sent for Calvanese.

❧ 4

SOME two and a half hours later Valdemarin was still in his office and still without his lunch, though a couple of empty beer bottles stood on his desk among the piled papers. He was engaged, for want of anything else to do, in upbraiding his assistant, who stood unhappily near the window, wishing that the heavy storm clouds piling up over the city in billowing masses of indigo and sulphur-tinged black would break in sheets of lightning and cannons of thunder and drown that sullen grumbling voice from behind the littered desk. ". . . had I not chanced to see it. What use do you suppose you and Fabrizi and the others are to me if you can't remember names or take in anything you read? One might just as well have evidence taken by a brainless tape-recording machine."

"But, Signor Maresciallo, you yourself did not believe Gualtierra to be in any way guilty, so—"

"So you didn't, either? It was much easier not to trouble your head over thinking for yourself so long as the *capo* was content, eh? In that case one wonders why you did not agree with Lieutenant Giacobelli. He was senior to me, after all."

"Well"—Calvanese looked down at his shoes—"he didn't seem to have a reasonable case to agree *with, signore*."

"But he was right, apparently, nonetheless." The Maresciallo's voice was grim. "The bullets match. The patrolman's description of his assassin fits D'Ambri. D'Ambri has almost certainly had—and doubtless still has—a bullet in his left arm. He would not dare go to a doctor so he's probably been trying to treat himself. The Gualtierra who worked in the O Sole Mio is the same boy we pulled in over that business. D'Ambri knew Gualtierra from the time they worked together in the restaurant." He paused. "The thing I find it most difficult to understand—or to overlook—is the way Fabrizi bungled his original investigation at the ITOLGAS plant. They told him that no one named Gualtierra had worked there, and he accepted their word—their *official* word! In Naples! And Fabrizi's a Neapolitan himself!"

Calvanese swallowed; he was Fabrizi's immediate superior and an attack on Fabrizi was an attack on himself—as, he realized, it was intended to be. "Since Commendatore De Santis has taken over, a whole new set of employment regulations has been put into operation. Only after medical examinations and psychological tests are workers taken on, and as all these are carefully recorded and as Gualtierra's name was not—"

"*Oh, per l'amor' di Dio,* Calvanese! What you're talking about are the *official* employment regulations! Fabrizi must have known perfectly well that there would be unofficial ways of being taken on. There are official and unofficial ways of doing everything in this city—you know that! If you want a job in ITOLGAS you still have to get it in the old way, whatever may be ruled by managing directors from Milan. You buy yourself in—buy yourself the right to take the new examinations, that's all. And before you do that you probably have a day's tryout to see if you and your future workmates are going to get on. Fabrizi merely accepted a simple statement from an office of clerks when, with a little more pressure, a little more patience, he could have done what you have just done and found out the truth."

"Signor Maresciallo, I went there this afternoon on your instructions to check on *D'Ambri's* possible employment." Calvanese's voice held a slightly timid resentment. "It was I myself who decided to recheck on Gualtierra while I was there. Consequently we now know that D'Ambri never worked for ITOLGAS but that Gualtierra was on a one-day trial—a system which, as you say, is unofficial but still apparently continues. In justice to Fabrizi I think I must say that he did not entirely accept the official negative to his inquiries, but he was side-tracked by the gate-keeper, Trulli. Today Trulli became alarmed and admitted that Gualtierra had been there. He pretended that he had forgotten this when approached earlier by Fabrizi. I indicated very plainly what happens to people who willfully mislead the police during their investigations—and he certainly won't do it again. The fact is, as he admitted, that he cheated Gualtierra out of his proper wages that day because Gualtierra had lied about his age. We now know that Gualtierra received five hundred lire in an ITOLGAS envelope but that Trulli, for obvious reasons, did not put it through the serial-stamper."

Valdemarin nodded gloomily. "Nothing goes right in this case. I'm as certain as you are that the piece of envelope we found was Gualtierra's pay envelope. But without a serial number we can never use it as evidence."

He pulled the fan closer toward him so that it blew directly on his face. Three sheets of paper lifted from the desk and fluttered to the floor from which Calvanese retrieved them. Valdemarin said slowly, "We have no more evidence—concrete evidence for use in court—against Gualtierra than we have ever had. You realize that, I suppose?"

"Yes. But perhaps we can find it."

"La Gobba?" The Maresciallo's great head nodded ponderously. "Yes, perhaps. Certainly Gualtierra was the one she saw. But we can't use her in court. It would be ridiculous—farcical. Or rather, we can only do so if Gualtierra confesses first, or in the most unlikely event of taking D'Ambri alive—which," added the Maresciallo slowly, "I do not want to do." He paused. "Turn on the light, Calvanese. It's getting dark. . . . No, but we can, if necessary, use La Gobba in place of that regrettable water experiment which our unfortunate Giacobelli used so disastrously last time. I can pull in Gualtierra, frighten him badly, threaten him with the water again and then suddenly confront him with La Gobba. He will probably confess after that. And then I'll make a deal with him. He can go completely free in exchange for telling us where D'Ambri is hiding. I'm not"—the Maresciallo shrugged his huge shoulders—"interested in Gualtierra anyway—except as a source of information concerning D'Ambri's whereabouts."

"*If* he knows." Calvanese's voice was dubious.

"He knows. D'Ambri has no one else to turn to since he killed Kovas. I think it very probable that D'Ambri's hiding out in Gualtierra's place. But if we've found nothing when we've searched it . . ." And then with a glance at his watch Valdemarin lumbered to his feet. "Why, in the name of God, does it take Fabrizi so long to get a warrant from the Procuratore's office? I gave him a special letter. I suppose"—the grumbling voice was heavy with sarcasm—"that's just one *more* thing I can't leave to my subordinates, eh? I've got to be my own office-boy and messenger too, it seems. Very well . . . Calvanese, my coat! I'll go around myself and explain things. I'll say 'Signor Procuratore, I apologize for troubling you, but since all my staff have become cretinous recently, and until I can replace them all—which I have every intention of doing at the earliest possible moment—it seems I must do even the simplest—' "

But from the window Calvanese hurriedly cut him short. "Here he is, *signore!* Fabrizi's just come back. He's getting out of the car. We can go now."

◄§ 5

FOR Crocifissa Buonafede that afternoon of the first of October was, in a sense, the last of her life. She was to live for a few years more, but to live only in the twilight world of the very old, the very worn—the world of those who have already surrendered to Death but, like the soldiers in a mass capitulation, must await their turn and their conqueror's convenience before being marched away into the oblivion of captivity.

As an Italian woman and a realist, surrender had seemed to her the best policy on so many previous occasions; surrender and resignation and a laying of one's personal subjugation at the feet of God. Fate was not something one fought with one's own weak weapons; it was something one deplored, requested the saints to mitigate, but ultimately accepted.

She had never wished to fight the eviction order in the first place. Not only her principles but her common sense had told her that it was wrong to do so. Like all Italians she had the greatest respect for personal property and, like the majority of

her generation born before the turn of the century, she revere[
those who were able to acquire much of it. But the poor had no
rights, and it was therefore seemly that they should demonstrate
qualities of submission and patience and industry. By so doing
some of them—the lucky ones—might improve their position
and in due course join the ranks of the affluent. She could not
comprehend the Communist theories propounded increasingly
among the younger generation of workers even though she could
understand, very well indeed, the workers themselves.

And because of this she realized something that so often
baffled others, particularly foreigners—the inexplicable and
long-lasting passion of a violently individualistic and undisci-
plined nation for an ideology based on the most rigid regimen-
tation, the sternest order. It was not, whatever its leaders might
say, a purely idealistic struggle to raise the poor, heal the sick
and comfort the old and lonely. . . . It was certainly not a desire to improve the national weal by modern centralization and
an efficient bureaucracy. It was an entirely destructive idea
based, not so much on malice or hatred, as upon the hurt vanity
and wounded self-esteem of a very large minority of Italian
men—naturally predatory men whose conception of worldly
success had a sexual implication quite unknown in other civilized
countries; with the corollary that worldly failure was at once
a sexual deprivation and a stain upon their vaunted and cherished virility.

Once, on an occasion when a long, low, gleaming sports car
had mistakenly strayed into the *piazza,* its owner had stopped
outside her shop to ask the way to the Corso and had been
quickly and politely directed by Renato Paolantonio. But as
the beautiful car had swept off into the Via Buonuomini, Crocifissa had seen the look of hungry frustration on Renato's face,
had heard him mutter, *"Dio!* With a car like that one could have
the Queen of England." Communism, even Renato could guess,
would not give him a sports car—but it would prevent others
from having them and thus bruising his self-respect with their
implications of a potency beyond his reach. All Italian women
knew what Crocifissa knew—which was why none of them were
Communists.

Crocifissa would never have agreed with this Signor Pietrini's
idea of resistance, not merely to Fate, but to the forces of social

law and order, had it not been for Gennaro. In the last few days she had tried determinedly to prise her mind away from a future without her substitute-son; the child who, five-and-a-half-years ago, had arrived to fill the void left by Dino. But it had been a painful and exhausting effort and as soon as Gennaro's own hopes had been raised by Renato and his friend she knew, try as she would to struggle against it, that her own were joined to them. Even so, the whole scheme seemed so wrong-headed and unlikely that only the determination of Iole Giansante, an educated and clever young woman, had eventually brought her into reluctant cooperation with the others.

As the hot, still morning wore on under its continually darkening sky and the demonstrators behind their banners had marched off to the Municipio, she had become more and more upset and flustered and frightened. In the end, merely to calm herself with a semblance of normal life, she had opened her shop and set Gigi to work, dusting and cleaning and rearranging the stock, until he had pleaded that his new duties as groom to Baldissera made it necessary for him to take the old horse out of its dark stable for half an hour.

And then—the ITOLGAS car had come with those two stern, angry men. "You realize that you are trespassing? That you're breaking the law? You're committing a serious offense, Signora Buonafede. We have given you ample notice to move out and you have done nothing."

Crocifissa had opened her mouth to reply and then shut it again. She had no words. The men before her were quite right. And then Iole Giansante had spoken. "We have not gone because we have nowhere to go. We have put in a *domanda* to the Municipio to halt the eviction. Until that is answered you have no right—"

But at that point the older and bigger of the men had interrupted. "Signora Buonafede is—or rather, was—the tenant-in-chief here. It is to her we speak. *Signora,* you must make arrangements to leave now. At once. If you do not, then you will be forcefully evicted. We have tried to avoid that solution, but you force our hands." Iole Giansante had begun to speak again but neither of the men took any notice of her. They had climbed quickly back into their van and driven away.

And then—then Renato and his friends had come across

the square and there had been interminable talk, argumentative and contradictory, indignant and repetitious, until the group around the shop had grown to almost the proportions of a large meeting, and one in which everyone seemed to be speaking at once and at the top of his voice. That swelling volume of noise had washed over Crocifissa like a wild sea, buffeting her and battering her with its breakers of sound. Red-faced, shrugging, lifting her hands in gestures of hopeless incomprehension, she had retreated further into her shop, and eventually into the small kitchen behind, to sit down in her old armchair, gather Otello into her lap and stroking him with trembling hands, to gaze upward at the shining picture of Dino.

It was thus that Gennaro found her more than an hour later. A pale-faced, dark-eyed Gennaro, his shirt stained with sweat, his jeans dusty and smeared with new varnish. "Crocifissa. I— I don't think it's going to be any good. Renato told me just now that the *domanda* has been refused. Pietrini says that they can't just refuse it in that way and that we can put in another to the Tribunale. But"—his hands opened in despair and fell to his sides—"I don't think it will work now." He paused and Crocifissa saw the strain apparent on his face. "But that's not what I've come for. Listen—I've got to take the hearse out and go somewhere. And I—"

But Crocifissa stared at him uncomprehendingly, and from outside, the shouts of the crowd seemed loud with menace. "But you can't! You have no license! And where would you want to go? And now, of all times! Gennarino, I knew this plan would not work. I tried to hope so for your sake. I tried to believe in it and I thought—I thought that Signora Giansante *must* know best. But inside me—in my heart—I never believed. . . ."

Gennaro wiped a hand across his mouth. "They're going to try to do something—I don't know what. Pietrini says he'll see we are all right if only we'll shut ourselves in and not come out. But—but I *can't* do that. I have to go now. And there's Quong—"

"But, Gennaro, I . . ."

Gennaro knelt down suddenly beside the old armchair and grasping Crocifissa's arm, stared up into her face. It was something he had not done for two or three years although it had been a common enough posture when he was still a little boy newly from Ferrara and wanting to ask questions or to confide in her. Absently, as she had done so often in the past, the old woman put out a trembling hand and stroked his springy black hair. But— "Listen, Crocifissa. I have to go. I *must*. I can't tell you why now. I haven't time and—and it's too difficult to explain. I'm not going to drive the hearse myself, of course. I'm going around now to the Porta Capuana to find someone to do it. But I will have to go with it, all the same. I'll be back tonight. I'll only be gone four or five hours I think. I want to get Quong down here and leave him with you in case anything—" He stopped abruptly and raised his head, his eyes widening, flaring with quick panic. And then Crocifissa heard it, too—the wailing lift-and-fall, growing louder, higher, shriller, of approaching police sirens.

✺ 6

THE shop's metal shutter was up and the long iron hook with which it could be unclipped and drawn down had somehow disappeared so that what, in Pietrini's plan, should have been a fortress lay open with its portcullis raised and therefore fell at once to the enemy.

These were twelve members of the Vigili Urbani, the Municipality's own city police, who roared into the square on their big red motorcycles with their sirens shrieking like banshees. They escorted a demolition truck carrying half a dozen workmen and —symbol of the power and prestige of the building's new owners—a great yellow ITOLGAS tanker.

Pietrini and Renato and two or three others were desperately trying to hook down the shop's shutter with sticks when the motorcycle cortège drew up at the curb and they were at once pushed aside by a Brigadiere and four uniformed policemen. "*Basta!* Out of here, all of you! Quick—if you don't want to spend tonight in the lock-up!"

Then they were inside the shop and brushing past the cans and bottles and boxes to enter Crocifissa's kitchen. "Signora Buonafede? And you, boy—who are you?"

"Quong's," said Gennaro unsteadily, licking his lips.

"All right." The Brigadiere grinned and drew the sleeve of

his white tunic across his hot face. "Well, I'm afraid it's no good. You've got to go—all of you. I'll read the eviction notice to you, although it has already been done by the new owners, I believe. And then we have orders to put you out. If you'll leave quietly and help us, your things will be safe enough. But if you make trouble I expect they'll get damaged and there will not be any redress—*capisce?*"

Gennaro said quickly, "You don't need to read the order. We'll go, Signor Brigadiere. We won't make any trouble— *veramente*" and felt Crocifissa squeeze his hand in agreement, perhaps in gratitude.

The police officer nodded contentedly. "Good. Then everything will be all right. They told us that there would probably be trouble, but if there is not it will be very much better for all concerned. We'll help you get your things outside and I'll put two men to guard them until you can get them away." He paused, smiling a little ruefully. "You know, it would have been much better if you'd gone when you were told to."

Then suddenly Iole was in the kitchen. She pushed past the policemen and seized Crocifissa's other hand; her face was white and miserable, her cheeks marked with tears. "Oh Crocifissa, you were right after all! It's no good. We'll have to go. I thought perhaps . . . But you were right and I was wrong. I've helped to get you into this trouble, too!"

Crocifissa's plump shoulders rose and she gave a small distracted smile. "You did what you could, *signora*. You were trying to help us, I know. You only did it for the best—"

And now the Brigadiere cut in soothingly. "There is no trouble, *signora*. No one is in trouble with us. And if Signora Buonafede and her—her friends will help us move their furniture and possessions outside there will be no trouble for anyone, I assure you."

Iole nodded. "I'll help. I'll do all I can" and, as the Brigadiere looked dubiously at her swollen body, "I can carry out light things and show you where to put them." Suddenly she turned to Gennaro. "What about Quong?"

"He's upstairs."

"We must get him down. Where can he——? I know! Gennaro, tell Gigi to take the *carròzza* out. He knows how to harness the horse, I've seen him do it. We can put Quong in the *carròzza* with

the hood up and then take him to the gateway beyond the
Annunziata. He can stay there with Gigi until—until we know
what we're going to do." She turned back to the police officer.
"There is an ill old man upstairs. He can hardly move at all.
We'll have to get him out first."

"Certainly, *signora*—just as you say. So long as there's no
trouble we'll do all we can to help."

But there was going to be trouble. Its threat had hung about
the *piazza,* indefinable yet ominous, since the wild red dawn. It
had drifted in little gusts of excitement and fear and hate up and
down the dark alleyways and tiny cobbled courts of the neigh-
borhood where children and loiterers and unemployed loafers
all sensed it and spoke of it; some openly, some allusively, some
only with a cocked eyebrow or the pulled-down corner of a
mouth. The long summer of rising prices and growing unem-
ployment, followed by the unusual heat of the last weeks, had
rasped and inflamed the prickly nerves of the San Lorenzini, leaving them with that sense of exasperated frustration which from
time immemorial had found its vent and its release in sudden
furious bursts of irrational violence. There were plenty of people
looking for trouble in San Lorenzo and the Forcella; mostly
young men and boys, *disoccupati*—penniless, bored, resentful
at a world which ignored them and left them to lounge, shirts
open to the waist, against grimy walls, fingering the crotches of
their tight jeans hungrily every time a woman passed.

They wanted trouble, not for its own sake or even from a
political motive, but to work off their nervous frustration, their
stifled emotions and self-pitying resentment, in a bout of furious
action. Pietrini's handbills had attracted some to the Piazza
Vittime Civili di Guerra that morning and though most of
them had trailed disappointedly away by early afternoon, the
arrival of the police cortège, gratuitously advertised by the
screaming sirens, had brought them running back, swarming
from the surrounding *bassi* and out of the *fondachi* like ants
who scent their food from afar and hurry instinctively toward it.

It started entirely spontaneously, without further prompting
from Pietrini or his colleagues, as Quong, tiny and impassive in
the old *carròzza,* rattled over to the shelter of the Annunziata
archway and the first policeman emerged from Crocifissa's shop
carrying her old armchair. A shout, a few undecided boos and

catcalls greeted him, and the quickly swelling crowd about the house heaved in a sudden angry wave. Then the next policeman came out with a bundle of blankets and an enamel jug. As he bent to deposit these on the cobbles a stone shot over his head and cracked viciously against the wall behind him. It was followed by another and the policemen on guard outside drew their heavy sticks from their belts and made a sudden dash at the crowd to drive it back. But they were too few. Amid a rising roar of shouts and screams and a volley of stones they were themselves driven back—back past the curb to the shopfront and into the shop itself. Here, wielding their heavy sticks shoulder to shoulder, they were comparatively safe; the crowd could not get at them and instead contented itself with destroying their motorcycles. These had been parked outside Baldissera's empty stable and now a gang of boys slashed their gas tanks with a butcher's cleaver, shouting with derision and delight as the contents splashed out over the flagstones. Only Gigi, who had been quite unable to stay with Quong on the other side of the square, and who had wormed his way to the forefront, caught some of the petrol in an old bucket he had found against the stable wall. He hoped to sell it later as lighter-fuel, but he was driven away before he had collected more than a few cupfuls.

Two of the policemen had already become casualties from the flying stones and were lying in Crocifissa's kitchen where Iole and the old woman staunched the blood from their broken faces and propped them against the wall with glasses of brandy in their hands. They were joined by two more before the Brigadiere managed to get the shutter down and then turned back, white, furious and frightened, into the interior of the shop. "No trouble, eh?" He grasped Gennaro by the shoulder and shook him savagely. "You said there would be no trouble, and now . . ."

"It's not our fault! We didn't—"

"Not your fault? They're your friends out there, aren't they? If you'd gone when you'd been told to this wouldn't have happened, would it?" The Brigadiere cast a quick glance over his shoulder—no one was looking—and hit Gennaro twice across the head with the full force of his arm. "And there'll be more later! Now—where's the telephone?"

"There—there isn't one." Dizzy, his head singing, Gennaro

swayed under the policeman's grip. "The *tabacchi* . . .
Tenerini's . . . the nearest . . ."

"On the other side of the *piazza? Mannaggia!* Can I get out at
the back of this place?"

"Yes."

"Quick, then—show me!"

For the next quarter of an hour Crocifissa, Gennaro and Iole
were imprisoned in the old house trying distractedly, and with
the sullen help of the remaining municipal policemen, to collect
and pack their possessions while outside the crowd, temporarily
balked, hooted and booed, surging undecidedly backwards and
forwards across the cobbles. The last of the motorcycles was
wrenched apart and a gang of boys tried to attack the ITOLGAS
tanker parked beside the stable, whose curved yellow sides were
already dented and scarred by a hail of stones. But the demolition men, who had so far shown themselves neutral and had
stood aside, now moved forward to guard their firm's property.
They were ITOLGAS employees with safe and steady jobs which
they had every intention of retaining and if possible improving.
Also they had been long enough under the rule of Commendatore De Santis to "identify"—if not personally with the firm itself, at least with its more tangible possessions as part of their
own prosperity.

And still men and youths poured in from the dark, arched
mouth of the Via Buonuomini and the narrow opening at the
end of the Vico dei Lepri to strengthen a mob that by now numbered more than a thousand and to swell its tumult with their
own raucous cries.

If the crowd had been smaller, or if the *piazza* had been larger
and possessed easier means of egress, many would probably
have dispersed when the riot vans of the Public Security police
arrived. But the vans—great, turreted monsters with hinged
flaps of armor-plating over their wheels and windshields caged
and barred with strong steel mesh—rumbled down both the
Via Buonuomini and the Vico dei Lepri so that the only ways of
escape from the *piazza* were into the two alleys on each side of
the Annunziata or down the tiny cul-de-sac beyond Tenerini's
tabacchi—lanes of retreat unknown to the mass of those who
now found themselves trapped in the square.

There were four trucks in all and they pressed purposefully through the crowd, which broke and heaved away in front of them as the bow-wave curves back before the stem of a ship, and then rolled to a halt side by side to discharge their load of helmeted riot police before the battered filigree screen of the public urinal.

For the first few minutes it seemed as if the newcomers had achieved the upper hand and would keep it. The mob, seeing the helmets, the guns and the wire shields, and cowed by the squat, ugly trucks, backed away and allowed the police easy access to the besieged building. Once more the shutter of Crocifissa's shop was raised and the gray-uniformed State Security men thrust into the interior. These were police very different from the municipal guards. Specially picked, specially trained and paid for their job, they were experts in every trick of that most ruthless and brutal of all forms of combat—hand-to-hand street-fighting. Their lieutenant, tall, burly, gun on hip and long, rubber-covered truncheon in hand, glanced quickly around the disordered kitchen at the piled furniture and the blood-spattered casualties until his eye came to rest on the small group of civilians—an old woman, a younger, pregnant one and a boy incongruously clutching a caged canary in one hand and an electric iron and a stamp album in the other. Then—"These are them?" he demanded curtly of a disheveled city policeman panting at his elbow.

"*Si*, Signor Tenente. The ones who must be put out."

"Then put them out—quick!"

Iole turned immediately toward him. "*Tenente*—what about our things? I've only got two suitcases of clothes, but the others—"

"Get out! Do you think you haven't caused enough trouble as it is?" The lieutenant seized her arm and dragged her through the kitchen toward the shopfront. Over his shoulder he called, "Bring the other two—hurry!"

And then they were together, outside in the roaring tumult of the *piazza*. For a moment they stood, three ill-assorted figures, dazed and frightened, on the small patch of cobbles between the police line and the crowd—a sort of no-man's-land from which there seemed no means of advancing or retreating—and then, before they had recovered their breath or had time to do more than stare around them, the crowd surged forward, caught them up in its front wave and drove them in against the line of police in a bloody whirl of stones and sticks, flailing boots and fists.

Gennaro saw Iole fall, saw Crocifissa sway and stumble, clutching her shoulder, screaming out in pain; then felt his own legs kicked from under him and fell to the cobbles, dropping his electric iron and crushing the brass birdcage beneath his chest. Pain, dizzying and fire-shot, yet through it all an anguish for the little yellow bird fluttering hopelessly between his body and the rough *piperno* of the roadway. He must keep his full weight off the wires, but even as he struggled to rise another body fell heavily upon his back to drive him face down on the stones over the flattened cage. Someone trod heavily on one hand and then, with an immense effort, he was on his feet and being pulled away in the backwash of the thundering crowd as it surged back toward the urinal.

Twenty meters of cobblestones lay empty before the old building save for some dozen sprawled bodies, mostly in jeans and cotton shirts but with the field-gray of at least one policeman entangled with them. The rest of the police were forming up for a charge, and seeing this the crowd hurled every stone and half-brick it possessed upon them—a shower of missiles which crashed off the wire shields and clanged on the helmets and stopped the charge before it had started. After all, there were still less than thirty policemen on the scene to face a crowd now perhaps numbering nearly fifteen hundred. Yet the threat of that charge had, as threats so often have in Italy, the effect of the action itself. The front ranks of the mob pressed backward, sullen and jeering, and widened the open area of the *piazza* to the whole extent between the doomed building and the urinal while the police, panting, triumphant, but very uncertain, lined out along the curb and sent in the demolition men to remove the rest of the furniture and goods.

Out came mattresses and chairs, bits of old carpeting, piles of women's magazines, Iole's suitcases, the photograph of Dino on a washstand, Crocifissa's dresser—the drawers were brought out separately to save weight and in one of them, beside some account books, it was possible to see a small, carved wooden box—Quong's bed, plaster statues of the Virgin and holy pictures, dull and dark now with the little lights behind their celluloid hearts no longer pulsing redly.

Everything was piled outside the housefront against the wall and while some of the workers began to dismantle the shop and remove the stock, others moved into Quong's Pompe Funebre. Soon they had the garage doors off their hinges and were manhandling the old hearse into the roadway. In the interior lay a newly varnished coffin half covered with a black velvet pall, some carpenter's tools and, incongruously, the spare wheel and a roll of baling wire. But there was still plenty of space and the workmen piled in everything which they found in the shop and the room above—Kwang-Yin, cans of varnish and glue, Gennaro's books, *Il Gatto degli Stivali, Cuore, Mastro Don Gesualdo, Nuda Ogni Giorno*—a Chinese scroll in a frame, pillows, blankets and the remains of a badly torn and stained lavender-colored suit. When the hearse was full the larger bits of furniture—the tables, chairs, cooking-stove and washstand—were set out on the curb. Very soon the old building would be nothing but an empty shell—even now the men were at work unscrewing the various fixtures, taking down window shutters and doors.

It was because these visible signs of eviction stirred the crowd to a new fury, and also because the nuclei of gang-boys from the Porta Capuana had found time to replenish their supply of missiles, that the fiercest battle of the lengthening afternoon was joined. The crowd rushed the police line in a solid mass, preceded by a furious barrage of stones, and drove them back, forcing them in until they were fighting amongst the piles of household goods and groceries along the curb. It was an indiscriminate and bloody melee of which for a long time the outcome seemed uncertain and it might well have ended with the destruction of the riot squad if their lieutenant had not shut his eyes, thrust his handkerchief over his nose and mouth, and burst the first tear-gas grenade almost at his feet. There was no wind, no touch of breeze from the thunderous sky to disperse the searing fumes, and as they lifted slowly from the *piperno* the front ranks of the crowd began to choke and cough and stagger back. The police had just time to drag their smoke-masks over their stinging eyes and noses before the lieutenant threw the second and third bombs and followed them up with an order to charge. Shoulder to shoulder behind their wire shields the riot police went forward and before that masked and helmeted phalanx, spluttering, screaming and coughing in the suddenly unbreathable air, the mob gave ground, reeled back and farther back again.

It was at this point that another vehicle entered the *piazza,* a heavy, khaki-painted van bearing army license-plates and the white grenade of the Carabinieri.

⊷§ 7

MARESCIALLO Valdemarin had left his office with Calvanese as soon as Fabrizi had reported with the signed search-warrant from the offices of the Procuratore della Repubblica. They had taken with them, besides their uniformed driver, two other plainclothes members of the Homicide Squad. All six men carried pistols in shoulder-holsters and Fabrizi and the driver were each equipped with submachine guns as well. It was not until they were halfway down the Via Buonuomini that the Maresciallo became aware that something was happening at its farther end. Seeing a khaki-uniformed Carabiniere on the sidewalk he ordered the car pulled in and demanded, "What's happening down there? What's going on?"

The man saluted and smiled slightly. "Signor Maresciallo, I think the *Pubblica Sicurezza* are having a little difficulty with the San Lorenzini."

"How?"

"I think they have started a riot. It appears to be their own doing, entirely. They were called in to help evict some people from an old house in the Piazza Vittime Civili di Guerra and seem to have performed the task in such a way as to anger the local populace."

The Maresciallo swore savagely and turned back to the driver. "On—go on. Quick!"

But it was easier to give the order than to obey it; that end of the Via Buonuomini which opened into the *piazza* was blocked by a screaming throng of people, mostly juveniles, who formed a mass of such density that no vehicle could penetrate it at more than a crawl without an impossibly ruthless disregard for human life. The Carabinieri van inched its way past the archway of the *piazza*'s main entrance but could progress no farther.

"All right! Stop, then!" The Maresciallo thrust open a door and extricated his great bulk from the seat beside the driver. "Come on—Calvanese, Fabrizi, and you two others! Driver— you stay here and guard the van. Give your machine gun to the Brigadiere." Then, on foot and using their fists and feet to clear a passage, the five plainclothes policemen forced their way forward into the *piazza*.

The sight that met Valdemarin's eyes then was to cause him from that day forth to regret bitterly the existence of two rival police forces in his country. Ever afterwards, throughout the remainder of his service and his years of retirement, he was to say, "We will never, as a nation, achieve proper law and order until the Carabinieri and the Public Security police agree to work together." No one was to take any notice of him, for the Italians had always preferred the present arrangement seeing, in the enmity and feuding of the two forces, a safeguard to their own liberties. Nor were his newfound views to be popular with his colleagues. Because of them the clock which was to have been presented to him on the completion of his service was reduced to a wristwatch and he was to be pointedly excluded from several reunion dinners.

For to Valdemarin, gazing with all the frustrated despair of Villeneuve upon the quarterdeck of the *Bucentaur,* across the heaving, swaying tumult in the *piazza* on that dark, autumnal afternoon, a moment of truth had dawned. Not only had the Public Security police deliberately refused to inform their military colleagues that an eviction and a consequent riot was taking place, but he himself had just as deliberately refused to tell them of the suspected presence of a murderer on the scene of their activities. There was no doubt in his mind, staring across that seething mob, that if D'Ambri had been hiding in the old house on the west side of the *piazza* he must by now have escaped. Even if the P.S. had found him there they would only have turned him out with the other tenants, since they had no idea who he was. And considering the state of the *piazza* and the excited turmoil in the neighboring streets, D'Ambri could have made off without the smallest difficulty—might, by now, be far away in a distant quarter of the city.

In that moment Valdemarin nearly called the whole thing off. He would go back to his office and start once more—but this time with fewer clues and less chances of success—to trace D'Ambri in the ordinary way. He was not unused to disappointments; he had suffered many such in his long career, but this one was particularly hard to bear. His great shoulders sagged in defeat and he began to move away.

Then Calvanese was grasping his arm. "Look, Maresciallo— over there, by the side of the house!" He had to shout at the top of his voice to make himself heard above the fearful din. "It's Gobba! At least we can bring her in and then, as soon as this is over, we can pick up Gualtierra and—"

The Maresciallo lifted his head and stared across the *piazza* at the bent old bundle of rags which, behind the line of police, was picking its way over the now deserted rubble of the bomb ruins beside the old stable, moving slowly, purposefully, apparently searching for something—its bucket, perhaps, since it only held its mop—toward the roadway and the scattered furniture and goods along the curb.

"All right. But it won't do much good. Gualtierra won't know where D'Ambri is now—how could he?"

"It's still worth trying, *signore*." Calvanese thrust determinedly into the backs of the crowd, forcing his way toward the police line with elbows and fists, watched by the Maresciallo and his remaining men—a little island of dark suits, collars and ties in a sea of vivid T-shirts, jeans and overalls. Their eyes were on Calvanese and not upon the old hunchback as she picked up a battered bucket and shuffled to the curb, searching the ground before her for cigarette butts.

It was the cigarette of one of the wounded municipal police which caused the disaster. He had emerged from the now dismantled shop, bandage around his head, to watch with revengeful satisfaction the beating back of the crowd under the sticks of the riot squad, when a waft of tear-gas caught him suddenly by the throat and, coughing and spluttering, he threw his lighted cigarette from him and retired quickly into the house. The cigarette landed almost under La Gobba's nose; she seized it and thrust it into her bucket—the bucket which Gigi had misappropriated earlier to collect petrol from the slashed gas-tanks of the police motorcycles—and was turned, in the space of a single second, into a mass of flames.

Everything happened, then, with such speed that, hours afterwards, the San Lorenzini were still inventing, retailing and believing the most unlikely and astonishing theories of spontaneous combustion, fiery meteorites, thunderbolts of vengeance hurled by San Gennaro from above—or, according to their political inclinations, deliberate sabotage by the police or the Communists. La Gobba let out one piercing howl and staggered toward the dripping standpipe beside the stable wall. But she never got there; the fiery mass of her rags and her own unaccustomed attempt at speed tripped her up five meters from the water and sent her, rolling and shrieking in agony, under the belly of the great yellow tanker-truck. The roar of the mob faded perceptibly. First one and then another of the gray-uniformed police turned, gazing incredulously over their shoulders. But no one did anything; no one dared approach that incendiary mass rolling under its ominous roof.

The kicking, screaming bundle of flames rocked hideously to and fro beneath the tanker and it seemed that the very ground took fire around it—the oil-soaked earth upon which the police motorcycles had been destroyed. Then—as the lieutenant shouted at the top of his voice for those inside the house to come out; as the wounded city policemen came to the doorway, gazed, took in the situation and ran for their lives—a thin snake of flame crawled up the side of the yellow tanker and was followed by another, then a third and a fourth.

There was no need for the police to force the crowd back now; every jeaned and overalled member of it was pressing backward for his life. Valdemarin, staring fascinated at the burning body of La Gobba, twitching faintly, then still and silent save for the leaping flames, was nearly swept away by the backwash and only his ponderous bulk, from which the lighter bodies of the San Lorenzini bumped and bounced like balls off a pneumatic buffer, saved him from being knocked to the ground.

Then the tanker exploded. It went up with a dull, rumbling boom in a pillar of yellow and scarlet flame which rose as high, and then higher, than the old building, drenching it from top to bottom in a mass of blazing gasoline. One moment the house

had stood, grimy, cracked, battered by the years, both ends falling away into rubble and weeds, but solidly enough, on the west
side of the *piazza*—the next it was nothing but a sheeted façade
of fire whose flaming breath reached out to scorch the faces of
police and rioters alike, thirty or more meters away.

There was no noise now in the *piazza*—or none audible over
the billowing furnace-roar of the fire. The mob stood silent and
appalled, their faces tinged hotly with red in the darkening thun-
der-light of the oncoming storm, or edging farther and farther
back as the increasing heat reached out toward them. The sucking draft of the fire swept up the last remains of the tear-gas,
fluttered the torn posters on the urinal walls and pulled inward
from the Via Buonuomini and the Vico dei Lepri currents of
warm air that stirred the hair and billowed the clothes of the
massed watchers in the square.

It was then that Maresciallo Valdemarin caught sight of a
grimy, bloodstained boy with a crushed canary cage in one hand
and what appeared to be half a stamp book in the other—Gualtierra. He was standing in the front ranks of the crowd close to
the urinal and about twenty meters from the Maresciallo.

"Fabrizi, Calvanese—quick! Come with me!" It was a last
chance and probably a hopeless one. With the death of La Gobba
there was now no evidence—unless a captured D'Ambri might
give it—of Gualtierra's complicity in the August murder. But
Valdemarin did not think of this. He knew only that there, within
a short distance of him, stood someone whom he was now certain knew where D'Ambri had been until so recently—until, perhaps, a few hours ago; someone who might even know where he
was now. Across his mind's eye flashed the picture of that long-
past evening in Genoa and the quiet supper table in his apartment before the door crashed open and the bullets flew—of
Nicola's pale face raised on his pillows, surveying his ruined life.
With a fearful urgency, and forgetting all the precepts of
strategic behavior toward a suspect which he constantly urged
upon his subordinates, Valdemarin ran heavily across the lava
blocks and reaching Gualtierra, grasped him by the arm and
shook him harshly. "Where is he? *Where is he?*" For a moment
he thought the boy was going to faint and fall down at his feet,
so appalled was the expression on that dirty, blood-smeared
face. Loosening his grip, calming his voice with an effort, he

said quickly, "Listen—I'm not after you, Gualtierra. You needn't worry. It's *him* I'm after—D'Ambri—Domenichelli. Where is he?"

But the look of horror did not leave the boy's face, the wide eyes stared with a fascinated incredulity past the Maresciallo at the blazing house. Then he lifted a hand and pointed. "There— he's in there."

"Where—in the house?" Valdemarin swung around and the full force of the heat hit him in the face, making his eyes water and close up.

"No—in the hearse! In—in that coffin!"

Incredulously the Maresciallo stared in the direction of Gennaro's pointing finger. The old motor-hearse lay where it had been manhandled by the demolition men, a few meters from the curbside and the blazing furniture that edged it. By some chance freak it had escaped the fiery rain of gasoline from the exploding tanker and was still intact, still untouched by the fire. Through its plate-glass sides could be seen a jumble of blankets and carpenters' tools, what seemed a wooden statue, and, jammed under a spare wheel and a roll of wire, a coffin partly draped in black.

"In *there*?" Once more Valdemarin glanced at the boy beside him but the expression on Gualtierra's face was proof enough of his veracity. "Calvanese! Fabrizi!" The Maresciallo swung round to his subordinates. "We've got to get that hearse clear—pull it away! Ropes—we'll need ropes. Somebody get ropes. . . ." He began to run toward the hearse and his two assistants ran with him. But after only five steps they were forced to throw up their arms to protect their faces from the searing heat, and after staggering three more they halted, wavered—drew back.

It was impossible to reach the hearse. No living man could approach nearer than ten meters to its sides, and the rapidly increasing heat was lengthening the distance every second. The Maresciallo, rubbing his eyes, fell back with his men beside him into the slowly retreating crowd. And now his gaze was fixed, was riveted upon that hearse. So close it lay to the billowing wall of flames that they seemed a crimson-yellow backdrop to its ornate and somber black. But what could the temperature be in that piled interior? What could it be in that coffin? For he saw that the whole vehicle was smoking, the black varnish bubbling and running down its sides. In a moment a tire burst and then the plate glass cracked with a report that could be heard over the roaring of the fire, and one great sculpted corner lantern suddenly crumpled and sagged sideways.

A small, thin smile slowly lifted the corners of Valdemarin's mouth as, step by step, he fell back with the crowd from the fierce breath of the fire. It was all over. There was to be no more shooting. D'Ambri had escaped perilously through a prison incinerator—escaped burning alive in the last days of May, only to burn alive on the first of October. The long account was closing fast—in minutes, seconds perhaps, it would be closed for good. He was patting something beside him with an unconscious, triumphant rhythm—the rhythm of the fire; he glanced down and saw that it was Gualtierra's shoulder, and as the boy looked up at him he smiled with a grim irony. Gualtierra was safe—doubly safe, for now the last and only remaining witness as to what had happened in the Vicolo Ciego di Pomodori was roasting alive before his very eyes. Sardonically he shrugged his shoulders. Tomorrow that particular file in his office cabinet would be closed forever.

He turned his gaze back to the smoking hearse and as he did so a low, warning rumble came from the heart of the fire and the crowd screamed and surged back in panic as the whole front of the building leaned slowly forward and then crashed into the roadway burying everything, the crackling furniture, the ruins of the tanker, the black hearse, under tons of blazing rubble. A column of white-hot fire roared in a huge billow of flame toward the darkening sky and to Gennaro, thrusting backward, scorched and seared by the terrific heat, it seemed for a single moment to rear upward in the shape of a great horse, pawing the air, tossing its glowing mane, above its incandescent pedestal.

But that crash, that rumble of falling masonry, continued after the ruined building had settled into a heaped and shapeless pyre. For suddenly a sizzling blue-white gash, brighter than any earthly light, tore the sky and the cannon-fire of thunder exploded in a convulsion of deafening sound directly overhead. Now lightning, forked and barbed like serpents' tongues, ripped open the bellies of the sagging clouds, and with a booming roar that thundered back from the slopes of Vesuvius and echoed hollowly away over the black waters of the gulf, the storm broke at last.

What the police had fought in vain to do throughout the afternoon the storm accomplished in a few minutes. Under the cataracting rain, deafened by the continuous ordnance-peals of thunder, blinded by the magnesium-glare of lightning, the crowd stampeded for shelter, leaping, shouting, falling—scurrying with the frenetic speed of mice before a pouncing cat. In less than five minutes the *piazza* was empty and the riot police, themselves soaked and breathless, had taken thankful refuge within the drumming interiors of their plated, saurian vehicles.

Only two figures remained in the square—a fat, gray-haired man who stood motionless under the sluicing rain staring at the blackened pile of steaming, smoking rubble, and a boy who limped slowly across the cobbles holding a few pages of colored stamps and a broken birdcage on whose floor lay a tiny bundle of yellow feathers.

A Cry in the Night

✦ 1

FOR two hours the storm raged over Naples and then boomed and flashed its way north and west, trailing behind it a tattered pall of ragged rain clouds which soaked out the last of summer as they blotted from view the stars of night.

Night and storm down the coast at Gaeta; cannonading the great castle with salvoes of thunder and penetrating, in split-second glares down the air vents and into the subterranean passages of Mont'Orlando—echo following flash, flash following echo.

Night and storm arriving in grim company over Caserta, over the Palazzo Colavolpe, empty now and shuttered. The lightning throwing the tossing pines around the Church of the Holy Tooth into black relief against the sudden, corpse-colored sky, gleaming on the sepulchral niches behind the vestry and on a new marble slab above the dirt and refuse—GALEAZZO ARCONOVALDO MARIA IGNACIO COLAVOLPE. . . . Night and storm.

✦ 2

IN the Villa Sanfelice at Posillipo the heavy curtains across the plate-glass windows shut out the darkness and the rain which bore in across the wave-torn gulf. In the bright fluorescent light of his study Commendatore De Santis sat with a glass of armagnac before him on the desk. He was not too dissatisfied with the outcome of the day, for since the old building in San Lorenzo had been demolished by accidental fire rather than by ITOLGAS employees the firm's public image could suffer little damage; but nonetheless it had vaguely depressed him with its implications that, whatever he might do or order, the Neapolitans were unlikely to become Milanese—at least in his lifetime. Such unnecessary excitement and raucous tumult over nothing was perturbing. Would these people never want to lead the civilized lives of industry and security which he was offering them? Did they really prefer stoning policemen and burning down property to playing football on his fields or racing bicycles on his tracks? There had been no water in the washrooms now for nearly four months and still no one had complained. It was difficult to know what to do about such people. Difficult, but not hopeless; Commendatore De Santis was not a man to give up hope.

Yet tonight he was tired and depressed—due, perhaps, to the heavy heat all day and the electric tension of the storm. There was a report lying on the desk before him for which he had waited impatiently and which he particularly wanted to study. It came from the firm's medical laboratories in Milan and dealt with the moderating influences of certain allegedly harmless chemicals on human fecundity. A small amount added to the canteen meals of the male workers might do something to halt the alarming rise in the birth rate of ITOLGAS's Neapolitan employees, and the consequent overcrowding of the firm's clinics and crèches. "Give them security," muttered De Santis, "and all they think of is imperiling it with more children than ever." But, if possible, the new drugs should not be actually spermicidal— there was always the possibility of trouble if the Church found out. . . .

⤳ 3

AND the flap of receding lightning through the rain over windy Vomero. The plane trees had suffered severely; their beautiful russet-and-gold leaves lay piled in the drains of the running gutters or were gummed damply to the roadway like children's transfers. On the Via Raffaele Morghen, in particular, even twigs and small branches had been torn off by the storm and the trees themselves still rocked and volleyed in the dying gusts.

A window at the front of a block of apartments had broken

open under the wind's force and banged angrily to and fro, its glass in splinters on the floor of the small kitchen within. Two tea towels, and a calendar depicting an English cottage garden bright with flowers which had been torn from the wall, lay in a pool of rainwater near the table. By tomorrow, when the porter came up with the master-key to have the window repaired, the calendar would be ruined—but it would not matter since the apartment's tenants were not returning before the next year's spring.

It was as well that the porter would not climb the stairs until morning for otherwise he might have received an unpleasant shock. Opposite the rattling frame, in the anatomy classroom of the medical school across the road, some students had pulled their skeleton up to the window and, slipping between its ribs a kitchen knife with a cardboard hilt painted to resemble a Nunzia-tella *spadino*, had lifted its stiff right hand to its bony forehead in a rigid military salute. It looked unpleasantly ironic as it alternately gleamed whitely and disappeared in the wide flaps of sheet lightning.

☙ 4

IN his small, brightly lit bedroom high up on the Via Michele Kerbaker, Nicola fitted together the last pieces of a large jigsaw puzzle to complete a picture of the Queen of England reviewing long ranks of red-coated guardsmen. It had arrived two days ago from London without a letter but with a small card bearing the picture of a black-and-white kitten very like the little cat which now lay curled up near the long-nosed Pinocchio doll on the bed beside him. Outside, the wind had fallen and the rain, no longer rattling on his window in spiteful gusts, descended with a steady, dripping persistence—a quiet, soothing sound. He had a new book to read tomorrow, and the next day he must begin the pencil sketch for another picture of his colored fowls—a cock crowing triumphantly with all its docile hens behind it. It would complete his series.

His father, soaked and exhausted, had returned some hours ago and, gulping brandy in the bedside chair, had told him the story of the afternoon's happenings in the city. It was not a story

Nicola had liked. He had listened, made the right remarks and ejaculations, but been secretly pleased when his father had finished and lumbered off wearily to change his wet clothes and get the supper.

But despite—perhaps because of—his aversion to what he had been told, Nicola had felt strangely content. Not so much because of the death of a man who had done him so grave a wrong, as through a vague feeling that perhaps—in a way—his life up here in his little room, or moving quietly through the small flat in his new wheelchair, had its compensations after all. Pictures to paint in colored inks, puzzles, books, games, a kitten to play with—a nursery life indeed, but secure, shut in and safe from all the fears and dangers of the jungle outside. And now—He pushed back the wheeled table on which the completed puzzle lay, took two sedative tablets from one of the array of bottles beside his bed, and easing his foreshortened body gently to a prone position, turned out the light and closed his eyes in the all-obscuring, all-covering blackness.

⋘ 5

BLACK as the pit; black as the nineteen hundred and sixty nails upon the Cross; a waste place of sagging railway viaducts, deserted sidings patched with cinders and weed-grown cumuli of long-decayed rubbish—it was here, beside a ruined arch of moldering, smoke-grimed stone, that they halted the old *carròzza* at last.

They did not know where they were save that it was somewhere far behind Pendino in the Rione Luzzatti, a place long since given up to the rusty, iron desolation of abandoned railway yards. At least they were far from the *piazza*, now cordoned off by police and closed to the public while the investigations and arrests consequent upon this afternoon's riot were under way.

The rain fell softly, persistently; tapping on the patched hood of the *carròzza* and running in thin streams down Baldissera's bony flanks. Quong had sat propped in his corner mute and motionless as they had crept along rain-swept streets ever more deserted, ever more sparsely lit; but Iole could not keep still, moaning and twisting with pain against Crocifissa's shoulder, and here at last they took her out, Gennaro and the old woman, and laid her on a horse-blanket under the dripping arch.

"It's coming, Gennà—her baby. They knocked her down, and the shock . . . You'll have to help me. Try to hold her still."

And wonderingly, patiently, Gennaro did as Crocifissa told him and soon it was accomplished—the birth of Iole's child—amongst that wasteland of cinders and abandoned sidings under the thin rain and by the light of the *carròzza*'s one flickering lamp. . . . Gennaro had had much to do with death during his short life but this was the first time he had assisted at a birth.

And somehow it filled him with a delighted wonder—a feeling of awed yet joyful reassurance and hope. There had been four people here under the broken viaduct arch—and now, suddenly, there were five. And the new one, the newcomer, was the most important of all, for he would go forward, leaving them behind, into a future which they would not see.

"Give him here," he said. "Give him to me."

Grinning he clasped the tiny newborn thing in his arms, and as its thin cry lifted faintly into the night he knew, suddenly, that it was the sign he had awaited. Not in the jubilation of pealing bells under the great roof of the Duomo, nor in the booming thunder of the storm, but in the first weak cry of this child had the saint answered him at last. Not "I will protect my Napoli" but "*You* will protect. . . ."

Kneeling with the child cradled in his arms, he lifted his dripping, laughing face to the darkness and the rain. Overhead, from pylon to post, in a great spider-net across Naples ten thousand city wires were stretched most cruelly against the city sky, but far above him the clouds had parted in a jagged rift and through them, calm and unchanging, shone a solitary star.

119   4.53
146   3.97
169₊   4.76
178   4.88
————   ————
6.11   18.14